OF
LOVE
AND
LIFE

OF
LOVE
AND
LIFE

Three novels selected and condensed
by Reader's Digest

CONDENSED BOOKS DIVISION

The Reader's Digest Association Limited, London

The Reader's Digest Association Limited
11 Westferry Circus, Canary Wharf, London E14 4HE

www.readersdigest.co.uk

ISBN 0-276-42540-5

CONTENTS

BOOKENDS

Jane Green

Cath and Si have been best friends since university even though they are total opposites—Cath is scatty, messy and scared of commitment, and Si is methodical, tidy, and desperately searching for a man of his own. They live close to each other in West Hampstead, close also to their married friends, Josh and Lucy.

Their friendship is complete, but when Cath and Lucy open a bookshop together, Portia, who knew them from their university days, attends the launch party and starts to threaten everything that the friends hold dear.

Chapter One

THE FIRST TIME I MET JOSH, I thought he was a nice guy but a transient friend. The first time I met Si I fell hopelessly in love and prayed I'd somehow be able to convert him.

But the first time I met Portia I thought I'd found my soulmate.

She was the sister I'd always longed for, the best friend I'd always wished I had, and I truly and honestly thought that, no matter what happened with our lives, we would stay friends for ever. And for ever feels a long time when you're eighteen and you're away from home for the first time in your life.

I met Josh right at the beginning, just a few weeks after the Freshers' Ball. I'd seen him in the Students' Union, propping up the bar after a rugby game, looking for all the world like the archetypal upper-class rugger-bugger twit. He—naturally—started chatting up Portia, alcohol giving him a confidence he lacked when sober (although I didn't know that at the time), and despite the rebuffs he kept going until his friends dragged him away to find easier prey.

I'm sure we would all have left it at that, but I bumped into him the next day, in the library, and he recognised me instantly and apologised for embarrassing us; and gradually we started to see him more and more, until he'd firmly established himself as one of the gang.

I'd already met Si by then, when I had gone to the audition for a production of *Cabaret*. Si was the only person who turned up in full costume. As Sally Bowles. In fishnet stockings, bowler hat and full make-up, he

9

didn't bat an eyelid as everyone else slouched down in their hard, wooden chairs, staring, jealous as hell of his initiative. And his legs.

He went in, bold as brass, and proceeded to give the worst possible rendition of *Cabaret* that I've ever heard, but with such brazen confidence you could almost forgive him for being entirely tone-deaf.

Everybody went crazy when he'd finished. They went crazy because he so obviously loved, *loved*, being centre stage. None of us had ever seen such enthusiasm, but even though Si knew every song, word for word, he had to be content with camping it up as the narrator, because Helen, the director, said she never wanted to hear him sing again.

Eddie was a friend of Josh. A gentle boy from Leeds who should probably have been overwhelmed by our combined personalities, but somehow wasn't. He was easy company, and always willing to do anything for anybody he cared about, which was mostly us, at the time.

And then of course there was Portia. So close that our names became intertwined: CatherineandPortia. Two for the price of one.

I met Portia on my very first day at university. We were sitting in the halls of residence common room, waiting for a talk to begin, when this stunningly elegant girl strode in on long, long, legs, crunching an apple and looking like she didn't have a care in the world.

Portia, with her mane of dark auburn hair and her cool green eyes and dirty laugh. Portia, who looked like she should have been a class-A bitch, but was soon to become the greatest friend I'd ever had.

Her confidence took my breath away, and, when she flung her bag down on the floor and sank into the empty chair next to mine, I prayed she'd be my friend. She stretched out, showing off buttersoft suede thigh-high boots, exactly the boots I'd dreamed of wearing if I ever got thin enough, and, taking a last bite of the apple, tossed it with an expert flick of the wrist into the dustbin on the other side of the room.

'Yesss!' she hissed triumphantly in a cut-glass accent. 'I *knew* all those years as goal shooter would pay off some time,' and then she turned to me. 'I'm Portia. When does this bloody thing start?'

Portia had more than enough confidence for both of us. We found, within minutes, that despite our different backgrounds we had the same vicious sense of humour, the same slightly ironic take on life. There never seemed to be a shortage of conversation with Portia.

She had a prime room—one of the most coveted in the building. A large bay window overlooked the main residential street, and Portia repositioned the armchairs so that they were in the bay, draping them with jewel-coloured crushed velvet throws. She sat there for hours at a time, watching people go by. Most of the time I'd be there too. We'd sit drinking bottles of Beck's, Marlboro Lights dripping coolly from our fingers, waiting for the men of our dreams to walk past and fall head over heels in love with us.

They frequently did. With Portia, at any rate.

Even then she had more style than anyone I'd ever met. It was obvious that she had money, but there was never anything snobbish or snooty about her. She'd been brought up in the country, in Gloucestershire, in a huge Jacobean manor house. Her mother was terribly beautiful, she said, and an alcoholic, but, Portia sighed, who could blame her when her father was sleeping with half of London. They had a *pied-à-terre* in Belgravia, to which Portia eventually decamped when she refused to go back to boarding school, opting to do her A-levels in a trendy tutorial college in London instead.

It was a world away from my own background. My life had started in deepest, darkest suburbia, in an ordinary prewar semi on a main road in North London. My dad, unlike Portia's landowning, gambling, semi-aristocratic father, is an accountant in a local firm. My mother is a housewife who works occasionally as a dinner lady in the local primary school.

As far back as I can remember I would escape from my humdrum world by burying myself in books—the one true love of my life when growing up.

I love Mum and Dad. Of course. They are my parents. But the day I went to university I realised that they had nothing to do with me any more, nothing to do with my life, with who I wanted to be, and never was I more aware of cutting the umbilical cord than when I met Portia.

I used to wonder whether style was something you were born with, or whether it was something you could buy. I'm sure that it's something you're born with, and Portia was just fortunate in being able to afford the very best as well. I still have no doubt, however, that she could have made a bin bag look sophisticated. But she was also funny, generous and kind. In fact Portia was the most sought-after girl at university, but underneath the designer trappings and *soigné* exterior, Portia was just like me. We were both eternal romantics, although we hid it well, and both desperately needed to be loved.

Portia had been practically abandoned by her parents since birth, and, though my background wasn't quite so dramatic, I was the product of people who should never have got married, of people who spent their lives arguing, shouting, who led me to believe, as a very young child, that it was all my fault.

My parents were still together, very much so, but I suppose every family has its problems, and mine no less than anyone else. We just don't talk about it. Everything is swept under the carpet.

Perhaps that's why I loved Portia so much. She was the first person I'd met with whom I felt able to be completely honest. Gradually we allowed more people to enter into our world. Only a select few, only the people who shared our humour, but eventually, by the end of the year, we were a small group of misfits, all from different walks of life, but all somehow feeling as if we had found another family.

So there was Eddie, Joshua, Portia and Si. Sarah entered halfway through the second year, by virtue of going out with Eddie, but, although we made her feel welcome, she never really belonged.

I longed to bring someone into the group in the way that Eddie had brought Sarah. And I had my fair share of flings. But the grand passion of which Portia and I talked, relentlessly, eluded me during those years, and one-night stands were the best I could get.

I'm ashamed to say that I slept with pretty much anyone who wanted me at university—my self-esteem so low, that show the faintest bit of interest in me, and I was yours.

I still vividly remember the craving for affection. It wasn't the sex I wanted, it was the cuddling afterwards. It was the lying in bed, arms around one another, softly murmuring as they stroked your hair. I would sleep with them, then wake up, eyes pleading for one more taste of the affection I had had the night before. But invariably the orgasm of the previous night had taken the intimacy with it, and I would either be ignored, or have to indulge in polite conversation before getting out of there as quickly as possible.

Portia had lost her virginity the summer before starting university, on holiday, with a strapping Swede on the Greek island of Mykonos, and had come to the conclusion that one-nighters weren't for her.

'I can't imagine why *anyone* would want to sleep with a stranger,' she would say.

There wasn't anyone good enough for Portia, I decided. Not here at the university. But then, towards the end of the second year, when we were sharing a house just off the high street with Josh, Si and Eddie—Sarah not yet having made her mark in the way she was evidently hoping to—Portia came home smiling. She said she'd met someone lovely at the library, and would we mind if he came over that night for supper?

I did mind a bit, actually. It was the first time Portia had ever seemed interested in anyone, and I suppose I must have been jealous, but as soon as Matt walked in, we all fell in love with him.

Matt really was the perfect man. He was funny, charming, kind, bright, and he adored Portia. *Adored* her. You know how some couples just look perfect together? That was Matt and Portia. And I didn't lose her. I gained another best friend.

But it didn't last. It never did, in those days, with Portia. For a year they were inseparable, and then, out of the blue, she split up with him. No reason, no explanation, nothing. She just decided it was time to move on, but what was an easy decision for her, left the rest of our tiny group devastated. And that was when it all started to go horribly wrong.

There was a girl called Elizabeth. A friend of Eddie. Someone with whom he had been to school, his best friend, who had opted for a job rather than university, and who had secured for herself the rather grand-sounding title of marketing assistant.

Eddie adored her. Throughout the first term we kept hearing about Elizabeth: Elizabeth this, Elizabeth that. Elizabeth began to take on mythical qualities. She was the elusive beauty that we had heard so much about, but none of us was entirely sure that she really existed, at least not in the way that Eddie had described.

We assumed that Eddie's crush had blinded him to her actual attributes. We assumed she'd be pretty. Striking, even. But unassuming.

And then Eddie announced she was coming to stay for the weekend. He was giving up his bed, he said, and would be staying the night at Sarah's so that Elizabeth would be comfortable.

'Yeah, yeah,' Josh ribbed him. 'Bet you'll be sneaking back into your bed in the middle of the night; Sarah won't be too happy about that.' Sarah was not, at that stage, a permanent fixture, but we could see that Eddie had, up until this visit from the infamous Elizabeth, fallen for her.

Eddie looked shocked. 'Absolutely not. You know how I feel about Sarah, and anyway Elizabeth is my friend. That's all.'

We all caught Eddie's excitement in the days before Elizabeth was due to arrive. All of us except Portia.

'Don't you want to meet this paragon of female loveliness?' I asked her, and Jesus, how clear this memory is. I remember asking that question. I remember exactly where we were, and the memory is so strong I can suddenly smell it.

I can smell the old seaside café, perched on the side of one of the narrow cobbled streets running up from the beach. Portia and I were sitting at a tiny table with our lighters precariously balanced on our packets of Marlboros, the air smelling of smoke, and freshly baked cakes, and salt from the sea. I remember saying I couldn't wait to meet Elizabeth. And Portia didn't say anything.

'You're coming with, aren't you?' I asked, having told her that all of us were going with Eddie to the train station to pick her up.

Portia shrugged. 'I've just got to go to the library, so I might have to miss the grand arrival.'

And it didn't occur to me that there might have been more to it.

'What do you think she's like?' I giggled. 'Do you think she's as perfect as Eddie makes out?'

'She's probably a total bitch,' Portia said, which seemed out of character and took me by surprise, but then I entered into the spirit of things.

'Or hugely fat,' I chuckled.

'Yup. She's probably put on ten stone since Eddie last saw her, eating for comfort now that he's gone. Either that or she's balding.'

I looked at Portia as if she were mad, and then we cracked up laughing.

Portia didn't come with to pick up Elizabeth, and in the end neither did I. Josh took Eddie and Sarah, as he was the only one of us with a car, and I sat in the kitchen at home, waiting for them, and waiting for Portia to come back from the library.

I'd just made some tea when the front door opened and I heard a babble of voices. As soon as Josh and Eddie walked into the kitchen, I could see they were both in love. Their eyes were alight and they were laughing, excitement making their cheeks flushed. Right behind them was Elizabeth, and I understood what had caused their reaction.

She was, simply, gorgeous. Not in the way that Portia was, in a slightly imperious, untouchable way. Elizabeth was the classic girl next door, and as soon as she saw me she came over with a huge smile and I could see how the others had fallen under her spell, even Sarah.

Si came back from a drama rehearsal soon after, and it didn't take long for her to work her magic on him, but the person who was quite clearly the most affected was Josh.

I hadn't seen Josh like that before. He couldn't take his eyes off her, and as the afternoon progressed I began to notice that she started paying him more and more attention. Soon she was laying a hand on his arm, begging him to stop teasing her. Because this was the only way that Josh, at nineteen, knew how to flirt.

'Isn't she amazing?' Si said, when we left to go to the corner shop and buy some more cigarettes.

'I didn't think I'd say this, but she is. She's just so nice, and natural, and funny! I've been in stitches all day.'

'And gorgeous,' Si said. 'If I were straight she'd be my perfect woman.'

'What about Portia?'

'Nope.' Si shook his head. 'Portia's beautiful, but there's something impenetrable about her, something slightly cold. Elizabeth's just so nat-ural. Jesus, what's Portia going to think of her?'

'What do you mean?'

'She's going to hate her,' he said smoothly as we went into the shop and picked up the cigarettes. 'She'll be eaten up with jealousy.'

I stood stock-still and stared at him. 'Portia? Jealous?'

'Cath, she won't be able to stand not being the centre of attention, and have you seen Josh? He's practically salivating over her. I adore Portia, but I wouldn't want to be the one pushing her off centre stage.'

When we got home Portia was there. She was sitting at the kitchen table, talking to Elizabeth, and, although I refused to admit that Si had been right, the atmosphere had definitely changed, and was I going crazy or did Portia suddenly seem to have a cold, flinty look in her eyes?

'So what's on the agenda for tonight, then?' Si put his shoes on the table as he slurped his Pot Noodles.

'We thought we'd do a pub crawl,' Eddie said, looking at Elizabeth for her approval.

'Fantastic,' she laughed. 'Haven't done a good pub crawl for ages.'

'Elizabeth pissed is not a pretty sight,' Eddie said as she hit him, but neither Portia nor I missed the fact that Josh had not joined in with the laughter, too busy gazing at Elizabeth's lovely face.

Portia came downstairs at seven o'clock, and Si nudged me to look at her as she stood in the hallway, shaking out her hair in the mirror.

'See?' he mouthed silently. 'She's dressed for battle.'

And she was. She was wearing a tight red dress that Josh once claimed gave him an instant orgasm just by looking at it, and what Si always referred to as her Fuck-me Shoes.

Si raised an eyebrow at me and I shook my head, because I really didn't want to believe Si, but all the evidence was pointing to Portia being very definitely up to something. I just didn't know what it was.

But it didn't take me long to find out.

We started out at the King's Head. Portia, as always, turned heads wherever we went, but Elizabeth generated a fair bit of attention too.

Nothing happened until we hit the club. At every pub we'd been to Josh had sat next to Elizabeth, and by the fifth pub they only seemed to have eyes for each other. Eddie shrugged resignedly, and Si and I just sat quietly, watching the blank look on Portia's face, wondering whether she would dare to say anything to Elizabeth.

Because of course Josh had always had a thing for Portia. From the moment we had all met, right through the first year, and on through the second. It had become a standing joke in our group, and even Josh was quite happy to be teased about it. Portia knew, and he knew that Portia knew, and he'd accepted that it was never going to happen.

Until that night, Portia had always laughed when Si and I joked about Josh's unrequited crush, saying that Josh was too nice for her, but tonight I could see that she couldn't deal with another woman in the picture.

And sure enough, in the last pub we went to, the last one before hitting the local nightclub, Portia literally shoved Elizabeth out of the way, sidled up next to Josh and started whispering things in his ear, her coat flung casually on the seat to prevent Elizabeth from coming close.

Poor Josh looked as if he'd been hit by a truck. Stunned. Here was the woman he'd lusted after coming on to him for the first time in his life, and yet here was this other woman, who was also gorgeous, who simply didn't know how to deal with Portia.

Elizabeth sat quietly next to Sarah, and Si tried to act as if everything were normal, even while Portia did her Mata Hari impersonation. In other words, as Si put it later, acting like a complete bitch.

As soon as we walked into the club, Elizabeth went to the toilet and I joined her to tame my hair and put on some more lipstick.

'Josh is lovely, isn't he?' Elizabeth said, as she washed her hands.

'He obviously likes you too,' I said, smiling, as she turned to me.

'Is there something going on with him and Portia, though? Eddie said absolutely not, but I feel like she's defending her territory or something.'

'Don't worry about it. Portia's fine, she's just not used to you, that's all, and no, there's nothing going on between her and Josh,' and we left to go back into the club.

Elizabeth saw it first. I heard this little gasp, and I turned to look at what she was looking at, and there was Portia. Well, Portia and Josh. Locked together in a passionate embrace in the middle of the dance floor, Portia entwined around him like a snake.

I couldn't tear my eyes off them, not least because I knew Portia wasn't a believer in public displays of affection, and it was an extraordinary sight, to see such blatant passion in public.

I knew Elizabeth was walking away, and I know I should have gone after her, but then Eddie and Sarah were tearing past me to reach her, and I found myself walking over to Si.

'See?' he said gravely, having to shout into my ear above the loud din of the Housemartins. He tried to look shocked, but the gossip inside him was completely loving this drama. 'Told you so.'

I watched as Portia and Josh finally broke apart, and I could see that Josh, while thrilled to have finally got together with Portia, was also completely bemused. He looked like a little boy lost, whereas Portia was positively triumphant.

She led him to our table by the hand and picked up a triple vodka, downing it in one before whispering something into Josh's ear, sucking Josh's earlobe as Si kicked me hard under the table.

'Where are the others?' she shouted above the din.

'Where do you think, Portia?' Si said, and Portia smiled, as a flash of what I swear must have been guilt passed over Josh's face.

'Oh well. May the best woman win,' she said, picking up another vodka before dragging Josh over to the dance floor and wrapping herself up in his arms.

That night we all got drunk, but what I do remember quite clearly, even to this day, was lying in bed and hearing Elizabeth's quiet sobbing coming from Eddie's room, and the rhythmic creaking of Josh's bed.

That old Victorian terraced house wasn't built to hide feelings of betrayal, of jealousy, of misplaced passion. I remember hearing Portia's soft moans, and feeling like a voyeur. I remember pulling the duvet over my head to block out the noise. Eventually I fell into a dreamless sleep.

Elizabeth had gone by the time I woke up. Eddie had left to take her to the station, and Si was already up, watching children's television with a plate of greasy fried eggs and toast balanced on his knees.

'What a night,' he said, in between mouthfuls.

'Is she OK do you know? Elizabeth?'

Si shrugged. 'Not particularly, but I'm sure she'll get over it. Eddie's taken her to the station. She couldn't face spending the weekend here, apparently, so she's gone.'

'How's Eddie about all of this?'

'Upset because Elizabeth's upset, and because he doesn't understand what was going on last night. He knew that Josh liked Elizabeth and that Elizabeth liked Josh, and he said he knew they were going to get it together and he didn't mind at all. Actually, he said he was bloody pleased it was Josh.

'But most of all he doesn't understand what happened with Josh and Portia. One minute they were just walking in the club, and the next Portia and Josh were all over each other.'

'God, poor Elizabeth. I have to say I don't really understand it either.'

'You're not serious?' Si looks at me in amazement as I shrug. 'Cath, don't be thick. Portia's chosen us as her friends because we're all a bit in love with her. She has to be the centre of attention, and she couldn't stand the threat that Elizabeth posed.

17

'It was bad enough that we all thought Elizabeth was fantastic, but the one thing she absolutely couldn't cope with would have been if Josh and Elizabeth had ended up together. She *had* to sabotage it.'

'Portia's not a bitch,' I said defensively. 'I can't believe she'd do that.'

'So you think that Portia's secretly been harbouring a massive crush on Josh, but now that she's finally found the courage to do something about it, they're going to live happily ever after?'

'They might.'

'Cath, Portia only slept with Josh to make sure he stays in love with her, and, providing he does, she'll never sleep with him again. Trust me,' he sighed. 'I'm the expert.'

And, sure enough, it was a one-night stand. Of course Portia didn't say that. She said that she adored Josh, had always fancied him too, but that they were better off as friends. She wouldn't be able to bear it if they got involved and then it ended, and she lost him as a friend.

Josh was bewildered by the whole thing: he just nodded mutely and seemed to agree with everything she was saying. And after that everything changed. Josh was bewildered, hurt and confused, and the worst thing was that she didn't just destroy him, she destroyed all of us.

She destroyed our friendships, and, although we tried to forgive her, she'd somehow driven a wedge into the heart of our group and we didn't trust her any more. We were still sharing a house, and Portia would make coffee in the mornings and bring it into my bedroom, curl up at the end of my bed like the old days, but a stiffness hung in the air, and after a while it became difficult to look one another in the eye.

'Where will you be living?' she asked, as we were packing up the house, graduating, getting ready to start our real lives in London.

'With some old school friends,' I lied, knowing that Portia would realise I was lying but not really caring. I never asked her where she was going to be living.

Eddie moved to Manchester, still unable to forgive Portia for hurting Elizabeth as much as she did, and Josh and Si moved to London with me. As we tried to forge ahead with our careers, we drifted further and further apart from Portia until suddenly I realised that I hadn't spoken to her in over three years. None of us had.

I had heard she was living in Clapham. I was in West Hampstead by that time, as were Josh and his wife, Lucy, and Si was in Kilburn, so I knew that with the North/South divide it was unlikely we'd see each other by chance. She'd gone into journalism, and after a while I gathered she'd joined the *Standard*. I'd see her by-line first in tiny letters, and then gradually bigger and bigger, eventually accompanied by a picture in which she looked absolutely stunning.

I was working in advertising. I started as an account executive for a big, buzzy trendy ad agency that had recently scooped armfuls of awards, and I loved it. And every night I'd get on the tube with my copy of the *Standard* and look out for Portia's pieces, savouring every word of my former friend, who was now almost famous.

But then, about two years ago, her by-line disappeared. I thought her name would pop up in another paper, but it never did, and after a while I gave up looking.

Josh and Lucy, and Si, were, are, my closest friends. Eddie is married to Sarah, and has become a hot-shot director for a television company, so we don't see him very often. He remains in touch with Elizabeth. She was at their wedding four years ago, as lovely as she had been back then, but even after all these years she avoided us.

Si is still on the hunt for the perfect man, as indeed was I up until a few years ago, but I've given up now, particularly given that Si is the perfect date for those social and work occasions I can't face on my own.

The funny thing is, if you had asked me whether we would all be friends ten years after graduating from university, I would have said yes, but only if Portia were included, because she was the star around which we all revolved. Yet even without her, it works.

We do talk about her, though. Do still miss her. They say time heals all wounds, but I find myself missing her more as the years go by, and if I'm honest I'd say she's always there, in the back of my mind

Chapter Two

'WHAT SHALL I WEAR?' Si is, as usual, moaning at me down the phone.

'Oh, for God's sake, Si. I'm busy. How come you don't understand the concept of work? Why do you never have anything to *do* except phone me a million times a day?'

I can almost see Si stick out his lower lip in a pretend sulk. 'Fine,' he says, in exactly the tone I would have expected. 'I'll leave you to your work, then, shall I?'

Before I can say anything I hear a click, then the dialling tone. I sigh wearily and punch out his number.

'Have I ever told you how much I hate you?' he says, picking up the phone before it has even rung.

'No you don't. You love me. That's why I'm allowed to say these things to you.'

'Oh, OK, then,' he grumbles. 'But what are *you* wearing? No, no! Let me guess. Black trousers perhaps? A large black tent-like jumper to cover your bum? Black boots?'

'Well, if you know so much, how come you're asking?'

'Cath, you're not a student any more. *Why* do you dress like one?'

'Darling Si. I'm just not interested in clothes, like you. I'm sorry.'

'One day I'll get you to Armani if it kills me.'

'Can I go now?' I say, in my usual exasperated tone. 'I *am* busy, Si. Seriously.'

'You're no fun,' he says. 'I'll come over to yours at seven thirty.'

'Fine, see you la—' and I stop with a sigh because he's already gone.

I smile to myself for a few minutes after I put the phone down, because it is extraordinary that Si manages to do this. He's supposed to be a film editor, although God knows exactly what that means. All I do know is that he works in Soho, which is, as he readily admits, completely perfect for him, because he can go out cruising every night, if he wants to.

He did throughout his twenties, and when Soho became the new gay village and all the seedy hostess bars were replaced with minimalist gay bars, Si thought he'd died and gone to heaven. But he seems to have settled down now and talks about finding someone to cook for, to make a home with, to share everything with. But he's so desperate for commitment, a relationship, anyone who comes even vaguely close is frightened off within days.

'It's my chocolate mousse, isn't it?' he says to me, humour doing a bad job of hiding the pain. 'I *knew* I'd over-whisked those egg whites.'

'Either that or the fact that you slid the onion ring onto the third finger of his left hand after half an hour,' I say, and we both sigh, because neither of us can understand why he can't find someone.

He's not drop-dead gorgeous, but he's certainly cute in a Matthew Broderick sort of way. He's funny, sensitive, kind, thoughtful and has a vicious sense of humour when he feels really comfortable with you.

Every New Year's Eve Si and I make a deal. If neither of us is married by the age of thirty-five, we'll marry each other. It used to be by thirty. And doubtless by the time we hit thirty-five it will move to forty.

I suppose I am slightly in love with him, if only in a platonic way, although there are plenty of times when I wish it could be different. We'd have a hell of a lot of fun, Si and I, if we were married. And I know he loves me more than anyone else in the world. But I also know that when Si goes to bed at night he closes his eyes and dreams of Brad Pitt, and he could never sacrifice that. Not even for me.

The phone rings again. My private line. Which means it's one of three people. My mother. Si. Or Josh. I'm always amazed that Josh manages to call me quite so regularly, but then again I'm not entirely sure I know exactly what he does, money and finance having always been something of an anathema to me. But I do know that he works for one of the big banks in the City. That he is in charge of a team of ten people, and that the only reason he manages to get back to his home in West Hampstead by seven o'clock every night is because he's in the office by 6.00am every morning.

Other than that, I think he has something to do with Mergers and Acquisitions, or M & A, as you're meant to call it in the trade, and I know he's doing well enough not to have to worry about money.

'You must work to live, not live to work,' Josh always laughs, when Si and I tease him about having such an easy life at the age of thirty-two. But, although I am constantly surprised by his lack of ties to the office, I am also impressed, and I know that his family is so important to him that he would never sacrifice his life purely for money.

My line is still ringing, and it could very well be Josh on the phone now, so I pick up, taking my chances.

'*Now* what do you want, Si?'

'Just to tell you that Mr Gorgeous Will has phoned!'

'Fantastic! So when's he coming over to break your heart? Oops, I mean, coming over for dinner?'

'And how do you know this one isn't The One?'

'I'm sorry, my darling. You're quite right. He might be. So you haven't invited him over, then? Let me guess, *he's* taking *you* to some fantabulously swanky restaurant for dinner tomorrow night?'

'Nearly,' he says brightly. '*I'm* cooking *him* a fantabulously swanky meal at my place tomorrow night.'

'You're hopeless,' I say.

'I know,' he replies, but his voice is bubbling over with excitement.

'No chocolate mousse, now,' I warn sternly.

'I know, I know. And I've buried the onion rings in the back garden.'

I get home at seven, cursing the fact that I haven't got a parking space at work, and fantasising about going freelance and never having to take the damn tube again. There are times when I really don't mind it, but then there are times, like tonight, when there are no seats, and you're all crushed together, and everyone is wet from the pouring rain so the carriage is filled with that awful damp smell.

I grab a towel from the bathroom and rub it vigorously over my head, rolling my eyes as I catch sight of myself in the mirror. I should not have been born with this hair. It is just not fair. It is a frizzy mess that used to circle my head rather like a fuzzy halo, and, now that I have tried to grow it, looks increasingly like Marsha Hunt's on a very bad day.

I used to make an effort. I used to wear make-up and have highlights and flirt with strange men in bars, but the older I get the less interested I am. I used to believe in love, in passion, but now I believe that the two cannot go hand in hand, because passion can never be love, and the one great passion of my life was someone I didn't even really like.

I was twenty-four when I met Martin. He really wasn't anything special, not that first time I met him, when he was running a four-day marketing course in Luton.

I remember he took the stage, bounding up to one of those flip charts, and I mentally wrote him off as a boring marketing man.

But by the end of the day I thought he was, quite simply, the most incredible man I had ever met. We all did. Then afterwards, at the drinks party, he singled me out, came over to talk to me. Looked deep into my eyes and told me I had interesting ideas. And all of a sudden I remember thinking that perhaps this was what it was like to fall in love.

Eventually we sat at a table in the corner, with other people who had paid fortunes to come on this course, and Martin fascinated all of us with his stories, his confidence, his charm. But I knew I was special. I knew that there was some sort of magical link between the two of us.

Our table-fellows gradually started to leave. 'Got an early start tomorrow,' they'd say with a wink at Martin, who would laugh politely. Eventually it was just the two of us, and Martin turned to me and said, 'Would you like to come up for a drink? It's rather noisy down here, don't you think? And I have a wonderful Scotch upstairs.'

Of course I knew that whisky meant sex, but I was somehow mesmerised by this man who was giving me his undivided attention and I meekly followed him upstairs.

We spent the next three nights together. I would sit in the front row during his lectures and feel a glow of warmth each time he looked at me, aware that the rumours were already circulating, but not caring.

I like to think that if I had met Martin with the wisdom and cynicism of my current thirty-one years, instead of the romanticism and dreams of twenty-four, there are two things that would have been different.

The first is that I would never have slept with him in the first place, because now I know that these course lecturers regularly look for someone as I was then: a young shy girl, preferably rather plain, who would be flattered and impressed with their false charm and attention.

The second certainty is that when the relationship continued after the four-day course, I would have known that those times when he said he couldn't see me because he was working, those nights when he'd rush out of bed after sex and leave, the fact that he never gave me his telephone number, only a pager, meant only one thing.

Of *course* I should have known he was married. But you see what you want to see, and you hear what you want to hear. I didn't know better. I was so flattered, so swept up by someone, *anyone*, telling me I was beautiful, I didn't stop to think about anything else.

Si knew. Although he didn't say anything at the time. He once tentatively asked me if I thought he might be married, and I was so furious with him he never brought it up again.

The whole *Martin Malarkey* (Si's expression, not mine) lasted two years. Two years that shattered my dreams of romance and love. Two years that taught me never to open myself up again for fear of getting hurt.

In fact the only good thing to come out of it was the weight loss. Even after he confessed he was married, I continued to believe that he loved her but wasn't *in love* with her. I believed that she had happily consented to his wishes to sleep in the spare room and that they hadn't had sex for two years. I believed that the only reason he was staying was because of the children, but as soon as they started school he would leave.

I believed this until I found out she was pregnant again. Don't ask how I found out—a long a complicated story—but I did, and Martin denied it until he could see I wasn't buying the lies any more, and then it was over.

So, as I was saying, the weight loss. I couldn't eat. Quite literally. Could. Not. Eat. For weeks.

'You know you're becoming a lollipop,' Si would say. 'You have this huge hair and a little sticky body. *Please* eat this,' he'd beg, proffering homemade coconut pie with chocolate sauce, or treacle tart, or salmon fishcakes. 'We're *worried* about you.'

Josh and Lucy would invite me over for dinner and exchange concerned glances when they thought I wasn't looking, too busy sighing and poking at pastry with my fork.

Eventually I started becoming happy again, and went back to my normal size. And since then I haven't really been involved with anyone.

There have been a few, but they've always been too short. Or too tall. Too handsome. Not handsome enough. Too young. Too old. Too rich. Too poor. Quite frankly these days I prefer a good book.

'What about Brad?' Si asked me one day.

'Brad who?' We were sitting at a café in West Hampstead, with Josh and Lucy, and a pile of the Sunday papers. It's become a bit of a tradition with us now. One o'clock at Dominique's, every Sunday, for coffee, croissants, scrambled eggs and papers.

'Brad who? Brad who?' he said indignantly. 'There is only one Brad,' he finally exclaimed, adding, 'Brad Pitt. That's who.' Si held up the *Sunday Times* magazine, and pointed to a picture of said man caught in a paparazzi snap coming out of a restaurant.

'What about him?' Lucy asked.

'What about him for Cath?'

'Yes,' I said slowly, as if talking to a child. 'Because Brad Pitt would dump Jennifer Aniston for a short, plain, mousy . . .'

'You're almost blonde,' Si interrupted. 'And he loves blondes! Remember Gwynnie.'

Josh put down his paper and looked at Si, shaking his head. 'Si, what on earth are we talking about? Have you gone mad?'

'No. I just meant that Cath finds fault with every man who even goes near her, and he's completely perfect, but she'd probably find something wrong with him too. Wouldn't you?' He looked at me.

''Course,' I said, examining the picture before exclaiming very seriously, 'his hair's too greasy.'

Josh and Lucy gave up introducing me to their friends a long time ago, but men never seemed to be much of a priority after Martin.

Not that I relished spending the rest of my life by myself, but I wasn't, not with Si, not with Josh and Lucy.

Damn. Si will be here in fifteen minutes and the place looks like a tip. As you would expect, Si's flat, despite being in the less than salubrious area of Kilburn, is immaculate.

Mine, on the other hand, is a mess. The flat itself is in a mansion block, and therefore lovely and large, but interiors have never been quite my thing, and the fact that most of the furniture was passed on by elderly relatives has never particularly bothered me.

It bothers Si, though. Every time he comes over he pulls books off the bookshelf and arranges them in neat little piles on the coffee table, together with whatever bowls he can find. He plumps up cushions and rummages around in my wardrobe for old scarves, which he drapes over furniture, to hide what he calls the 'hideous pieces of crap'. He collects mugs that are gathering mould, and, shooting me filthy looks, takes them into the kitchen, stands them in the sink and covers them in hot, soapy water.

Now I run around the living room, gathering papers, videos, books, and stack them in a precarious pile next to the sofa, well out of Si's view. The mugs are literally thrown into the sink.

At seven thirty on the dot the doorbell rings. I haven't had time for a bath, and I run to the door tugging a cream cardigan over my head because I can't be bothered to undo the buttons.

'Are my eyes deceiving me? Could that be . . . cream?' says Si. 'That's adventurous. What happened to basic black? I don't think I've seen you in a colour for years.'

'It's not a colour,' I say grumpily. 'It's *cream*.' I grab my coat, turning to see Si watching me.

'Sweets,' he says. 'You really should make more of an effort. Put on just a tiny bit of make-up on this gorgeous spring evening. What if Mr Perfect turns up?'

'I don't need Mr Perfect,' I say, closing the door behind us and tucking my arm cosily into Si's. 'I already have you.'

Josh comes to the door with a tea towel in one hand and Max in the other, looking, it has to be said, extremely cute in his little striped pyjamas. That is if you didn't know better.

Even Josh looks rather cute, come to that, with his dirty blond hair mussed up, his shirtsleeves rolled up to show off rather strong and sexy tanned forearms (well, they would be if they didn't belong to Josh).

It's funny how I've never thought of Josh in that way. Maybe it's just that he's too much of an older brother to me now, or maybe it's because I don't believe he's got any sex appeal, but I have never, could never, think of Josh as anything other than a friend.

And yet, looking at him now, purely objectively, he's a good-looking man. He is the sort of man who grows into his looks, who is just now, at thirty-two, starting to look seriously handsome in a boy-next-door kind of way. The deep laughter lines and creases at the corners of his eyes make him look worldly, as if he's been around the block a few times, which God knows he needed, because Josh was, still is, the straightest of all of us.

'Look!' Josh says to Max, after rolling his eyes at me briefly. 'Aunty

Cath and Uncle Si! Do you want to give Aunty Cath a cuddle?' he says brightly, swiftly passing Max to me.

'No!' wails Max, turning back to Josh with a look of sheer panic on his face. 'I want Daddy!'

'Come to Uncle Si,' says Si soothingly, as he effortlessly lifts Max up and starts making him laugh immediately by pulling funny faces. 'Shall we go upstairs and find Tinky Winky?'

Max nods his head vigorously, as Si disappears up the stairs, concentrating hard on Max, who is now chatting away merrily. Josh sighs and leans down to give me a hug. 'Lucy's in the kitchen and I'm supposed to be helping her, but Max has been a bugger today.'

'Kids, eh?' I sigh. 'Who'd have 'em?'

'Tell me about it,' Josh says, but, tired as he looks tonight, I know that he adores Max, that although he might pretend to be unhappy about having to take Max out of Lucy's hair, he secretly loves it.

Josh and Lucy live in a terraced Victorian house that is always messy, always noisy. Most of the activity is focused around the large kitchen at the rear, which wasn't a large kitchen when they moved in two years ago, but, thanks to a smart conservatory extension, is now large enough for a huge dining table that usually has at least three people sitting round it, drinking coffee.

Tonight there is a man I don't recognise sitting there, strange only because I know most of Josh and Lucy's friends, and because I thought it was just going to be the four of us tonight.

Lucy has her back to us, chatting away, finishing an anecdote about work; she trained as an illustrator but seems to have done less and less since having Max. When she does have free time, she seems to spend it doing other things—displacement activity, Si always says. Her latest venture is a course in counselling, and I can hear, from the conversation, that the other person sitting at the table is from the course as well.

Lucy stops mid-sentence as she hears my footsteps. Her face lights up as she puts down a lethal-looking knife, and she gives me a huge hug.

Lucy is one of those people who is always radiant, sickeningly healthy-looking, always smiling, and is the best possible person to talk to if you ever have problems.

I love the fact that this is who Josh chose to marry. For a while Si and I were slightly terrified he was going to pop the question to one of an endless stream of identikit girls with streaky blonde hair, braying laughs and a lack of brain cells, but then he went and surprised us by going on a skiing trip to France and falling madly in love with Lucy. Lucy was the sexy, funny and down-to-earth chalet girl who nursed him back to life with endless mugs of coffee when he fell and twisted his ankle skiing. Lucy, with her ruddy cheeks and raucous laugh, with her rounded figure in faded dungarees, with her winks as she ruffled Josh's hair and told him, repeatedly, that she was built for comfort and not for speed. Lucy, whose maternal instincts were such they were almost oozing out of every pore, who gave birth to Max five months after their wedding.

'Cath! So lovely to see you,' she is exclaiming now. 'Look at you, you look as fresh as a daisy in that sumptuous sweater. Sit! Sit! What are you having? Red? White? Or vodka? Gin?' Lucy bubbles away as she manoeuvres me into a chair, bustling away to open another bottle of red and pour me a glass.

'Where's that wicked Si? Not corrupting my Maxy I hope. Josh!' she screams, 'come and be sociable! Oh God. So rude. You haven't met,' and finally she stops to take a breath and grins at us.

'Cath. Dan. Dan. Cath.'

We smile warmly at one another, and I hope that this will not be one of those awkward evenings where strangers make small talk and ask questions like, 'How long have you known Josh and Lucy?'

'We're all on the course together,' Lucy explains, 'Dan lives in Camden and he gave me a lift, so it was the least I could do.

'Here,' says Lucy, thrusting a knife into my hand. 'You're on cucumber duty.' Dan is given red peppers, which might be an odd way of treating your dinner guests, but it breaks the ice and within minutes we are all laughing like old friends.

'I'm missing out on all the fun, aren't I?' says Si, rushing into the room behind Josh. 'Lucy, darling. You look gorgeous.' Si sweeps Lucy into a big hug, and Lucy blushes, gesturing at her faded apron, her hair tied back with a fraying old scrunchy. 'I look terrible,' she says, but she's delighted, as she always is, when Si compliments her.

'Hello. I'm Si.' He grins cheerfully at Dan, leaning over his shoulder to grab a piece of red pepper.

'Oi!' I dart over, covering Dan's pile of peppers protectively, hunger making me, as always, incredibly territorial about food. 'Hands off.'

'You can't speak to me like that,' Si says, in mock horror. 'You're not even in charge of peppers, so M.Y.O.B.'

'I've got my hands full with one child, thankyouverymuch,' Lucy says, grimacing. 'I don't need another two this evening.'

'It wasn't me, it was her.' Si pours himself a glass of red wine, grinning at Dan, who's laughing at this ridiculous exchange, before going to the stove and lifting lids off pots and sniffing.

I wish I could be more like Si at times. I know how insecure he is deep down, as insecure as the rest of us, and yet he has this ability to meet complete strangers and instantly put them at ease, make them feel as if they have known, and loved, Si for ever.

He wanders over to the fridge and busies himself doing something, while the rest of us keep chopping.

'So how is the course?' I throw into the room.

Lucy and Dan groan at the same time.

'It was fine,' says Lucy.

'Until Jeremy,' says Dan.

'And now we can't wait until the bloody thing's over,' finishes Lucy.

'Jeremy?' I ask.

'Jeremy,' says Josh, in the tone of voice that says I ought to know who Jeremy is. 'Jeremy the class bore,' he continues, rolling his eyes, evidently having heard more than enough about him from Lucy. 'Who monopolises every group session by talking about himself, having temper tantrums if he feels he's being ignored.'

'Oh, that sounds so mean,' says Lucy. 'I feel awful talking about him behind his back. It's not right. We actually shouldn't be doing this.'

'You're right.' Dan sounds contrite, for about two seconds. 'But fuck it. He is a major pain in the arse.'

Lucy remembers something, jumps up, checks her recipe book and pushes Si out of the way to get to the fridge. She pulls the butter out, then stops as she closes the fridge door and squints at a point on the upper left side of the door.

'Si!' She shrieks with laughter as Si skulks over to the table, trying to look innocent. 'Luscious Sexy Smells Excite My Potent a r m p I t s'

'Armpits?' Josh looks bemused. 'That magnetic poetry kit doesn't have the word "armpits".'

'I spelt it out myself,' Si says proudly, and within seconds we are all clamouring round the fridge trying to out-do one another with ridiculously flowery poems.

'Come on, then, guys, who's going to set the table?' Lucy says, handing me the cutlery, glasses to Dan, and napkins to Si, who instantly arranges them into little swans, prompting much oohing and aahing from Lucy. 'It's so pretty I don't want to undo it,' she says, placing it gently down on her plate.

The five of us sit down and help ourselves to Caesar salad.

'Bugger.' Lucy jumps up and runs to the oven, bringing out a familiar-looking silver loaf.

'Lucy, I love you!' Si blows her Parmesany kisses from the other side of the table. 'You never forget.'

'Si, I only do this for you, you know. I'd never *dream* of serving garlic bread to anyone else. It's just so seventies.'

'Seventies is in again now,' says Josh, shaking his head at Si, who's licking dripping butter off his fingers. 'God, do you remember that seventies party Portia had, Si?' he laughs. 'When you and Cath set fire to my Afro wig?'

'It practically stuck to your head.' I smile at the memory. 'I haven't thought about that in years.'

'Portia,' says Dan. 'I know a Portia. What's her surname?'

'Fairley,' say Si, Josh and I simultaneously.

Dan smiles as the rest of the table freezes. 'I knew that wasn't a common name. How do you all know Portia?'

How can a name from the past still have such an impact on the three people in this room who knew her way back when? Time seems to stand still, and I'm too lost in memories to notice that Josh and Si are diving into those memories at the same time.

And the thing is, I can't help but wonder if she's forgiven us. I forgave her, forgave her for breaking Josh's heart, a long time ago. I figured that she must have had her reasons, that she wasn't doing it intentionally, but I've always wondered whether she has forgiven us for abandoning her friendship as a result.

'We were at university together,' I eventually tell a bemused Dan, because he can see his words have had some effect, only he is not sure what it is. 'And you? How do you know Portia?' I say doing my best to keep the excitement contained.

'She bought my old flat,' he laughs. 'Nice flat in Sutherland Avenue. I miss it. Wish I didn't have to sell but there it is. Give up your job in the City for psychotherapy and bach pad goes with it, I'm afraid.' He shrugs and smiles at Si and Lucy, who offer him sympathetic smiles in return.

'She was beautiful,' Si says dreamily. 'One of those girls whose life was perfect. She had money, class, beauty, kindness. Born with a golden spoon in her mouth. We followed her career as a journalist for a while, but lost track. Do you know what she's up to now?'

'Sure,' says Dan. 'I'm surprised you didn't know. Haven't you seen that series on TV?' He mentions the name of a series we all love. A weekly drama that follows the lives of a group of thirty-somethings. Suddenly I realise that she is the writer. She could not be anything other than the writer because, and I know this should have occurred to me before, because all of the characters are based on us.

I look at the others and see Josh's mouth hanging open, Si's eyes wide with shock, both having had the same realisation.

'Oh my God, she writes it!' Si snorts, half in wonderment, half aghast.

'She doesn't just write it,' Dan says. 'She came up with the concept, sold it to the network, does all the writing and to top it all has sold it on to seventeen countries worldwide. She's making a fortune.'

Si looks at Josh, and coughs, attempting to regain some composure. 'Excuse me, can you pass the salt please, *Jacob*.'

'Don't be ridiculous,' says Lucy, 'they're not u—' and she stops, because in the split second it took for her to verbalise that thought, she had another. A memory. She remembered the characters.

The central character is Mercedes (good joke, I thought). Mercedes is the daughter of a millionaire who has spent her life struggling for independence. Mercedes looks like she ought to be a bitch. But of course she's not. She's adorable, although she can't seem to find a man who looks beyond the physical, who is interested in getting to know her.

There's Jacob, world-weary, kind, but rather weak, who's married to Lisa, an overbearing Sloane who's too busy shopping and lunching to take much care of their toddler, Marty.

Steen is the perfect gay best friend, who keeps the laughs coming in with his curt one-liners.

And Mark. Gorgeous, sensitive Mark, who loves Mercedes unrequitedly, for he is far too nice for Mercedes to love in return, and he, of course, could only be Matt, Portia's boyfriend from university.

And then, I realise with horror, there's Katy. Katy, who is plain, dowdy, but completely self-obsessed. Katy who only wears black. Or occasionally sludge-green. Katy, whose hair looks like it could house a few hundred sparrows in it if they were really stuck for accommodation.

Lucy suddenly chokes, and we all look at one another in panic, terrified she's choked with shock, but she has a sip of water and then starts laughing. And laughing. And laughing.

'It's hysterical,' she says, as we slowly see the funny side. 'You're Katy!' and she points at me and goes off into peals of laughter again, almost falling off her chair, arms weak with mirth.

'You can laugh,' I say in a nasty tone. 'She hasn't even met you. She's obviously just heard that Josh married someone who's name begins with an L, who has a son whose name begins with an M. I'm Katy, for God's sake. Katy, who's a selfish cow. I can't believe she'd do that to me.'

'Are you sure about this?' Dan says, looking more than a little worried about all this. 'Are you sure the characters are you?'

'Look at us,' says Josh with a shrug.

'I'm happy,' Si says brightly. 'Steen's gorgeous.'

'Don't you mind?' says Dan suddenly. 'Don't you mind that someone whom you knew has written your life stories down and shown them to thousands of people?'

'Millions, according to the ratings,' adds Josh. Quietly.

'Not quite our life stories.' Lucy gets up to check the pudding. 'Josh really isn't Jacob. Josh is far stronger than that. And Katy isn't Cath. She's gorgeous, for starters.' She gives me a quick squeeze as she passes, which is supposed to make me feel better. And does, as it happens. 'As for Steen'—she eyes Si up and down—'Si's far sweeter than Steen.'

'Not to mention far more handsome,' prompts Si.

'Of course,' she laughs. 'And far more handsome.'

'You know what it is,' muses Josh, staring into his glass of wine as if it holds all the answers. 'This is sort of her revenge, isn't it? She's taken the worst aspects of our characters and magnified them. But the weird thing is, she's taken our characters as she knew them then, and I for one think I've changed immeasurably. We all have.'

'Revenge for what?' asks Dan, intrigued, as a silence falls and we all start to look slightly shifty.

'It's a long story,' Lucy says matter-of-factly, able to do so because she wasn't involved, she simply heard all about it many years later. 'A story for another time.' The disappointment shows on Dan's face, but he's polite enough not to push the point.

'So what about Portia?' Si asks finally. 'Is she the breathtaking Mercedes? Perfect on the outside but unable to find lurrve?'

'Who knows,' shrugs Dan. 'She's very beautiful, but I only met her the few times she came to my flat with interior designers and stuff.'

'Interior designers,' I smile. 'So Portia.'

'I can give you my old number if you like,' Dan says suddenly. 'I don't think she changed it.'

'No, no,' says Josh. 'It was all a long time ago.' I see him shoot a worried glance at Lucy, but she doesn't look bothered in the slightest.

'We were just curious.' Si's voice is nonchalant. 'That's all.'

'I'd like her number,' I find myself saying, even though I hadn't planned for those words to come out of my mouth.

And later, as Si and I walk back to my flat in silence, we both find ourselves immersed in thoughts of Portia, memories of our gang, the strength of our love for one another.

'I do still miss her,' Si says softly as he hugs me goodbye.

I pull back and look at him. 'Maybe that's why we met Dan tonight. Everything happens for a reason, doesn't it, Si? Maybe I was supposed to get her number. Maybe none of us is supposed to miss her any more.'

Chapter Three

I LOSE MY NERVE. It's not that I don't try, I do. For the last two weeks I've picked up the phone at least twice a day, Portia's scribbled number on a scrap of paper, mocking me from the table next to the telephone. I've even got as far as dialling all seven digits, but as soon as the phone starts to ring, I slam it down, not knowing what to say.

'Well?' Si asks, as he asks on a daily basis. 'Have you done it yet?'

'Yes,' I say earnestly, slowly. 'And I decided not to tell you that in fact I saw her last week, because I didn't think you'd be interested.'

'God, you're being such a wimp,' Si says. 'If it were me, I'd just pick up the phone and call her.'

'Go on, then,' I push the phone towards him. 'Do it.'

It's a Thursday night, the night of Portia's series, which Si has been coming over to watch for months, since our newfound discovery. Earlier on this evening, instead of laughing our way through the show as we usually do, we are glued to the flickering blue screen, desperately searching for clues to our own characters.

'I'd *never* say that,' Si exclaimed indignantly, after Steen emerged with a particularly bitchy line.

'No one's saying you would.' I rubbed his back gently, eyes still fixed on the show, waiting for Katy to come back in.

'Jesus,' I whistled a few minutes later. 'I know it's meant to be funny, but she is so selfish. I'm not like that, am I?'

'Sssh,' urged Si. 'Here comes Steen again.'

And now it's over, and Si grabs the phone and dials the number, giving away nothing, looking as if he's phoning Josh, just for a chat.

I watch his face intently, waiting for him to become animated, but he shakes his head after a few seconds and says, 'Answerphone.'

I grab the phone from him and listen to Portia's voice.

I'm so sorry neither of us can get to the phone. Leave a message and we'll get back to you. Thanks for calling.

'Neither of us?' I look at Si. 'That means she's married.'

'And what decade are *you* living in?' Si is horrified. 'The fifties?'

'OK, not necessarily married, but living with someone, then.'

'Look,' Si says, gesturing at the phone, 'this is the perfect opportunity to find out. You want to talk to her, but you don't actually want to *talk* to her, and I know you're terrified of how she'll react. I am too. This way you can leave a message, and then it's up to her. She may not call, but at least if she does you'll know it's because she wants to.'

I grab the phone, hit the redial button and listen to her message again, trying to smile so that I sound cheerful, happy and successful.

Beeeeeep.

'Portia, hi. Umm. This is, umm, quite strange, hearing your voice on the machine.' Si rolls his eyes at me. 'I mean, because we haven't spoken for ages. Years. Your name came up the other night at dinner—we met Dan, the guy who sold you his flat, and it's just that we were wondering how you were, and it would be really nice to see you. Anyway, give me a call, if you want. Oh. It's Cath, by the way . . . *beeep.*'

'Shit! her machine cut me off.' I said, feeling like an idiot.

'There,' says Si. 'That's done, then.'

'Do you think she'll call?'

'If she hasn't changed, she will.'

'You're right.' I nod thoughtfully. 'If she hasn't changed, she'll call.'

Ever since I can remember I have loved books. Not just loved, but been passionate about. I regularly spend hours at a time browsing in bookshops, losing track of time, losing myself in another world.

My dream has always been to own a bookshop. Actually, my dream has always been to own a bookshop that also encompasses a café. I envision it as the sort of place that would attract regulars, lovable eccentrics who would step in to make the cappuccinos if I needed a hand.

It would be a laid-back kind of place. There would be beaten-up old leather sofas, squashy armchairs, possibly a fireplace in winter. Of course, when it's summer I envision it in a completely different light. Then it's light, bright, breezy with stripped pine floors, huge glass windows and Mediterranean-blue walls.

I indulge in this fantasy more frequently as I get older. I used to think that I would work until I had enough money in the bank to open my bookshop, and when I did, I would hand in my notice and get going.

But, of course, enough money is never quite enough, and even although I seem to have amassed a fairly sizeable amount (thanks largely to my lovely grandmother, who died and left me her flat in Wembley a couple of years ago), I know it will never be enough to allow me to jump ship, because actually it's not about the money at all.

Si says I'm scared, and of course he's right. I haven't got the nerve.

'Cath, darling! We need to meet. When are you free?' Lucy's voice is bubbling over with excitement, making me smile.

'Why? What's happened? You're not pregnant again, are you?'

Lucy shrieks. 'God, no. Not yet. This is much more important. I have a proposal to put to you.'

'I can't marry you,' I laugh. 'I'd love to, but you're already married.'

'If I were a big strapping chap, I would certainly marry you, but this, Cath, is something else entirely.'

'Go on, give me a clue.'

'Can't. Not on the phone. Can you meet me this afternoon?'

I flick open my work diary on the desk and check the rest of the day. Thankfully there are no more meetings, and, although I don't do this often, I agree to scoot off early to go to meet Lucy.

'Hoorah!' she says, when I agree. 'Come over to me, then, and we'll have a coffee. See you later. Bye bye.'

'Hello, Max. It looks like you've been eating something yummy.' Max stands in the doorway, blocking my path, looking at me with a mixture of disdain and pity, which is quite extraordinary, bearing in mind he's three years old and half his face is covered in chocolate.

I'm not, as you may have gathered, a natural with children. In fact I'd go so far as to say that when God created me, he seemed to have forgotten all about my maternal instinct.

'If you're a good boy, Cath will give you a present. Would you like that?' I feel ridiculous, saying these things to him, but I don't know how else to talk to a three-year-old.

I've watched Si with envy, because Si doesn't treat Max like a child, he treats him like an adult. I've actually seen Si walk in, sit down next to Max and say, 'God, what a terrible day I've had a work. Do you want to hear about my day?' And Max will nod very seriously, as Si proceeds to talk at him about film rushes and editing, and things being left on the cutting-room floor.

But what's even more ridiculous, is that Max *loves* it. *Adores* it. He cannot take his eyes off Si during these conversations, yet no matter what I say to Max, how large my bribes, he never seems to change the way he acts with me.

I bring a lollipop out of my pocket and extend it to Max, who takes it out of my hand, turns his back, and disappears down the hallway.

'Max!' Lucy shouts, running after him and sweeping him up. 'I saw that! Don't be so rude. You must say thank you when someone gives you something.' She rolls her eyes at me, and drops Max at my feet.

'Fank you.' He looks at the floor, lollipop already in his mouth.

'You're welcome,' I say, as he trundles off again. I follow Lucy into the kitchen, the smell of freshly baked biscuits making me salivate. 'He does hate me, you know,' I say, pulling off my coat and throwing it on a chair.

'He doesn't hate you, he's just at that difficult age,' she says.

'He's been at that difficult age since he was born.'

'Bloody men,' she laughs. 'They're all the same. Now, have some homemade, fresh-from-the-oven, apple-and-cinnamon biscuits.'

I rub my stomach and take one from the plate Lucy sets on the table, not bothering to wait for the tea that ought to be the accompaniment.

'Lucy,' I mumble, mouth full, trying to catch the buttery crumbs that fall as I speak. 'These are amazing.'

'You're so sweet.' Lucy breaks into one of her dazzling smiles. 'That's why I adore having you over. I just can't bear all these sticklike girls who eat only lettuce. Have some more.'

I happily comply, knowing that even those sticklike girls would have trouble finding will-power if they had a friend who could cook like Lucy.

Lucy brings the teapot to the table. 'Cath, are you happy?'

'What? What do you mean?'

'I mean at work. Do you enjoy what you're doing?'

'I love my work,' I say, suddenly realising that I am only saying this because, up until recently, it is what I have always said. Except now my words sound hollow and empty, even to me.

I start again. 'Well, I quite enjoy it, but not like I used to. What a strange question, what are you up to?'

Lucy sighs. 'I've just been thinking an awful lot recently, about why we're here. For years I always thought I wanted to help people, which is why I'm doing this bloody counselling course, although thank God it's practically over.' She pauses to drink some tea.

'But the thing is,' she continues, 'I haven't done any proper illustrating since Max was born, and to be totally honest I don't think I want to do it any more. This is going to sound awful.' She looks at me sheepishly, then smiles. 'But I feel like I've devoted these last few years to helping other people, looking after other people, being Josh's wife and Max's mother, and, although I adore looking after my boys, I think that now I need to do something for myself.' There's a long pause. 'What do you think?'

'I think that if that's what you want to do, then that's what you should do. Absolutely.' Even as I say it I know I should be applying those rules to myself, but then I haven't got a husband who would pick up the pieces if everything went horribly wrong. Who could afford to take on the entire mortgage if my money ran out. 'So what are you thinking of doing?' I ask, curiosity getting the better of me.

'Ah,' she says, breaking into a smile. 'Now that's where, hopefully, you come in.' She stands up. 'Grab your coat. We're going for a walk.'

As we reach the bottom of the stairs, Lucy yells out to the au pair, 'Ingriiiiiiiid? I'm going out. Won't be long.'

Ingrid appears at the top of the stairs. 'OK, Lucy,' she says stonily, ignoring the fact that Max appears to be wrapping a lasso around her left leg. 'See you.'

'She is a godsend,' Lucy says, closing the front door, which slightly surprises me, as personally I think she's a cow.

'So where are we going?' I walk alongside Lucy, up her road, on to West End Lane, smiling because it's impossible not to feel good when the sun is shining and the pavements outside the cafés are crowded with tables and chairs, with people enjoying the sunshine.

'Surprise,' she says. 'But you'll see when we get there.'

'**H**ere we are,' says Lucy, stopping in front of an empty shop on West End Lane and turning to look at me expectantly.

I look at what she's looking at. An empty shop in between the organic deli and the shop that sells strange wooden carvings. A shop that you can't see into because all the windows are obliterated by huge, multi-coloured posters advertising bands, concerts, gigs.

'And we are here why?' I ask.

'Oh, Cath, darling. You're being thick. This is the perfect place for my new business. Well, actually, hopefully, our new business.'

'What business is this?'

'Your bookshop and my coffee shop.'

I look at Lucy, at her beaming eyes, expectant face, and I am amazed that she has remembered my dream, and more amazed that she wants to do it with me.

'How on earth did you remember that? I must have told you years ago.'

She links her arm through mine as we stand next to one another, trying to see into the shop.

'The thing is,' she says, 'it actually wouldn't be that difficult, and Josh would help, and we'd only have to employ, say, two other people to make it work, and Cath, please say yes, because I think we could do it. I *know* we could do it.'

'You're serious, aren't you?' I stop and look at Lucy's shining face with amazement, feeling nervous and excited, and not sure whether we could actually pull this off.

Because isn't that the thing with fantasies? Fantasies are absolutely safe, as long as you never try to make them a reality.

But, as I look into Lucy's eyes, behind the sparkle I can see steely determination, and God knows Lucy could do it. There really wouldn't be anything to be frightened of if Lucy were a partner.

'Have I convinced you yet?' Lucy grins.

'God, Lucy.' I shake my head. 'It's not as easy as that. There's so much to think about. My flat, the mortgage, my job. I mean, Christ, could I just walk out? My savings, because this would be it . . .' I'm so caught up in my world of problems I don't even realise that Lucy has steered me across the road and into an estate agent's. 'Come on,' she says. 'I found this site and I think it might be ideal, even though I haven't seen the inside, so I thought it might help to convince you.'

The door closes behind us as a young man in a navy suit looks up from where he's perched on the corner of a desk, sifting through papers.

'Hi.' He looks up, smiling broadly, putting the papers onto a desk and brushing a lock of mousy brown hair out of eyes that are surprisingly twinkly. 'Can I help at all?' His voice is deep, with just a hint of an accent that I can't quite place. Definitely south of England, possibly Dorset or Wiltshire. Whatever it is he looks far too *normal* to be an estate agent.

I always imagine estate agents to be smart and slick, dressed in sharp suits with mobile phones surgically attached to their ears, and though this man is wearing a navy suit, he looks as if he'd be far more comfortable in a chunky woollen sweater and a pair of faded jeans.

I realise I'm staring and look away quickly, pretending to be absorbed in the grains of wood on the floorboards.

'We're looking for James,' Lucy says, as the man stands up.

'Let me guess. You're Lucy Portman.' His laughter lines grow deeper, and I comprehend with a shock that this is a seriously attractive man.

'James?'

'None other.' They shake hands, as I try to be as unobtrusive as possible. I glance up to see him looking at me with an eyebrow raised.

'Hi, I'm Cath, er, Catherine Warner,' I mumble, awkwardly.

'Nice to meet you, Cath,' he says, looking directly into my eyes. He releases my hand and walks over to another desk, picking up a set of keys. 'Shall we go?'

We cross the road again to the empty shop, me still in shock.

'You know, the more I think about it the more I think it's a brilliant idea,' James says, as he unlocks the door. 'A café/bookshop. Just what this area needs, and wait until you see inside. The space you're looking at is perfect.'

'You don't know of any others, do you?' says Lucy, vaguely anxiously. 'I've tried to find out, but I don't think there are any.'

'There is a bookshop, and there are plenty of cafés, but this area's so young and buzzy, the combination's bound to go down well.'

Now I know he's only an estate agent, and I know he's got no experience of running a café/bookshop, but because he has somehow validated this idea, I start to feel excited.

Lucy takes my hand, giving it a quick, reassuring squeeze, as we both gingerly step in. We don't say anything for a while, just wander around, trying to envisage whether it could be what we're looking for. What, in fact, I wasn't looking for up until an hour ago, but still. What the hell.

But as our eyes adjust to the gloom, lit by a solitary light bulb in each room, Lucy and I gasp, because the only thing this place is, it could ever have been, is a bookshop.

Surrounding the walls are beautifully made wooden shelves, stretching from floor to ceiling, the shelves acting as partitions, forming an open library. The craftsmanship is superb, and I realise how absolutely perfect this place is.

And the space is huge. The ceilings go up for ever, and, as my eyes adjust to the one swinging lamp bulb, I can see that there is a gallery in the larger room.

'Can you believe it?' Lucy keeps whispering. 'Can you believe it?'

There's one large L-shaped room with a huge picture window at the back, and a slightly smaller room next door.

Lucy starts reading the details James has brought with him, and excitedly walks to the back of the shop, where she pushes open a door.

'Look! Cath! The kitchen!' And then she runs into the larger room and, sure enough, off the L-shape is another room.

'Let me guess.' I smile wryly. 'Stock room?'

'Isn't it perfect, Cath?' she says, whirling around. 'Close your eyes and can't you hear those pages rustling? Smell the coffee?'

I smile at her, swaying gently in the middle of the floor, eyes squeezed tight, able to see exactly what it will be like. And of course it is perfect. It would make the perfect café/bookshop. I'm just not sure that I have the nerve to get involved with something entirely different.

'What was it before? It must have been a bookshop, but I don't remember.'

'Believe it or not it's been empty for about twenty years,' James says. 'It was owned by one of the local eccentrics. He died last year in his nineties, but up until the week he died he used to go to work every day, dressed in a three-piece suit, immaculately turned out.'

'And?' Lucy's eager to hear what happens, loving nothing more than a good story.

'We all thought Harry was a bit of a chancer.' James smiles fondly at the memory. 'He used to come into the office to talk about property, and we'd indulge him because we thought it made him feel good. But he turned out to be worth millions.'

'No!' Lucy breathes in awe. 'Really?'

'I'm not kidding,' James said. 'He lived in a hovel of a flat. Really disgusting. Threadbare carpets, chairs held together by string; but he owned about half of the commercial property in the area.'

'But didn't you know?' I asked. 'You must have known?'

'That's the ridiculous thing,' James says. 'He just leased them all out for next to nothing. When they were going through his estate they realised that he had been sitting on a fortune.'

'So they sold them off,' he continues. 'And this one had just been sitting here for years. We'd tried to find out who owned it. Everyone in the area had, but this was the one property he'd never leased out.'

'Oooh. How fascinating. Why do you think?' Lucy squeals.

James shrugs. 'All sorts of rumours have flown about. Allegedly it was a bookshop, and the previous owner was a woman he'd had an affair with. She was supposed to be the one great love of his life, but she was already married and wouldn't leave her husband. He never got over it, or so they say.' He grins at us. 'But you never know with rumours.'

'How romantic, how wonderful,' Lucy says, hugging herself with happiness.

'It's crying out for some TLC,' James says, looking at me. 'But, as I explained to Lucy the other day, all the basics are here. Stick in a new kitchen, a bar in the middle here, and a coat of paint, and I really can't imagine a more perfect spot for your business.'

'Have you had much interest?' I ask casually.

'We've only just got it,' he says. 'So we haven't started marketing it properly yet, but we're putting ads in the trade press next week. It will go like a shot.'

Lucy looks dispirited. 'That means we must act quickly, Cath,' she advises sternly. 'Come on now.' She grabs my arm and turns to James, flashing him a dazzling smile. 'James, you are an absolute angel for showing us at such short notice. We'll ring you in the morning.'

James, still stunned by the radiance of Lucy's smile, nods, and we leave him basking in the excitement and joy Lucy has left behind.

'Low-halogen spots, lots of pale wood, very sunny. What do you think?' Lucy's pacing round the kitchen, words tumbling out of her mouth.

'I think,' Josh says slowly, looking at me, 'you should (a) stop pacing round the floor, and (b) ask Cath what she thinks.'

Lucy stops in mid-step and looks at me, mortified. 'Cath! Darling! I'm so sorry.' She runs over and gives me a big hug. 'I just haven't stopped talking. God, I'm so selfish. Tell me. What do you think?'

'It's all a bit much for me,' I say. 'I mean, it's not that I don't want to do it, it's my life's dream, but I just don't know if I could really leave my job and do this. What if it were a massive failure? What if we lost all our money? I'd have to put my life savings into this.'

'Not necessarily,' Josh says slowly.

'Come on, Joshy,' Lucy says. 'You're the clever banker. How could we minimise the risk?'

'You could go with a backer,' he says thoughtfully. 'But then again, maybe it's best to keep the investors to a minimum.' He sits in silence for a while as Lucy makes faces at me. 'You know,' he says eventually, 'it might actually be far less than you think. I'd say around a hundred thousand pounds once you've sorted out builders, alterations, stock cost, etc. One of the guys at work has parents who own a bookshop. It's in Derbyshire or somewhere. I'll have a word with him.'

He walks over to the dresser and pulls out some plates, napkins, and lays them on the table. 'But as for the idea—I do actually think it will work. You'll have to do your research, of course, but the cafés that are already there seem to be full all the time, so there's obviously room for one more, and we need a populist bookshop, one that stocks a good range of books across the board. You can't compete with Waterstone's or Books Etc., but you can offer a next-day delivery from the wholesalers.'

Lucy's looking at him with affection. 'Darling husband of mine, tell me how you know all this?'

Josh shrugs. 'And the other thing,' he continues, 'is that as far as I know most books are stocked in bookshops on a sale or return basis, so apart from the refurbishment of the shop, and the catering outlay, it wouldn't be as much risk as, say, a clothes shop.

'Plus, Lucy, we could always remortgage the house. God knows I'd rather use the money for a business venture than for a holiday.'

'What about your son's schooling?'

'We'll cross that bridge when we come to it. And Cath, what about that money from your grandma?'

I gasp. 'How do you know about that?'

'Because you told me, Cath. You asked my advice on investing it, then promptly ignored it, and I bet it's been sitting in the bank all these years gaining nothing on interest.'

I choose to stay silent.

'Exactly. It's about time you made that money work for you. God, between the two of you, you can do this thing, no problem.'

'Have I ever told you how much I love you?' Lucy says suddenly, flinging her arms around Josh and planting a smacker on his cheek.

'Yes,' Josh smiles. 'Does that mean you love me enough to serve me dinner?'

Lucy flops into a chair with a grin. 'Nope,' she says happily. 'You cooked, you serve. That's the deal.'

'So let me get this straight. You're thinking of leaving your super-duper, high-powered fantastic job that pays you a fortune, to set up your own business with Lucy?'

'What's wrong with Lucy?'

Si begged and pleaded for me to meet him for a drink after work in Soho, and, even though it's a pain trying to find a black cab when it's going-home time, I could do with a fun night out, so what the hell. Is this a sign of getting old? That going out for dinner now usually means going home after work, then popping up the road to a comfortable, cosy local restaurant? That I never have to even consider making an effort with my clothes? That not only am I always home by eleven o'clock, but that if I weren't I might possibly die of exhaustion?

I wasn't always like this. Honestly. In the early days, post Martin, I threw myself into the club scene with wild abandon. Si would come and pick me up at midnight, and we'd hit the one-nighters all over town, ending up sipping coffee at Bar Italia in the early hours of the morning.

To be honest, I've been feeling for some time that I'm slightly stuck in a rut. I love my friends. Would die for them. But part of me would quite like to meet a man, and unless I manage either to convert Si or to steal Josh from Lucy, neither of which is a particularly appealing option, I think it's highly unlikely, unless I drastically change my life.

So Lucy's plan seems to have come at exactly the right time. Think of all the new people I'd meet! Think about what it would be like to have my own business! To—oh joy of joys—go to work almost on the doorstep of my home and never go on the tube again.

It was all I could think about at work today. Work? I didn't do any. I sat in my office, closed the door and fantasised the day away. By mid-morning I'd planned the lighting. By lunchtime Lucy and I were playing the convivial hosts, loved and adored by the entire community, and by the end of the day we were being written up in the *Ham & High*.

'So what *is* wrong with Lucy?' I ask again, when Si refuses to answer.

'It's not for me to say.'

'Right,' I mock. 'If not you, then who?'

'Oh, OK,' he sighs. 'If you insist. It's just that Lucy's wonderful, and we all adore her, but she's not a businesswoman.'

'But that's the point, Si. That's why Josh is looking into it before we do anything, but anyway I'm the one with the common sense. Lucy's the creative person. She'll help with the design, the concept, and, let's face it, she is the best cook in London.'

'That's true,' he agrees. 'So what exactly would you be doing?'

'What do you mean?'

'Cath, sweets, I know you have good business acumen, but it's in advertising, not in bookshops. It's all very well Lucy being the creative person, but you know next to nothing about running a bookshop, and I'm not sure if this isn't too big a challenge for you.'

'Actually, I think you're wrong,' I say with certainty, slightly pissed off at Si for pointing out the obvious, but pleased that it is firing my determination. 'I mean, I'm sure Lucy wouldn't have asked me if she didn't think I could contribute something, and there's no way Josh would let either of us do it if he didn't think it was a viable proposition.'

'Cath,' Si says, suddenly serious. 'Do you want my honest opinion?'

I nod.

'My honest opinion, and remember I'm only giving you this because I love you and I want you to be careful, but my honest opinion is that you should become involved on some level, but certainly not throw in your job until it's established and it's successful. Lucy doesn't really have anything to lose, and if it went horribly wrong, then Josh could always pick up the pieces. You are the one with the most at stake here, and you'd stand to lose the most.

'I'm not saying don't do it, I'm saying think about it. Hell, work in the shop at weekends, organise reading groups, events, anything you want. Just don't give everything up yet, that's all.'

I know what he's saying makes sense. But I also know that there's no way on earth I will let Lucy fulfil my lifelong dream without me in it. I just won't tell Si. That's all.

'And by the way,' he adds with a twinkle, secure in the knowledge that I've listened to him and taken his advice, 'if I gave Lucy my application form for a Saturday job, would you make sure I got it?'

'Only if you pay me enough.' I squeeze a smile, and we sit in silence for a few moments, then Si looks at me and lets out a big sigh.

'I know you too bloody well.' He shakes his head.

'What?'

'You're sitting there thinking; Screw Si, I'm going to do it anyway.'

I know I'm not supposed to be smiling at this, but I can't help it: a grin flashes up.

I cannot believe how quickly this all seems to be happening. Six weeks ago there I was, stuck in my job, wondering if there would ever be an end to all of this, and praying for summer to arrive early just to make me feel better.

The next minute I'm caught up in Lucy's whirlwind of interior design, recipe ideas, hurried phone calls to the estate agent to make sure it's still ours. And God, am I glad I didn't take Si's advice. I cannot think of anything worse than watching Lucy do this without me, because I have loved, am loving, every minute of it.

The scariest bit was actually handing in my notice at the agency. They offered me more money to stay, but my mind was well and truly made up. That first Monday morning, when I didn't have to get up at the crack of dawn and catch the tube to work, I suddenly realised what I'd done and panic set in. But then, later that day, Lucy dragged me to a meeting with the carpenter in the shop, and once we'd spent half an hour talking about bars and counters and display shelves, it started to feel real again and, more importantly, started to feel right.

And then the meetings started. We were hoping we wouldn't have to do a business plan, Lucy and I managing to raise £120,000 between us, but we hadn't banked on working capital: paying employees; paying the bills; managing the inventory; petty cash and all the other minor day-to-day expenses that you never think about when it's still just a fantasy.

So Josh said we had to go to the bank. We set aside the best part of a week and drew up a business plan, and every night, when Josh got home, we'd run it by him, moaning and groaning because he kept telling us we had to make it more businesslike.

But eventually we got it right. We took it to the bank, and they agreed to lend us a further £100,000, which was far more than we'd even dreamed. And Josh and Lucy remortgaged their house, which meant we could buy the shop in the first place.

One day Lucy and I travelled up to Derbyshire and spent the day with Ted and Linda, the people Josh had told us about who own a bookshop, and their advice was invaluable.

And eventually contracts were exchanged, with the completion date amazingly set for the same day, and we could actually start work. It was touch and go for a while, us getting the shop, but James managed to swing it our way, despite the competition that suddenly appeared.

James has been fantastic, and the more I know him, the more I like him. I know I shouldn't be that surprised, but he really does seem to be honest, straight, to have integrity. Lucy's also pointed out that he's rather dishy, but to be perfectly honest he's not my type. If I have a type any more, that is.

The snowball appears to be gathering momentum with every passing minute, and last week, when the builders had finally moved out, Lucy and I were able to do the one job we'd been looking forward to since the beginning—painting Bookends ourselves. Corny name, I know, but it seemed to fit.

Lucy and I have been to Homebase. Have selected the perfect shade of sunshine yellow for the walls. Have contacted local hire companies for huge, professional sanding machines to sand down the floor ourselves. Have found a 'carpenter from heaven'—Lucy's words—who's building the bar for a knockdown price.

Lucy's been developing new recipes, although no one's allowed to taste until she's absolutely ready, and I've run up huge phone bills calling Edward—a distant cousin who works in sales at one of the major publishers—and picking his brains about the how, what, when and where of stocking a bookshop.

Even Si, loath though he is to admit it, is impressed, although I know he won't actually come out and say so until we're up and running.

'**H**ave you seen their house? Have you seen what's happened to their house?' Si's borrowed a huge, shaggy mutt called Mouse to walk in the park. Except we're not walking in the park simply to enjoy the pleasures that nature can offer. It means that Si's on the hunt for Mr Right. Si has this theory that every woman, and/or gay man, should have a dog. This is because, he says, most men go weak at the knees over dogs. Not small dogs, though. Big, strapping dogs. Alsatians, Labradors, Retrievers. Real dogs.

Mouse belongs to Steve and Joe, and Si discovered the joys of Mouse when Steve and Joe bought a holiday home in Tenerife and Si was enlisted to dog-sit while they were away.

Si phoned me after he'd taken Mouse for his first walk. He was breathless with excitement. 'I have to get a dog of my own,' he said.

'Because?'

'Because I've never met so many gorgeous men in my life!'

Apparently Si and Mouse had been minding their own business, walking up Frith Street, when three—three!—gorgeous men stopped to pat Mouse and say what a handsome dog he was. Never mind the fact that none of them had gone on to invite Si out on a date. It was enough, and Si decided that the only thing standing between him and Mr Right was the lack of a canine friend.

Of course a week later it all changed. 'Oh my God,' Si hissed down the phone. 'The bloody hair gets *everywhere*. Christ. I've spent the last week hoovering and it still hasn't helped. *Mouse! Get Down!*'

'So you're not going out to buy Mouse Junior, then?'

'I don't think so.'

Si no longer dog-sits for Mouse, but he does take him out regularly for walks, trying to guess where the gay population of North London might be. And yes, I know you're thinking behind Spaniards Inn at the top of Hampstead Heath, but, as Si says, he's not looking for a quick fuck. Plus, he wouldn't want to corrupt Mouse.

'What's happened to their house?' I ask Si, as I pull off my cardigan and tie it round my waist, as the sun has finally managed to break through the clouds and it's turning into a beautiful day.

'The place looks like a bomb's hit it. Those book catalogues! Piles and piles of the bloody things. You can hardly move in there.'

I shrug. 'That's the new business, I'm afraid.'

We slow down a bit to catch our breath, because beautiful as Primrose Hill is it's not called Primrose Hill for nothing, and when we reach the top we collapse on a bench to admire the view.

'So.' Si reaches into his pocket for a treat for Mouse, who gobbles it up, then bounds over to a mad Old English Sheepdog called Dylan for a spot of harassment. 'Aren't you going to ask me about my date?'

'Oh my God!' I'm absolutely mortified that I've forgotten—that last night Si saw the gorgeous Will again, and that, despite Si having cooked him dinner, Will does seem to be rather interested after all.

'I'm sorry. I want to know everything.'

'Everything?'

I roll my eyes. 'Leave out the gory details. Start with your menu.'

'Fresh asparagus to start with. Garlic bread, naturally . . .'

'God, Si, you really must learn to outgrow that, it seriously is becoming increasingly naff. Wait! Let me guess. You consulted Queen Delia for the main course.'

'But of course,' he sniffs. 'Since when have I consulted anyone other than Queen Delia for my seduction dinners?'

'Hmm. Let me think. I'm guessing . . . fish?'

A faint smile spreads over Si's face.

'OK. So . . . it was either the coulibiac or the salmon with a cous cous crust.'

'Good,' he says, eyebrows raised. 'But which one?'

'Well, I know you would have wanted to impress him, and, although both are equally impressive, the coulibiac is one step ahead on the presentation front, so I'm guessing coulibiac.'

Si laughs. 'If you're so bloody clever, what did I make for pudding?'

'OK,' I say, thinking hard. I suddenly remember Si's last Queen Delia success, and I smile to myself as I say breezily, 'It was hot last night, wasn't it? Hot enough for'—I pause dramatically—'a *strawberry granita*.'

'God, you really are a witch, aren't you?' Si hits me and we both snort with laughter.

'So we didn't stop talking all night,' Si says, itching to keep on the subject of Will. 'He is fantastic, you know. He's handsome, and funny, and charming. You'd love him. And he works in PR, so you'd have something in common.'

'Si, how many times do I have to tell you that PR and advertising have practically nothing in common.'

'He's creative. You're creative. He has black shoes. You have black everything. You're bound to get on.'

'And what's his relationship history?'

Si takes my arm, and we start to walk down the other side of the hill, Mouse and Dylan happily tearing around the field, chasing one another. 'Darling, Cath,' he says. 'He's a gay man with twinkling blue eyes and a body to die for. I'll have to assume he's been shagging for Britain, and is now tired of it and looking for security.'

'But didn't you ask? That's always your first question.'

'He would have lied. They always do.'

We walk in silence for a while, then Si asks, 'If you could meet anyone walking round this field right now, who would it be?'

'Dead or alive?'

'Alive, sweets. This has to be a fantasy that has potential. Otherwise what's the point.'

'OK, OK, sorry.' We trudge along while I try to think of someone, but, as each name flicks into my head, I mentally cross them off, knowing that they're not the person I'd really like to meet. Eventually I'm left with only one name.

'Portia.'

Si looks at me with horror. 'God, Cath. You're so sad. I thought you'd say Brad Pitt. At the very least I would have accepted Tom Cruise, but Portia? You really are obsessed, aren't you?'

Actually I'm not obsessed. In fact, I've hardly thought about her since I left that message on her machine.

I was pissed off that she didn't call back. Pissed off that she'd obviously rejected us, but other than that I really didn't mind, it was just that there were so many unanswered questions. I suppose what I'm trying to say is that there never seemed to be closure with Portia.

I remember Lucy once saying that the relationships she carried with her, the ones that hadn't seemed to die, no matter how far in the past they were, were always the ones that didn't actually have an end. They were the ones that were cut short before their life span was up. The relationships where one person decided they'd had enough—invariably the men—and the other person never had a chance to say their piece, to explain how they felt. Lucy was using this analogy to talk about relationships she'd had before Josh, but I see no reason why you can't extend this analogy to female friendship? Without the sex, of course.

And relationship does sum it up far better than friendship: I remember feeling, at times, that Portia and I were locked into such an intense, emotional relationship, something incredibly special and pure, that it wasn't unusual for us to joke that we felt like lovers, except we didn't want to sleep together.

'If I could find a man like you,' she'd say, 'I'd marry him tomorrow.' And I'd say the same thing back to her.

There were occasions when I felt quite simply overwhelmed with love for Portia. She was like the sister I never had. The best friend, mother, father, brother, the everything, and I do not believe that you can simply walk away from friendships like that. You cannot simply drift apart and get on with your lives, never giving one another a second thought.

Which was perhaps what upset me, pissed me off most, about Portia not returning the phone call. So when Si makes the comment about being obsessed with Portia, I shrug regretfully and explain lightly, 'Unfinished business, Si. I'd just like to see her again.'

'You know that if she does happen to call you'd be duty bound to tell her about the bookshop? Just to make sure she includes it in the series. She'd have to rework her storylines to give you a dusty little bookshop called something like Fully Booked.'

'And Steen would presumably be called in to do the decorating. Chintz armchairs and gingham cushions.'

Si laughs. 'Anyway. My turn. Now who, other than Will, would I most want to bump into right here, right now. Hmm. Let me think. Rupert Everett or John Travolta? Eeny Meeny Miny Mo . . .'

'No, Max,' Lucy says. 'Go and wash your hands before touching anything.' She turns back to the fridge and Max walks over to me with a grin, which I take to be a good sign.

'Hello, Max. Have you been at school today?'

Max doesn't say anything, revolting Damien devilspawn that he is, but, still grinning, he reaches out two chocolatey hands and grabs my cream cardigan, before running out of the room chuckling to himself, leaving me open-mouthed with shock. Not because I care about the cream cardigan, but because that child is a monster.

'He is a monster,' I shriek, proffering my cardigan to Lucy, who starts to clean it with an old dishcloth while screaming for Ingrid.

A shadow falls in the hallway and I smile faintly, wondering how on earth an au pair girl can manage to look so immaculately groomed, my immediate second thought being how on earth Lucy can trust Josh with Ingrid in the house, because isn't that always the classic scenario? Wife comes back to find husband in bed with nubile Scandinavian tottie?

Ingrid runs her fingers lazily through her hair and steps gingerly into the kitchen. 'Were you calling me?' she asks, which is an extraordinary question, given that Lucy has been shrieking her name for three minutes.

'Ingrid. Yes. Look, would you mind keeping Max with you? Playing a game with him? Staying in the playroom? Something? Anything?'

Ingrid shrugs and walks off down the corridor.

'How do you put up with her?' I whisper, when the coast is clear.

'Oh, she's all right. Rather sweet, actually. Maxy adores her, and that's all I care about.'

'But don't you worry about having someone like that in the house?'

'Worry? Why on earth would I worry?'

'Well, how does Josh get on with her?'

Lucy looks at me, confused, and then starts to roar with laughter. 'Oh, Cath. Now that is funny. Josh and Ingrid! Ingrid and Josh!'

'So glad I've amused you,' I say grumpily, wondering what the joke is.

'I'm sorry,' Lucy says finally, giving my hand a squeeze. 'It's just that I didn't know what you were talking about. As far as Josh is concerned, Ingrid's a naive young girl, far away from home, who's doing a fairly good job of looking after Maxy. And she probably thinks Josh is old enough to be her father, anyway. Oh dear, Cath. You have made me laugh. Anyway,' she says, slipping her glasses on and sitting opposite me at the table, pulling a large notebook towards her. 'I've been trying out recipes for weeks, so here's the final list.' She passes me a copy

'These sound amazing, Lucy.'

'I know the virtually fat-free, sugar-free, chocolate-chip banana

muffins are probably desperately unhealthy, but they taste delicious.'
Lucy looks at me closely, then takes off her glasses again.

'I thought you might give me a pre-session opinion. Well? Will you?'

'You'll finally allow me to have a taste?' My eyes light up.

Lucy laughs and goes to the fridge. 'Other than myself, I've never met anyone who loves their food as much as you do.'

'I know,' I say regretfully, mouth already full of delicious chocolate-chip banana muffin. 'I just wish it wasn't quite so obvious.'

'What are you talking about?'

I start to laugh. 'Having a face stuffed with chocolate muffin is not the time to start bemoaning a weight problem, is it.'

'Weight problem?' says Lucy. 'What weight problem? You're a woman, Cath, and that's what women are supposed to look like. You're gorgeous and I don't ever want to hear you say anything else.'

Amid sounds of ecstasy I finish the muffin, only to see Lucy looking at me sadly. 'What's the matter?' I say. 'You look like you're about to cry.'

Lucy shakes the expression off her face. 'No, no. I was just thinking how wonderful it is that we're finally fulfilling this dream, and the only thing that would make this complete would be if you found yourself a wonderful man. I just don't understand why you haven't got anyone.'

'I'm not that interested,' I say. 'I'm quite happy with you, Josh and Si.'

'I know,' she says with a smile. 'That's what worries me.'

Chapter Four

SUNDAYS HAVE ALWAYS BEEN my take-it-easy day. The one day when I'll allow myself a lie-in, scooping up the papers to take out to brunch with the rest of the gang.

But today Josh and Lucy are taking Max to friends in the country, and Si is all loved-up with Will, so there won't be a brunch. Instead, Si has decided that Will is definitely more than a fling, and that therefore it is time to seek my approval, so Si has decided he wll bring Will over for tea.

I did say that tea might be better at his house, particularly given that Si's flat is so much nicer than mine, but they are going antiquing—

'revoltingly coupley', said Si, with glee I might add—and Si has decided they will come over on their way home.

I do not understand how, in the space of two weeks, Si has found someone with whom he can go *antiquing*. Isn't that the prerogative of long-term couples? Of people who are used to one another, who know all of one another's foibles?

But perhaps I shouldn't be so surprised, because Si has always done this. He always decides, within minutes, that this time he has met the right one, and instantly attempts to create the intimacy that you don't usually have for at least six months. And of course this always frightens them away. I hope this time it's different. I hope that Will could turn out to be someone special, and I suspect that after this afternoon I'll have a pretty clear idea of his intentions.

I clamber out of bed, pull on a pair of tracksuit bottoms, a baggy sweater and trainers, and shake my hair out on the way to the bathroom to get washed.

I know what Si's expecting. He'll be expecting Mr Kipling's finest, but today I'm going to surprise him. I plan to put on a proper English tea. Not quite scones and cream, but certainly cucumber sandwiches.

And, oddly enough, I'm in the mood for baking. Not that I actually know how to, but, in his quest to turn me into something vaguely resembling a female, Si has bought me a few cookery books over the years, and before I leave I pull out a few and look at the recipes.

Chocolate sponge. Not too difficult. I list the ingredients, shove the piece of paper in my pocket, and walk up to Waitrose.

'Oh my God!' Si's mouth is hanging open with shock, as Will and I stand in the doorway, watching him with amusement.

'Catherine Warner, I do not believe this.' Si's frozen by the coffee table, on which are piled plates of dainty cucumber sandwiches, a teapot that rarely sees the light of day, and bone china cups and saucers.

Si sniffs. 'Something smells good too. What have you made?'

'Shit!' I run back into the kitchen just in time to stop the chocolate sponge from burning. Si follows me in.

'Well?' he whispers. 'What d'you think? Do you like him?'

'Si!' I start laughing. 'Give me a chance. I know you think I'm a witch, but my powers only start working after twenty minutes, OK? Ask me again in twenty minutes.' Si makes a face at me before dashing back into the living room to look after Will.

I bring the cake in, to find Si sitting on the sofa next to Will, holding hands and looking like a match made in heaven. They do look good together—Will has floppy blond hair and classic good looks, but there's something cold behind his eyes, and I'm not sure why I think this, but I am pretty damn certain that Si's going to come out of this one very hurt.

'Tea?' I start to pour for Will, who says, 'Do you have Earl Grey?'

'You're lucky she's got PG Tips, her kitchen's so badly stocked,' laughs Si, while I apologise frantically for not having Earl Grey, suddenly feeling very inadequate at only being able to offer boring old breakfast tea.

'Sandwich?' I pass the plate to Si, who shoves one in his mouth while putting another three on his plate, and then watch as Will takes one sandwich and puts it on his plate, which he then places on the floor.

Does this man think I have fleas?

'So,' I say, rubbing my hands together because suddenly there seems to be an awkward atmosphere, which is ridiculous given that Si is one of my best friends. 'Did you find anything good today?'

'I found a wonderful Victorian washstand,' Will says. 'So beautiful *and* he took a good offer, so a bit of a win for me.'

'Si?'

'Nah.' Si shakes his head, as Will starts laughing.

'He tried to buy a huge Victorian dresser, but it was obviously repro.'

Will looks smug, and I wonder what gives him the right to patronise Si in this way.

'Will knows far more than I do,' Si says finally, deferring to his new partner. 'About antiques, that is. Not much else.' Si gives Will an affectionate squeeze, but this last comment doesn't seem to go down all that well with Will.

'So, Will. What do you do, then?' Now I really hate asking that question. Not because I'm not interested in what people do, but because it really does epitomise small talk, which I loathe and detest. Very occasionally you will ask that question to discover that the askee has a fascinating job, and you, the asker, can then fall into a deep discussion with them for hours. But more often than not they'll say something like, 'I work in computer programming' or 'I'm a lawyer', and you quickly have to think of more questions that you don't really want to know the answers to, except you don't want to appear rude.

'He works in PR,' Si says impatiently. 'Remember? I told you.'

'Oh yes, of course.' I try to think of the next question. 'Who do you work for?'

'I'm the head of press at Select FM.'

'Really? How interesting!' I strive for enthusiasm, trying to catch Si's eye to make a slight face, but Si's gazing at Will in rapt adoration.

'It's actually a huge responsibility, but I enjoy it.'

'How long have you been there?' Jesus, this is like pulling teeth.

'I joined two years ago as a senior press officer, and when the head of press left I was the obvious choice.'

'He's very important,' Si says, pride shining out of every pore. 'Aren't you?'

Will shrugs, too full of his own self-importance to give an answer.

Si leans forward and helps himself to more sandwiches.

'Have some,' I encourage Will, because if they don't go I'll be eating cucumber bloody sandwiches for the next week.

'I'm fine,' Will says disdainfully, still not having touched the sandwich on his plate.

'Oh God,' Si groans. 'I'll have to make a confession now. I'm sorry, Cath, but we had a huge lunch. That's why Will can't eat anything.'

'Don't worry,' I say, 'not a problem,' although if this lunch were so huge, how come Si can still manage to stuff himself?

I wish I could tell you that it got better. It didn't. It got worse. Even Si started to look vaguely uncomfortable and took the first opportunity he could to whisk me into the kitchen.

'You just hate him, don't you?'

I sigh and look at my lovely friend, wishing I could like Will, wishing, at the very least, I could lie about it, but I just can't. But nor can I be entirely honest.

'He seems very nice.' I grit my teeth.

'Oh, come on, sweets. You can do better than that. Be honest. Tell me what you really, really think?'

'Really really?'

'If I can't rely on my best friend to tell me the truth, who can I rely on?'

'OK.' I take a deep breath. 'It's just that he seems a bit arrogant.' I pause, checking that Si's OK with this. 'And you know that arrogance doesn't go down particularly well with me.'

'He's not usually like that,' Si whispers quickly, watching the door to make sure Will doesn't surprise us both by coming in. 'I swear, Cath. I haven't seen him like this before.'

'So you mean even you think he's a wanker today, then?' I say, smiling.

'I didn't say that. I just meant that he's normally very laid-back.'

I thank God that Si doesn't ask me any more questions about what I think, whether I might change my mind, whether I think they will make a good couple.

Once they've gone, I flick through the TV guide to check the evening's viewing, then put the kettle on before realising I've run out of milk. I head towards the door but turn back, because, typical English summer, there's now a chill in the evening air, and a T-shirt isn't enough to keep me warm.

I walk out to the corner shop, and just as I've picked up the milk I hear my name.

'Cath! Hi!'

I turn round to see James the estate agent standing there, beaming at me, and I almost start to laugh. He is wearing exactly what I would have expected him to wear, exactly what I pictured him in the first time we met, except the sweater isn't chunky and cableknit, but a fine grey lambswool.

'Oh, hi, James. How are you?' I'm amazed that my voice sounds so normal, because I had forgotten how attractive this man is, how unsettling I find it to be around someone who might make me feel things I didn't think I could feel any more.

'Fine,' he says, at which point I sneak a glance at his shopping basket and note that it contains a packet of fresh pasta, one lemon, a packet of Parmesan cheese, one can of Coke and some salad stuff. One can of Coke? Interesting. James didn't strike me as the sort of bloke who would be single, and, unless my powers of deduction have deserted me, I'd say the Coke proves he's having dinner alone.

'Dinner,' he says, gesturing to the basket with a smile and running his fingers through his hair in a distinctly endearing manner.

'I can see,' I say, smiling back. 'I thought all you estate agents would have cupboards full of Marks and Sparks ready-made gourmet food.'

'You've forgotten, I'm not really an estate agent,' he grins, resting the basket down on the floor in front of his mountain boots, which, I note, are covered with splashes of paint. 'The struggling artist deep down still feels guilty about spending that much money on food,' he says with a shrug and an apologetic smile.

'I know Lucy lives locally, but I didn't know you did as well,' he continues. 'Whereabouts are you?'

'St James's Mansions?' It comes out with a question mark, but of course James knows exactly where it is.

'I sold a flat there last month, so I know it quite well. You know what's great about those flats? Most of them still have the original mouldings, and the ceiling heights are fantastic.'

I start to laugh and James stops abruptly.

'What?'

'I'm sorry. It's just that you sound so like an estate agent.'

He groans. 'Oh God. Thank you for pointing it out. If I ever do it again, a swift sharp kick should shut me up.'

We stand chatting in the middle of the tiny corner shop, as people squeeze past us, murmuring 'excuse me', and I realise that, even though this isn't exactly a social situation, I'm enjoying myself.

There's something incredibly down-to-earth about James. He looks like he'd be completely at home in a pair of old green wellies on a farm, so it's no surprise when he admits, during the conversation, that his real home is in fact a farm in Wiltshire.

After a while James looks at his watch, and I actually feel disappointed that he's going to leave. As I said before, he's a genuinely nice guy, not to mention frighteningly gorgeous. Did I say that? I can't have done. Ignore that.

'Do you want to go for a coffee or something?' James suddenly says, 'it's just that it seems crazy to stand here in everyone's way.'

'Sure,' I find myself saying. 'Great.'

James grins, and we both head to the checkout, where we're given the evil eye by the bloke behind the counter for blocking his precious aisle for the last fifteen minutes, and we escape outside, laughing.

'La Brioche?' we both say at exactly the same time, and we head off up West End Lane.

'You know,' James says, as we walk along, 'if we'd bumped into one another in six weeks' time, we'd be going to the bookshop for a coffee. Word's got round, you know,' James says, holding the door of the café open for me.

'And what's the reaction?'

James shrugs. 'Most people think it's a brilliant idea. Oh.' The waitress is standing by the table, waiting to take our order. James looks at me. 'Cappuccino?'

I nod. 'You know, it was the best thing I've ever done, handing in my notice, although I'm pretty apprehensive. But even if the bookshop doesn't work, although God knows I hope it does, I'll never be able to look back and regret not having done it.'

James's face lights up. 'I know exactly what you mean. I've always thought that the one thing I would hate most in life would be to reach the age of seventy, look back over my life, and think "if only".

'We have to fulfil our dreams, and I think you're incredibly lucky having a dream in the first place, and then being able to fulfil it.'

'So if your dream is to be an artist,' I say, trying to steer the conversation away from me, 'how come you're still an estate agent at the ripe old age of . . . how old are you anyway?'

James laughs. 'Thirty-six.' I practically fall off the chair. 'I know, I know.' He rolls his eyes and tries not to look exasperated as he says what he must say to everyone who accuses him of the same thing: 'I look ten years younger,' and then he laughs. 'But I've got it all worked out. Why do you think I'm not spending fortunes at M and S? I'm stashing every penny away so that when I'm forty I can chuck it all in and spend the rest of my days painting.'

I'm impressed. Impressed by his passion and commitment. By his confidence in everything turning out fine.

'I'd love to see your work,' I say.

'Would you really?' Suddenly he seems shy.

'I really would. I'm assuming you still paint.'

'God, all the time. My only extravagance these last few years has been the studio.' He smiles. 'Why don't you come over some time? Maybe you'll even persuade me to cook.' He smiles, then looks slightly worried. 'Only if you want to. You're probably very busy.'

You know, if those words came from anyone else, I'd think I was being asked out on a date, but I know, quite categorically, that this isn't the case. I am definitely not his type. Which is quite a relief, really, because at least it means I don't have to worry about anything. He's just an interesting man with an interesting hobby. And I did say I wanted to meet some new people . . .

Chapter Five

'I CAN'T WAIT TO START decorating,' Lucy groans eagerly, stepping into her professional painters' dungarees, while George the carpenter looks at her as if she's gone completely mad.

'You're not going to do it, are you, love?' he says. 'You'll have to get some men in to do that. This is a huge job. Too much for you ladies.'

This immediately gets my goat, even though I know it's only George being George, but nevertheless I speak up on Lucy's behalf, telling them that they're talking nonsense, and ladies such as ourselves would do a far better job than some big oafish blokes.

Sam the Spark—as we've come to know the electrician—smiles to himself without saying anything, as Lucy and I inspect their work.

'I can't believe it,' Lucy says, stroking a single kitchen unit that is currently sitting in the middle of the café area. 'It's going to be wonderful.'

We look around, at the low-halogen spotlights that instantly bring the appearance of bright daylight into the room, at the sleek modern counter in the centre, solid maple with glossy granite surfaces, from behind which Lucy will reign as queen of the cakes. And as soon as the decorating's finished, the floor will go down. It's almost D-Day.

And it's only now that everyone can start to enjoy it. Because it's been hell. Everyone said it would be, but Lucy and I thought we knew better. The first set of builders we had turned up at seven o'clock every morning, on the dot, which we thought was pretty damn amazing. Until we realised that they were stopping for tea breaks every fifteen minutes, and that at lunchtime they were off for the rest of the day.

Fortunately Lucy found George soon after that. She'd asked his advice in Homebase, thinking that he looked like a man who knew what he was talking about. George not only turned out to be a fantastic chippy, he also had a team of people who worked with him, all of them reliable, hard-working and nice.

In short, George was a godsend—despite being the sort of man who believes that men are the hunters, and their job in life is to protect women, who should, incidentally, be feminine, giggly and hopeless at anything other than cooking, sewing and bringing up children.

I have never met a harder worker than George. Lucy literally had to force him to stop for coffee by bringing in huge slabs of cake and delicious sandwiches every day, trying to tempt him to take a break.

So today is the first D-Day, as Lucy put it. In other words, decorating day. Josh is turning up later, and even Si has invested in some decorators' overalls to help out, but for now it's just Lucy and I.

We wait until George and Sam have packed up and headed off to the pub for a well-earned drink, before tugging off the lids of the paint pots and starting to paint. Select FM is keeping us company, even though I'm tempted not to listen any more due to the ghastly Will, who seems to have slightly come between Si and me, if only by virtue of the fact that Si seems to spend all his time with him.

I do feel incredibly selfish, disliking Will as much as I do, because surely I should be thrilled that Si has finally found someone, but I can't shake the feeling that Will is going to hurt Si—and he deserves to find someone so much better.

After an hour my arm starts killing me. Lucy on the other hand seems to be thriving, and one wall's almost done, so I keep my moans to myself, figuring that I'm not going to be the first to crack.

Two hours later I climb off the stepladder and stretch, grinning as Lucy does the same thing.

'Cath?' Lucy says, leaning her head on my shoulder. 'Whose blasted idea was this?'

I start laughing. 'Thank goodness,' I say. 'I thought I was the only one thinking this is a bloody nightmare.'

'It's not quite a nightmare,' she sighs, 'but it's not half as much fun as in all those adverts on the box, where young couples smile adoringly at one another while they're decorating the nursery.' Then Lucy starts to laugh. 'Tell me I don't look as bad as you.'

'What? What's wrong with the way I look?'

'Go and look in the mirror.' Lucy sternly orders me to the tiny loo off the stock room. I look like a slightly less *soigné* version of Cruella de Vil. In other words, my brown hair now has a sunshine yellow streak running along one side, about four inches thick, and there are smears of yellow on my forehead where I've obviously got some paint on my fingers, and without realizing have pushed my hair back.

In other words, I look a mess.

'I see what you mean,' I shout out to Lucy, who still looks as clean and shining as when she arrived.

'Why don't we have a break?' Lucy says. 'I'll go up the road to the takeaway and get a couple of coffees. You'd better stay here. You can't go out like that!'

'Fine,' I say, shrugging, and off she goes.

With nothing else to do, I pick up the paint roller and carry on, and don't even turn round when I hear the door open five minutes later.

'Just put mine on the table,' I shout. 'I'll be down in a sec.'

'No rush,' says a voice that is definitely not Lucy's.

I turn round to see James standing there, although for a second I don't quite recognise him because he's in his weekend gear again and I've grown used to seeing him in the neighbourhood in his navy suit. Not that we've had time to chat—we've been far too busy for that—but we manage a wave and a grin through a window.

'Is this a bad time?' He's already apologising, backing out, thinking he's made a mistake, but I clamber down the ladder telling him not to be ridiculous, we're only painting.

'I can see,' he laughs, and I laugh with him, frankly not caring that I look like a dog's dinner.

'Anyway'—I point my roller at him sternly—'you should be offering to help. You'd probably do a much better job than me.'

'I doubt that,' he says, 'but I'd certainly do a cleaner one.'

'Yes, well, I'm sure that wouldn't be difficult.' I peer at him closely because he seems to be carrying something in his right hand. 'What are you doing here anyway?'

'I walked past earlier and saw you both in here, and I remembered that I had something for the shop, so I thought I'd drop it in.'

'For the shop? What is it?'

James hands over the package just as Lucy walks through the door.

'James! How lovely to see you!' She puts down the polystyrene cups of coffee and gives him a hug, which would normally surprise me, given that she hardly knows him, but it's typical Lucy behaviour and only seems to faze James very slightly.

'Oh damn!' She looks at the two cups of coffee. 'Let me run out and get another one for you.'

'Don't be silly,' James says. 'I'll go.'

'Are you sure?'

James nods.

'OK,' she says. 'But come straight back and we can all have some strudel together.'

'Strudel?' I roll my eyes to the ceiling, wondering how on earth I'm going to manage to retain my voluptuous, yet normal size 14, when Lucy's bringing in these delicious things all the time.

'So why is the handsome young James visiting our humble abode?' Lucy says slyly, when he's safely out of view.

I shrug.

'Might it be that he has a little bit of a soft spot for the lovely Cath?'

'You know what?' I turn round and give Lucy my innocent wide-eyed look. 'I think you're absolutely right. Because what man wouldn't adore me with canary-yellow paint all over my face?' And I give my head an expert Jerry Hall style toss, thus causing the Afro to vibrate slightly.

Lucy starts to laugh, stopping only when she notices the package on the table. 'What's this?' she asks, examining it more closely.

'James brought it. It's for the shop.'

'For the shop? But this looks like a present. What on earth can it be?' As she shakes the parcel James walks back in and Lucy drops it guiltily.

'Caught me red-handed,' she blushes. 'I'm so sorry, James.'

'Don't be,' he smiles. 'It's for you.' He looks at Lucy and then at me as he says this. 'But if you don't like it then you must tell me.'

'Go on, Cath,' Lucy says, suddenly making herself very busy with a tin of paint. 'You open it.'

I wipe the residue of wet paint from my hands on to my overalls and gently open the package to reveal a tiny painting in a simple wooden frame. It's an incredibly delicate abstract watercolour, deep royal blues fading into turquoise, strips of colour criss-crossing one another, the layers built up until they shimmer richly from the paper.

'This is beautiful,' I say, because it truly is.

'Are you sure?' James cannot hide the look of relief on his face. 'I just wanted to bring you something for the shop, a sort of good-luck token if you like, and I thought the colours were very sunny, it reminds me of summer, so I thought you might like to put it up somewhere.'

Lucy puts down the paint pot and comes over, gasping when she sees the picture. 'Goodness, how extraordinarily beautiful. What a stunning painting. But James, you didn't . . . It's not *yours* . . .?'

But of course it is. And I have to say, I'm shocked. Shocked because I didn't expect he'd be quite this talented? Well, yes, possibly. And shocked because this is such an incredibly kind thing to do. To bring a painting to people he hardly knows. To treat us as something other than just another business deal.

'You really like it?' James is now beaming.

'We love it,' Lucy says, and gives him a kiss, which means that I have to give him a kiss too, which is fine, except I'm not all that big on touching people I barely know.

But I cast my inhibitions aside and give James a kiss on his left cheek, pulling away sharply afterwards because I do find these situations so awkward, but then Lucy thankfully breaks the ice by loudly ripping open the cover on the strudel and cutting each of us a huge slab.

'It looks fantastic in here,' James says, admiring our counter, our shelves, our etched glass windows. 'Seriously.'

'Thank you,' Lucy smiles. 'So, James, given that you're not just any old artist, but in fact a deeply talented and wonderful one, how would you feel if we had some paintings for the shop? We could give you a sort of mini-exhibition. What do you think?'

James looks thrilled as Lucy continues. 'Look. We can't promise anything, because it may not even be a viable idea, but even if we don't display them in the shop I'd love to buy some for home.'

'I'm astounded,' James says. 'And embarrassed. You must think I came here to try and wangle an exhibition, or . . .'

Lucy cuts him off mid-sentence. 'James,' she says gently. 'I am not a people pleaser. I am not a person who says things because she thinks it will make the other person happy, nor am I a person who offers things she cannot deliver because I want the other person to like me.'

James nods. 'OK.'

Then, to my astonishment she says, 'I think that Cath and I should come over this evening when we've finished and have a look at your work. How does that sound?'

James gulps. 'This evening? OK. Why not? Fine.'

'Oh bugger!' Lucy says immediately. 'I can't make it this evening. I forgot, I have to go for dinner with some boring colleague of Josh's. Never mind, Cath, you don't mind going by yourself do you?'

'Mind? Why should I mind?' I say. 'I'll just cancel the dinner party I was having.'

James looks completely stricken while Lucy lets out a snort. 'She's joking,' she says. 'She'll see you at . . . seven?'

James nods, and I try to catch Lucy's eye to let her know she's about to get a severe bollocking. After all, this is supposed to be a joint business venture, and what the hell is Lucy thinking of, offering him a show without discussing it with me first? Not to mention press-ganging me into going over there later. But Lucy refuses to look at me, just chats animatedly to James about the plans for the shop until he gets up to leave.

'It's not funny,' I hiss down the phone at Si, who's laughing hysterically at Lucy's conniving. 'And I can't get this bloody paint out of my hair.'

Si snorts again. 'God, it's amazing what Lucy hides behind that innocent face of hers. So, what are you going to wear?'

'The usual,' I say, smiling, waiting for Si's predictable reaction.

'Oh Christ. Not bloody black again. At least try. Please? For me?'

'All right, then,' I mutter. 'Brown. But for God's sake, Si, I don't know why you're getting so worked up. I told you before, this isn't a date.'

'Not yet,' he says, 'but give it time.'

'You and Lucy,' I sigh. 'You're both as bad as each other.'

I've never heard of his road before, which is odd because I thought I knew West Hampstead pretty well by now.

'It's off Sherriff Road,' he'd said earlier, writing down the address while Lucy practically exploded with pent-up excitement. 'It looks a bit dodgy from the front, but the house is back to front, so follow the path round to the back and you'll see the front door.'

I realise while trudging up the path that I haven't eaten anything since the slab of strudel earlier, and although I very much doubt that food will play even the tiniest of roles this evening, because it's purely a business arrangement, I am praying that James will not keep me long, so I can grab something on the way back home.

The back of the house is almost pitch black, but I can just about make out that almost the entire back wall is a huge arched window, and next to that is a front door. I stumble over a stone and feel around the door frame for a doorbell, but before I can find one the door opens and James is standing there grinning. 'You found it,' he says.

'I found it.' I find myself grinning back at him, noting that he is holding a corkscrew in one hand and immediately regretting that I had not brought a bottle of wine with me.

'Come in, come in.' James gestures inside, and I shuffle in, apologising for coming empty-handed.

'Don't be silly,' he says. 'I've got plenty of wine. What would you like? Red or white?'

I'm about to answer him, but, as I walk inside, I just stand there, open-mouthed, too dumbstruck to say anything, because out of all the scenarios I had imagined for James's studio, this was definitely not one of them.

The room is enormous. Vast. At least double height, the entire ceiling is glass, and, although all you can see now is velvety blackness, it must be like the playground of the sun during the day.

It seems to be divided into three sections. The section closest to the door is obviously where James paints. The white varnished floors are splattered with paint, and everywhere there are canvases propped up against the wall, some finished, some blank, waiting to be started. Pots of paint are dotted around, brushes, rags, the smell of turpentine.

'Have a wander,' James says gently, enjoying my amazement. 'I don't mind. Oh, and take your shoes off, it's probably safer.' I kick them off, noticing that James is wearing thick red socks.

I pick my way through the pots of paint, purposefully not looking at James's paintings, wanting to save the best until last. I walk through the large opening into the second section, the open-plan kitchen, and through again to what is evidently the living room.

Sea-grass rugs cover the scrubbed floorboards, while huge white squashy sofas dominate the room. An old wooden chair sits at an angle by an enormous stone fireplace. It is, in short, spectacular. And yet, despite the all designer-type furnishings, it is a house in which I feel immediately comfortable. Then it dawns on me why. The mess. Piles of papers dotted around, just out of sight, but nevertheless there.

In the kitchen sink there is a pile of washing-up, waiting to be tackled, and on the kitchen table there are distinct rings left by coffee cups.

James notices me noticing. 'God, I'm sorry,' he sighs. 'I'm just so bloody messy. You're horrified, aren't you?'

I laugh. 'You'll be happy to hear you're not half as disgusting as I am.'

'Really?' His face shows the beginnings of relief.

'Really.'

James breaks into a grin. 'Red OK?' I nod, and he pours me a glass of wine as I wander back into his studio.

'This place truly is incredible.' I turn to him. 'It's the sort of home we all dream of living in but none of us could ever afford.'

'The one perk of being an estate agent,' he says with a smile. 'You get to hear about things way before anyone else.' He pulls out a chair for me in the kitchen and I sit down, wanting to hear more.

'How did you find this, then?'

'It was about four years ago,' he says, taking a sip of the wine and murmuring with pleasure, his expression inviting me to do the same. 'It was one of those ridiculous situations where this had been on the market for ages and the owner was desperate.

'He didn't live here, he'd moved to the country years before, and this place was slowly falling down. Everyone knew about it, but nobody wanted to touch it because somehow word got round that there were problems of some kind. So it just sat here slowly rotting.'

'Until you came in and saved the day?'

'Well, sort of,' he grins. 'I'd always been curious, but I'd heard all the negative stuff. Then one day I overheard a couple of other agents talking about it and I decided to come along and have a look.'

'And was it love at first sight?'

'Yes and no. I couldn't believe the building. The potential. But it was disgusting. There were rats here, rubbish that had been left for years. It had been lived in by squatters for a while, and you could hardly walk around for the smell.' He gestures up at the gallery. 'That was completely rotten, you couldn't even walk up the stairs to see what was there.'

'So did you get it for a knock-down price?'

'Yup.' He grins. 'And a week after I exchanged I was offered double for it.'

'You're joking!'

'Nope. That's property for you. As soon as one person's interested, everyone wants it.'

'But double the price? Weren't you tempted?'

'Are you kidding? This was my dream home. And now I love it. I can't imagine living anywhere else. Do you want the guided tour?'

'You mean there's more?' And as I say this I suddenly blush slightly because I realise I haven't seen any bedrooms, and there is something uncomfortably intimate about going into a strange man's bedroom.

James stands up and walks to the arched window, flicking a switch to the left. Suddenly the outside lights up, and he opens two double doors hidden in the window, and we walk outside.

And I realise that the pitch blackness outside through which I stumbled to get here is in fact a huge garden, not particularly well tended, but breathtaking by the sheer fact of its size.

'Bit of a mess, but at least I get to grow my own tomatoes.'

'You are joking?' I start to laugh.

'No, I'm serious.' He points to a patch at the back where I can just about make out large black shapes that are evidently tomato plants. 'What else would you expect from a farmer's son?'

We go back indoors, James pours me another glass of wine—I didn't realise I'd finished the last quite so quickly—and makes me laugh with stories of drunken rides on tractors and escaping the clutches of braying horsy women at Young Farmers events, saying how moving to London when he was twenty-one felt much like winning the lottery.

'So where's your yokel accent, then?' I ask, after a while.

'You mean my Worzel Gummidge accent?' he says, doing a perfect impression as I splutter out my wine with laughter. 'I haven't spoken like that since my first day in London,' he laughs. 'It took about five minutes to realise that I didn't have a hope in hell of surviving here unless I changed the accent.'

'Did you really speak like that?' I'm amazed.

He raises an eyebrow and grins, pushing his hair out of his eyes. 'You'll never know now, will you?'

'Come and see the rest of the house,' he says, and I follow him upstairs, where he proudly shows me two bedrooms and a bathroom, and I manage to control any lascivious thoughts that may or may not have been lurking somewhere in the depths of my mind.

And then it's back downstairs to sit in the kitchen, still chattering away.

'Look, I don't know about you,' James says after a while, 'but I'm starving. Do you fancy getting takeout?'

'Whatever you want,' I say. 'I really don't mind.'

'Curry?'

'Great.'

James picks up a sheaf of papers from the kitchen counter and leafs through them. 'What do you fancy?' he says bringing a leaflet over to me.

'What are you having?'

'Maybe a Vindaloo. You?'

'Chicken korma, I think.'

'OK. Plain rice?'

I nod as he picks up the phone. 'Hello,' he says, 'it's Mr Painting here.' I stifle a laugh as he shrugs his shoulders in resignation at the name they've evidently given him. 'I'd like to order a delivery. No, no. Not the usual. We'll have a chicken korma . . .'

I watch him with a smile, because he's the most un-estate-agency estate agent I've ever met. James is so normal. So nice. And it's been so long since I've met someone new with whom I immediately bond. And although it might be a little early to jump to conclusions, I would say that James is exactly the sort of new friend I've been looking for.

It's not just that he seems to fit in with me, I think, as I watch him put the plates in the oven to warm. It's that I could also see him fitting in with my friends.

'Onion bhaji?' He looks at me for approval and I shrug my shoulders. 'A nan and a peshwari nan. Oh, and vegetables. Maybe a sag aloo?' I throw caution to the winds and just nod, slightly bewildered at the amount he's ordering, but he must be a man with a big appetite.

Oh, and by the way. Just in case you're wondering, I do mean all that stuff about James fitting in—platonically. OK?

'I've got a stomach ache,' I groan, undoing the button on my waistband and rubbing my stomach to try to ease the pain of over-stuffing.

'Oh God, me too,' says James, grinning.

'I know this is a bit weird,' I say, downing the last glass of our second bottle of wine, 'especially as I hardly know you, but it is weird that I feel comfortable enough to make a pig of myself in front of you.'

'That is weird,' James says. 'Does that mean that if you didn't feel comfortable with me you would only have eaten six grains of rice and a thimbleful of chicken korma?'

'Quite probably,' I say sternly. Then I remember with horror that this is supposed to be a business evening.

'Oh God.' I manage to force myself upright. 'We've been having far too much fun. I'm supposed to be here on business.'

'Are you?' James looks completely bemused, which isn't surprising, bearing in mind he's matched me mouthful for mouthful.

'I'm supposed to be looking at your paintings.' I stand up, in my best impression of an imperious gallery owner. 'In fact, as you already know, Lucy and I are considering giving you the opportunity to exhibit your work in our super new gallery café/bookshop type thing. And I'—I pause dramatically—'am here to decide whether to give you a chance.'

'Right-oh,' James says, trooping into the studio bit, as I stumble in after him. 'Let's see what you think, then.'

One by one he starts gently pulling canvases out, laying them against walls, standing back to look at them, and as he pulls them out my heart starts beating faster and faster.

'James,' I say finally, when there are nearly twenty paintings displayed in front of me. 'What the fuck are you doing working as an estate agent?'

James turns to look at me in confusion. 'What are you talking about?'

'These are the most beautiful, subtle, inspiring paintings I've seen for years. And I don't even know what I'm talking about.'

James looks embarrassed. 'Does that mean you like them?'

I start to laugh. 'Jesus Christ, James. I love them. In fact, to quote Woody Allen, I don't just love them, I lurrrve them. We'll take 'em.'

'Are you serious?'

I ignore the fact that I've just done exactly what Lucy did earlier and have taken a decision without consulting Lucy. But what the hell.

'More serious,' I say, 'than I've ever been in my life.' Unfortunately I ruin that last statement somewhat by hiccuping at the end of it, but nevertheless the sentiment remains the same.

'James,' I say, extending my right hand, 'it's been a pleasure doing business with you.'

'And where the hell have you been until this time on a Sunday night?'

'Having sex.' I keep a straight face for a while but the silence becomes too much for me and I collapse with amusement at my little joke.

'That's not your line, that's my line. I hope you're joking.'

'Why? What would be so terrible if I wasn't?'

'It wouldn't be terrible, as it happens,' Si muses. 'It would be pretty bloody cataclysmic, that's all.'

'Si! That's not nice. Anyway. No sex. I've been with James.' I slur ever so slightly, but enough for Si to pick up on.

'James? James who?' Si plays the innocent as I laugh, knowing that he'll have been sitting by his phone for hours, waiting for me to call him back, to give him the full report on my evening.

'But more to the point,' he continues, 'you, Catherine Warner, are drunk as a skunk, aren't you? Aren't you?'

'Shut up, Mum,' I intone in my best truculent teenager impression. 'Leave me alone.'

'Good God. Wonders will never cease. You don't mean to tell me, Cath, that you've been out having a good time? With a man, no less?'

'Yup.'

'So tell me about the evening from heaven with James the hunky estate agent who's got a crush on you? Was it heavenly?'

'Someone's been talking to Lucy. He's not hunky and neither does he have a crush on me. He's just nice. And a fantastic artist.'

'Methinks the lady doth protest too much . . .'

'Si!' I stop him.

'So tell me more about James. Is he a boxer shorts or briefs kind of guy?'

'I think probably a boxer shorts kind of guy.'

'You think? You think? You mean you didn't find out?'

'Forgive me. Next time I go to his house I promise I'll rifle through his underwear drawers.'

'Next time you go to his house I expect you to strip him personally. So what's his house like anyway?'

'Oh, Si.' I snuggle down under the duvet and get ready for a long gossip. 'You would have loved it.' And off I go.

You're impossible,' I say, raising my eyes to the sky, as Si rolls down the window of his car and urges me to hurry up.

'Come on, come on,' he says, pressing the horn to irritate me further, but I speed up and open the door of the Beetle.

'God, I love this,' he says, leaning over to give me a kiss. 'I can't believe it's September, look at that sun. On days like this I wish I had a convertible. Anyway, I can't believe you actually agreed to let me take you shopping. We haven't done this since . . .'

'Since I was thin?' I finish off his sentence for him and we both laugh.

'*You* might say that,' he says, pulling away from the kerb, 'but I could-n't possibly comment.'

'So, where are we off to?

'We are going to Bond Street, and before you say anthing, you are going to have to trust my judgment on this one. It's the opening party for the shop and you, my darling, will go to the ball.'

Although Emporio Armani is not a shop I would ever normally enter, the clothes are actually pretty nice. Si has picked out a selection of trouser suits, and this one, the black velvet one with the long fitted jacket and the beautifully cut trousers, looks pretty damn impressive, even if I say so myself.

Si whistles as I step out of the changing room.

'Jesus, Cath.' He's practically rubbing his hands with glee. 'You look gorgeous. If I didn't know better, I'd say you were a size ten.'

The very thin, very chic, very French sales assistant was obviously just about to agree, but stops suddenly, not quite knowing what to say. 'Yes,' she says uncertainly, 'it is very flattering.'

'Oh, fuck off,' I say, turning to Si, as the sales assistant pretends to spot something very important on the other side of the shop.

'It's pretty nice, isn't it?' I continue, twirling while I marvel at how cleverly the jacket manages to conceal my rather Rubenesque thighs.

'No question about it. It was positively made for you. Now, if only you'd let me do something with your hair.'

'My darling Si, even you know that's pushing it too far.'

'OK, OK,' he grumbles. 'But you can't blame a guy for trying.'

We get to the cash desk and the assistant rings it up, then turns to me and says nonchalantly, 'That's four hundred and fifty-five pounds.'

I turn white as Si grabs my arm to steady me.

'How much?' It comes out in a whisper but, before the assistant has a chance to repeat herself, Si drags me to one side. 'Cath,' he says sternly. 'I'm sorry, but for a suit that divine, that's how much you have to pay.'

'No way, Si.' I shake my head. 'I'm not paying over four hundred quid for a bit of black velvet when I can get exactly the same in Top Shop for a hundred and fifty. Forget it.'

'Fine,' Si says. 'Let's go to Top Shop and see how we do.'

'Fine,' I say, as Si goes back to the sales assistant, presumably to apologise as I head out of the door and wait outside.

We do Top Shop. We do Miss Selfridge, now seemingly renamed the funkier Spirit. We do Hennes. We do French Connection. We push through the Saturday crowds to do Oasis.

Three hours later we're back in shop number one, grinning rather sheepishly at the same sales assistant, who smiles without saying a word, then pulls out the velvet suit from behind the desk.

'As my grandmother always used to say, if you pay peanuts, you get monkeys.'

'The stuff we've been trying on wasn't bad,' I say, doing my best to stick up for the chain stores.

'I'm not saying it was,' Si says smoothly, watching me physically wince as I pull out my Visa card, 'I was just saying that once you'd tried this on, you'd never find anything as nice.'

'God, it kills me to tell you you're right,' I say, shaking my head.

'But?'

'But you're right. OK?'

We go back to the car and five minutes into the journey back he pulls up sharply outside an Italian menswear shop.

'Why are we stopping here?'

'And who says Cinderella is the only one allowed to buy a new outfit for the ball?'

'Hi, I'm Laura. I'm the baby sitter.' Si stands back and lets Laura in, as he mouths to me, 'Baby sitter?' in a question, then rapidly smiles as she turns round and catches him.

'Lucy's in the kitchen,' he says, showing her through before turning to me and saying, 'What the hell have they got a baby sitter for?'

I shrug. 'Maybe it's Ingrid's night off.' Si wanders into the living room, where Josh is adjusting his tie in the mirror above the fireplace, and I go to help Lucy in the kitchen.

'Cath, be an angel and put some Cling Film on this, would you?' She hands me a bowl of baby ricotta-and-spinach tarts that she's made for our opening party. 'And then can you take those boxes into the car for me? Max!' she shrieks. 'Come and say hello to Laura.'

The next thing I hear is a clattering downstairs as Max runs in and whacks Laura on the thigh with a wooden fork. 'Hello, Max,' she says, beaming through her gritted teeth. 'Do you remember me? I came to baby-sit and we watched *The Lion King* together.'

Max stares at her uncomprehendingly, then runs out of the room, while I smile widely, grateful that I'm not the only one.

Lucy sighs. 'He's just impossible at the moment. I'm so sorry.'

Laura smiles. 'Don't worry. I'll go after him, shall I?' Lucy nods gratefully, and Laura follows Max upstairs. We do our best to ignore the ensuing shrieks as Max realises we're all leaving him.

I enlist Si's help and we load up both cars with food and drink, then we go back inside and collapse around the kitchen table to toast ourselves with champagne.

'So, where's the lovely Ingrid tonight?' Si ventures.

'Coming to the party, of course,' Lucy says. 'I couldn't not invite her.'

'That's very nice of you,' I say, as Ingrid herself waltzes into the kitchen, whereupon my mouth drops open a few notches in amazement. Ingrid, while being one of those incredibly striking naturally blonde Scandinavian stereotypes, is usually to be found in a pair of faded jeans, a T-shirt and trainers. But tonight even Lucy stops in amazement as we survey Ingrid's get-up of tiny black mini skirt, plunging jacket and super-high strappy sandals that, quite frankly, wouldn't look out of place in a brothel specialising in S & M.

Ingrid, on the other hand, looks completely relaxed as she totters over to get a glass of water. Lucy gulps and looks at me.

'Ingrid,' she says eventually, and rather cheerfully. 'Looking ever so glamorous. How on earth do you manage to walk in those marvellous shoes?'

'I am used to them,' she says, as Max comes running in and falls at her feet, clutching her calves. She raises one leg and for one happy second I think she might aim a sharp kick at Max with one of her killer shoes, but no, she just gives him a disdainful look and shakes him off.

'Ingriiiiiiiiid,' Max wails, going in for the cling again. 'Don't go. Stay here with me.'

'No, Max,' Ingrid says, walking across the kitchen and thereby dragging Max with her across the floor, 'I am going out tonight to party.'

'She can say that again,' Si whispers, doing a double take at Ingrid disappearing up the stairs.

'Blimey,' Josh says, with a huge grin on his face. 'Old Ingrid, eh? Who would have thought she'd scrub up like a sex kitten?'

'Sex kitten?' splutters Si. 'More like cheap hooker.'

'WHAT'S A HOOKER?' Max's voice reverberates around the house, and we all turn to stare at him in horror, Ingrid evidently having managed to disengage him from her leg just halfway up the stairs.

'Oh God,' Josh says, managing to shut Max up by offering him a handful of chocolate, 'do you think she heard?'

'And what if she did?' Si sniffs. 'Face it, she does look as if she's on her way to a street corner in Westbourne Park Road.'

'Oh, she's only young,' Lucy says. 'That's obviously all the fashion.'

'In Scandinavian porn films,' Si says, 'perhaps.'

Josh quickly stuffs some more chocolate into Max's face, then whisks him into the other room to distract him with the video of *Mulan*. Thankfully he manages this before Max can utter those immortal shrieks: WHAT'S A PORN FILM?

'Thank God.' Lucy rolls her eyes. 'Peace and quiet. Now, Si.' She turns to face him. 'Is your new man coming tonight, and if not, why not?'

'I did ask him, but he said he had other plans.'

'What other plans?'

Si shrugs. 'He didn't say. But anyway, much better that it's the old gang. To be honest I'm not sure how comfortable I'd be if he were here now. Not that I think you wouldn't like him—well,' and he shoots me a dirty look, 'other than Cath, of course—it's just that I'd be worrying about what you all thought about him, and what he thought of you, and quite honestly I just want to have a good time tonight. And of course,' he goes over to Lucy and puts his arm around her, 'give both of you my undying love and support.'

'I can't believe it,' I say. 'I can't believe this is the opening party. God, Lucy. Do you think it's going to be fine?'

'You tell me, my love,' Lucy says with a grin. 'You're the one who keeps saying we're going to be a huge success.'

'I know,' I groan. 'I was hoping the power of positive thinking would work, but now that it's actually here I'm so nervous.'

'Here.' Lucy pops a prawn satay stick into my mouth to shut me up. 'The food's great, the shop looks amazing, and the local support has been extraordinary. You just wait, Bookends is going to be a huge hit.'

We get ready to leave, and, as I walk out the front door, I almost have to kick myself to remember that this isn't all a dream.

But the truth is, it's all been so easy. Hard work, but lovely work, because it's ours. We've employed two young local people, Bill and Rachel, to work in the shop with us—Bill will be on the till, while Rachel will take control of the stock and help Lucy in the kitchen. I, naturally, am in charge of the accounts.

The four of us have slaved to get the shop ready in time. Bill and Rachel took over the responsibility of organising the bookshop, and between the two of them they skilfully divided the shop into sections: fiction, biography, cookery, travel, etc, etc. All the orders have come from wholesalers—thank God—so I haven't had to deal with a million invoices and deliveries from all the different publishers, which, quite frankly, would have done my head in.

There's still a lot to learn, but we're learning fast, and thankfully Bill had a summer job at Waterstone's when he was at university, so he's been unbelievable, to put it mildly.

Now I used to go to parties quite a lot for work, and most of the time they weren't much fun. Even the ones that are supposed to be 'trendy' and 'media' were usually trivial and boring, and a couple of years ago I decided that parties were no longer my thing.

But look at this place! Look at the people squeezed into every available bit of floor space in the shop! Listen to the buzz of conversation that's growing steadily louder and louder as people's tongues are loosened with champagne.

And watch their faces as they groan in ecstasy at Lucy's canapés—her delicious bite-sized morsels of food that, quite literally, melt in the mouth; and watch Lucy, weaving through the hordes, beaming with heat, pride and happiness.

A handful of local authors are here, each in turn being interviewed by the *Ham & High*, and each saying how thrilled they are that Bookends has opened, and what a great idea it is.

'Cath?'

I turn round and James is standing there, smiling. He's wearing his navy suit and a tie that is covered with tiny jewel-coloured books.

'James!' I give him a big kiss, not feeling the slightest bit self-conscious. 'I love your tie!' I shriek, over the din.

'Thanks.' His lips brush my ear as he leans forward to be heard, and I shiver. 'I painted it myself. Appropriate, I thought.'

I laugh as I link my arm through his and lead him slightly unsteadily towards Lucy. 'Lucy! Look! It's James!' I shout.

Lucy's face lights up and she too plants a large kiss on his cheek, as Si rises up behind her.

'Hel-Lo,' he says, in his best Leslie Phillips impression, eyeing James up and down, then raising his eyebrows practically to the ceiling as he notes my arm linked through James's. I hurriedly unlink it and introduce them.

'Oh,' Si says. 'Now I've heard *all* about you.'

James looks surprised as Lucy starts to drag Si away. 'What a load of rubbish,' she shouts over her shoulder to James. 'He knows nothing about you. Nothing. He's just drunk.'

'Sorry.' I now feel slightly awkward, unsure what there is to talk about, when I remember the paintings. 'Look!' I gesture around the room. 'Don't they look wonderful? I think they've even sold one or two.'

'Are you serious?' James's face lights up. 'That's amazing. Will you come with me to see which ones?'

I nod happily as James suddenly seems to look at me again. He stands back and shakes his head slightly. 'God, Cath,' he says, the smile disappearing from his face. 'You look fantastic.'

'I do? I mean, no, I don't. But thanks.' It's been so long since I last had a compliment I haven't the faintest idea what to do with it.

'Come on.' I take his arm again, if only to stop myself from fainting with happiness. I don't remember the last time I had such a great time. I'm high on champagne and life. My dream of opening a bookshop has come true, and could I be . . . am I . . . oh my God! I'm actually flirting with James, and what's more, I'm enjoying it. Christ, this feels good.

'Cath, have you seen Josh?' I turn and see Ingrid, towering above me.

'Nope. But I'm sure he's around here somewhere.'

'Hello.' Ingrid suddenly extends an arm to James. 'I am Ingrid.'

'Hello,' he says, taking in her twelve-foot legs, three-inch waist and pneumatic breasts. 'I'm James.'

'Nice to meet you, James,' she breathes, in what I'm convinced is a deliberate take-off of Marilyn Monroe.

'Umm, yes. Nice to meet you too.'

'So what are you doing here, James?' Ingrid says, and I give up. My bubble deflates in a split second, and as I back away from the pair of them neither notices, each completely wrapped up in the other.

How is it that you can go from feeling on top of the world to feeling like shit in less than a minute? If this weren't our party, weren't the opening of my dream, I'd leave right now and go to bed. But of course I can't do that, so I choose the only other option available. Booze.

I drink and I drink and I'm about to drink a bit more, when Lucy comes over and, giving me a stern look, introduces me to yet another potential customer to charm. I give her a grateful look, because tonight, the opening of our shop, is not the time to be disgracing myself.

At some point I become aware that Si is trying very gently to steer me into the stock room, and then I look over his shoulder and do a double take. Because walking this way is someone who looks very like Portia.

'Hello, Cath,' she says coolly. 'Long time no see.'

Chapter Six

IT'S VERY STRANGE TO SEE someone again after ten years. Strange to see how that person has changed, whether they have, in fact, changed.

I can see that somehow Portia has. Her face seems harder, and, even though she is still tremendously beautiful, there seems to be something brittle about her. We stand there for a few seconds, both half smiling, both unsure of how to greet one another after all this time.

And though I know my face doesn't give it away, I'm nervous as hell and I can feel my heart beating wildly, and I just hope that when I speak I'm not completely breathless with nerves.

'Oh my God!' Si's shrieking breaks the reverie, and he flings his arms around her in a bear hug before she can say anything. She laughs and gently disengages herself, then gives me a kiss on the cheek.

'But how did you . . .? What are you . . .?' Si is as surprised as I am, and I realise that this isn't his set-up, his surprise.

'Don't ask,' she smiles. 'I got your message, but you never left your phone number. I read about this in the local paper and it mentioned your name, so I thought I'd pop in to say hello.'

'You look amazing,' I find myself saying, because she does, she looks as if she has just stepped from the pages of a glossy magazine. Make that an expensive glossy magazine. Her hair is a rich curtain of mahogany, her eyes bright and clear, and her voice rings with a confidence that has evidently developed tenthousandfold over the years.

'Thank you,' she smiles. 'And it's a relief to find you look exactly the same. The same old Cath. Still presumably as disinterested in fashion as ever, although,' and she fingers my jacket and takes a close look, 'do I detect a hint of Emporio in here?'

Si gasps with pleasure. 'I told you,' he nudges me. 'Told you it was worth the money. I've been trying, Portia'—he looks at her with a shrug—'but you know Cath. This is the first decent thing she's worn in the last ten years.' It's odd to hear his tone of voice, friendly, light, familiar. Almost as if it has only been a week since we last saw her.

'You look good too,' she says to Si. 'This is so weird, coming here and finding that you're all here and still friends and still looking the same.'

'Because you've had to imagine us these last few years?'

Portia looks bemused. 'What are you talking about?'

'I should be angry, but actually I'm rather flattered. Steen is gorgeous.'

Portia laughs. 'God, you wouldn't believe the number of times I've heard people say they *know* it's about them. Si, I hate to disappoint, but they are fiction.'

'Portia, we're not stupid,' I interject gently at this point, guessing that she'll refuse to admit anything, for fear of being sued.

'Anyway,' I say brightly, 'you've done so well. We had no idea the show was yours.'

'Thank you,' she smiles. 'I haven't done too badly.' She looks around the room and says, 'Josh must be here. I'd love to see him.'

'And Lucy, you haven't even met Lucy,' Si says, shooting me a warning look. 'You'll love her. Let's go and find them.'

As I lead Portia through the room, towards Lucy and Josh, I briefly remember Elizabeth. I remember Portia entwining Josh like a snake, before cruelly dumping him, and I think of Lucy's shining face and bright eyes.

And as I walk I thank God that these ten years have passed, and that Portia is not, presumably, the insecure girl she was at university, and that Josh and Lucy are the stongest couple you could ever hope to find.

By the time we manage to reach the other side of the room, the party has thinned considerably. People have come, as they said they would, to show their support and have now moved on to feed families, step into local restaurants, and even, in a few cases, continue drinking elsewhere.

Lucy is perched on one of the stools at the bar, talking animatedly to a reporter from the *Kilburn Herald*, and, as I walk past, Lucy grabs me and pulls me over. 'This is Cath,' she says, 'and this is Keith, who's promised to write lovely things about us, haven't you, Keith?'

Keith smiles, and disappears to find another drink.

'Lucy,' I say, as Si and Portia stand behind me, waiting to be introduced. 'There's someone here I'd like you to meet.'

'More people?' Lucy laughs. 'I thought I'd met everyone in this room.'

'Not everyone.' Portia steps forward, her right hand extended, and Lucy beams at her and shakes her hand.

'I'm Portia. And you must be Lucy.'

'Now this,' Lucy says, her gentle face breaking into a broad smile, 'is truly a surprise.' Lucy pats the stool next to her and Portia obediently sits down, her posture, her poise making Lucy appear rounder and plumper than ever, but Lucy wouldn't notice, wouldn't care: too intrigued by this apparition from a past she never knew.

'So do you like my bookshop, Portia? Will it be a huge success?'

'Yes and yes. I think it's wonderful,' Portia says. 'Although I haven't been here long. Just long enough to see Cath, and Si, and now to meet you. You're not what I expected.'

Lucy, to her credit, doesn't ask what Portia might have expected. She just smiles and says, 'And you, Portia, are far more beautiful, now that you have actually appeared in the flesh. Has my Josh seen you yet? He'll be, well, I don't know. Thrilled? Certainly. Speechless? Far more likely. Shall we go and find him?' and Lucy stands up, links her arm through Portia's and leads her off, as Si and I watch them, open-mouthed.

'What do you reckon?'

'What do you mean?' I look at Si in surprise.

'Is she or isn't she up to something?'

'Oh, for God's sake, Si. Why do you always have to be so bloody negative when it comes to Portia?' Which perhaps isn't entirely fair, given that it's been ten years since we've seen her, but it is true that after that night with Elizabeth, none of us quite trusted her again. 'Come on. Let's go and see the reunion.'

We cross the room to find Lucy beaming at Josh, who does, as she predicted, look completely lost for words.

Lucy is making conversation for both of them. 'Do you know what would be lovely?' she says, surveying the room. 'A proper reunion. We're all dying to know what you've been doing, and I'd love to get to know you properly. Would you come for supper one night, Portia?'

Portia nods and I realise that she probably doesn't know quite how to handle Lucy, because even in the short space of time since they have been introduced, it is clear that Lucy is not intimidated by anyone, and certainly not by Portia.

But how could even calm, sophisticated Portia not respond to Lucy? Lucy is so warm, so welcoming, Portia cannot help but be swept away by her charm, and she tells Lucy that supper sounds wonderful and that there is so much to catch up on.

Josh doesn't really say anything, but then again he doesn't need to, and once Lucy has pressed their phone number into Portia's hand, and Portia has handed over a thick cream business card of her own, Josh shakes Portia's hand awkwardly and says he'll look forward to seeing her soon. And then he excuses himself to help clear up.

Portia turns to Si.

Si has been watching this from a distance, observing as if it were a play. 'Come on you,' she says, nudging him. 'What's been happening in your life? Tell me everything.'

The three of us go to one of the leather sofas, recently vacated, and collapse gratefully on it as Si starts talking to Portia about work. She is fascinated, and it doesn't take long before they find people in common, television and film being so closely linked.

And, as cautious as Si has been, I can see him warm up, and the more he talks the more Portia concentrates, and you could honestly believe that she has never met anyone more fascinating than Si.

'And what about your love life?' she asks finally, and Si gives her a blow by blow account of his relationship with Will, insisting that this time it may well be The One.

'What about you?' he says. 'You don't look married, and'—he picks up her left hand before letting it drop gently down into her lap again—'there's no ring. So are there any potential Mr Fairleys on the scene?'

'God, no,' she groans. 'The only men I seem to meet these days are middle-aged television executives who are all married and desperate for a glamorous bit on the side. I've lost count of how many times I've been invited for a "quick drink after work".'

'Do you ever go?'

Portia laughs. 'I did in the beginning. Back when I was naive and desperate for my big break. Before I understood that a quick drink after work meant a quick bonk in the shabby hotel around the corner.'

'Oh,' I say, trying to picture Portia in a shabby anything, anywhere.

'They could at least have booked Claridge's,' sniffs Si, and we all start laughing.

'So how does it feel to be this huge success?' I ask. 'Do you love it? Has it changed your life?'

'Absolutely.' She looks at me. 'And it's wonderful, but it's also very strange. I always used to think that the one thing I wanted more than anything in the world was to be famous. I used to have daydreams about being a film star, being recognised, being loved by everyone.'

I catch Si's eye, and I know immediately what he's thinking. That of course Portia would have wanted fame, that the only thing she thought would make her feel secure would be the adulation of strangers.

'Not that I'm famous now,' she says quickly, 'but I am *known*. I've gone from being the journalist, the one who does all the interviews and has the power to rip someone apart if she so chooses, to being the vulnerable one, and I'm not sure how much I like it.'

'But I would have thought you'd love it.' Si echoes my thoughts.

She smiles. 'I never expected to feel so vulnerable. You never know what someone's agenda is. And when the series first took off I did lots of interviews. I let people into my home, trusted them in my personal space, opened up to them and was as honest as I knew how, and then I'd open the paper a week later to see that they'd torn me apart. And I know I used to do the same thing, but then I thought that this was the price people paid for being in the public eye, and that it wasn't personal. Except most of the time it is.'

'Jesus,' whistles Si. 'Sounds like a nightmare.'

'It's amazing how quickly you develop a shut-off mechanism,' she says. 'But it never really stops hurting. You just try to avoid the negative pieces because all it's going to do is upset you, and it's not as if anyone's giving you constructive criticism, they're just slagging you off because they don't like you and because they can.'

'But what about the good things? Aren't you going off to amazingly glamorous parties and hobnobbing with the stars and things?'

'Sometimes,' she says, shrugging, 'but actually it's not very exciting at all. You go to two or three things a night, air kiss the same people, do a few lines of coke to keep you going, and have the same vacuous conversations as the ones you had the night before.'

'If you ever need an escort, I'm usually free,' Si grins, throwing up his hands and saying, 'Only joking,' when he sees the look on my face.

'I would have thought the trick is to surround yourself with people you trust. Just the really good friends,' I say. 'So you can go to all these things, but you know that it's not real, and that the real people, the true friends, are the ones you spend your real time with.'

Portia thinks for a while. 'You're absolutely right, Cath. But I suppose I've just been so busy with my career I haven't had a chance to find the sort of people I'd want to surround myself with.' There's a pause. 'I haven't found those sorts of people since university,' and with that she looks first at me, and then at Si, and guiltily I pray that my blush doesn't become any more fierce, for we, after all, chose to lose contact with her when we had all graduated.

'God, I'm boring you!' she says suddenly, turning to me and laying a hand on my arm. 'Cath, you will never know how good it is to see you after all this time. It's your turn. Tell me everything.' And I do.

Half an hour later, or possibly an hour, Lucy comes over with a tray of steaming *lattes* for us, refusing to sit down because there are still a handful of people here who need looking after.

'Oh, damn,' she says, turning round just as she's started to walk off. 'Cath, I forgot. The gorgeous James was looking for you.'

'Was he?' I perk up for a second as Portia raises an eyebrow.

'I thought you said there weren't any men in your life.'

'There aren't,' I say quickly, as Lucy laughs and shouts over her shoulder, 'Not yet, but he's definitely her not-so-secret admirer.'

'I don't think so,' I said, remembering what happened earlier.

'What's he like?' Portia asks.

'Gorgeous,' Si says. 'Young sexy Farmer Giles type.'

'Rather like him?' she says, gesturing to the door.

'Yes.' I watch in a deep gloom as James guides Ingrid out of the door, her face lighting up in a most uncharacteristic way as she turns her head to laugh at something he has said. 'Exactly like him.'

I didn't mean to get drunk last night. In fact I think I was doing incredibly well. Lucy stopped me going hell for leather, and then I'd been knocked sideways by Portia turning up, which definitely sobered me up, and then, after all that, I had to deal with my admirer not actually admiring me in the slightest.

But once the guests had gone, once Portia had left with strict instructions to be at Lucy and Josh's house on Saturday the 18th (instructions from Lucy, needless to say, Josh having gone back home to pay the baby sitter), once it was just Lucy, Si and I, I really let my hair down.

Bill and Rachel attempted to clear up, but Lucy and I shooed them home with a bottle of champagne each.

I was ready to drop, but Si and Lucy were so high on the success of the party, turning the volume of the CD up loud, dancing on top of the bar, that it was impossible not to join in. And Lucy, wisely (or perhaps unwisely), had stashed a few bottles of champagne in the office for exactly this reason.

So we cracked one open, we danced, and we started drinking again.

Properly. Before the champagne appeared, I was desperate to do the Portia post-mortem with Si, but I could see that it would have to wait until the next day, so I pushed all my questions aside, and Lucy and I toasted one another. Over and over and over again.

Josh walked in at some point. I think he was fairly shocked to find Lucy and I lying head to head on the bar, while Si attempted to pour hazelnut syrup into our mouths. Si said it was supposed to be done with tequila, but, since we didn't have any, the syrups used to flavour the coffees would have to be the next best thing.

He didn't seem to be very happy to find Lucy with sugar syrup smeared all over her face and hair.

'Now that,' he said disapprovingly, 'is the most disgusting thing I've ever seen. Look at the pair of you.'

'You're an old killjoy,' I shouted.

'Well, one of us has to act their age, and you're going to have a hell of a job clearing this up tomorrow. I would suggest that unless you plan to spend the whole day in bed with the largest hangovers you've ever had, it's time to go home.'

'I think, troops,' said Lucy, as we struggled up off the counter, 'that much as I hate to admit my boring old husband is right, we should all call it a night.' And although we all moaned and groaned, today I could kiss Josh for being so stern, because if we had carried on drinking all night, I think my liver might well have collapsed.

I wake up the next morning to the doorbell ringing. What the hell does anybody want at this godforsaken hour on a Sunday, and why the hell don't they shut up?

I stumble out of bed, groan as my head pounds like a drum, and walk as quickly as I can to the hallway.

'Hang on,' I shriek, cringing at the loudness of my own voice. 'I'm coming.' And mercifully, the doorbell stops.

I make my way gingerly back to the bedroom and grab the towelling robe from behind the door.

'Who is it?' My voice is back to normal now, I just wish that I were back to normal. My eyes feel like pinheads, my throat is dry and scratchy, and, as if the headache weren't bad enough, waves of nausea are threatening every few seconds.

'Flower delivery,' a voice says, and through the frosted glass I can just make out a huge bouquet of flowers. Strange. Who the hell's sending me flowers on a Sunday?

I open the door quickly, hoping that no one's around to see me, because I don't even have to look in the mirror to know I look like shit.

'Thanks,' I mumble, reaching for the flowers, and as I take them they reveal the face of the delivery man. I stand paralysed with horror.

'Hi!' James's smile fades as he gets his first good look at me. 'Umm, I didn't wake you, did I?'

'What? What do you want?' I don't mean to be rude, but what the hell is his game? He left last night with Ingrid, doubtless took her back to his amazing studio, probably shagged her senseless, and I'm supposed to be pleased to see him?

'Just leave me alone.' I ignore the bewildered expression on his face, shove the flowers back into his hand and slam the door, groaning as the bang reverberates through my poor thumping head.

Oh shit. I make my way slowly to the bathroom, and go to the medicine cabinet. To Nurofen Plus. To redemption. I take three pills just to be on the safe side and stumble back into the bedroom, turning down the volume on the phone on the way. I draw the duvet over my head.

Why should I care if James and Ingrid got it together? Why do I actually feel upset about this? Enough. I'm not going to do this any more.

This time I refuse to wake up until my head, my heart and my life have all returned to normal.

'I can't move,' I groan, eyes still closed, phone lying on the pillow beside my head. 'Leave me alone. I've already been disturbed by that bloody James coming over this morning, and now you. Just go away.'

'Nope.' Si's voice is as dodgy as mine. 'I feel like hell too, but we've got to do the post-mortem, and we've got to do it before we clean the shop. And anyway, the best way of curing a hangover is a fry-up. We need fried eggs, chips, sausages swimming in grease and baked bea . . .' Before he finishes his sentence I've jumped out of bed, run to the bathroom and shoved my head down the bowl of the loo.

I lean my hands on the sink and look at my reflection, marvelling at the face that stares back. I haven't had a hangover this bad for years, and I'm sure I never used to look this awful the morning after. I splash my face, groaning with relief at the cold water.

And as I walk back to the bedroom I hear muffled shouts coming from the telephone. I pick it up in amazement.

'You're still here?'

'I refuse to put the phone down until you agree to meet me for breakfast. And I got the message about the fry-up, so we can just go for a cup of coffee. You have to come.'

What can I do? I give in and we arrange to meet in an hour's time.

An hour later I'm sitting by the window of a cosy café off the high street in Hampstead, nursing a large black coffee and a thumping head.

Si walks in and comes to sit at the table.

He scrapes the chair away from the table, as I grimace and lift my hands to my tender temples.

'Sorry,' he whispers, leaning over to give me a kiss, then sits down. 'Now, we both need to order Cokes,' he says. He goes off into this long explanation of why Coke is the best cure for a hangover, and, true enough, once it arrives and I start sipping it slowly, it's extraordinary how much better I feel.

'First, James,' Si says, and I tell him what happened last night, up to the point I saw him leave with Ingrid.

'But I thought you weren't interested,' Si smirks, as I jump on the defensive.

'I wasn't. I mean, I'm not. It's just that everyone was so convinced he was interested in me, and to be honest it was hugely flattering. And he is a nice guy. At least I thought so until last night, and I suppose I just feel let down.' More than let down, actually.

'But you don't know that anything happened,' Si said.

'You saw Ingrid last night. She looked up for anything, and no man can resist that.'

'True, but if he's as nice a guy as you think he is, then he's not the type to jump into bed with her on the first night.'

'Not "think he is". Thought he was. The only thing I think right now is that I was wrong.'

Si shakes his head and laughs. 'I can't even believe we're having this conversation. This is Cath-the-celibate-one I'm talking to, isn't it?'

'I'm still celibate,' I grunt. 'Just in case you hadn't noticed.'

'I had noticed actually, but I still think it's strange,' he says pensively. 'Portia only re-entered our lives last night, but already I feel unsettled, that the dynamic suddenly seems to be changing.'

'What do you mean?'

'Well, that we should be having this conversation, for starters. I don't remember talking to you like this about men since we were third years. I feel as if I've regressed ten years, as if we all have. And then did you see Josh's face last night? If I didn't know better I'd say he was a lovestruck undergraduate. I almost expected Portia to wind herself round him like a snake and put her tongue in his ear.'

'Jesus!' My mouth drops open. 'I can't believe you just said that. That's exactly what went through my mind.'

'And, pissed as I was, I noticed Josh was not a happy bunny when he came back. I can't help but wonder what else is going to change?'

'Si, you're being a touch overdramatic, don't you think? Anyone would think she's spent the last ten years plotting her revenge and she's come back to steal all our husbands.

'Well, Lucy's husband, because obviously you and I are husbandless,' I continue. 'But still, Si, I do think that's slightly ridiculous. The only time she's ever been interested in Josh was one night, ten years ago. She could have had him permanently then, but she didn't want him, and I don't believe she wants him now.'

'You don't think she could be jealous because he's the only one out of all of us who's actually happily married with a gorgeous child?'

'Did I just hear you use the word "gorgeous" in relation to Max Damien Devilspawn?'

Si grins.

'Look, if we hadn't phoned her that day, we wouldn't have seen her last night. You're reading far too much into it.'

'I don't know.' Si shakes his head. 'I hope I'm wrong. Anyway, I suppose we'll have to watch this space when she comes to Josh and Lucy for dinner. So, back to Farmer James the gorgeous estate agent. What was he doing coming over this morning, or is there something you haven't been telling me?'

Si has arranged to meet Will for a walk on the heath and he persuades me to walk him up to the tube to meet him.

'You don't have to stay,' he begs. 'Pleeeeaaaase,' he pleads. 'I'll be your best friend for ever and ever, and I'll invite you to my party.'

How can I resist? I do, however, clearly state that I will just stay long enough to say hello, and then I will be off.

The gorgeous warm sunshine of yesterday has well and truly disappeared, leaving the weather cold and windy, and truly autumnal, and as we stride slowly up the hill, my breath is visible in the crisp air.

'I love this weather,' Si says, taking a deep breath and exhaling with a look of intense satisfaction on his face.

'Are you serious? Give me the summer any time. People in short sleeves, carefree, everyone smiling and milling round outside.'

'Nope.' Si shakes his head. 'Give me cold, windy winters. Or, even better, this time of year. Autumn. Kicking through the leaves across the heath, then going home to snuggle up under thick blankets with a roaring fire to keep you warm.' He sighs with pleasure.

'God.' I shake my head in wonder. 'You really are an old romantic, aren't you? No wonder you haven't managed to settle down with anyone. Who could live up to those expectations?'

Si thinks for a second. 'Rupert Everett,' he offers finally, smacking his lips together before licking them lasciviously. 'That's who.'

We reach the station five minutes late, and there's no sign of Will. Si immediately worries that we've missed him, that he's been and gone.

'Don't be ridiculous,' I say. 'He's probably late himself.'

And, although it's really far too cold to be standing around a chilly tube station, that's exactly what we do. For half a bloody hour.

'Hasn't he got a mobile?' I ask eventually, and Si nods, so we troop down to the payphone down the hill, Si having forgotten to recharge his. I lean outside, while he phones Will.

I want to eavesdrop desperately, but I don't want to look as if I want to eavesdrop, so I walk over to a shoe shop and try to appear interested in shoes, which isn't exactly a realistic proposition, but it's the best I can do.

Eventually I hear the door to the phone box open, and Si comes out looking completely dejected.

'How do you fancy coming for a walk?' he says finally, his voice flat.

I look at my watch and shrug apologetically, because I have to get to the shop, but Si and I walk back to the tube station together, in silence, as I wait for him to explain. Eventually he lets out a long sigh and says, 'He forgot.'

'He what?' I'm flabbergasted. And horrified.

'He's with friends in some brasserie somewhere, and he said he completely forgot.'

I look at Si's sweet, loving face, and I just want to kill that man for treating Si as if he's disposable. How dare he?

'Bastard!' I spit.

Si doesn't say anything, he just shrugs, so I take his hand and say, 'Just remember what you always used to say to me? That I deserved the best and when was I going to get enough self-esteem to realise that if somebody didn't appreciate me, then it was time to simply walk away.'

Si nods.

'Well, remember that you're old enough to start listening to your own advice? Because, if someone gets away with it once, if they know they can treat you like that, then it sets the pattern for the future.'

'You forgot to say ugly enough,' Si says, with the vestige of a smile.

'What?'

'You said remember I was old enough. You forgot to say "and ugly enough" too.'

'I thought that went without saying,' I grin.

'Thanks,' he says, 'you're the best friend a girl could ever ask for.'

I arrive back home, change into my oldest, most disgusting clothes, grab a bucket of cleaning stuff and dash to the shop.

Lucy's already there, cleaning up the kitchen, and she makes us both strong cappuccinos before we start work. We sit at one of the cleaner tables to drink our coffee and gossip about the night before.

And then, Jesus, do we work. We scrub, sweep, mop and polish, until the shop is positively gleaming, until you wouldn't have a clue that last night there were well over a hundred people crammed in here.

And eventually, when we've finished, Lucy asks me over to have supper with them.

Lucy's kitchen is even more disorganised than usual. The dustbin lid is wide open like a gaping mouth as rubbish threatens to spill out all over the kitchen floor, the sink is overflowing with dishes, and the fridge is now evidently doubling up as a noticeboard, the magnetic poetry kit having been completely hidden by scraps of paper clinging onto the fridge with the help of some rather dusty hamburger-shaped magnets.

Christ. I know I've been neglecting my flat for the past few weeks, but this takes neglect on to a whole other level.

But Lucy is, as always, the port of calm in the storm, blissfully unaware of the chaos around her. I follow her into the kitchen, and she sits down at the kitchen table to slice tomatoes.

Max climbs onto her lap and attempts to grab the knife, while Lucy smiles and gently brushes him aside.

'Don't be silly, darling,' she says, 'you know knives are bad for you,' and I wonder again how she manages to stay so serene in the face of all this noise and mayhem. 'Go and tell Ingrid to get you ready for bed, and Cath, why don't you open that bottle of red on the side,' she continues, as I bristle at the very mention of Ingrid's name. Max runs upstairs shrieking for Ingrid, and minutes later there she is, Ingrid, coming down the stairs looking as sullen as ever. I examine her face closely, trying to see whether she had sex last night. She certainly doesn't *seem* to have any sort of post-coital glow, which is what people always talk about. Not that I think I've ever actually *seen* a post-coital glow, but I'm sure I'd recognise one if I looked hard enough.

I am still examining Ingrid's face as she strides into the kitchen and stops in front of Lucy, left hand planted aggressively on her hip. 'I would like to know where you think Max's blue pyjamas are,' she says.

'The wash?' Lucy says hopefully, as Ingrid shakes her head. 'Ironing pile?' Ingrid shakes her head and pulls her right hand from behind her back. 'They are here,' she says. 'In the laundry basket. Where they have been now for more than one week.'

Lucy grimaces at me, then starts to apologise to Ingrid, who merely says, 'He is your son and tonight he will have to sleep in his day clothes,' before heading for the fridge and helping herself to a yoghurt.

I haven't taken my eyes off her, but I've stopped examining her for the post-coital glow and now I'm just looking at her in amazement, astounded by how she can talk to her employer like that. When she turns round again, she catches me looking at her, and she just stands there watching me, obviously trying to embarrass me for staring at her. I look quickly away as she smirks and leaves the room.

'So.' I stand up and put the kettle on to hide the expression on my face. 'What do you think about James and Ingrid last night, then?'

Lucy looks bewildered. 'What do I think about James and Ingrid what?'

'Well, they left together. I'm assuming she didn't come home?'

Lucy laughs. 'Sweet Cath, do you think that Josh would have come to rescue us from a night of debauchery if Max had been here alone?'

Why didn't I think of that? Thank God.

'But they did leave together,' I continue. 'And James looked as if he were practically salivating.' This last bit isn't quite true, as I couldn't actually see his face when they left, but, if I had been able to, I'm pretty sure that's what he would have looked like.

'Really? I would have thought she was far too obvious for him.' Lucy puts the knife down and smiles. 'Does this mean that you're admitting that you might have some feelings for the lovely James after all?'

'Absolutely not,' I say. 'We're just friends. Well, we were, anyway.' And with that I busy myself with the intricate task of making a cup of tea.

Chapter Seven

BILL'S BEHIND THE TILL, Lucy's busy arranging fresh pastries and croissants in baskets on the counter, and Rachel and I are racing round the shop checking that all the books are exactly where they should be.

'I don't believe it,' I say, turning to the door with a grin as it rattles, and already there are two people outside, ignoring the fact that the closed sign is up, attempting to open the locked door.

'Must be a good omen,' Lucy laughs.

'What do you think?' I check my watch. 'Shall we do it? Shall we let them be our first customers?'

The two women don't show any sign of giving up, so Lucy nods and I go to the door to let them in, the smile on my face completely obliterating the fact that I'm as nervous as hell. Our first customers! I swing the door open and welcome the women in.

'Sorry we're so early,' one of them says, 'it's just that we've been watching this for weeks and we were dying to have a look round.'

'What do you think, Shirley?' The shorter one turns to her friend. 'Coffee first or browsing first?'

Shirley sniffs, then looks over at the counter, where Lucy is beaming.

'We've got delicious homemade Danish pastries,' Lucy says, and the pair of them succumb to Lucy's smile and sit in the café area.

'I must say,' Shirley says, 'you've done a beautiful job here. Look at how lovely and sunny it is. Just what this area needed.'

'I hope everyone feels the same way,' Lucy says.

'Just as long as I don't walk out without *Angela's Ashes*,' Shirley says. 'I've been meaning to read it for ages.' Lucy winks at me from behind the counter, and I scurry off to dig out the Frank McCourt, and take it over to Shirley.

'Oh, what an angel you are,' Shirley says. 'I wish more shops would take a leaf out of your book,' and I walk away feeling a deep satisfaction.

An hour later and there have already been six more people in the shop. Four of them are still here, quietly turning pages, two on the sofas and two in the café, and the others just ran in to buy new titles.

Everyone seems to agree with Shirley, or perhaps they're just saying it to be polite, but people seem genuinely impressed, and by the end of the day we've sold twenty-one paperbacks and sixteen hardbacks, plus taken orders for four more books that we haven't got in stock, which is pretty marvellous.

Not to mention the fact that every single one of Lucy's homemade cakes and pastries has been eaten, and there hasn't been a single minute during the day when the shop has been completely empty.

'I've got to tell you,' I say, turning to Lucy as we're closing up the shop, having shared a bottle of wine with Bill and Rachel to celebrate. 'I think we're on to a winner here.'

'As if you could ever have thought anything different!' Lucy laughs. 'Oh, Cath, you're such a worrier. It's going to be fine.'

And for the first time I understand that she is right after all.

But the fact that she is right does not mean that she is not completely mad. Two weeks later she is busy organising this dinner party on Saturday, when any normal person (ie, me) would be (is, in fact) completely shattered.

And the shop? Well, as everyone predicted, so far it seems to be doing OK. Despite the initial flurry of interest things have settled down, and there have been a couple of very quiet afternoons. It's not what you might call a runaway success, but then we are talking about a bookshop here, and you can't expect people to come in and spend thousands.

As I said, in a rather embarrassing interview in the *Ham & High*, we can't compete with the huge Books Etc. up the road, but then we're not trying to. This was always going to be more of a community bookshop, somewhere for people to meet, chat, have a snack, and then stop on the way out as an interesting book catches their eye.

And the partnership between Lucy and I really seems to be working, despite the reservations Si had.

I love the feeling of waking up every morning and knowing that I'm doing the job I've always dreamed of, and it's my own business. And Lucy's doing what she does best—cooking and playing the convivial host, and she's completely adoring it. She's on her feet all day, which always makes me feel slightly guilty, as I tend to be either sitting behind the till or sitting in the stockroom, but she just laughs and says she doesn't mind. It's worth every second of sore feet.

And now it's time for Lucy's dinner party. I spoke to Portia once last week. She phoned me after Lucy had invited her, and she said I should go to her flat for a drink first, and that it would be lovely to see me on my own after all these years, and how excited she was about seeing me properly, talking to me properly.

You know how I felt after that phone call? I felt exactly the same as I used to feel when we were at university. Honoured by Portia's interest. And although I've relished breaking free from Portia's shadow over the last ten years, there's something about stepping into this old role that feels very familiar, very comfortable, and I wonder whether I'm happiest in the shadows after all.

'What about that lovely James?' Lucy asked last Tuesday when we were closing up the shop. 'I'd love to invite him over, and the two of you seemed to get on so well. Can't I ask him, Cath, my love?'

'No!' I practically barked at her, almost dropping the pile of books I was carrying up from the stockroom.

'You know,' she said carefully, 'there is nothing going on between him and Ingrid.'

'Oh?' I have to admit, my interest was piqued, particularly because I hadn't actually been in touch with him since the day he brought the flowers round, which I still felt fairly guilty about.

'Nope. I asked her.'

'You asked her? What did she say?'

'Well, it was most peculiar, actually. For a moment she looked completely stunned, and then she looked at me as if I'd gone completely mad and laughed uproariously for about five minutes.'

'Are you serious?' I was horrified. 'That's appalling. Jesus, I mean James isn't exactly Mr Universe, but she'd be bloody lucky to get someone like James. Who does she think she is?'

'I know,' Lucy said. 'I mean, James is divine. He may not be her type, but still, there was no need to laugh like that.'

'Lucy, when are you going to realise that the woman is completely vile?'

'Cath, as long as Max is happy I don't really care. Anyway, the point is that obviously nothing happened between them, and I would love to ask him round, and please, please, please say that you wouldn't mind.'

'OK,' I grumbled. 'But don't think this means I've given you my blessing.'

'Fine,' she said, grinning. 'I'm ringing him as soon as I get home.'

Now you know and I know that clothes have never exactly been a big thing for me, but I think I do kind of owe it to James to make something of an effort after the last time he laid eyes on me.

In fact, every time I think about opening the door and seeing him standing there, and more importantly him seeing me, with my wild woman of Borneo hair, my bleary eyes and grey skin, I feel ashamed.

So tonight I want to show James that I can look nice, and maybe, if I try really hard, I'll manage to wipe the image of me from the other morning out of his mind and replace it with one infinitely better.

So I did something this morning that I haven't done for years. I took a day off from the shop—only possible because Si is now dying of jealousy and wants to get in on the act and couldn't wait to take my place for the day—turned a blind eye to the Saturday crowds and hit the Oxford Street shops, even though I didn't have a clue what I was looking for.

But in the first shop I went into I found a pair of grey flannel trousers that would have made Si proud, and then a few doors up I had to stop and admire a window display that made even me want to step inside.

I walked past, hesitated, then stepped back and caught the eye of one of the sales assistants, who smiled at me, encouraging me to go in.

I strode in and walked towards the back of the shop and an array of gorgeous pastel sweaters.

'Why don't you just try one on?' the assistant said with a smile, picking up the one I'd been tentatively fingering—as soft as butter, a delicate baby pink, it was the most beautiful sweater I'd ever seen.

I went into the changing room and when I pulled the sweater over my head and came out, even I had to admit that it was probably the nicest thing I'd ever worn in my entire life. It looked amazing. I couldn't believe how much this simple sweater cost, but I figured that it would be worth it after all. Because, to be honest, what would be the point in revealing your new image in the same old overstretched black sweater that you've worn almost daily for the last five years?

I went, I tried, I paid through the nose. And I was intending to go straight back home, really I was, but as I was walking down the street a trendy-looking girl pressed a paper flier into my hand.

'We're doing a special offer,' she said brightly. 'At Snippers. Everything's half-price today and you get a free consultation.'

On any other day I would have smiled vaguely at her and walked straight past, but today I stopped in front of her, listened, and then looked at the flier. 'Bored with the same haircut?' it proclaimed. 'Looking for a new image? At Snippers we have a team of top experienced hairstylists ready to show you the new YOU!'

What's a girl supposed to do when something like that is thrust into her hand? Up the steps of Snippers I went, and into the hands of— hopefully—top experienced hairstylist, Pezz.

'Mmm,' he said, picking up handfuls of hair and looking distinctly unimpressed. 'Yays, I see. Eet is very deefeecult to handle, no?'

I nodded meekly.

'You would like to have seelky smooth hair, no?'

I nodded again.

'We will give you the hair of Jennifer Lopez,' he said triumphantly. 'But maybe you don't like the colour of theese hairs, hmm?'

Actually I wasn't that bothered. Pezz, on the other hand, was.

'I am theenking vegetable rinse, yes? I theenk nice reech brown. Strong warm tones weeth leettle beet of red, hmm?'

Two hours later I'm sitting in the chair at Snippers looking into the face of someone who does look like me, only a far better version.

Because I would never have believed that *my* hair could be silky, smooth and actually *shiny*! My hair is *shiny*! Pezz has worked wonders. I seem to have a chestnut mane falling to slightly below my shoulders.

It looks amazing. I love it. I can't stop smiling at myself. The only problem is, and I only realise this as I keep looking at myself in the mirror, it's exactly the same as Portia's. Shit. And how the hell am I supposed to pass this off as coincidence?

'Cath, you look wonderful.' Portia comes to the door of her apartment, air kisses me on each cheek and beckons me inside, through a wide, airy corridor to an enormous living room with huge windows overlooking communal gardens off Sutherland Avenue.

On the glass coffee table, next to the enormous bowl of white lilies, is a bottle of champagne, already opened, and two glasses. Portia pours me a glass and collapses elegantly on a terrifyingly expensive-looking white sofa. I sit next to her, her knee-length skinny skirt more than adequately showing off the length of her legs, helped somewhat by high strappy sandals.

Portia looks rich. She looks as if she doesn't have a care in the world. And, although I am in my new grey flannel trousers, my new pink cashmere-mix sweater, with my glossy locks falling sleekly on my shoulders, next to Portia I feel even more frumpy than I did this morning.

There is something about her appearance that looks effortless. If you look closely you will see that she *is* wearing make-up, and quite a lot of it at that, but unless you are standing nose to nose, she looks as if she has just fallen out of bed, brushed her hair, slicked on some lip gloss and run out of the door.

She raises her glass to mine and smiles. 'Cheers,' she says, and then sips some champagne, looking for all the world as if she should be in a film or, at the very least, a television advert.

'Your flat's amazing,' I say. 'I can't believe how huge it is, how high these ceilings are.'

'I know. The first time I came into this room I just fell in love with the proportions. Do you want the guided tour?'

I nod, and she leads me through into the kitchen, the dining room, and the bedroom. All of it is beautiful, and at the last door Portia hesitates and grins before turning the knob.

'This,' she says, 'is the real me. It's the room I never show people because it's in such an appalling state, so here goes. 'My study.'

No wonder she manages to keep her flat immaculate. All the junk, all the papers, all the books, are in here.

'I do all my read-throughs on here,' she says. 'My favourite place in the world.' She flops down onto a navy blue sofa and for a second I catch a glimpse of Portia before she felt she had to play a role, before she became the well-honed sophisticated adult she is today. Portia was always sophisticated; you always knew she came from a wealthy family, but you didn't *know*. Now she wears it like a coat of armour.

We go back to the living room and I ask her whether she is comfortable playing this role, and for a second she looks hurt, but she swiftly regains her composure and lets out a small laugh. 'What sort of role do you think I'm playing?'

'God, I'm sorry, Portia, I didn't mean to offend you. It's just that everything about you is so perfect, so polished. It looks like it must be such hard work, living like this.'

She shrugs. 'Not hard work. You get used to it, and this is, I suppose, what's expected of me.'

'What do you mean?'

'Well, every time anyone writes about the new league of single superwomen, I'm usually in there at the top of the list, and they always want to photograph me at home and examine the contents of my fridge, and quite frankly I wouldn't want to disappoint.'

'So what does a single superwoman keep in the fridge?'

Portia laughs. 'Help yourself,' she says, and I go and open the fridge. 'Portia,' I start to laugh. 'Lucy would have a fit if she saw this.' Because there is, quite simply, nothing remotely edible in the fridge. There are two shelves devoted to champagne and white wine, another devoted to mineral water, and a few tins at the back which on closer inspection reveal themselves to be—surprise, surprise—caviar.

'What do you live on?' I come back into the living room, shaking my head in amazement.

'I eat out mostly,' she says. 'And occasionally I'll pick something up on my way home from work.'

'What if you have dinner parties?'

'Darling,' she says, fixing me with a mocking look, 'what do you think caterers were invented for?'

I smile, and then a question occurs to me. 'Portia, I can see why you're portrayed as a single superwoman, but why are you?'

'Why am I what?'

'Why are you single? I just don't understand it.'

Is it my imagination or does Portia suddenly look slightly uncomfortable? 'I just haven't found the right person yet,' she says breezily, but somehow I don't believe her. Then again, this is typical of Portia. She probably has some terrible tale of loss and heartbreak, but, when she doesn't want to talk about something, she switches off.

She pours some more champagne for us both, and then sits back, looking at me over the rim of her glass, and before I have a chance to ask more questions she deftly changes the subject.

'How have these last few years been for all of you?' she says, continuing without waiting for an answer. 'You and Si told me a bit about your lives at the bookshop the other week, but what about Josh? Is he happy? I must say that Lucy seems . . . she seems *charming*. Not perhaps what I expected, but obviously the relationship works . . . Does it?'

'Josh and Lucy? God, they're amazing. Well, you'll see for yourself later on, but they're the most perfect couple imaginable. I know what you mean about Lucy not being what you'd expect—you should have seen the horrors he kept picking up throughout his early twenties. All these identical Sloanes called Serena who were desperate to get Josh into Daddy's business.'

'Lucy definitely doesn't fit into that category,' Portia says. 'So how come he ended up falling for Lucy?'

I tell Portia the story of how Josh and Lucy met on a skiing trip, that Lucy was the chalet girl who looked after him when he fell and injured his ankle. And then I look at my watch and let out a yelp, and we order a minicab and dash over to Josh and Lucy's.

And throughout the entire cab journey, Portia asks me questions about Josh, about Lucy, about Max, and I'm not entirely sure why, but I find myself clamming up slightly. Perhaps I'm not entirely comfortable with her interest. Perhaps I'm starting to think that Si might be right, that she might be up to something after all.

As usual, Si opens the door to Josh and Lucy's house and welcomes us in, giving Portia a brief hug before turning to me and leaning forward to give me a kiss. And then he stops.

'Oh my God!'

I smile.

'Oh my God, oh my God, oh my God!'

Lucy comes running out of the kitchen, and Josh comes running out of the living room, and within seconds all three of them are staring at me open-mouthed.

'Can I touch it?' Si whispers reverently, as he reaches out and softly strokes my head as if I were a cat.

'Look at our Cath!' Lucy beams proudly. 'Quite the supermodel! Cath, you look gorgeous, look at your fantastic hair, and your sweater!'

'You look amazing,' Josh says, when he finally recovers, and he catches Portia's eye and immediately goes over to welcome her.

I watch, and I can see Si watching out of the corner of his eye as Josh leans down to give her a kiss, and Portia, instead of kissing the air as she has done with the rest of us, plants her lips softly, but very definitely, on Josh's cheek, and I look at Si in alarm as he raises an eyebrow.

We go into the living room, and because we're so late I'm certain that James will already be in there, so imagine my surprise when the vile Will turns round from examining the bookshelves.

'Hello, Catherine,' he says, extending a hand, which I take reluctantly. 'Nice to meet you again.'

'And you,' I say, nodding, extracting my hand and shooting a filthy look at Si for not telling me Will was coming. 'This is Portia.' I introduce them, and edge towards the door, so that I can sneak into the kitchen to try to discover what has happened to James.

Lucy hands me a bowl of Indonesian crisps and instructs me to take them into the living room, and just as I head out of the room I turn my head and say in a nonchalant manner, 'Isn't James coming tonight?'

'Oh bugger!' Lucy slaps her forehead. 'Oh blast! Oh damn! I knew there was something I'd forgotten.' She looks mortified. 'Oh, Cath, I'm sorry, can you forgive me?'

I feel a flash of anger at her because this is just typical of her to be so scatty and to forget. This is exactly what Si was talking about, why he warned me off going into business with her.

'Bugger. And you look so gorgeous, I can't believe it.' She's genuinely devastated and I start to forgive her. It's not the end of the world. I'm just disappointed. 'What happened?' I say.

'I phoned him and then the machine picked up just as my call waiting went and so I left it and I just completely forgot to call him back.'

'Don't worry,' I say, but I feel like laying my head on my arms and sinking into a deep sleep. It's not even as if I'm terribly upset, I'm just weary. Weary of this whole relationship game. Weary even though I've only taken one tiny tentative step back into the lion's den, and already I'm learning that I'm just not equipped to win this one.

I take the bowl into the living room and sink miserably into the sofa, as Josh looks at me with a worried expression, then leaves the room, presumably to find out what's wrong.

Portia and Will are deep in discussion, and, bizarre as this may sound, it almost looks as if he's flirting with her. I watch Si trying to push his way into the conversation, only to be ignored, and eventually he comes over to me with a shrug and an apologetic smile.

'They seem to be getting on like a house on fire,' I say.

'I know. At last someone seems to like him. Look, sweets, I know you don't like him, but please try to make an effort. It would make me so happy.'

'OK,' I grumble as Josh and Lucy walk in, having finally got the food in the oven and the devilspawn into bed.

'Will.' Josh pours him some more wine. 'Si tells us you live in Clerkenwell. How do you find it?'

'I love it,' Will says. 'I've got the most incredible loft in probably the best building in Clerkenwell, and there's always something going on in the neighbourhood.'

'Will's been thinking about moving to Soho, though,' Si interjects in his best husbandly way.

'Really? Why?'

'I'm not seriously thinking, it's just that the only problem with Clerkenwell is it's pretty much in the back of beyond and I miss being in the centre of things. Don't you feel the same way living here?'

The hairs on my back bristle, but luckily he wasn't talking to me and I leave it to Lucy to deal with that last comment.

'Here? Why on earth should we feel that living *here*. It's West Hampstead. We're practically in town.'

'Oh, come on,' Will sneers. 'This is the nineties version of suburbia. A high street lined with cafés and local ethnic restaurants, and the whole area filled to bursting with young marrieds like yourself with their 2.4 children and a four-wheel drive. It's the updated version of Abigail's Party. Mike Leigh would have a ball.'

I'm dying to open my mouth, but I'm frightened that if I do the damage will be irreparable, not only to my future relationship with Will, but more importantly to the relationship I have with Si.

'You are joking?' Lucy says very quietly, as Will shrugs and says he's not. 'First of all, *Will*,' and I can tell by the inflection on his name that Lucy is seriously pissed off, which is something that doesn't happen all that often, 'West Hampstead is a fifteen-minute drive to the West End, and a ten-minute ride on the Thameslink to the City, which I think you'll find would not merit a labelling of suburbia anywhere.

'Secondly, what exactly is wrong with an area that caters to the needs of, as you put it, *young marrieds*?'

Will shrugs disdainfully. 'It's just, well. Look at you all. You think you're so cutting-edge and trendy, with your stainless-steel top-of-the-range kitchen equipment and your Alessi corkscrews, but it's all just the nineties version of suburbia.'

'I'm not entirely sure of the point you're making,' Lucy says, her voice ice-cold. 'So what if we have Alessi corkscrews and four-wheel drives . . .' She takes a breath and is about to carry on, but Portia steps in and expertly changes the subject to calm everyone down.

'Speaking of four-wheel drives,' she says coolly, 'I've been thinking about trading in my car for one of those jeeps. I quite fancy the idea of being so high up on the road—it adds a whole new perspective to my superiority complex.'

Everyone laughs and the tension is shattered, and I wonder how I had forgotten Portia's ability to do this—to diffuse situations, to calm things down, to take control—for which I am immensely grateful.

We somehow manage to sit and make small talk, and I watch Si watching Will with big, adoring eyes, and I can't help but note that Will barely even turns to look at him.

If I were to give him the benefit of the doubt I'd say that Will was trying so hard to make a good impression on everyone else that he was temporarily abandoning Si, but somehow I don't think it is that. I just don't think he's interested, really, but God, how I hope I'm wrong.

Eventually we stand up and all file into the dining room, as I give Lucy's arm a squeeze, because none of us has even been into the dining room for about two years—we always eat in the kitchen—and I find myself seated next to Josh at the top and then, thank God, next to Si.

Will walks past my chair on his way to his place, and as he passes he leans down and touches my sleeve. 'Very nice,' he says, and I open my mouth to thank him for such an unexpected compliment. 'Shame it's not pure cashmere.' And with that he walks off round the table.

Portia is on the other side of Josh, opposite me, and thankfully next to Will, and in the commotion as people take their seats Si leans over and whispers, 'Bet you a fiver she flirts with Josh all night.'

But Si is wrong. Not, perhaps, through choice, but for lack of opportunity. Will has evidently decided that Portia is the only person at this table worthy of his attention and monopolises her totally.

The rest of us fall into our easy conversations. We talk about the bookshop, and I make everyone laugh with tales of mad customers. Already three people have come in and asked for a book, and, on being told it isn't stocked but it could be here the next day, have gone on to ask if Waterstone's have the book.

Lucy chuckles, as I apparently kept smiling through gritted teeth, even as I politely told them to go and find out for themselves. And where, the customers wanted to know, would they find the book? On which floor?

The conversation dies down as Lucy brings in the chicken dish, and we all make the appropriate noises of delight at the smell as Lucy lifts the lid to release the steam.

All, that is, except for Will. He says nothing until he is served, and when we all start eating, all groaning with pleasure, Will chews for a while, then pushes his plate aside. We all stop and stare.

'Is everything OK?' Lucy asks.

Will sneers at the food. 'Not really, no. This is *supposed* to be a River Café recipe, isn't it?' he says, as Lucy nods and looks worried. 'I can't put my finger on it, but there's something not right about it. You've changed the herbs or something, what is it?'

Lucy's face falls, and I look at Si in exasperation, as he simply looks crestfallen.

'Well,' Lucy says uncertainly, 'I don't usually stick to recipes all that precisely any more. I'm not sure what I did differently, but I just used that recipe as a guideline, a base. You don't like it?'

'Put it like this,' Will says. 'Inedible would be one of the nicer things I would say about it.'

Nobody says anything for what feels like an interminably long time, then Josh stands up and the silence that has already descended on the table grows even more fraught.

'Enough,' Josh says slowly, and we all turn to look at him. 'Will, I would like you to leave.'

'You're not serious,' Will says, half smiling, picking up his fork and prodding the chicken on his plate.

'Put. That. Fork. Down.' Josh says, and my eyes widen because I don't think I have ever seen Josh that angry before.

'I welcomed you into my home as a guest, and you have spent the entire evening making me regret ever allowing you across the threshold. You have insulted my wife, my friends and me. You are not welcome here, and I want you to leave this instant.'

Finally Will seems to realise that he's not joking. Si's face is purple with embarrassment, and, as Will scrapes his chair back, Si stands up as well, but he can't look any of us in the eye.

'Fine,' Will says, as he walks out of the room, Si scuttling behind him. 'I was here on sufferance anyway.' I keep my eyes glued to the table-cloth, terrified that if he catches my eye he'll start on me.

Will storms out, slamming the front door, Si hovers in the hallway apologising to Josh. And from what I hear, Josh is telling Si that it's not his fault, and that Si is welcome to stay, of course he is, but if he wants to leave we'll all understand.

Of course Si, loving, lovely, needy, insecure Si, leaves. And as soon as the door quietly closes behind him and we are all just about to breathe a sigh of relief, a familiar clattering comes down the stairs.

'Lucy.' Ingrid towers in the doorway. 'Why are there doors being slammed when Max is asleep.'

'God, I'm sorry Ingrid,' Lucy apologises. 'It was one of our guests, he left in a bit of a hurry.' She pauses. 'Ingrid, would you like some supper? We've got masses of this chicken left over.'

'And it's delicious,' I add, just in case there's any doubt.

'No,' Ingrid says, scanning the room. 'I have eaten already.'

'You know Cath, of course,' Lucy says, as Ingrid barely nods in my direction. 'And this is Portia, an old friend of Josh. Portia, this is Ingrid, our wonderful au pair.'

Portia smiles at Ingrid, and, Christ, does this woman's charm never cease, Ingrid smiles back. If I didn't know better I'd think Ingrid was as sweet as sugar from the beatific smile she now bestows upon Portia.

'It's nice to meet you, Portia. I hope you all have a nice evening,' she says, and goes upstairs.

'You're unbelievable,' I say to Portia once she's gone. 'You're like one of those Indian snake charmers. You just manage to charm everyone.'

Portia laughs. 'What do you mean?'

'Oh, come on.' Even Josh is laughing. 'She's right. First of all you were the only one who managed to charm that awful Will bloke, and then you manage to charm'—and at this point he lowers his voice to a whisper—'the scary Ingrid.'

'Is she scary?' Portia laughs, also whispering.

'God, yes,' Josh whispers back. 'Ask anyone.'

Lucy's watching us with a broad smile. 'Yes, but how terrifying do you find the fact that Si seems to be completely enamoured with that . . . that *pig*?'

'He's disgusting,' I moan.

Portia looks pained. 'He wasn't that bad,' and my jaw hits the floor.

'Oh, come on,' Josh starts laughing. 'You've got to be joking.'

'No,' she says earnestly. 'I know too many people like that, and all that arrogance hides tremendous insecurity. He wasted no time in telling me he'd spent the afternoon looking at company cars and that he was thinking of getting a Porsche Boxster, which I don't believe for a second.'

'Prick,' Josh says, as we all nod in agreement.

'But you know,' Lucy says, doling out second helpings. 'I'm not sure that insecurity is a good enough excuse for that sort of behaviour. We're all insecure, and he's old enough to have discovered the reasons behind his insecurity, and do something about them.'

'Darling,' Josh says affectionately, 'not everyone is a budding psychotherapist. He probably doesn't even care what the reasons are.'

'I bet I can tell you what the reasons are,' Portia says suddenly.

'Go on.' I'm fascinated.

'Well, there were some obvious clues. First, he speaks in very polished tones. Too polished. If you listened closely there were some definite northern inflections, and after I'd asked him he confessed—reluctantly—that he was from Yorkshire.'

We're all very impressed and stay silent for her to continue.

'Before that he said his father was a bigwig at one of the City banks, and changed the subject when I asked which one. And then a while later he said that since he's lived in London he goes home to his parents for the odd weekend to help his dad with his accounts.

'So his father clearly doesn't work in the City. He's probably a dentist or something, in a sleepy northern village, and Will thinks that in order to run with the fast crowd in London he has to make up a pack of lies that he thinks will impress people.'

'But at the end of the day, even if he's from a family who didn't have a bean, it doesn't give him the right to be arrogant, superior and, well, as Josh put it, a prick.'

'True, Cath,' Portia says. 'But I think he's terrified of people discovering who he really is and where he's really from.'

'OK, clever clogs.' I give Portia a challenging smile. 'You're proving to be the witch tonight. Is Si going to stay with him for ever?'

'I have a feeling,' she says with a sigh, 'that it won't be long before we all find out.'

Next day at around 11.00am, I get a sheepish phone call.

'It's me.'

'I know,' I say, surprised he's taken so long. 'How are you?'

'Embarrassed,' he admits. 'I know I've got to phone Josh and Lucy and apologise, but I don't know what to say to them.'

'Why are you apologising? It's your arse of a boyfriend who should be saying sorry. He behaved appallingly.'

'I know.' And he does know, because I have never heard Si sound this contrite before. 'But he won't apologise. He doesn't think he needs to, because he'll never be seeing any of you again.'

'Charming. I take it he liked us as much as we liked him, then?'

'More, possibly. Except for Portia, whom he raved about all the way home, but then again she is a semi-celebrity, which seems to turn him on somewhat.' His voice sounds slightly bitter.

'So I take it all is not rosy in the garden of Eden?'

'God, I don't know, Cath.' He lets out a deep sigh. 'I went back to Will's flat, and he basically ignored me the whole night, and I was appalled by his behaviour at Josh and Lucy's. I just don't understand it.'

'Si, what are you doing with him?'

'He's not all bad, you know, Cath. He can be incredibly sweet and loving, but . . .' and he stops and sighs again.

'So it's not over yet?'

'Not until the fat lady sings.' And with a sad smile that I can picture as he speaks, we say goodbye.

And when I get home the next evening there is a message from Lucy, three messages from Si, and finally, James's voice comes on the machine.

'Hi, umm, Cath. It's James. Look, I'm not sure what I've done to upset you, but whatever it is I'm really, really sorry. I'd really like it if you called me . . .' and he leaves the number. I replay the message a few times, trying to work out if there is a subliminal message lurking in between the lines, but there's nothing.

I kick off my shoes and wander into the kitchen. I make myself a coffee and take it into the living room with the food to think about James and whether I should call him back.

The problem is that I do like James and if I were to even contemplate getting involved with anyone at this time in my life, James is probably exactly the sort of man I'd choose.

But the bigger problem is that I can't get involved. I can't go through all the shit that Si's going through now with Will—the hassle of introducing someone to all my friends and praying that they'll like him and that he'll like them. Although I suppose that bit's already been taken care of with James.

Look at me. I'm sprawled on the sofa, one leg flung over the back, crap sit-coms that I'd never admit to watching blaring from the television screen, and I'm slurping my coffee because it's too hot.

I wouldn't be able to do any of this if I were with James, with *anyone*. And even if I could, the risk of hurt, or loss, is always there, and right now I'm happy. I don't want anyone to come and spoil that.

'Not even if you could be a thousand times happier?' Lucy once asked.

'Nope.' I shook my head with a grin. 'Not when I've got all of you.'

'You can't grow as a person,' she said sadly, ignoring my joke, 'when you close yourself off emotionally. It's all well and good saying you avoid pain by avoiding relationships, but what about the wonderful things you're avoiding as well? What about the joy and the intimacy and the trust that come with finding someone you love?'

'I don't need to find someone I love to have that,' I remember saying. 'I have joy and intimacy and trust with my friends. What I don't have is heartache and insecurity and the loss of my *self*.'

I head back into the kitchen and open the fridge to see if there's anything vaguely edible, again, but no luck there. Aha! The freezer! I thank God, and thank Si, that nestling in among the frozen peas is the one thing that's guaranteed to make my night.

A Sara Lee frozen Cinnamon Danish that Si brought over one Sunday but that we never got around to eating. Licking my lips, I set the microwave to DEFROST and linger in the kitchen, smelling the delicious cinnamony, almondy smells wafting around.

I can't wait for the ping. I open the door ten seconds before it's ready and pull the Danish out, tearing off a large chunk. Oh God, this is delicious. I take the plate inside, vowing to eat only half and settle back into the sofa, plate balanced on my knees.

Ten minutes later I'm groaning with disgust, but even as I groan I'm licking my index finger and sweeping it around the plate to catch any crumbs I missed earlier. I've eaten the whole thing, and it was delicious.

And let's face it. I'd never be able to do this if I had a boyfriend, would I? But James is a nice guy. James could be a good friend. I've always said I don't need any more friends, but that's mostly because Si has filled the role of boyfriend/brother/best friend better than anyone else. But since Will has come on the scene, maybe I have been feeling just a tiny bit lonely.

I resolve to phone James back, because he would be the perfect friend. But right now, with bulging belly and lethargy inflicting every bone in my body, I can't be bothered. But I *will* ring him tomorrow.

The TV stays on for the rest of the evening. I mute it temporarily to phone Lucy, and I leave a message for Si, then carry on mindlessly watching, and find myself becoming really quite engrossed in one of those detective drama series when the doorbell rings.

Shit. Now I know I said that James would be a perfect friend, but this habit he has of turning up with no warning is beginning to seriously get on my nerves.

I stomp down the hallway and open the front door, trying to smile so that I don't frighten him off permanently, and on my doorstep is Si.

'Si! I was just thinking about you! What a gorgeous surprise,' I exclaim happily, giving him a hug, and when we pull apart Si gives me a wobbly smile and proceeds to burst into tears.

'Oh shit.' I usher him in and lead him to the sofa, sitting down next to him and rubbing his back until the first bout of tears has subsided.

I ask if it's over, and again he nods, and along comes a fresh spurt of tears. Eventually he manages to calm down enough to tell me.

Will had phoned Si at work today, and after a brief chat in which Si now says he could tell something was wrong, Si asked if they would be seeing one another later. Will said that Si could come over if he wanted, and that he'd be in around eight.

So Si duly went over, planning to have a talk with Will. Not *The Talk*, he said, just a talk about how important his friends were to him, and how important Will was becoming, and how life would be so much easier if he could try to get along with Si's friends, even though he understood they weren't Will's types.

But Si never got the chance to have any sort of conversation. Will opened the front door, then ignored Si as he walked back into the living room. And there, on the sofa, was Steve—a guy they'd met together in a pub a couple of weeks back.

Steve was exactly the sort of man that Si always runs miles from. Good-looking, arrogant, dismissive. Exactly, I thought to myself, like Will, except this Steve obviously didn't bother with the charm act at all.

Will went to sit back down on the sofa, pressed up next to Steve, and the pair of them sat there drinking their beers, giggling like teenagers at jokes that Si was clearly not in on.

So Si sat there for a while, watching them flirt, hoping this was some horrible nightmare that would be over any second, when Will looked up and said, 'Are you still here?'

Shocked, Si stood up, as Steve snorted in amusement and Will buried his head in his shoulder to hide the laughter.

'Not interested,' Si heard Will say as he stumbled out of the flat. '*You're* boring as fuck, your *friends* are boring as fuck, and as for your *fucking* . . .' and he heard the laughter as he slammed the door.

It wasn't that Will was the love of his life, Si sniffs, but the humiliation was awful. 'I can't cope with the rejection. Why does this always have to happen to me? Why? What have I done?'

And what can I say? What is there to say? Eventually I come out with a feeble, 'He wasn't good enough to even lick your bloody shoes. Si, you're gorgeous. He's just an arse for not recognising it.'

'Do you think that somebody, someday will recognise it?'

'Absolutely, one hundred per cent, definitely.'

'Thanks, sweets.' He gives me a wobbly smile and I give him a hug until he starts to sniffle again, warning that I mustn't be too nice or it will set him off again.

'You know what will definitely make me feel better?' he says suddenly with a faint twinkle in his eye. 'Ice cream. Come on, get your shoes on. We're going out.'

On any other night I'd tell Si to get stuffed because going out this late in the freezing cold is the very last thing I feel like doing, particularly after the entire cinnamon Danish, but tonight I have to show what friends are made of, so I pull some boots on and head out of the door.

Half an hour later we're sitting in the window of Haagen-Dazs, rain splattering the glass, my wonderfully smooth locks having now, thanks to the rain, frizzed up to the usual Cath mess.

Si's spooning out the last of a tub of Strawberry Cheesecake ice-cream, and I'm watching him, doing my best not to be sick.

'Are you sure you don't want my last spoonful?' Si says, holding the spoon to my mouth.

'Absolutely not.' I shake my head as the Danish threatens to rise once more. 'But I'm glad you love me enough to ask.'

Chapter Eight

'CATH, MY LOVE, do you think anyone would ever understand how much we appreciate a Sunday off? I don't know about you but I am absolutely exhausted.' Lucy kicks off her shoes and stretches her arms up to the ceiling, rolling her shoulders and sighing. 'I wish someone had told me quite how many hours we'd have to be working.'

'But think of all the benefits . . .' I make sympathetic noises just as the front door slams, and Ingrid and Max arrive back from the park.

'MUmmyyyyyy!' Max comes hurtling down the hallway and flings himself into Lucy's arms, as she covers him with kisses, and whatever animosity I may have felt towards Max in the past, my heart warms.

'What's that, my love?' Lucy says, gently detaching herself enough to take the piece of paper clutched in Max's hand.

'Darling, that's wonderful. Is that you with Mummy and Daddy? Why have I got blonde hair?'

'Because,' Max says, 'it's me, Daddy and Ingrid. I was going to draw you, but Ingrid plays with me more,' and with that he climbs down, too young to see the hurt in Lucy's eyes. She waits until he's run upstairs, and then rubs her temples with her hands.

'You see?' she says finally, looking at me. 'I can't blame him for that. I hardly see him, and Josh and I feel like ships passing in the night right now. In the mornings I pass him in the kitchen as I'm making a cup of coffee and he's grabbing his briefcase and running out the door, and if I'm lucky we have a chance to have a quick two-minute chat at night before I hit the sack.'

'Lucy, I don't know what to say, because I haven't got anyone to worry about other than me, and quite honestly I love the fact that it keeps me so busy. It stops me worrying about not having a social life.' And it's true. I have never been happier in my life than this last month, since the bookshop opened.

I love getting to know my local community, because although I've lived here for years, I never really knew anyone outside my immediate social circle. I love getting to know the regulars, chatting about books with them. And I don't mind in the slightest the fact that I am working late almost every night, and that whatever social life I might have had has flown out the window without a backward glance.

Lucy looks at me with a smile. 'No social life? What are we, then?' and she laughs. 'The problem, my darling Cath,' she says eventually, 'is that I love it too. I love Bookends and I love the fact that I'm a person again, not just Josh's wife, or Max's mother. I love the fact that I'm working with you and that I'm meeting people every day. I'm getting out there, achieving something.'

'So how do you think you can resolve it?'

'On the rare occasions I've managed to catch Josh he's said these are just teething problems. He says that hopefully we'll be able to take on more staff soon and just be in the shop for normal opening hours. I hope he's right.' Suddenly the light comes back on in her eyes and she flashes her megawatt smile at me. 'Anyway,' she continues, 'that's enough about my boring old life. I've been so wrapped up in myself I haven't even asked you anything. So what's all this about you and the lovely James going out next week?'

I called James back. I decided the best way of proceeding would be, rather than apologising for slamming the door in his face and shoving the flowers back at him, to pretend that everything was fine and nothing out of the ordinary had happened. Obviously, as Lucy pointed out, I was running the risk of him thinking I was completely round the bend, but I'd prefer that to having him know I was furious because I thought he'd gone off with Ingrid.

He sounded guarded at the beginning of the conversation, but I can hardly blame him for that, and within the first two minutes I made him laugh by telling him about the dinner party he was supposed to have gone to, and then everything was fine.

Suddenly I realise that half an hour has flown by without me even thinking about it, and then James asks me out for dinner, and I find myself saying yes, which I suppose means I'll be going out on a date.

A date! Why do I feel like such a teenager at the very mention of the word? But a date! I have to talk to someone about this, have to share it with someone.

Now, usually Si would have been my first port of call when asking advice, but right now he has done what he always does when he is dumped, which is immediately come round to me to have a good cry, and then hibernate for a while to get his strength back. Once upon a time I used to feel shut out when he did that, but I'm used to it now, and I know that the only way to get the old Si back, when he's been truly hurt, is to leave him be, as he spends his evenings alone in his flat, listening to old love songs and feeling sorry for himself, until suddenly he snaps out of it and demands we accompany him to some club or bar.

So who am I supposed to share this with? Si is incommunicado, Lucy is far too busy with the shop to pay any attention, and Josh? Josh seems a bit distracted right now. Apparently—and Lucy says this is the only reason why she doesn't feel quite so guilty not getting home until late— he's got some huge deal going on at the office, and he's having to work all the hours God sends.

So I suppose the only person that really leaves is Portia.

'Why don't we have a long girly lunch?' she says, when I phone her a couple of days later on the pretext of finding out how she is, but really to talk to her about James. 'My treat.'

Well, how could I resist?

I arrive at Kensington Place at exactly one o'clock, and I'm shown to a table next to the window, where I sit looking at my watch, wondering when exactly Portia will turn up.

At ten past one I order a glass of white wine, and at quarter past I start studying the menu, deciding what I'm going to order.

At twenty past one, just when I've given up hope, I look up to see Portia grinning at me outside the window, and I grin back and relax my shoulders because she's finally here, although it takes a good five minutes for her to actually walk through the restaurant, because it seems she knows *everyone* in here.

Eventually she reaches the table and envelops me in a warm hug, apologising profusely for being so late. 'I got carried away with a script for the new series,' she laughs, 'and had no idea what time it was.'

'Don't worry,' I say, not bothering to add that I had pretty much used up my lunchbreak travelling all the way to Kensington.

'So,' she says, when she'd ordered a sparkling mineral water. 'You look wonderful.'

'You liar,' I laugh, because my hair is back to the wild woman of Borneo, and I'm in my usual old black gear today, saving my pink sweater and grey trousers for the date.

'No, seriously,' she laughs. 'I mean, you looked fab the other night, but you weren't you.' My face falls. 'No, no,' she says quickly, 'don't be offended, but sitting here now, with your curly hair and no make-up, this is the Cath that we all know and love.'

'So what do you think I should do for my date with James?'

'Be yourself. Make-up and hairdressers are lovely for special occasions, but this is the Cath that he fell for, so why change anything?'

I start to laugh. 'Portia! That's all well and good, but look at you, for Christ's sake! You're immaculate!'

'But that's different.' She rolls her eyes. 'Didn't I ever tell you that my mother says I emerged into the world wearing high heels and lipstick?'

I laugh with her, but she can see there's something in my eyes and that all is not completely well.

'What's the matter?'

I sigh for a bit, then try to explain the way I feel. How I've managed to protect myself by surrounding myself with people I know and trust and love, and that anything outside that group feels very dangerous, and very frightening, feelings I'm not used to.

'I do understand,' she says, smiling, when I finish. 'Better than you might think. I know what it's like to want something very badly but to be too frightened of going after it because it feels dangerous. But Cath, I don't need to tell you of all the good things you could be missing out on. I'm sure Lucy's already told you.'

I smile, because of course Portia's right.

'But you know, if this helps at all, I've always thought that the one thing I would regret more than anything else in life is to reach the ripe old age of, say, eighty, look back on my life and think, "What if?" What if I'd done something differently, what if I'd followed my heart?

'And you know, even at thirty-one, I have regrets. There are things I wish I'd done, things I wish I'd said, and things'—her eyes become increasingly wistful—'I wish I hadn't said, hadn't done.'

'It's not too late, though? You're *only* thirty-one, Portia,' I laugh, trying to lighten things.

'I don't know,' she sighs, then pushes a smile on to her face. 'I can't turn the clock back, but hopefully I can right some wrongs, and who knows, maybe even give myself some happier endings . . .'

There's a silence for a while, and eventually I pluck up enough courage to say tentatively, 'Portia, we've never talked about those days when we were all at university, and then, after that night, with Josh, how we all lost touch.'

She laughs. 'Oh, that. That was nothing. I was just a silly little girl demanding some attention, and there's nothing to talk about.'

Relief seeps through me. 'Do you know, I've thought about that for years. I always felt guilty that we all drifted apart.'

'Cath, it was a long time ago and I can barely remember it. Really, it's not necessary to apologise. It's over. Forgotten.'

She smiles and shrugs, and I know from days of old that it's the end of the subject: she won't talk about it any more.

'How's the bookshop going?' she asks, changing the subject.

'Fantastic. Truly unbelievable. I'm loving every minute of it, but poor Lucy's working like a demon in the café bit and she's absolutely exhausted. And then, to make matters worse, she got home the other night to find that evil little Max had drawn a picture of the family while he was at nursery or somewhere, and instead of drawing Lucy he'd drawn Ingrid.'

Portia starts to laugh. 'Oh God, sorry,' she says, seeing that I'm not laughing. 'I mean, that must be awful for her, particularly because Ingrid's so gorgeous. I can never understand these women. Aren't they just asking for trouble by employing some stunning Swedish blonde as an au pair girl? Particularly when they're out working late every night.

'I just always think that the easiest thing in the world would be to turn to the au pair for a bit of comfort during those lonely evenings. Especially when she looks like Ingrid.'

'Well, no possibility of that,' I say. 'First of all, Ingrid's the prize bitch from hell.' Portia arches an eyebrow in surprise. 'Oh, come on, you saw her the other night, she's a nightmare, and as far as I can see her only saving grace is that Max loves her. Anyway, despite what you may think, Josh *adores* Lucy.'

'Does he?' Portia looks interested.

Now at this point it occurs to me to have a little gossip about Josh and Lucy passing like ships in the night, but, however tempting it might be, it really wouldn't be fair to Lucy, so I mentally zip the lip and decide that no matter what Portia says I will not be drawn.

'God, yes! Josh can't keep his hands off her. Really, it's quite ridiculous, I mean after all these years together you'd think some of the passion would die, but if anything it's the reverse.'

I'm not entirely sure what makes me go so over the top, but something in my gut tells me it's the right thing to do.

'They didn't strike me as being particularly affectionate to one another,' Portia says, after considering what I've just said. 'Oh well, I must have been wrong.' She sits back as our rocket and Parmesan salads arrive. 'I like Lucy, you know. She's not at all what I expected, as you know, but I've surprised myself by how much I like her. And she's certainly a wonderful cook. That food was amazing. Oh God, I haven't even asked about Si. You said on the phone that he and Will had broken up. How is he?'

'He's probably about three-quarters on the road to recovery,' I tell her. 'Hopefully about to come out of isolation and join the real world again.'

'Maybe when he does you'll all come to me for dinner. How does that sound?'

'Would *you* cook,' I say doubtfully, remembering her inability to even make a toasted cheese sandwich at university, 'or would it be catered?'

'Don't be silly, darling. Catered of course.'

'In that case it sounds fantastic,' I say, grinning, and she laughs, and I realise that I'm having a much better time today than I thought I'd be having, and when Portia says, at the end, that we must do this again soon, I find myself agreeing.

'I'm back!'

'From where? Ibiza? Majorca? South Beach?'

'Oh ha bloody ha. From the land of lamenting and feeling sorry for myself. Oh, and by the way, I could kiss you for the videos. So clichéd, but absolutely perfect for squeezing out those last few tears.'

'Oh, Si, I've missed you.'

'I know, sweets, and I've missed you too. So, what's been going on since I've been gone? Has Portia run off with Josh yet?'

'Si! That's a terrible thing to say!'

'Joke, joke.' A pause. 'Well, has she?'

'God, Si, you are incorrigible. Of course she hasn't, although—'

'Although what?' he snaps, just in case I'm withholding some vital gossip from him.

'Although I did have lunch with her last week, and she was saying that she wouldn't be surprised if Josh ran off with, wait for it, Ingrid! Can you believe she said that? Ingrid!'

'I can actually.' Si's not laughing. 'She was probably just testing the waters to see if Josh has it in him to be unfaithful, checking to see if he flirts with Ingrid or something. After all, if Portia is after Josh, and I still think it's a distinct possibility, then it would make her job a hell of a lot easier if she found out that he'd already had an affair or two during their married life.'

'Well, I don't think that. When we had lunch she said that she had regrets, and she hoped she could right some wrongs and maybe give herself a happy ending, or something like that.'

'Uh oh. Doesn't sound too good to me. Anyway, sweets, how about a movie tonight?'

'Oh, Si, I would have loved to, but actually, I've sort of got a date . . .'

'A what?'

'Well, Lucy's calling it a date, but it's probably not, it's just that James and I are going out for supper.'

'Oh my God! Oh my God!' I can hear Si doing a little victory dance at the end of the phone. 'Where are you going? What time is he picking you up? What are you wearing? Oh my God! What are you wearing?'

I start laughing.

'Tell you what,' Si continues, 'why don't I whizz over and help you get ready? I promise I won't embarrass you, and if I'm not gone by the time he comes over, I'll hide in the bathroom.'

'Si, I love you and I know you mean well, but . . .'

'See you in ten minutes!' he whoops, and the phone is slammed down.

'Oh, come on, James,' I laugh, 'I don't look that different.' He's standing on the doorstep and his mouth is hanging open as he stares at me.

'James?'

He shakes his head. 'Cath, I'm really sorry,' and he peers at me closely. 'It is Cath, isn't it?' And he grins.

'The new Cath,' I say. 'Improved, I hope.'

'You just don't look like *you*,' he says uncertainly, and my face falls as I begin to regret letting Si loose on my hair with the hair irons and de-frizz serum.

'You know,' James says finally, 'I think you actually look very lovely, it just takes a couple of minutes to get used to.' I relax and we go straight out to James's car. We drive through London, chatting quietly, although it's hard to hear over the sound of the windscreen wipers swishing through the October rain. I twist my body in the passenger seat so I can look at James's profile, and I marvel, despite not having done this for years, at how familiar this whole scenario is—the nerves, the excitement, the apprehension—how going on a date hasn't changed since I was a teenager.

We seem to be driving for ever, on the Westway, down to Hammersmith and eventually into Barnes, where James parks the car and we walk round the corner to a chic little French restaurant.

'I hope this is OK,' he says nervously. 'I used to come here a lot when I lived in Hammersmith and I thought it would be perfect and the food's delicious.'

I realise that he's talking so much through nerves, and the realisation that he's as nervous as I am makes me relax, and I smile my approval as we walk through the door.

We are shown to a secluded corner table, and although we are in Barnes—outside the trendy epicentre of London—the rest of the clientele look surprisingly smart, and I feel an overwhelming burst of gratitude to Si for doing a number on me, because I'm quite sure I would have been intimidated had I not had glossy locks and shining lips.

'Is this OK?'

I smile at James. 'Better than OK. It's perfect.'

'Good. I'd offer you champagne, but you don't strike me as the champagne type. What would you like to drink?'

'What do you mean, not a champagne type? What kind of type do I strike you as, then? A few pints of beer?' I start to laugh.

'Nah.' He looks horrified. 'Not beer. Lager, perhaps.' And from that point on, I start to relax.

Halfway through my second glass of wine I start to have a good time. Not that I wasn't having one before, but the alcohol loosens my inhibitions, and the more we talk, the more James smiles at me, the more attractive I start to feel.

And suddenly I realise what Lucy, and Portia, have been banging on about. *This* is what it's all about. *This* is what I've been missing out on. And no matter how much I love Si, Josh and Lucy, it's not a patch on *this*.

I'm in the middle of telling James why Geminis should never be trusted, and he's laughing even though he's already admitted that he thinks all this star sign stuff is a load of rubbish, when the door of the restaurant opens, and I can just about see through the smoked glass someone handing their coat in, and, as I carry on talking, the someone steps into the restaurant and it's Portia.

I stop in the middle of the story, and James turns round to see what

I'm looking at. 'I don't believe it,' I say. 'It's my friend Portia.'

I am about to call her over when the door opens again, and Portia's mystery date shakes the rain off his umbrella.

The manager greets them effusively before leading them to their table. Portia's companion has his arm around her, and they look at one another tenderly and laugh.

And when he looks at her I sit back down with a bump because the mystery man with his arm round Portia, looking at her with an extraordinary amount of tenderness and—dare I say it—love, is Josh.

'Oh fuck,' I whisper, unable to tear my eyes off them, even as they disappear into the back room. 'He was right.'

Extraordinary how magic can disappear in a split second. I, we, had been having such an incredible time, but the minute I see Josh and Portia together, my evening is ruined.

And poor James. It's not his fault and later, when he spots Josh and Portia, he understands what I'm feeling, but the only person I really want to talk to is Si, because he, after all, was the one who predicted this would happen right from the start.

So this is what she meant by giving herself a happier ending. This is why she kept asking the questions about Josh and Lucy. But Josh? I just can't believe Josh would do this. I can't believe he would treat Lucy like this. And if this can go wrong, this marriage, this partnership that seemed so perfect, then what in the hell hope is there for the rest of us?

James tries to keep the conversation going on the journey home, but my heart just isn't in it, and after a while he gives up and switches the radio on.

We pull up outside my house and I know I ought to invite him in for coffee, to try to make amends, as the last part of the evening has disintegrated so badly, but the only thing I want to do right now is talk to Si, quickly, because he's the only person who will know what to do.

'Are you going to be OK?' James says, and I nod. 'You're not going to do anything rash, are you?' his voice slightly more nervous. 'Like call Lucy or anything?'

'God, no! I need to get this clear in my head first.'

I give him a distracted wave and let myself into the flat, heading straight for the phone.

'Si, it's me.'

'And what are you doing home at this early hour? Unless of course the gorgeous James is in your bedroom, pulling off his boxers at this very moment.'

'We saw them. Josh and Portia together. You were right.'

There's a gasp on the other end of the phone, then silence for what feels like a very long time. 'What?'

'I know. I can't believe it either.'

I proceed to tell Si the story, and when I've finished I realise from the silence that he's as shocked as I am.

'Jesus, Si. Say something. You were the one who said she was after Josh from the beginning.'

'I know, but I didn't think she'd actually succeed. I mean, Josh loves *Lucy*. What the hell is he thinking of?'

'I know. But more to the point, what the fuck are we going to do?'

'Well, I know what we can't do and that's tell Lucy.'

'But we can't just sit back and watch the marriage of our best friends disintegrate. This is just horrific. I can't believe how horrific this is.'

'Look, we're just going to have to sleep on it tonight. Maybe by the morning we'll have a plan of action.'

But of course we don't have a plan of action the next morning, and that's despite me having hardly slept a wink, tossing and turning, too busy thinking about Josh and Portia to get a decent night's sleep.

This whole fiasco has brought out something incredibly protective in me towards Lucy; I feel that I ought to be close to her, to somehow try to shield her, and I follow her around the shop the next day, making sure she's OK, although we're so busy we hardly have time to speak.

'Cath, darling!' Lucy calls from the bar some time that afternoon, and for a second I think that last night must have been a nightmare; it feels so unrealistic when Lucy's voice is still exactly the same. 'I can't believe we haven't had a chance to speak today. Give me a hand with these cups, and then you can tell me how last night went with the lovely James.'

'Lovely.' I try to make my voice sound as normal as possible. 'I'll tell you all about it later.'

'I've got a better idea,' she laughs. 'Josh has another meeting tonight, so I'm on my own again. Why don't we order pizza and you can tell me all about it. How does that sound?'

Scary, is how it sounds, because the memory of Portia and Josh together will loom all evening, but the desire to see Lucy out of the work environment outweighs the fear. 'Great,' I say. 'I'll supply the wine.'

So that evening I stand on the doorstep of Lucy's house, place a hand over my heart to calm it down, and ring the doorbell. It's ridiculous to feel even more nervous about seeing Lucy socially, as opposed to in the shop, than I did last night when I saw James, but it's the truth.

I hear footsteps, and Ingrid comes to the door, followed closely by Max. 'Hello, Cath,' she says, with what looks like, unless I'm very much mistaken, a suspiciously warm smile. I give her a faint smile in return.

'Lucy has popped out to get some vegetables. She said she would be back by half past. How are you?' she says over her shoulder as I follow her down the hallway, trying very hard not to step on Max, who is jumping from side to side in front of me.

'Fine,' I say slowly. 'Umm, and you?'

'Oh, fine,' she says breezily. 'Would you like a glass of wine? We are having one.'

'We?' I follow her into the kitchen, and I swear to God I'm not exaggerating this, but I actually gasp because sitting at the table, as cool as a cucumber, is Portia.

I stand, frozen, in the doorway, doing a very good goldfish impersonation. What the fuck is she doing here? Oh Christ, oh no. Please tell me she's not here to tell Lucy that she and Josh are in love and Lucy should leave. Oh Christ. Get her out of here. Get me out of here.

'Hi, Cath,' she says warmly—bitch—standing up and coming over to give me a kiss. 'I was just leaving.'

'Here to see Josh, were you?' The words are out before I have a chance to think about what I'm saying, and I can't hide the sarcastic, bitter tone in my voice.

'What?' she says carefully, looking at me strangely, and I know she doesn't think I know. 'I was just passing, so I thought I'd pop in and see if Lucy was home,' she says. 'I brought her this recipe book from Italy I'd told her about,' and she gestures to a cookery book lying on the kitchen table.

Ha. A likely bloody story. But what's really weird is that I've heard of unfaithful husbands buying their wives unexpected gifts when they're having an affair, to appease their guilt, but I've never heard of the mistress doing it.

'Right,' I say slowly, nodding at Portia to let her know I know she's lying.

'Anyway,' she says, smiling brightly at Ingrid and slightly less brightly at me, 'got to go. Big night out tonight.'

'I'll just bet,' I say, and she stops and stares at me, then shakes her head as if I'm the one who's mad, and Ingrid shows her to the door. I can hear the two of them whispering in muffled voices, and Jesus Christ, I can't believe Portia is whispering about me to the bloody bitch of an au pair girl.

'Are you feeling OK?' Ingrid says, walking back into the kitchen after the front door slams, and pouring an orange juice for Max.

'I'm not the one you should be asking,' I say pointedly, and Ingrid shrugs nonchalantly and goes out to call Max just as—thank God—I hear the key turn in the front door and Lucy walks in, only to be practically knocked over by Max jumping into her arms.

'That wasn't Portia I just saw driving off, was it?' she says, cuddling Max as she walks into the kitchen.

'Yup. She was dropping off a cookery book.' I point to the book as Lucy shrieks and immediately starts flicking the pages.

'Oh, I can't believe she remembered this, how lovely. I must remember to phone her and thank her. She's such an angel!'

Oh bugger, I think. If only you knew.

Chapter Nine

A WEEK LATER and I'm convinced Lucy thinks I'm completely mad. All day yesterday she kept catching me watching her with, as she put it, these big worried eyes, but every time she asked me what was wrong I just sighed, apparently, and said it was nothing.

Now, tonight, half an hour after closing time, I'm walking round the shop, putting the books back where they belong as I do at the end of each day, and I'm watching Lucy untying her apron and collapsing into a chair, smiling wearily. 'How are you doing, my darling Cath? And more importantly, what are you up to tonight?' she asks. 'Seeing James again or is it too soon?'

'Much too soon. I haven't even thanked him for last week. Damn. I meant to phone today. I'll do it when I get home.'

Lucy's smile disappears for a while and she stares into space, her mind obviously on other things. Oh God. Do you think she knows?

'Lucy? Are you OK?'

She looks at me and nods, but her expression is one of sadness.

'Are you sure?'

'Well, no,' she says finally, and I mentally brace myself because if she actually asks me if I know anything, I just don't know what I'm going to say. Lie. You must lie. But I'm a hopeless liar. My face is, as Si always says, exactly like an open book.

'What's the matter?' As if I don't already know.

'It's us, I suppose. Josh and I,' and the smile has well and truly disappeared, which is when I realise that I never see Lucy's face in repose. She is always so animated, that seeing her like this makes it look as if all the stuffing has been knocked out of her. 'Things just aren't right,' she continues after a long pause, looking up at me to see if I'm still listening.

'I know that things have changed, what with me working here, and Josh having this really big deal, and that we're not spending as much time together, but Josh seems to have taken it personally, and the less time he spends at home, the less time he seems to want to spend at home. If I didn't know better I'd think he was up to something.'

I can't stop my sharp intake of breath, but luckily Lucy's looking at the table and she neither hears nor sees.

'Do you think he's having an affair?' I ask.

'Josh? Absolutely not,' and she starts laughing. 'It's just not up his street, although God knows I wouldn't blame him, given the state of our sex life. I don't even remember the last time we had sex, and Cath, this is so awful, but I'm just too blasted tired.

'You know,' she says, looking up at me, 'often during the day I feel really rather sexy. I'll read something or think about something, and I'll think, how lucky I am to be going home to a man that I still really fancy, and I spend the rest of the day looking forward to seeing him and maybe making love.'

'And?'

'And then by the time I've got home and spent some time with Max, and had something to eat and jumped into a hot bath, I'm so exhausted it's all I can do to fling back the duvet and climb into bed. That uses up any surplus energy I might have had, and then that's it. I'm fast asleep as soon as my head touches the pillow.'

'Lucy, if it's any consolation, it's exactly the same for me. I'm exhausted, too, but don't the benefits outweigh the negatives?'

'In your case, my darling, yes, because, and don't take this the wrong way, but because you haven't got a family, but in my case, I just don't know any more.' She sighs deeply. 'I didn't mean that. I suppose it's just a question of finding the right balance.'

There's a silence for a while and I try to lighten the tone. 'Well, they always say that you stop having sex when you get married. You're just proving the rule.'

'But Josh and I always had the most marvellous sex life. Oh, Cath, I'm not embarrassing you, am I? It's just that I have to talk to someone or I'm simply going to explode, or implode,' she says sadly, 'which is infinitely worse.' And she smiles.

'It's fine. I don't mind at all. But did you mean what you said about not blaming him if he were to have an affair?'

'No,' she sighs. 'Of course I didn't mean that. I'd be devastated if he were having an affair. But I honestly don't believe he would do that. I think, I hope, it's just a phase we're going through.'

'All marriages have their ups and downs,' I state sagely, praying that soon this will be over and Portia will have moved on.

'I know,' she says sadly. 'It's just that we've never hit a down like this before, and it's pretty bloody miserable when you're stuck in it.'

'What about pulling a big seduction number?' I say suddenly, as Lucy looks puzzled. 'You know, sexy underwear, stockings, the whole works. Why not try it?'

'You're not serious?' Lucy starts to laugh.

'Yes, I am.' I start liking this idea more and more. 'How about if Si and I took you on a shopping expedition? If nothing else we'd have a laugh.'

'I'd feel ridiculous,' Lucy laughs, but I can tell her resistance is wearing thin. 'Anyway, what on earth do you suppose I'd buy?'

'I don't know,' I chuckle. 'How about a nurse's uniform?'

'God no!' Lucy starts to giggle. 'How impossibly naff.'

'But sexy,' I wink, and the pair of us snort coffee out through our noses.

'Si really isn't that keen on Portia, is he?' A few days later it's a slow afternoon in Bookends, and Lucy's helping me tidy up the stockroom.

All the colour drains out of my face, and, I swear, my heart actually misses a beat. 'What do you mean?'

'Oh, come on, Cath! There's something going on, isn't there?'

'What do you mean?' I say again, trying to keep my voice steady.

'For starters, you look like a ghost every time Portia's name is mentioned, and Si looks as if he's about to murder someone, probably Portia. What on earth is going on with her?'

Oh God, what do I do? Do I tell her? Should I confess? Or maybe I should just pray that it is, after all, a phase, and just cross my fingers and hope that it's all over soon.

I take a deep breath and look into Lucy's eyes, and I know immediately that I will not be the one to tell her, to hurt her in this way.

'What's going on with Portia?' I repeat, stalling for time.

'Yes, have the three of you had some kind of falling out?'

My relief is palpable.

'It's ridiculous that you and Si were so excited about seeing her again after all this time, and suddenly she's become *persona non grata*.'

I shrug. 'You know,' I say, after a while, 'it isn't anything tangible. Ten years is a long time, and I just don't think Si and I have that much in common with her any more.'

Lucy's about to say something else when the door creaks open and Si staggers in, clutching his head and groaning in mock agony.

'Fine, thank you,' I laugh. 'Nice to see you too.'

'Sssh,' he says. 'Hangover.'

'Let me guess . . . Turnmills *again*?'

He nods, and a grin spreads all over his face.

'Uh oh,' Lucy laughs. 'I hope he was worth it.'

'Well, you know what they say,' Si says, brightly. 'The best way of getting over someone is to find someone new.'

'No! Already?'

'Well, not permanently,' Si says. 'Definitely not relationship material, but gorgeous, gorgeous, gorgeous, and let's just say a good time was had by all. Meanwhile back at the ranch, how did the new sexy Lucy go down on Friday night?'

Lucy sighs. 'I tried. Really, I did, but he didn't want to know . . .'

'Oh, Lucy,' I stroke her arm, and, fuelled by cappuccinos and carrot cake, the full story comes out.

Josh phoned Friday afternoon and said he had a meeting but wouldn't be back later than eight thirty. So Lucy slapped on a cucumber face mask and started chopping and peeling, switching the radio on in the kitchen and dancing around in time with the music, feeling, for the first time in a long time, as if she were getting ready for something special.

At six o'clock, when the casserole was firmly in the oven, the pastry had been carefully laid out over the tarte tatin, Lucy poured four capfuls of luxurious and horrendously expensive bubble bath into the hot running water, and lay back feeling excited, and sensuous, and completely relaxed.

Max, for once, seemed to be on his best behaviour, and after dinner and a story he climbed into bed, had a goodnight cuddle, and went straight off to sleep, leaving Lucy to finish her preparations.

She tipped her head upside-down once her hair was dry and sprayed hairspray all over, so when she tipped her head back she looked wanton and sexy, in the way that Josh had always said he loved, although she could never be bothered to do it these days.

She stood in front of the bathroom mirror and carefully applied some make-up before slipping on the sexy new Agent Provocateur underwear she'd splashed out on.

115

And sliding her feet into her highest heels, she opened the wardrobe door back as far as it would go, and examined herself in the full-length mirror hanging on the inside of the door.

'Well, hello, big boy,' she said to herself, in an accent as close to Mae West's as she could manage, a slow kitten-like smile spreading on her face. 'Why don't you come up and see me some time?'

Si laughs briefly, breaking the spell, and even Lucy has to join in. 'I bet you looked fantastic, though,' he says.

'You know what?' A genuine smile breaks through. 'I actually did, although I didn't look like me in the slightest. I looked in the mirror and there was this sexy, curvaceous glamour puss staring back.'

'What do you mean, it didn't look like you? You are a sexy, curvaceous glamour puss.'

'Oh, Si, I do love you. No, I'm not, nor would I normally want to be.'

'Anyway, go on, what happened?' I'm getting impatient.

Lucy slipped a little black dress over the top and went downstairs to pour herself a glass of champagne, which always gets her in the mood for romance. The table looked beautiful. No kitchen, not tonight. The dining room was sparkling, candlelight glinting off crystal, and sleek silver candlesticks. Everything was perfect.

At twenty past eight Lucy took the casserole out of the oven, lit the scented candles in the living room, put Nina Simone on low, and waited in the living room for the front door to open.

After fifteen minutes she picked up a magazine lying on the coffee table and started idly flicking through. Fifteen minutes is nothing, she told herself. Who could, after all, predict exactly when a business meeting was going to end?

She was telling herself the same thing at ten o'clock.

But at a quarter past ten she stopped waiting. She put the casserole into the fridge, the empty champagne bottle went in the bin, and the tarte tatin—Josh's favourite pudding—was tipped on top of it. And just as she finished clearing the dining room, the front door opened.

'Sorry I'm so late,' Josh said, hardly glancing at Lucy. 'The bloody meeting went on for hours.' He was pulling his tie off as he put his briefcase down in the hallway, and finally looked at Lucy as she stood in the doorway in her little black dress and stockinged feet.

'You don't mind if I go straight to bed?' Josh said, looking at her but most definitely not seeing her.

Lucy shrugged, sighed, and took the champagne flutes into the kitchen, whereupon she threw them against the back door.

'Jesus!' Josh thundered back downstairs to survey the shards of crystal on the kitchen floor. 'God, you must be more careful. Look, leave it for Ingrid to clear up in the morning. I'm off to bed. Night.' And he kissed her distractedly on the forehead, then went to bed.

'God, Lucy, it sounds horrific.' I take her hand and squeeze it, as Lucy rubs her eyes as if to rub out the memory, and I can see that she is hurting far more than she is letting on.

'We could always go to plan B,' Si says, after a while.

'And plan B is?'

Si shrugs. 'God knows, but give me five minutes and I'm sure I'll be able to think of something.'

Lucy gets up and goes to the loo, and as soon as she's out of earshot I lean forward towards Si. 'I think maybe you should talk to him.'

'Me? Why me?' Si sits back in his chair, pointing at his chest indignantly before leaning forward again conspiratorially. 'Why not you? Josh has always listened to you.'

And it's true, Josh has. I'm not sure why, but perhaps because I've always had a proper job (as opposed to Si's sporadic bursts of creativity), because he knows I'm independent, he has somehow trusted me, and, although I do not want to do this, I think that Si may have a point. Because I can no longer sit back and watch his marriage disintegrate.

Since I saw him and Portia together, we haven't actually had a proper conversation. He used to call me in the office for long, cosy chats, but now that I'm in the bookshop, with Lucy, he only ever phones to speak to her, and even when I pick up the phone he usually sounds far too busy to talk. I don't even remember the last time Josh phoned me at home for a long chat, but then again I suppose I haven't exactly made much of an effort either.

'I don't know if we should get involved at all, but I love Josh and Lucy too much to ignore this, so I'll do the only thing I can.'

'Which is?'

'Tell Josh that we know, and remind him of what he'd be losing if he and Lucy broke up.' But the very thought makes me feel sick.

'And what if he says that Portia's the love of his life and she's the only thing he cares about?'

'I just don't believe Josh would do that, I just can't believe that.'

Lucy comes back with a bottle of champagne that's part of our secret stash, well hidden in the stockroom, and gets out some glasses. 'Look at you two whispering furtively. If I didn't know better, I'd say you were planning a secret rendezvous.'

'You might say that,' Si sniffs, 'but I couldn't possibly comment,' and with that he pops the cork and we start to drink.

Thank God my life seems to have found its equilibrium again. This whole Josh and Lucy thing has been so upsetting, that even when I tried to get on with things and forget about it, I still felt unsettled all the time, as if something terrible were about to happen, something I couldn't control, couldn't get away from.

I suppose it could just have been the fact that Portia had come back at all. Irrespective of her affair with Josh, I suppose it is bound to be unsettling when somebody new enters your world, changes the dynamic, disturbs the balance.

She's called me a few times, left messages, and I've managed to avoid the calls, telling Bill and Rachel to say I'm out, and screening my calls at home. I know this sounds wimpish, but it's so much easier to withdraw from the friendship than it would be to confront her. Plus, as Si keeps pointing out to me, she isn't the only bad guy in this scenario. I know it takes two to tango and all that, yet I can't help but feel that however clever and sharp Josh may be, he's also weak. I've always known that, but I still can't blame him as much for giving in to temptation, as I blame Portia for tempting him in the first place.

And the funny thing is that for the last week or so, Lucy seems much happier. She made me laugh this morning, telling me about Ingrid, who seems to be acting more and more strangely. Lucy told me how she got home last night, kicked off her shoes, poured herself a whisky and sat down at the kitchen table, only for her mouth to drop open as Ingrid walked nonchalantly in and picked up her keys from off the table.

She had, Lucy giggled, outdone even herself. She was wearing a red PVC catsuit, which showed off her extraordinary figure extraordinarily, and her hair was scraped into a slick ponytail.

'Off to an S & M club?' Lucy enquired politely, which is completely out of character, but, as Lucy admitted, she was too damned tired to keep up the good old British reserve.

'No,' Ingrid said, all sweet smiles that didn't, somehow, seem to go with her outfit. 'I have a hot date.' She then added, 'If I am not back tonight, you will not worry?'

'Well, uh, I suppose not, not if you tell me you won't be. Should I lock the front door, then?'

'I think so,' Ingrid said, waving goodbye and practically floating out of the room, as Lucy blinked a few times to check she wasn't dreaming.

'God,' I laughed, listening to the story. 'She sounds like Denise Van Outen on Viagra. I hope he's worth it.'

'Oh shut up.' Lucy and I both giggled. 'You're just jealous. I bet you wish you looked that good in a red PVC catsuit. I certainly do.' And then her voice suddenly became serious. 'I know this sounds ridiculous,' she said slowly, 'you don't think . . . ?' She tailed off as I mentally willed my heart to slow down.

'I mean, it's just that Ingrid seems far happier suddenly, and she obviously is seeing someone, and you don't think that . . . well, you don't think Josh and Ingrid are having an affair?'

'God, no!' I practically shouted. 'Not in a million years!'

Lucy looked relieved. 'Oh, OK, then, if you're sure. Anyway, as it happens Josh was an absolute sweetie last night. He turned up with a huge bunch of flowers and whisked me off to Julie's for dinner.'

And apparently it was the first normal evening they'd had in ages. Josh had arranged for Laura to come and baby-sit, and once they were in the restaurant they sat and actually talked. Not about the bookshop, not about Max, not about Josh's work, but just talked. It was, Lucy said, a beam breaking out on her face, wonderful. Not romantic, it didn't lead to passionate sex or anything, but she felt married again. And happy.

Si rang earlier and I told him about Lucy's evening, and he said it was a good sign, although it didn't mean it's over with Portia.

But I don't know any more. I think that maybe it was just a passing fling. That perhaps, like that one night all those years ago at university, it's over. After all, would Josh really be happy hanging out with media junkies at Soho House, nibbling Thai spiced fish cakes in restaurants, only ever going home to sleep. Remember, I have sat on Portia's sofa, and trust me, it is not a sofa that inspires you to kick off your shoes and curl up with the remote control while shovelling down a curry, which is Josh's favoured way of spending an evening.

And while I know there are some women who are prepared to compromise their entire beings for their man, Portia isn't one of them. Maybe once upon a time she would have made a few sacrifices, but now, in her thirties, I realise that Portia has grown hard, and if a man did choose to enter her life on a permanent basis, it would be on her terms or not at all.

So, I hope, I hope and I pray, that this is a passing fling, and that Josh somehow has to exorcise Portia completely before moving on with his life. With Lucy.

A week later and I could almost have believed that it really was over with Portia, because ever since that night at Julie's, Josh and Lucy have been, well, they've been Josh and Lucy again. Even to the point where Lucy phoned this morning to say how about Sunday lunch, usual table, usual time? And without even thinking about it, I said yes.

As soon as I walk in the unsettled feeling I've been carrying with me disappears, because there, in the corner, are the usual gang, and the scene is so familiar it is as comforting as travelling back to the womb.

A cafetière fights for space among the piles of papers, and I know exactly what papers will be there, and who brought what. A basket of croissants sits in the centre of the table, and Josh is buried in the Money section of the *Sunday Times*; Si is stuffing his face with croissant while simultaneously pointing out pictures in the *News of the World* magazine, and Lucy is sipping her coffee, laughing at Si's outrageous comments.

I pull off my jacket and scarf, rubbing my hands together to warm them up as they're almost blue from the cold November air, and I drape everything over the back of the chair and sit down, as Lucy calls the waitress over and orders more coffee and an extra cup.

'So,' Si says when I've had some coffee. 'Heard the latest gossip?'

'Let me guess. Prime Minister run off with Meg Ryan? Queen pregnant again?'

Si raises an eyebrow. '*Real* gossip, sweets. Ingrid, it seems, has a'— and he pauses to roll his r's significantly—'lurverrrr.'

'Oh, Si!' Lucy slaps him playfully. 'You are so beastly about poor Ingrid. I shouldn't have said anything.'

'So what else is new?' I shrug my shoulders. 'She did say she had a hot date the night of the red catsuit, so what's the big deal?'

'OK, no big deal,' Si says nonchalantly, 'it's just that it's been confirmed now. She's going away with him next weekend.'

'Have you met him?' I ask Lucy. 'What's he like?'

'You know how private she is,' Lucy says. 'She hasn't said a word, other than to say her new lover is taking her to the George V in Paris for the weekend, and would we mind if she were gone for four days.'

'What did you say?'

'What *could* I say? Of course I said yes.'

'So does this new lurrve,' I pick up Si's inflection, 'mean that the dreaded Ingrid has become a nicer person?'

Lucy laughs. 'I'm not sure that nicer is the right word, but at least she seems a bit happier, which certainly makes life easier for the rest of us. But as you know, the only reason I keep her is because Max adores her.'

'That boy really has no taste,' Si says acidly, with no shadow of a smile. 'Reminds me of his father.'

'Si!' Lucy and I exclaim at once, and Josh looks at Si in amazement, because there was more than a hint of viciousness in that remark, and although I know what he means, that he's talking about Portia, he has no right to be that obvious in front of Lucy.

'Si!' Lucy says again. 'Are you saying Josh picked me in bad taste?'

Si recovers masterfully. 'My gorgeous Lucy,' he says, kissing her on the cheek, 'the one time in his life Josh has shown impeccable taste was in choosing you.'

After lunch, we wander up to the O2 centre on Finchley Road for a lazy afternoon film, our breath visible in the cold air, and it feels lovely, it feels normal. I love this time of year. Early November, just as everyone is getting ready for the full force of winter, and the perfect time to disguise yourself with layers of snuggly warm clothes.

When Si walks me home I say goodbye knowing that this has been a perfect Sunday. Si is off to see a friend up the road, although he says if he's not there he'll pop back and we can have supper together.

Luckily for Si I have managed to go shopping this week. Unfortunately I went shopping when I was completely starving, and instead of ending up with healthy, nourishing food that would have lasted a week, I ended up with a basket of terrible fast food that had almost gone by the end of that night.

So if he comes back, he can look forward to a double cheese and pepperoni pizza, half a packet of onion bhajis, eight (I've only eaten two) pitta breads, the obligatory houmous and taramasalata, a full and unopened packet of Chinese chicken wings, and a four-pack of white chocolate mousse.

Not a bad feast for a Sunday night, I think you'll agree.

I open up the Culture section, grab an old biro and circle my evening's viewing, and then, feeling absurdly decadent, start running a hot bath, even though it's only six o'clock in the evening. I think a glass of wine is called for, and I pour myself a glass of chilled Chardonnay and pad back into the bathroom.

And, soaking back into the hot water, I think how lovely today was. Even though we have spent our Sundays like this for years, it is only when you take a break, or when something threatens to disturb the routine, that you fully appreciate it when it is back to normal.

I soak my head under water, then reaching for the shampoo bottle, I come up for breath and lather up my head.

I dip under again and, as I emerge, shampoo still clinging to my hair, I keep very quiet because I'm sure I just heard the doorbell ring. A few seconds go by and there it is again. Definitely the doorbell.

Oh Christ. I grab a towel from the bath rail and, shivering, jump out of the bath, frantically rubbing the shampoo now dripping into my eyes, and stumble to the front door.

Now I know you should never open the door without asking who it is first, particularly not when you're half-naked and wrapped in a towel. But I was convinced it was going to be Si, so I didn't think twice.

Now I know you're not stupid, even though I, quite obviously am, but there on the doorstep, surprise surprise, is James.

'**Ah**,' I say, still squinting through the shampoo, slowly bringing James into focus.

'Ah,' he says, looking, it has to be said, slightly horrified by my appearance. 'I suppose I ought not to just drop in like this.'

'Actually I rather like people just dropping in. Except when I look like this of course. Do you want to come in and give me a few minutes?'

'No, no, don't worry.' He starts backing off. 'I'll ring you later.'

'James! Just come in, for God's sake.' I practically pull him through the front door, push him onto the sofa and scurry into the bedroom.

Shit. It's worse than I thought, but, shoving the embarrassment aside, I run back into the bathroom, rinse my hair of the shampoo, wash the mascara off my face, grab a hairbrush and run back into the bedroom, frantically pulling my hair back into an elastic band. And finally, I shove on some leggings and a baggy old sweatshirt, pausing before I walk out serenely to dash to the cupboard and pull on a bra because I do not need to hoist my boobs up from around my kneecaps in James's presence.

And eventually I walk sheepishly into the kitchen, as I shout at James over my shoulder, asking whether he wants a cup of tea. I hear him get up to join me in the kitchen, saying he would love one.

He comes in and sits down as I pick up the dirty plates that are covering almost every available inch of workspace and pile them in the sink, then dig around for a bit until I find two mugs to wash up for us.

'It feels like ages since I've seen you,' I say brightly, as I open the fridge and tentatively smell the milk that, thank God, is still fine. 'What have you been up to?'

'Actually I've been incredibly busy painting,' he says, grinning, lifting an arm up from the table and examining the honey stain on his sleeve.

'Oh Christ! Sorry.' I run over with a cloth and clean the table, but James just laughs.

'Jesus, Cath. I remember that night you came over to the studio and it was a pigsty, you said you were worse than me, but I thought you were just joking to try to make me feel less embarrassed. But you really are more of a pig than I am, aren't you?'

'I can't help it,' I say, shrugging. 'I try so hard to be clean and tidy, but the pig inside just won't stay down. She's too strong. At least the mugs are now clean.' I grin, showing off the sparkling mugs. 'So . . . painting. What are you working on now?'

'You probably won't believe it. God, I can hardly believe it, but after you exhibited my stuff in the shop, *North West* magazine came over and did a feature on me, and suddenly I've got phone calls left, right and centre, asking where people can buy my work.'

'Oh, James! That's amazing!' I sit opposite him, beaming, genuinely thrilled for him. 'Does this mean you'll be able to retire before forty?'

He grins. 'I don't think I've reached quite that level of success yet, but you never know . . .'

'Listen, today Bookends, tomorrow the Saatchi Gallery.'

'God, don't I bloody wish! Anyway, that's enough about me, what about you? How's everything with you?'

'The same.' I shrug, longing to be able to make him laugh with witty tales of hanging out in glamorous places, but there's very little to tell.

'Had any more mad people in the bookshop lately?'

'Nah, and I'm slightly worried about it. I'm sure every bookshop should have its token eccentric.'

'I could always put an ad in the paper for you?' James grins. '"Wanted: true eccentric, sixty-plus, pink or blue hair, to add character and charm to local bookshop. No pay, but all the cappuccino you can drink." What d'you reckon?'

'I reckon you'd have to hire coaches to bring in all the lonely old dears who'd answer the ad,' I laugh.

'You could always borrow my nan,' he says. 'She's lonely.'

'But is she eccentric?'

'Not yet. But I'm sure she could learn. She could sit in the corner and screech at everyone in her thick Yorkshire accent.'

I shake my head as I start to laugh. 'James, you do paint the most extraordinary mental pictures.'

'Thank you. That's the best compliment I've had all year. Now, there was something else I'd been meaning to talk to you about.'

'Yes?'

'My grandad.'

'You are joking?'

'Yes, actually. I know it's a bit of a pain in the arse, that I keep dropping in like this, but it's so much easier to talk to someone in person, and anyway I hate the phone. Plus this is getting ridiculous now.

'The last time I tried to take you out for dinner it all ended up in a shambles, and I would really like to see you properly.'

'What do you mean, "properly"?' Although I know what he means, and he knows that I know, because there's a huge grin on my face.

'I mean go out for dinner. Get to know you *properly*.'

'We could always start tonight,' I say coquettishly. 'I mean have dinner.'

James looks delighted. 'Tell you what,' he says, looking at his watch and standing up. 'I'll come back here at eight o'clock to pick you up. So you can get dressed and stuff. How does that sound?'

'Perfect.' I walk him to the door, and then a thought occurs to me. 'James, you know the last time we had dinner, when we saw Josh and . . . well, you know. Aren't you going to ask about Josh and Lucy?'

'Not my business, Cath.' He shrugs and says, 'If you want to talk about it with someone, then I'm happy to listen, or try to help, but you should only tell me if you want to,' he says.

'James,' I laugh. 'You're just too good to be true. I'll see you at eight.' And I close the front door behind him and squeal to myself for a bit, suddenly feeling things I thought I was incapable of feeling any more—excitement, exhilaration and more than a touch of anticipation.

I dry my hair, change, and when, at twenty to eight, the doorbell rings, I curse James silently for being so early, but thank God I am ready.

But it's not James, it's Si, and I have completely forgotten that he would be coming round for supper if his friend wasn't in, and I start to apologise, start to explain, when I notice that Si is as white as a sheet and looks suspiciously like he's about to throw up.

'Si? What is it? What's the matter?' I clutch him in alarm as he threatens to topple over, and then lead him inside, terrified of his shaking.

He sits down as if in a daze, and then turns to me. 'Will's not well.'

'Oh, Si.' My face crumples in sympathy, because, hate Will though I do, I can see that this is hurting Si, and that hurts me. 'I'm so sorry. Is it something serious?'

Si turns to me. 'Cath,' he whispers, showing me the fear in his eyes. 'He's got AIDS.'

'What?' I never really knew what people meant when they talked about their blood running cold. Until now.

'He said he was fine. We talked about it because you know how completely paranoid I am, and he said he'd had a test last year and it was negative, and that if I was negative too, there was no reason to . . . well . . . you know.'

'Oh my God. Oh my God. Si.' My breath catches in my throat and I'm so angry, so frightened, I want to start shaking him. Because although I knew Si had had plenty of one-night stands, lots of brief encouters, I was certain that he had never, ever practised unsafe sex. 'Please tell me you used condoms. Please tell me you didn't . . .'

Si looks at me and then starts to cry, and I reach out and put my arms around him, rocking him to and fro as his body heaves with the sobs. The doorbell goes. Oh Christ. James. Si looks at me questioningly and I whisper that I'll be back in a second. I go to the front door, feeling ridiculous for having to cancel again, but knowing that there's no way on earth I will leave Si like this.

And James can see immediately that there's something wrong.

'I don't believe it,' he sighs, visibly annoyed. 'You're cancelling me again, aren't you?' he says flatly, and I can see that he really is pissed off.

'I'm so sorry, James, something has come up. I can't explain now. I'll have to explain later. Can I call you tomorrow?'

'You know what, Cath?' he says, and his voice is hard, and although I'd like to tell him why I'm doing this, I can't. He turns to go. 'Just forget it. Let's just forget it,' he says.

'James?' I plead softly as he looks at the floor. 'I am so, so sorry. I was so looking forward to this evening, but it's going to have to wait. I'm not cancelling, James, I'm just postponing.'

'How long,' he finally sighs, looking up at me and forcing a smile, 'do you suppose I will wait? Because I have to tell you, Cath, my patience has pretty much run out.'

'I promise I'll call you tomorrow,' I say, and this time he does turn to leave, and I shut the door and go back into the living room, to Si.

Chapter Ten

I KNOW THIS ISN'T THE TIME for recriminations, and I know that Si, above all else, needs support and understanding, but I'm in shock. I still can't understand how Si, the Condom Queen of North London (his expression, not mine), could have risked everything for Will. Especially because we've always laughed in the past when Si's been told that people are fine—as Si has always said, 'He would say that, wouldn't he?' and it has never stopped Si from practising safe sex.

'I don't understand,' I keep saying. 'How? Why?'

After a while Si calms down and starts to breathe normally, and soon he even makes a joke or two. I make tea, and I can see the warmth flow slowly back into his veins, and suddenly I think that we are being ridiculous. We are being overdramatic, we don't know anything for sure, and surely we should not be making these assumptions. Not yet. Not when this life feels so normal.

'Si,' I start, 'I know this might sound crazy, but you couldn't possibly have it. You're as healthy as an ox, and so you slept with Will a handful of times without using anything, it doesn't mean you've got HIV.'

'Cath,' he says slowly, 'I have no idea whether you'll be able to understand this, but I've got it. I know I'm HIV positive.'

'Si, that's ridiculous. That's you being overdramatic. You can't possibly know that . . .' And I tail off because of course there is then only one question left for me to ask. 'What are you going to do?'

Si looks into his mug for a long time, and then looks back at me. 'Cath, this is something that I've thought about for years. I've often wondered what I would I do if my glands swelled up for no apparent reason and then refused to go down. What I would do if a cold refused to go away, sticking around until it got worse and worse. And I always thought that unless I absolutely had to, I would live in blissful ignorance because I never thought I'd be able to handle the results.'

'And now? How do you feel now?' My voice is gentle, but I'm still trying to take this in.

'If I am positive, then the best thing I can do is to know now, to deal with it now, to take whatever drugs I might need. But you know what the worst thing is?'

I shake my head.

'There's an incubation period of three months, and the last time we slept together was the beginning of October, only a month ago, so it might not even show yet.'

'Oh God, Si.' I can feel my own tears welling up. 'You can't have it. Please say you haven't got it.'

'Cath,' and he tries to smile. 'It's only a virus, for God's sake. I'm going to go to the clinic tomorrow.'

'Can I come with you?'

'That's what I was going to ask. I don't think I could handle getting the results on my own. I want you to come.'

'Where will you go?'

He mentions the name of a GUM clinic at a local hospital. A clinic that specialises in testing for sexually transmitted diseases. A clinic that gives you the results within an hour.

'You know, Cath, it doesn't mean AIDS,' he says with amazing calmness. 'Not necessarily. People can go for years and years being absolutely fine. Now, with all these new drugs, they're talking about twenty years, no problem, and who knows, by then they may have found a cure.'

'Si.' I shiver. 'Stop talking as if you already have it.'

All of a sudden he looks lost again, like a little boy, and I put my arm around his shoulders and give him a squeeze.

'I'm scared, Cath,' he says. 'I'm really, really scared.'

Si stays until midnight and we talk softly about the implications of being HIV positive, about what he might do, how he might tell people, how it will affect his life.

When he eventually leaves, I sit for a very long time on my sofa, and I do something I have not done for years. I pray. I, who have not believed in God since I was a little girl, who do not believe in religion, sit there with my eyes clenched tightly shut, and I pray that if there is someone out there, then he must make Si be negative.

I pray and I pray, and I offer a few disjointed lines from the Lord's Prayer, half remembered from school assembly all those years ago, in the hope that this will appease any God that may be up there.

When there is nothing more to be said, I climb into bed and pray for a quick and dreamless sleep, but nobody hears that particular prayer, and I lie wide awake for hours, thinking about Si.

The phone rings at eight o'clock the next morning. Si tells me to get my skates on, as he'll be picking me up in fifteen minutes to go to the clinic. I ring the bookshop and leave a message on the answerphone, telling Lucy I'm going to be in late as I'm not feeling well and am off to the doctors, but that I'll call her later.

Si sounded suspiciously cheerful when he phoned, and when he eventually arrives I look at him with concern, my head slightly cocked to one side, and I ask gently, 'How *are* you?'

'Oh God,' he moans, raising his eyes to the heavens. 'Don't you start.'

'What? What have I done?'

'That sympathetic look. The cocked head. "How *are* you?"' He imitates cruelly, accurately, and I apologise and laugh.

And all the way to the clinic Si seems in great spirits, and it is only as we climb slowly up the steps to the clinic entrance and ring on the doorbell, that the colour drains from his face.

We are shown into a front-facing waiting room. Slightly shabby, rather gloomy. A nurse comes in. Australian. She is bustling, matter-of-fact, smiling, and I think that whoever employed her is a wise person indeed, for she is exactly the sort to make you feel comfortable. Despite her youth she clucks like a mother hen, even while handing Si a form on a clipboard to fill in.

When he has completed the form, he stands up and hands it to the nurse just outside the door.

'The doctor won't be a moment, love,' she says.

And less than a minute later a door at the other end of the waiting room opens, and a young, dark-haired man in a white coat comes out, clutching the clipboard and looking at Si with a smile. The doctor.

'Please come in.' Si stands up and just as he turns to go he holds my gaze and I nod because there is nothing to say, and he walks to the door, which shuts behind him.

I flick through a faded copy of *Hello!*, glancing at the photographs but barely taking them in.

The door of the clinic opens again, and a girl comes in, young, pretty, trendy, and the nurse hands her the clipboard and she sits opposite me, head down, deep in concentration, and she looks so calm, so together, I wonder what circumstances might have brought someone like her here.

But of course, I mentally kick myself. AIDS, HIV, does not necessarily choose its victims because of their sex or their sexuality. I am reminded of a story I heard a long time ago, when we had just left university, when everyone laughed at the government campaign, the warnings of a worldwide epidemic. Not us, we thought. Never us.

A student from our university, a friend of a friend. She had had two lovers. One, a long-term relationship of two years, and then, just after they broke up, a summer fling with a boy a couple of years older.

And then, a year or so later, she started to feel ill. Nothing serious, just tiredness, a few headaches, swollen glands. The doctor offered her an HIV test, just so they could rule out the possibility, he said, and she laughed, because how on earth could she possibly have HIV?

The test came back positive. It seems the summer fling had unknowingly contracted it from someone who had slept with someone who had caught it from who knows where.

I don't remember the girl's name. She was not someone I actually knew, but someone I could well have known. Someone who would have been at the same balls, the same parties as me.

Someone, in fact, much like me. And mostly I remember being shocked that someone like me could contract HIV, because of course that wasn't supposed to happen.

But we now know it does happen. I sneak furtive peeks at the girl and I know that she is just as susceptible as Si.

I check my watch. Twenty minutes. Why is this taking so long? And, just as I think that, Si walks back into the waiting room.

'Well?' I try to gauge the result from his expression, but there is no result, not for another hour or so.

'What did he tell you?' I ask gently.

Si glances at the girl still filling in her form, then back at me. 'Look, shall we go for a walk? I need some air.'

'Good idea.' I grab my coat and we walk out into the cold crisp air.

'So?' I say, taking Si's arm and falling into step.

'So nothing I didn't know already. We talked about the impact if I'm positive. How I would deal with it, what I would do in terms of counselling, what's available to me. He said that HIV is a virus, not an instant death sentence, and that people can live completely normal lives, and there are drugs that blah blah blah.'

I stop and look at him. 'Blah blah blah? Now there's an interesting medical definition.'

'I'm sorry.' A big sigh. 'It's just that I've heard it all before, and I know it's true, but it still means that I am probably not going to see old age, and that when I die it will be horrible and painful and degrading.'

'Oh, Si,' I groan, stroking his arm, because I cannot think of anything else to say.

We go back to the clinic and again, as we ascend those steps, a feeling of gloom overtakes me. We sit in the waiting room, and I manage to entice Si back to a semblance of his normal self by showing him a picture of Courtney Cox in a particularly disgusting dress, and in the middle of our laughter the surgery door opens and the doctor appears.

He comes over to us and again says, 'Please come in.' And although the words themselves are completely innocuous, there is something about his expression, his lack of smile, the sympathy lurking just behind his eyes, that makes my heart start to pound.

'Back in a sec, my darling,' Si says, winking at me, putting on his old self in a bid to cover the fear, then, just as he goes, he leans down and kisses my cheek, and that is when I feel the tears burning, but I will not let them out. I will be strong for Si.

I look up, and the girl, the trendy, pretty girl who is presumably now waiting for her results, smiles at me. 'Awful, isn't it?' she says softly, and I nod, not daring myself to speak, because her sympathy will ensure the tears come thick and fast if I so much as open my mouth.

Twenty minutes go by, and then the door opens and Si reappears, smiling brightly, and, if I didn't know him as well as I do, I would think that the smile means everything is fine, but I know that smile. That is his false smile. His forced smile. He is stuffing leaflets into his pocket, and I stand up and follow him out into the cold sunshine.

'Si?' I stand in front of him on the pavement, and only then does his smile start to fade.

'Positive,' he whispers, and I put my arms around him and feel his stiffness, his resistance, but whether he needs this or not, I need to do it.

'Regent's Park?' I whisper, because it's not far, and because I know he loves the rose garden, and because I sense that he needs to be reminded of things that he loves.

We get in the car, not saying anything, and drive to Regent's Park, then walk through the gate. My arm is linked through his, and as we walk beside the boating lake I squeeze him tightly, reassuring myself that he is still the same old Si, and although the temptation is to keep looking at him, to check if he's OK, I know this would infuriate him and so I resist.

And finally, when we reach the rose garden, Si gestures towards a bench and we sit down, and he starts to speak.

'I have to make an appointment with a counsellor,' he says, drawing the leaflets out from his pocket and looking at them blankly. 'And I have to go for regular check-ups, my CD4 count and Viral Load Tests. I have to go back in a week for the first round of tests. And my diet probably needs looking at, although he said there were courses I could do to learn about all of this stuff, to get support, and . . .' He stops, sighing.

I say nothing, just stroke his arm.

'Oh, Cath,' he says, and his voice sounds incredibly sad. 'How can my life have changed so drastically in one day? How can everything have been fine yesterday morning, and everything be so awful today? How can we even be sitting here talking about check-ups and drugs. I mean, why me? Why did this have to happen to me?'

'Nothing has changed,' I say, putting my arms around him. 'You are exactly the same person today as you were yesterday. And you'll be exactly the same person tomorrow, and the day after that. The only thing that's changed is that you've caught a virus, and you have to be more careful with your health.

'But Si,' I continue, 'you have friends who love you and, touch wood'—I slip off a glove to stroke the bench—'your health. It's a virus, Si, it's not the end of the world.'

And then we both sit there, holding hands, looking out over the park, and we stay there for a very long time.

Chapter Eleven

I CALL LUCY IN THE SHOP, and luckily I do sound terrible, and she thinks I'm ill before I even have a chance to deliver a made-up excuse. She tells me to tuck up in bed and not to worry about anything, which is what I wanted to hear, as I need to spend the rest of the day with Si, but it nevertheless strikes me as slightly ironic, given that I'm the one who is absolutely fine. In shock, certainly, but fine.

But Si is fine too. Or should that be too fine. After we leave the rose garden he tells me he really feels OK about this; he says that, bizarre as it may seem, it somehow already feels a part of him, that he can deal with it.

I don't know what to do with Si today. He is too calm, too quiet. I drag him down to Marylebone High Street and we find a small café and tuck ourselves away in the corner, ordering cappuccinos and baguettes. But as soon as the food arrives I know that I couldn't eat this if you forced me, and of course Si pushes it away.

So we sit and drink our coffee, and Si draws out the leaflets again and this time we really look at them, read them, read about courses for the recently diagnosed, the importance of regular check-ups, the life expectancy growing longer and longer.

And when we have finished the leaflets I pull my diary from my bag and rip out a clean page, and we write down the places Si is going to contact this afternoon, the support centres he will visit, the names of books to read.

'Doubtless the doctor at the clinic will go through all of this with me next week,' he sighs at one point, but I ignore him because I can see that this is helping, to actually do something practical, to make a list, and even if it is not helping Si, it is helping me.

Eventually we leave and Si drops me off. I practically beg him to let me come over in the evening, but he says he will be fine.

'You won't do anything . . . well . . . you know . . .' I can't help but ask the question.

'Anything stupid?' he says, grinning. 'No, Cath. I'm fine. Well, I'm not, but I'm certainly not unfine enough to down a bottle of paracetamol, if that's what you're thinking.'

'Will you ring me later?'

He nods. 'And, sweets? I don't know how to tell Josh and Lucy. I know I have to, but I need to do it in my own time, in my own way. Is that OK?'

'God, yes!' I'm mortified that he thinks I would take it upon myself to tell them, almost as if this were mere gossip.

'I'm sorry,' he says. 'I didn't mean to offend you, my love. Listen, I'm going to go home now, have a quiet day, an early night, give myself time to digest everything. I'll ring you later, I promise.'

I do the same thing in my flat. I curl up on the sofa and open a novel I've been meaning to read for weeks. I scan the first page, desperate for some form of escapism, desperate for something to take me out of myself, but every time I reach the bottom of page four I realise I haven't got a clue what I've just read, and I have to start all over again.

Eventually I put the book down and wonder how I'm going to kill the hours before bedtime, wishing today had never happened.

I do manage to kill some of the hours before bedtime. Some, but not all. I speak to Si a couple of times and he sounds fine.

But I can't sleep, and when, at twenty past one in the morning, the phone rings, it doesn't surprise me in the slightest, and I pick up the phone to hear jagged sobs at the other end.

'Ssh, ssh,' I try to soothe, feeling Si's pain as if it were my own.

'I don't want this to be happening,' he sobs, his voice blurred with alcohol. 'Why is this happening to me? What have I ever done?'

'I'm coming over,' I say, and without giving him the time to say no, I pull a coat over my pyjamas, grab my car keys, and I'm out of the door.

Six minutes later I'm on his doorstep, and he opens the door, his T-shirt wet with tears, his face puffy and blotchy, hiccuping as he tries to stop crying, and I put my arms around him and start crying too.

I stay the night, although we don't really sleep. We sit up, still talking, still trying to make sense of it all, and eventually, at around seven, we both fall asleep on the sofa.

Obviously I can't go into work the next day. I phone the shop and when Lucy comes to the phone I'm astonished by the exuberance in her voice. 'Darling Cath!' she says. 'We are worried about you. Rachel says take lots of echinacea. Tell me you're feeling better?'

'Yes, I'm feeling much better, even though I hardly slept last night. How is everything in the shop? You sound positively ecstatic.'

And Lucy, bless her, drops her voice and I can almost see her checking that no one's listening. 'Actually, I didn't sleep much myself last night,' and her voice is positively purring.

'Lucy! You didn't! You and Josh? SEX?,' at which Lucy giggles.

'God, Lucy! That's amazing! No wonder you sound ecstatic. How was it, or need I ask?'

Lucy sighs with pleasure at the memory. 'Oh, Cath, it was so lovely. So unexpected and so, so lovely.'

She tells me that Josh had been just like his old self all day yesterday. That getting together as a gang to have our regular Sunday lunch seemed to have somehow brought them back together again, reminded them of how things used to be before she opened the shop.

They went home last night and Ingrid went out, as she always does these days, and Max went to bed, as he rarely ever does, and, instead of burying himself in a pile of paperwork in his study, Josh opened a bottle of wine and sat down at the kitchen table to talk.

And they found themselves laughing together over some silly story Lucy was telling, and Josh put the dishes in the dishwasher after supper and then stood behind Lucy as she finished clearing the table, put his arms around her and gently kissed the nape of her neck, 'Which,' she said guiltily, 'always turns me to jelly.'

And that, as they say, was that, but God, what a pleasure it is to hear Lucy laughing again. It is a welcome and uplifting distraction, and what a relief to know that whatever was going on between Josh and Portia must surely now be over.

'Oh, Cath,' Lucy sighs. 'I feel that everything's back to normal. It's all been so upside down for so long, but now I've got this feeling that life is back on track. Now, sweet Cath, to change the subject entirely, or rather to get back to the original subject, what is happening with the lovely James?'

I don't know where to start. 'You know how some things are just meant to be?'

'Yes?' She is eager, expectant.

'This, unfortunately, isn't one of them. Every time we try and get it together, something happens to pull us apart, and I can't help but feel that this just isn't meant to be.'

'Nope. I refuse to accept that.' She is determined. 'If things keep going horribly wrong when James invites you for dinner, why don't you try to reverse your luck by inviting him?'

'What?'

'Make dinner for him. Every man adores a home-cooked meal.'

'Dinner? At my place?' God, now there's something I haven't done for at least five years.

'Yes. It's perfect. If I were you, I'd drop in and ask him just as soon as you're back on your feet. He'll be over the moon.'

133

By Friday I figure Si is doing just about OK, or at least OK enough not to need me on permanent standby, but I still feel incredibly fragile. I know I should be going back to the shop, but if Lucy starts being all warm and maternal towards me, I'll probably just lose it.

But by Friday afternoon the guilt takes over, and I do go in to Bookends, and everything's fine. Lucy's fine. Bill and Rachel have been working like demons, and Lucy's so busy chatting up the regulars she doesn't really have time to fuss over me, which is truly a relief.

At the end of the day I cross over the road and push open the door of the estate agent's and, much like a Wild West saloon, the room goes quiet as five pairs of eyes eye me up and down, presumably assessing how much I would be willing to spend on a property.

The silence lasts a second. A second that is evidently enough for them to realise I won't be buying that eight-bedroom house in Aberdare. Nor even the three-bedroom conversion in Greencroft. Nope. I am not a buyer to get excited about.

I have never seen the office this busy before. Five men seated behind five large, trendy beech desks, all talking into their phones. And these men all look identical. All short, young and dark, neatly packaged in slick dark suits, their voices filled with a confidence their age would not suggest.

And then I see James, right at the back, looking completely out of place, with his laid-back manner, lazy smile and tousled brown hair.

'Can I help you?' the bimbo-esque receptionist enquires. I smile and shake my head. James wipes the smile from his face and looks at me sternly as I walk towards the back of the office to talk to him, trying to ignore the eyes that appear to be watching my every move.

'Hello.' His voice is guarded. 'What can I do for you, Cath?' Oh God. Have I blown it? Have I been so completely stupid and blown it? I look at his arm where the sleeve is rolled up, exposing strong muscles and light brown hair, and my stomach lurches as I realise that I do, in fact, desire this man. That I have not felt desire for anyone for a very long time. And that I cannot blow it again. I bite my lip as I start to speak.

'Well . . .' I'm nervous, and I don't want to blurt out a dinner invitation in front of the receptionist, who is now hovering near by.

Thankfully James picks up on my discomfort, and he ushers me into a room at the back of the office, where there's a large sofa, and I sit down as he stands in front of me and raises an eyebrow, still as cold as before.

'James,' I say. 'I have to apologise. I don't know why things come up every time we try to get together, but I feel terrible about it and I was just passing and . . .' I am about to ask him for dinner, but I can't quite manage it. '. . . and I just wanted to come in and say how sorry I am.'

'God, Cath,' he sighs. 'This is just so exhausting. All I'm trying to do is take you out for dinner and you're just making it so bloody difficult.'

'I . . . er . . .' I'm floored. I don't know what to say, and the emotion that I've been suppressing is suddenly threatening to spill out all over this lovely white sofa. I try to blink back the tears that well up out of nowhere, but they don't go away.

'Cath?' James sits down next to me, concerned, trying to look into my eyes, which are busy failing to stop the tears trickling down my cheek. 'Jesus, Cath. You're not OK, are you?' And his voice is so gentle, so caring, that I find myself reduced to a sobbing, wailing heap.

I'm aware that this is the most exciting thing everyone in the office has ever seen at work, but he stands up and pulls the door closed, and when he comes back he sits and rubs my back, just as I did with Si.

And it works. It is soothing and calming, and after a while I take a deep breath and James says, 'Can you talk about it?'

I start to shake my head, but then the tears start rolling down my cheeks, and I know that I can't keep this to myself any more. And I know it's selfish, but I need someone to confide in.

I wouldn't tell Lucy. Nor Josh. They are our closest friends, and it is up to Si to tell them, but I trust James, I don't know why. Perhaps because that night we saw Josh and Portia together he never asked about it, was so obviously not interested in the potential for gossip.

And slowly the story comes out. I don't refer to Si by name. A friend is what I say, although it is clear from what I say, from the closeness of our friendship, that it could only ever be Si.

'Can I make a suggestion?' James says gently, quietly, when I finish. 'I think that first of all you should also go to see someone. I don't know what exists for friends and family of people with HIV, but there are bound to be groups, counsellors, people who can talk to you, help you, because you need to learn to deal with it as well.'

I nod mutely.

'But you're the only one who knows right now, is that right?' I nod. 'Do you think your friend is planning to tell more people? Because it's a hell of a burden to shoulder on your own.'

'I don't know. I don't think he's thought that far ahead.'

'Where is he now?'

'Oh shit.' I check my watch and stand up, grabbing my bag. 'He must be home from the hospital. I've got to go.'

'You're sure you're OK?'

I nod, heading for the door.

'Cath?' I turn just as I'm stepping out. 'You know that if you ever need to talk, you can just pick up the phone or come over.'

'You know, James, you're amazing. I don't know what to say, thank you just doesn't seem enough.'

He smiles. 'Don't be silly, that's what friends are for,' and he leans forward and kisses my cheek, squeezing my arm at the same time. I walk into the street and go home to phone Si, having completely forgotten that I was supposed to have proposed dinner.

The nights are not good. Si seems to get far more frightened at night.

During the daytime I'm there, on the end of the phone, to keep him sane, to remind him of what the doctor told him at the clinic: that at last there are effective treatments, that the average prognosis, before people became ill, used to be ten to twelve years, but that now, with these new treatments, that has been significantly extended.

So, as I say, the daytimes are not quite so bad. During the day we even manage to have occasional conversations in which the words HIV or AIDS don't even figure. But it's during the night that he gets the fear.

During the night when he phones me up, either crying softly, or the weight of the fear pressing down on him so much he can hardly speak, just needing to know that someone is there for him.

Lucy asked me yesterday if everything was OK with Si, because he hasn't returned her calls. What could I say? I told her that he was fine, very busy, and that I hadn't spoken to him much either. But when I get home I ring Si and ask him whether he's thought any more about telling Josh and Lucy. This, apparently, is one of the issues the doctor brought up in his first counselling session. Whom he should tell, and how.

Si has decided, he tells me, that he does want Josh and Lucy to know because we, after all (and at this point he puts on a cheesy American accent), are his 'family of choice'. He hasn't, on the other hand, decided quite how to tell them, but is thinking of throwing some kind of dinner party, a miniature version of the film Peter's Friends, to break the news. Except, he says, right now he can't think of anything more terrifying.

His real family, he says, do not need to know. They live far away, they wouldn't understand, and it took them years to come to terms with the fact that he's gay, never mind being diagnosed as having HIV to boot. 'If I'm not ill, what's to tell?' he says. And I agree.

He has not taken drastic steps to change his life, not yet. He has not done any of the courses, or started regular counselling, but he has been to the clinic, had his CD4 count checked to measure the strength of his immune system, and had his first Viral Load Test to measure the amount of virus in the blood.

At the moment his Viral Load is huge, but apparently that is to be expected, given that he has contracted the virus so recently, or at least any time between July and October. It will take a while for his immune system to settle down.

But, all in all, so far, so good.

It is a Thursday night and Si has come over to watch Portia's series. We have ordered a Chinese takeaway, as we have always done, and Si is bemoaning the fact that we've slipped these last few weeks and have, you might say, somewhat lost the plot.

'How much do you want to bet,' Si smirks, just as the titles start, 'there's a new character called John, or Joe, or Jason, something like that, and he's a local estate agent with a crush on Katy? Oh, and he's a fabulously talented artist on the side.'

'Oh fuck off.' I throw a cushion at him and he ducks, chuckling, but it's true, the thought has occurred to me that she may well take her revenge on me for not returning her calls via the television programme.

And then we both settle down to watch. Jacob and Lisa are having marriage problems, but, astoundingly, Jacob hasn't turned to Mercedes's arms for comfort.

'Well, he couldn't in the TV series, could he?' Si sniffs. 'Mercedes is an angel who could never do anything as evil as split up a marriage.'

No, in the series Mercedes is there to offer support to Jacob, a shoulder to lean on.

'Oh shit.' I turn to Si in the commercial break. 'Have we got it horribly wrong? Do you think we've completely misinterpreted everything?'

'Jesus,' Si says, turning to me. 'I don't know. I mean, Portia would never portray herself as the marriage wrecker on TV, but . . .' he says, tailing off.

'Then again,' he says, 'what was she doing at Josh and Lucy's all the time? Remember all those times you pitched up to see Lucy, and Portia was sitting at the kitchen table, being all smug?'

'Yeah. Good point.'

Si makes a worried face at me. 'God, I hope we weren't wrong. I'd feel awful if we were.'

'Oh, I shouldn't worry,' I say breezily. 'I'm sure she'll get her revenge on the show. Sssh, sssh, here it comes.'

For the next fifteen minutes we sit there transfixed as Jacob makes a pass at Lena, the gorgeous Danish au pair, after they both find themselves in the kitchen in the middle of the night, both unable to sleep.

'Jeeee-sus,' Si whistles, as we watch them tumble to the floor in a fit of passion.

'No way,' I whisper. 'Josh and Ingrid? It can't be.'

And Si raises an eyebrow.

'Well, it could be,' I mutter reluctantly.

'Bugger,' Si says, getting up to go to the loo during the next commercial break. 'You know what this means, don't you?'

'What?'

'We're going to have to start hating Josh again. Oh God. What a total nightmare. Thank God there are only fifteen minutes left. I mean, what else could happen?' And he disappears into the bathroom.

When he comes back he sits down with a sigh. 'This is ridiculous, Cath. You and I sit here speculating about the state of Josh's love life, and the only person who seems to know what's going on, other than Josh, who would never tell us, is Portia. You've got to confront her.'

'Me? Why the hell must I do it?'

'Because you were always closer to Portia than I was.'

'Si, there's no way I'm doing this on my own. I'll only confront her if you come too. We could ask her straight out, because the one thing about Portia is she's a crap liar, and your bullshit detector's far better than mine.'

I ring Portia mid-afternoon, when Lucy's furiously busy serving the rush of customers that always seems to appear from nowhere on a Friday afternoon. We arrange to get together for a drink on Monday evening, and I manage to make my voice sound as normal as possible. Even though I'm convinced she knows why I'm phoning, she doesn't give anything away, doesn't even mention the fact that I've obviously been avoiding her. She sounds genuinely thrilled to hear from me, and as soon as I mention getting together she suggests Monday, which is rather keen, even for Portia.

At the end of the day Lucy brings me over a pile of books that have been left in the café. 'Cath, my love, are you going to be around the weekend of the 27th? You and Si, actually. It's just that's the weekend Ingrid's off to Paris with the grand passion, and Josh has just announced that he's got to go to Manchester for a meeting, so I thought the three of us could have a lovely cosy evening on the Saturday and maybe you'd stay?' She pauses for breath, and my blood runs cold.

I think back to last night. To Jacob and Lena grappling on the kitchen floor in the TV series. Ingrid and Josh. It can't just be a coincidence, that they're both away at the same time. Oh God. Oh no.

'Cath? Are you listening to me?' Lucy's voice filters through as I try to collect my thoughts, and I manage to tell her that the 27th sounds fine, and I'd have to check with Si, but even if he couldn't make it I'd definitely be there.

And she walks off back to the café as I stand there feeling sick. I don't understand what's going on. I feel confused—first Portia, now Ingrid—confused and hurt, so I do what I always do when life throws these obstacles in my path—I go home and ring Si.

He picks up the phone sounding morose, and I start by telling him about Portia, that we're meeting her at the Groucho on Monday at seven, and then I tell him about Josh being away on the 27th, when he interrupts.

'I couldn't actually give a fuck about Josh being away,' he starts, the coldness in his voice almost making me jump. 'I've got AIDS, Cath.'

I am about to interrupt and tell him that he hasn't got AIDS, that he is HIV positive, which is very different, when I realise that he has been drinking, and that now would not be the time to say anything at all.

'And before you say the usual shit about me not having AIDS, you know and I know that it is just a matter of time. All I ever wanted from life was to be happy, and what bloody chance do I have of meeting Mr Right now? No bloody chance, that's what, and there's no point in you saying anything because you don't know the first bloody thing about it.

'You have no idea how it feels to be me right now. You don't know what it's like to have this death sentence hanging over you. God,' he snorts with drunken laughter, and I wonder whether I should just put down the phone. But no, I am a friend, I will be here for him.

'At least you, Cath,' he continues, 'don't have to worry about AIDS. Jesus, your legs are stuck so tightly together it would take a man a lot stronger than that bloody James to prise them apart.

'And relationship? You don't know the meaning of the word. You're so frightened of getting hurt you attach yourself to me, Josh and Lucy, like a fucking limpet, just so you don't actually have to put yourself out there in the big bad world and risk finding love. You don't have a clue.'

I have had enough. The tears have already started to drip down my face, but Si doesn't need to know that. He just needs to know that I won't take this abuse from him.

'I'm not going to listen to you any more, Si,' I say gently.

'Why? Because the truth hurts?'

'I gently place the phone back in the cradle, I can hear Si shouting, 'Cath? Cath?' but I then unplug the phone.

And I curl up on the sofa, hugging my knees to my chest, and I let the tears stream down my face, because I know that Si would never have said those things if he wasn't drunk, and frightened, and filled with rage, but I also know that everything he said he believed, but just never told me before because he didn't want to hurt me.

And the worst part is that I know he's right. He's right about me closing off from the world. Running away from anything that isn't safe and familiar. Running away from James.

After a while I get up, splash cold water on my face and pick up the phone to ring James. I listen to his answerphone, and then, after the bleep goes, I still haven't formulated anything to say, so I gently put the phone down.

Si was right. The truth does hurt. But sometimes hearing the truth can inspire you to do things differently. I am going to get hold of James, invite him over for dinner and seduce him.

And just because I put it off until tomorrow because I suddenly realise that the emotions of the day have severely taken their toll, doesn't mean that I'm not going to do it.

Trust me.

Chapter Twelve

AT HALF PAST FOUR on Monday a woman walks into the shop with a large bunch of flowers and asks for me by name before handing me the flowers. This is vaguely cheering because today has been the day from hell.

I just feel that everything is going wrong in my life. Too much is changing too quickly. I can't blame Portia for that, but her return has damaged the equilibrium far more than I could ever have anticipated.

Which I know is ridiculous, because Si would still have met Will and would still have contracted the virus, but nothing feels safe any more, and I just seem to be waiting for the next bomb to fall.

Just for a change I didn't sleep well over the weekend. I spent the entire two days on my own, unable to face anyone, and at night everything that Si had said kept going through my mind.

And I haven't called him. Perhaps I should have done, because he, after all, is the one who is truly going through hell, whereas I am just experiencing it second hand, but I need some time and space to forgive him, and I'm hoping that a few days will be enough.

He won't be coming tonight. Won't turn up after the conversation the other night, if, that is, he remembers anything at all, because God knows how much alcohol he had, in fact, consumed.

And now I have to deal with Portia myself, which is fine, especially given that she was clearly not the object of Josh's affections. I drop the flowers off at home, waiting until I'm in a cab on the way to Soho before opening the card, although I already know they'll be from Si. Sure enough: *For Cath. I'm so, so sorry. You're a far better friend than I could ever hope for, and I need you. Please forgive me. Will explain when you call. Will you? Soon? Love you, sweets. S.*

It doesn't even bring a smile to my face, not yet, not when the hurt is so raw.

I am shown into the bar at the Groucho, where I see Portia instantly, sitting in a corner, sipping a gin and tonic, looking stunning.

I walk over and she stands to greet me, her face lighting up when she first sees me, the smile fading as she realises I am not smiling in return, or not, at least, with quite the same brilliance.

'Cath.' She opts for the double kiss on the cheek, her voice warm but businesslike. 'You're looking great. It feels like ages. What can I get you?'

A gin and tonic arrives and we make small talk for a while. I talk about the shop and how busy we've been, and she tells me she has just come back from New York.

We talk about New York. About where she stays. I say that it is somewhere I have always wanted to go, but I am quite sure that if I went, I would never return, because my love for the city would be so strong.

'How do you know that?' she laughs.

'Because of Woody Allen and *NYPD Blue*,' I reply, in all seriousness, and even as she's laughing I wonder whether she is mentally filing this away, only for the phrase to pop up in a future episode of the series.

The series. How can I sit here and pretend that I am here merely on a social call, a catch-up, an innocent girls' night out, when she is exposing all our secrets in her series, when we don't even know what some of those secrets are?

'Portia,' I interrupt her gently, mid-flow. 'There's something I need to talk to you about.'

'Ah,' she sits back. 'I thought there was something,' and she shrugs. 'I thought, when you phoned, that perhaps I had been going mad, that perhaps you weren't avoiding me. I wasn't going mad was I?'

I shake my head. 'No, but that's not what I want to talk to you about, that was Si and me thinking that you and Josh were having an affair, because I saw you in Barnes one night, in a restaurant, and I was so furious with you, but now, obviously, we know that's not true, and anyway, that's irrelevant, that's not what I wanted to talk to you about.'

'Hang on, hang on. You saw us in that restaurant?'

I nod.

'Oh, Cath, I didn't know. No wonder you and Si had been so awful to me. I can't blame you. But you know we didn't have an affair, Josh and I, although not for want of trying, on my part, anyway.'

I stop, astonished at Portia giving away so much information. 'What do you mean?'

She sighs. 'I mean that for years I had always thought that Josh was the one to get away. A lost love? I convinced myself it was Josh, and that if Josh and I were together, then I would live happily ever after.'

Aha. Her happy ending. So there was an ulterior motive behind it all.

'I managed to persuade him to come to that restaurant that night, and I only managed it because he was tired and lonely, and things, as you probably know, weren't going that well with Lucy, and I thought it would be the perfect opportunity to seduce him.'

Jesus. What a bitch.

'I know what you're thinking,' she says. 'And I agree. It was disgusting behaviour, but I hardly knew Lucy then, and I'd spent ten years thinking about Josh. Ten years thinking that he was the only man who could ever make me happy, and here he was, telling me he was unhappy. God, Cath. I'm only human.'

I don't say anything, just wait for her to continue.

'But it didn't take long for me to realise that Josh saw me as an old friend who was concerned, who would be there to listen, and that was it. He sat there and talked about his marriage all night. He talked about Lucy, about how much he loved her, how special their relationship was, and how he couldn't understand why they seemed to be drifting apart since Bookends.'

'So you didn't try to seduce him?'

'Even at the beginning of the evening I still thought I would. But the more he talked the more I realised that he really loved Lucy, and that I'd be wrecking a marriage that had been perfectly happy apart from this one glitch that would soon sort itself out.'

I sit there in silence for a while, stunned. Stunned at her honesty, and the courage it must have taken to walk away. 'But you know,' she says, after a while, 'life works in very mysterious ways.'

'What do you mean?'

'Just because Josh wasn't The One, doesn't mean that things won't work out, just not in the way that I'd actually planned . . . well . . .' She is about to say something more but evidently changes her mind, and picks up her drink with a smile and a small shrug.

We sit and talk softly, and another hour goes by, and there is such an air of intimacy, of trust, that when Portia asks about Si, asks how he is, where he is, I almost find myself telling her. But I don't. Not quite.

We carry on talking, and the conversation moves on to sex, and we start laughing as we remember exploits of old, and then sex becomes safe sex, which becomes AIDS—always Portia's greatest fear.

And I tell her I have a friend who has just been diagnosed HIV positive. I don't mention names. I just say a friend. And Portia becomes very quiet. Too quiet. And I suspect she knows, but she won't say anything.

'How is your friend taking it?' she says quietly.

'Nobody knows yet, except me. And you now, obviously. How is he taking it? Not great. At times I think he's fine, he's accepted it, realised that it doesn't mean death. And then he phones me in the middle of the night, drunk, frightened, furious, and I know that he feels it's the end of the world.'

'Has he started counselling?'

'Not really. He's been to the HIV clinic, and he's got all the leaflets, but he hasn't joined a group, although God knows he needs to.'

Portia appears to be deep in thought, and eventually she asks, 'Cath, do you think he'd talk to a friend of mine?'

'What for?'

'I have this friend, Eva. She's a bit older than us, mid-thirties, but she's been diagnosed as HIV positive for thirteen years, picked up during her early twenties in New York, and she's the most amazing woman I know.'

I sit forward in my chair, interested.

'I think that your friend should meet her, because she's incredibly inspirational. She turned her life around when she was diagnosed, and she has this extraordinary outlook on having HIV.'

'How did she turn her life around?'

Portia smiles. 'It's a long story, but I think she's someone he should definitely meet. We should put them in touch with one another, and she could tell him her story herself. It might help your friend see things from another perspective, turn him around, if you like.'

'Portia, I don't know what to say. That would be wonderful.'

'Don't be silly,' she says, giving me a sad smile. 'It's the least I can do.'

And it's only the next day that I realise I didn't even mention Josh and Ingrid, the very reason for meeting her in the first place. Somehow I never got around to it. So I'm still in the dark, but quite frankly there are far more important things to deal with right now.

I'm not sure what I expected from Portia, but I'm pretty sure I didn't expect this from her. Not in a million years did I ever think she would be the one to dive in and rescue Si, but by introducing him to Eva, this is precisely what she has done.

I told Si what Portia had said, and Si said I could tell her, as long as I swore her to secrecy. Of course she said she already knew it was Si, and that she wouldn't dream of telling a soul, other than Eva, of course.

And I can't help but feel that Si and I have been far too unfair on her—have misjudged her enormously, because every time we think she has betrayed us, we end up being wrong.

Si phoned me on the Wednesday night, immediately after dinner at Portia's, and he was buzzing. He told me that already, after spending an evening with this woman Eva, this woman who was HIV positive, he felt entirely different. She was tiny, he said. Tiny, dark, very pretty, and the picture of health. She sat there drinking sparkling mineral water, listening to Si, before quietly telling her story.

In 1980, when she was fifteen, she fell in with the dope-smoking crowd at school. No big deal. She did it because everyone else was doing it, but unlike most people, Eva didn't grow out of it. Within a couple of years she had progressed to speed, and soon, because other people did, and because she fancied one of the boys in her crowd who did, she was using heroin. The remainder of her school days were blurred by heroin. At twenty she took herself off to New York, hoping for a drug-free stay and a fresh start.

Within two days of arriving at JFK she was living with a coke dealer, and using again. This time she started hanging out in 'shooting galleries'. Grotty rooms in old brownstones in the wrong part of town, havens for the junkies who would use these rooms as safe places to shoot up. And Eva, the youngest of them all, would be given their leftovers, together with the dirty needles that had been passed around the entire room. And of course she didn't know. No one did.

Back home, two years later, Eva went to university. Middle class, bright, she was studying Philosophy, Politics and Economics, and trying, unsuccessfully, to give up heroin.

And then the 'tombstone' adverts appeared. Adverts warning about AIDS and HIV, warning of the dangers of unprotected sex, of not knowing your partners' sexual history. Of shared needles and drug use.

It couldn't be me, she thought. Things like that don't happen to middle-class girls like me. To rule it out, she went to her doctor and requested a test. It was positive.

Twenty-one years old, HIV positive, perhaps she should have felt that her life was over, but Eva didn't feel that. She knew she had to make a choice. She realised that by giving in to HIV, by expecting it to take her life, she was removing all choice, and that, for her, was untenable. She didn't choose to die, she suddenly realised. She chose to live, and she refused to give in to the fear, because fear is the most toxic thing of all.

A year after being diagnosed, Eva set up an illness and recovery group working with AIDS awareness groups, teaching, helping, advising. Then one day she woke up, and, in spite of everything, she still felt that one day this thing, AIDS, was going to get her.

And that was when she decided it wasn't. She turned to Buddhism, to believing in one day at a time. She stopped believing there was no point in training in anything worthwhile because her life was about to end, and started to train in cranio-sacral therapy.

And she found a therapist who refused to allow her to become a victim. If she had a cough, her therapist would turn to her and say: 'So you've got a cough? So what?' He didn't say it would be the onset of PCP pneumonia. He didn't say it was a symptom of full-blown AIDS. He said it was just a cough, and you know what? He was right, and she learned that even when you have been diagnosed, not everything is HIV related.

Now, thirteen years on, she is the picture of health. It may not work for everyone, she told Si, as she was coming to the end of her story, but what works for her is to believe she's fine.

'And she really is,' Si told me, in wonder, in awe.

Chapter Thirteen

'CATH, MY LOVE?' Si and I are walking Mouse on Primrose Hill, and Si is almost, almost, back to his usual self. Of course he's not the same, he says that something inside him has shifted, but the clouds have passed and his outlook is sunny again.

Soon after that evening Eva took him to Body Positive in Greek

Street, where she seemed to know everyone. They made him feel welcome, and persuaded him to sign up on the Recently Diagnosed course.

His first session was last Saturday, and he called the next morning to tell me about the course: about how they were told about Body Positive as an organisation; about HIV, the immune system, the tests that they would come to expect. They were told what would happen on the rest of the course: about meeting dentists, dieticians, complementary therapists; about dealing with transmission, reinfection and the practicalities of living with HIV.

'Cath,' he said, sounding brighter than he had for ages, 'I feel like I can finally see the light at the end of the tunnel. Christ, I can't even begin to tell you how much better I feel. How normal I feel, now that I know I have this support.'

For a Saturday, Primrose Hill isn't too crowded, the darkness of the sky with the impending threat of rain evidently putting people off, and Mouse is happy to run around looking for fellow four-legged playmates.

We huff and puff our way up the hill (well, me, because Si's a damn sight fitter), and when we reach the top I collapse, as usual, on one of the benches and beg for mercy as Si agrees to give me five minutes' rest.

'Has Portia told you about Marcus?' he says, after we've been sitting for a while.

'No.'

'Well, she has this friend, Marcus, and he's got an apartment in Tenerife, and apparently he lets his friends use it when he's not there.

'He's offered it to Portia in a couple of weeks, but she can't go, too much work, so she thought I might like to go.'

'It sounds amazing! Who would you go with?'

'Actually, I thought I might go on my own . . .'

I shoot him a worried look, but he starts laughing. 'No, no, don't worry, I'm not going to sink into a deep depression and throw myself off a cliff or anything. Actually I'd just love some peace and quiet, and I think the sea would be incredibly healing for me.'

'Si, come on, you'd be lonely as hell.'

'You know, six months ago I would have agreed with you, but everything's changed now, and, bizarre as this sounds, given all that's happened, I feel incredibly serene at the moment.

'I just want to go by myself, read my self-help books, sunbathe and sit on the terrace at night, breathing in the smell of the pine forest and listening to the sea.'

I snort with laughter and press my palm on to his forehead. 'Pine forest? Simon Nelson, are you sure you're feeling all right?'

'Oh ha bloody ha. Meanwhile, how about moving that big bum of yours and getting some exercise?'

'Yeah, yeah,' I mutter, 'I see that some things, like insults, never change.'

We carry on walking round the field, Si picking up sticks and branches that are just beginning to fall off the trees, and throwing them for an ecstatic Mouse.

'There's something else I've been meaning to tell you,' he says. 'I think it's time I told the others, now that I'm coming to terms with it. What do you think?'

'I think that if you're ready, and you're sure, it would be the right thing to do.'

'I've decided to hold a dinner party,' he announces grandly. 'Well, actually I thought it would just be us, you, me, Josh and Lucy. I thought when I'm back from Tenerife, but definitely before Christmas. Give me a chance to dust off Queen Delia, because God knows she hasn't seen the light of day for a while.' He sighs. 'The thing is that I'm sure Lucy will be fine with it, but what about Josh? You know how straight he is, I think this might completely freak him out, and I couldn't bear it if he suddenly started dragging Max away or something because he thinks I'm infectious.'

'Sounds like heaven to me,' I mutter, but then I compose myself. 'First of all,' I say, 'I'm sure Josh wouldn't react like that, and secondly, would you really care what that unfaithful sod thinks?'

'I suppose not. So you really think I'm doing the right thing?'

'I really think you're doing the right thing.'

When I finally get home, I am about to listen to my messages when the phone rings. It's James.

'And what are you up to now?' he asks, when I have finished burbling my news down the phone, trying hard to push the picture of his forearms out of my mind. 'I hope you're doing something extra special.'

'Actually I'm staying in,' I laugh. 'I'm treating myself to a lovely lazy night in.'

'Cath, you can't possibly stay in tonight. It's not allowed. You are, on the other hand, allowed to have a lovely lazy night in, but I'm afraid it will have to be at my place, because I'm bored too and I want some company. Say, eight-ish?'

How could I possibly refuse?

Just before I leave the house I check myself in the mirror and grin at my reflection, which, thanks to the stress of the last few weeks with Si, is looking just the tiniest bit smaller, and are those . . . could they possibly be . . . cheekbones?

Ten minutes later I'm standing outside James's door, and when he opens it he gives me a big hug and immediately hands me a glass of champagne.

'Are we celebrating something?' I say, raising the champagne glass together with an eyebrow.

'The fact that you haven't cancelled me, perhaps?' he says, grinning, as he sits next to me on the sofa.

'Now, now. The night is still young. Give me half an hour and I'll be doing another runner.'

'You had so better not do that,' he says sternly. I apologise and tell him that really is the last thing on earth I will be doing tonight.

'So.' He reaches for his glass on the table.

'So.' I smile, as we toast one another.

'How's your friend,' he says, putting the glass down. 'Is he dealing with it better now?'

'He's really OK, actually.' I flush slightly at the memory of the state I was in the last time I saw James, but he doesn't mention it, and I push the thought out of my mind and carry on. 'He's started doing a course for people who have been recently diagnosed, and he's met this amazing woman. She's had it for thirteen years, and it's just completely changed her life, for the better. So he seems to have started coming to terms with it now, which is extraordinary, given the state he was in.'

James shivers. 'Horrible thought. Here we all are, thinking it couldn't happen to us, and boom, suddenly someone you know gets it and it completely changes your opinion.'

'God, I know. Tell me about it,' and I lapse into silence. Luckily James changes the subject before I start getting morose.

'Just keep still!' he says suddenly, and I freeze, expecting him to brush off an insect of some kind, but he reaches down and pulls a sketchbook out from under the sofa. 'Keep still!' he says, starting to sketch.

'Wonderful, wonderful,' he murmurs in a crap French accent that makes me laugh, even as he stares at me intently, glancing at the paper as he scribbles away, then back to me. 'Beautiful, beautiful.'

I sip the champagne awkwardly, trying to keep my face as still as possible, until eventually James puts the pencil down, closes the sketchbook and picks up his glass again.

'So how's everything at Bookends?'

'What!' I practically shriek as I dive for the sketchbook, and he leaps out of my way as I open up the page to reveal a beautiful little sketch that looks exactly like me, only far, far prettier. 'This is beautiful!' I gasp, 'even if it is the most flattering thing I've ever seen.'

'Rubbish,' James says. 'That's exactly what you look like. Trust me. I'm an artist.' And I start to laugh.

Soon we have relaxed into the sofa, talking softly, about relationships, marriage, and then, after a while, about Josh and Lucy.

I tell him how hurt I am by Josh's behaviour, that it's putting me in an impossible situation, and that I wouldn't wish this upon anyone, to know about an affair and not to be able to tell. The weekend that Josh is going away with Ingrid, I tell him, Si and I are spending Saturday night with Lucy, and I don't know how good either of us will be at pretending that everything is normal.

And James surprises me yet again. He surprises me because he is so incredibly wise and sensitive.

He thinks that, however much we love Lucy, and love Lucy and Josh as a couple, it is not our place to interfere. He says that he knows it must hurt, but that whatever will be, will be, and that nothing we say or do will resolve things. It may in fact make things worse. I think about it and know he's right.

He goes to the kitchen, pulls another bottle of champagne out of the fridge (which is slightly worrying only because I haven't eaten anything and I'm beginning to get seriously light-headed), then sits down again, a few centimetres closer.

Now this, I have to admit, would normally startle me, but the champagne is definitely starting to have an effect, and I note the closing distance between us with nothing other than amusement.

But then he really startles me.

'How come you're still single?' he says, out of the blue.

I start to laugh. 'That's like asking how come the sun is yellow. It just is. It's a fact of life. I've just always been incredibly happy with my friends, and I suppose I never have really needed anybody.'

'It's funny.' He shakes his head. 'When I first met you I thought you were incredibly tough, but you're really soft inside, vulnerable. Oh God, I've gone too far. That sounded so naff, I'm sorry.'

I start to blush, he starts to blush, and we both start speaking at the same time. I stop to let him carry on, and he does, looking at his glass rather than at me.

'You ought to let that softness show more often. You're far more attractive when you do.'

I laugh nervously, because no one's called me attractive in a very long time, and then, without even realising it's happening, he's kissing me.

Or I'm kissing him. Either way, we're kissing, and once I've got over the shock, because I cannot even remember the last time I had a proper, passionate kiss (although this is far more gentle than passionate), we pull apart and I cannot wipe the smile off my face.

'Is this OK?' James whispers, and I nod, wondering whether it's the champagne or the kiss that's keeping this dopey grin on my face, but then not wondering for too much longer as he kisses me again.

'Shit!' I jump away as champagne pours onto my trousers, my having become so carried away the glass just flopped from my hand.

'Let me get a cloth,' I say, but James smiles and shakes his head. Then he takes me by the hand and leads me up the stairs.

I follow him mutely, feeling as if I'm in a dream, because this surely can't be happening, not to me. I just don't do this any more. I don't have sex. Aaargh! Sex! Oh God. He's leading me to the bedroom.

Fortunately the grin is still plastered to my face, hiding this inner turmoil, but anyway, my body doesn't seem to be listening, as it follows him up the stairs and into his bedroom as if on auto-pilot.

The grin disappears pronto as he starts undressing me. Oh God, I pray, as he unbuttons my cardigan. Please let my bra not be too old, please let it not be too grey, and I furiously try to remember which bra I put on this morning.

Two minutes later I breathe a sigh of relief as James switches off the main lights, a soft glow coming from the small lamp on what is obviously his—right—side of the bed, and I make a mental note to stick to the shadows on the left.

And then I don't have to think any more, because what has felt like a film, suddenly starts to feel very real indeed, and I close my eyes, wrap myself around James and . . .

. . . beautiful, tender, loving, warm, comfortable . . . shall I go on? How could I have forgotten? How could I have lived without this? How could I have run away from this for so many years, when it isn't scary at all, it's absolutely right, and lovely.

It's so lovely that just after James has entered me (condom-encased, of course), just after he's whispered, 'Is this OK?', just as he's starting to move inside me, I start to cry. Not like that time in James's office. Crying this time with pleasure. With sheer and utter bliss, and despite the tears I'm smiling, and although James is concerned, I reassure him and soon there's nothing left to say. Because it feels so wonderful.

Better than wonderful. Perfect.

Si and I stop at the corner shop en route to Lucy's to pick up some wine, and a couple of giant bars of Cadbury's Dairy Milk, because there's no better sustenance for a Saturday night in than chocolate, and then we roll up at Lucy's.

I haven't said anything about James. Ridiculous as this may sound, this is my secret right now, and I want to keep it precious and safe, at least until I know it's not just a quick fling.

'Who is it?' Max's voice wafts through the door, loud and clear.

'Hello, Max. It's Auntie Cath and Uncle Si.' Si leans down and says, 'Do you want to see what I've got for you?'

A pause, then, 'Yes.'

'You can't see it if you won't open the door, can you?'

Brilliant. Si and I stand on the doorstep listening to Max's thought process, and then, when Max decides that in fact Si's plan is not flawed, the door slowly opens, and we look down into Max's expectant face.

'OK, Max.' Si crouches down and looks him in the eye. 'Which would you prefer? A fire engine or . . . a piece of chocolate?'

'A fire engine,' Max says eventually, and I start to laugh.

'Oh well. Chocolate will just have to do.' Si shrugs and hands him a small Dairy Milk, which doesn't seem to go down at all badly.

'Cath! Si! I'm in the kitchen!'

Lucy appears in the doorway. 'Quick, quick, big gossip! Huge!' She hurries us into the kitchen. 'You've got to sit down because you're never going to believe this!' Lucy is bursting, bursting to tell us something, and I'm assuming it's good news, because if she'd found out about Josh there's no way she'd have this mischievous look on her face.

'Pour some wine, quick. OK. Listen. This weekend is the weekend that, as you know, Ingrid's away with the mystery lover.'

'Yes?' Si and I both say simultaneously.

'Well, Ingrid had said the mystery lover was picking her up this evening and I was supposed to be at work and we'd got Laura to baby-sit, but I got home earlier than I'd planned, and you're never going to believe what I walked in on . . .'

Si and I shoot each other worried glances.

Lucy is grinning like the cat that got the cream. 'I walked in on Ingrid and the mystery lover locked in a passionate embrace.'

'And?' Si's now starting to look bored. 'Some swarthy Italian? Playboy type? Medallion and hairy chest?'

Lucy's smile is growing wider. 'Nope,' and she pauses dramatically until even Si starts to look interested. 'It's *Portia*!'

'WHAT?' Si knocks his wine glass over.

'You *are* joking?' I leave it to Si to speak, as I am, for possibly the first time in my life, completely speechless.

'Nope.' Lucy shakes her head. 'I know! *Portia!* Isn't it *extraordinary!*'

'Extraordinary.'

Portia? Ingrid? How? When? Oh Christ. This is just too much for me. 'Christ, how did this happen?'

She shrugs. 'Ingrid's hardly likely to tell me the whole story, is she?'

'But Portia?' It hits me again. 'It's just unbelievable.'

'You should have seen Josh's face!' Lucy starts to laugh.

'Josh?' Si and I say together, and I suddenly think, God, were we wrong *again*? And a deep shame engulfs me as I realise that yet again Si and I have jumped to conclusions and shunned Josh for something he evidently hasn't done.

'I thought Josh was away?' Si manages to sound breezily nonchalant as Lucy's busy concentrating on unwrapping the Dairy Milk.

'He was supposed to be, but it got cancelled at the last minute. He's upstairs in his study, still working on his big deal.'

I for one, am still completely speechless, and I can see that Si is also lost for words, but thankfully Max chooses that moment to disrupt the shamed atmosphere in the kitchen by zooming around the kitchen table with Pokémon in hand, making a huge amount of noise, until Si scoops him up and asks whether he'd like a story.

Lucy looks at him gratefully, and Si carries Max out of the room, with me following closely behind.

At the foot of the stairs, just out of earshot, Si waves frantically for me to come over.

'OK, I'm coming.' As soon as we're upstairs Si sends Max off to find last year's Furby, telling him that the Pokémon wants to destroy it, and then whispers to me, 'Christ, we've got to apologise to Josh.'

'I know. But what are we supposed to say?'

'Oh, God knows, but I think we just have to do it.' He shoots a glance at Max, who's on his hands and knees rifling through the toy chest.

'Will he be all right?'

'He'll be hours,' Si says, pulling his sweater up to reveal a small brown Furby nestling in his waistband. 'Come on, let's go and find Josh.'

As we walk up to the study door we can hear the sounds of typing. Si knocks on the door. The typing stops. 'Yup?'

'Josh? It's Si. And Cath. Can we come in?' Si is already opening the door as he asks this, making it a purely rhetorical question.

Josh swivels round from his desk. 'Hi, guys,' he says nonchalantly, which, if you didn't know any better, you might think was a sign that there was nothing wrong, but there is a warmth missing in his voice, and I suddenly realise how awful this must have been for Josh. We are, after all, two of his best friends, and for weeks now we've been giving him the cold shoulder without letting him know the reason why, and poor, poor Josh, with all his insecurities, must have felt terrible. Why did I not think of this before?

'Josh, we need to talk to you,' I start, then stop, because how on earth do you explain, or justify, or apologise for what we've done?

'The thing is,' Si says, sitting down on a futon pushed against the wall. 'We thought you were having an affair with Portia—'

'Well, actually that was my fault, because I saw you in Barnes one night with Portia and I immediately jumped to the wrong conclusion, but then we discovered you weren't,' I interrupt.

Si continues, 'But only because we then thought you were having an affair with Ingrid.'

'And now we know that you weren't, and we feel terrible because we've been so awful to you, but we were only trying to protect Lucy,' I say.

There's a long silence, then Josh says, 'What made you think I would be unfaithful to Lucy?'

'Well, you kept having these late meetings and then, when you were here, you weren't interested in sex . . .' Whoops. I think I've gone too far, and I see Josh clench his teeth, which means he is seriously pissed off, but, repressed as he is, he won't let it out, which is a relief.

I shrug apologetically. 'I'm sorry, Josh. We both are. We were just so angry at the thought of you hurting Lucy.' We hang our heads in shame.

And Josh shakes his head, looks at the floor. 'I didn't know what it was,' he says eventually. 'At least now I know why the pair of you had just switched off.'

'Oh, Josh, please forgive us?' I can feel my eyes welling up.

'What can I say?' Josh looks first at me, then at Si. 'You're my oldest friends, and I suppose, at least, you've been honest with me. But why didn't you say something before? If you thought I was having an affair, why didn't you confront me with it instead of just cutting me dead? Christ, we're not children any more.'

'With hindsight we were wrong in what we did,' Si says. 'If we ever have a problem in the future I swear to you we'll sit down and talk about it.'

'You mean, if you ever think I'm having an affair again?' but Josh's voice is soft and I can see he's forgiven us.

But before Si has a chance to answer, the study door is pushed open and Max stands there, eyes alert, the war between the Pokémon and Furby completely forgotten.

'Daddy?' he says, climbing on to Josh's lap. 'Can I go to affair too? And can I have a toffee apple and a candy floss?' The three of us start to laugh, and it is the first time I have ever wanted to kiss Max.

Chapter Fourteen

'NOT . . . SEX!' SI SQUEALS, when I finally admit everything. 'You witch! You complete witch! I can't believe you waited a week to tell me. I knew it. I knew you looked different! So how do you feel?'

'Amazing.'

'And you've seen him how many times since?'

'Almost every night,' I admit sheepishly.

'OH MY GOD!' he shouts so loudly my eardrums practically pop, but then he recovers and says seriously, 'Now, Cath. Don't jump in feet first looking for a big relationship. You must take it slowly.'

'Oh fuck off,' I snort, and he laughs, because this is, of course, what I have always said to Si.

'Details, details,' Si says, 'I want details. Oh no. Oh bugger. I've got to go or I'll miss my flight.'

'I know,' I chuckle maniacally. 'That's why I left it until now to call. Oh well,' I say, letting out a dramatic sigh. 'You'll just have to wait for the details until you get back from Tenerife. Have a lovely time. Bye.'

'CATH!' he shrieks. 'Don't you dare. Oh God, oh God, I can't bear this. I have to wait a whole week.'

'Look, you. You're going to miss your flight. Look after yourself, and I'll see you the weekend after next and I love you.'

'I know, sweets.' He blows me a kiss down the phone. 'I love you too.'

For someone who has spent years erecting barriers around her love life, I'm doing a remarkably good job of letting them down.

But perhaps the strangest thing of all is that it simply doesn't feel scary. If I didn't know better, I'd say it felt *right*, but of course I do know better, so instead I'll say it feels easy.

So, so easy. Although it's been years, I well remember the men who didn't call, who'd phone to cancel ten minutes before I was due to see them, who'd say they would phone and then never would. But James is different. When he says he's going to phone, he phones. If he says he'll pick me up at seven thirty, he's on the doorstep at seven twenty-nine. There is no messing about with James, and I always, *always* know exactly where I stand.

And we get on so well. I feel totally, completely, one hundred per cent relaxed in his company. There are no games, no insecurities.

And the loveliest thing about him is that he thinks I'm perfect. He lies in bed at night, stroking my thighs, not even flinching at the orange peel effect of cellulite under his hands, and he thinks I'm beautiful.

And having him think I'm beautiful has started to make me feel beautiful, and this is perhaps the biggest change of all, because I've never felt beautiful before.

He calls me in the shop every day, at least twice a day, and we've been, as I already said, together every night. I know it's slightly early to say this, but it does seem that already we're settling into a pattern. Lucy, of course, is over the moon; she was almost bursting with excitement when I first told her, and now I can't wait for Si to get back so I can fill him in.

So here I am at Heathrow, waiting at Arrivals to surprise Si. There are hundreds of people milling around, and it's far too early in the morning for me to be doing this.

He is almost the first one through, which doesn't surprise me, as he's such an orderly and neat packer that he usually manages to get away with hand luggage only. I push my way to the front so he can see me.

He's sharing his trolley with another man, around the same age, and they're both laughing and talking animatedly as they walk through, so animatedly they don't see me until I'm practically on top of the trolley.

'CATH!' Si throws his arms around me. 'I can't believe you're here!' He turns to the man with him, 'And there we were, about to jump on the train to Paddington. Thank heavens for large mercies.'

'Not that large.' I smack him, and he winces in mock pain.

'Cath, this is Paul,' he says, standing aside for me to have a good look at his companion, who grins at me, showing rather gorgeous dimples in his cheeks, and shakes my hand. 'I suppose you won't believe me if I tell you I've heard all about you and all of it's good?' he says, smiling.

'You were doing so well until the last bit,' I say, grinning back.

'Paul was staying in the apartment next to mine,' Si explains. 'We met on the first day . . .'

'And haven't been apart since.' Paul squeezes Si's arm as he looks at him affectionately, and I feel a jolt of excitement.

And Si looks fantastic. Not that I was expecting anything less, but he looks tanned, healthy, positively *glowing*, and I know that sun, sea and sand alone haven't given him this glow.

I grab the trolley and the three of us walk to the car park, leaving Paul in charge of the bags because Si insists on accompanying me to the car-park pay machine. 'Well?' he hisses, just as soon as we're out of earshot. 'Isn't he *gorgeous*?'

'Gorgeous,' I echo, laughing. 'I can't believe you. I mean, I expected you to come back looking all lovely and tanned, but I certainly didn't expect you to have some beefcake on your arm.'

'Well, sweets. Neither did I!' I look at him slyly as I feed the coins into the machine. 'I *swear*! But we've had an incredible time, and he's sweet, and bright, and funny, and for the first time in years I haven't fallen head over heels.'

'Yeah, right.'

'No, I'm serious, Cath. If anything he's been the one doing all the chasing. I kept telling him I wasn't interested in a relationship, but he didn't want to hear it.'

'Does he . . . ?' My sentence tails off, because I'm not sure whether I should be asking this question.

Si shrugs and nods. 'That's the thing. I kept saying no, and he kept saying why not, and in the end I just told him, and he was fine about it. Said he'd already sort of figured it out.'

'And?'

Si shoves me playfully. 'And he'd brought condoms. Thank God.'

I hold up a hand, putting on my best schoolmistress voice. 'Too much information, Mr Nelson.' And he laughs.

'Christ, come on, he'll think we've done a runner,' and we both rush back to see Paul smiling as we approach.

'Done the post-mortem,' Si pants, as we move off towards the car. 'And you, Paul, will be glad to hear you pass with flying colours.'

'I don't remember saying that,' I say, mock-indignant.

'You didn't have to,' he says triumphantly, and Paul looks at me and shakes his head, as if to say, What can we do?

I haven't spoken to Portia since that night at the Groucho, but not because I haven't wanted to. I so valued that night, when she reminded me of why we were friends, and why I loved her so much, but I didn't want her to think I was prying, and I didn't know what to say about Ingrid, so I've just avoided the situation altogether.

I've thought about her, of course, and thought how strange it is that life should turn out like this, and how Portia is the last person I would have expected to have a relationship with a woman.

Looking back, over the years, I remember how inseparable we used to be, how much I worshipped her, and I wonder what I would have done had there ever been a time when our friendship might have progressed to more. I know this sounds ridiculous, but now I almost feel rejected, and I keep thinking, how come she never made a pass at me?

And I've really tried to think, to remember whether she had, but maybe she hadn't admitted anything to herself then.

But however much I loved her then, however close I felt to her that one night when she explained her affair-that-never-was with Josh, however indebted I feel to her, she simply doesn't have a place in my life any more. She talked of happy endings, and before she came back I always subconsciously thought that I wouldn't be able to have a happy ending unless Portia was around, but now I think I was wrong.

I think that all those years of thinking about her, talking about her, building her up into something she couldn't possibly have lived up to, weren't so much about missing her as about needing to have some kind of ending. Lucy has called it closure, and that feels exactly right. It feels that finally I am able to close the chapter on Portia, to sever the ties that have bound me to her all these years.

Which is not to say I won't see her. She and Si are growing closer, and I'm sure she'll be there, at his dinner party, tonight, although I'm not sure how often Josh and Lucy will want to see her, Ingrid now spending almost every night at Portia's, which is, as Lucy keeps saying, not what they're paying her for, given that Ingrid is still their au pair.

Perhaps I am over-analysing all of this. Perhaps it is merely as simple as my life moving on: I have the career of my dreams now that I have Bookends; I have a relationship with James, and I am happy. No, more than happy. Content. Deeply content, and perhaps it is this that is allowing me to let go of the old life and welcome the new.

Because God knows a lot has changed. Not that I was unhappy before, but I can see now that Si is right when he says that I was in a rut, that we all were. Bizarre as it seems, Si thinks that there is a reason for him being diagnosed positive. He has started to involve himself far more in the world of alternative therapies, and has been talking about training in acupressure massage himself.

As for Paul, it actually does seem to be materialising into something important, and Si does have a point when he says he would never have met Paul had he not been diagnosed. I popped in to see them the other night and Paul was clucking round Si like a mother hen, which Si was pretending to find irritating, but of course he was loving every second.

Even Josh and Lucy have changed, grown far closer, since the 'affair that never was'. It may not have actually happened, but there's no denying that the pair of them had drifted apart. They make time for one another now. They talk to one another, and at least twice a week they ensure they have dinner alone, just the two of them, to keep the romance alive (incidentally, the Agent Provocateur gear hasn't been wasted after all).

'Crisis, crisis.' Si's on the phone, sounding desperate. 'I need lemons. Cath, can you bring me lemons?'

'Now?' I'm standing in the living room, water dripping into a big puddle on the carpet, as I still have this ridiculous thing about taking a phone call, even when you're in the bath and have an answerphone that functions perfectly normally.

Si grumbles to himself for a few seconds. 'Oh, OK,' he mutters eventually. 'I suppose you can bring them with, but you *must* be first. Seven thirty sharp. Can you do that?'

'Okay. Where's Paul? Can't he get lemons?'

'Nope. He's gone to get some more crackers and his mobile's not on.'

I already know that tonight will be the dinner party to end all dinner parties, and not because Si has told me he intends to reveal his *coup de grâce* in what will doubtless be the most dramatic way possible. I know because Si has been planning this for days. He has planned the menu, the flowers, even the place settings. Paul has borrowed a trestle table from a friend, to be covered with a crisp damask tablecloth and tiny tea lights in glasses ('Candles, my darling Cath,' said Si, the other day, 'are just so *done*.'). The champagne will be on ice, and Si's beloved opera will be playing softly in the background as we take our seats.

Portia was invited to come tonight, but it turns out that she had accepted an invitation to some media do with Ingrid, and although part of me is fascinated to see them together, the other part is relieved they won't be coming, because Ingrid is not exactly my favourite person.

Paul, naturally, will be there, having been Johnny to Si's Fanny Craddock all week, and James has been invited as well. James knows about Si, he would have had to be stupid not to guess, and he knows that tonight is the night he is planning to tell Josh and Lucy.

'Is there not something slightly ghoulish about announcing it in this way?' he asked the other morning, and I was surprised to find myself saying that it is, in fact, quite the reverse. It will be a celebration of life. Of friendships, both new and old.

'Cath! Look at you! You look all gorgeous and sparkly, like a film star!' Lucy is as exuberant as ever as we approach them, shivering on the doorstep in the cold December air.

'Look at me? Look at you!' I laugh, admiring her slinky red dress and tiny glittering beads threaded through her hair.

Josh leans down and gives me a kiss, and I am relieved to see that he has truly forgiven me, and the twinkle in his eye tells me everything is back to normal. He shakes James's hand as Lucy links her arms through James's and smiles up at him with a wink.

'Could it be you, young James, making our Cath look so sparkly?'

'I'm certainly trying,' he laughs, as the buzzer finally lets us in, and we all fall into the hallway and up the stairs.

Paul answers the door, and I introduce him to James, Josh and Lucy, who are all instantly won over by that large, open smile and those trusting eyes. Si runs out of the kitchen to greet us, then runs back in to stir the soup, and Paul opens a bottle of champagne and pours it, shouting for Si to come in and join us for a toast.

'To old friends,' Si says, as we all raise our glasses and echo his words, and as I take a sip I catch sight of Lucy, who has a huge smile on her face, and she stands up.

'And to new arrivals,' she says, as we all say 'new arrivals', and Si puts an arm round Paul as I squeeze James's leg.

'Tiny new arrivals,' Lucy says, stressing the word 'tiny' and looking around the room at each of us, as Si squeals and runs over to her.

'Are you trying to tell us there's a tiny bun in there?' he says, patting her stomach. She nods and he throws his arms around her.

'Lucy, I'm thrilled,' I say, although quite frankly, given how I feel about Max, I'm hardly relishing the prospect of yet another devilspawn-child-from-hell, although I am thrilled that they're thrilled.

'Oh bugger. The canapés.' Si stands up and puts down his champagne, but Paul jumps up. 'Don't worry,' Paul says. 'I'll get it. You stay and chat.'

I catch Lucy's eye and she raises an eyebrow, and I know we are thinking exactly the same thing: that all these years we thought that Si was waiting to be someone's wife, but not only does he now appear to have found a wife of his own, he's obviously thrilled to pieces with the arrangement.

A bell goes off in the kitchen, and Si stands up and calls everyone to the table, where we stand for a while, oohing and aahing over the crystal rose bowl in the middle, the beautiful calligraphy on the name cards, the candlelight flickering off the silver.

'I must say, I do feel special,' Lucy says, pulling out her chair. 'This feels like we ought to be in some rather grand castle somewhere—'

'Instead of in a poky one-bedroomed flat in Kilburn?' I say.

'Poky? Did I hear you describe my palace as poky?' Si looks at me in mock anger.

'Moi? I wouldn't dream of it. Mmm, something smells gorgeous.'

Si dashes into the kitchen and emerges with a tureen of soup. 'I wish I could take credit for this—' he says, placing it on the table.

'But Queen Delia got there first?' I say, unable to resist.

'Actually, Paul got there first,' and we all turn to look at Paul, who pretends to look humble and then laughs.

'Before you call me Queen Paul, I have to say I'd be happier as Prince Charming.'

'Prince Charming it is.' Si looks at him affectionately, and, given that the champagne has already had its desired effect, we all loudly raise our glasses and toast Prince Charming, who duly bows his way back into the kitchen to fetch the croutons.

James starts off quietly, getting used to the whole crowd in all their boisterous glory, but the alcohol keeps flowing, the conversation starts rising, and soon he is as loud as the rest of us.

I watch him, watch him banter with Lucy, with Si, and I smile to myself as I sip from my glass of red wine, delighted at how he fits in.

We are so busy having a good time that I completely forget that there is a reason for tonight, and it is only when we are all groaning and complaining about the amount of food we have consumed, that I wonder whether Si is still planning to make his announcement tonight. For he looks so calm. So content. And the Si I know, the Si I knew, would be having a huge anxiety attack right now, palms sweating at the prospect of revealing his innermost secret.

But then Si comes into the living room bearing a cafetière, and calls for silence.

'Speech, speech!' Josh calls drunkenly, as Si shushes him with a benevolent smile.

'Believe it or not,' he says, 'there is a reason for this little dinner.'

'To drink fine wine and get pissed?' Josh has, as he always does when drunk, regressed back to his student days, and Lucy puts a hand on his arm to silence him, because the atmosphere is now changed, and it is no longer appropriate for Josh to shout out anything.

'I have an announcement to make, but first I want to say I'm absolutely thrilled that Max will have a little brother or sister, and the fact that such a lovely and unexpected announcement was made earlier this evening, makes what I'm about to tell you much easier.'

My heart starts pounding, and I can't even imagine how difficult this must be for Si. James reaches for my hand under the table, and I squeeze it hard, staring intently at Si's face.

'But I want you to know that it really isn't a big deal. I mean, I thought it was, at first, obviously. But being diagnosed as HIV positive only means I have a virus, not that I'm going to die. Well, hopefully not yet, however much you might want to kill me at times.'

If you weren't concentrating, you'd almost miss it, so casually does Si weave this into his sentence, but then I look at Josh, who suddenly looks completely pale, and at Lucy, whose eyes are already brimming over as she stands up and runs over to Si to give him a hug.

'It's OK, Lucy,' Si murmurs, rubbing her back, then letting her go.

'The thing is, you're basically my family. Sorry, James, I know you're the latest addition and you probably weren't expecting to be drawn into a drama quite so soon.' James smiles at Si and shrugs as if to say it doesn't matter, and I love him for that. 'But I need you all to know, and I need your support.

'Lucy, Josh, you probably have things you want to ask me, and I've started going to a course for, well, for people like me, and one of the things I've learned is that it's incredibly important to be honest with one another, so if there's anything you want to ask me . . .'

The questions come thick and fast. Mostly from Lucy, once she has recovered from her tears. How long had he been ill, how had he caught it, what did it mean, were there new treatments . . . Si answers them quietly and patiently, and it is only when he has said all that he has to say, that I realise Josh still hasn't said a word.

'Josh?' Si speaks gently, as Josh raises his eyes, looking completely shell-shocked. Josh starts to say something, but then leaps to his feet, walks to the door and slams it behind him, without a word.

Lucy, stricken, apologises for him, then runs after him, the door slamming behind her. The four of us who remain speak in hushed voices, concern for Si mingling with outrage at Josh, and fury.

Half an hour later the doorbell rings and I open the door to find Josh standing there with Lucy. Both of them have swollen faces, and eyes puffy with crying, and they walk in wordlessly, Lucy coming to sit down with us, and Josh walking over to Si.

And I see something I never thought I'd see Josh do. He puts his arms around Si and starts to cry, and Si comforts him, patting his back and telling him it's OK, as the rest of us decide to go into the kitchen to start the washing-up.

'Is Josh OK?' I whisper to Lucy, as James and Paul busy themselves putting more coffee on.

'Shocked,' Lucy says. 'You know what Josh is like. He thinks HIV means AIDS, which he thinks means death, and he just went into shock. I've been sitting out there with him for the last half an hour, trying to explain what it really means.'

'Lucy, did you know?' I don't know what makes me ask this question. She shrugs. 'I guessed. Si hadn't been his usual self, and I woke up one morning and just knew. Although I kept hoping I was wrong. But I knew something was wrong with you as well, and you stopped talking about Si for a while . . . ' She stops and sighs. 'Is it going to be OK?'

And I stand in the kitchen, listening to James and Paul clattering about with coffee cups, looking at Lucy's puffy face, turning so I can just see, through the doorway, Si and Josh sitting together on the sofa, talking softly, and I feel an incredible peace come over me. In the heart of— as Si would put it—my family of choice.

'Do you know,' I say, smiling, seeing Lucy's face relax as she looks into my eyes, as I suddenly know what the answer is. 'I really think it is.'

JANE GREEN

When I arranged to meet Jane Green we chose to have lunch at the same cosy, hidden-away Italian restaurant in Hampstead where we had met after the publication of her previous novel, *Mr Maybe*. At that time Jane was heavily pregnant and now has a son, Harrison, and she had mentioned that she might bring him to lunch with her so I was quite disappointed when she appeared without him.

'Well, I suddenly thought, it's not very professional is it?' Jane said with a smile. 'But don't worry, I have brought photos.' After looking at the photographs of a very handsome Harrison and chatting about the challenges of motherhood, we finally got down to talking about Jane Green the writer.

'I really feel I have moved on in my novels,' she told me. 'I started writing about single girls and their loves but I am not living that kind of life any more and I can't write about it. I'm married now, with a delicious son. My life has changed and therefore my novels have too. In fact,' she says with a wry look, 'I went to a gallery opening last night with a girlfriend and we decided to go party-hopping. But I quickly realised how glad I am that I'm no longer part of the single scene.'

Jane Green was writing *Bookends* when she was pregnant. 'Perhaps because I had a new life growing inside me, I wanted to write a real-life novel, with genuine warmth and characters you would want as friends.' In fact, Jane's original plan for her character Si was to give him just an HIV scare, but as she developed the story, she knew that that would be taking the easy way out. Jane talked to many people who are living with HIV but there was one story that affected her deeply. 'I spent the day with a woman who was HIV positive and when I met her it almost took my breath away because she could have been me. She was my age, came from the same area of London, same sort of background, wore the same sort of clothes. She just got in with the wrong kind of people and has been living with HIV for fifteen years. I found her story incredibly moving.'

Since the birth of her son, Jane finds it much harder to stick to her writing regime, but even so she is working on her next novel to be published in June. 'Since I've had Harrison I have become an expert at procrastination. Even when I do sit in front of my computer I will run back down to smother him with kisses far too regularly. I can't help it. I hear a gurgle or a cry and I have to go and see him. But I love the fact that I am at home working and around all the time. That's definitely one of the major advantages of being a novelist.'

Jane Eastgate

Katie Fforde
Thyme Out

When market gardener, Perdita Dylan,

makes her daily delivery of produce to

Grantly Manor, she is horrified to find

her ex-husband, Lucas Gillespie, in charge

of the kitchen. Then she learns that he

is about to become a television chef and

would like to borrow her picturesque,

if primitive, cottage kitchen for the

production, as well as her skills as an

assistant. It seems she can't escape him—

but can she resist him?

Chapter One

'WELL? ARE YOU GOING to come in? Or just stand in the doorway with your trug, looking picturesque?'

Perdita was almost paralysed with shock and confusion. How could short, plump, amiable and easy-going Enzo have, almost overnight, turned into the tall, black-browed monster she had divorced ten years before? Somehow she got herself across the threshold.

'And take off those bloody gumboots! This is a professional kitchen, not a farmyard!'

Perdita looked down at her feet and noticed that the floor was a lot cleaner than usual. She looked up at her ex-husband. 'No.'

'So you've got bolshi in your old age, have you? You always were difficult.'

'I'm not at all difficult. Where's Enzo?'

'Fucked off to sunny Napoli, I expect. How the hell should I know?'

Perdita suddenly became aware that it wasn't only Enzo that had undergone a hideous transformation. The rest of the kitchen had been affected too. The friendly, busy place she had been delivering veg to for five years had metamorphosed into something akin to an operating theatre. The noise and clutter had gone, as had the cheery hum of Radio One, a Greek chorus to the hubbub of the kitchen. No one was singing, swearing, or clattering pans. In fact no one seemed to be doing anything.

The other two occupants of the kitchen were still just recognisable, but looked completely different. Instead of a pair of brightly coloured cotton trousers, besloganed sweatshirt and a striped apron in one case, and a pair of ripped jeans and grubby T-shirt in the other, they wore white overalls and chef's trousers. Janey, the young sous-chef, who looked about seventeen, had tried to confine her Pre-Raphaelite hair under a white cap, but like its owner, Perdita suspected, it was desperately trying to escape.

Enzo's regime had come to an end: an evil dictator had dethroned him.

Aware that she had become the focus of attention, and that the evil dictator was wearing a very familiar scowl, Perdita decided to pretend everything was normal. 'Hi, Janey, Greg. How are you?'

Greg and Janey nodded stiffly but didn't speak. Janey had taken on the appearance of a rabbit in thrall to a stoat and didn't offer to put the kettle on or make toast. Greg, the washer-up and general dogsbody, had his long hair tied back in a ponytail under a white cap instead of a bandanna, and didn't make one of his politically incorrect jokes. The kitchen seemed under a strange, sinister enchantment—like Narnia under its blanket of snow. It was not hard to find the warlock responsible: Lucas Gillespie.

'You will have gathered,' he addressed his work force, 'that Perdita and I used to know each other.' He gave her a slanting glance and she stiffened. 'It was years ago, when we were both very young.'

She relaxed. Lucas didn't want his failed marriage known about either. 'I still am young,' she said.

He shrugged. 'So, what have you got there?'

Perdita looked down at the contents of her trug. 'Your—Enzo's usual order. Lamb's lettuce, some Ragged Jack kale, the usual saladinis, lettuces and some pea plants.'

'Pea plants?'

'Yes. An excellent crop.' She broke him off a leaf.

He crunched it up. 'Mmm. Does it stand well?'

'Of course. Everything I sell stands.'

'I suppose that explains the exorbitant prices you charge.' He raised an eyebrow. 'I've been looking at the accounts,' he added.

Perdita was offended. 'My prices may seem high, but I offer very good value. And if you don't want to use me, feel free to stop. I've got plenty of chefs I just can't supply at the moment.'

'And you reckon you can grow anything?'

'Well, I won't grow anything it doesn't pay me to grow.'

'What about capsicums?'

She shook her head. 'Too much heat. Too expensive.'

Lucas frowned contemplatively. 'Stay here!' he commanded, and strode off towards the cold store.

The moment he was out of the room, she asked, 'What on earth's happened to Enzo? And how did you get lumbered with *him*?'

'Enzo's retired,' Janey whispered back nervously. 'We're very lucky to have Chef. He's very well thought of.'

Perdita humphed. 'What do you think of him, Greg?'

Greg shrugged. 'Not laid back like Enzo was.'

Lucas came back into the kitchen.

'Here.' He handed Perdita a small segmented tuber, about the size of a prawn. It was dark brown. 'Can you grow these?'

Perdita was a professional. She reckoned to know her veg—the more obscure the better—but she was flummoxed this time. 'Er—what is it?'

'It's a crosnes.'

'I thought that was a disease,' said Perdita.

'It's named after a French town, but you can call it a Chinese artichoke if you like. It's like a dead nettle with roots you can eat. I brought it back from France. If you can grow it, I'll buy every bit you can produce.'

She examined the tuber he put into her hand. 'Well, I'll give it a go. Have you any idea what it needs?'

'You're the gardener. But if you're in any doubt, I'll take it back. They're expensive'

Perdita's fingers closed around it, as she put it in her pocket. 'No, no. I'm sure I'll have no trouble. I'll just go and get the rest of your order.'

No one seemed to move while she went back to her van, piled three crates of veg into her arms and came back into the kitchen with them. She took them through to the cold room and put them away. When she came back Lucas was inspecting some ducklings with signs of distaste, Janey was chopping onions, and Greg was pulling trays out of the oven, prior to cleaning it. It was something Perdita hadn't seen before. Which didn't mean that the oven was never cleaned when Enzo was in charge, she told herself, just that she'd never been there when it happened. This happy realisation was banished by Greg's obscene and unwitting exclamation as he looked inside.

'So,' said Perdita, 'is there anything you want specially for next week?'

'I'll see how good this lot turns out to be first.'

Perdita gave him a snarl disguised as a smile. 'Will you give me a ring?'

He saw through the disguise. 'Yes, but I don't seem to have your mobile number.'

'I don't have a mobile. My home and work number are the same.'

'I can't believe you're running a business without a mobile. Still, if you want to stay in the Dark Ages, don't let me try to stop you.'

'Oh, I won't.'

'And don't let anything bad happen to that crosnes.'

Perdita patted her pocket to check that it was still there. 'Well, if you don't want to order anything now, I'll be off. I've got a van full of baby vegetables for the health farm.'

'Then you'd better go. I'm sure they don't like being kept waiting for supplies any more than I do.'

Perdita ignored the dig. 'I don't suppose Janey could—'

'No she couldn't. She's got a lot to do. If she wants to keep her job. Which at the rate she's going, doesn't seem likely.'

Perdita shuddered, and swore to herself that she would get Janey out of that kitchen as soon as she possibly could. Janey reminded her of herself at that age and she would never have survived working for Lucas. Greg, she hoped, was tough enough to look after himself.

She gave Lucas a nod, and her two friends a tentative wave. A roar from behind her as she fled indicated she had left mud on the floor. Her satisfaction was slightly marred by the knowledge that Lucas wouldn't be the one to clear it up.

She clambered into her van in a confusion of emotions, none of them happy. Had Enzo gone willingly? And what the hell was Lucas doing as a chef? When they'd been married, he had been a thrusting young stockbroker, determined to become a millionaire before he was thirty. She had been a dreamy art student, who just wanted to paint. The ten intervening years had apparently affected Lucas's dreams and ambitions as much as they had her own.

'Well, at least I'm completely over him,' she murmured as she kicked off her Wellington boots so she could drive. She switched on the engine. Over him or not, she was forced to acknowledge that seeing him, with no warning, had been a dreadful shock. She turned the key another couple of times, praying that she wouldn't have to go back into the kitchen to ask for a push. 'Come on, baby,' she crooned. 'Start for Mummy.' Her woollen socks hanging over her toes, she pressed gently on the accelerator, and the van grumbled into life.

The health farm, Perdita's second biggest customer, which took pretty much everything and anything she could produce, was reassuringly the same as it had been on her last visit.

'Hello, ducks,' said Ronnie the manager, as she staggered into the kitchen under a pile of plastic crates. 'Got your usual array of slugs and aphids, have you?'

'Now you know you have far more time to clean them than I do,' replied Perdita amiably. 'Besides, I would have thought the guests here would be glad of the extra protein.'

'You know perfectly well we don't starve anybody here, even if they are on detox . . .'

'Which is why you want my fresh-out-of-the-ground veg, full of vitamins and minerals. Anyway, never mind about that. Have you heard about the new chef at Grantly House? I nearly had a fit when I saw Enzo had gone.'

Ronnie, always glad of a gossip, inclined his head in a knowing way. 'Want a coffee, dear? You look a bit peaky.'

Perdita did feel a little shaky. 'Yes, please. Black. Lots of sugar.'

'We'll take it through to the office, so we can talk in peace.'

'So?' demanded Perdita, the moment the door was closed behind them.

'Oh, don't sit on that stool, love; it wobbles,' said Ronnie, taking the swivel chair by the desk, refusing to be hurried.

'Oh, Ronnie! Don't keep me in suspense! You're always like this when you've got something really good to tell me.'

'OK, OK. Well, the story is that Mr Grantly was in France and he met this new young chef . . .'

'Not that young, surely?' Lucas must be about thirty-five by now. In chefs' terms, that was ancient.

'Younger than Enzo, anyway. And Mr Grantly thought he was just the person to get Grantly House a Michelin star, so he paid off Enzo and got this bloke over.'

'But that's terrible! Kicking Enzo out so—this new chef—can sweep in and take over!' Perdita was outraged as well as mystified.

'No need to look like that about it,' Ronnie went on. 'Enzo's delighted.'

'Is he? How do you know?'

'He rang me before he left. Said he'd got a very good golden handshake out of it. And, of course, he's been talking about going back to Italy for years. You know that. He's no spring chicken.'

Perdita took a sip of coffee. 'So what's this new one like, then?'

'Well, you've seen him, so you tell me. But by all accounts he's gorgeous. All smouldery and dark.' Ronnie gave Perdita a sideways glance. 'Obviously not your type, then?'

'Well, no. Actually, we sort of know each other. Years ago, in a previous reincarnation. He was a stockbroker.' Better to tell Ronnie and hope his sixth sense for old scandal wouldn't be aroused.

'And you didn't get on?'

'No. He was a pig. Um—did Enzo say anything about his wife?'

'Who? Enzo's?'

'No! Lucas Gillespie's. He was married when I knew him.' Which was true.

171

'Oh? Well, Enzo didn't say anything about whether he was married or not. Apparently he's staying with Mr Grantly until his staff flat is ready, but I've not heard tell of any wife. What was she like, then?'

Perdita hesitated only a millisecond before abdicating from the role of spouse, giving it instead to the woman for whom she had been abandoned. 'Well, I didn't know her well.' Perdita had met the other woman in her husband's life only once. 'But she was older than me.' That had seemed the ultimate insult—he left her playing with her toys while he went off with the grown-ups. 'And very sophisticated.'

'So how did you meet the evil Mr Gillespie?'

'Oh, at a party. I'd only just left school. I hardly knew him at all, really.' This was also true. They had met and married within three months. 'But who I'm worried about is Janey. He'll bully her to bits!'

'If you didn't know him that well, how do you know that?'

'I know Janey. She's young and innocent—'

'And pretty. Remind you of anyone?'

'Stop teasing me, Ronnie. This is serious. We must get her out of there!'

'Perdita, love, I hope you don't mind me being personal . . .'

'But you're going to be, anyway.'

'But don't you think you spend too much time worrying about other people, and not enough time worrying about yourself? You should get yourself a nice boyfriend, have some fun.'

Perdita looked at Ronnie as if she had never heard this from him before, when in fact he said it nearly every time they met. But this time it raised an important question: what would Lucas think when he found out, as he inevitably would, that she hadn't got so much as a sniff of a boyfriend, let alone a husband? He would think, conceited bastard that he was, that she was carrying a torch for him.

Ronnie, surprised that Perdita wasn't protesting as usual, followed up his opening. 'You're really a lovely girl, just a little bit unkempt. I mean, look at your clothes.'

For once, Perdita looked. The ancient fair-isle sweater, which was warm and comfortable and, to her eyes, attractive, hung halfway down her thighs and the hem was partially unravelled. There was a panel of mud on the inside of her leg running from her Wellingtons to above her knees.

'And your hair . . .' Ronnie, seeing that for once his words were having an effect, pressed on. 'A good cut and a few highlights would make all the difference—carry you over the hump between light mouse and dark blonde. Why don't you come here for a make-over?'

Perdita shuddered. 'If you've got in mind some wonderful man who'd make it all worth while, I might just consider it.'

'You won't find a man looking like Orphan Annie. But no,' he went on, defeated, 'I'm afraid I haven't got anyone up my sleeve. It's no good looking among our clientele. We get mostly women, as you know, and enough of them are single to make any man a sitting target.'

'Tell you what. If anyone lovely, male and straight comes in, let me know and I'll submit to every torture you think I need to make myself beautiful.'

'Perdita, love,' Ronnie said sharply, 'this wouldn't be anything to do with the new chef at Grantly's, would it?'

Perdita felt herself blush and knew that Ronnie would have noticed it. 'Only indirectly. Seeing him unexpectedly like that made me look back to how I'd been the last time I'd seen him.' A wreck, but no need to tell Ronnie that. 'I've come on a lot. I'm independent, I've got my own business going, but I haven't got a partner. I've spent so much time and energy getting my market garden going, I haven't had a date for years. I don't mind ending my life as an old maid, but I want it to be through choice, not because I never had an opportunity for marriage.'

This fairly grown-up-sounding statement seemed to satisfy the eagle-eyed Ronnie. 'You don't get the opportunity because you spend all your spare time looking after Mrs Anson. How is she, by the way?'

'Kitty? Oh, she's fine. She's always telling me I ought to have children of my own, and not waste my time treating her life a child. As if I'd dare!'

'She's right, you know, Perdita. That old lady's got a lot of sense.' Ronnie patted her knee paternally, and got up. 'Now, must get on.'

'So must I. Thanks for the coffee and the chat, Ronnie.'

'Any time, love. And let me know if you fancy a make-over.'

'I will.' A make-over, much as the idea horrified her, would be worth the agony if it helped her get a man before Lucas could find out that she hadn't already got one.

Although Kitty and Perdita lived so close that their gardens backed on to each other, Perdita drove to Kitty's on her way home, parked her van outside the house and knocked on the back door.

'Kitty? Are you there? It's only me!' She walked down into the garden where she found her quarry in the vegetable plot, pulling out bean sticks.

'Hello, darling, how are you?' The elderly lady removed her pipe from between her teeth and kissed Perdita's cheek fondly. 'Here, take these and come and look at my wintersweet. I think it's going to flower at last.' Perdita took the bean sticks and followed her friend down into the shrubbery. Once there, they studied the emerging blossom.

'You are patient. I would have got fed up and thrown it out if it hadn't flowered before now.'

'By my age you've learned patience, dear, and it smells heavenly.' Kitty stripped off the surgical gloves she wore for gardening and rummaged in one of the many pockets of her body warmer for her tobacco. Eventually, she found the plastic pouch in the pocket of her combat trousers and with it a postcard, which she handed to Perdita before pinning a slipping plait back round her head with a hairpin retrieved from another pocket. She gestured to the postcard.

'It's from your father. The places they get to! I expect there's one for you at home.'

Perdita glanced at the picture of a waterfall in the Andes for a moment. 'Kitty, what did the doctor say?'

Kitty opened the pouch and found a tamper. She emptied the pipe with a firm knock against the fence and then began to scrape out the bowl of it with the tool. 'Oh, the usual. It was only a routine check-up. There's nothing wrong with me.'

'Did he say you should give up your pipe?'

'No, he didn't,' said Kitty firmly. 'He said that at my age there was no point in giving up my little pleasures. It's quality of life they go for now. Longevity is out of fashion.'

Perdita laughed. 'Pity they didn't know that when you hit eighty-five!'

Kitty chuckled. 'I could have been hygienically euthanased. Now come in and let me get you some lunch. I know you won't eat unless I make you.'

'Nonsense! You're the one who stays out in the garden until it's dark and then is too tired to cook!'

Perdita and Kitty constantly accused each other of not eating properly while denying they were both equally guilty. One Christmas they had, coincidentally, given each other microwaves. Perdita used hers for heating up frozen pizzas and Kitty used hers to sterilise soil.

Perdita sat herself down at the large mahogany kitchen table and flicked through the junk mail, marvelling at how fit her old friend seemed. Kitty was eighty-seven and more sprightly than many people half her age. She was Perdita's favourite person in the world.

Perdita's parents lived abroad, having worked their whole careers in the diplomatic service. Perdita had spent her holidays from boarding school with Kitty, who was her mother's godmother, and had been more than that to Perdita. She vividly remembered the first time she had met Kitty. Sent by train to stay with her for the Easter holidays, Perdita had been terrified. For a start, she had no idea how to address the person her mother referred to as Aunt Kitty, because no one had remembered to tell her Kitty's surname. She had managed to avoid calling her anything for nearly the whole of the first day.

She was shown her room, a large first-floor bedroom with windows in two walls. 'This is always going to be your room now, my dear,' Kitty had said. 'My other guests can have the attic. If you're going to stay with me during the holidays, you'll need somewhere that is permanently yours. Can't think it's going to be much fun for you, staying with an old lady like me, but your mother said there was no one else she trusted to look after you.' Although she had no children of her own, Kitty instinctively knew how to make Perdita feel at home. She just treated her like an adult who needed cosseting a little. The name thing was got over very quickly when they were saying good night. Perdita started on the 'Aunt' and Kitty stopped her immediately. 'Call me Kitty, dear. All my friends do, and I think we're going to become very good friends.'

Many years had passed since that first meeting, and the love between the two of them had grown and developed. When Perdita's marriage had broken up, her first instinct had been to go to Kitty, who hadn't said, 'I told you so,' although she had warned against Perdita marrying a man she had known for such a short time. She had simply said, 'Men are *bastards*!' and given her a stiff drink.

'So, any news from the outside world?' asked Kitty, when she had put bowls of tinned tomato soup and a plate of bread and butter down in front of them both.

'Enzo's gone from Grantly House!'

'Michael Grantly never did know when he was on to a good thing. I thought Enzo cooked jolly well. On his good days.'

'Exactly! And you'll never guess who has replaced him!'

'Then just tell me. You seem very excited about it.'

'It's Lucas! Lucas Gillespie! My ex-husband!'

There was a moment's silence. 'I know quite well who Lucas Gillespie is, dear. But he isn't a cook, he's a stockbroker.'

Perdita was concentrating hard on sounding upbeat. 'He's a chef now. Apparently. Ronnie told me that Michael Grantly found him in France, and has sacked Enzo so Lucas can sweep Grantly House into all the gourmet food guides.'

Kitty frowned. 'Well, you seem perfectly happy about it, but I can't see it as a good thing.'

'Of course I'm not *happy* about it, exactly. But nor am I traumatised. After all, it's years since we parted and, thanks to you, I'm now an independent woman. Not the little mouse he left weeping in heap.'

It had been Kitty who had insisted that Perdita stop weeping and, as much as a distraction as anything else, help her in the garden. Later, when Perdita's green fingers became apparent, she had suggested she had some formal horticultural training. Eventually Kitty persuaded Perdita's father to give Perdita the fifteen grand he would have spent on her wedding had Perdita's mother had her way. With that capital, Perdita had started Bonyhayes Salads. Now it was a thriving, if not exactly lucrative, business.

'No. You've done marvellously, but I can't help feeling it would be nice if you had a man as well as a smallholding.'

'You've managed without one for nearly forty years.'

'True,' Kitty said, producing a plate of rather sweaty cheese from the refrigerator. 'Lionel dying like he did left me manless for the rest of my life. But you're a different matter altogether.'

Perdita was indignant. 'Am I? Why?'

'Because although my marriage was short, it was satisfying. You've only known that swine. You should have another bash at it. And you don't want him thinking you've been pining all these years, do you?"

Perdita extracted a catalogue from the pile at one end of the huge mahogany dining table that was the hub around which Kitty's life revolved, partly to avoid Kitty's direct gaze. 'These clothes are quite nice. Have you ordered anything?'

Kitty ignored the change of subject. 'He will think you've been pining because he's arrogant. You need a man to throw him off the scent. After all, you don't want him thinking he can pick up where he left off.'

Perdita shook her head. 'I really don't think he'd even dream of it. But you're right, I don't want him thinking I've been carrying a torch. I'd better find a man. Trouble is, there aren't any round here.' Her eye was caught by 'Derek, Vet', who was advertising sailing trousers in the catalogue. 'He's nice. Do you think you can buy the men, or is it just the clothes?'

The next time Perdita went to deliver at Grantly House she was prepared. She hadn't exactly put make-up on, or worn her best clothes, but she had made sure her hair was clean and that her jeans were freshly washed. Lucas had greatly increased the order, which pleased her.

She piled up the plastic crates and carried them carefully into the kitchen. There were several people standing round Lucas, who was storming about, throwing his hands up in frustration.

'This is a professional kitchen. I don't see why it can't be used!'

'But our programme isn't for professionals,' said a well-spoken young man with floppy hair and an anxious expression. 'It's for entertainment.'

Lucas opened his mouth to shout, and Perdita decided to announce her presence.

'Hi, everyone!' she said over the top of her crates. 'I've just brought the veg.' Everyone turned towards her. 'I'll just put it all in the cold store, shall I? You're obviously busy.' Nobody moved or spoke, so she picked her way through the group until she got to the other door. 'I don't suppose anyone could possibly open that for me?'

The man who had spoken sprang into action and opened the door for her. 'Who is that lovely creature?' said someone else, making Perdita glad of the cool of the cold store.

'That's Perdita, from Bonyhayes Salads,' she heard Lucas answer.

'I think we really must use her. She'd make a lovely contrast to Lucas. A sort of angel and devil thing.'

Perdita swung the door to, so she couldn't overhear Lucas's reply. She stayed in the cold store, stacking boxes as long as she could without risking hypothermia, taking in what she'd heard. So Lucas wasn't satisfied with morphing from a City slicker into a chef, he had to be on television as well. When she emerged from the cold store, the kitchen was still full of people.

And Lucas, his arms folded, was still scowling, but this time the scowl was directed at her. The man with the floppy hair was also looking at her, but he was smiling, extremely charmingly.

'Perdita?' He took hold of her hand. 'I'm David Winter, and I think you may be the answer to our prayers. What sort of house do you live in?'

'Oh, it's a small cottage—'

'Perfect! Is it picturesque?'

'Well, I think it's very pretty, but it's not at all done up, or restored, or anything.' She had a feeling these people thought all cottages were candidates for *Country Living.* 'I don't seem to get much time for decorating,' she added, emphasising her point.

'Do you think we could go and see it?' asked David. 'We're looking for a location, near here, to use for our cookery programme.' He frowned, seeing that she needed more explanation. 'It's a pilot for a series where professional chefs cook in real kitchens . . .'

'This is a real kitchen,' snapped Lucas.

'But it's completely lacking in heart. I'm sorry, Lucas, but the viewers want a good location nowadays.'

'I really don't think my cottage would be suitable,' said Perdita. 'It's tiny, not at all convenient, and the kitchen is . . .' How to describe the dank, irregular space with little light and almost no working surface? 'Primitive, to put it politely.'

'It sounds *perfect*! After all, most viewers have tiny kitchens.'

'Really,' Perdita persisted valiantly, 'my kitchen is *not* suitable.'

'Couldn't we just look at it?' asked David Winter.

'Of course, but I promise you, you'll be disappointed. It's tiny, it's dark and it smells of damp. But I'll take you there if you insist.'

'Don't you usually visit your aunt at lunch time?' said Lucas.

Perdita wondered briefly how on earth he knew that and then realised that anyone could have told him. 'Well, actually it's her bridge afternoon, so I'm not going to today.'

'I expect she's got a lovely big kitchen,' said Lucas, with enough despair in his voice to inspire reluctant sympathy even in Perdita.

'I'm not having her involved in this,' she snapped, to hide it. 'And anyway, she's not my aunt.'

'So we can go and look at your kitchen.' David Winter sounded pleased. 'I've got such a good feeling about this.'

Perdita groaned. 'Promise not to cry when you see how wrong you are.'

'If we're going, let's go,' said Lucas impatiently. 'Even though it'll be a complete waste of time. I'll come with you, Perdita.'

Perdita considered refusing to take him, but she decided that her van might be just what he needed to bring him down off his pedestal.

'Now, listen to me, Lucas,' said Perdita, when she'd cleared the front seat of rubbish and Lucas had clambered in. 'You will hate my kitchen. I'm not fond of it myself, and I don't ever do any cooking, but it's not my fault. It's you who want to be on television so don't blame me for any of this fiasco. OK?' She switched on the ignition, and, reliably, the van failed to start. Lucas sat in silence while she tried another couple of times. 'Now would you mind getting out and giving me a push?'

Perdita disappeared into the coal shed and came out with a large key. As she did so she heard mutterings of 'adorable', 'perfect', and 'don't you just love those diamond panes?' issuing from the carload of television people.

'It's a bit cramped in the hall,' she said, opening the door and going in first. She led the way into the sitting room so that the half-dozen people could all get in through the front door.

The sitting room was the one place Perdita had made comfortable. There was a large wood-burning stove in the stone fireplace, and weak November sunshine shone in through the windows, catching a small collection of copper items that stood around the fireside.

'But it's charming!' declared David Winter.

'You haven't seen the kitchen yet,' said Perdita doggedly.

'How did you come to live here?' asked David, eager for details.

Perdita sighed. She didn't really want Lucas knowing her life story since he left her, but she had nothing to be ashamed of. 'It was adjoining

the land I had for my salads. When it came on the market, I bought it.'
She saw Lucas's eyebrow shoot up, desperate to ask, 'What with?'

'I see. And it was unrestored?' David Winter went on.

'It was pretty much as it is now. I had the stove put in, and it does the
hot water and a couple of radiators. But as I said, I don't have much time
for decorating.'

She knew most women would have been waxing the floors, sponging
and stencilling the walls and covering the chairs with petit point, but all
her creative energy went into her garden. Home for her was where she
flopped for a couple of hours before falling into the bath and into bed.

'So let's see the kitchen,' said Lucas glumly.

The kitchen was a later addition. It was a lean-to at the back of the
house and was small and badly arranged. The room was full of trays of
soil, sprouting seeds and tottering heaps of flowerpots waiting to be
washed. The sink was stacked with unwashed saucepans and grubby
plant labels. The only thing obviously used for its purpose was the
microwave, which took up most of the work surface.

'I did warn you,' she said as her guests stood open-mouthed in the
doorway. There wasn't room for more than Perdita and Lucas in the
kitchen at the same time.

'But it's ideal! Just needs tidying up a bit!' said David. 'Look at that
lovely deep windowsill! And the beam!'

'That's not a beam, it's a railway sleeper,' said Perdita, perturbed that
David was not put off. 'It was just stuck in to stop the house falling down.'

'Presumably all beams were just "stuck in to stop the house falling
down",' Lucas retorted acidly.

Perdita turned on him. 'Do you really want to cook in this kitchen?'

'Do you two know each other?' asked David.

'Of course,' said Perdita quickly. 'I deliver veg to Grantly House.'

'I know, but there seems to be some sort of . . . chemistry between you.'

'If you mean a hearty dislike, you've got it about right,' said Lucas.

'Hmm.' David stroked his chin thoughtfully. 'You know, people are
beginning to get tired of perfect-every-time cookery programmes. A
little frisson . . .' He narrowed his eyes as some creative and ground-
breaking idea occurred to him.

It made Perdita nervous. 'Honestly, this kitchen is not at all suitable.
It would be quite impossible to do a television programme in here.
Lucas would hate it, wouldn't you, Lucas? And he's your star!'

'Actually,' said an annoying individual, 'we could all be out in the passage and still get good shots. If it was cleared up, it would be perfect.'

'Well, it's not going to be cleared up! This is my home and where I work, and I'm not going to tart it all up for you lot!' Perdita wanted to cry.

'Temper, temper,' said Lucas.

Perdita turned on him again. 'Are you really telling me that you would be willing to do a cookery programme in a kitchen where there's barely space to boil a kettle?'

'If it wasn't full of junk there'd be plenty of room,' said Lucas.

Perdita stopped wanting to cry and started wanting to kill Lucas, slowly and painfully.

'And you'll be in it, too. You can tell us all about the wonderful things you grow,' said David Winter, as if offering her a treat.

'I don't want to be on television. I have a job,' said Perdita crossly.

'We will pay to use your cottage as a location,' David went on.

'And you do need a new van,' said Lucas.

David frowned, not wanting to give anyone the impression they'd pay huge amounts. 'Possibly not quite enough for that, but it'd be marvellous publicity for your business,' he added.

Perdita took a deep breath. 'I don't need any more business, and I don't suppose you'd start filming for ages. I will have bought a new van without your contribution by then.'

'Actually, we want to start pretty much right away. The programme's due to go out in the spring.'

Later, while she was washing up six dirty mugs and a few bowls, Perdita found it impossible not to think back to her short, turbulent marriage to Lucas Gillespie, and how she had picked herself up afterwards.

Kitty had been marvellous. She had fought Perdita's corner against her parents, insisting that their daughter didn't share their passion for travel and so didn't want to backpack round the world to get over her heartbreak. She convinced them that living quietly with Kitty, gardening, reading and eating nourishing meals, was what Perdita needed. And much later, when Perdita had done her horticulture course, she encouraged her to buy her first polythene tunnel and set up in business.

Kitty then sectioned off half an acre of her own enormous garden and gave it to Perdita—'So I don't have to feel guilty about not looking after it.'

Later, Perdita had found herself in a position to buy the tiny cottage at the end of the lane, which had once housed the gamekeeper of Grantly House, as well as enough land for two more tunnels.

There were a few spectacular arguments about money; Kitty wanted to finance the whole thing, the idea being that Perdita was going to inherit all Kitty's money anyway.

With a stubbornness that had surprised them both, Perdita refused.

She arranged a mortgage and a bank loan. 'So I'll have more to inherit,' she told Kitty.

It was at college that she had learned about markets. She realised that she could never make enough to keep herself by growing carrots and potatoes. She needed to grow specialist vegetables for specialist cooks. She went to the nearby health farm and persuaded Ronnie's predecessor that he needed to provide vegetables fresh out of the ground, and if he would only tell her what he wanted she would grow it and deliver it.

She did the same with Enzo at Grantly House. His requirements had been more esoteric and included specialist herbs, flat-leaved parsley, chervil, coriander, every sort of basil, tarragon, thyme, parsley and dill. He wanted baby leeks the size of her little finger, sprouted fenugreek, alfalfa and sweet seasoning peppers. Her business had flourished.

Now, five years on, certain that all wounds from her marriage had healed, Perdita's first concern was Janey. Lucas was obviously the sort of chef who thought humiliating one's staff was the way to get the best out of them. Even without her own personal knowledge of just how cruel Lucas could be, Perdita would have been worried about Janey, especially when a couple of telephone conversations with her made it clear she was developing a crush on Lucas. Janey must be rescued. Perdita liked rescuing things, and if it thoroughly annoyed Lucas in the process, well, all the better.

With these happy thoughts in mind, she didn't know whether to be pleased or sorry when, the next day, she received a fax order from Grantly House that was even bigger than the last one. She had no way of knowing how Lucas felt about her personally, but he was a big fan of what she produced.

When she delivered the order a couple of days later she dutifully removed her gumboots and padded into the kitchen in her woolly socks.

'Hi, everyone! How's things?' she carolled gaily, in an attempt to sound as she had before Enzo's departure. 'Oh, he's not here,' she went on, more naturally. 'What a relief.'

Greg was scrubbing the bars of the oven, giving Perdita the impression that he'd done nothing but clean it since she was last here. Janey was making potato balls with raw potatoes and a melon baller, a process that looked both tedious and painful to the palm of the hand.

'So where's your lord and master?' asked Perdita.

'He's having a conference with Mr Grantly,' said Janey, throwing down her baller in a gesture of rebellion. 'Let's have a cup of tea!'

'Oh, let's. I'll get the stuff.' She went to the door and put her boots back on. Such a relief not to have to take them off when she returned.

'Is it hell? Is he a bastard?' Perdita, having unloaded six crates of salad and put them in the cold store, helped herself to a biscuit, and heaved herself onto the counter.

'Don't sit there!' Janey screamed. 'He'll go mad! I've just sterilised it. He says he doesn't know how we weren't closed down when Enzo was in charge.'

'Oh, sod him,' Perdita said, rebelliously staying put.

'I suppose things had got a bit slack,' Janey went on, reluctantly picking up her melon baller.

'You haven't said much,' Perdita said, turning to Greg. 'How do you like working with him?'

'I don't,' he growled. 'I think I'll go back to college and get some qualifications. Anything's better than being bossed around by that bastard.'

'You could get another job. So could you, Janey.'

Janey sighed. 'It's very good experience, working with someone with such a good reputation. It'll look very good on my c.v.'

'And how come he's got such a good reputation? He's not famous, is he?' Perdita, aware that she led a rather narrow existence, wanted to make sure there was nothing about her ex-husband she ought to know.

'Well, you know about the television thing . . .'

She shook her head. 'Actually, I haven't heard a word since they all trooped out of my kitchen. I sort of hoped the idea was off.'

'Not according to Mr Grantly. CMG doesn't talk about it,' said Greg.

'CMG?' asked Perdita.

'Call Me God,' Greg explained. 'It's how he likes to be addressed.'

'Not really?'

'Well no, we leave out the Call Me part.'

'Oh dear. So working with him isn't much fun, then?'

Janey sighed. 'I'm just glad I'm not making a TV programme with him.'

'Oh, that's so unfair!' said Perdita, recognising the disappointment in Janey's tones. 'Who are they getting?'

'Well, you, of course,' said Janey. 'I thought you knew.'

'Oh no! I thought that was just that man's whim, not a serious suggestion. I won't do it.'

'But you must!' said Janey. 'It's such a wonderful opportunity. And they're dead set on your cottage.'

'For God's sake! You know my kitchen, Janey. Would you set a cookery programme in it?'

'I don't know anything about television,' said Janey unhelpfully. 'If they think it's suitable, it probably is.'

'Nonsense. I think they should find another chef and another set and

182

leave us to get on with our work.' Perdita drained her tea. 'And if Lucas is a swine, you should tell Mr Grantly. He's probably got no idea.'

'Sure,' said Greg. 'Mr Grantly thinks the sun shines out of Lucas's—'

'Out of my what?' demanded the man in question, appearing like a dark cloud on a sunny day, in the corner of the kitchen.

Perdita jumped off the work surface, jarring her feet in her hurry. 'You don't want to know, Lucas,' she said. 'I've brought your veg.'

'Well, I didn't think you'd come here solely to distract my staff from their work.'

'Hadn't you better go and check it?' said Perdita, who would have been furious if he had suggested that such a thing was necessary.

Lucas snarled, and disappeared into the cold store.

Taking advantage of his absence, Perdita hissed at Janey: 'He's a bastard. Don't work for him.'

Janey, aware that she'd got behind with her tasks, frantically dug into a potato. 'I know I shouldn't, but he's so gorgeous! Knowing he's going to be here, however horrible he's going to be, makes me look forward to coming into work in the morning.'

It was no good trying to argue Janey out of her lunacy. What Janey needed was another man to have a crush on. And at that moment, the very chap occurred to her. William, who worked for her.

'Janey, you don't work on Sundays, do you? Come to Sunday lunch.'

'But Perdita!' Janey was surprised. 'You don't cook!'

'No,' said Perdita with dignity. 'But I heat up very well.' Lucas reappeared. 'Was everything in order with the veg?'

'No. You left the cold store in complete chaos.'

She smiled. 'There are rather a lot of crates to take back. I wonder if Janey could give me a hand? I see Greg's busy.'

'And as Janey obviously isn't, she's no loss if she helps you. Don't be long, Janey; you're not paid to shift boxes for the greengrocer.'

'Specialist greengrocer, if you don't mind,' Perdita corrected haughtily, as she went into the cold store to collect the first load of crates.

She went back for a second load. 'I can manage these, Janey. Now don't forget, Sunday. Come about one.'

'Cooking Sunday lunch can't be that difficult,' she said to Kitty later as she helped her stack flowerpots. Kitty sucked on her pipe doubtfully.

'Hell in a bucket, my love. You have to get everything cooked at the same time and the oven's never hot enough for the potatoes.'

Perdita thought about her oven for a second. 'Oh God. Do you have to have roast potatoes? Baked ones wouldn't do?'

'Men like roast potatoes,' said Kitty. 'But anyway, who are you going to ask to be your man?'

'No one. I don't need a man.'

'Darling, won't it be a bit obvious? If you invite Janey and William and no one else?'

'The only unattached man I know of within fifty miles is Lucas, and it's him I'm trying to lure Janey away from.' Perdita thought for a moment. 'You come, Kitty. You can help me.' Perdita watched her friend searching for a reason to refuse. 'Come on, it'll be fun.'

William was as reluctant a guest as Kitty.

'You're not doing anything much this Sunday, are you, William?'

'Why? Do you want me to do some overtime?'

'No, I want to invite you to lunch.' William seemed genuinely confused. His boss did take him to the pub occasionally but she had never asked him for anything that could be described as a meal.

Perdita decided that she had better come clean. 'There's this girl I want you to meet.' William didn't respond. 'The trouble is,' Perdita went on rather desperately, 'she has a tendency to fall in love with bastards. I want her to see that there are lots of other men out there who are perfectly nice and just as attractive.'

She saw the beginnings of a blush steal from William's beard to his hair and she hoped he wasn't taking her remarks too personally. It would be dreadful if William decided that she, Perdita, had developed a crush on him. I must find myself a man, thought Perdita, seriously.

'So you'll come?' she persevered.

William nodded somewhat anxiously.

Chapter Two

PERDITA HAD ACCEPTED that roast potatoes were essential, and had borrowed a Delia Smith from Kitty to tell her how to do them. As she handed Perdita the book, Kitty had said, 'If all else fails, stick them under the grill.' It was sound advice, which Perdita would have willingly taken had her grill worked.

Tidying the kitchen had been the worst part, it was so full of horticultural paraphernalia. Eventually, Perdita filled a corner with as many non-cookery items as it would take and flung a faded Indian bedspread over them. Thank goodness it was only Janey, William and Kitty, who all knew her well, and had better reasons for loving her than her culinary skills. Kitty was bringing sherry and wine, as she didn't share Perdita's opinion that, for wine, good value meant cheap.

The lamb smelt delicious. Perdita had studded it with sprigs of rosemary and a clove of elephant garlic, which, sliced up, was enough to ensure that the lamb both looked like the picture in her recipe book and would taste distinctly Mediterranean.

She swept the sitting-room floor, and took a stiff broom to the worn and faded rugs that covered it. Perdita didn't own a vacuum cleaner, convinced that, not having fitted carpets, she didn't need one. Having dusted the mantelpiece with her sleeve she dashed out into the garden and picked a huge bunch of late asters and chrysanthemums. They looked wonderfully opulent in her copper jug, which, she told herself, was better tarnished, more subtle.

It took her a while to work out how to seat four people round her little gate-leg table without anyone sitting with the leg inelegantly between their knees. Eventually she managed it, providing that William wouldn't mind having his knee pressed up against the leg.

In a washing-up bowl, usually used to sprout pea seeds, was a hotch-potch of all she had in the garden and in her poly-tunnels—broccoli, cauliflower, spinach, beet tops, Swiss chard and some Good King Henry, in fact everything she could find that looked like green veg.

For pudding, Perdita had made Kitty's version of trifle, which took a maximum of ten minutes to prepare and tasted delicious, even if it was very liquid and alcoholic.

Perdita was collapsed in front of the wood-burning stove, which was blazing well, when Kitty arrived. She had walked over with a basket containing the promised sherry and wine, but also some ground coffee and a box of chocolates.

Perdita kissed the wrinkled cheek offered her, and then hugged Kitty hard. She took the basket. 'You shouldn't have carried all those heavy things. You should have let me collect you in the van.'

'My dear child,' replied Kitty, allowing Perdita to relieve her of her coat, 'when I can't walk a few hundred yards with a couple of bottles of wine and a box of chocolates, I hope you'll have me humanely put to sleep. Now, have I time for a quick pipe before the others come? Then I'll see what a muddle you've got into in the kitchen.'

Kitty smoked her pipe looking at Perdita's flower garden, taking the opportunity to do a bit of dead heading while she was about it, and then went into the kitchen.

'What time are they coming?' she asked, after surveying the scene.

'In about ten minutes,' said Perdita, having shot an anguished glance at her watch.

'Have you got those *big* sherry glasses I gave you?'

Perdita, correctly interpreting this as indication that her kitchen and its contents were past praying for, dutifully retrieved the glasses from the back of a cupboard and gave them a cursory dust with a tea towel.

Before Kitty had taken more than a sip of sherry, the door knocker rattled loudly. Perdita answered it.

On the doorstep was a distraught Janey with Lucas on her heels.

Lucas saved Janey the trouble of explaining. 'I invited myself. It wasn't Janey's fault.'

'I could have worked that out.' Perdita stood in the doorway, not letting either Lucas or Janey across the threshold.

'I wanted to see how your kitchen functioned when it wasn't full of garden rubbish.' Lucas pushed forward slightly.

'You're welcome to another time,' said Perdita, untruthfully. 'But this is a private lunch party. I'm terribly sorry, but you can't come.'

'Don't be ridiculous! If you're cooking a joint you can stretch it. I'll carve if you can't.' Lucas took a couple of steps forward. Janey's anxious expression made Perdita sigh and step aside to let them both through.

'I suppose I'll have to let you in,' she said grudgingly, adding to Janey, 'How *could* you?'

'Mrs . . . Anson. . . .' said Lucas. 'We haven't met for some years.'

Kitty, who had seated herself in the one armchair, regarded him through narrowed eyes. 'No. Well, I don't suppose it'll be a pleasure seeing you again, but I dare say it'll be interesting.'

Perdita was aware of a shudder from Janey and decided, for her sake, to keep lunch as explosion-free as possible. 'Well, do sit down everyone, and I'll get us a glass of sherry.' After they had all taken their first sip and were looking to her for the next step, she said, 'I'm just going to have a peep at what's going on in the kitchen and then I'll see if I can fit another place round the table.'

'I don't mind eating separately,' said Lucas, who, she noted, had put on an extremely smart suit for the occasion. She hoped William wouldn't feel out of place when he turned up in corduroys, flannel shirt and sweater.

Perdita went into the kitchen, more for a moment to herself than because she thought she could do anything about the chaos that met her there. Fury with Lucas for turning up uninvited tempted her to throw her carefully grown vegetables into a pot and boil them to destruction.

She peered into the oven and saw that the lamb was brown on top, and the garlic and rosemary at least smelt nice. The potatoes were the colour of church candles and showed no inclination to change. 'Sod it,' she said, slamming the oven door.

On her way back to join the others she bumped into Lucas. 'Can I help?' he asked.

'Only by leaving the country,' said Perdita, pushing him backwards out of the room. 'Or you could get the chair down from the bathroom.'

It was only after she had dispatched him thence that she remembered that her bathroom chair was loaded with unwashed clothes. Oh well, if he would invite himself to lunch, it was his lookout.

William arrived while Lucas was still upstairs. He looked clean but crumpled, and extremely dubious.

'William, how lovely. Let me give you a drink. You know my friend Mrs Anson.' Kitty nodded benignly. 'And Janey. She works at Grantly House. I don't think you've met.'

William glanced at Janey from under his eyebrows.

Lucas and the chair announced their imminent arrival with banging and muted swearings as they came down the stairs. 'And this is Lucas, who also works at Grantly House.'

'Hello,' said Lucas. 'Where do you want this chair?'

It had taken Perdita long enough to fit four chairs round the table, she didn't intend to struggle with a fifth. 'If you wouldn't mind just fitting it in somewhere . . . And try to make it so that no one's sitting in front of a leg,' she said, knowing this was impossible, but feeling it a just punishment for him.

The room was silent apart from the shifting of chairs and more muted swearing from Lucas. Perdita perched on the arm of Kitty's chair, trying frantically to think of something to say. 'Nuts, anyone?' she said at last. 'I'm sure I've got some somewhere.'

Janey followed her into the kitchen. 'Knives and forks. We'll need some for Lucas. Oh God!' she went on, when they were out of earshot. 'I'm just so sorry! But he heard you invite me and I just found him outside my door when I set off to walk here. It was kind of him to give me a lift. And you must admit,' Janey went on, 'he does look lovely in a suit. I do like smartly dressed men.'

This didn't bode well for Perdita's matchmaking plans. William had many admirable qualities, but sartorial elegance was not among them. 'I could have arranged for William to pick you up.' Though he would have taken some persuading. 'You haven't met him before, have you?'

'Not to speak to, but I have seen him playing skittles down the pub. He's a bit older than me, you know.'

'But *decades* younger than Lucas!'

'So?'

'Oh, never mind.' Her matchmaking doomed to failure, Perdita took another look at her potatoes. 'Do you think they're a little bit brown?'

Janey shook her head. 'Well, I dare say they were whiter than that before, but no one could call them brown.'

'Oh bloody hell! What am I to do with the wretched things? I haven't got a grill to put them under.'

'You could put them in their tin on the hot plate and sort of fry them,' suggested Janey.

When tested, the lamb oozed pink fluid. 'What shall I do? It's probably completely raw. I'll poison us all.'

'It's OK,' said Janey. 'Lamb is supposed to be pink.'

'Everything all right in here?' Lucas's voice boomed from behind them, making both women jump.

'Fine!' snapped Perdita.

'Mrs Anson wants to know if you want her to cook the vegetables,' Lucas persisted, peering over Perdita's shoulder at the mess beyond.

'No. Tell her, thank you, but I'm managing just fine. Now everybody get out of my way and let me get on!'

After Janey and Lucas had gone back to the sitting room, Perdita put all the vegetables into her wok, stirring them violently with a wooden spoon. Then she took Janey's advice about the potatoes and stuck them in their tin on her hottest ring at its highest heat. While everything spat and cracked behind her, she drained the meat juices into a saucepan.

All three plates of her ancient electric cooker were going full bat, but Perdita concentrated on the gravy, flinging a handful of flour into the pan with the meat juices, adding salt and pepper, and the heeltap of a bottle of wine she had opened rather a long time ago. It thickened, and turned a purplish colour. She added the vegetable juices from the wok, which did nothing for the colour. She turned over the potatoes and was gratified to see faint singeing at the edges of some of them, but the gravy was still an unattractive pinky-beige colour. In desperation she found some soy sauce and tipped in a large quantity. She knew it would make the sauce dreadfully salty, but anything that meant she didn't have to serve gravy the colour of raw sausages was OK by her.

To her huge relief it worked. It even tasted all right. Perdita decided to quit while she was ahead and declare the meal ready. She stood in the doorway of the sitting room. The gathering didn't look like a hive of social intercourse. Lucas was reading a book, Kitty had produced her needlepoint, and Janey and William were exchanging stilted sentences, but not appreciative glances. Perdita sighed.

'Janey—give me a hand?' she asked.

Janey, glad to get away, came at once.

'It's the carving,' said Perdita. 'Do you think you could do it? The table's not big enough so we'll have to do it in here. Do you mind?'

'Perdita, I don't *mind* giving it a go, but why don't you ask Lucas?'

'No. I'll carve myself. It can't be that hard.' She picked up the knife and made a pass at the leg of lamb. The knife bounced off it and landed on the top of her thumb. 'Bugger!' she muttered.

'Why don't you let me?' asked Lucas, from the doorway.

'OK,' said Perdita, deciding that copping out was better than taking more bits off herself than off the joint.

While she and Janey brought through plates, gravy, serving spoons and the vegetables, Perdita spotted Lucas sharpening the knife on the back doorstep. Then, while she was finding space for everything on the table, he turned the leg of lamb into a row of tidy pink slices, which he laid out on the somewhat stained and chipped serving plate she had dusted down for it. He brought it in and stood holding it.

'Wow,' she said, forgetting for a moment who she was talking to. 'That looks really nice.'

'Goodness knows what it tastes like,' said Lucas.

'Now, where is everyone going to sit?' asked Perdita rhetorically. 'Kitty, you sit there, with William on one side. Now Janey, sit next to William, and Lucas next to Janey. I'll sit next to Kitty.'

When at last everyone was served, Perdita and Lucas squashed into their places. 'Do please start, everyone,' said Perdita, too tired to care if she could reach her plate or not.

'Well, here's to our hostess,' said Lucas blandly, his sarcasm as silent as it was obvious. Perdita took a huge gulp of wine and was pleased to note that Kitty's dear departed husband had not let them down; the wine Kitty had found in his cellar was delicious.

And so, by some miracle, was the food. 'Darling! This is *delicious*,' said Kitty. 'I didn't think I liked lamb rare, but this is really tender.'

'No thanks to me. That was the organic butcher,' said Perdita.

'Well, the veggies are down to you,' said Janey. 'And cooked just right.' She blushed and glanced at Lucas.

'The vegetables are fine,' agreed Lucas. 'No marks for presentation, but they taste fresh.'

'So, what about the gravy?' Perdita demanded provocatively.

Lucas regarded her. 'Let's not spoil a pleasant occasion by discussing it.'

'I think it's jolly good,' said William. 'Is there any more?'

'And what is this?' asked Lucas, as Perdita handed him a glass dish.

'It's trifle,' said Perdita.

'I was afraid it might be,' said Lucas.

'Now, now, young man. Don't criticise until you've tried it,' said Kitty. 'That's a family recipe, handed down the generations.'

'I thought you and Perdita weren't actually related?'

'Oh, shut up and eat it,' muttered Perdita, rather to Janey's surprise.

'Oh,' he said, after a spoonful. 'No jelly. I'm almost disappointed.'

'It's delish,' said Janey. 'Can I have the recipe?'

'If you promise not to give it to Lucas,' Perdita replied. 'I don't want it turning up on the Grantly House menu as one of his creations.'

Eventually the meal drew to a close. Coffee and various sorts of tea were made and drunk, and Kitty's chocolates were handed round, and Perdita was just racking her brains for some neutral topic of conversation when Kitty got slowly to her feet.

'Well, I think I should be going . . .'

'I'll give you a lift back,' said Perdita, jumping up.

'Nonsense. No need to break up the party. It's only a step.'

'I'll drive Mrs Anson back,' said Lucas firmly. 'Then you don't have to leave your guests, Perdita.'

'Very well,' said Kitty. 'If you will be so kind, I would be glad to accept your generous offer. No need to see me out, Perdita dear. Lucas will look after me.'

While reluctant to see Kitty driven away by the Demon King, Perdita didn't feel she could object, so she just kissed her friend goodbye and thanked her again for the wine and sherry.

'Right,' said Janey. 'Let's do the washing-up.'

William got to his feet, obviously dying to go home and watch some sport, and added, 'Yes.'

'Certainly not! I wouldn't dream of allowing you to wash a thing. But it you're going, William, perhaps you wouldn't mind giving Janey a lift? She came with Lucas and although I could run her back . . .'

'Of course I can give Janey a lift.'

Janey didn't look terribly enthusiastic. 'Well, if you really won't let us wash up, let us just take some of these things out.'

When they were alone in the kitchen, Perdita said, 'He's nice, isn't he?'

'Oh yes,' said Janey immediately. 'He's lovely. I really like him.'

'He's much nicer than Lucas, isn't he?'

'*Nicer*, yes, but nothing *like* as sexy.'

Perdita saw them both into William's car, knowing her matchmaking had not come off. She felt tempted to do what she knew Kitty was now doing, curling up in a chair with her eyes shut, but the washing-up would be even less appealing if she waited until dark to do it.

The kitchen looked like it had been turned over by a particularly untidy gang of burglars, only instead of taking things they had brought dirty dishes with them. There was more crockery than Perdita knew she owned, and every glass, plate, cup, jug or dish had been used.

She attached a length of hose pipe to her hot tap. This she led into a black plastic bucket on the floor and added a squirt of washing-up liquid. While she filled a second bucket, she loaded the first with dirty plates. When she heard a loud bang on the front door she muttered an expletive and turned off the tap.

Her annoyance was rapidly replaced by anxiety when she saw it was Lucas. 'Oh my God! Is Kitty all right?'

'Yes, of course! She's indestructible. She got me to clean out the gutter before I left. No, I came back to help with the washing-up,' he said.

'Well, you can't.' Relief gave Perdita confidence. 'It's kind of you to offer, but I'm better off doing it on my own.' She took hold of her door. 'Now if you wouldn't mind—my water's getting cold.'

This would have disposed of the most dogged doorstep salesman, but Lucas pushed his way into the house with a combination of force and determination. 'I need to talk to you about the kitchen,' he said.

Perdita, having failed to keep him out of the house, was determined to keep him out of that devil's brew of grease and dirty crockery. 'You can't!' she repeated, barring his way. 'At least, not in it, and not now. Say what you want to say out here, and be very quick.'

'You're forgetting that I carved the lamb. I know exactly what state the kitchen is in.' Perdita found herself swept aside and watched helplessly as he opened the kitchen door. 'What on earth are you doing?' he demanded, seeing the buckets.

'The washing-up,' snapped Perdita. 'What's it look like?'

'Good God! You're not camping. Why don't you use a bowl, like everybody else?'

'Because I hate washing-up bowls! A bucket is far more efficient. I have one bucket for washing and another for rinsing.'

Lucas shook his head. 'You're mad. Why can't you do anything the same way as anyone else?'

191

'Why can't you tell when you're not wanted? I'm quite happy with my washing-up. It's nothing to do with you how I choose to do it. I didn't ask you to come back and help me!'

Lucas looked about him. 'No, I know. But you must admit it'll take you hours on your own. And why don't you put the light on?'

'The light *is* on,' sighed Perdita. 'Can't you see it?'

Lucas saw the single, naked bulb dangling from the ceiling. 'For Christ's sake! No wonder you don't like cooking, if you try to do it in this black hole!'

'I don't try to do it in this black hole! I don't try to do it, full stop! Today was a one-off, never-to-be-repeated experience.'

'I can see why.'

'Well, I'm glad you can see something, because after the sun goes down, I can't! So would you mind buggering off so I can do the washing up by feel.'

'Why don't you get some lighting in there?' called Lucas from the sitting room. He came back with a table lamp. 'Where can I plug this in?'

Perdita sighed. 'Unplug the microwave.'

Lucas swept up the large quantity of post, junk mail and important letters that sat on top of the microwave and put it in a pile on a chair.

'Don't put it there! It'll get lost!'

'It's only junk mail anyway,' said Lucas disdainfully.

Perdita shrugged. 'I like junk mail. It gives me something to read over breakfast, and I don't have to do anything about it.'

Lucas tutted explosively. 'For God's sake, woman, get a grip!'

Perdita took a breath in order to tell him, in no uncertain terms, exactly how hard a grip she had on life, and no thanks to him, when she observed that he was getting stuck into the washing-up with a speed and efficiency her kitchen had not previously witnessed. 'You're slopping water on the floor. Let me do it.' She elbowed him out of the way and sank to her knees. 'Put the kettle on, if you want to be useful. This water's gone cold.'

With a growl of irritation, Lucas filled the kettle and switched it on. 'I need to talk to you about the cooker. It won't do for the programme, you know. The kitchen is fine, but the cooker is a disaster.'

'Well, I'm sorry, but it's the only one I've got, and even if I could afford to I wouldn't dream of replacing it just to please you and your television company.' She sank the last plate into the bucket of rinsing water.

'No. *I* want to replace it.'

'What do you mean?' She retrieved the plate, and got up.

'I mean, I will buy you a new cooker, so I don't have to use that one.'

'Don't be silly. You may be a prima-donna chef these days, but surely even you can't be so prissy you can't use an ordinary electric cooker.'

'That cooker is not ordinary! It should be in a museum.' He stepped round her in order to inspect it. 'It's only got three burners, the grill doesn't seem to work, it wobbles, and I doubt you can get the oven very hot.'

'It was hot enough to cook the lamb!' she said.

'But not hot enough to roast the potatoes.'

Perdita toyed with the idea of pretending they weren't meant to be roast potatoes but rejected it. 'It's all cheating, anyway, isn't it? I'm sure they just paint things with varnish to make them look brown. Perhaps you're too scrupulous to be a television cook, Lucas.'

He heard the laughter in her voice and strode towards her, bringing his hands down on her shoulders. 'I suppose you think this is funny!'

'Well, of course I do! It's hilarious! You coming into my house, *my* *kitchen*, to do a cookery programme. You must see the funny side! Or have you completely lost your sense of humour?'

Having Lucas's hands on her shoulders was unsettling. He always had had the ability to arouse her with the most innocent of touches. It seemed that he still had.

His mouth twitched, first in one corner, and then it curled into a grin made more attractive by the fact that he tried to suppress it. 'I suppose it is a little bizarre, and not something I would have imagined happening six months ago.' His hands slipped off her shoulders. 'It must have been a shock for you, seeing me again after all these years.'

'Well, yes. But it must have been just as much of a shock for you.'

'Not really. I knew Kitty lived in the area, after all. And I saw your name under Bonyhayes Salads.'

'Of course. But if I hadn't delivered salads to you, you wouldn't have looked me up.'

'Why not? I know we parted on bad terms, but I would have hoped we could have got over that.'

She turned away from him and put her hands into the sink, trying to make it look as if she was doing something. 'Bad terms doesn't really cover it, Lucas. You abandoned me for another woman, in the most hurtful circumstances possible.'

'I know, and I'm not proud of it. But you've got over it, haven't you? You seem fine.'

She turned back to him. 'Yes, of course I'm fine. But it's no thanks to you, and you really couldn't expect to swan back into my life and for me to forgive and forget.'

'I didn't say anything about coming back into your life, Perdita. Just that I would have looked you up and hoped we could have been civil to each other.'

'Then it's a shame that's obviously quite impossible, particularly as you've got yourself involved in a television fiasco that seems to need my cooperation!'

'I can do without your cooperation! I can easily find another picturesque cottage. But can you do without the money? They'll pay you for using your kitchen and pay for all the vegetables they use.'

'I run a flourishing business. I don't need my life messed around by a television crew.'

'If your business is so flourishing, why don't you drive a decent van?'

'If I really needed a new van I could use the money you gave me.' She hadn't meant to mention this money. It was a symbol of a time of failure and misery in her life, and she had tried to blot it out.

Lucas frowned. 'Then why don't you?'

'Because I would rather deliver my vegetables in a wheelbarrow or in a sack on my back than use a penny of the money you sent me to make yourself feel better about ditching me!'

'I sent it because I thought you might need it! I could ill afford to do without it at the time! I should have known that you would have fled back to dear Auntie Kitty and she would have picked up the pieces and put your life back together for you!'

This statement—though pretty much the truth—sent Perdita's anger to heights it previously hadn't known. She stormed out of the kitchen in search of her handbag. By the time she stormed back into the kitchen with a cheque, the saucepans were draining in the sink.

'Here's your money! I hope it comes in useful!' She thrust the cheque at him, knowing she would have to do some very rapid financial fiddling to get the money into her current account before her bank manager summoned her for an explanation.

Lucas handed it back. 'I don't want it. It's yours. Why don't you do something useful with it?'

She refused to touch it. 'I've told you why!'

'Then give it to charity!' He stuffed it into the neck of her jumper.

She snatched it out and thrust it deep into his breast pocket. 'You give it to charity! I'm sure there must be a benevolent fund for trainee chefs suffering from nervous breakdowns caused by tyrants like you!'

'I think I should tell you that, in chef terms, I am a pussycat. I don't hit my staff with ladles, or throw boiling water over them. And if I shout a bit, or let slip the occasional four-letter word, they're all adults, they don't have to stay.'

'Enzo never shouted and he was a brilliant chef.' This wasn't entirely true. Enzo *could* cook like an angel, but more often didn't.

'He was the most hopeless idiot ever let loose in a kitchen!'

'How would you know? You didn't see him cook.'

'Yes I did, and I ate his food. When I came to look the place over. I've never seen anything so unprofessional in my life.'

'Well, anyway, at least he was happily married!' she shot at him, wishing she hadn't a moment later. She didn't know that he hadn't married again. 'Though, perhaps you are too,' she added more quietly.

'No, I'm still divorced.'

'So the woman you left me for left you, did she?'

'No, I left her, actually.'

'Oh.' Perdita suddenly needed to get away from the kitchen, with its sodden floor, crowded surfaces and memories of the stress of cooking.

He followed her into the sitting room and sat down in the armchair, while Perdita knelt before the wood-burning stove, and delicately coaxed back some flames.

'So, is there a man in your life?'

Perdita had a log in her hand. 'That is absolutely none of your business!'

'You asked me if I was married!'

'No I didn't! You volunteered the information!'

'You volunteer it too, then.'

Perdita sighed sharply and got to her feet before collapsing into the Windsor chair opposite his. 'Like you, I'm still divorced.'

'And not engaged, I see.' She looked quizzically at him. 'No ring,' he added. 'Knocking thirty and no man on the scene. Dear, dear. Lovely girl like you. What is wrong with young men these days?'

She narrowed her furious gaze. 'I do have a boyfriend, if you must know. But he lives quite a long way away, and I don't see him often.' That should shut him up.

'Oh, I am glad.' Clearly, he didn't believe a word of it. 'Then could I invite you both to dinner with me at Grantly House?'

'Does that mean you'd be eating with us?'

'I'd be in the kitchen. I'd come and talk to you, of course, since you would be my guests, but I wouldn't spoil your romantic evening.'

'Of course, I can't make arrangements without consulting . . . him.' If she made up a name, it might lead to all sorts of complications.

'Of course not. But in principle you'd like to come?'

'Oh, yes. We'd love it.' Like a snowflake enjoys a visit to hell.

'Good.' He got to his feet. 'Well then, since you're not going to offer me tea—'

'No, I'm not.'

'I'd better get back. Thank you for lunch. It was very interesting.'

'Thank you so much for coming. It wouldn't have been nearly so much fun without you,' she said, opening the front door.

'No need to be sarcastic, Perdita. I did help with the washing-up.'

'That was the worst part.'

'Let me change your mind about that.' Before she could think what he was doing, he took the cheque out of his pocket and thrust it down the front of her jumper. Before she could react, he got one arm round her shoulders and then kissed her, so hard and so long that she would have fallen over if he hadn't been holding her up.

'You bastard! How dare you?' she hurled at him, the moment she could speak.

He turned, from halfway down the path on the way to his car. 'The advantage of being the wicked ex-husband is that you don't have a reputation to lose. Goodbye, Perdita. See you soon.'

She was so outraged by the kiss and his subsequent remark that she only remembered the cheque when she heard a crackling sound as she turned to stomp indoors. By that time his car had roared off.

She stood, simmering quietly, then slumped into the armchair and stared at the flames, which flickered behind their glass doors.

'I'll get the bloody cheque to Lucas if it's the last thing I do,' she said aloud. 'Then I have to find a boyfriend. A big one. Who looks likely to punch him on the nose if he so much as thinks about touching me.' Her indignation was not, she knew, because of his rapine kiss, but because of her reaction to it. She hadn't felt revolted or violated, or indeed any of the proper, politically correct emotions felt by women when men forced themselves on them. In fact she had responded to the feeling of a strong man's arms around her.

'It's my hormones, letting me down,' she muttered. 'I have to find a boyfriend—not only to punch Lucas, but for *me*! I need a man to hug me. Because, however much you love them, you can't cuddle lettuces!'

It was a few days after the lunch party that Perdita came across Kitty, poring over catalogues. 'Hello, what's all this,' Perdita asked. 'I thought you hated shopping by mail order?'

'I do. It's environmentally unsound, but I've just realised that if I look through these I can do all my Christmas shopping without going out.'

'Don't you feel up to going out?'

'I feel up to going out,' Kitty explained, irritated by the concern in Perdita's voice, 'but not inclined to thrash my way through the crowds.'

As Perdita often felt like this herself, she stopped worrying and looked across at the selection of catalogues Kitty was going through. 'They're mostly plants. Do your friends want plants for presents?'

'Of course. Everyone loves plants.'

'Well, don't give me anything in a plug I can't make money out of.'

'So, what would you like?'

Perdita sighed. 'A man. Or, better than that, a table lamp. I've put one in the kitchen now, which does improve things a bit, but it means I haven't one in the sitting room.'

'That's easy. I'm sure there's a catalogue here with them in. You could choose your own.'

Perdita chuckled. 'What do you want for Christmas, then?'

'Oh, I don't know, but I do want to talk to you about it.'

'Talk then. But you will have to think of something. Otherwise I'll order you some surfinias or whatever they're called.'

'The Ledham-Golds have invited me for Christmas,' said Kitty. 'I wasn't going to say if I would go until I'd talked to you about it.'

Perdita felt a bit flat. She and Kitty usually spent Christmas together, and while neither of them felt it was their favourite time, exactly, it was at least familiar. 'Well, I think you should go. It would make a nice change.'

'I could ask them if they could have you as well, but they are all awfully elderly. It wouldn't be a lot of fun for you, but I don't want to leave you on your own.'

'I wouldn't mind, honestly. I think I'd quite like having it on my own if I couldn't have it with you, of course. You tell the Ledham-Golds you'll go. They probably need cheering up. Doesn't his sister live with them, or something?'

'That's right. She does the garden and Veronica does the house. Bernard does the crossword and watches *Countdown*. Now, are you sure you don't mind having Christmas on your own?'

The thought of being on her own at Christmas really didn't bother Perdita, but she knew it bothered Kitty. No amount of telling would persuade Kitty that a day spent pottering about at home, dipping in and out of the Christmas specials, was an attractive prospect to Perdita. She worked hard, and had very little time to mooch about and refresh her batteries. But she couldn't convince Kitty.

The problem was solved a few days later when Perdita got an early Christmas card from an old school friend, Lucy, who had married shortly after Perdita and subsequently disappeared off to the Caribbean. Unlike Perdita she had stayed married, even when an island in the Caribbean had turned into an island off the north coast of Scotland.

'I'm really organised this year as, you will see from the address, we are supposed to be moving to Shropshire next week,' it said, in gold pen. *'It should have been October, but house sales never go to plan. I know the house will be wonderful eventually, but at the moment it's crumbling and ancient and will cost megabucks to get habitable. I don't suppose you fancy spending Christmas with us? Seriously, it would be lovely to see you some time.'*

Lucy had always been what she liked to call spontaneous, which other people felt meant unpredictable, and her throwaway invitation could be a godsend. Perdita gave her a ring.

After a lot of shrieks, how-are-yous, and I-can't-believe-the-children-are-that-bigs, Perdita said, 'I don't suppose you meant it when you asked me to spend Christmas with you?'

'You're not saying that you want to come? Oh, Perdita! It would be marvellous. I mean, there'll be no hot water or carpets or curtains, or anything, but we'd love to have you!'

'And I'd love to come. It would be such fun to see you again.'

'Are you sure? Jake's brother is coming. His marriage has just broken up. Can you really cope? There's an Aga, but we're not sure if we'll be able to get it lit in time.'

Having assured Lucy that her new house would be considered luxury by some people who had seen hers, Perdita rang off, suddenly looking forward to the festive season.

Kitty, of course, was thrilled. 'Lovely for you to be with some young people for a change. Pity they live so far away. Moving to Shropshire, you said? Will the van get that far?'

'It will do if you pay to have it serviced as my Christmas present.'

'Of course, darling. I've ordered you a table lamp, but Father Christmas can give you that.'

The next fortnight was extremely hectic for Perdita. Both the health farm and Grantly House were particularly busy, and other restaurants that were not regular customers wanted things at Christmas. Aware she was likely to get a furious phone call from Lucas when he found it, she decided to bury the cheque she had so far failed to give him in her delivery box, among some handsome but not very appetising cardoons.

Then she rang Janey to find out when would be a good time to deliver—in other words, when Lucas wouldn't be there. Having been assured that he never appeared before ten o'clock, she got up even earlier than usual and ignored her chores, so she could arrive seconds after the kitchen opened. When Lucas leapt out from behind a door at ten past nine, she couldn't help screaming.

'Ah! What did you do that for? You gave me such a fright! Honestly!' Perdita hoped her indignation and surprise would conceal her anxiety about the hidden cheque. He hadn't ordered cardoons, either.

'What have you fobbed off on me this time? Not what I ordered, that's for sure. Oh my God! Cardoons!'

Knowing the cheque was right at the bottom of the bunch of spiky, acanthus-shaped leaves, she managed to look him straight in the eye. 'Oh?' she asked sweetly. '*Can't* you handle them, then?'

He leant against the cold store door and narrowed his eyes. 'Bitch.'

Perdita took this both as a compliment and as an acceptance of the culinary challenge, thrust the box into his arms and went to fetch the next lot. She was on her way out after the final delivery when Lucas stopped her.

'Don't run away. You usually have time to waste my staff's time, so you can stay for a minute. Can you get us both a coffee, Janey?'

'Say please,' muttered Perdita, on Janey's behalf.

'So, what are you doing for Christmas?' Lucas asked, having carried the two mugs into the office.

Reluctantly, Perdita had followed the coffee. 'Oh, I'm going to an old school friend's. In Shropshire.' This made her sound like a proper person, not a sad divorcee without a social life.

'And I expect you'll be seeing your boyfriend while you're there?'

Perdita had forgotten about her fictional boyfriend. 'Oh, yes.'

'What does he do? I can't remember if you said.'

Perdita couldn't either. 'He's a vet,' she said, remembering the catalogue that Kitty was still mulling over.

'Oh. Well, don't forget my invitation. Perhaps you'd like to bring him for New Year's Eve? We're doing a special dinner dance.'

'Sounds fun. I'll have to ask him, of course.'

She took a few sips of coffee. 'So, what did you want to see me about? Not just to check out my holiday arrangements, surely?'

'No. It's about this cooker. I really need to replace yours. I can probably even get a cooker firm to give me one, as an advertising stunt: "As used by Lucas Gillespie in the award-winning programme . . ." '

Perdita shook her head. 'If they did that they'd want you to use their biggest, fanciest model, not something small enough to fit into my kitchen. No, Lucas. You have to manage with the cooker I've got, or do the programme somewhere else.'

She stalked out of his office, hearing his low growl and feeling his furious gaze on her back. She tried hard not to appear to hurry.

'How are you, love?' asked Ronnie, when she staggered into the kitchen at Abbotsford Health Resort. 'Haven't seen you to talk to for ages. What's all this about a television programme with Count Dracula from Grantly House?'

'You wouldn't have a biscuit, would you? I'm starving.'

'I've got KitKats, but don't let anyone know, and you can only have one if you tell me everything.'

'I will, but there isn't much to tell, honestly. The television company that's filming Lucas—Count Dracula—decided, for some inexplicable reason that they want to do the series in my kitchen, with me.'

Ronnie's shriek was gratifyingly loud. 'But it's titchy!'

'Exactly. I expect they'll see sense before anything actually happens. But Lucas is in a froth because my cooker's not up to much. He wants to buy me a new one.'

'Well, let him!'

'I can't—for all sorts of reasons.' Perdita realised how nearly she had let slip that she and Lucas had once been married. 'I mean, one wouldn't want to be beholden to a man like that.'

'I'll take your word for it. But promise me one thing: if you are going to be on telly, let the girls sort you out first.'

'But, Ronnie! I'm a woman of the soil!'

'There's no need to look like one! You could be a real beauty if you weren't so . . .'

'Grubby?'

'No! Well, I'd have said unkempt, badly groomed.'

'Leave me alone, I'm all right as I am.' She gulped down a last mouthful of coffee. 'Now, I must go, I've got an appointment with Derek at the garage, and you know what a ray of sunshine he is.'

Derek, her grudging but long-standing garage man, had declared her van unfit to go to Shropshire without a major overhaul, which, of course, he couldn't possibly do before Christmas. 'You need a new van, love, that's the top and bottom of it. It's not worth spending money on, see?' He had kicked its rotting underparts and Perdita had seen.

She had faked gratitude as best she could and taken her unreliable, unrepairable but strangely dear vehicle back home, depressed. She would have to tell Lucy that she couldn't come for Christmas, and face up to the fact that she would have to find the money for a better van.

Lucy, who still hadn't moved, took the news badly. 'But, Perdita! You must come! I was depending on you!' Then she burst into tears.

Perdita, realising that there was a lot more behind this than one less pair of hands to do the sprouts, listened until the sobs had stopped long enough for her to speak. 'I really hate to let you down. But honestly, if the van's not going to make it, I really don't think I can come.'

Lucy sniffed loudly. 'No, of course not. Sorry to be so silly. Moving is such hell—*Christmas* is such hell—and to have them both together is too awful for words—I keep crying. My mother's coming . . .'

'That'll be a help then—' began Perdita.

'But I don't want her to have to do a thing. She always had Christmas at her house, but Daddy died last year, and I want to do all the things she always did, for her.'

'But Lucy, you're moving house! She won't expect you to do the Full Turkey! When do you move, by the way?'

'Oh, the day after tomorrow, and I'm still not properly packed.'

'I'm so sorry,' Perdita said.

'I've just had a brilliant idea!' Lucy sounded distinctly happier. 'Geoff can collect you! He's Jake's brother, the one whose marriage has just broken up. He lives in Cornwall. That's not far from you, is it?'

'Only about a couple of hundred miles away . . .'

'But it's on the way, isn't it? I'll ring and ask him if he can pick you up. I'm sure he'll be delighted.'

'You're not taking that rust-bucket to Shropshire, are you?' Lucas demanded, when Perdita delivered the last salads he was going to get before the New Year.

'No, I'm getting a lift.'

'With your boyfriend? That's nice. What kind of a car has he got?'

'I don't know,' said Perdita without thinking, and then added quickly, 'he's changed it recently.'

Janey, who was making roses out of butter with a potato peeler, gave Perdita a curious look.

'Perhaps you'd like to bring him here for lunch?'

'Oh no, he'll be in a frightful hurry. We won't have time for lunch.'

Lucas's steely gaze narrowed. 'I don't believe in this boyfriend of yours. I think you've just made him up.'

Perdita blushed. 'How ridiculous. Why would I do a thing like that?'

'To prove something to someone—me, perhaps.'

'I've never heard anything so silly in my life. And I'm not going to disrupt his plans just to show you he's real!'

Lucas shrugged. 'Fair enough, but don't forget, seeing is believing.'

Perdita, elated at having got herself out of trouble, smiled sweetly at him. 'What are you doing for Christmas, then?' she asked.

'I'm working, except on Christmas Day.'

'Oh.' Perdita's compassion warred with relief that she and Kitty were both going away, so she couldn't possibly feel guilty for not inviting him to spend Christmas Day with them. Or worse, with her on her own. 'But you'll have somewhere nice to go for the day, won't you?'

'Oh, no need to worry about me, Perdita. I expect I can conjure up a "girlfriend"'—he said the word in inverted commas—'from somewhere.'

'Oh, good. Happy Christmas then, Lucas. Janey, we must go for a drink together, or something. I'll see you before then, anyway.'

'Just a minute. I've got a card for you,' said Lucas. He handed her an impressively large envelope.

'Oh.' Perdita was horribly caught out. 'I'm afraid I only send them to people if they've sent me them, as they come in. And it's a bit late, now.'

'So I'm even cut off your Christmas card list? How sad,' he murmured softly, so Janey wouldn't hear.

When Perdita got home and opened the card, inside it, as well as a beautiful Madonna, were neatly shredded strips of cheque.

Janey, whom Perdita ran into in the post office, was bubbling with Christmas spirit and enthusiasm. 'When I found out that Lucas was going to be on his own for Christmas, I invited him round.'

'To have Christmas with your family? How kind.' How brave, how foolhardy, she thought. And how surprising that he accepted.

'We'll all have Christmas lunch together, of course, but in the evening we usually go round to my auntie's. I thought me and Lucas could stay behind. He's not going to want to have tea with my Auntie Susan, is he?'

'Possibly not. But what will you do with him?'

Janey blushed. 'I thought we could watch the film on telly.'

'Really, Janey, don't you think Lucas is a bit old for you?'

'No. He's gorgeous. And I'm sure he's just grumpy because he's lonely.'

Perdita sacrificed her place in the queue, so she could keep talking to Janey. 'You wouldn't do anything silly, would you?'

'It's up to me what I do, Perdita. And anyway, what's all this about a boyfriend? You didn't tell me about him! And spending Christmas together! It must be serious!'

Perdita took a deep breath. 'We really can't talk here,' she said. 'Let's meet for a drink, and I'll tell you all about it.'

'OK. White Horse, Thursday night, eight o'clock? We can both walk there, and I'm not working then.'

Perdita retreated to the back of the queue to speculate about whether she could trust Janey with the truth about her fictional boyfriend, or if there was a risk she might let something slip to Lucas.

As things turned out, Perdita was spared the decision. Geoff, her broken-hearted chauffeur, rang to ask if he could pick her up the night she had arranged to go for a drink with Janey. Perdita couldn't do anything but agree, and rang Janey to cancel.

'I wasn't expecting him before about midday on Friday,' she explained. 'But he managed to get away early.'

'But where does he come from?'

'Honey, I really can't tell you all about it now. I've got to finish my Christmas shopping, but I promise I'll give you a blow-by-blow, when I come back. Now you won't do anything stupid with Lucas, will you? I mean, I know he's terribly sexy and everything—'

'How do you know?' Janey interrupted. 'I thought you hated him!'

'I do, I do! But I can tell you find him sexy, and I just don't want you seduced by a bastard, that's all.'

'OK, Agony Aunt. I won't do anything foolish. Well, I mean, I would if I thought Lucas was up for it, but I don't think he fancies me. Now you'd better run along to the supermarket, which will be the only shop left open, and do your Christmas shopping.'

By about five o'clock on the day before Christmas Eve, Perdita had dispatched Kitty safely into the friendly hire car and driver who took her about if Perdita couldn't. Kitty, dressed in her best coat and skirt, made for her in the war by her husband's tailor, looked timeless and very fit.

'Goodbye, darling,' said Kitty, kissing Perdita. 'I do hope this Geoff turns out to be a dish.'

Perdita hugged as well as kissed the old lady. 'I don't suppose he will for a minute, but it'll be fun. And don't you run off with anyone without letting me check they don't just want you for your money.'

'Silly child. Now goodbye, and don't worry about me.'

'I won't,' said Perdita, knowing she would. Having waved the car out of sight, Perdita walked back to her own house to wait for her lift.

Geoff knocked on her door an hour and a half after he had arranged to. He was full of apologies, but Perdita felt certain he blamed her directions. He was tall and stooping and had floppy brown hair, which would have been attractive had it been washed more recently.

'I'm so sorry you had such a dreadful time getting here,' said Perdita, pulling on her ancient sheepskin coat. 'How long will it take to get to Shropshire, I wonder?'

'Another couple of hours, I expect.'

It was after ten. They wouldn't arrive at Lucy's until well past midnight.

'Does Lucy know we're going to be so late?' she asked, as they drove out of the village.

'No. You'd better ring her. My mobile's on the back seat. The number's in the memory.'

Mobile phones were a wonderful invention, thought Perdita, for those who knew how to use them.

Chapter Three

LUCY'S FACE SEEMED to be wearing every one of the seven years since Perdita had last seen her. Then, she had been tanned and relaxed from living in the Caribbean; now, she had dark circles under her eyes and looked far too thin.

'Perdita! It's so lovely to see you! You haven't changed a bit, damn you. I'm so glad you could come. And you, Geoff, of course. We only got in the house yesterday, and hardly anything's unpacked. Mummy's arriving tomorrow, and we must get at least her room in some sort of order. It's her first Christmas since Daddy died, and I want it to be *perfect* for her.' Lucy cleared her throat and swallowed hard.

Remembering how much she had cried on the phone, Perdita put a sympathetic hand on Lucy's arm. 'It must be quite upsetting for you, the first Christmas without your father.'

'Well, yes, it is. But that's not why I'm crying. It's just a hormonal thing. Don't take any notice. Have you met Jake?'

'Only at your wedding. It's very kind of you to invite me,' said Perdita to the large, amiable man before her.

Jake's hand enveloped hers. 'The favour is all on your side. If you can stop Lucy getting thoroughly overwrought you can stay until spring. Come and have a drink.'

'But it's nearly two o'clock in the morning,' said Perdita, suddenly desperate for alcohol. 'Don't you want to go to bed?'

'The children are in our bed,' said Jake, leading the way into a vast sitting room, which would be wonderful with curtains, paint and floor covering and more than the few bits of furniture that were dotted about.

'Their cots are still dismantled, and so we can't go to bed until we've put them up. Whisky punch? It's guaranteed to kill off any cold bugs that may be lurking.'

'It's terribly important we don't give Mummy a cold,' explained Lucy. 'It goes to her chest. I really don't want her getting bronchitis.'

'Of course not,' agreed Perdita, suddenly wondering how Kitty was.

'The trouble is she will overdo things so. She lets the children exhaust her. She's a bit of a perfectionist.'

'It runs in the family,' said Jake, casting his wife a significant, reproachful glance.

'I'm not a perfectionist usually,' Lucy protested. 'It's just I want this Christmas to be right.'

'But you were up until after one making the pies.' Jake yawned. 'I hope you two don't mind sharing a bedroom,' he went on. 'There are only three habitable rooms upstairs, the roof leaks in all the others. Ma-in-law's got the master bedroom with the dodgy en suite. Us and the children are crammed into the nursery, so that only leaves one room for you.'

'It's very big, though,' added Lucy. 'And it's got two beds. You don't mind sleeping-bags, do you?'

Perdita felt that if she drank any more whisky punch she'd fall asleep where she sat. 'Er, not at all,' she said.

'I hope I don't disturb any of you in the night,' said Lucy apologetically. 'I have to get up to go to the loo rather a lot at the moment. I'm pregnant. Don't tell Mummy. That's why I'm so tearful. I'm perfectly all right if people don't draw attention to it.'

Perdita thought that unless Lucy's mother was both blind and deaf she couldn't fail to notice, but didn't like to mention it.

'I don't suppose Perdita really wants to share a room with me,' said Geoff, getting up. 'Perhaps I'd better sleep down here.'

Lucy frowned. 'OK, but you'll have to promise to get rid of all your bedding before Mummy's up, when she gets here. It's so studenty, having people sleeping on the sofa.'

'I really don't mind sharing, Geoff, but if you'd feel happier sleeping down here . . .' Briefly, Perdita wondered how she'd have felt if she'd had to share a bedroom with Lucas. She drained her drink. 'Well, let's go and get these cots organised. Lucy looks done in.'

Christmas Eve, with its own share of rituals, found Perdita in the kitchen, offering to cook a meal.

'Not that I'm much of a cook,' she said to Jake.

'Doesn't matter! I've got to go and assemble a bloody doll's house!

'Why Lucy insists on giving them a doll's house, when there's no time to build it except when they're asleep, which hardly ever happens . . .'

'It's so they've got their own house to move into,' said Lucy, coming into the kitchen. 'Oh, Jake! I thought you agreed with me on this!'

'I'm going to cook supper,' said Perdita, quickly, before Lucy could burst into tears. 'I've explained to Jake. I'm not much of a cook, but I've had a lot of experience with less than perfect kitchens.' Unlike the others, she was unfazed by the camping-gas stove, which was all there was until the solid-fuel stove was persuaded to light. And the lack of any gadgets, except a rather unhygienic wooden spoon and a rusty knife, didn't faze her either. 'It's pretty much a home from home for me,' she explained.

Her long-neglected artistic skills were also called upon. The house was huge, filthy and empty, but it had beautiful proportions, and a garden full of wonderful evergreens. Asked to 'do something about the sitting room, please!' by a tearful Lucy, she let herself go.

Having sent Geoff to the nearest town to raid it for fairy lights, Perdita ripped ivy off the outside walls of the house, and sellotaped it above the picture rail. She found a twisted willow in the garden, and made a designer Christmas tree out of it, decorated with the lights Geoff had brought back.

'It looks *stupendous*,' said Lucy, in tears again. 'You've both been brill. Don't take any notice of me. I'm always like this when I'm pregnant.'

'Then how are you going to keep it from your mother?' Perdita felt that for everyone's sake it would be better if things were out in the open.

'Oh, I don't know, just keep a stiff upper lip, I suppose.'

'But why don't you want her to know?'

'Oh, I don't know. It just seems so selfish of us, having sex when she's in mourning and can never have sex again. Can you imagine that, never having sex again?'

Until recently, Perdita could have faced the prospect with equanimity, but lately she had found herself wondering a bit about it.

'But your mother would be horrified if she felt you weren't having a proper marriage because your father died.'

Lucy sighed. 'I suppose that's true. But I really would rather not tell her about it just yet. She does worry about me when I'm pregnant.'

Perdita felt that Lucy's mother's fears were probably justified. Moving house, Christmas and pregnancy seemed a combination likely to bring on something dreadful—miscarriage, a nervous breakdown, at the very least.

'So what about your love life, Perdita? No one since Lucas? Not that I was surprised you split up.'

'Oh?'

'Well, I mean, it was just too hot and passionate to survive, wasn't it?'

'I did at least remain faithful for those few short months, but I had no idea how to handle him.' She wasn't exactly a dab hand at it now.

'I don't suppose you ever hear from Lucas?'

'Funnily enough, I do, sort of. He's become a chef at the local hotel and moved into our village. I sell him salads.'

'A chef? I thought he was something in the City?'

'He was. But he gave it up and became a chef.'

'How bizarre! What on earth made him change direction like that?'

'I have no idea.'

'But is it awkward? Dealing with him?'

'Well . . .'

'Oh, go on, do tell,' pleaded Lucy, looking more cheerful than Perdita had yet seen her. 'I haven't had a good gossip for yonks.'

'He keeps asking me if I've got another man in my life and, of course, I haven't. So I pretended I was spending Christmas with my boyfriend.'

'You didn't want him to know you weren't attached?'

'No! He left me for an *older* woman. A girl has her pride.'

'But is he still with this woman?'

'No, but it's only a matter of time before he breaks some other poor schmuck's heart.'

Lucy's mother was a small, kindly, undemanding woman. Her little car was filled with baskets and boxes and suitcases. After the prolonged greetings, a relay of people unloaded it for her.

'I've brought ready-prepared sprouts,' Mrs Heptonstall confided to Perdita. 'Lucy's a dear, sweet girl, and so good to me, but she does tend to fuss, especially at Christmas.'

'I know she wants this Christmas to go well, for your sake,' said Perdita, from behind a huge cardboard box, en route to the kitchen.

'Oh, dear! I knew this would happen. She's only just moved house and she's going to get upset if we can't find the cranberry sauce.'

'Oh no,' said Perdita. 'That'll be all right. She's made some from a special recipe. I know where it is.'

Mrs Heptonstall tutted. 'Honestly! And between you, me and the gatepost, I think she's pregnant. But don't say a word because I don't think she's realised it herself yet.'

Christmas Day passed far more calmly than Perdita would have predicted, thanks to Mrs Heptonstall convincing Lucy that the world wouldn't end if not every detail was as it was in the magazines.

Everyone went for a long walk after the stockings had been opened and a boozy breakfast had been consumed. The turkey was timed to be cooked at three o'clock, so no one needed to rush, and after a light buffet lunch they opened presents.

Perdita immediately draped herself in the huge, creamy white shawl her mother had sent her, and earmarked the cheque from her father to go towards a better van. Thus her pile was quickly dispensed with, as she hadn't brought Kitty's table lamp with her.

Her presents to other people were surprisingly successful. The green nail varnish was extremely popular with its six-year-old recipient, although less so with her parents. The four-year-old was thrilled with the plastic bubble filled with miniature chocolate footballs. Lucy genuinely liked the selection of herb vinegars, which Perdita had made herself, and the lavender bags, which she hadn't, and Jake looked at the wine, which had come from Kitty's husband's cellar, with quiet reverence. Geoff had a similar bottle and they exchanged glances that said, 'How did that rather scatty woman come up with such bloody good wine?' Perdita smiled, and said nothing.

'Do feel free to ring Kitty,' said Lucy, yawning. 'You must be worrying about her.'

Perdita, who hadn't been, suddenly did. 'That would be nice. Just to say Happy Christmas.'

'We're not actually on the phone yet. Jake, give Perdita your mobile.'

'I'll do it,' said Geoff resignedly. He reached behind him and produced his phone. 'If you've got the number, I'll punch it in for you. It'll take for ever, otherwise.'

Perdita felt herself go pink. 'I am sorry about erasing all those numbers. I'll just run up and find Kitty's.'

Kitty was, as expected, perfectly fine, although annoyed to be rung up when she had a very good hand of bridge. 'Now my partner will take advantage of my absence and play it for me.'

Having no knowledge of bridge, Perdita could make no comment. They chatted on about meals and presents and eventually rang off.

'She's fine' said Perdita. 'Now, should we be doing anything in the kitchen?'

She went in to see and found Lucy's mother searing the roast potatoes with a blowtorch.

On Boxing Day evening, Perdita had fallen asleep on the sofa in front of the fire when Lucy whispered sharply in her ear, 'Perdita? Wake up. Someone's at the door for you. I think it's Lucas.'

Perdita woke up with a start. 'What on earth is he doing here? And how did he find me?'

'I don't know! I only know he's asking for you!'

'Well, you'd better bring him in, then.'

Lucas came in looking tired, with an air of unaccustomed concern.

'Lucas?' said Perdita, getting up. 'What is it?'

'I'm terribly sorry,' he said. 'It's Kitty.'

Perdita felt a rough hand at the back of her neck, pushing her head between her knees. Then she came back to reality and panic.

'It's all right,' Lucas was saying. 'She's not very ill. She's not even in hospital, but the people she's staying with thought you should be informed.'

'So what's wrong with her?' Perdita's mouth was stiff and her voice sounded croaky, as if she'd been ill herself.

'She's had a TIA—transient ischaemic attack,' said Lucas.

'What's that? It sounds dreadful.' Lucy glanced at Perdita, concerned.

'It's a very mild stroke, one that has left no aftereffects. As I said, she's not even in hospital. There's really no need for you to panic.'

'But I must come now,' said Perdita. It wasn't a question.

He nodded.

'I'll just go and pack.'

Lucy came up with her, leaving her mother to tend to Lucas. 'I'm so sorry, Perdita. I know what you must be going through. When Daddy died . . . It's a very growing-up experience.'

And Lucy's daddy, Perdita couldn't help remembering, was much younger than Kitty. 'Well, Lucas says she's not that ill . . .'

Rather to her surprise, Lucy put her arms round Perdita and hugged her, very hard. 'You'll never get all this in that holdall,' she said after a minute. 'I'll get you some carrier bags.'

Later, in the car, Perdita felt the need to talk. 'I know Kitty's very old. She's going to die some time, and soon. I just don't want her to do it when I'm hundreds of miles away . . .'

'Of course not,' said Lucas. 'But she's not going to die for a while.'

'I know.' She paused. 'It was very kind of you to come and get me.'

'It seemed the least I could do, in the circumstances.'

'Which were?'

'A frantic phone call from the people Kitty is staying with. A Mrs Lettum-Havvit, or something.'

'Ledham-Gold.' Perdita sighed.

'Something like that. She'd got my number from Michael Grantly.'

'But how on earth . . .? Why you?'

Lucas shrugged and changed gear to overtake the car in front. 'Apparently I was the only person Kitty could think of who might be able to get in touch with you.'

'So she wanted me to be with her, did she?' This did not bode well. Kitty hated causing anyone any trouble.

'I don't think she did, particularly. But her hostess did.' He hesitated for a moment. 'I gather the doctor thought it was a good idea.'

Perdita digested this, trying to work out if it was good news or bad. 'It really was very, very kind of you to come and find me.'

'Bloody right it was kind. God knows what's happening in the kitchen. Those idiots have probably ruined my reputation by now.'

'What idiots?'

'Greg and Janey.'

'Surely you're not open on Boxing Day? Poor Greg, poor Janey.'

'There aren't many in, just a few staying at the hotel for Christmas. Those two'll make a complete bollocks of it, but who cares? The guests have absolutely no appreciation of good food anyway.'

'They didn't ask for ketchup?' Perdita's horror was a little exaggerated.

'No.' He shot her a glance. 'They weren't keen on the cardoons, though.'

Perdita thought it best to ignore this. 'So what did they do about Christmas dinner? You had the day off, didn't you?'

'We gave them their meal in the evening. I was back to cook that.'

'So you spent the day with Janey's family?'

'You know I did.'

'Well, did you have a nice time?'

'It was very pleasant.' He sighed again. 'And no, I didn't seduce Janey, if that's what you're worrying about. Sleeping with half-fledged ducklings does not come under the heading of pleasure.'

'It did at one time,' she said, blushing in the darkness.

'That was a long time ago, and that was you.'

Lucas filled the sudden silence with some rather complicated jazz, which Perdita's tired and shocked brain found difficult to unravel. She closed her eyes and dozed.

'So,' asked Lucas a little later, when she had woken up. 'Which one of those men was your boyfriend? The fat one or the one with dirty hair?'

With Kitty ill, perhaps dying, the lying and subterfuge just seemed silly. Perdita sighed. 'Neither of them. There is no boyfriend. Geoff, who gave me a lift up, is Jake's brother. I'd never met him before.'

Lucas nodded, but didn't look at her. 'And you told me a bundle of complete untruths. Why was that, I wonder?'

'Why do you think? You and I were married once. You left me—'

'For an older woman.' He sounded bored.

'And I was on my own, years later. I didn't want you to think I was car-rying a torch for you, that's all. Of course, in some ways, you coming back has done me a favour. It made me aware that I didn't have a man, and made me wonder if perhaps there isn't something missing in my life.'

'Oh? What?'

'Well, you know. Sex, companionship, that sort of thing.'

'Unfortunately, as there's such a shortage of single, eligible men, and apparently none at all locally, it might be quite difficult for you to find a boyfriend.' He shot her a provocative glance. 'Maybe *I* should try my chances with you.'

Perdita continued to look straight ahead. 'Not if you ever want to be able to father children, no. And "eligible" is the operative word, Lucas.'

Lucas laughed in a way that Perdita hadn't heard for years.

'I need a cup of coffee,' he said. 'I'll stop at the next service station.'

'I wouldn't have thought you'd consider what they serve as coffee.'

He laughed again. 'Beggars can't be choosers. I need something, or I'll fall asleep.'

Perdita let her breath out sharply, suddenly aware of what he had sac-rificed to fetch her. It would amount to a drive of not less than three hundred miles. On Boxing Day.

'I really am so grateful to you for fetching me. I don't know how I can ever make it up to you.'

'Oh, that's quite easy. You can agree to make a television cookery pro-gramme. In your house. With a brand-new cooker. Provided by me.'

'That wasn't the reason you came for me, was it? Blackmail?'

'Of course. The minute I got the phone call I didn't wonder why the hell she didn't have a mobile phone, so she could be contacted, I thought: What a brilliant opportunity to get Perdita to be cooperative! I'll play on her anxieties over Kitty to manipulate her into giving me my way.'

Perdita blushed in the darkness. 'I'm terribly sorry. That was quite out of order.' She gulped. 'And of course I'll do the television programme.'

'Don't overdo the gratitude or I might be tempted to hold you to it. Here's the turn-off. Do you want to go to the loo? I'll meet you in the café. I want to look at the map.'

'It's going to be terribly late when we get there. It's past ten now,' said Perdita, when they were back on the road.

'Mrs—'

'Ledham-Gold—'

'—said she'd stay up for us. And we should be there soon after eleven. They sounded very kind, and very concerned about Kitty. Not because she's that ill,' he went on slightly impatiently, as Perdita frowned with anxiety, 'but because they're so fond of her.'

'Talking of kind,' she said, 'thank you for sending my cheque back, but I'm afraid I really can't accept it. I don't need your money—'

Lucas braked sharply and pulled onto the hard shoulder. 'If you ever mention that cheque again, or make any further attempts to give it to me, I will come and find you in whatever distant corner of the earth you've hidden yourself, and beat you. Do you understand?'

He sounded more genuinely angry than she had ever heard him. 'OK, OK.' Perdita hoped he couldn't hear the tremble in her voice.

He paused a moment, to let his feelings on the matter sink in, then flicked the indicator, looked over his shoulder, and pulled back out onto the road. Perdita was shaking. If she wanted to touch that particular nerve again she must do it when she was in a position to escape.

A security light flashed on as they approached the gates of the house, which were open. The front door also opened before they had time to knock, and they were ushered very kindly inside.

Perdita felt tears spring to her eyes as she saw Kitty, looking suddenly very small and old, lying in a vast double bed.

It was obviously the best bedroom, and Kitty was surrounded by coordinated floral fabric, frilled table lamps, valances and mirrors.

'Darling, how lovely to see you! I told them not to bother you.'

'I'm so glad they—you'—she glanced up at Kitty's hostess, whose name she suddenly couldn't remember—'did bother me. I couldn't have lived with myself if you'd been ill, and I hadn't known.'

'And did that nice man bring you down? The one who drove you to Shropshire?'

Perdita hesitated for a second. 'Lucas came and fetched me.'

Kitty frowned. 'Oh, my goodness. Why?'

Had Kitty really forgotten that she'd given Lucas's name as a contact? Perhaps she'd lost a bit of her memory. 'Because you—because he heard you were ill, and I hadn't left a telephone number.'

'Oh dear. I know I suggested they asked him how to get in touch with you, but I never dreamt he'd go all that way to fetch you. I hope it wasn't awkward for you.'

Relief that Kitty's memory was as sound as ever made Perdita lie gaily. 'Not at all. He was very kind. He's being given turkey sandwiches in the kitchen. He drives extremely fast.'

'Since he got you here safely, I won't grumble about that. They say I might have to give up my pipe.' Kitty frowned.

'We've spoken to Kitty's doctor,' said Mrs Ledham-Gold. 'He wants to see her the minute she gets back home, and she's not to go home unless there's someone there.'

'I'll be there.'

'I thought you would be, though of course Kitty grumbled like anything . . .' Kitty made a sound confirming this. 'And he also wants to see you, to discuss Kitty's aftercare.'

'I'm perfectly capable of taking care of myself!' Kitty's firm assertion cheered Perdita. There would be lively arguments ahead.

Perdita eventually kissed Kitty good night, promising to collect her in a few days. She then spent a long time thanking the Ledham-Golds.

'You've looked after Kitty so well. I am so grateful to you.'

'She really needs someone living in, in case it happens again,' said Mrs Ledham-Gold. 'Has she got any relations who might oblige?'

'I'm all she's got and we're not related, but I'll live with Kitty.'

'But haven't you got other commitments?' She glanced at Lucas.

'Only my business and I can run that just as well from Kitty's house as mine. We live very close.'

'Kitty's very lucky to have a lovely girl like you to keep an eye on her.'

Lucas coughed in the background, obviously itching to leave. 'And I'm very lucky to have a friend like Lucas to fetch me,' said Perdita.

'Friend? Oh, I thought you were married.' Mrs Ledham-Gold sounded disappointed.

'That was years ago,' growled Lucas. 'Now, I don't want to hurry you, but could we please get on?'

'What time do you have to be at work in the morning?' They were in the village now, and Perdita tried not to sound as guilty as she felt.

'Eleven.'

'But who cooks breakfast?'

'We've taken on a breakfast chef who surpervises Greg and Janey doing the prep. And if they don't know how I like things done by now they can look elsewhere for a job.'

'That's terrible! Talking like that, when Janey had you for Christmas!'

'Janey did not "have" me for Christmas. Much as she might have liked to. But actually, Janey is shaping up very well.'

'I hope you tell her so. People do far better on praise than on criticism, you know.'

Lucas thought this highly amusing. 'That's not how things work in restaurant kitchens.' He slowed the car and drew up outside Perdita's house. 'Do you want me to stay for what's left of the night, or will you be all right?' He pulled on the handbrake. 'I'm not inviting myself into your bed, Perdita, just offering to stay with you if you need company.'

Perdita was shocked, mostly because she did need company, and the thought of sharing her bed with Lucas was far from unpleasant. 'No, no, I'll be fine. I'm perfectly used to living on my own, you know,' she added sharply. She opened the car door and clambered out. He got out his side and went round to the boot.

'You take the carrier bags, I'll take this,' he said. He waited while she found her key, and then followed her indoors. The house was cold and smelt of wood ash. 'Are you sure you'll be all right on your own?'

'Oh yes. I'll have a hot-water bottle and some hot milk with brandy in it, and I'll be asleep in minutes.' He studied her carefully, obviously not convinced. 'Really, Lucas. I'll be fine.'

'I'll be off then.'

Perdita put down her bags. 'I really can't thank you enough, Lucas . . .'

'Please don't thank me any more, or I'll die of boredom. Give me a hug instead.'

It wasn't hard to go to him and put her arms round his tall figure, made bulky by his overcoat. His arms round her were very strong, he held her very tightly for a very long time. She felt some of the stresses leach out of her body into the warmth of his. He bent forward and kissed her on the cheek. 'Good night, Perdita. I'll be seeing you. And please, for everybody's sake, get a mobile phone.'

It took Perdita ages to get to sleep that night. She had left her hot-water bottle in Shropshire and there hadn't been any heat in the house for days, so she was very, very cold. And although she had long-life milk, she didn't have enough brandy to do more than give it a very slight taste.

She wrapped her feet in a mohair shawl and eventually warmed up, but it was the knowledge that she was by no means indifferent to Lucas that made it so difficult to drift off. Of course, she wasn't in love with him, she didn't even have a crush, like poor Janey, but she had been grateful for his presence, and his arms around her had been more than just comforting. They had felt right, as if no other arms would do.

Because Christmas fell at the weekend, the day after Boxing Day, when Perdita was foodless, hot-water-bottleless and lonely, was a bank holiday. Fortunately her van got her to the nearest town, and after much searching of empty streets, she found an emergency chemist. She bought herself a new hot-water bottle, one with a furry cover, because it was Christmas, and she was alone.

Back at home, Perdita lit her wood burner, waited until it could be safely left, and then went out to inspect her poly-tunnels. In the shed she glanced towards the pot in which she had buried the crosnes Lucas had given her to grow. She had found a book that told her how to grow it, and was waiting until March to plant it. Until then, it had to be kept safe, not allowed to rot or dry up.

She picked a selection of salads to go with a baked potato and went back into the house to ring Janey. Janey, extremely surprised to hear that Perdita was not still in Shropshire, was off duty unexpectedly, without plans, and more than willing to come and visit.

'Tell me everything,' she demanded, before the first glass of wine was even poured, let alone drunk. 'Why did you come back so early? Did you have a row with your boyfriend? I want to know everything.'

'You tell me about how you got on with Lucas first,' said Perdita cravenly. 'You know I've been worrying about it.'

'There's nothing to tell, really. He was very sweet to Mum and Dad, took over the carving because Dad had had one too many, but he didn't do anything when we were alone, watching telly.' Janey took a determined slug of her wine. 'But I'll get him somehow. I'll dazzle him with my cooking, and one day he'll look up and see what a jewel I am, and pounce.'

'Ooh. Very romantic.' Perdita was relieved. It didn't look as if Lucas was likely to take Janey up on what she offered.

'So? What about you then?' Janey looked at Perdita expectantly.

Perdita decided to just tell the truth—everything except the closeness of her relationship with Lucas. 'Well, to be honest with you, I haven't got a boyfriend. The man who took me to stay with my friend at Christmas was just her brother-in-law. I came back early because Kitty was ill.'

'Oh. I'm really sorry about Kitty.'

'She's not that bad, really. She should be home quite soon.'

Relieved that she could get back to the subject really of interest to her, Janey went on, 'But why did you pretend to have a boyfriend?'

'Well, it's terribly silly I know, but it's because of Lucas. You know we knew each other, years and years ago?'

'Yes?'

'Well, he always made me feel sort of inferior. I didn't want to seem on the shelf, or available or anything.'

'Oh.' Janey seemed more disappointed than shocked. 'And I was so thrilled for you.'

'I'm sorry. It was sort of a fantasy, I suppose. You know, being whisked away to a glamorous location for Christmas, in a fast car.'

'And was it glamorous, where you went?'

'Not at all. It was very primitive. They'd only just moved in and nothing was unpacked, and it was freezing cold.'

'No opportunities to dress up, then?'

'Only in layers of jumpers. Just as well I'd packed my thermal vest.'

Janey was suddenly aware that Perdita was pushing thirty. 'Oh,' she sighed, 'I sort of pine for the sort of Christmas you read about in magazines, where everyone dresses for dinner.'

Perdita chuckled. 'That was the sort of Christmas Lucy wanted—a perfect magazine one. Poor old Lucy. It wasn't at all like that, but I think she had a nice time in the end. Her kids did, anyway.'

'Christmas is for children really.' Janey sighed. Her moment of nostalgia lasted about a second before she went back to Perdita's love life, or lack of. 'So, what was the brother-in-law like, then? Still married?'

'Separated, but not fanciable, and too broken-hearted, even if he was.'

'Oh.' Janey drained her glass and helped them both to more wine. 'We're both a couple of silly cows—you for pretending you had a boyfriend, and me for having a crush on a man who'll never want me.' They clashed glasses. 'Cheers!'

'Cheers.' Then came another tricky moment for Perdita. Did Janey and Greg know why Lucas left them so suddenly on Boxing Day? 'So did you have to work on Boxing Day or were you free then?'

'Had to work, which is why I'm off now. Lucas had to go flying off somewhere for some reason, which left me and Greg in charge. Well, me, really. Everyone was very pleased with what I did.'

'What, even Lucas?' Perdita could smile now she knew Lucas had been discreet.

'Well, no. He wasn't there, was he? But when I went into work this morning, he said I could have today off because of having to take over yesterday. He can be really kind at times.'

Perdita, who knew this, took refuge in a gulp of wine. 'Let's go and see if the spuds are cooked. We need something solid like a baked potato to put our feet back on the ground. You especially.'

'He's just so gorgeous. I can't help being in love with him. Even if he never looks at me.'

'Come on, Janey!' said Perdita, not confident that Lucas's lack of interest in 'half-fledged ducklings' would last for ever. She led the way to the kitchen. 'Lovely girl like you should have a real man, not a fantasy. Leave that to the old birds like me.'

'You're not old!' Janey indignantly followed Perdita into the kitchen. 'And you'd be lovely if . . .'

Perdita turned round with a sigh. 'Don't tell me. If I did something about myself. Ronnie says something of the sort every time I see him.'

'I know!' said Janey. 'But promise that if this television thing comes off you'll get done up? That's fair enough, isn't it?'

Perdita and Mrs Welford, Kitty's favourite taxi driver, went up to collect Kitty from the Ledham-Golds. It was only after Mrs Welford, having been given tea and tea cakes and discreetly paid, was sent on her way that Kitty and Perdita had a row. It was, as usual, a ladylike row. No one shouted but Kitty flatly refused to let Perdita move back in with her.

'You cannot give up your life to look after me,' Kitty said. 'It's not necessary and it would drive me mad, having you hovering round me all day looking to see if I was telling the truth when I said I was perfectly fine.'

'Supposing you had another TIA?'

'Don't talk to me in initials.'

'Transient ischaemic attack. If you'd been alone when you had that one—'

'My dear Perdita, do let's have a drink. I don't think I can stand all this concern without one.'

Perdita didn't say a word about alcohol being bad for her, nor did she protest when Kitty lit her pipe. 'Mrs Ledham-Gold distinctly told me that your doctor said you weren't to go home unless there was someone there.'

'Very well, if you insist on bullying me, you can stay here tonight, but tomorrow I'll ask Dr Edwards to talk some sense into you.'

'OK.' Perdita took a sip of whisky, which she only drank in emergencies. 'If he says I can go home, I'll go home. But if he doesn't, you're stuck with me, like it or not. Now I'll go and get us some supper.'

Kitty arranged for Dr Edwards to visit the following afternoon. Perdita rushed through her jobs so she could be there, not daring to be a second late in case Kitty bullied the doctor into saying what she wanted him to.

Dr Edwards, a tall, well-set-up man in his forties, was courteous and pleasant, and Kitty was very fond of him.

Today, when he arrived, Kitty offered him sherry, although it was tea time. It was, Perdita knew, to give Kitty a little Dutch courage; the thought of losing her independence reminded her of her old age. The doctor accepted the sherry gracefully and seated himself on the sofa.

'Have a cheese straw,' said Kitty. 'Not home-made, I'm afraid, but just about edible. Perdita, dear, help yourself to sherry and pour me one.'

When they all clutched cut-glass glasses, and the cheese straws had done the rounds, the doctor got down to the point. 'Mrs Anson asked me to come here this afternoon to tell you, Perdita, that she can live perfectly well by herself.'

Perdita nodded, hoping fervently that he could see through Kitty's ability to put on a brave face, and appear heartier than she really was.

'For her age,' he glanced at Kitty, apologetic for discussing her health in front of her, 'she's really in very good form. But she has had this TIA, and she could have another one. However,' Dr Edwards went on, 'I don't think there is any need for Perdita to move in with you at the moment.' Sunshine radiated from Kitty's wrinkled face. 'But you will have to make some compromises.' He turned sternly to her.

'Well, of course, anything within reason . . .'

'I'm not going to ask you to give up your pipe. But you must have a personal alarm, a button you wear round your neck and can press if anything happens. The signal is picked up by the ambulance station who'll get in touch with Perdita, or whoever is nearest. If they can't they send an ambulance.'

'Really,' muttered Kitty, 'it sounds quite unnecessary to me. I can't bear newfangled gadgetry.'

'It's that or contact a private nursing agency and have carers in day and night,' said the doctor smoothly.

Kitty and the doctor locked eyes, both determined. Kitty backed down first. 'Oh, very well, I'll have your gadget then.'

'And I'll get a mobile phone. That way I can guarantee to be there if it goes off,' said Perdita. If Kitty was willing to take on 'gadgetry' it was only fair that Perdita should too.

'What happens if Kitty has another TIA?' Perdita asked.

'Then we have to consider the likelihood of her—you'—he smiled again at Kitty—'having a full-blown stroke. If that happens—'

'I'm not going into a home.'

'Of course you're not,' said Perdita firmly. 'There's no question of it.'

'Besides, you haven't had the stroke yet,' said the doctor. 'You might get run over by a bus.'

Kitty snorted. 'Precious little chance of that around here! Do you know how infrequent the buses are in the village? You could die of exposure waiting for one.'

Perdita showed the doctor out. When she went back, Kitty was in the sitting room, looking far more tired than she'd allowed the doctor to guess. Perdita cooked her an omelette and told her that she was staying the night, in spite of what the doctor had said. Kitty accepted this without argument, an indication that the doctor hadn't been unnecessarily pessimistic. Kitty seemed to feel this too.

'To misquote dear Winston,' she said, 'it's not the beginning of the end, but I have a feeling it's the end of the beginning.'

Perdita hugged Kitty very hard. 'I expect you're right. But I promise you won't go into a home while I have breath in my body.'

Not usually much given to physical contact, Kitty returned the hug. 'Thank you for that.'

Kitty went over to the mantelpiece in the kitchen and produced an envelope from behind the clock. 'To save you the trouble of opening it, it's the money for a new van. Don't argue. If all my money goes on private nurses, and I assure you I do have plenty of money, I want you to have something. Save on death duties.'

'It doesn't have to be new-from-the-shop new,' said Perdita, when she had opened the envelope, and seen the vastness of the amount written.

'Yes it does. Buy the best and it will last you longer. Now do go to bed. You have to be up early, and Veronica lent me a book I've been wanting to read for ages.'

Once New Year was over and the shops had reopened properly, Perdita bought a mobile phone. Completely at the mercy of the man in the shop, she did exactly what he told her, signed on for the arrangement he thought best, and generally put up no resistance. Nor did she make much effort to learn how to use it; she was much more excited about her new van. She had to wait three weeks, and when it finally arrived she found driving it such a different experience she hardly knew herself.

Lucas must have been waiting for her the first time she took it to Grantly House, because he appeared as she opened the back doors.

'You've got a new van, then,' he said.

'Ten out of ten for observation,' she said glibly. 'Kitty paid for it,' she added more seriously.

'So how is Kitty, now she's home?' Lucas took a tray of salads from Perdita's hands.

'She seems fine. She wouldn't let me go and live with her, though. But at least she's got an alarm now.' She took another box out and put it on top of the one Lucas was holding. 'And I've got a mobile phone.'

'Welcome to the twentieth century. And is the alarm system working OK?' he asked.

'Well, yes. I was contacted a couple of times, and rushed over only to find Kitty in the garden, fit as a flea. She kept setting it off by mistake.'

Perdita heaved out another box and made to follow Lucas.

'She does wear it, then?' he asked, when they were through the kitchen.

'She did protest when I kept jumping up out of nowhere, as she put it. But I threatened her with twenty-four-hour care if she didn't persevere with it, so she agreed.' She watched Lucas reverse into the cold store, holding the door open for her to follow. 'It'll probably come to that though.'

He peered into the first box, frowning. 'What is this muck you've brought me? We have our own compost heap, you know. We don't need contributions from yours.'

'There's absolutely nothing wrong with it!' she snapped, after a few moments' tense inspection. 'You're so bloody fussy.'

'I have standards I like to maintain, that's all.'

'Well, do you want the other boxes, or not?'

'I might find something salvageable in them, I suppose.'

As Perdita stormed back to her van she realised that Lucas had probably made her angry on purpose, to stop her feeling depressed about Kitty. If so, his plan had worked.

Chapter Four

PERDITA WENT BACK to her tunnels. Lucas had ordered some Witloof chicory, and she wanted to check if it was doing something under its flowerpot. She also wanted to see if the crosnes had survived its hibernation, and would be ready to plant in March. William was digging in some alfalfa that had become tough.

'Hi, William. How's it going?'

'Work, or life in general?'

As his fork seemed to be working just fine, she said, 'Life in general.'

'OK, I suppose, but I'm meant to be going to a college reunion. Formal do.'

'That sounds fun. Do you need extra time off?'

'No, I need a partner. I don't suppose . . .' He looked at her.

'No, certainly not. What would all your college pals think if you turned up with an older woman on your arm?'

'That I'd got lucky.' He chuckled to hide his embarrassment.

'Why don't you ask Janey? I'm sure she'd love to go with you.'

'I don't know her well enough.'

'Of course you do! Tell you what, I'll ask her for you. She'll understand about you being shy because she's quite shy herself.'

'She's cool, but I don't suppose she'd want to go with me.'

'Rubbish! Of course she would. And she'd love an opportunity to dress up. Where is it, and how will you get there?'

'We're all staying over in a guesthouse. Dad said I could take the car.'

'So it'll be a whole weekend thing?'

'Well, yes. You'll be all right here, won't you?'

'Oh yes, fine.' Even if she hadn't been fine, Perdita would have accommodated William's time off if it meant getting Janey away from Lucas. 'So you'd really like me to ask her?'

'Oh yes. I like Janey. She's dead pretty, and she makes me laugh.'

'But you don't want to ask her yourself?'

William blushed, undecided.

'Tell you what,' said Perdita, 'I'll tell her that you've got this lush ball to go to, and want to take someone with you, and are thinking about asking her. I'll see if she seems keen or not, and tell you. Then you don't have to worry about being turned down.'

'Really, Perdita? That'd be top.'

As Perdita had anticipated, Janey was enthusiastic about going to a ball with William. An excuse to really dress up, a weekend away, and if William wasn't the man of her dreams he was at least available, and was quite nice-looking.

'After all, it doesn't look as if Lucas is ever going to ask me anywhere,' she added. 'Give William my number.'

Feeling very pleased with herself, Perdita rang William, then did a little cleaning while waiting to hear the results of her manipulations. She was delighted when Janey finally called back and told her she was all set to go to the ball.

Her satisfaction in playing fairy godmother was short-lived, however. Lucas was looking particularly grumpy when she delivered the next day. A glance at Janey told her she wasn't happy either.

'Hi, Lucas, I've got your Witloof chicory.' She didn't expect a bunch of flowers but would have liked a little more than the grunt she received. 'In the cold store, or shall I leave it here?'

'Cold store,' he said.

'So, how are you, Janey? Looking forward to your ball?'

'She's not going to any ball,' said Lucas. 'At least, not on that particular Saturday. We've got a very big event on. I need everyone I can lay my hands on. Especially Janey.'

'Surely you could get a sous-chef from an agency?' Perdita was as disappointed as Janey was and William would be.

'Why should I? Janey's on the rota for that night. I need her and she can't have the time off. Unless she wants to look for another job.'

Janey, and a new girl Perdita didn't know, quailed in the face of his fury. He was obviously in a foul mood. Perdita decided she would ask him again when he was feeling happier. She was determined that Janey should go to the ball. The Demon King wasn't going to stop her.

'I tried asking him again,' said Janey, on the phone, 'but he flatly refused. He says why should he pay an agency for inferior staff?' She paused. 'I suppose it is quite flattering that he feels like that about me.'

'But you did want to go to the ball?'

'Yes, but not if it means my losing my job.'

'Janey, run it by me what you *do*, exactly?'

'Puddings, mostly. Lots of prep. I cook the veg sometimes.'

'Well, I'm sure I could do that.'

'What do you *mean*? You can't cook to save your life.'

'I don't have to. All I have to do is stand in for you on the night of the ball. If I make it clear it's my fault, he won't blame you.'

'He'll *kill* you! And probably me too.'

'Honestly, Janey, I don't see why you're making so much fuss. I'll turn up in your place, and if Lucas breaks a few plates, he breaks a few plates. It's only one evening, and it can't be that important.'

'I can't do it, Perdita. It's not fair on Lucas. And I have my own professional pride.'

'Oh, stuff! It's one evening! You've got a whole lifetime to build up your reputation. And if Lucas is as shit-hot as everyone says he is, he'll be able to manage with me instead of you.'

'Lucas will sack me.'

'No he won't, because if he does I won't do his television programme.'

'That's blackmail!'

'I know.' Actually, it was worse than blackmail, as Perdita had already promised she'd do the programme. She'd have to rely on Lucas's sense of fair play—a very uncertain commodity—to stop him blaming Janey for something that wasn't at all her fault.

'OK,' Janey sighed, still very doubtful. 'But if I lose my job—'

'You won't!' Perdita crossed her fingers. 'I promise!'

'What the hell are you doing here?' demanded Lucas, as Perdita entered the kitchen. 'We've got all the garnishes we need.'

She had got there a good half-hour early so she could familiarise herself with her surroundings, but although Janey had told her that Lucas wouldn't appear before six, here he was. 'I'm your sous-chef for the night.'

'*What?*'

For a moment, Perdita wanted to run out of the kitchen and never come back as his expression darkened from its habitual irascibility to incandescent rage. There was a terrible silence.

'I don't believe even you could be so fucking silly! There's more to being a sous-chef than peeling potatoes! Where's Janey?'

'On her way to a college reunion.' Perdita found herself backed up against the freezer. 'It's not her fault! It was all my idea. I'm here in her place. You won't even have to pay me.'

'Pay you? *Pay you?*' He was almost whispering. 'You'll be lucky if I don't *murder* you. Don't you know that we've got a dinner for thirty and a bloody Michelin inspector coming?'

Perdita didn't, and nor had Janey, or she would never have agreed to go to the ball.

He let out a loud, frustrated breath and then went on at normal volume. 'I didn't tell Janey she couldn't have the evening off to be awkward! I would have let her go if I could have! I've got a lot of agency staff coming. She's the only permanent staff member on tonight! I'm going to be left with a load of people who haven't worked for me before.'

'Oh dear. I know Janey wouldn't have gone if she'd known about the Michelin man.'

'Well, Janey had better start job hunting.'

'You can't sack Janey.' Outrage at his injustice gave her courage. 'Because if you do, I won't let them use my house for the TV programme.'

'I don't think the prospect of cooking in your kitchen is sufficiently alluring for me to keep on a member of staff who's proved so outstandingly disloyal.'

'She's *not* disloyal! She worships you! You can do anything you like to me, but don't take it out on Janey.'

'Anything I like? Really? I'm almost tempted, but then I don't think there's anything I can do to you that would make up for me not getting my Michelin star.'

She bit her lip and closed her eyes. 'Lucas?' she pleaded.

'Well, we'll have to see, won't we?' he said after minutes had become hours. 'If you do a good job, Janey can keep hers. But if you fuck up, Janey's out of here. Fair enough?'

Relief restored Perdita's powers of speech. 'It's not fair at all, Lucas. But that's not such a surprise, is it? Fairness never was you strong suit.'

'Then you'd better perform, sweetheart. Though what the hell I'll find for you to do, God knows.' He looked up as the kitchen door opened and other people began to drift in. 'I need a sous for tonight,' he said to the two men and two women who stood there warily. 'You!' he stabbed an accusing finger at a tall boy who looked very smart in his whites. 'What are your qualifications?' The boy mumbled something. 'You'll do. What's your name? What? Tom? You're sous.'

'Yes, Chef. Thank you, Chef.'

'Right! Listen, everybody. There's a party of thirty due in at eight. It's a party of hoteliers. They're not here on business, but they know about food and service, and I don't want any cockups. Understood?'

Everyone nodded.

'I have also heard a rumour, which might be quite unfounded, that there's a Michelin inspector coming in. You won't know which one he is, so I want everyone, but everyone, to receive first-class service. We're a member of staff short tonight,' he gave Perdita a glance that let her know she would never reach the status of 'staff', 'so we need to keep our minds on the job.' More nods. 'OK, let's party.'

Perdita went and stood next to a boy who was boiling sliced potatoes in a pan. 'Can I help you?'

'OK, but don't let them go too far. They've got to be sautéed.'

Perdita stood over them with a knife, poking at them occasionally. Then she heard a scream in the corner and saw that a girl had dropped a cold poached egg on the floor, and a bowl of them teetered on the edge of the counter. Perdita ran to rescue the bowl and help her clean up before Lucas noticed. She knew where the roll of kitchen paper was, and and was back with her potatoes within moments. But not before Lucas.

'What are these?' he demanded. He picked up the pan and a sieve and took them over to the sink. He tipped the potatoes into the sieve, his eyes never leaving Perdita's, then dumped them onto the floor. 'Clear that up,' he ordered her. 'It's complete mush. We are not running a pie shop here.'

Then he strode back to the boy who had prepared the potatoes. 'They were your responsibility, you had no right to off-load it on to that girl, who knows jack-shit about cooking.'

'No, Chef, sorry, Chef.'

Perdita, having dealt with the potatoes, took a deep breath and went up to Lucas. 'I think I'd better just go,' she said.

'You go, Janey goes,' he replied, not looking up.

'This is intolerable!'

'You put yourself here. If you don't like it, you can't blame me.' He sighed and looked up. 'Keep out of the bloody way. Go into the corner and chop parsley.'

It's nice to spend time with a friend, she thought, finding a bunch of parsley she'd grown herself. She took it as far away from Lucas as possible, found a board and a knife and started chopping.

A worried-looking waitress came in. 'The party of thirty are starting to arrive. They're having drinks in the bar. Shall I take them menus now, or wait until they're all here?'

'Better wait. Now, are we ready, people?'

A hush fell over the usually noisy room. Tension and heat seemed to increase by the second. Perdita shuffled deeper into her corner and crouched over her task.

There was a stillness, while everyone stood at their places waiting to spring into action. No one could do anything until the first script came in, but the moment it did, they would be flying to get the order cooked, plated and garnished as quickly as possible.

Lucas, in the middle of the working area, was conductor, director, but also lead singer. The light shining down on him enhanced his jutting nose and strong chin, making him look devilish under the bandanna knotted into a rope and tied round his head, to catch the sweat. Perdita was glad Janey couldn't see him. Even to her jaded gaze he looked dangerous and extremely attractive in his double-fronted white jacket. She hoped fervently that William looked half as good in his dinner jacket, otherwise this evening in Hell's Kitchen would have been for nothing.

Soon the waitress came in with the orders.

Perdita didn't allow herself to look over her shoulder often, but when she did, Lucas seemed to be everywhere, shaking pans, creating delicate towers of rösti, aubergines, puréed swede, which he heaped about with slices of crimson lamb or duck, and then drizzled with gravy. Every serving had to be as pleasing to the eye as it was to the palate.

He seemed to know what was going on in every pan and where each order had got to in its preparation. He shouted commands in a voice that would have turned Perdita to jelly if she hadn't been jelly already.

'Get that fillet out of the pan! You're not at McDonald's now, and he wants it rare. Is that fingerprint on the plate edible? If not get it off!'

Perdita kept her head well down in her corner. Then the waitress who'd been dealing with the dining room and the dirty plates came into the kitchen. She cleared her throat nervously.

'The dishwasher's broken down!' she called, then stood well back and looked ready to duck. Lucas took this news surprisingly coolly and turned to the kitchen porter, a vacant young man with virulent acne. 'Right, John, you stop doing pans and start doing plates. The glasses can wait. Perdita! Where the hell are you, when you're wanted? There's a number on the board. Ring the company and get them to come out right away.'

A few moments later, Perdita had to break the news that the dishwasher couldn't be mended until tomorrow, certain that this time Lucas would surely throw something, or somebody, probably her. But he didn't.

'Right, you keep the draining area clear for John, Perdita. Becky will give you drying-up cloths. Have you chopped that parsley yet?'

'Yes, mountains of it.'

He swooped into her corner and picked up some parsley between finger and thumb and tossed it into his mouth. He spat it out. 'Gritty.' Then he swept the whole lot onto the floor with his hand. 'You didn't wash it, did you? Wash, dry, chop. Clear it up and then help John.'

'You can't do that! You can't treat me or anyone like that! I have spent hours chopping that parsley. You never told me to wash it! How was I supposed to know you had to?'

'Yes, I suppose I just forgot, for a moment, that you have you own rules about cleanliness, food and hygiene. Foolish of me. Still, it won't happen again. Could you dry the plates and stack them, that is, put one on top of the other, in the pantry? Thank you so much.'

This quiet sarcasm was worse than his shouting had been. If only Janey hadn't been so wedded to this job Perdita would have walked out.

Becky, the waitress, came in excitedly. 'I think I've spotted the inspector,' she said. 'He's balding, has got a French accent and is alone. Do you want to do his order first?'

Lucas turned on the poor woman. 'What the hell are you thinking of? No way do we take orders out of sequence!'

Becky scurried away, accustomed but not inured to such outbursts.

The evening went on, too fast for Perdita to follow. Becky brought in pile after pile of plates, so that it seemed that John washed and Perdita dried enough plates for each customer to have used ten of the things. Eventually the pace of the kitchen slowed. Now it was only coffee, various types of tea, and plates of handmade chocolates that were going out, although there was a lot of cleaning-up going on. What seemed like hours passed, then at last, Lucas seemed satisfied with the state of the kitchen.

'OK, you lot, you can push off now. Bring me your time sheets. Good service, Tom.' He patted the boy's shoulder. 'Work with you again.'

Perdita limped to the passageway where she had hung her coat.

226

'Where do you think you're going?' Lucas, hands on hips, made her feel like a cat burglar, stealing into the night.

'Home.' She took off her apron. 'I've done my night's work.'

'No you haven't. What about the pans? The glasses?'

'You said those could wait.'

'They have waited. Now you've got to wash them.'

'But the dishwasher's going to be fixed tomorrow!'

'The machine can't do pans, and I'm not risking the man not coming. It's Sunday tomorrow: twenty-four-hour service or not, he may not turn up. Get back in here.'

There was no point in protesting further; he would only threaten Janey again. William would have to be showering her in diamonds and giving her multiple orgasms to make this agony worth while.

Lucas stayed in the kitchen, tidying up, writing notes and cleaning the ovens. But by the time she'd got to the glasses, he had finished and was leaning against the worktop, watching her.

'These are smeary,' he said, picking up a glass from the side. 'And this one's got lipstick on it. Would you like to be given a glass with someone else's lipstick on it? Empty the sink and do them again. And this time, wash and rinse them in really hot water.'

That was it. Perdita had kept a lid on her temper all evening, but now there were no witnesses she could let rip without inhibitions. 'I've had enough. You can wash the rest of the glasses yourself!'

She stood, still clutching a glass, waiting for the explosion. She was in the mood to throw things.

'Listen! If you play games with other people's lives, you've got to stick to the rules! You set up Janey and your friend to try and stop her having a crush on me! Well, Janey and I don't need your interference! If we choose to have an affair that's our business, and if I choose to sack her, that's mine. Now get on and finish those glasses. Some of us have to work in the morning.'

The glass left her hand, sailed through the air, glanced off his shoulder and landed with a satisfying smash on the floor. 'You are such a bastard! I believe you'd seduce Janey, break her heart, just like you did mine, just to spite me! Well, I'm not going to stand by and let you!'

'So what are you going to do to stop me? Janey's a very pretty girl, very like you were. I think I might like to have her, after all.'

His row of knives, neatly laid out by his chopping board caught her eye. One appeared in her hand without her knowing how it had got there. She rushed at him but he caught her wrist, causing the knife to join the broken glass with a clatter. She kicked his shin as hard as she could.

'Bitch!' He grabbed her waist and pulled her to him. She kicked out again, but he was ready for her, hooked his leg behind the one she was standing on, making her lose her balance. She pulled him down on top of her as she fell, trying to roll so that he was underneath as they landed. They were both breathing hard. Perdita felt a deep, primitive satisfaction in grappling with him physically, releasing her anger by inflicting as much pain as possible. She tried to move but couldn't. Lucas was looking down into her eyes, not moving, not letting her move.

'You,' she said, breathless from the weight of his body on hers, 'are the biggest, most bloody, most hateful bastard in all the world.'

'And you, in spite of being the most useless, irrational, temperamental woman I have ever had the misfortune to have in my kitchen, still drive me to distraction.'

She closed her eyes, not wanting to see if there was desire or just exasperation in his, but when she felt his breath come nearer, she said, 'If you try to kiss me, I shall bite you.'

'I have no intention of kissing you, wildcat, and if I did, you wouldn't be able to do a thing I didn't want you to do.'

She couldn't help it. She felt herself reach up to snap at him, like a terrier. Her teeth had dug into the soft tissue of his lip before he could pull out of reach.

'You bitch!'

He whispered the words, but she saw the fire in his eyes and wondered if he would bite her back, or knock her senseless with the back of his hand. She had never had a violent thought before, but now all her suppressed aggression came to the surface. The sight of his blood on his lip, the taste of it on her own, turned her into a savage.

She closed her eyes, fighting her feelings, trying to cling on to some remnant of civilisation. 'I'm not staying here all night!' she hissed. 'Let me up!'

'Not until I can be sure you won't try and savage me again. I warn you, don't do anything to me you don't want me to do right back.' He let this sink in. 'I'm going to help you up now.' His soothing tone heightened her madness. The moment she was standing she flew at his neck, unable to bear his patronising attitude any more than she could tolerate the maelstrom of conflicting feelings that made her dizzy, wild, miserable, and yet elated.

This time he didn't spare her. He grabbed her wrists and lifted her so that she was half sitting, half lying on the worktop, then he stood over her legs so she couldn't hurt him, gathered her into his arms and kissed her, in a teeth-clashing, lip-bruising kiss that was as painful and passionate as it was arousing. Suddenly she found herself kissing him back, and she didn't want it to stop, ever. By some mysterious alchemy, all her hatred had turned to desire. She no longer wanted to kill him, she just wanted to make violent love to him, to have him make violent love to her.

Her fingers flew at the buttons of his jacket, ripping them open, baring his chest. He hesitated only for a second before he returned the favour, tugging her shirt out of her jeans, undoing the buttons almost as fast as she was undoing his. When they stopped for breath his jacket hung open, exposing his naked chest, and Perdita's shirt was falling off her shoulders, joining her bra straps halfway down her arms.

'Not here,' he said. 'Not on the workbench. Come with me.'

As if not trusting her to follow him, he picked her up and carried her out of the kitchen, through the deserted foyer of the hotel and into the Ladies, kicking open the door. He rested her on the broad, mirror-backed Formica counter used as a dressing table, and, still holding her, swept everything off it. Potpourri, hand towels, hand cream and bottles of scent landed on the floor unheeded.

Cold air touched her bare flesh, cooling her. Back there, under the hot lights of the kitchen, where tempers and passions were heated beyond reason, the fieriness of her emotions seemed reasonable. Here, in the cool, soothing surroundings of a ladies' powder room, they seemed suddenly inappropriate.

And how did he know about the ladies' loo? How did he know there was a counter top suitable for making love on? Had he taken other members of staff there? Sanity began to push through her dying passion.

'Lucas—I really don't think we should be doing this.' Her voice seemed to separate her from her desires, reminding her of the sensible, down-to-earth person she usually was.

He swallowed. 'There's no should about it. Do you want to?'

She did want to. She wanted very much to make love to Lucas, to have him make love to her. But she knew it would take her years to get back to being the contented, fulfilled person she had been, if they did make love. For her, lovemaking could never just be a simple release of sexual tension, and for Lucas she doubted if it would ever be anything else. She'd make herself vulnerable to him again, and this time she might not recover. But nor could she be anything but honest with him.

'I do want to, Lucas. You know I do. But not here, not like this—and I don't mean not in the ladies' lavatories, for God's sake! I'd have made love on the kitchen floor a moment ago . . .' She closed her eyes, briefly regretting that they hadn't done just that.

'But not now?'

She shook her head. 'I got very carried away. I did—want you. I wanted to hurt you, tear you apart, scratch and bite and leave bruises.' She noticed some marks on his torso. 'I probably have left bruises,' she smiled, 'not that you didn't deserve it, but sex isn't about revenge. For me, it's about love. I'm terribly sorry if I led you on.'

He turned away from her and gave a brief laugh, starting to do up his buttons. 'I suppose I've only myself to blame. As usual.'

'I don't usually mind contradicting you, Lucas, but I think I have to take my share of responsibility.' She watched him in silence for a few moments. Then she said, 'What about the mess?' She indicated the pot-pourri, the towels and the bottles. 'Shall I get a dustpan and brush?'

'If I see you in close proximity to the floor, it's unlikely you'll get out of here with your virtue intact. Wait here and I'll get your coat.'

When he came back he looked weary, and a little cynical. 'I think I should warn you I wouldn't have made love to you for revenge, or to punish you—I've done enough of that this evening—but because I wanted you, very much. Now go away before I remember I'm the villain of the piece, and ravish you.'

'So,' asked Kitty, the following lunch time, 'what was it like working for Lucas?' She had made Sunday lunch—roast beef and Yorkshire pudding.

'Hell. The sooner I get Janey out of there, the better.' Perdita drained her sherry glass and refilled it. 'Shall I set the table?'

'Yes, just clear one end of it. That'll do.'

As Kitty's kitchen table had never been seen clear by anyone, this proviso was unnecessary. Perdita picked up the book that was open face-down in front of Kitty's chair. She found a leaflet offering cheap car insurance and slipped it between the pages. Then, to distract herself, she opened the book and looked inside. The name Lucas Gillespie, written in thick black ink, shouted at her.

'Kitty?' she demanded. 'Who lent you this?'

'Oh—I can't remember. Can you put some mats down for the vegetable dishes?'

Kitty wasn't usually vague. 'It was Lucas, wasn't it?'

'If you know the answer, why are you asking?'

'Why didn't you tell me he'd lent you a book? Why did you keep it from me?'

'Well, I would have told you, but he asked me not to, thought you might feel betrayed.'

'But I didn't know you knew him! Socially!'

'I didn't, but he came to see me shortly after I got back from the

Ledham-Golds, to see how I was. We got talking about books and he lent me some. Now, do start, or it'll get cold.'

Perdita sawed at her meat somewhat savagely, wondering if she was being totally unjust suspecting Lucas of having an ulterior motive for visiting Kitty. 'But when does he have the time to visit you?'

'It's just the odd afternoon. He rings to check you're not here, and not likely to be. He thought you wouldn't like it. I thought he was talking nonsense, but he obviously wasn't. I can see you're quite put out.'

Janey rang Perdita on Sunday night. She was ecstatic, she had had a wonderful weekend and was determined to give Perdita a drink-by-drink account of it. Somewhat unwillingly, Perdita agreed to meet Janey at the pub. She listened patiently, but it felt like a Pyrrhic victory. Soon, no doubt, she would revel in Janey's happiness, and not think her own peace of mind was too great a sacrifice. Just now, she felt too raw.

'. . . So William turned out to be a really nice person when he'd had a few beers. He's just really shy, isn't he?'

'Mmm.'

'Anyway, the journey was a bit awkward, but it turned out we both like Mogwai, and he had some tapes, so that helped. When we got there, I felt dreadfully shy, although William had warmed up a bit by then, and I must say, he was ace about introducing me to everyone. He seemed sort of—proud of me—know what I mean?'

Perdita suppressed a yawn, not so much because other people's accounts of splendid evenings are less entertaining than tales of disaster, but because she was very short of sleep. 'So did you get off with each other?' she asked, in an attempt to cut to the chase.

'Well, we didn't go to bed. In fact—he didn't even suggest it, which I thought was sweet. And I must say he looked lush in his dinner jacket.'

This was good news, but it wasn't quite enough. For some reason Perdita very much needed Janey to have gone further along the road to destruction than she and Lucas had. 'But you did kiss?'

'Oh yes. A lot. How about you?'

'What do you mean?' Perdita's voice was sharp with guilt.

'I mean, how did your evening in the kitchen go? What on earth did you think I meant?'

'Oh, nothing, it's just you were talking about kissing and then you said what about me.' She managed a laugh. 'Lucas is such a bastard! The dishwasher broke down and he made me wash all the pans and glasses. I don't know how you work with him, Janey, I really don't.'

'I hope you looked after him, all right, Perdita. I mean, I know he is a bit of a pig, but he's so talented. And all the great chefs are—'

'Pigs?'

'Well—yes. But it's so exciting, isn't it? Watching everything happen, all that chaos, and then, beautiful plates go out as if there was all the time in the world to do it.'

'He threw my parsley on the floor. He said it was gritty.'

'I don't suppose you washed it in enough changes of water. Didn't Lucas tell you about the washed and dried parsley in the fridge?'

'He didn't say a word. He hated me being there, in fact I would have walked out—' Just in time Perdita stopped herself announcing that the reason she didn't was because Lucas had threatened to sack Janey; it wasn't fair to put that responsibility on her.

'Yes?'

'Except you're right. It is very exciting, and there was supposed to be a Michelin inspector in that night.'

'What! Oh, no! Oh God, I hope everything was all right. It's so important for Lucas to get his star.'

'Why?'

'A Michelin star is such an accolade. I mean, they're really difficult to get and everything, and it'll give the hotel such kudos. It's a public declaration that you're cooking to a certain, enormously high, standard.'

Perdita began to feel twinges of guilt. It would be a shame if Lucas failed to get his star because of Janey having the night off. 'So, this star. Is it all or nothing? I mean, if you fail when the inspector comes, is that it?'

'Well, it's more like, if you succeed on one night, that isn't it. You have to prove you're consistent. The inspector will come several times. You don't know how many. Nothing went wrong on Saturday, did it?'

'No, no, not that I know of.'

'If I'd known there was the smallest chance of an inspector coming, I would never have skived off like that.'

'Oh well, can't be helped. When will you know, anyway?'

'Not until the beginning of January.'

'A whole year away? Oh that's all right, then.'

'No it's not!'

'Oh, come on, Janey. We can't be worrying about next January now. Forget the Michelin thing and tell me about William. Are you going to see him again?'

'I bloody well hope so! If he doesn't ring me—'

'I'll sack him. Now, I must go, Janey, my feet are still killing me from last night. I can walk for miles and dig all day, but standing about on those hard floors . . .'

It was when she was in bed that Perdita's troubles really began. She yearned for Lucas, not only for the passionate, red-hot sex she remembered, but for the comfort of hearing him breathing next to her— snoring, even. Inevitably, her mind returned to their honeymoon, so many lifetimes ago. They had had a small, informal wedding, and then driven in Lucas's battered and noisy sports car up to Scotland, to where his family owned a shack on the shores of a loch.

It was very primitive. It had no electricity, running water came from the burn by the side of the building, and there was no loo. It was May, and the surrounding woods were full of bluebells, scenting the air. They ate every meal they could outside, looking at the stars, anticipating the night to come. Because they spent so much of the night making love, they caught up on their sleep at odd times during the day. Perdita got used to washing her hair in rainwater, brushing her teeth in the burn, and finding pretty, private spots to relieve herself. Lucas was so kind, teaching her to row, reading to her while she dozed, hunting among the stones for jewels for her.

He gave her a perfectly egg-shaped piece of rose quartz, which she still had, somewhere. The honeymoon was a summer idyll that vanished when they got back to London. Lucas had a high-powered job he was too inexperienced and young for. To keep on top of it, he worked long hours and when he came back to find Perdita had spent the day painting rather derivative watercolours, he grew angry. With hindsight Perdita realised that her paintings really were awful, and it was probably the job that made him angry, but he took his feelings out on her. He invited his high- powered colleagues home for meals, but Perdita couldn't cook, and her fey, romantic looks seemed childish and unsophisticated set against the sleek, well-paid women he mixed with. Perdita didn't even try to com- pete with them. She adored Lucas unrestrainedly, but even the sex, which had been so wonderful in Scotland, never worked for her again.

She never refused him, but she faked every orgasm, and though it was utterly devastating when it happened, she wasn't surprised when he found someone else.

'Bugger Lucas,' she said aloud when, heavy-headed and still tired, she got up the following morning. But she knew that the person she really held responsible was herself.

William was humming to himself when Perdita tracked him down later. While he wasn't actually grinning from ear to ear, his happiness was apparent.

'So, it went well then?' she asked him. 'You had a good time?'

'Oh yes. It was great.'

Envious, in spite of herself, she decided he could spare her the embarrassment of seeing Lucas again so soon. 'Well, I'm glad it went so well. I want you to deliver to Grantly House today. It's very straightforward. You drive the van round the back, go in through the kitchen entrance and bring the boxes with you. It'll be three loads today, I think. I've got some pea plants he ordered last week, but didn't get. He might as well have them today.'

'But supposing he doesn't want them?'

'Then he'll tell you, and you can take them back. It's no problem offloading them; I can take them to Ronnie later. Come on, William. You haven't had much opportunity to drive the new van.'

'Oh, OK.'

'Thank you, William. You're a star.'

Perdita planned to catch up on her missed sleep in front of the television. So she cursed when there was a knock at the door. Her feelings when she saw it was Lucas, were not so much mixed as homogenised. She couldn't tell if she was angry, pleased or plain terrified.

'What do you want?' she demanded, standing in the opening of the door so he couldn't get past her.

'I need to speak to you.'

'There's really no need to apologise.'

He scowled. 'I have no intention of apologising! I bitterly regret what happened, but I'm bloody well not going to say I'm sorry!' He glared at her. 'Passions run high in professional kitchens, you know.'

'Oh. So you'd've behaved like that with any of the people working there, or Janey, would you?' The thought was chilling, for lots of reasons.

He sighed. 'Perdita, you threw a glass at me, you tried to pull a knife on me, you bit me, you kicked me several times and I lost my temper—justifiably. You behaved extremely badly, and I wasn't much better, but as I said, these things happen in kitchens. Now, can I please come in!'

She held fast to the door. 'Why? You've said your piece, now go away.'

'Perdita! I've come about the cooker. You know? The one I'm having put in your kitchen so there's something half decent for me to cook on?'

'Oh God! I thought you'd forgotten about the cooker.' She meant that she'd forgotten all about it.

'How could I? And can I please come in? It's bloody cold out here.'

Perdita sighed and opened the door. It was strangely comforting to find Lucas the same ornery pig he always had been. 'I came because it's arriving today,' he said. 'I'll help you clear a space for it.'

'Hang on! Why didn't you warn me? You can't expect me to take delivery of a cooker without notice.'

'I would have warned you this morning if you'd been brave enough to show up. But actually, I only knew about it myself on Friday.'

'I saw you on Saturday. Why didn't you tell me then?'

He shot her a searing glance that reminded her only too well. 'Other things on my mind. Now can we please find room for it?'

Perdita, unclear if she had in fact told Lucas that he could put a new cooker in her kitchen, frowned. 'There's no need. There'll be space when they take the old one out.'

'The new one's a bit bigger than the old one.' Lucas took out a tape measure from his pocket. 'We many need to get rid of this shelving.'

'Well you can't!'

'Yes I can, easy. Look, it's rotten.'

'Lucas! Stop demolishing my kitchen!' A piece of rotting melamine bent like cardboard before tearing. Woodlice and silverfish darted and dived, looking for cover.

'I'll get a carpenter to come and make good,' Lucas said. 'And you'd have plenty of storage space if you didn't keep so much clutter. Here, take these.' He handed her a pile of Pyrex dishes, all opaque and edged with brown, from long-ago burnt pastry.

Perdita put the pile in the sink, not because she intended to wash them, but because the sink was, for once, empty. 'I'll go and find some boxes to put these things in. But you'd better make sure I've got some cupboard space.'

She returned ten minutes later to find the entire contents of her kitchen in her sitting room.

'I thought you might as well have a clear-out,' said Lucas, 'while we wait for the cooker.'

Perdita felt strangely detached, and watched as Lucas filled the boxes. 'What do you want done with it? Charity shop? Jumble sale?'

'Kitty gave me most of those things. I may want to keep them to remember her by when she's gone.'

'If you need this junk to remember Kitty by, your memory must have deteriorated more than hers has.'

Knowing he was right, she decided to attack him on another issue. 'Well, you'd know all about Kitty's memory, seeing as you've been visit-ing her.' She just stopped herself adding 'behind my back'.

'You found out about that, did you? I knew you'd be upset, but I wanted to see if she was better, and she seemed to enjoy my company. I think she gets a little bored of women gushing over her all the time.'

'I am not at all upset. And I do not gush over her.'

'I didn't mean you, idiot, I meant all those visitors who treat her like a little old lady.' He kicked the boxes nearer the door with his foot. 'I'll put this lot in the car, to get them out of the way. The men'll be here with the cooker in a minute.'

She perched on the window seat, watching Lucas putting boxes of her possessions into the boot of his car. She tutted at herself for her apathy. Really, she should block Lucas at every stand. Perhaps, she decided, if she wasn't so short of sleep she would have.

When she spotted a van driving up the road she set off for her poly-tunnels via the back door.

Only when she was certain that the delivery men had gone did she go back and see what Lucas had inflicted on her. It seemed to take up an entire wall. 'How am I to manage without any cupboard space or working surface? There's only the draining board left.'

'I've got a joiner friend of mine coming tomorrow. He's going to build you a counter with shelves underneath. He's going to use recycled iroko and put a bit of slate next to the cooker to put hot pans on.'

'It sounds very expensive.'

'Actually, it's not. And I'm paying anyway.'

'Actually, you're not.'

'Perdita! Don't be silly. You can't afford all this. And you would never have bought a new cooker in a thousand years.'

'You're probably right. But for whatever reason, I've got a new cooker, and I refuse to let anyone else pay for it. Anyway, how do you know I can't afford it?'

'Perdita, I perfectly appreciate how you feel. I left you in a very hurtful way, and it's very understandable if you hate me. But think about it logically. I am doing a television cookery programme because I want to. To further my career, to get publicity for Grantly House so, eventually, I can ask Michael Grantly for mega amounts of money. You must see that it's only fair that I pay for the damn cooker!'

'Yes, I see it's fair, but you don't have the monopoly on being *unfair*, you know, Lucas. And either I pay for the cooker, and all the work needed to make the kitchen habitable, or there isn't going to be a television programme. OK?'

Perdita's delight in getting her own way with Lucas was a little spoilt by the fact that Lucas had paid for the cooker already and he wouldn't tell her how much it cost. With a new cooker and kitchen confronting her every day, she could no longer keep the TV programme at the back of her mind and she was hoping Lucas would mention it when she next delivered. But he just glanced up at her when she came in with the first boxes and said, 'Janey, give Perdita a hand.'

'That's a turn-up for the books,' said Perdita, while she and Janey unloaded the van. 'Fancy Lucas letting you escape for a few seconds.'

'He's been making a real effort to be nice lately. You must have said something to him when you worked here that evening. Either that or he's practising being nice for the television cameras.'

Perdita was reorganising the cold store, so it was no longer necessary to climb over several pints of cream and a brie the size of a cartwheel to reach the lettuce, when a persistent ringing penetrated her consciousness. Unfortunately it took her a few moments to realise it was her phone, and by the time she had worked out how to answer it, it had stopped ringing. She took it through to the kitchen and sidled up to Greg.

'My phone's just gone and I didn't answer it in time. What do I do?' she murmured to him, hoping Lucas wouldn't notice.

Greg took the phone and frowned at it. 'I haven't got a mobile,' he said.

Lucas strode over and snatched it out of Greg's hands. 'You should be able to see who rung you.' He pressed buttons, producing little beeps and squeaks. 'There you are. Missed call—it shows the number.' He handed back the phone to Perdita.

The number on it meant nothing to her. 'It's probably a client. I'll go home and ring them back.'

Lucas tutted in exasperation. 'Why don't you ring them from here? That's the point of a mobile, you know. You don't have to be at your desk.'

'I need to have my order books with me, though,' she said sharply.

He ignored this. 'Are you going to be at home this afternoon? I need to have a word.'

'Can't you have a word now? That's the point of having people you want to speak to right in front of you. It saves making appointments.'

'Are you going to be in, or aren't you?'

'I'm going to see Kitty for lunch, but I'll be back early afternoon.'

'I'll call round then.'

Perdita stalked out, forgetting that she had left the cold store floor covered with boxes of salad and tubs of cream.

After she had dealt with her missed call, she went round to see Kitty and wasn't surprised to find the house empty. It was a chilly day, but the sky was bright and shot through with sunshine. Kitty, she knew, would be inspecting the progress of the bulbs she had put in the previous autumn.

Kitty was lying on her back in a lake of crocuses. Perdita hardly had time to react before she spoke.

'Hello, darling. You're late.' The words were understandable, but slow, and only one side of Kitty's mouth moved.

Perdita swallowed hard, trying not to show how upset she was. 'Kitty, what are you doing here?'

'Fell.' Kitty tried to smile.

'Why didn't you press your alarm?'

'Don't want ambulance. Ring doctor.' Kitty had obviously had a stroke, and should be got into hospital straight away. 'Please.'

Her sudden vulnerability caught at Perdita. She couldn't ignore Kitty's wishes; her being ill automatically robbed Perdita of choice. 'I'll have to go into the house and find the number.' It was in her phone memory, she knew, but it would take her too long to retrieve it. Perdita ran into the house, found the number, and pressed it into her mobile phone. Then, while she waited to be connected, she ran upstairs to the airing cupboard, gathered up a pile of blankets, and went back to Kitty. She had just dropped them on top of her friend when the phone was answered.

'Hello, it's Perdita Dylan. Kitty Anson has had a stroke.'

The receptionist was wonderful. Having checked the address, she said, 'Hang on. Dr Edwards has been visiting near there. I'll beep him.'

Perdita tried to appear cheerful as she arranged the blankets over Kitty, and folded one to put under her head. 'They're going to ring Dr Edwards on his mobile. I hope he's better with it than I am with mine.'

Half of Kitty's mouth moved. 'Gadget.'

'I know. But it would have been useful if you'd pressed your alarm. I could have been here ages ago. Are you cold?' she asked her friend. Kitty was in her winter gardening uniform of several layers of coats. Now she was covered with blankets, too. 'No? Well, at least you're well wrapped up, or you'd have died of hypothermia.'

'Good thing if I had.'

'Rubbish. If you are going to die, you want a good deathbed scene, with all the family round you, and some golden-haired children weeping. Though I suppose we'd have to hire them specially.'

Perdita kept up the chatter, managing to sound light-hearted until the doctor arrived. Then she had to turn away while he examined Kitty. He was so gentle and kind.

'I'm afraid you're going to have to have a spell in hospital,' he said.

'Damn,' said Kitty.

Dr Edwards took out his mobile phone and moved a little way away to make his call. It seemed to Perdita that Kitty was finding it harder to speak now than she had done earlier. And her eyes, which had been tranquil, had taken on a look of anxiety.

Dr Edwards came back. 'Listen, I think we are going to have to move Mrs Anson. I was hoping that if the ambulance came straight away they could do it, but it's going to be a good thirty minutes. Is there anyone you could ask to give us a hand? A neighbour, or something?'

No one was in. Perdita banged on every door. When she got back to the house, breathless and beginning to panic, she saw Lucas's car in the drive.

'Oh, Lucas! Thank God!' Perdita said, pulling him round the house into the orchard. 'Kitty's had a stroke and we need to move her, but I can't find anyone to help.'

'Oh, well done,' said the doctor, seeing Lucas. 'Well, now we've got a half-decent stretcher party, let's get you into the house, Mrs Anson.'

Kitty turned out to be surprisingly heavy. Lucas got hold of her head end, and the doctor took the other. Perdita tried to take some of the weight in the middle, but it was awkward.

When they had finally got Kitty into the house and onto the sofa, Perdita went to Kitty's bedroom to pack a few things.

Now she was alone, she let herself weep as she moved about the room, hunting in drawers for a clean nightdress, underwear, pills and reading matter. She found an ancient holdall and piled things into it.

Eventually, she rejoined the others, and the reality of Kitty's illness confronted her again.

'I'll make some tea,' she said. 'While we wait for the ambulance.'

The kitchen was still the same as ever—the gardening catalogues covered one end of the table, and the remains of Kitty's breakfast egg stood on the drainer. A pipe lay in a chunky glass ashtray, purloined from some French station café many years ago.

The doctor came into the kitchen to see how she was getting on. He caught her with tears in her eyes. Perdita hoped he wouldn't comment, but he put a hand on her arm.

'Mrs Anson is very old. She might make a full recovery, but she might not. You will have to think about how to go on from here. Unless we're very lucky she won't be able to live alone again.'

'But she will survive?'

'Of course I can't make promises. But the signs are good. It seems to be only the left side of her body that is affected, which means the right side of her brain is OK. Her speech is slow, but she isn't suffering from dysphasia—when speech and comprehension are damaged. Whether she'll ever come home again is another matter.'

'I want her here. Even if she has to have twenty-four-hour nursing. I don't want her in a nursing home.'

'Perdita, my dear, that is a major commitment. Even if Kitty can afford it, the organisation involved is a nightmare.'

'I can move back here. My business is only over the other side of the garden. I can just shut up my house and come here.'

'It may not be necessary, but it's very reassuring to know Kitty has you batting for her. Now, is that tea ready? I'm gasping.'

Kitty had made it quite clear that she didn't want Perdita to travel in the ambulance, and while Kitty was being manoeuvred onto a stretcher, Lucas offered to drive Perdita to the hospital.

'No, don't be silly! You've got a restaurant to run, and I'll be fine. I don't need to be driven.'

Lucas frowned, torn between the desire to disagree with her and the knowledge that she was right. He had got a restaurant to run.

'Really, Lucas. You don't need to worry about us. You've been marvellous. But you've got your own life to lead.'

He grunted. 'I'll ring you later, then, and promise to call me if you need me. For anything. I'm very fond of Kitty.'

'I know you are. And she's very fond of you too.'

Chapter Five

FOUR HOURS, a thousand questions and answers and a million forms later, Perdita drove her van into the gateway of her house and turned off the ignition. She was exhausted. She had left Kitty lying on a high, narrow hospital bed, looking small and frail and light years older than she had when Perdita had seen her just the day before.

She let herself into her house, planning what to say to her parents on the phone. She had her address book open and was ready to dial when there was a very quiet knock on the door.

'Who is it?' she called.

'It's me, Lucas.' She opened the door. 'I came to see if everything was all right,' he explained.

'You'd better come in. I've just got to ring my parents. If you listen, then I won't have to say it all twice.' Perdita swayed with fatigue, and Lucas steadied her elbow.

'When did you last eat?'

Perdita had answered enough questions. She flapped her hand at him, went to the phone and started dialling.

Her mother, who had never accepted that Perdita was grown up, wanted to drop everything and fly over to be there for Perdita and Kitty. Perdita, who would have liked that in many ways, refused, as she knew her mother drove Kitty mad.

'But, darling,' her mother persisted, 'it's a lot for you to cope with on your own. Old people can be so difficult.'

Perdita didn't like Kitty being lumped together with her mother's idea of 'old people'. 'Honestly, Mum, I can manage. I'd rather keep you for when I can't than have you coming over now.'

'Well, if you're sure . . . I've never got on with Kitty in the way that you seem to. But you've got to promise to tell me if she gets difficult, and we'll find a nice home for her.'

Perdita managed not to say that Kitty had a nice home, and that Kitty would stay in it while she and Perdita had breath in their bodies. 'We hope it won't come to that,' she said instead.

'And Kitty told me that Lucas Gillespie is in the area. I do hope it's not awkward for you.'

'No, not at all.' Lucas was in the kitchen, so wouldn't overhear. 'He's been very helpful with Kitty, actually.'

'So she said in her letter. But you're not going to let yourself get tangled up with him again, are you?'

'Of course not! I'm not a complete idiot!' Lucas came back into the room with a plate of sandwiches. 'But, Mum, I must go. I'm completely exhausted. I'll give you a ring tomorrow with a progress report.'

'OK, love. But don't do anything foolish, will you? Kitty has been very good to you, but you don't have to sacrifice your life to looking after her. She's not actually a relation, after all. I'm sure there must be a distant cousin or other who could be made to take responsibility.'

Perdita put the phone down before she could express her feelings on this matter.

There was cocoa to go with the sandwiches. Lucas handed her a mug and the plate without speaking. Too tired to do more than murmur her thanks, Perdita sank into the armchair and started eating.

'Right, now I know you've at least eaten something, I'll get back. I'd offer to stay, but I know you'd refuse. Let me know how Kitty is when you've seen her. When are you going in?'

'Tomorrow afternoon. But they say it'll be about a week before they will do a full assessment. They can do a lot with physio these days.'

'But she's unlikely to do her garden again?'

Perdita nodded.

'Well, I'll go. Ring me if you need me.'

She nodded again. 'Thank you for the sandwiches.'

'That's OK. I see the kitchen's reverted to being a potting shed again.'

This time, when Perdita nodded, she felt less desolate. If Lucas was still sniping at her, the world hadn't completely fallen off its axis.

When Perdita got to hospital the next day she found Kitty in a ward with three other women, lying propped up in bed. Her left hand rested on the sheet, looking as if it was no longer part of her. Her long hair was in a plait over her shoulder and she looked tiny and very frail.

'Darling,' Kitty's voice was croaky, as if she hadn't yet spoken that day. 'Lovely to see you,' she said slowly.

Perdita gulped back the tears. 'Lovely to see you, too. How are you?'

Kitty smiled with half her mouth. 'Don't know. Won't tell me. You find out.'

'I will in a minute. Let me check you over myself first. Here, I've got the regulation bag of grapes.' Perdita chatted and joked, fighting her desire to weep. When Kitty seemed to tire, Perdita went in search of information. The nurse she asked told her to wait while she fetched Sister. When the sister finally appeared, looking younger than Perdita and four times as tired, she couldn't give her much information.

'It's very early days yet. Mrs Anson had quite a severe stroke.'

'But she's not going to die, or anything, is she?'

The sister smiled wanly. 'We're all going to die—sorry, who are you again?'

'A friend—it's a long story. Mrs Anson is my nearest relative, in a way, though we're not actually related.'

'Oh. I'm not sure I should be telling you about her condition. Who is her next of kin?'

'Kin doesn't come into it. Mrs Anson hasn't got any living relatives that we know about. She's my mother's godmother, and she looked after me during the school holidays. We look after each other now.'

'Oh well, if she's got no family—she's lucky she's got you, isn't she?'

'Actually, I'm lucky I've got her. And I would like to keep her as long as possible, or at least get her home.'

'I'm afraid it's far too early to be thinking about that.'

Perdita left the hospital feeling tired and depressed. She drove her van home, heated a tin of soup and tried to have an early night. Lying there in the dark, she realised that although she was no more alone now that she had been for years, it was the first time she'd felt alone. The difference between solitude and loneliness, she said into the blackness, was that solitude was voluntary, and could be ended at will. Perhaps I should get a cat, she thought, as she curled onto her side.

The next day, Perdita decided to go to Grantly House first, in theory so she could bring Lucas up to date, but also so she could have some contact with the young and fit.

'So, how is she? Why didn't you ring?' Lucas demanded.

Perdita found herself smiling at him. His abruptness was such a relief after the hushed voices of the hospital. 'They won't commit themselves; they just keep saying, "It's very early days."'

'Is she eating?'

'I don't know. I shouldn't think she has much of an appetite.'

'I expect it needs tempting. They're probably offering her slop.'

'You don't know that. I don't know when you were last in hospital, but I expect the meals are lovely.'

He looked at her dubiously. 'I know you, too ladylike to find out whether the food is edible. I'll go in this afternoon and ask her.'

When Perdita arrived at the hospital that evening, armed with clean clothes, she found her elderly friend looking much better. The reason, she soon found out, was Lucas.

'He told the sister he was my long-lost nephew,' Kitty explained slowly, but highly amused.

'But why?'

'Sister said I could only have family members to visit. Lucas said he was family.' Kitty chuckled laboriously. 'Sister said, couldn't be. You'd said I had no relatives.' The chuckles became so strong Perdita feared her old friend might actually die laughing. 'He said you didn't know about him, he was a black sheep denied by all family members.'

'But how did he find out you were ill if he really was a black sheep?'

'Telepathy!' Kitty would have been speechless with mirth even if she hadn't just had a major stroke.

Perdita was laughing too. She could appreciate the funny side of the situation, but was more pleased with Kitty's upturn in spirits.

'He brought food,' Kitty went on, still delighted.

'Well, I don't suppose a clean nightie can really compete,' she said. 'Though I did bring "a wee dram". If Dr Edwards approves it, you might be allowed an occasional sniff of the cork!'

'How kind, dear,' said Kitty, suddenly tired after all her laughter. 'Do you know, I'm not missing my pipe at all. Do you think that means I'm getting old?'

When she got home later that evening, Perdita found an array of little pots and a note on her kitchen worktop.

You must make your house more secure and give me a key. It's far too easy to break in. Eat this for your supper, I know you won't have anything decent otherwise. Love, your friendly neighbourhood house-breaker and counterfeit nephew to the stars.

Smiling in spite of herself, Perdita inspected the pots. There was a little ramekin of some very strong-smelling pâté, a pile of matchstick carrots with threads of courgettes sprinkled with herbs and blobbed with mayonnaise, and some soup. There was a pot of chocolate mousse with a large dollop of cream on it.

Perdita ate ravenously and then glanced at the clock: half past ten. The kitchen would be quiet now. She rang the number. Lucas answered.

'Hi. Thanks for the food.'

'How did you get on at the hospital?'

'Kitty was delighted with your performance. She could hardly speak for laughing. Will you be able to get in and see her again, do you think?'

'Of course! You don't think I'd miss an opportunity to mix with all those lovely, desperate nurse, in uniform, do you?'

'It was kind of you to visit Kitty and bring her nice things to eat. And to leave me a midnight feast.'

'I know you don't eat properly, and you'll need your strength.'

Perdita did need her strength. It was hard work running her business and keeping Kitty well visited, cheerful and in clean clothes. Then one evening, after a particularly hard day, there was a man sitting by Kitty's bedside as she arrived. It could only be a doctor, and Perdita's heart sank.

'Hello, are you the specialist?' She tried to smile as he got up. 'I'm Perdita Dylan. I'm not actually related to Mrs Anson, but I look after her.'

He put out his hand. He was a pleasant-looking man, probably in his early thirties, smartly dressed with a tie and shiny shoes. 'No, no. I'm not a doctor,' he said, smiling. 'I'm Roger Owen. Unlike you, I am related to Aunt Kitty, although only very distantly. Do sit down, I'll get another chair. We can chat while Aunt Kitty doses.'

Perdita did as she was told, wondering simultaneously why on earth she'd never heard of him before, and how the nursing staff had coped with a second long-lost relative.

Roger Owen came back with another plastic chair. 'I don't suppose you've ever heard of me. I'm the son of a distant cousin of Aunt Kitty's, but they didn't speak. After my mother died I found some correspondence relating to Aunt Kitty, and I was just thinking about looking her up when a Mrs Dylan—would that be your mother?—rang me and told me about Aunt Kitty being ill.'

'It probably was my mother, but how did she know about you?' And why did she get in touch with you without telling me? Perdita wanted to add, furious that her mother had gone on a relative hunt without consulting her.

'I don't know, but she told me you were dealing with the situation all on your own.' He smiled. 'You're probably not at all pleased to see me, and have everything in hand.'

Because this was what she was thinking, she found herself smiling. 'No, no, it's nice to meet you, and I expect Kitty was pleased you came.'

He smiled back. 'She was rather surprised, and the nurses insisted I produced documentary evidence of our relationship. Fortunately I'd brought some, for Aunt Kitty, but apparently there's another nephew who's been visiting.'

'Yes, it's complicated. But how long can you stay? I'm sure we could wake Kitty if you've got to get off somewhere.'

'Actually, I'm hoping to do a little work while I'm around, so I've booked in at a hotel here in town.'

'Oh.' Perdita was just struggling to think of something to say when Kitty stirred.

'Oh, hello, Perdita, darling. How nice to see you. Have you met . . .?'

'Roger—Roger Owen.'

'Yes,' said Perdita. 'We've just been introducing ourselves.'

'Poor Roger,' said Kitty. 'I'd forgotten all about him. I never got on with his grandmother, and so lost touch.'

'Apparently Mummy got in touch with him,' said Perdita.

'Clever of her, wasn't it? I expect she thought it was too much for you, looking after me all by yourself. Quite right too. You're looking dreadfully tired. I keep telling you, you don't need to visit every day.'

'But, darling, you need some contact from the outside world.'

'Lucas can come and see me on the days you don't. One visitor a day is more than most of these poor old things get.'

'And now I'm here, I can visit too,' Roger added.

Both women regarded him thoughtfully. 'You're probably far too busy,' they said, more or less together.

'Not at all,' he said with another smile. 'I'd be delighted.'

A couple of days later, Dr Edwards summoned Perdita. 'Kitty's done extremely well. She's determined to get home. But what she doesn't quite realise is that she'll never be able to cope on her own again.'

'I can look after her . . .'

'I'm afraid you're not going to be able to manage on your own either. You'll have to have a professional carer full time.' He paused. 'It might, of course, be cheaper to put her in a home.'

Perdita took a deep breath. 'Not while—'

'I knew you'd say that,' said Dr Edwards, before Perdita had time to finish. 'You'll need to organise enduring power of attorney. You are her next of kin, aren't you?'

'I'm not sure. I'm not kin at all, really, and now she's got Roger— Roger Owen. He's some distant cousin, and visiting regularly.'

'I'd heard about a couple of long-lost nephews. Why two?'

Perdita grinned. 'One's genuine, and the other's Lucas, the chef at Grantly House. You remember? He helped us carry Kitty into the house when she had her stroke. He told them he was a nephew so he could visit.'

'Well, if he's the one bringing her all those delicious titbits it doesn't matter who he is. Eating well has greatly improved her recovery. Now,' he became more businesslike, 'Kitty's going to be able to come home in about a month. Here's a list of numbers, the district nurse, et cetera. And here's a couple of numbers of nursing agencies. It's not going to be easy for you, but if you're determined we'll give you all the support we can.'

Perdita decided to ask Ronnie for help in transforming Kitty's elegant drawing room into a bedroom fit for an invalid, or, as Ronnie remarked when he saw the task before them, turning it into 'a cross between *Casualty* and *The Antiques Roadshow*'.

'Well,' he said. 'That sofa's got to go. It's huge, probably not very comfortable, and without it we could put the bed along here.'

'She and her husband first made love on that sofa,' Perdita said.

'Well, if she wants to make love now, she'll have to use the bed, like everyone else. You said the bed had to be by a wall?'

'So the lifting gear can be fixed to it.' She gave the wall an experimental knock. 'It has to be a good wall, too.'

Ronnie gave the wall a thump. 'Solid as a rock. The bed goes here. You'll have to redecorate a bit when they put the grab handles in. Now, where is the nearest bathroom?'

'Upstairs. There's a cloakroom down here. I'm going to knock through that alcove,' she pointed to where several shelves of china were tastefully displayed, 'so you can get straight into the downstairs loo, which will become a bathroom.'

'Wow!' Ronnie was impressed. 'I bet that took a bit of persuading, to get the old lady to agree to that.'

'It was hell. Fortunately I had support from Roger—did I tell you about him? Long-lost nephew?'

'You did mention it. Nice-looking, is he?'

'All right, I suppose. Anyway, he turned up just at the right moment.' She sighed. 'I felt awful having to bully her. It's such a dreadful upheaval for her—mentally more than anything. Eventually I said if she didn't agree to pay the builders, I'd sell my own furniture and pay for them myself.'

'It's horrid having to take charge of someone's life when they've always taken charge of yours. I felt just the same when my mother died.'

They were sharing a consoling hug when they heard a car draw up outside.

'That'll be Roger. He's coming for lunch.'

'Well, I'll have a quick butcher's at him, and then leave you to it.'

Perdita offered Roger a glass of sherry. He accepted with a pleasant smile. 'I never knew Aunt Kitty when she was well, but I imagine she liked a glass of sherry.'

Perdita returned the smile. 'Well, she really preferred whisky.'

Roger frowned slightly. 'Whisky? I would have thought she was too much of a lady to drink spirits.'

Perdita laughed, bringing a bowl of salad to the table. 'She wouldn't care about things like that. She smoked a pipe, after all.'

He appeared disconcerted by this information. 'Um—is there anything I can do to help?'

'If you'd just bring the breadboard over . . . I'll get the butter. Do sit down. It's only tinned soup, I'm afraid, but I've dolled it up a bit with sherry and cream, à la Kitty.'

Roger picked up his spoon. 'It's really very nice,' he said after trying it

Perdita decided that he was, too. 'Have some butter on your bread.'

He shook his head. 'Better not. I have to watch the waistline.'

'It looks fine to me,' said Perdita, having checked.

'Only because I watch what I eat and work out.'

'Have some salad. It hasn't got dressing on it.'

'I can tell you either watch what you eat or take lots of exercise. What do you do? Jog?'

'No, dig,' said Perdita, chuckling. 'I'm a market gardener, don't forget.'

'Of course, and do you do that near by?'

'Just over the fence, really. You must come and have a look after lunch.'

'I must say I would like to see Aunt Kitty's garden. I gather it was all she really cared about,' said Roger.

'She still does care about it.'

Roger put out his hand to cover Perdita's. 'Of course she does, and I hope she will do for a very long time.'

Perdita put her hand back in her lap. 'It's easy to talk about her in the past tense because she's not here. Would you like some more soup?'

'I think I've had enough, thank you. Now,' he got up briskly, 'shall we tackle the washing-up?'

'Oh no. Let's go and see the garden.'

Roger was regarding the orchard at the bottom of the plot with narrowed eyes, and Perdita felt Kitty's reputation as a great gardener was on the line. 'It's nothing like as good now as it was years ago, when Kitty was really well, but it's jolly good considering.'

'Oh no, it's fine. How big is it, do you think?'

'I'm not sure. About an acre, I suppose. There was more before she gave me a chunk. Those are my poly-tunnels, over there.'

'I see. I expect she let the undergrowth develop to screen them.'

'I suppose they are rather an eyesore, now you point it out. I don't come to this bit of the garden much.'

'I'm sure Aunt Kitty wouldn't have minded them being there. After all, she gave you the land, didn't she? Or did she just suggest you use it?'

Perdita bit her lip. 'I don't know. Is there a difference?'

'Only technically. You may need to get the boundaries sorted out. Later.' He smiled. 'I know we've agreed not to talk about Aunt Kitty as if she was already dead, but when the time comes, do call on me if you need help sorting out those sorts of details.'

His gaze lingered on her for a second before he went on briskly, 'Now, do show me where you grow your salads.'

'Of course.' Perdita had meant to ask him what he did for a living, but now had lost her chance.

The carer assigned to Kitty was of the school of nursing that Perdita would have assumed would have gone out of fashion before Florence Nightingale's time. She appeared to be in late middle age, but had probably looked the same since her twenties.

'As the agency will have told you,' she addressed Perdita coldly, 'I am a qualified nurse, unlike most of those on our books.'

The agency had also explained that Nurse Stritch was a lot more expensive than the other carers, but that until a routine was established it was a good idea to have a fully qualified nurse.

'Would you like to come upstairs?' Perdita asked. 'Let me help you with your bags.'

Nurse Stritch inspected the bedroom that Perdita and Miriam, Kitty's cleaner, had prepared for her. It had its own washbasin, was pleasantly furnished, and had an excellent view of the garden. Perdita had washed and ironed the curtains, provided a lace mat for the dressing table as well as a huge selection of towels and a carefully arranged vase of flowers.

Nurse Stritch's lack of comment offended Perdita. 'I hope you'll be comfortable here,' she said stiffly.

'There isn't a television. Could you arrange to have one installed?'

'Of course,' Perdita replied, knowing she would have to bring her own television from home. Kitty, if applied to for funds for a television for the carer, would just say, 'Nonsense,' which might make Nurse Stritch hate her.

Kitty's arrival home lacked a fanfare and bunting, but it had all the other trappings of a state visit. To begin with, much to everyone's disapproval, she insisted on being carried round the upper garden on a stretcher, the wheelchair not being up to it.

Fortunately, Perdita had removed some of the weeds that had appeared with the spring sunshine, and once Kitty had caught up with everything accessible in the garden, she consented to be brought inside.

Kitty was appalled at the sight of her drawing room, although the builders had made a very attractive arch round the door to the new bathroom. 'It's not that it's unattractive, dear,' she said, almost apologetically, 'but it's just not mine.'

'I think you should be getting into bed now, Mrs Anson,' said Nurse Stritch. 'If you get overtired, you won't be up to your physiotherapy.'

'I'm going to put the kettle on. I'm sure we could all do with a cuppa,' said Perdita, wanting to be well clear of any flak that might start to fly.

While Perdita was making the tea, Roger arrived. She let him in through the back door.

'Hi, just come to say hello to Aunt Kitty. It's so wonderful that you've managed to get her home. I never thought she'd leave that hospital alive.'

Perdita, who had been feeling quite cheerful, suddenly found herself depressed. 'Well, she's very much alive. Go and say hello before the scary nurse puts her to bed.'

Roger seemed to get on very well with Nurse Stritch. Unlike Perdita, he seemed able to make her smile. He even coaxed her to eat a biscuit.

When Perdita went back in later with more hot water for the teapot, Kitty said, 'Perdita, my love, Roger's just been telling us that the hotel where he's been staying have asked him to leave.'

Perdita looked at him with new interest. Had he been thrown out for rowdy behaviour?

'Yes,' he said. 'They've got a big wedding coming up, which they'd told me about, and as I didn't expect to be here this long I said it was fine. Now I've got to find somewhere else.'

'I've asked Roger if he'd like to stay here,' said Kitty, 'if that's all right with you, darling?'

'Of course he can stay, if you want him to,' Perdita said brightly. 'He could have the room I've been sleeping in. Then I can go home, and Nurse Stritch will have company.'

Nurse Stritch, who had been looking quite cheerful, shook her head. 'I can't possibly look after house guests. My duties are clearly laid down.'

'But you wouldn't have to look after me,' said Roger. 'I'll just make myself at home and look after myself.'

Kitty's expression became anguished. 'I can't have you to stay if you're not properly looked after,' she said. 'Who'd give you your breakfast?'

Perdita smiled. 'Don't worry, Kitty. I'll make up another room, and I'll give him breakfast. I don't do other meals,' she said, turning her gaze to Roger. 'But I can put a packet of cereal on the table.'

Why do I feel strange about him? she asked herself. He's perfectly nice and pleasant, Kitty obviously likes him. Why aren't I thrilled that he's turned up to cheer Kitty's last years?

Perdita looked out of the window at the little patch of garden that bordered the poly-tunnels. Suddenly, the sight of some crocus foliage reminded her of something. 'I never planted the crosnes thingy that Lucas gave me,' she said to herself. 'It said I had to in March.'

She ran downstairs, picking up her book on how to grow oriental vegetables on the way.

'Now, crosnes. Rich soil, plenty of water, gross feeders. Where did I put you?' She found the pot with the tuber in it and carefully unburied it. It seemed perfect. It hadn't rotted, and still looked like a very fat brown caterpillar. Feeling this was a good omen, she spent a happy ten minutes planting it, referring to her book and muttering endearments.

When she got back to Kitty's house, Nurse Stritch looked pointedly at Perdita's fingernails. Perdita went to the new bathroom to scrub them, before she could be told to.

Roger fitted surprisingly easily into the household. He was out most of the day, wiped his feet when he came in, was tidy in the bathroom, and never left the seat up in the loo. Nurse Stritch thought he was perfect, mostly because of the loo seat.

Nurse Stritch was excellent at her job. She was gentle but firm with

Kitty, making sure she did her physiotherapy every day, and by the end of the week, when Nurse Stritch was due to leave Kitty to a lesser mortal, Kitty had improved a lot. In a strange way, Perdita was quite sorry to see her leave.

'She wasn't exactly entertaining,' said Kitty, while Nurse Stritch was giving Eileen, her South African replacement, a hand-over session, 'but she was a natural at nursing, and you have to respect that.'

'Yes, and we'll miss the physio, although she has shown me what you should be doing, so I'll be able to bully you now.'

Kitty sighed. Perdita had meant it as a joke, and Kitty knew that, but she had not yet settled into her role as patient. 'Where's Lucas?' she said, changing the subject. 'I haven't seen him for ages.'

'Well, I haven't seen him either. I gather he's away.'

'Perhaps he's sorting out that television programme business. He did say something about it.'

Perdita shrugged. 'You know more about it than I do, then. And I'm supposed to be in it!'

'I know, it's so exciting. By the way, darling, did Roger mention to you that he's got to go away for a few days?'

'Yes he did. You've enjoyed having him around, haven't you?'

'I have, rather. And with him here to fuss over me, you do get a bit more time to yourself.'

Perdita was about to protest when Nurse Stritch came in with Eileen to say goodbye. Kitty thanked her warmly and sincerely, but the two women kept up their formality, even after a week of living together.

Eileen promised to be much more fun. Although only just twenty, she had nursed a dear and sick aunt through a terminal illness, and had a maturity that offset her youth. She was also reluctant to sleep in the house with only a bedridden old lady for protection, so Perdita decided to cut her losses and went home and fetched her house plants.

A routine was soon established. Various friends of Kitty's arranged between them when they could be either at her side, or within easy earshot, so Perdita could work in the afternoons. When Roger was with them, he took on the early evenings so she could work later. If Kitty was asleep by the time she got back, he would wait up for her in the kitchen and chat. Although she knew she should be grateful, she really preferred it when he was away, so she could rush home early and have some time alone with Kitty. Now, to Perdita's secret relief, Roger had a contract somewhere the other side of the country, leaving Perdita to establish a relationship with the carers.

They worked for a week or, at most, a fortnight at a stretch to give everyone a break. There were three regulars. There was Eileen, who got on well with Perdita. She and Perdita shared the cooking, at which they were both very bad, and played three-handed bridge with Kitty, at which they were worse.

There was Thomas, an ex-merchant-navy steward, whose first appearance had Kitty and Perdita in a froth of indignation. Neither of them liked the idea of Kitty being nursed by a man. Fortuitously, Kitty needed the bathroom urgently while Perdita was making tea. Thomas, possibly aware of Kitty's uncertainty, wheeled her to the lavatory before she could protest. His masculine strength made the transfer from chair to loo much easier than usual, and Kitty very quickly learned to value him.

The last in the trio was Beverley. Beverley had never married, but had nursed first her mother and then her sister. She had a rather coy manner, which irritated Kitty, but she was so good-natured that it was impossible not to love her.

Only Thomas was happy to sleep alone in the house with Kitty, but by this time Perdita felt it was hardly worth going back home.

She mentioned this to Kitty while they had a drink together. Perdita was tired, and trying not to show it. Kitty was observing her keenly, but not making any comment.

'I could sleep at home tonight,' said Perdita. 'But I don't think I'll bother. I always leave something I really want over here. I might as well just stay put for the time being.'

'That's what I said to Lucas.'

'Lucas?' Perdita hadn't seen him for ages as William was now doing all the deliveries.

'I didn't mention it because we hardly have a moment alone, but he does visit me in the afternoons, quite often.'

'Oh—well, that's nice of him.'

'It is. Which is why it seems a good idea for him to sleep in your house.'

'What!' Perdita was outraged.

'Don't get all worked up. His flat is being treated for woodworm.'

'But how dare he suggest such a thing?'

'He didn't. It was my idea. But he said he couldn't possibly sleep in your house without your permission.'

Partially mollified, Perdita said, 'Oh.'

'Perhaps he'll pop round one evening and talk to you about it. He has turned out to be a nice man, you know.'

'So nice, in fact, that you've offered him my house.' She smiled to disguise the snap in her tone.

'Only for a short time. And it's not as if you're in it. I wouldn't want him sleeping there if it wasn't empty.' Kitty regarded Perdita over her glasses. 'I'm sorry, I shouldn't have offered a house that's not mine to offer. I would have invited him to stay here, only I feel the carers and Miriam have enough to do without having Lucas to look after.'

Perdita smiled tightly, feeling petty for minding about Lucas when he was so marvellous with Kitty.

The garden seemed to be the only place she could be on her own these days, and she made the excuse of picking some purple-sprouting broccoli to get away. On the way to the vegetable patch, she asked herself why she was reacting like this to the thought of Lucas sleeping in her house without her, when the thought of him sleeping there *with* her didn't have the same effect at all.

'But that's lust,' she said, apologising to the cluster of aphids she squashed as she picked the broccoli.

When she got back to the kitchen with her colander, she was greeted with the news that Lucas had rung to say he'd be over to see her that evening, at about eight.

'He probably wants to talk about living in your house,' said Kitty, regarding Perdita as if trying to read her mind.

Perdita smiled blandly. She didn't want to discuss her feelings for Lucas just now.

'Take her for a drink, Lucas!' demanded Kitty, the moment he arrived. 'She never goes out. She'll go green and fall over if she doesn't see daylight occasionally.'

'I get plenty of daylight,' said Perdita, unusually annoyed with Kitty.

Lucas eyed Perdita. 'I think we should go out. We can't have a good row here.'

In the pub, Lucas bought Perdita half a pint of cider. 'I expect you know why I want to talk to you,' he said.

'You want to move into my house,' she said, trying to sound noncommittal, but not managing it. 'Kitty told me.'

'I'm already moving into your kitchen—'

'And I was fine about that, was I?'

'You know you kicked up like hell about it. And you obviously feel the same about me using the rest of your space.'

'I'm not thrilled by the idea, no.'

Lucas narrowed his gaze over his pint of Old Snout. 'Why not? Kitty tells me you're not living there yourself. My presence wouldn't really make any difference to you.'

'That's not really the point. I don't like the idea of my bolt hole being occupied. Kitty's house is full of people and I'm used to living on my own. It's nothing personal.' Perdita took a gulp of cider.

'Yes, it is. If it was Janey, or her bloke William, you'd say yes like a shot. It's me you don't want there.'

Perdita contemplated continuing with the lie but decided not to. Lucas was too good at seeing through her. 'Well, can you blame me?'

'Tell me, then I'll tell you if I blame you or not.'

She took a deep breath. 'You don't need reminding of the circumstances we parted in, and I'm sure you're aware of how completely and utterly devastated I was.' He nodded. 'Well, that house represents my recovery. By the time I was in it, I was better, I'd got up off the floor, I'd made a new life for myself, I'd bought somewhere to live and I was OK. If you lived there, to me it would be like winning a prize and having to give the cup to my opponent.'

He considered this for some time. 'OK, then,' said Lucas. 'I'll find somewhere else to stay.'

Perversely, because Lucas wouldn't argue with her, she had to argue with herself. 'Where else would you go? There's not room at Kitty's with me, the carer and Roger there most of the time. She's got so much furniture and not many of the rooms are habitable.'

'Roger? Oh, the real long-lost nephew? I met him a couple of times at the hospital. What's he hanging around for?'

'He's working in the area and Kitty asked him to stay.'

'I expect he's after Kitty's money.'

'You don't really think so, do you? Anyway, why shouldn't he be? He's Kitty's only remaining blood relative.'

Lucas didn't speak for a moment. 'I'm sure he's fine.'

Perdita's drink was strong and it enhanced her tiredness. 'You probably think I'm pathetic, not wanting you to stay in my house.'

He stared into his pint to avoid agreeing that he did.

'I know it's the logical solution. In fact, it would probably be good for someone to be there. Keep burglars away.'

He put down his glass and cleared his throat. 'Peri— Perdita . . .'

He corrected himself hastily and Perdita started at the sound of his pet name for her, a name that no one else used.

'I do know how much I hurt you,' he went on. 'And there hasn't been a day since I did it that I haven't felt terrible remorse.'

This admission made Perdita feel even worse about not wanting him in her house.

'Also anger,' he added.

'*Anger?*' She felt angry now. 'How have you felt anger about me? You were the one—'

'Yes, I know all that, but while I actually ended the marriage, you have to accept that the fact it went wrong wasn't only my fault.'

Perdita had not accepted that, and, as a concept, this was actually entirely new to her.

'I don't know what you mean. How can I possibly have had anything to do with it? I loved you, I was faithful to you. How can it have been my fault, in any way?'

'You didn't fight back, Perdita. You didn't demand that I was faithful, you didn't curse me for bringing colleagues home unexpectedly. You let me get away with murder.'

'But you can't blame me for any of that! I was only eighteen.'

'If you hadn't put up with so much bad behaviour, I might have stopped behaving badly. You should have thrown me out when I came home smelling of other women, made me see what I stood to lose by abusing our relationship.'

'That's so unfair! I can't believe you're blaming me for all that.'

'I'm not blaming you for my bad behaviour, I'm blaming you for not reacting to it.'

'But how was I supposed to react? Hit you over the head with a rolling pin?'

'That's what you'd do now. You wouldn't be so bloody passive.' He looked at her with something that could have been respect. 'You've changed so much, Perdita.'

'I was so young—and young for my age. I didn't realise I had any control over my own destiny until after you left me.' She glared at him as a thought occurred to her. 'I suppose you'd say I should be grateful.'

He smiled back. 'Too right! If I hadn't left you, I'd have bullied you to death, and I expect our six children would have bullied you too. You had a lucky escape.'

'Not so lucky that I didn't avoid meeting you in the first place.'

He met her gaze with an expression that was rueful, challenging and a little amused. 'You owe me your independence, everything about you that makes you the successful businesswoman you are—*if* you are. But I don't want you to feel obliged to let me sleep in your empty house. And thinking about it, I don't want to sleep in a bed that you've watered with a million tears, because of me. I don't suppose I *could* sleep.'

Suddenly Perdita decided the whole thing was silly. If she was over him, she was over him, and if him leaving her had turned her from a mouse into a mover and shaker, perhaps she did owe him something.

'It's all right, Lucas. At first I couldn't hack it, but I realise now that nothing you can do to me can hurt me any more. Have my bed. Feel free.'

Lucas frowned. 'I don't know if that makes me feel better, or profoundly depressed. Do you want another drink?'

Perdita shook her head. 'I don't think I should. I feel sleepy enough as it is. Could you please take me home?'

The following Saturday Roger was due to return from his business trip, and Perdita wondered if she should take Lucas's comments about Roger being after Kitty's money seriously. She decided not to, and as she had a lot to do in her tunnels, she put it out of her mind. It was also change-over day.

Thomas was leaving, and Beverley was taking over. Having signed Thomas's form, Perdita left them to it and went across to the poly-tunnels. When she came back she was exhausted and longed to sink into a bath with a bad book and a glass of whisky, but Roger was there, so she felt obliged to drink sherry with him and Kitty. She made Beverley join them so she wouldn't have to talk.

'While you were out,' said Beverley, 'someone called Ronnie phoned. He was very insistent that you had agreed to have your hair cut this evening, at about half seven. Is that right? Did you have that arrangement?'

'No! Honestly, that Ronnie. He's so bossy.'

'He said he'd cut my hair too.'

'Well, what about mine?' said Kitty. 'Will he leave me out?'

They all laughed. The idea of Kitty having her hair in any way different from the two plaits around her head was totally unthinkable.

'You couldn't do that, Aunt Kitty,' said Roger. 'What would people think?'

Kitty didn't answer this question.

'Surely,' said Perdita, thinking aloud, 'Lucas would have said something if the television show was that imminent? I'll have to get the kitchen sorted out a bit and things.'

'Well, let's have our hair cut, anyway,' said Beverley. 'As I said to that Ronnie, I haven't had a chance to get mine done for ages. I would appreciate the opportunity.'

Perdita glanced at her watch. It was nearly seven now. 'Well, I must have a quick bath first. I'm covered in grime and probably stink. Let me grab a sandwich, I'm starving.'

'You're not going to eat a sandwich in the bath?' protested Roger.

Perdita nodded, heaving herself to her feet. 'If I fall asleep, Ronnie can start on you.'

When Perdita got downstairs, nearly an hour later, she found Ronnie in the sitting room. Roger was nowhere to be seen, but Beverley was sitting on a stool with a cape round her neck. Kitty was sitting in her wheelchair watching with apparent interest as Ronnie wielded the scissors. Something about her was different. Then Perdita gasped.

'Kitty! You've had your hair cut!'

'I thought it was time for a new look,' she explained, somewhat smug. 'Do you like it?' Kitty had had her hair in a plaited coronet about her head ever since Perdita had known her. Now it curved softly round her face with a short, feathery fringe. It looked wonderful.

'It's amazing! What on earth made you decide to get Ronnie to cut it?'

'I told you, I thought it was time for a new style. And it saves the carers and you having to plait it all the time.'

'I hope you didn't do it because of that,' said Perdita. Beverley was looking concerned, too.

'She did it because she wanted a new look,' said Ronnie. 'She's told you. I think she looks ten years younger.'

Perdita smiled. 'He's right, Kitty. You don't look a day more than seventy-nine.'

'Which means Perdita will look nineteen again,' said Kitty, 'when Ronnie's had a go at her.'

When Perdita's turn came, Beverley took Kitty to the bathroom to get her ready for bed.

'You'll be done by the time we get back,' said Kitty, 'the amount of washing Beverley makes me do.'

Ronnie tugged a wide-toothed comb through Perdita's curls. 'So, Perdita. What do you want? Something young and sexy to attract that man you were going to get yourself?'

'Was I really?' She bit her lip. 'Getting to know someone new is just so much effort.' She was thinking of Roger.

'Especially when Mr Wonderful is on your doorstep in the shape of Mr Michelin Star.'

'What?'

'So, take to an inch all over? An urchin cut would really suit you.'

'Ronnie! What are you thinking about? If you take off more than an inch, I'll sue you! And as for Mr Michelin Star, I don't think you know him very well.'

'Calm down, love. I was only joking. Two inches should do it.'

She closed her eyes while he combed her hair. 'That feels wonderful. Would you mind if I had a little nap while you worked?'

'Go ahead. It'll give me a free hand. But keep your head up.'

Chapter Six

IN SPITE OF HER FEARS, Perdita was pleased with her new hairstyle. It was a bit shorter, so it bounced round her face in a way that was at once youthful and sophisticated, but if she had been hoping for admiring comments from Lucas, she was disappointed.

'The television people are going to start next week,' he said when she delivered to Grantly House the following Monday. 'Can you be ready?'

'What do I have to do?'

'I'll give you a list of veg I'll need.'

'Well, don't go setting your heart on anything out of season.'

He scowled at her. 'I pretty much know what's available and when, but I would like a chance to go and have a look.'

'Come this afternoon then. You can have a tour.'

'I like your hair,' whispered Janey, as Perdita walked out of the door. 'It suits you shorter.'

'Janey! You're not here to gossip! Get on with your work!'

'There's no need to be so rude, Lucas. How are you going to cope with all those television people if you can't even be civil to your own staff?' muttered Perdita.

Lucas sighed. 'God knows!'

The sight of Perdita's poly-tunnels, filled with such delights as chrysanthemum greens, Chinese box thorn, edible burdock, purple-flowering pak choi, as well as more conventional crops, made Lucas glance at Perdita in admiration as he took notes, walking along tasting as he went.

'This lot is quite inspiring, I must say. I'll make up a list.' He sighed. 'Although I dare say they'll only let me use bog-standard ingredients you can buy at the supermarket.'

'Then they won't want me. You can buy your lollo rosso in town.'

'Oh no, they definitely want you involved. The producer was on the phone the other night. They've slightly changed their original idea.'

'Oh? Do you want to tell me over a cup of tea?'

'You haven't been in your house lately, have you, Perdita?' he asked, as they walked back together.

'No. I don't have much time to be in it, what with one thing and another.' Then she remembered that Lucas was going to stay in it while his flat was deloused. 'Why? Do you know something I don't, like, my kettle's gone missing?'

'Oh, your kettle's still there. I think.'

Alerted by his tone, Perdita hurried along the walkway to her back door and opened it.

Perdita's kitchen looked like something out of a magazine. Everything in it that she ever used had vanished. There was now a three-tiered wooden plate rack attached to the wall, next to a bar from which butcher's hooks supported a selection of copper cooking implements. There were ladles, tiny frying pans, a conical colander, a nutmeg grater, a cream-skimmer and a set of cream measures. A wire egg basket in the shape of a chicken hung next to upside-down bunches of dried flowers.

'Oh my God!' she breathed. 'It's gone all *Country Living*.'

'I know you hate it. I couldn't stop them. They are set on having it look all antiquified, and when they heard you weren't living in the house, a set designer came down and went mad.'

Perdita looked about her. 'Well, it does look pretty, I must admit. But can you work in among all this clutter?'

He laughed. 'You don't usually have a problem with clutter.'

'No, but I'm me. You're—you.'

'I shall do my best. Let's hunt out your kettle and I'll make a cup of tea. Don't go in the sitting room.'

She needed no other invitation. It was as transformed as the kitchen. It was as if the pages of a magazine had settled over her old house like a mantle. Looking carefully, she spotted a few of her own possessions, hidden under kilims and throws and log baskets, but her papers, her clutter, and all signs of her personality had been waxed, polished and dusted out of sight.

She went back into the kitchen. 'Where's all my stuff? You didn't let them throw it away?'

'Of course not. It's all in that container at the end of the drive.'

A little groan escaped her. 'And what about upstairs? Did they trash that too, or did you?'

He seemed offended. 'I wouldn't let them go upstairs. I said I had to live here and couldn't have it messed with.'

'Oh. Are you living here? I didn't notice any of your stuff around.'

'Some of us manage not to go through life scattering litter as we pass, although it must seem strange to you. Now, come and have your tea and I'll tell you what's going on. By the way, whatever else happens, and it probably will, I think we both agree that we mustn't let them find out we were once married. They'd have a field day.'

'As much as I hate to agree with you, ever, I think I have to this time.'

They perched on some wobbly but rustic stools and he opened a battered antique tin that had once, according to the advertising on the outside, contained shortbread. Now it was full of florentines.

'Have one. I'm trying them out as a base for fruit and ice cream, but they may be too dominant.'

'If this is dominant, I like it,' said Perdita, biting into a wafer of flaked almonds, glacé cherries and dried fruits coated on one side with chocolate.

'Now,' he went on briskly. 'Filming starts this Friday. It's only a half-hour programme at the moment, but it'll take three days to shoot, at the least. Will you be able to manage that, with Kitty?'

'Oh, yes. All her sitters are primed to be on call whenever they're needed. And Kitty is looking forward to hearing all about the television.'

'They want this show to be more real, with a few failures on view. And they want interaction between us. They want me to talk to you about the veg, say what it's used for and what it tastes like.'

'Hell! I know what it tastes like, but I don't know what to do with the bloody stuff! I just grow it!'

'That's what I told them. They said, "Never mind, she could have fewer brain cells than her pak choi and we'd still want her for her looks."'

Perdita found herself blushing. Whether it was because of the slur on her intelligence, or the reference to her appearance, she didn't know. 'How soon will you know what you want?'

'Go play in the garden for ten minutes, and I'll give you a list now.'

Perdita took another couple of florentines and her mug of tea, and went out into her shed. When she came back for more, he was ready. She read through it.

'I'm afraid you can't have purslane until the end of next month, claytonia's fine. Ditto sorrel, lamb's lettuce and mizuna. You can have sprouted lentils if I start now, and you can have celery leaf, but not a lot, so you'll have to be careful. You won't be able to mess it up and start again.'

He looked affronted, and she patted his knee placatingly.

'May I have another biscuit?'

He handed her the tin. 'Just as well I didn't want to use these. Do you eat proper meals, ever?'

'Of course. Whatever the carer puts in front of me. Anyway, what are my eating habits to do with you?'

'I don't want you fainting on set, or anything. The lights will be quite powerful, you know.'

'Well, I promise to eat more when we start.'

'Do it now! You can't do what you're doing, living two lives, and not have proper nourishment! From now on you'll have a proper breakfast every time you make a delivery to Grantly House.'

'Well, that would be very kind. But I won't be making any deliveries between now and the show.'

'Then I'll send William back with breakfast on a plate! But after the show, if you don't turn up, I'll come and find you and feed you myself!'

Perdita opened her mouth to make some scathing remark, but didn't. Lucas's form of caring was nannyish and overbearing, but it was also strangely welcome.

'Hi! Lucas!'

'Hello, Perdita. What have you got in your basket? Anything nice?'

Perdita felt that if she had to come in through her own back door, smiling, with a trug of now somewhat wilting vegetables on her arm again, she would tell the world she had slugs and snails and puppydogs' tails, and see what the star chef made of that.

'Well, I've got some mizuna, which is a sort of mustard leaf, some cress, some nettle tops and some Good King Henry. And over there'— she gestured to a copper bowl—'I have some sprouted lentils.'

'And did you sprout these yourself?' asked Lucas.

'No, the fairies did it,' she muttered, she thought, inaudibly.

'Heard that!' said the sound man. He was a taciturn young man in black, who held his endearingly fluffy mike like a fishing rod.

'Cut!' called George, the producer. He had replaced the charming, floppy-haired David Winter

'For God's sake, Perdita,' snapped Lucas, 'stick to the script.'

Perdita had opened her back door, smiled, and said hello to Lucas possibly twenty times. Something was wrong every time. Her patience had suffered more than her vegetables. 'But it's so artificial! Lucas asks me if I've got anything nice, as if I'm likely to say, no, I was on my way to the compost heap with this lot! It's silly!'

'There does seem to be a bit of an edge between you two,' said George. 'Or is it just the script?'

'It's just the script,' said Lucas.

'We hate each other,' snapped Perdita.

'Doesn't look like hate to me. Let's try again.'

A girl came up and powdered Perdita's nose. 'Getting a bit of shine, there,' she said.

'Actually,' said George, who had been looking at Perdita through narrowed eyes, 'I think she's got too much make-up on. I think the natural, dryad look would be better.'

Perdita, who had never worn so much make-up at one time in her life, had been rather pleased with the effect. 'We spent hours putting it all on, and I like it. Can't we just leave it as it is?'

'Just do as you're told, Perdita! You're a natural beauty, you don't need all that crap,' said Lucas.

Perdita and Sukie, the make-up girl, who'd had plenty of time to become friends, railed against the unreasonableness of the male sex together. They were in Perdita's bedroom, which had been turned into a dressing room.

'There.' Sukie flicked Perdita's face with a brush. 'That should please them, now we'd better get back or they'll go mad.'

'There's been a change of plan,' said George. 'We're abandoning the script. Perdita will come in and show Lucas her basket. He'll say something spontaneous—like, "What's this load of rubbish?"—'

'And I hit him?' asked Perdita, hopefully.

'No. You tell him what you've got, but in a light-hearted way, and he'll take a bit of each thing and tell us what it tastes like.'

'So do we need to practise this spontaneity?' asked Lucas. 'Or can we just make it up?'

'Make it up,' said George, 'but quickly; it's nearly lunch time.'

The lighting was altered, the microphone lowered, and everyone got out of the kitchen and squeezed themselves into the passage, several of them crouching down behind the table.

'Action!'

'Five, four, three, two, one—'

'Well, Perdita, what have you got in that trug of yours? Anything edible? Or do they all just have indigestible names, but no flavour?'

Perdita smiled sweetly. She had nipped back to her tunnels to fetch something Lucas hadn't asked for. 'Well, here's something that could have been grown with you in mind, Lucas.'

His brows narrowed suspiciously. 'What is it? It looks like spinach.'

'It's something you really, really need, Lucas . . .' Perdita could feel the heat of the lights on her face, she knew the camera was trained on her face. She gave a brilliant smile. 'Herb patience.'

Perdita left Lucas and the crew at four o'clock. He was cooking trout fry, which were like whitebait and looked enchanting peeping from the crust of miniature star-gazy pies. Perdita felt sorry for the tiny fish, though she agreed with everyone, they were extremely decorative.

Almost as decorative were the people who crammed her sitting room. There was a producer, an assistant, a sound man, a cameraman, his assistant, and, to Lucas's chagrin, two home economists, who had done all the preparation, and had previously cooked all the food, to every possible stage, so Lucas's genius fingers were shown doing comparatively little.

Perdita was completely exhausted and her face was stiff from smiling. Now, she collapsed into the chair by Kitty's wheelchair, grateful that the ubiquitous Roger seemed to be absent.

'I need a very large drink, then I'll tell you all about it.'

Beverley came in with the whisky bottle, two glasses and a slightly disapproving expression. She didn't think women should drink neat spirits.

'I told you about my house being turned into something out of a magazine, all bunches of flowers in inconvenient places, and piles of packing cases where they catch your shins as you turn round the corner? Well, at first the script was just as artificial, but then we asked if we couldn't just say what we were meant to say, and not use the words they'd given us. That worked quite well for a while, but I can't see Lucas putting up with it all for long.'

'Don't say any more until I've got the supper!' said Beverley. 'Roger's not coming back tonight, so we can have it on our laps, and I don't want to miss a word.'

Perdita took advantage of her absence to close her eyes for a few moments, wondering why they ate formally for Roger, when they didn't want to.

'Well,' said Beverley, putting a plate of cod-in-sauce, green beans and new potatoes on Kitty's table, and handing one to Perdita. 'Did they make you wear make-up?'

'To begin with I had the works. But then they made me take it all off.' Perdita took a forkful and had a moment of longing for the duck that had been cooking on and off all day, in a way that meant they couldn't eat it. It had ended up being sprayed with glycerine, to give it the shine it had lost since nine o'clock that morning.

'Lucas didn't wear make-up, did he?' Kitty sounded horrified.

'I'm not sure,' said Perdita. 'What he does have is women, home economists who do the food, the producer's assistant—'

'What do the home economists do?' asked Kitty. 'If they want Lucas to cook, why do they need them?'

'To save Lucas's valuable time. They prepare everything, cook it to every different stage, so you might have a shot of Lucas putting a bit of duck into a pan, but then he won't go on cooking it. Everyone faffs around Lucas like anything, because he's the star, and the more they do the more he smoulders, and the more he smoulders the more they seem to like it.' She took a large sip of the small whisky that Beverley had poured her. 'It's quite funny, really. Only everything takes so long to set up, my poor veg keep wilting under the lights.'

'It sounds terrific fun, darling. Did you eat Lucas's delicious cooking?'

'No, because it had all been kept hanging around too long. His women wouldn't let us eat it. They said it had probably picked up all sorts of bugs.'

She sighed. Now the excitement of telling Kitty and Beverley about it all had worn off, she felt exhausted. 'Would you think I was an awful spoilsport if I had a bath and a really early night? I've got to be up God knows when tomorrow, to get the day's veg organised. And I ought to send a few things to Ronnie. It's not fair to forget all about him.'

She was up at four the next morning, stealing downstairs in the dark, putting on her boots and going across Kitty's land to her own. She felt better after her long night's sleep, but she wanted to spend time in her tunnels, to remind herself what real life was like before spending another day in front of hot lights, people, and Lucas.

On the final day of filming, her energy and therefore her temper were running out. She found Lucas infuriating. He was being a bully, shouting at one of his women for cutting something up into too small cubes, and throwing a batch of alfalfa into the sink because it had gone brown.

'He's so brilliant,' said Karen, the assistant producer, and one of Lucas's biggest fans. 'He really cares about the food, which is what makes him temperamental.'

'You can care about food without having tantrums,' said Perdita, who was sorting out more lamb's lettuce, originally earmarked for Ronnie.

'He's an artist. More to the point, he's eye candy. The women will love this programme.'

'Huh! What about the men?'

'Oh, they've got you.'

Perdita muttered a rude word.

It was when 'Eye Candy' reduced one of his women to tears that Perdita lost her temper completely.

'For crying out loud, Lucas! You are such a bastard! She's trying her best, doing her job, chopping and slicing her socks off, but it's never good enough, is it? If you're not used to cooking with sorrel, you don't know it loses its acidity if it hangs around too long. You can't blame her for not knowing! You were always fucking arrogant, but now you're so up yourself, it's not true!'

Everyone was silent. Lucas didn't seem to notice the effect Perdita's outburst had had, he just went right on and had his own.

'Will you butt out? This is none of your business. She doesn't need Saint Perdita to rush to her rescue, saving every woman within fifty miles from Wicked Lucas, just because he once broke your heart. She happens to be a professional, not like you, playing about with your mustard and cress farm.'

'Children, children, what is going on?'

George rose from behind the table like a jack-in-the-box. He was staring in amazement. 'I mean, I know you two know each other, but this is looking very like a domestic!'

'Well, that's hardly surprising,' said Lucas. 'Considering—'

Their eyes locked. At the same moment they realised that Lucas had nearly announced to the world via television that which they most wanted to keep secret. Laughter sparkled in his eyes and his mouth twitched convulsively.

'Considering what, Lucas?' asked Perdita, her expression solemn with the effort of trying not to laugh.

'Considering what a very—very—exasperating woman you can be.'

Perdita got herself out of the way as quickly as possible. Beverley wasn't in the kitchen and was unaware of Perdita's arrival and, for the first time ever, Perdita didn't immediately go in to see Kitty. She slipped upstairs to one of the attics, from which she knew the view was both magnificent and calming. She needed to get a sense of perspective.

She was more shocked than annoyed to find Roger. He had a notebook and pen and was sorting through a cupboard of china.

'Hello,' she asked, somewhat breathlessly. 'What are you doing? Has Kitty persuaded you to look for something?'

He hesitated for the merest second. 'Er, yes—I mean, in a way. She did mention some photographs the other day, and I thought I'd see if I could find them for her.' He sensed her unease. 'There'll be a lot of sorting to be done when the time comes.'

'What do you mean? What time?'

'When Kitty dies. This'll all have to be itemised and a proper inventory made.'

'I expect you're right, but she hasn't died yet.'

'But it won't be long now, will it? She's very frail.'

'She's not particularly frail. She's made a brilliant recovery from her stroke. She may last for years.'

He exhaled sharply. 'Oh, come on! I don't want to seem harsh, but she's going to die soon. You have to face it.'

'I know, but I don't have to face it until it happens.'

'You need to make some preparation,' he persisted gently. 'Because I don't think things'll be quite as you expect them when she does die.'

'What are you talking about?'

'I think I should warn you—so it doesn't come as a shock—that Aunt Kitty has made it clear to me I'm going to feature in her will. With a substantial legacy.'

'But why should I need to prepare myself just because Kitty wants to leave you something?'

'You still don't get it, do you? I'm not talking a nominal hundred pounds, or whatever old ladies think is generous these days, I'm talking about most, if not all, the estate going to me.'

Perdita perched on a tea chest. Her mouth had gone stiff with shock and her heart had begun to pound. She was appalled, not because he might be Kitty's sole heir but because he was thinking about it now, before she was even in her grave. Perdita knew her knees would have failed her if she'd tried to stand. 'Roger—'

'I know she's led you to believe you're entitled to everything, but I'm her own flesh and blood, you're not even her goddaughter.' He let this sink in. 'And she already feels bad about the way my grandmother's family treated my mother.'

Perdita still felt weak. How could anyone be so mercenary? 'Oh, I know,' she said, trying to sound normal. 'She told me.'

'What did she tell you?'

'That she felt bad about the way your family had been treated, and that she meant to put things right.'

He nodded. 'She does have a strong sense of justice. But will it convert to reality?'

'How do you mean, exactly?'

'I mean, will she get round to changing her will? She could have had no idea of my existence when she made it.'

'If she wants to change it, she will. She's not gaga, you know.'

'I know this is a bolt from the blue for you, but I will see you're all right.' He got hold of her wrist and held it between caressing fingers. 'Do you know where she keeps it, by the way? Her will?'

Perdita pulled her hand away and shook her head. 'I'm afraid I haven't a clue. It's probably in the bank, or something. But what makes you think she didn't know about you before? If my mother knew about you, why shouldn't Kitty?'

'It's possible, but I'm afraid I can't take the risk.' He brushed the dust off his hands. 'We don't want Aunt Kitty's wishes ignored because we couldn't find the will.'

Perdita clenched her teeth to stop herself shouting that if Roger referred to Kitty as Aunt once more, she wouldn't be answerable for the consequences.

'I know you'll want to do what's right, and if you help me, I'll let you have anything that's of sentimental value. I'm not greedy, I just want what's mine by right.' He reached out and squeezed her upper arm.

'Let's go downstairs,' said Perdita hoarsely. 'I need a drink.'

Somehow she got through the evening with an appearance of normality. But all the time her brain was chewing over Roger's revelations about his motives. Should she tell Kitty what had happened? If Kitty had been fit and able, she would have like a shot. But she wasn't fit and able, and if she wanted to leave everything to Roger, that was her right.

Eventually she decided she'd have to think long and hard to decide what to do, and made an excuse to go to bed early.

Next morning, it was a huge relief to discover a note from Roger on the kitchen table saying he'd been called away.

The filming, scheduled for three days, went on for five. Perdita began to find it difficult to keep her business going. Ronnie and Lucas had both agreed to have whatever she wanted to give them, so she was able to cut swathes through anything that threatened to bolt, and dispatch William with a vanload. But when, on the third day of filming, she went to one of her seed tins, and discovered that the little bag of silica gel had gone pink, indicating dampness, she began to worry. She saved a lot of seed from year to year, but if she was to keep producing new salads to tempt the jaded palates of chef and bon viveur, she had to buy in expensive seed from other sources.

Her anxiety about Roger didn't help. She got up the moment it was light, did as much as she could in the poly-tunnels, and then came home to check that the Kitty-sitters were arranged for the afternoon. Then it was back to her cottage, to have her make-up put on and taken off again. After the day's filming, she rushed back to Kitty, to regale her and Beverley with amusing tales about Lucas's tantrums and the enormity of the producer's demands. On the final day she asked Sukie if she could paint on a smile for her, to save her face muscles.

Sukie laughed. 'You are looking tired, I must say. It will be better when we've all gone.'

'Yes, but I have enjoyed it. Really. It was an experience. And Kitty and

Beverley have loved hearing about it all. In fact, Kitty wants to invite everyone back for a drink before you all go home.'

'If we finish early—and we've overrun by two days, so we might—I'm sure the crew would be delighted. They've all heard so much about Kitty, from you and Lucas, it would be lovely to actually meet her.'

So, after a successful day of Lucas and Perdita fencing with words and (almost) cooking utensils, the entire crew, except Lucas, who had to go back to Grantly House, trooped into Kitty's sitting room.

She enchanted them. She found something pertinent to say to each one, she made everyone feel flattered and talented, and by the time they all left to go home, the producer was begging Kitty to let him make a documentary about her.

Perdita, who was delighted to see Kitty so happy, was also anxious about her. Her colour was heightened, which could just have meant she was having a lovely time and had had a glass of champagne too many, or it could mean she was running a fever. Oh please, God, she prayed silently, don't let Kitty die until I've found how she wants things left!

'Are you feeling all right? Not overtired by those media types?'

'No, they were delightful. I thoroughly enjoyed myself.' Kitty sounded a little cross. 'What a pity Lucas couldn't come. I haven't seen him for ages.'

'He's been dreadfully busy—filming all day and then rushing back to cook at night. He says you can lose your star if you appear on too many television programmes and seem to have dropped the ball.'

'He hasn't got his star yet, has he?' Kitty frowned.

'No—the book doesn't come out until January. But if he does get it, and the telly thing's a success, and they want to make a series with him, he wants to be able to do both.'

'Would you do a series, if they asked you?'

'Oh, I don't know. It was huge fun, but terribly time-consuming. They probably won't ask me to do another one.'

'You and Lucas are good friends now, anyway.'

'Are we? First I've heard of it. I threw a bowl of lentils at him yesterday.'

'My dear child! I don't know how he puts up with you. Still, when you're in love, you're in love.'

Perdita felt the blood rush to her face. 'What *are* you talking about?'

'Oh dear, have I said something I shouldn't? I thought you must know. It's so obvious to everyone else.'

Perdita wiped her forehead on her sleeve. 'Kitty darling, I hate to be rude to an old lady, but you're talking complete rubbish.'

'I've spoken out of turn, and I shouldn't have. It's not as if Lucas has actually said anything to me. It's just the way he talks about you.'

'Oh, Kitty, I'm sure you've got your wires crossed.'

'I'm sure I haven't. It will give me great satisfaction to see you remarried from whatever cloud they allocate me.'

'You're very sure of yourself! How do you know it won't be a red-hot tufa rock?'

'Don't change the subject. I know it's too much to hope to see you married while I'm still alive, but I'll be there in spirit.'

'Oh, Kitty!' Should she choose this moment to talk about Roger? She decided not to spoil the moment; memories of such times might be all she had of Kitty soon.

The following morning Kitty couldn't be got out of bed. Dr Edwards, visiting before morning surgery, told them, Kitty in bed, and Beverley and Perdita hovering anxiously round, 'It's another stroke, I'm afraid.'

Kitty groaned, Beverley tutted and Perdita said, 'How bad?'

'It's hard to say at this early stage and, as you know, physiotherapy can do a lot to help. But it might be a while before Kitty's able to get into her chair again. I'll arrange for the district nurse to come and see her later this morning, if I can.'

'You don't sound very optimistic.' Perdita, who was feeling near despair herself, had been hoping for something a little more bracing.

'We'll do everything we can, Perdita, but we've got to be realistic. Kitty is a very old lady. She's had one stroke, another was inevitable.'

It was hard for Perdita not to feel depressed. The amount of time spent in either nursing Kitty herself, or arranging for others to do it, was inordinate. She decided to tell Roger he wouldn't be able to stay with them when he came back from his trip. She phoned his mobile.

'I'm terribly sorry, but I'm sure you understand,' she said.

'Well, I can't say I'm surprised,' he said. 'It was bound to happen. Have you told Aunt Kitty?'

'No. I thought I'd better tell you first.'

'Then tell her I can go back to the hotel where I was before, and that I'll still be able to come and see her often, probably every day.'

Perdita subdued the suspicion that the message was really for her, not Kitty. 'I'm sure she'll be very pleased.'

'I'll call in to collect my stuff, then.'

'Oh no, don't worry about that! Just give me the address of the hotel and I'll send everything on.'

Kitty wasn't greatly put out that Roger was no longer going to be living with them. 'You must do whatever you think is right, my dear. I'm causing you all quite enough trouble as it is.'

The summer rushed past in a blur of ever-changing visitors for Kitty. The professionals: health visitors, nurses, doctors, and various carers; and then there were the social visits. Roger visited mostly when Perdita was out of the way. Whether this was tact or serendipity, she didn't know, but it did mean she could avoid confrontation. If she and Roger did coincide, he treated her with unpleasant familiarity. She almost expected him to give her an exaggerated wink and tell her 'he'd see her right'. She knew that if Kitty had been herself, she wouldn't have been able to stand him either. Although she rarely saw him herself, Lucas was one of the most frequent visitors. He brought food: morsels of duck breast, truffle mashed potato, buttered spinach, all in tiny portions, beautifully presented. Kitty, whose appetite was poor, ate every mouthful.

Caring for Kitty became more difficult. Bathing her required two people, and she became incontinent. The doctor told Perdita that Kitty really needed two nurses now, as all the kindly neighbours in the world couldn't put her on a bedpan, and Kitty often woke in the night.

Roger called almost every day, sending Perdita fleeing to her tunnels for sanctuary.

One morning Janey came to visit her there.

'Since William's been doing the deliveries I never see you.'

Perdita stuck her fork into the ground. 'I know. I never see anybody these days except carers, health professionals, and Kitty and her mates. And Roger.' She shuddered. 'Sorry!'

'It's all right. I know how busy you've been. Lucas says you're never in when he goes. I've just come to ask you a favour.'

Perdita sighed. 'As long as it doesn't require any of my time, the answer's probably yes. What is it?'

'It's about your house. You're not living there at the moment, are you?'

'Well, no. I'm at Kitty's. I only use it to make coffee and tea in. Talking of which, would you like one?'

'If you're not too busy, I'd love it.'

Perdita's kitchen and sitting room had been shorn of their borrowed finery, all of which had gone back to the various antique shops from whence it had come, but Perdita's own, familiar clutter had not yet replaced it. The kitchen still had its new cooker and worktop, and a bowl of peas soaking in the sink, and there were various bowls of lentils sprouting, but there was nothing more personal there. The sitting room was still unnaturally empty.

Perdita put the kettle on. 'So, what about my house?'

'It's me and William,' said Janey. 'We want to live together.'

'Oh.' It was hard to believe that they had reached this stage so soon,

but then she realised that half the summer had gone without her noticing, and they had got together in the winter. 'I had no idea my matchmaking had been that successful. I'm really pleased.'

Janey laughed. 'The trouble is there aren't many places round here to
rent. Not that we can afford, anyway.'

'So you want to rent my house?'

Janey nodded. 'But you could go on using it during the day. I
wouldn't want to cut off your bolt hole.' Janey nibbled a biscuit. 'I was
talking to Lucas about it, and he explained about you needing somewhere during the day, where you could get away from everybody.'

She was silent for a moment. Lucas was surprisingly perceptive for
a bully.

'But Janey, look at all this stuff.' Perdita waved a hand towards the
plastic bowls, filled with water and sprouting pulses. 'There's nowhere
else I could do it, especially not when it starts to get colder.'

'We wouldn't care about that. We wouldn't mind if you used the
kitchen—or any of the house if you wanted to.'

Perdita stirred the coffee. 'It wouldn't be fair to take money from you
when I'm still cluttering up the place. I tell you what, you can borrow
the house while you save up for somewhere else.'

'Oh, I couldn't possibly do that!'

Perdita silenced Janey's protests. 'I feel guilty leaving my little house
unlived in.' She smiled. 'So, when would you like to move in?'

The next evening, Perdita was tossing up between having an early bath,
and joining Kitty and whatever visitor it was for a drink, when Lucas
appeared. She hadn't seen him since the television programme, though
he'd visited Kitty almost every afternoon.

'Oh, hi!' said Perdita, her foot on the stairs. 'How are you?'

'Better than you are, obviously. You look dreadful. Janey told me
you did.'

She didn't feel strong enough to discuss her looks, so she attacked
him on another front. 'Oh. Was that why you let her have time off in the
morning, so she could spy on me and report back?'

'It was her morning off, but I didn't come here to argue, just to take
you out for a meal.' His raised hand to shut her up before she'd opened
her mouth. 'You never go out, you live a punishing routine of work and
caring, and you have no fun at all.'

The corner of her mouth twitched. 'And going out with you is supposed to be fun, is it?'

He saw the twitch and answered it with one of his own. 'It is. Go and have a quick shower while I see Kitty. Be ready in half an hour. OK?'

As Perdita stood under Kitty's shower, which didn't know the meaning of the word 'quick', preferring to distribute its water droplets slowly, on only carefully selected parts of the body, she realised it was quite nice to be bullied occasionally.

When her entire body had been at least cursorily washed, she stepped out of the shower and blotted herself, wondering if she should take the opportunity to unburden to Lucas about Roger. No, she'd keep Lucas as a backstop if she couldn't take care of Roger herself. Now, she'd stop worrying about things that might not happen and prepare to go out with Lucas. With him, she could be as rude as she liked, and know she didn't have to face any unpleasant consequences in the morning. She pulled on the first summer dress she found that didn't need ironing, and went to join Lucas and Kitty.

'Darling, you look lovely, doesn't she, Lucas?'

'Much better. Clean, even.'

'Isn't he kind? Lucas is going to take you out for a nice meal so you can get away from the sick room for a bit. Now, do you want a drink first? So much cheaper than paying those ridiculous prices in restaurants.'

'If you and Kitty start gossiping we'll never get away. I want to check out a colleague's place over towards Oxford, so we have to leave now.'

'It's only six thirty!' protested Perdita. 'I haven't said hello to Kitty yet.'

'Oh, do what the man says,' said Kitty. 'I've spent all day being sociable, I really don't have the energy to talk to you.' She smiled fondly, making the words into a caress.

'Very well, you grumpy old woman.' Perdita kissed Kitty's cheek. 'But I've got my mobile. If you need me, get Beverley to give me a ring.'

Once in Lucas's leather-seated car, Perdita knew she should lay into him on the matter of his overbearing nature, or some such, but she didn't have the energy.

'I hope you're not expecting scintillating conversation, or anything, Lucas,' she said, with her head back and her eyes closed. 'Wake me up when we get there.'

She woke up of her own accord before they got there, feeling refreshed after her nap. 'So, where are we going? Our local restaurants not good enough for you, then?'

'Not good enough for *you*, my sweet.' He laughed at her surprise. 'Don't worry, I just want to call on an old colleague of mine who's recently taken over a little place in the Cotswolds.'

L'Escargot was tucked between an antique shop and a shop that sold gingham napkins, rope angels and shaker-style hatboxes. From the outside the restaurant looked small, but inside it was much bigger, and although it was a weekday the place was nearly full.

Lucas murmured to the beautiful woman who came to greet them. She hurried away and came back with an elegantly dressed man who greeted Lucas with hugs and back slapping.

'You've made it at last, you old bastard! About bloody time! And who's this lovely woman you've brought with you?'

'This is Perdita. She costarred with me on the TV programme. This is Bruce.'

Bruce grinned. 'Actually, it's Anthony, but they call me Bruce because I come from Australia. Names always get changed in kitchens.' He embraced her warmly.

'Put her down, Bruce, she's spoken for.'

'Pity,' said Bruce, 'I'd better find you guys a table. Follow me.'

'Well, he seems like a nice man,' said Perdita, feeling girlish for the first time in months. 'Is he going to bring us some menus?'

'I doubt it. I expect he'll bring us some aperitifs and some canapés, and then whatever they've got that's best.'

'You mean, I won't get to choose what I eat? Supposing they give me something disgusting, like sweetbreads, or brains?'

'You must learn to educate your palate. After all, you might become a cooking celebrity.'

'Might I? Why? It was just a pilot.'

'Wait until you see the programme. They're seriously considering doing a series, with us both.'

'I shall demand a huge increase in salary, then.'

'But you'd do it?'

'Oh, I'll do anything for money.' She laughed.

Although certainly not a gourmet, and not usually very interested in food, Perdita thoroughly enjoyed herself. Lucas had been right when he'd told her the L'Escargot people would just bring what they thought were their best dishes. Perdita never thought she'd manage to eat it all. Starting with hand-dived scallops and finishing with an assiette of puddings, there were about seven courses in all. They were all tiny, beautifully presented, and in Perdita's opinion, with the exception of the salad, which she pronounced unimaginative, it was all delicious.

Bruce brought each dish to Lucas, and stood over him while he tasted it. Lucas chewed each first mouthful with the concentration of a man who was reading something it was imperative that he understood and remembered. Bruce stopped his wisecracking until he had received the verdict. Perdita had expected Lucas to be critical, but he was surprisingly generous with his praise.

After the first time, when Bruce had gone away, smiling broadly, Perdita said, 'I'm surprised you were so polite about that. I thought you'd be really picky. You're so bloody fussy in your own kitchen.'

'Because I have high standards, it doesn't mean I don't appreciate other people's good cooking when I come across it.'

'Glad to hear it. Although I think these scallops are a bit chewy.'

He narrowed his eyes over his wine glass. 'Oh really? Well, don't tell the chef, he'd be heartbroken.'

She chuckled, enjoying herself more and more. Bruce joined them whenever he could and his presence took away any awkwardness Perdita could have felt about being alone with Lucas. Their relationship was so strange nowadays. They weren't quite 'just friends', although 'friends' most nearly described their relationship, and they certainly weren't anything else.

For tonight, Perdita put all such complications, all other concerns, aside. Both men flirted with her shamelessly, making her feel witty and attractive; she enjoyed the food and the surroundings. While they were toying with the cheese, finishing up the last of a very good red wine, Lucas pronounced himself impressed with the meal.

By this time Perdita had had rather a lot to drink. Each course had been accompanied by a different wine and, as Lucas was driving, he had taken only one critical, crunching, swilling sip from each one. She had happily consumed a full glass each time. Now she gathered up a few biscuit crumbs with her finger, suddenly melancholy, aware that her freedom from responsibility was nearly over. 'It was so kind of you to bring me, Lucas. I've had a lovely time.'

'Kind! Not at all. I wanted you to come.'

Perdita shook her head. 'After the telly programme is out, you won't need the likes of me. You'll have women after you in droves.'

'Then I'll beat them off with a big stick. I don't want women after me in droves.'

'Of course you do. All men do.'

He shook his head. 'No. Some of us just want a lifetime of commitment with the right woman.'

The sudden seriousness of his tone unsettled her. She took refuge in sarcasm. 'Oh, really?'

'Yes, really. People do change, you know. Years pass, stuff happens, people want different things.' He looked at her intently. 'Don't look so anxious. I'm not about to make any embarrassing declarations.'

274

'I'm not looking anxious,' she lied. 'I've just got indigestion. I've had more to eat this evening than in the last fortnight put together.' This was probably true.

Perdita slept all the way home. When she got out of the car, and they were both standing by the gate, she forgot it was Lucas, forgot all the many complicated strands of their relationship, gave him a hug and kissed him on the cheek.

'Thank you, that was absolutely wonderful. I had a brilliant time.'

Although his arms came round her, he didn't hold on when she pulled away. 'So did I, Perdita.'

He sounded wistful, as if he had been dismissed.

She tiptoed in to check on Kitty and found her awake.

'Not waiting up for me, I hope?' said Perdita.

'Of course not. You're old enough to stay out as long as you like. I just want a bedpan.'

While she was dealing with Kitty, Perdita realised that her skin felt warmer than usual. 'Do you feel all right?'

'I'm fine,' said Kitty unconvincingly.

'Let's take your temperature.'

Kitty made token grumbling noises while Perdita searched for the thermometer, but she didn't protest when Perdita stuck it under her tongue.

'Now, while it cooks I'll tell you about this evening. The food was superb! I think I could get into this gourmet lifestyle.' She chatted on, fetching the bedpan, lifting Kitty onto it and afterwards straightening the bed and plumping up the pillows. When she came to look at it, the thermometer told her she was right, Kitty's temperature was up.

'OK,' she told Kitty. 'I can either wake Beverley, who'll know if I can safely give you a couple of paracetamol with all the stuff you have to take anyway, or I can just pop you a couple of pills, and see how you are in the morning. What do you think?'

'Beverley will want the doctor, and I'm not having him disturbed in the night. Just give me the pills. I'm sure I'll be fine in the morning.'

'Do you want me to stay with you?'

'Of course not! I've got the bell. I'll ring if I need you. I'll be fine now I've been to the lav.'

Perdita was woken by Beverley banging on her door. It had taken her a little time to drop off after seeing to Kitty, and so she was in the depths of sleep at seven o'clock, an hour later than she usually woke up.

'I think it's time you were up, dear,' called Beverley. 'I've made tea. It's downstairs. Mrs Anson isn't well, I'm afraid. The doctor's on his way.'

Perdita was overcome with guilt. If she'd woken Beverley, or even called the doctor herself, Kitty's chest infection might not have got so bad. If she hadn't gone out she would have been aware of Kitty becoming ill during the evening, and the antibiotics could have been started immediately. The chest infection might not have got a hold.

Dr Edwards spent precious minutes reassuring Perdita that Kitty was probably perfectly well at bedtime, and only developed the infection later. 'Don't worry about it more than you can help, and for God's sake don't feel guilty about going out for an evening. You have to have some time off, Perdita, or you'll get ill yourself.'

She rang Lucas. 'Hi, it's me. Thank you so much for last night. It was brilliant, but I'm afraid Kitty's got a chest infection.'

'Oh, I am sorry. Is she going to be all right?'

'The doctor says so. But I thought I'd let you know in case you were going to call this afternoon.'

'I'll pop over anyway. I've got some news for her.'

'Oh? What?'

'We've got a date for the transmission of the telly programme. A couple of weeks from now.'

'I can't wait to see it. Or can I? It might be desperately embarrassing.'

'Not a bit of it. You'll look lovely, I assure you.'

Kitty's chest infection got better, but she didn't seem to improve with it. Her appetite disappeared and she had to be tempted into eating every mouthful. She woke more often in the night—so often that Perdita made up a bed on the floor in Kitty's room, to save having to drag herself awake and almost fall downstairs.

Perdita and the doctor discussed her prognosis.

'You're not going to be able to manage with her like this for long, Perdita. You're going to have to think about either employing more nurses—and I mean nurses, not just carers—or a home.'

'It'll have to be nurses. I won't let her go into a home.'

'It'll cost a fortune.'

Should she voice her concerns about Roger to the doctor? There wasn't anything he could do about it. 'Not if she doesn't live very long.'

'She could go on for months, even years like this. You, on the other hand, can't. Not when you've got your business to run.'

She opened her mouth to say that the business could go hang, but didn't. 'I wish I had someone I could ask,' she said instead.

'You could ask a solicitor. Did you ever arrange enduring power of attorney, like I suggested?'

'No.' She sighed. 'I know it's silly, but at the moment Kitty still has all her wits. I don't want to treat her like a dependent relative, incapable of making her own decisions.'

'I'm sure Kitty appreciates your discretion, Perdita, but she could have another stroke tomorrow, be unable to speak, or write, or communicate in any way. What are you going to do then?'

'Whatever I have to, I suppose.'

'You won't be able to access her money, you know. You'd have to go to the Court of Protection for permission. She could be a millionaire, and have to moulder away in a hospital for months, before you could get permission to put her somewhere more comfortable. I'm sorry to be so harsh, Perdita, especially at a time like this, but you have to face facts.'

Perdita did get as far as finding out who Kitty's solicitor was but he was on holiday. As she didn't want to speak to anyone else about Kitty's affairs, it still wasn't organised before the TV programme was broadcast.

The morning it was due to be shown, Roger rang. He wanted to check what time the programme was so he could see it with Kitty. When Perdita got the message she bit back a cry of rage and frustration and sighed instead. There was no point in wishing she and Kitty could just watch the programme on their own because they couldn't. No amount of hysterics would alter that.

Thomas was the carer at the time, which was somewhat of a relief. Beverley had done two weeks, and although she was pure gold, she got on Perdita's nerves. Perdita suspected she got on Kitty's too, but Kitty wouldn't confess it. She complained less the iller she became. She was sinking into herself, perfectly lucid, polite, yet somehow diminished.

But the thought of seeing the television programme she had heard so much about cheered her immensely. She greeted Roger quite warmly, and then turned to Thomas. 'Be a kind man and go and look in the cellar and root about for some champagne. Put a couple of bottles in the freezer, we'll have them while we watch the show.'

They all sat together in Kitty's room. Thomas distributed glasses of champagne and packets of crisps, and they settled back to watch.

First of all came a long shot of Perdita's cottage. It looked more fairy tale than ever, and she could see why they had been determined to use it. Then up came the titles: *A Gourmet and a Gardener*.

'I had no idea they were calling it that,' said Perdita. 'How embarrassing!'

'Shush, dear. Have some more champagne.'

Kitty was sitting up in bed, more attentive than she had been for a long time. Perdita decided to stop being embarrassed, and just enjoy the show. She hadn't realised how photogenic Lucas would turn out to be. His smouldering bad temper was punctuated with dazzling smiles. No wonder all the female crew had idolised him.

Lucas gave a short spiel about what he was going to cook, and then Perdita watched herself come in through her own back door—except it wasn't herself, or her back door, it was this dreamy, girl-woman, and her back door was the entrance to a quaint old cottage, bursting with charm. But it was when they started to speak to each other that the show really took off. They sparkled and sparred, responding to each other's offhand remarks, throwing out challenges. Everything he cooked, or appeared to cook, shone with the same brilliance. Her vegetables were fresh and pretty and appetising.

'Wow,' said Thomas, when the show was over. 'I think you girls should have another glass of champagne.'

'It was marvellous, darling. You look so beautiful and Lucas looks so handsome. You really are a lovely couple.'

'Yes, they are, or were,' said Roger, producing something from his pocket. 'Look what I found.' He laughed. 'I wonder if I could sell it to the tabloids and make my fortune.'

'What have you got there, dear?' asked Kitty innocently.

'It's a picture of Perdita and Lucas, outside a register office—proof that they were once married. It might cause quite a scandal if I let that cat out of the bag, mightn't it?' Again he laughed, but this time it didn't look as if he was joking.

Thomas said nothing. Perdita tensed.

'Show me,' demanded Kitty.

Roger handed over the picture. 'Mmm,' Kitty said thoughtfully. 'You were a pretty girl then, but much better-looking now. Where did you find the picture?'

Roger was a little thrown by this reaction. He'd expected a scene and hadn't had one. 'Oh, in the attic, in a box marked PERDITA.'

'And what made you want to go up to the attic? Did you have business there?'

'Perhaps he went up to look at the sunset,' suggested Perdita drily.

'That was it. I met Perdita on the same errand.' He smirked at her, implying an assignation. He plucked the photograph from off the bed and tucked it back into his wallet.

Perdita, who was watching his every move, noticed, as he dealt with the photograph, a business card with the name of Kitty's solicitors on it.

'Now, Roger, dear,' said Kitty, still in that same calm, nannyish tone, 'I think you'd better go now. I'm really quite tired. Thomas, would you be so kind as to show Roger out?'

When they were alone, Kitty said, 'That side of the family were always frightfully common.'

Perdita drew breath to tell Kitty that being common wasn't their only fault, but then she saw that Kitty had fallen asleep.

Chapter Seven

SOMETHING TOLD PERDITA that Kitty was dead even before she opened her eyes. She had not got Perdita up in the night at all, and unlike with many of the dying, Kitty's breathing had not become laboured. But it might have been the silence that woke Perdita. She wriggled out of her sleeping-bag to check the time. It was a quarter past five in the morning. Perdita waited to cry, to feel a rush of tragic emotion, but none came. She felt perfectly calm, and relieved for Kitty. From her point of view, being totally dead was better than being mostly dead, full of drips and tubes and medicine that would keep her alive, but not well, for another few weeks.

It was also wonderful that Kitty had seen the television programme. She had thoroughly enjoyed watching Perdita and Lucas setting sparks off each other, noticing every time the show had been cut to avoid offending the viewers with violence and bad language.

And now she was dead.

Perdita sat on the chair where she had sat to feed Kitty, to read to her, to gossip with her, and silently to pray for her. Perdita had been dreading Kitty dying, both consciously and subconsciously, for years. Now it had happened and she was alone in the world. She had her jet-setting parents, of course, but Kitty had always been *here*, constant, reliable.

Still perfectly calm, Perdita wondered which aspect of Kitty she would miss most: the supportive sage, adviser and comforter, or the witty, interesting friend. Instantly, she decided it was her friendship that would leave the biggest gap. Now Kitty was actually dead, who could she share jokes with, make cutting little remarks to, remarks she would be ashamed to let anyone else hear? Lucas came into her mind, probably put there by Kitty, whose spirit seemed to hover around. That was an area where Perdita was bound to disappoint Kitty. Her romantic old heart, heavily disguised by a crust of cynicism, had wanted them to put aside their differences, fall in love and get married. But Lucas had broken Perdita's heart once, and once was enough, thank you very much.

Perdita sat with Kitty until six o'clock, when Thomas came in. 'Morning,' he said in a low voice. 'How's the patient? Oh.' He looked anxiously at Perdita, who felt oddly detached and calm, but otherwise tranquil. 'I'll make us a cuppa. Have you been up long?'

She shook her head. She didn't feel in the least like crying but she didn't trust her voice. Thomas seemed to understand. 'Back in a tick.'

Perdita sighed. She would have to ring her parents, and they would come flying back, her mother trying hard to take over. They would fill the house with funeral etiquette, they would panic about the amount of books and furniture to sort out, and try to get Perdita to call in a house-clearance firm, all before poor Kitty was buried.

It's not, she told herself, nearly out loud to make it more convincing, that I don't love Mum and Dad, because I do, very dearly. But this had been Kitty's space, and her own, and she didn't want them moving in on it, tidying Kitty's personality away.

And then there was Lucas. She'd never persuade Lucas, even if she dared to ask him, to behave as if he was not an intimate of the household. When her mother saw this was the case, she would descend into paroxysms of maternal anxiety. Luckily for Lucas, Perdita's mother was unlikely to say anything to him about the unsuitability of his presence, but Perdita would not be spared.

Perdita got up and stretched. She seemed to have been sitting a long time. She went to the window, and looked out across the lawn, newly cut by Thomas, and dew-spangled. The garden looked lovely, although Perdita always felt a little sad when summer began to turn to autumn. She never quite knew why this should be; as she always told Kitty, it wasn't as if she minded winter. It was just the turn of the year that made her melancholy. The tiny purple and white cyclamen, which Kitty and Perdita both loved, were a sign that summer was over. Their appearance always caused Perdita's heart to sink a little

Thomas came in with tea and shortbread biscuits. Kitty always had a shortbread with her early morning tea and it seemed right that Thomas and Perdita should have them now.

'You'll have to start ringing people. The doctor, and then your parents.' He was quite firm about this, as if he knew she would have preferred to get the arrangements under way before telling them. 'If they're halfway across the world, it'll take them a few days to get here. You will have got it all sorted before they arrive.'

She nodded. 'I'll make a list.'

'And Roger. Otherwise he'll turn up as usual. Talk about an ambulance chaser!'

Perdita chuckled gently. 'OK, I'll ring him.' She shook her head as she reached for a pad and pen from Kitty's bedside table. 'Now, who else? Doctor, undertaker, newspapers for an announcement—'

'Lucas,' he interrupted firmly. 'He loved Kitty. You can't let him hear it from anyone else.'

On the dot of eight, Perdita rang Lucas. She didn't need to say anything. The moment he heard her voice he knew what had happened. 'Are you all right? I'll be there as soon as I've got some clothes on.'

Still Perdita couldn't cry.

By the time Lucas got there, the doctor and the undertaker had been telephoned. Lucas stood on the back doorstep, with his arms half opened, ready to receive a sobbing Perdita. Only Perdita wasn't sobbing, didn't want to start, and felt that being hugged might release a lot of emotion she didn't have time to indulge in.

'Hello, Lucas. Do you want to see her? Or would you rather not?'

'No, I'd like to, otherwise I'll never believe it's really happened. Come with me.'

Together they stood and looked at the woman they had both loved.

'You know,' said Perdita, 'of all the things I admired her for, and there were a lot of them, one of the things I thought was bravest was having her hair cut. She hadn't changed her hairstyle for about seventy years.'

'It suits her,' said Lucas.

'She wants—wanted—you to have her books, you know. As many as you have room for, at least. She didn't want to burden you with them.'

'Of course I don't have room for many, but there are some I'd treasure. Is it in her will?'

Perdita shook her head. 'I shouldn't think so. I don't know what's in her will, to be honest.' She frowned.

'But surely she'll leave everything to you, won't she?'

'Not according to Roger. He was very intent on getting her to leave it all to him, as a blood relative, you understand.'

'Bastard!' he whispered. 'But surely you'd know if she'd changed it?'

Perdita shrugged. 'He was here a lot, and I was out a lot. I wouldn't necessarily know about it.'

'And you never asked Kitty?'

'No. The moment was never right, and by the time it was, she'd gone to sleep. That was last night.'

'I see.'

'I don't care about Kitty's money, although I do care a little about this house; it was home for such a long time. But what really bothers me is that Roger knows that Kitty never gave me my land officially. I just use it, but I'm pretty sure she won't have had the deeds altered, or anything.'

'And he'd take that land away from you?'

'With the utmost of pleasure.'

Lucas bit his lip, struggling to keep back his anger. 'Jesus, Peri, I wish you'd told me about this, when I could have done something about it!'

'I probably would have told you sooner or later, but I didn't expect her to die so soon.'

He put his hand on her shoulder. 'No. We none of us did. Is the doctor coming to do the death certificate?'

'Before morning surgery. The undertaker's coming later.'

'Are you going to leave her here for a bit?'

'I don't know. What do you think?'

'I think it's up to you. But somehow I don't think Kitty would like people looking at her when she's not at her best. You could get out lots of photographs of when she was alive and well, instead.'

'That's what I'll do. I'll let the undertakers take her away, and get out photos. There are some lovely ones. She was very photogenic.'

Perdita sent Lucas away when the doctor and the undertaker had been. Like the doctor, the undertaker had looked at her dry eyes suspiciously. Perdita, painfully aware that she was not behaving as expected, hoped she didn't appear hard-hearted. She said as much to Thomas.

'No one who's known you for more than five seconds could think you were hard-hearted, love. You just do what you feel you need to, and don't worry about what people think. Have you rung your parents?'

She changed the subject. 'Thomas, would you be willing to stay on until after the funeral? I know you're paid to look after Kitty, but could you look after me, too? I'll never get the house organised on my own.'

'I wouldn't leave you now, Perdita, love. As long as you don't think Lucas will mind us being alone in the house together.'

Perdita frowned. 'Lucas? What on earth has he got to do with it? I'll ring Roger and get that over, and then I'll call my parents.'

Roger was nauseatingly sentimental about it, referring to Kitty's 'passing over', and then he mentioned the funeral. 'Just a few sandwiches and cups of tea for anyone who comes back to the house, but I don't think we should encourage it. No point in spending money unnecessarily.'

Perdita drew a deep breath. 'Roger, I don't care if Kitty's left you every penny in her will, but she is going to have the sort of funeral I know she would have wanted. If you think we're going to fob people off with tea and sandwiches, you don't know me or Kitty very well.' Elated by this outburst, she felt more than able to handle her mother.

Perdita's mother was very good on the phone. She checked that Perdita was all right, and said that she and Perdita's father would be over within three days. 'Will you be OK on your own until then?'

'Oh, yes. I've got Thomas, the carer. I thought he might as well stay and help me get ready for the funeral next Thursday.'

'But what about Roger? Couldn't he do all that?'

'He's got a bad back,' Perdita lied.

'Well, I'm sure you know best,' she said, meaning just the opposite.

'I do. Thomas is brilliant and as strong as a horse, and we've got lots of furniture to move before the funeral.'

'Now, Perdita, dear, you must be sensible about the furniture. I'm sure none of it's as valuable as Kitty thought. Just get a house-clearance man in and get him to give you a good price.'

Should she break it to her mother about Roger now? No, it was a long-distance phone call and not worth the uproar the news would cause. 'It's OK, Mum. When the time comes to sort out the house, I will be sensible. But Kitty's only just died. I won't be getting in the removers for a while yet.'

'Oh, darling, how tactless of me. Now you go and have a good cry, and I'll ring you tonight to tell you our arrangements.'

Perdita didn't have a good cry, she dashed across to her poly-tunnels and did some work. She sorted out the deliveries, and when William arrived, told him about Kitty.

'Of course, it is sad, but it would have been sadder if she'd lingered too much longer. Her quality of life was going every day. It's a relief, really.'

William nodded. His relief was at the fact that Perdita wasn't sobbing and he didn't have to feel obliged to comfort her.

'I will have to depend on you rather a lot, I'm afraid, as I will be a bit frantic until after the funeral, but you've been so great already. I think you actually like making deliveries.'

'It's all right when you get used to it. Janey always checks the order for Lucas, and Ronnie's OK when you get to know him.'

'I'd be grateful if you'd tell Ronnie about Kitty. He'll want to know, but I'm a bit tired of telling people over the phone.'

'He'll be sad. She was much loved, your—Kitty.'

Perdita nodded. 'She was. Now, I must get on. Is Janey in the kitchen, or has she gone?'

'No, she's there. She'll make you a nice cup of tea.'

She shared breakfast with Janey, but got away as quickly as she could. While she was working, Perdita could forget that Kitty had died, and all that that entailed. But she couldn't stop thinking about Kitty as a person: Kitty when Perdita had first met her; Kitty in the garden, pipe between her teeth, muttering curses on the aphids; Kitty with a glass of whisky in her hand, looking at the sunset, a smudge of earth on her cheek. That was the real Kitty.

Perdita's positive attitude lasted until she went back to Kitty's house. Thomas had cooked her a lunch of sausages, mashed potatoes and green beans. 'Now, get that down you. Have you arranged to see the vicar?'

Perdita nodded. 'I'm a bit nervous about it. Kitty wasn't religious in a conventional way. He's popping over at tea time.' She looked at her watch. 'Which means I must finish this and be off.'

Thomas tutted. 'You eat your lunch. You'll do yourself no good gulping it down. You'll get a hiatus hernia, and you don't want that at your age.'

'I'm sure I don't want that at any age,' she said with her mouth full.

'I did meet Mrs Anson,' said the vicar, who was young and untidy, and asked Perdita to call him John. 'It was at a coffee morning in the village. She was wonderful—absolutely charming.'

'Her beliefs weren't exactly conventional, I'm afraid.'

'Don't be afraid. We had a long talk about her beliefs, and I must say I enjoyed the conversation, even if she did challenge me on rather a lot of my best points.'

Perdita chuckled.

'Would you like to read something? Or say something? You could write a bit about her life. I bet it was interesting.'

'It was, of course, and I wouldn't mind writing something, but there's no way I could read it out loud in church.'

'That's OK. Get someone else to read it.'

'But who? Would you do it?'

'Of course, but it would be better if someone else did, someone who knew her well. Why don't we talk about music, and perhaps you'll think of someone, or someone will volunteer?'

The vicar left Perdita with the task of writing an essay on Kitty, and worse, of finding someone to read it. Should she find someone of Kitty's generation to do it? Or should she ask Lucas, who would be unlikely to break down in tears, and of whom Kitty was very, very fond?

'I don't suppose you'd do it, Thomas?' she asked him at supper.

He shook his head. 'Ask Lucas. He's the obvious choice. And I'm sure he'll be chuffed to be asked.'

Perdita took a sip of the wine that Thomas insisted she drank. 'I'll think about it. I'll move out of Kitty's room now, and into somewhere smaller. Then we could put a couple in her room. We're bound to have to put lots of people up.'

'Would you put your parents in there?'

'No. I thought I'd put them in my house.'

'But aren't Janey and William living there?'

'Oh my God! I'd completely forgotten! And I can't face having my parents here.'

'Well, don't worry. Give Janey a ring and tell her. I'm sure it won't be a problem for them to move back home for a week or so.'

Janey was just as understanding as Thomas said she would be. 'Of course I understand, Perdita! And I'll make sure we leave the place absolutely gleaming. No condom wrappers on the floor, or anything.'

Perdita was chuckling as she put the phone down. 'Janey promises she'll leave everything tidy,' she said to Thomas, 'but I'll go and check.'

'Your parents should be able to cope with a bit of dust.'

Perdita shook her head. 'If I don't appear to be in control of everything, my mother will just take over.'

Thomas frowned. 'Well, in her absence, I'll tell you it's time for bed. I'll clear up. No arguing. You're paying for a carer, just be cared for! OK?'

Perdita felt impossibly tired. She climbed into Kitty's bed upstairs, in spite of her intention to make herself a space somewhere else. She fell asleep the moment she put out the light, and woke again four hours later. She lay, listening to the World Service until six, when she got up, left a note to Thomas, and went to her poly-tunnels. When she'd sorted out the day's deliveries for William, she went back to the house and organised furniture, telephoned people, received condolences and burrowed in the airing cupboard, searching for sheets and pillowcases and duvet covers.

Between them, she and Thomas cleared Kitty's mahogany kitchen table for the first time in years.

'Keep it clear at least until after the funeral,' said Thomas, rubbing the table with polish. 'We'll need somewhere to give people meals.'

Perdita nodded. 'Kitty's cleaner will be delighted. She's been polishing it in sections for years, and Kitty always just put the junk back on it. Now it can be admired properly.'

On Friday evening, the day before her parents were due to arrive, Perdita went across to her own house to sort out her bedroom for them. In spite of Thomas telling her it was fine to leave it to Janey, she had to make sure for herself that everything was in order. It would be the first time she'd been upstairs in her own home since Kitty's death.

Her kitchen, which she'd been using to soak and sort her pea plants, looked empty and strange. Janey had removed all traces of her and William's domestic bliss.

The sitting room was also unnaturally empty, and she dumped her armful of clean bed linen on the back of a chair. She was rummaging in the cupboard under the stairs for a duster and some polish when the back door opened. She jumped as Lucas appeared.

'Sorry, did I give you a fright?'

'Yes you did! What on earth are you doing here?'

'Actually I came to make sure Janey and William had left the place reasonably tidy. Janey told me your parents were going to stay here.'

Perdita relaxed. 'How kind. I was on the same errand.'

'I was coming to see you afterwards. How are you?'

Perdita was becoming accustomed to this question. It was always followed by the sort of peering look that at normal times would be considered rude. 'I'm fine. I just wanted to put clean sheets on the bed and stuff, but I have only one set of things, so I brought some of Kitty's.'

'How do you usually manage?'

'Oh, I choose a fine day and wash them and dry them and put them straight back on the bed.' She made a face. 'Don't tell my mother; she'd be horrified.'

'Don't worry, I don't expect she'll ask me. I never was her favourite person, was I?'

'You're still not.'

He was silent for a moment. 'Do you want a hand with the bed?'

'Probably.' She sighed and picked up the bedding. 'Come on. It might be a dreadful mess up there.' She bit her lip. 'I never checked it before you had it. Was it OK?'

'I don't know. I never went upstairs. I just slept down here, on a camping mat. I thought you'd have known that.' He smiled ruefully, biting his lip. 'There was me, going to so much trouble to be sensitive, not to intrude on your space, and you didn't even notice.'

She smiled back. 'And there was me, making such a fuss when Kitty offered you this house, and I wasn't even aware of you being here.'

There was a moment's silence. All their quarrels suddenly seemed childish. 'Come on. Let's get this done.'

Before Kitty's death, she would have felt awkward going into her bedroom with Lucas. Now she felt perfectly matter of fact about him catching the opposite side of the sheet and lowering it onto the bed.

'Lucas, I wonder if I could ask you a favour?'

'Anything. I'm yours to command, Perdita.'

She smiled. 'This is for Kitty, really.'

'What is?'

'The vicar suggested I wrote about her, so that people who didn't know her when she was young would know something of her. I couldn't possibly read it myself. I was wondering if you would.'

'Shouldn't you ask someone like your father?'

Perdita shook her head as she stuffed a pillow into a clean case. 'He and Kitty never really got on. It should be someone who knew her well, and who loved her.' There was a tiny pause. 'Also, someone Kitty loved.'

Lucas didn't answer immediately. He pulled off the duvet cover and started to put on the new one.

'So, will you read my thing about Kitty, or not?'

Lucas emerged from inside the cover of the duvet. 'If you want me to.'

'I said, it's not for me, it's for Kitty.'

'But do *you* want me to read it, Perdita?'

There was a moment's silence in which something intangible and unspecific hung. Perdita wanted to tell him that yes, she did want him to. Instead, she nodded, and put her hand on his wrist. 'Mmm.'

He put his hand on top of hers but still hesitated. 'Then I'm flattered to be asked. After all, although Kitty was fond of me, I don't expect I'm your favourite person any more than I am your parents'.'

Perdita cleared her throat. 'Oh, I expect you are. In a way. Now tuck in your side of the sheet and I'll sort out towels.'

Later, when Lucas had walked her back through the garden, and shared a nightcap with her and Thomas in the kitchen, Perdita wondered if Lucas had noticed what she'd said about him being her favourite person. She hadn't meant to say anything like that. With luck, he'd put it down to Kitty's death, and not think too much about it.

Perdita was a little light-headed when her parents arrived at lunch time the following day. After her usual chores, she'd spent the morning emptying drawers in her bedroom for her mother and pushing her horticultural activities to one end of the kitchen so her parents would have room to make themselves breakfast. When she'd done that, she'd made a start on the speech. She was still working on the second sentence when she heard their taxi arrive. She rushed out to greet them.

'*Darling!*'

Her mother's familiar-smelling kiss nearly undid Perdita. She hugged her hard, clinging in a way she hadn't clung since boarding-school days.

'Are you all right? You look exhausted! And what have you done to your hair? It suits you.'

Her father hugged her just as hard. 'How's my brave girl?'

'Not very brave at the moment, but coping. Come into the kitchen and meet Thomas. I don't suppose you've had lunch.'

'Only a stale baguette on the train down,' said her father.

On the table was a whole poached salmon, potato salad, green salad, and a salad of fine green beans and salted almonds.

'Oh, Thomas!' said Perdita, who'd been expecting bread and cheese, and with luck, soup. 'You've excelled yourself.'

'No I haven't. Lucas sent this over.'

'Lucas!' said her parents, practically in unison.

'He's been wonderful since Kitty died,' said Perdita.

'He was pretty wonderful when she was alive,' said Thomas. 'Reading to her, sitting with her, taking her to the lav and everything.'

Lucas assisting an old lady to the lavatory was hard to imagine, even for Perdita, who'd seen it happen. Her parents visibly struggled with the idea and regarded her accusingly.

'Didn't I mention how good he'd been? Well, never mind. This is Thomas, Thomas Hallam. Thomas, my parents, Mr and Mrs Dylan.'

'How do?' said Thomas. 'Now, wine everybody? Or there's sherry? Unless anyone wants anything stronger?'

Perdita's mother looked a little askance at the paid help making free with Kitty's drinks cupboard, but when her husband said, 'I must say, I could murder a gin and tonic,' she agreed that so could she.

'I'll do it,' said Perdita.

'I'll just go up and wash my hands,' said Perdita's mother. 'Come up and talk to me when you've mixed the drinks.'

Perdita brought drinks up for them both and she joined her mother in Kitty's bedroom. Her mother was crouched in front of the dressing table, trying to see her reflection in the mirror.

'Here you are, Mum. This'll make you feel better.' She took a fortifying sip of her drink. 'By the way, I thought you and Daddy would be happier in my house. It's going to be a bit chaotic here, as we'll have to offer beds to the other two carers, at least, and possibly the Ledham-Golds. You'll have a bit of peace and quiet over there.'

'I think it would be much better if you had the peace and quiet, and we were on the spot to organise things.'

'No, I really need to be on hand to keep an eye on things.'

'But, darling, we've come to do that.'

'It's lovely of you, really, but I've started this, and it's easier for me to finish it. And don't get too comfortable up here. Daddy's starving.'

'He can't be. Besides, I must have a few words with you alone. How are you? I suppose you've closed down the business for a bit? People will understand.'

'Oh, no. I can't do that. I get up early and sort it out for the day, and go over again in the evening if I've got the chance.'

'No wonder you're looking so exhausted.' She opened her mouth to say something else, but changed her mind. 'What about Kitty's nephew, Roger? Is he coming to the funeral?'

Perdita gripped her glass. 'I've no idea. I can't stop him, I suppose, but he certainly won't be particularly welcome.'

'Why on earth not? He seemed perfectly pleasant on the phone.'

'Oh, he's pleasant, all right, it's just that he's after Kitty's money and property, including the bit I've got my tunnels on.'

It was a moment before Perdita's mother took in what her daughter had said. 'Oh my God! Oh, darling! What have I done? I never would have found him if I'd known.'

'It's all right, Mummy. There's no need to panic. We don't know he's got Kitty to change her will, and if he has, well, it's too late to worry about it now.'

'We could contest the will—do something!'

'Only when we know what the will says. Until then, I'd really rather not talk about it.'

'If that's the way you feel, but I must say I wouldn't have thought—'

'Mum, please!'

'OK, tell me about Lucas. I mean, I know you did the television thing together, but it must have been awkward for you, to have him insinuate himself into the household.'

Perdita shut her eyes briefly, trying not to let the gin reveal her anger. 'Lucas does not insinuate,' she said tensely. 'He loved Kitty. When she was in hospital he made special meals for her, so she wouldn't have to eat hospital food. He's been so supportive, and brilliant.'

Perdita's mother regarded her daughter, a little startled. 'He must have changed an awful lot since I last saw him, then.'

Perdita was suddenly aghast at her outburst. 'I'm sorry. I was forgetting that you hadn't seen him since—'

'Your wedding.'

'And he has changed. A lot, really.'

Her mother's mouth crinkled with anxiety. 'Darling, he's not—you know . . .' She struggled for the right words.

Perdita laughed. 'Don't worry. I've no intention in getting involved with him again. He's just been a kind friend, that's all.'

Felicity Dylan got to her feet and patted her daughter's hand. 'You've turned into a woman, all of a sudden.'

'About time too, Mum! I'm nearly thirty! And I'm sorry if I seemed a bit snappy. I am a bit preoccupied with everything.'

'Don't worry about it, darling, and don't forget, we're here now.' She hesitated. 'We'll help you with anything you want.'

Perdita gently kissed her mother's cheek. 'Thank you for being so understanding.'

'I can be, you know,' said her mother. 'Now, let's go down before your father's low blood sugar makes him bad-tempered.'

After lunch, for which Perdita insisted Thomas joined them, Perdita took her parents over to her cottage to settle in and have a lie-down. She wandered back to Kitty's house, aware that she was swaying a bit.

Thomas took a quick look at her, removed the crystal glass she was drying from her hand, and sent her upstairs for a nap. When she came down again, it was tea time, and her parents were in the sitting room. Sitting with them was Lucas.

'Oh. Hi, everyone,' said Perdita, scanning faces for signs of disharmony. 'Sorry, I've been asleep.'

Lucas, who had got up, came over to her. 'We can tell: your hair's sticking up at the back.' He smoothed it down for her.

'I'd better go and brush it,' said Perdita, wanting a chance to interpret this tender gesture and to ask Thomas if everyone was getting on OK. Reluctantly, Lucas allowed her to leave, and she fled to the kitchen.

'What's Lucas doing here?' she demanded from Thomas. 'And are they getting on?'

'I think so,' said Thomas, who'd found cups with matching saucers and was putting them on a tray. 'Why shouldn't they?'

Perdita exhaled loudly. 'They didn't like him while we were married, and hated him afterwards. They think he's the arch enemy, and to be fair to them, so did I until I got to know him again.'

'So you don't think you and Lucas will get back together again?'

'No. We separated on very bad terms. We couldn't possibly get together again.'

'But he so obviously—'

'Who does what obviously?' asked Lucas, who wandered into the kitchen. 'Where's the tea? I can't make polite conversation any longer.'

'Never mind, I'm sure my parents will have been impressed by just a couple of minutes,' said Perdita.

'It's been twenty at least, and you still haven't brushed your hair.'

Perdita made a face. 'Take the tray, and I'll go and do it. Are you joining us, Thomas?'

'Not likely. I'm going to get this larder sorted before your mother finds the tins of bully beef left over from the war.'

'I just came over to check the details of the food,' said Lucas. He handed Perdita a menu. 'Is there anything else you think we should have?'

'Looks fine to me.' Perdita passed the menu to her mother, who produced her reading glasses from her bag and examined the card.

Perdita's mother frowned. 'It seems very lavish for a funeral. What's wrong with sandwiches and fruitcake?'

'One of your fruitcakes would be nice,' said Perdita, 'if you had time to make one. But Kitty was always very sniffy about the food at funerals. She said she wanted proper party food. But substantial, so people don't have to drive miles back home after only a couple of bits of soggy bread and butter wrapped round tinned asparagus.'

'I can hear her saying it,' said Perdita's father. 'I dare say you'll have to serve whisky, as well.'

'And champagne,' acknowledged Perdita.

'And tea, I hope,' said her mother. 'With the funeral at two, people will be wanting tea, not alcohol.'

'We're having tea, too. Thomas and I have sorted out dozens of cups and saucers. Kitty used to get them from jumble sales to use when she opened the garden to the public.'

Perdita's mother sighed deeply and opened her mouth to protest.

'Well, I think that menu will be fine,' said Lucas, quickly, before she could. 'But a good homemade fruitcake would just finish it off, for people who want something more traditional. Would you have time to make one, Mrs Dylan?'

Perdita's mother turned to him. 'Well of course, if you think it would go down well,' she said.'

'That would be brilliant, Mum,' said Perdita. 'Does it matter if the fruit is a bit old? Kitty's had cupboards of it for years. Does it go off?'

A couple of pained seconds later, Lucas answered.

'I'll bring you round some dried fruit, Mrs Dylan. Perdita, give Kitty's old fruit to the birds. For someone who hated waste, Kitty was a dreadful stockpiler,' he added.

Perdita's parents waited for their daughter to fly at Lucas for daring to criticise her beloved Kitty.

She didn't. 'It must have been something to do with the war. She always wanted to be able to feed an army if she had to.'

'I'd still be grateful if I didn't have to use ten-year-old fruit for my cake,' said Perdita's mother somewhat tersely.

Perdita still hadn't cried by the morning of the funeral. She got up at five to finish the flower arrangement for the coffin. When she finally came in from the old stable where she was doing the flowers, she found her parents in the kitchen. They looked smart in their funeral clothes.

'We thought we'd come over early to give you a hand,' said her mother. 'What are you going to wear?'

'There's a lovely old black dress of Kitty's,' said Perdita. 'I thought I'd wear that.'

'I know Kitty was keen on recycling,' said her mother, implying that Kitty was in fact just stingy, 'but don't you think that's taking economy too far? There's time for us to go into town together and buy something suitable. A nice suit, perhaps.' Perdita shook her head. 'I couldn't possibly. I haven't time, apart from anything else. And I really want to wear this dress of Kitty's.' It wasn't only because she didn't want to spend a lot of money on something she'd never wear again, but because she wanted to have a bit of Kitty with her at her funeral. 'Come up and see.'

The dress was on a hanger in a cupboard in one of the rooms she had prepared for guests. 'There it is. I've always liked it, but when I tried to get Kitty to give it to me, she said I could wear it at her funeral if I liked, but otherwise it was too gothic for words.'

Her mother sighed. 'Well, put it on and let's have a look.'

'You wouldn't be very kind and see if Thomas is up? I'm longing for a cup of tea.'

While her mother was safely out of the room, Perdita quickly got undressed and put on the dress before she could see, and therefore comment on, the state of her underwear.

Her mother came up with a mug of tea, saw Perdita in the dress and said nothing. The dress was made of some extremely fine material and was lined with satin. It was high-waisted and fell in handkerchief points to just above Perdita's ankles. It had a boat neck and the sleeves were fitted until the elbow where they widened out into a trumpet shape.

'It does look stunning, I must say. But is it suitable for a funeral?'

'Why ever shouldn't it be? It's black, smart and I'm sure it was wildly expensive.'

'Come and show your father. I still think a suit would be better.'

Her father was reading the paper. 'Edward, don't you think this dress is quite unsuitable for a funeral? I mean, Perdita does look heavenly in it, but don't you think it's a bit—well—over the top?'

Edward Dylan looked up. 'She looks sensational. In fact, I don't think I've seen her look so lovely since her wedding day.'

Perdita smiled. 'I'm obviously destined to look good only on tragic occasions.'

Perdita, hatless and chilly in her unaccustomed clothes, detached herself from the occasion by admiring the flowers. The church flower lady had done two huge arrangements, which seemed to incorporate whole trees and certainly included giant hemlock.

Her own arrangement on the coffin gave Perdita a certain amount of satisfaction. Even her mother had been impressed. The *pièce de résistance* was the miniature cabbages on wires which looked like tiny green roses. Kitty would have said they were too young to die, and it was wasteful to put edible plants into arrangements that weren't going to get eaten. Well, too bad, Kitty, thought Perdita. If you feel that strongly about it, you shouldn't have gone and died.

When Lucas got up to speak, Perdita felt overcome with nerves. After struggling with the speech for ages, she had finally given up. She just gave Lucas her many failed attempts and told him a few anecdotes. The rest was up to him.

In spite of such poor material it was a wonderful eulogy. He managed to re-create the spirit of Kitty, letting everyone know that she had achieved far more in life than just a great age. He even made people laugh, which pleased Perdita. She had wanted people to remember the fit, healthy and alive Kitty, and not think too much about the one who had died. She was aware that people were watching her, expecting her to cry. Still the tears wouldn't come. She seemed to have lost the mechanism. People will think I'm so hard, she thought. They'll think I don't care, that I'm glad she's dead so I can inherit her money. Perhaps I should borrow Dad's hanky, and blow my nose. But she couldn't pretend to cry, either.

Afterwards, at the house, she was a charming hostess. The sitting room, full of more flowers, looked magnificent. Food, whisky and champagne did their magic, and soon everyone was talking hard. Perdita spotted Roger looking disapprovingly into his champagne glass, obviously wondering if he was going to have to pay for it. It made Perdita wish she'd asked Lucas to provide oysters and caviar, vintage champagne instead of ordinary, and malt whisky instead of blended.

It was lovely to see Beverley and Eileen and Thomas gassing away to each other. They were all staying the night, and Perdita knew she'd have plenty of help with the clearing up.

'Is Mrs Anson's solicitor here?' asked Beverley.

'I don't think so,' said Perdita. 'He wasn't a personal friend.'

Beverley frowned. 'Oh. It's just that he called on her while she was ill, I thought he must be. And Roger was asking if he was here.'

Perdita's heart dipped. 'And was Roger staying with us at the time?'

'Oh, yes. He was with Mrs Anson while the solicitor was there. Did I do something wrong?'

Perdita forced a smile. 'No, of course not. Now, do eat up, everyone. Lucas has gone to so much trouble with the food.'

She moved away. There was no point in having a fit: what was done was done. Roger had either got Kitty to change her will or he hadn't. She would find out soon enough.

The Ledham-Gold trio spent a long time talking to Perdita's parents, looking at her so often that Perdita knew she was being talked about. Lucas was putting himself out to be pleasant, and accepting a lot of compliments on the food and the television programme with equal grace. Roger smiled blandly at everyone, doing his devoted nephew impression. Janey and William were there, so much a couple that Perdita wondered if they would have got together without her machinations, they were so clearly destined for each other.

But the person who seemed to Perdita to be having the most fun was Kitty. She's so nearly here, she thought. It's as if she's in the kitchen, or showing someone something in the garden, or finding a book to check a reference. It's only just a trick of the light that I can't see her. Perhaps that's why I can't cry. I don't believe she's dead.

'Now, are you sure you'll be all right? I really think I should stay and help you sort out the house.'

'Yes, Mum. I've got to get used to living on my own. Only I can sort out Kitty's things. You've had this holiday booked for ages.'

'I'd never forgive myself if anything happened to you. What about that dreadful Roger?'

'I can deal with him, and when it's all over and we . . . know how Kitty's left things, and we've got probate and everything, I'll come and have a long holiday with you. But for now, I must get on with it.' Whoever Kitty had left her money to, Perdita wasn't going to have her friend's personal possessions sorted by anyone but herself.

Getting Thomas to leave was harder because in some ways, in spite of her longing to be alone, Perdita would have liked him to stay. He was supportive but not bossy. He was also worried about leaving Perdita.

'I just don't want you turning into a dotty old lady, never going out, never seeing anybody.'

'I promise you I won't get any dottier than I am already. If I get stuck without you, I'll summon you back, as long as I can afford to pay you.' She raised a hand to silence his protest. 'You know you can't afford to work for nothing, and I know you lied to the agency about how long you stayed, telling them you went home the day after Kitty died.' She pressed an envelope of bank notes into his hand. 'I'm an heiress, I can afford it,' she said, although she knew that until Kitty's estate was settled, one way or the other, that she couldn't.

Perdita found it quite impossible to ring the solicitors to find out what was in Kitty's will. She knew it was irrational, but she didn't feel she could face the possibility of having to lose her poly-tunnels. While she was in ignorance, she could cope.

She had boundless energy, she hardly slept, and when she wasn't working, she sorted Kitty's things. She was in the attic reading through a file of newspaper cuttings when Lucas found her.

'What the hell are you doing up here?' he demanded.

'Sorting through Kitty's papers. And how did you get in?'

'Through the front door, like any self-respecting burglar.' He was angry and trying to conceal it. 'I've brought you an answering machine. I'm fed up with you never being in when I ring you.'

'Oh, sorry. I should of course be waiting by the phone night and day in case you phone me. Why would you want to phone me, anyway?'

'To find out how you are! Hell and damnation, Perdita! You're recently bereaved, no one ever sees you, even William says you mostly just leave notes, and you wonder why I'm worried! Have you resigned your membership of the human race?'

'Of course not! I've just got a lot of sorting out to do. Kitty was a terrible hoarder.'

'I know. And she was constantly cutting bits out of newspapers to read again later. But you don't need to read them all too. Either keep them, or throw them away.'

'But I can't. They might be important.'

'You're in no fit state to decide that.'

'What do you mean? I can read, can't I?'

'Well, I suppose so, but Janey told me that William said you threw away all the good peas and sprouted the damaged ones the other day. And she also said that William is having to watch you like a hawk in case you pull up the good lettuces and try to sell the stuff that's bolted.'

'Oh. Well, perhaps I am a little tired. I probably just need a few early nights to sort me out.'

Lucas removed a cobweb from her hair. 'I daren't ask when you last ate. You look awful, you've got shadows under your eyes, although that could be dust, and your clothes are hanging off you. And I don't know what Ronnie would say if he saw your hair.'

Perdita smiled weakly. 'I expect I can guess.'

'He's worried sick about you. He wants to book you in at the health farm, for a fortnight's rest cure.'

'And how does he think I'm going to pay for it?'

'He thinks you're an heiress. Everyone does. Janey, William, the whole village.'

She almost told him that, far from being an heiress, she might have to sell her business. Bonyhayes Salads barely made a profit as it was now; without Kitty's land it wouldn't be viable. Instead, she said, 'And do *you* think I'm an heiress?'

'I have better things to do with my time than speculate on other people's money. And for your personal interest, I don't give a fuck if Kitty didn't leave you a red cent.'

'Oh.' This was strangely consoling.

'So come down and eat something while I fix up the answerphone.'

The following week Perdita had had three messages from the surgery on her answerphone, the last one from Dr Edwards personally, before she finally rang back and made an appointment.

She felt bullied, and complained about it to William.

'I think you should go, Perdita,' he said seriously. 'We've all been worried about you. Lucas especially.'

'Oh? What makes you say that?'

'He keeps nagging Janey about you, that's what.'

'If he's worried, he could come and see for himself that I'm all right. He doesn't need to bother Janey about it.'

William gave her a rather odd look. She was used to odd looks—they were all she got these days, from the few people she saw—but this was a different kind of odd.

'I expect he's frightened of gossip.'

'Gossip! When has Lucas ever given a damn about what people say about him?'

William took on the expression of a messenger, about to be killed. 'Since they started saying that now you're an heiress, he's going to marry you and open his own restaurant with the money.'

'*What?*' How would people react if and when they discovered she was anything but an heiress? 'Oh God! I can't cope with all this nonsense as well as everything else.'

'Do you want me to run you to the doctor's then?'

The doctor started off with easy questions she could answer, like when did Kitty die. That date was engraved on her heart, she'd had to put it on so many forms. Then the questions got more difficult.

'So, are your parents at home at the moment?'

'My parents? No. They're walking somewhere. With rucksacks and sherpas and stuff.'

'And when are they due back?'

'I really don't know. They travel a lot. I can't keep track.'

'Have you got anyone else you could go and stay with? Some friends your own age, perhaps?'

After some moments reading the eye chart on the wall, Perdita remembered Lucy 'Umm, well, there is the friend I spent Christmas with, but she cried a lot, because she was pregnant. She's probably had the baby by now.'

'Haven't you heard?'

'No.' Perdita didn't mention that she'd stopped opening letters.

'Is she the sort of person you could go and stay with, and sleep a lot?'

She cast her mind back to the neurotic, dependent woman addicted to perfect Christmases. 'Not going on what she was like when I last saw her, and the house was in need of a very major make-over. I suppose Kitty's is, too.'

'It's your house now, Perdita.'

'Not necessarily. Kitty had a nephew—or he may be a great-nephew.'

'But she always told me she was leaving everything to you.'

'Yes, but that was before Roger turned up. *I'm* not related to her.'

'And you haven't rung the solicitor to ask what's in the will?'

'Why should he tell me? Supposing I'm not mentioned? He'd just ask me what the hell it was to do with me.'

The doctor frowned.

'I'd rather not know, anyway. If Kitty has left everything to Roger, I might lose the land my tunnels are on. I can't cope with the thought of winding up my business and trying to find some other way of earning a living just now.' She smiled weakly.

The doctor sat in silence, regarding her in that respectful, listening sort of way that always made Perdita feel very stupid.

'I'm going to give you something to help you sleep.'

'I never said I couldn't sleep!'

'You didn't need to. Now, these are very mild, they're not addictive. I'm going to ring through to the desk to make you another appointment next week.'

'Oh, I can do that on my way out.' She was already on her feet.

'You could, but you won't. Just sit back down.' He made the call.

'You can go now,' said the doctor. 'Don't forget to take this to the chemist. The receptionist will give you a card with your appointment time on it.' He gave her a look she'd seen him use on Kitty. 'And if you don't turn up, I'll have to make a house call.'

Perdita was delivered back home by William, who was going on to make some deliveries. She made herself a cup of tea and stared at the pile of post on the kitchen table. She ought to check there were no final demands lurking among the letters of condolence, and those addressed to Kitty from organisations who didn't know she was dead.

Perdita got up a little stiffly. Nothing about her seemed to work quite as well as it used to. She decided to go and clean the windows in the old stables. She picked up the cleaning stuff and some rags, but somehow she found herself in among the lettuces with William.

'What did the doctor say? Janey was furious with me for not asking before.'

'You can tell Janey that the doctor didn't say anything much, except I've got to go back next week.'

'Have you made an appointment?'

'Yes! Look!' She pulled the appointment card out of her jeans and waved it at him. With it came the prescription. He picked it up.

'Do you want me to get this filled out for you?'

'No, it's OK. I've got to go into town soon. I'll do it then.'

William gave her a strange look and went back to his digging. 'I've got a friend who needs a job,' he said. 'He's done an agricultural course. Just qualified. You wouldn't need to pay him much.'

It took Perdita some moments to grasp that William wasn't just passing on chitchat about his mate, but wanted her to offer him a job. It was probably because she had got so batty, he was scared to be alone with her. She gave him what she hoped was a reassuring smile. 'We're managing, aren't we?' She picked a leaf at random.

'Not really. I need some help.' William addressed some lettuces.

She frowned. 'We've always managed before. I know I've been busy at the house, but I still put in the hours here. And I just don't think I can justify taking on any more staff at the moment.'

'It's not to help my friend out,' he muttered. 'It's to help me.' Then, louder, he said, 'You've inherited Mrs Anson's money, haven't you?'

'I don't know, William. Possibly not. But even if I have, it'll be a while before I get probate. I can't just hire staff on a whim.' She didn't like to tell him what might happen to her existing staff if she didn't inherit.

A week later William came to her door at five to ten in the morning, and told her it was time to go to the doctor's. 'I'll see you get home OK,' he said, 'so just wait, if you come out early.'

Perdita was surprised when she came out of the surgery to see Lucas's car in the car park. He got out when she walked across to the car.

'I've come to pick you up,' he said.

She shook her head. She knew William had said he would come for her. 'It's all right, Lucas. I've got a lift.'

'William is busy. I've told him I'm going to take you away for a while. He's going to hold the fort while you're gone. Now, jump in.'

She stood there, confused. 'I don't think so.'

'It's either that or drive you to the nearest loony bin so you can have a nervous breakdown.'

'That's nonsense!'

'I'm only quoting Dr Edwards, though I do agree with him. He said if you don't get away you'll have a breakdown. So I'm taking you away. Now do get in, people are watching us.'

Perdita got in. 'Where are we going? I don't think I could face a hotel or anything like that.' Just pulling on her jeans and sweater had become enough of a chore. The thought of dressing up for breakfast made her want to weep.

'The bothy. Now go to sleep. I'll wake you when we stop for lunch.'

Obeying him was frighteningly easy. She was so tired, a long, built-up tiredness that had become part of her. She had no energy to fight or protest, she just felt grateful that the decision was made for her. She closed her eyes and fell into unconsciousness.

When he woke her, they were parked in a motorway service station. 'Pee break, also I need food and fuel. Come along.'

She found herself biting into a hamburger with all the trimmings. It was surprisingly tasty, though after a few mouthfuls she was full. Lucas finished her fries and then steered her to the Ladies.

'I'll wait for you outside,' said Lucas, seeing her try to open the door the wrong way.

She was asleep again before he'd finished filling the tank.

They stopped again, just before the motorway ended, and had tea and fruitcake. This time she was awake enough to ask a few questions.

'Surely you can't take time off just now, Lucas? Isn't it your busy time?'

'I've got minions. Janey's very good, and there's another young chef I'm training up, Tom. The lad who was sous for me that time you—worked in the kitchen.'

Perdita decided to ignore this reference. 'Well, I'm not at all sure I can take time off.'

'Yes you can. I've given William permission to take on that friend of his, and anyone else he needs. And he's got Janey to tell him what people need.'

She sighed. 'William can't run the business without me.'

'Yes he can. Apparently you haven't been a lot of use, lately. Pulling up the wrong things, cutting weeds instead of salads—you won't have a business soon, unless you take some time out. The doctor made no bones about it.'

'Well, I probably am cracking up, but I'm not happy about William hiring extra people. The business won't stand it.'

'It won't stand without it. Besides, you can afford the wages.'

She sighed. 'Not someone else assuming I'm a heiress. I'd have thought you'd know better.'

He was silent for a few moments. 'But I do. Know better, that is. I know that you are an heiress, quite a considerable one.'

'What? How do you know? I might not inherit anything. I might even lose the land Kitty gave me.'

He shook his head. 'You inherited almost all Kitty's worldly goods.'

'Have I? But what about Roger?'

'I don't know about the odd individual bequest, but you get the bulk.'

This was an enormous relief. 'Hang on. How do you know all this?'

'Because Kitty showed me her will. She wanted me to be an executor, but I refused.'

'But when was this? Roger got the solicitor to visit one day when I wasn't there. Just before we made the television programme.'

'Really?' Lucas took time to think this over.

'Yes! And Roger had told me he was going to get Kitty to change her will in his favour. I didn't think he'd done it until Beverley told me about the solicitor at the funeral.'

'And you've been carrying this anxiety around on your own?'

Perdita chewed her lip. 'Oh, and he was going to tell the tabloids we were once married. I meant to warn you, but then Kitty died and I forgot all about it.'

'Bastard! Not that it would have mattered, really.' Lucas leaned forward and put a large warm hand on her chilly ones. 'And I wouldn't worry about Kitty changing her will. She may have fiddled with it, but I'm sure she won't have changed her mind about the bulk of it.'

Perdita, feeling better than she had for ages, chuckled. 'Bulk might not be the right word. She bought me a van at Christmas, don't forget, and then we had carers for ages.'

'That won't have even dented it.'

Perdita rubbed her forehead. 'Can you tell me how you've got time to suddenly shoot off?'

'Would you have preferred it to be your parents? I did wonder if I should try to get in touch with them.'

'No! But I don't think it's fair that you should just drop everything, to take me away . . .'

'Oh God, Perdita, don't be so dense! I love you! If you need me to take you away, of course I'll drop everything!'

'What?' She felt she was watching a film and had fallen asleep, missing a vital bit of plot.

Lucas was unsympathetic. 'Oh, for God's sake, Peri! Why are you the only person in the whole village, the whole viewing public of *A Gourmet and a Gardener*, who doesn't know how I feel about you?'

She blinked at him in confusion. 'Possibly because you never said anything about it.'

'The others didn't need to be told, and how could I come near you when Kitty had just died, and the whole village are assuming I'm going to muscle in on you so I can open my own restaurant?'

'Lucas . . .'

'Never mind, don't think about it now. Let's get back on the road. You can do some more sleeping.'

Perdita, bewildered, and feeling as if an ant could push her over if it had a mind to, agreed that this was the best course. When she next woke up, Lucas was opening the gate to the track that led down to the bothy. It was ten o'clock at night.

'Welcome back.' Lucas pulled on the handbrake and smiled. 'You can wait in the car while I light the fire, if you like.'

'No, I'll come in.' She was still very tired, and a totally different person from the innocent young bride she had been when he'd first brought her here, but she felt the same bubble of excitement at having arrived as she had all those years ago.

She followed him into the little wooden building. It was pitch-dark outside. He struck a match and lit a camping-gas lamp.

'Now, is there any kindling left?' He rummaged in an old fishing creel that hung on the wall of the shack. 'Never mind, I've a secret supply somewhere. You wait here.'

While she waited for him, she looked around, wondering how much was different from the last time she had been here. Very little, she decided. But she noted that there was now a fridge under the table.

Lucas came back with a box of kindling. 'The trouble with a family property is that not all members of the family are as good at leaving the place as you'd wish to find it as others. That's why I always leave some kindling and some whisky well hidden.'

In no time the stove was crackling with flame, and although no heat came from it as yet, it was a wonderfully welcoming sound.

'Oh.' He regarded the two single beds, which had been pushed together to make a double. 'I'll sort them out in a minute. It takes a bit of shifting about, but I can soon separate them. I'll see if there's a can of soup, or something. Or aren't you hungry?'

'I'm not hungry, and please don't bother about the beds now. It's late, and you've been driving for hours. Let's leave it until morning.'

'Fine. Er—you remember about the loo situation, don't you?'

'Like, there isn't one?'

He nodded. 'You need a torch, a spade and paper. Luckily the ground's very soft. Go now, before you get comfortable and can't face it.'

Perdita groped her way round the back of the bothy, shone the torch for stinging nettles, and found, rather to her surprise, a strange pleasure in sitting under the stars. Back in the bothy, she found that Lucas had boiled a kettle, and there was a bowl of hot water for her to wash in.

'Now, whisky? Or shall I make a hot toddy?'

'You haven't got lemons, you can't make a toddy.'

'That's what you think, Miss Know-it-all.' He dug into his pockets and produced a lemon from each one. 'I grabbed them just as I left the flat.'

Perdita chuckled, and realised that it was the first time she had laughed for ages, although a polite smile had been pinned to her face seemingly for ever. 'I'll still make do with whisky. I haven't the energy to wait for you to faff around.'

He made a face at her. 'Your clothes, those I could find, are in that bag. I bought you a toothbrush and toothpaste, because they weren't in your washbag. You get ready for bed. I'll be back in a moment.'

She was huddled under the duvet, shivering violently, when he returned. 'I'll get you a hot-water bottle,' he said, seeing her teeth chatter.

He opened a cupboard. 'It won't take long to bring the kettle to the boil. The fire's going really well now and will have heated the kettle quite a lot.' He filled her a hot-water bottle, wrapped it in a scarf and handed it to her. It was wonderfully soothing. When the whisky kicked in and she was drowsy once more, she snuggled down deep under the duvet, heard him turn out the gaslight and felt him clamber into bed.

She didn't have the energy to think about what he'd said about loving her. It was too complicated. But it was also a little golden casket, something to be taken out and dreamt over, in private.

It was very quiet. Only the sound of the burn and the wind in the trees broke the silence of the deep countryside. She felt relaxed, and was starting to warm up. Then suddenly, unexpectedly, she started to cry. She was appalled. It was so embarrassing. She hadn't cried since before Kitty died, and had no idea why she was doing it now. She tried to keep quiet. Lucas had been wonderful, looking after her so well, she didn't want to keep him from his well-deserved sleep with her stupid tears. She managed not to sniff or sob as the tears ran wetly down her face, over her nose and into the pillow, but she couldn't stop shaking.

In spite of there being separate mattresses, Lucas felt it. He lay still for a moment, and then he put out an arm and pulled her towards him. 'Come on.'

He heaved her over the join so she was sharing his bed. He put his arm round her and her body remembered what her mind had long forgotten, how to lie alongside him. She laid her head on his shoulder and her arm across his chest, one leg slid between his, and, like the last piece of a jigsaw puzzle, she settled comfortably into position.

She awoke some time later, boiling hot. She kicked at the hot-water bottle until it landed on the floor with a thump. She had felt she would never get warm, and now she was sweating. Her pyjama bottoms had tangled themselves round her legs, tying them together. Could she sort out the situation without waking Lucas?

He was lying on his back, on the join between the two beds, snoring. It wasn't very loud and she found the sound comforting. She eased herself from under his arm, and, trying not to disturb him, slithered out of bed and out of the pyjama bottoms. Now, she wondered if she should get in the other side, to give them both more room, but as she cooled down she decided just to get back in.

His arm came round her, and she turned onto her right side, so it was on her waist. It was funny, she thought, as she settled herself, I couldn't have told anyone how we used to lie together, I wouldn't have known. But my body knows. Which is a good thing, she added prosaically, because it means we can both get some much-needed sleep.

The next time she woke his hand wasn't on her waist, in a chaste, companionable way, it was on her breast.

'Lucas,' she whispered.

There was no answer, but his fingers began circling her nipple. It was difficult to believe he was really asleep. She decided to give the matter a little thought. Should she stop him, or should she do what she'd been wanting to do for ever?

She moved away half an inch. 'Lucas,' she spoke out loud. 'Your hand. It's on my breast.'

Still no answer, but there was no possibility of him being asleep, he was just pretending to be so he could take her past the point of no return. He knew just how to do it, he was nearly there already. Perdita sighed. 'Lucas, you're not taking advantage of a recently bereaved woman, are you?'

'Peri, if you don't know how much I love you by now, I don't know what I can do to convince you.'

She smiled. Both his hands were working hard now, but she still had her back to him. 'You could try telling me.'

'I love you more than life itself. I love you more than I want sex with you. Here,' he shuffled backwards, abandoning her breasts. 'I'll get up and go and swim in the loch to prove it.'

This was taking it all too far. 'There's no need to do that.'

He laughed. 'No, I think I should prove to you that I don't just want you for your body.' He moved onto his mattress, and it seemed a long way off.

'What if I just want you for your body?' demanded Perdita, beginning to enjoy herself. 'Are you denying me a single girl's right to a sex life?'

She turned to peer at him in the dim light. He made an attractive silhouette, with his hair ruffled up at the back, moonlight catching his shoulder and upper arm.

'Yes I am. I don't think you should be a single girl with a sex life. I think you should be a married woman with one. Married to me.'

Perdita sighed. 'Do you think that's a good idea, after last time?'

'Yes I do!'

He reared up and leaned over her so she collapsed backwards.

'Supposing I don't agree with you?'

'You know me. I'll either torture you, or bully you until you submit.' He freed a hand to start unbuttoning her pyjama jacket. 'You'll soon give in.' Her chest was bare now, and he looked down longingly at where the moonlight lit her breasts.

'Does it have to be marriage? Couldn't we just have an affair?' she countered. After all she didn't want him to think she was desperate for him, even if she was.

'No we can't. We have to get married properly, preferably in church. I'm not risking losing you again.'

'You didn't lose me last time, you threw me away.'

'I was such a bloody fool. Why didn't I realise that you were the one, and always would be?'

'Because you were young, and I was even younger, and very silly. We've both changed.'

'Except that some things are wonderfully the same.' He ran his thumb down from her collarbone to the top of her rib cage. 'Do you still like that?'

'Mmm.' She nodded.

'So, will you marry me?'

Perdita turned her head to one side. 'Make love to me first, I'll decide afterwards. After all, you may not be as—'

He roared and leapt on her, taking her in his arms and rolling with her so she lay on top of him. 'If you agree to marry me,' he said, 'we can go into Perth and buy a double mattress.'

She gave an ecstatic sigh. 'Oh, all right then . . .'

In the morning, when, sated at last, Lucas got up to rekindle the embers in the wood-burner and make a cup of tea, Perdita sat up in bed and pulled the pyjama jacket back on.

Lucas was crouching naked on the hearth, breaking sticks and posting them into the fire. He looked very primitive, and beautiful. 'I think we should talk,' he said, getting to his feet. 'It's raining, and although I want to get back into bed and make love just as much as you do, there are a few things I think you should know.' He picked up his clothes and started to dress.

'Oh.'

'Nothing to look worried about. Just some things I need to get off my chest. I want you to know everything, so you can trust me. This time.'

She didn't think she'd have a problem trusting him, this time, but then she'd trusted him before. 'Then speak.'

'I'm going to tell you about Kitty's money and everything in a minute, but first I want to tell you all the stuff that happened before.'

'Before when?'

'Before I came to Grantly House. It wasn't coincidence. I knew you lived near by.'

'Oh?'

'I came back to find you.'

'That sounds very romantic.' But she knew it wasn't.

'I wish I could say, now, that I came back because I knew I still loved you and wanted to claim you as my own. But it wasn't quite like that.'

'So, what was it like?'

'I wanted to make sure I hadn't made a mistake, leaving you. I wanted to find out that you'd turned into someone I wouldn't want to be married to in a thousand years. But I didn't.' He poured water from the kettle on the wood-burner into the kettle on the gas stove, and lit it. 'You came into my kitchen, and either I fell in love with you all over again, or I was still in love with you from before. I don't know which it was, but it was bloody inconvenient, I can tell you.'

'I suppose you're going to tell me I was always "bloody inconvenient".'

'Well, you were—are! First of all, we meet when we're both far too young to know how to handle a relationship. Then you crop up again, a beautiful, successful, confident, irresistible woman, just when I'm starting to succeed in a new career.'

'It's hardly my fault you chose to succeed in the village where I live! Where you knew I lived! You could have fallen in love with another—of those women.'

'There aren't any more of those women. There's only you.' He squatted down to the fridge and took out a packet of bacon. 'And I do know it's my fault I came back, like everything is my fault.' He ripped open the packet with his teeth and started peeling rashers from it, laying them carefully in a frying pan.

'Not everything,' said Perdita. 'Something, or someone—you or Kitty, probably—made me realise there are always two sides to a relationship.' She shuddered, troubled by the ghost of failure. 'Do you think we'll make it, if we get married again?'

'There's no "if" about it!'

'But supposing it doesn't work? I don't think I could go through that again . . .'

'Without Kitty?'

She put her arms round her hunched-up knees. 'No. Kitty has nothing to do with this. I don't need her any longer.' She bit her lip. 'Oh, I *want* her, I miss her terribly, but I don't *need* her. I've come to realise that these last weeks.'

'I'm glad. Kitty would be so proud to hear you talk like that.'

Perdita cleared the tears from her throat and wiped her eyes.

'You were in the middle of a confession, Lucas.'

'Not really a confession—more a short talk on why I think our marriage would work this time when it failed so spectacularly before.' He turned down the gas under the pan. 'When we got married before, we were all sex and no substance. We've both grown up a hell of a lot, and been through a lot together. I've learned so much from that, so much about you I might never have known.'

'And I've learned that under your grumpy exterior, you're extremely kind, but you don't want people to know it. You disguise it as self-interest. You were wonderful to Kitty.'

He looked up. 'Actually, when I first called on Kitty, it *was* self-interest. I called on her so I could either get closer to you. Would you like an egg, or just a tomato?'

'Egg, please.' She hesitated for a second, but then decided to ask her question; if their marriage was to work, there must be no doubts between them. 'Lucas, why were you unfaithful to me? The first time? And how did you get to be a chef?'

Lucas thought for a few moments, trying to work out what to say. 'I was frightened. I was in a marriage I couldn't make work, a job I couldn't do, and wasn't suited for. Celia was senior to me, older than me and her attention was flattering. She came on to me when she'd summoned me into her office to give me a bollocking.'

'Instead she gave you a rollicking?'

He frowned. 'She took off all her clothes and then started on mine. I'm not saying I shouldn't have resisted, but I'd stopped giving you orgasms—'

'It's all right, you've started again.'

'Don't interrupt. Celia wanted me so blatantly. It seemed easier to abandon you and carry on with her. God! I was such a shit! I don't know how I lived with myself!'

'What about Celia? Did you live with her?'

'For a bit, until she got bored with me. Then she kicked me out.'

'I thought you said you left her!'

'I did; my possessions followed rapidly behind.'

Perdita chuckled. 'Go on.'

He added butter to the pan, and put in the halved tomatoes. 'I bummed around the City for a while, making money, sleeping with older women. Then I saw a girl I thought was you. It brought me up short. Some mates had hired a house in France, asked me to go with them.' He paused to add the eggs to the pan.

'Go on. How did you get to be a chef?'

'We got talking to one, one night. Strangely, he was English. He came through into the bar for a coffee. We'd had a bloody good meal, and told him so. I asked him a couple of questions, he saw I was interested, and said if I wanted to learn more I could sign up at the hotel down the road.' He looked at Perdita, his expression rueful and self-deprecating. 'I don't know if the chef was a sadist or a genius or both. But he taught me about food.'

'So when you got to be a chef, you modelled yourself on him?'

He shook his head. 'You think I'm a bastard? *That* bastard nearly took the end of my finger off with a knife.'

'So why did you stay?'

He shrugged, and got two plates out from the cupboard. 'He knew about food, he took me on completely untrained. I was learning a lot. Now, do you want breakfast in bed? Or will you get up?'

She slid out of bed. 'I'll get up.'

'Then please put some knickers on. That jacket is long, but not quite long enough for my peace of mind.'

She giggled and rummaged in her bag. When she was dressed, below the waist at least, she joined him at the table. 'So how did you get from scullery boy to shit-hot chef?'

'Eat your breakfast, it's getting cold.'

Obediently, she sawed at a piece of bacon. 'Don't you want to tell me? Surely this is the good bit of the story?'

He frowned, pulling the skin of his tomato as if it required great skill. 'You really want to know? Well, I poisoned him.'

'What!'

'Not badly, only enough to give him dreadful diarrhoea. The sous was drunk—I'd arranged that, too—and so I had the restaurant to myself for the night, apart from the other skivvies, of course.'

He shot her a look that reminded her of the night she had worked for him, and what had nearly happened afterwards.

'So, what happened?'

'Well, the owner came in. That I hadn't arranged, and wouldn't have done. But he liked my work and offered me a better job in his restaurant in Paris.'

'And the rest is history?'

'More or less. Now, eat up, you know how offended chefs get if people let their meals get cold.'

'I've just had a dreadful thought,' said Perdita, when they'd reached the toast and marmalade stage. 'What are my parents going to say when I tell them we're going to get married again?'

He balanced a large piece of peel on his crust of toast. 'I don't think that'll be a problem.'

'Lucas, you didn't ask my father's permission for my hand, did you?'

'No! Of course I didn't. But before they left, they asked me to keep an eye on you. And your mother . . . intimated that she'd be glad if we got married again. Now Kitty's gone, she thinks she might have to be a mother to you herself.'

'She did the best she could. I've turned out all right, haven't I?'

'More than all right.' He sighed. 'Now, have you had enough breakfast? Have we talked enough? Or can we do what we were put on earth to do?' He came round the table and pulled her to her feet.

'You haven't told me about me being an heiress, yet.'

'Later.'

'So Kitty said, would I mind looking at her will, even if I didn't want to be an executor.'

Perdita could imagine her saying it. *'Cast your eye down that, darling, and check I haven't lost my marbles and left it all to a cats' home.'*

'Her husband left her very well provided for, she's had some extremely good financial advice and she's lived frugally most of her life. You'll inherit an unencumbered house, an excellent portfolio of shares, and some valuable jewellery and pictures, which have lived in the bank for years.'

'But when was this? Unless it was very recent, there was still time for her to change it.'

'It was before she had the first TIA.'

'Then it might all have changed. It might be Roger who's the heiress, not me.' She smiled to hide her anxiety.

He shook his head. 'She wouldn't do that. She wasn't taken in by Roger any more than I was. I dare say she's left him something, but she'd never disinherit you.'

'I do hope not—not because of the money, but—'

'The land. You told me. And Kitty wanted you to be well provided for.' He smiled. 'If the worst comes to the worst, and she has left it all to Roger, you'll just have to be a kept woman, and live off your husband.'

She frowned. 'I wouldn't want to do that.'

'Seriously, though,' he went on, 'we could raise the money to buy the land off Roger, and if he was dealing with me he wouldn't dare to ask over the odds.'

She was forced to laugh. 'So you think my fortune is safe?'

'Yup. So do you want to sell the house?'

Perdita sat perched on a low three-legged stool. 'No,' she said. Until that moment she hadn't allowed herself to think about what she might want to do with Kitty's house. Now she felt she wanted to live in it, fill it with children, stop the roof from leaking and revamp the kitchen. And now suddenly, it wasn't only her decision. 'But where do you want to live?'

He didn't hesitate. 'Where you want to live. With you. By your side.' He gazed at her, for once letting his feelings for her shine through his eyes. 'I don't care where I live. I can do what I do anywhere.'

'But supposing you get fed up with Grantly House? Supposing you want to open your own place somewhere?'

'Then we'll sort out how later, when it happens. Let's just concentrate on getting married and being happy. Oh—' he paused guiltily.

'What?'

'I've just remembered. They want us to make a TV series together.'

The days that followed were like their honeymoon had been, only better. The weather was golden. The short October days were filled with sunshine, and the mornings with mist. Lucas swam naked in the loch, insistent that at the end of the summer the top few feet were warm enough to do so. Perdita was happy to watch him, especially when he came out, dripping like Poseidon, and swept her wetly into his arms, but she kept her own ablutions to the minimum, depending heavily on the public lavatories in the local town, and any pub they visited. If the evening was fine, Lucas put the bars of an old oven shelf over the remnants of the fire they'd used for their billycan tea and had a barbecue.

On the last afternoon, before they were due to go back, he took her to a spot where, if you were lucky, you might see golden eagles and harriers, mountain hares and distant flocks of deer.

They spent a lot of time gazing across the valley to the mountains beyond, watching the sky darken to the colour of duck eggs, tinged with pink. Perdita hadn't spoken for a long time and eventually Lucas asked her if she was all right.

'I was just remembering something Kitty once said to me about bereavement.'

'What?'

'It was years ago, when I was still at school, and I asked her about Lionel, her husband. She said when you lose someone you love, the days go by so slowly, and the loss leaves a vast, immeasurable hole in your life. But gradually the hole begins to close. It's like darning, she said. Slowly, slowly, you place threads across the hole and weave them together, until eventually, after decades, maybe, you find the hole has gone.' She found herself laughing and crying at the same time. 'Kitty told me this and then said, "I don't know how you'll cope, darling. I've never managed to teach you to darn."'

He buried her in his arms and held her very tightly. Eventually he said, 'I'll help you. I'm good at darning.'

Perdita was half excited, half terrified as they swept round the drive and stopped in front of Kitty's house. She had been partly expecting to be confronted with a couple of pantechnicons and Roger filling them with antiques.

She felt as if she'd been away for months, not just a couple of weeks. Cobwebs and rats, possibly even weasels and stoats, could have taken the place over in her absence. They had spent the night in a motel, halfway home, so that they wouldn't arrive in the dark, and now everything looked in surprisingly good order. The front was clearer of weeds than it had ever been, even in Kitty's day.

'Someone's been doing the garden,' Perdita said, pleased, but anxious lest something precious had been tidied onto the compost heap. She found the key and unlocked the front door. Instantly the smell of polish greeted them. A huge vase of chrysanthemums stood on the hall table. Everything looked shiny and cared for.

'I wonder where all the boxes of papers are.'

Lucas opened the door to the library. 'They're in here. In fact, I think Miriam must have raided the local public records office for extra supplies.'

Perdita peered in over his shoulder and saw row upon row of boxes, obviously gleaned from the local wine merchant. 'Let's go into the kitchen. That's where Miriam will have put the post.'

The kitchen also gleamed. The table, cleared of extraneous items, made a lovely centrepiece. There was a note from Miriam leaning up against a little silver jug full of garden cyclamen.

Nothing has been thrown away, it's all still there for you to sort out. I'll be in tomorrow. I've made a note of my extra hours. The post is on the sideboard.

'I gave her permission to do extra hours,' said Lucas, as Perdita picked up the pile of letters and took them to the table.

'Spending my money for me before I've even got it, are you?' She flicked through the post, identifying the letter from the solicitor. 'Well, I'd better find out if I've got any.'

Perdita opened the thick manila envelope and withdrew a sheaf of papers. She scanned the letter that was on top.

'"Dear Miss Dylan,"' she read aloud. '"I am happy to enclose the papers . . ." Oh, why don't they cut to the chase?'

'Let me look.' Lucas took the bundle and riffled through it. He handed her a copy of the will. Perdita took a deep breath and glanced down the page. Then she closed her eyes and handed it to Lucas. 'It's all right. It is all mine.'

'Not quite,' said Lucas after a moment. 'There's a legacy for Roger here. "To my great-nephew Roger Owen,"' he read, '"I bequeath the entire contents of the cupboard on the landing outside the attic." What on earth's in there, I wonder?'

Perdita started to laugh. 'I know. It's all the cups and saucers Kitty got from jumble sales. We used them for the funeral. Remember?'

'Well, I'm sure it's a very handsome legacy,' said Lucas, obviously a little confused.

'No it's not! It's probably worth about a fiver! God, she was a wily old bird! Even when she was in her death throes she was on to Roger and his interest in her Meissen collection! That has cheered me up. I hated the thought of Kitty being bullied when I wasn't there to protect her.' She dumped all the papers onto the table. 'Come on, let's explore the rest of the house.'

'I didn't think that table would stay clear for long,' said Lucas.

It was quite different looking at the house, knowing it was to be their home, and the home of their children. Kitty was still there, in every book and picture, piece of silver or china, but the house no longer seemed to be in decline. Perdita and Lucas had plans for its future.

'I might have a sort through and see if there's any other stuff I can fob off on Roger.' Perdita paused. 'I would like to keep the blue sofa. Kitty felt so sentimental about it.'

'Only if it's comfortable. She wouldn't want us to be burdened by her sentiments when she knows we'll have enough of our own.'

'Shall we test it now?' Perdita asked with mock innocence.

'No,' said Lucas firmly. 'Let's go back to the kitchen.'

Back there, Perdita surveyed the room with a critical eye she had never used before. For years and years this had been Kitty's kitchen, the way she liked it. Now it was hers and Lucas's.

'I think an Aga, don't you? A four door one. Middle-class-lefty-trendy red,' said Perdita.

'Not while I live and breathe! If you think that I'm going to cook on something that takes half an hour to boil an egg, you can think again! No, we need a professional range, something that gets up to a decent temperature.'

'I wanted to make the kitchen a bit more like they made my kitchen in the programme, with a few bits of copper and stuff hanging from the ceiling.' She glanced at Lucas, to see if he was reacting.

'Darling, do you really want a kitchen like they turned yours into on the programme?' He seemed to have given up fighting and wanted to please her. But on the other hand, he didn't want to share what he considered to be a work space with a lot of clutter.

'It's all right. I'm teasing. We'll keep the cooking end of the kitchen strictly business, as long as it's pretty, and make the dining end all fancy. Shall we go upstairs now?'

He shook his head. 'I don't think we'd better. We're bound to feel obliged to test the beds and there are probably rather a lot of them.'

She chuckled. 'Let's go and see my poly-tunnels then. I hope everything's not dead.'

'Well, let's just give William a ring first. Janey might be there and they haven't been together long. We don't want to embarrass them.'

Perdita bit her lip in horror. 'Imagine being caught *in flagrante* by both your bosses!'

'Exactly. We'll take the car round the front, like proper visitors.'

William and Janey weren't in bed; they were waiting by the gate, rather anxiously, holding hands.

Perdita jumped out of the car and ran to them, embracing them both. 'Hi! How are you? How are my poly-tunnels? How is everything? We've brought you some honey and some genuine Scotch whisky. Thank you so much for holding the fort while I just ran away.'

The anxiety faded and was replaced with tentative expectation. Janey let go of Perdita and said, 'Well? Are you two . . . well, you know?'

'We're going to get married, if that's what you want to know,' said Lucas. 'And I'm not planning to use her great fortune to open a new restaurant. Things'll carry on as before, until Perdita gets pregnant.' He glanced at her. 'If she isn't already.'

Perdita ignored this. 'And we're going to live in Kitty's house, so you can have this one as long as you like.'

'That's great,' said William. 'We thought we ought to get married, too.'

'Brilliant! I wonder if we've used up all Kitty's champagne? If not, we'll have to buy some and have a celebration!'

Perdita suddenly grabbed Lucas's hand. 'I've just thought of something. Come along.'

She dragged him into one of the poly-tunnels and along the rows to the back. 'I've no idea what I'm going to find, but, if we're lucky . . .' She lifted out a large pot. There was nothing much to show from the top except something that looked like faded mint. She took a dibber from a ledge and very, very gently, began stirring the surface of the soil. 'Yes!' Carefully, she dug her fingers into the loosened soil and brought out a curious spiral shape, like an extremely plump maggot. It had a wonderfully pearlescent surface.

Lucas pushed her aside. 'I don't believe it! Crosnes! You've managed to grow crosnes! You little beauty! This is fantastic!'

'Crosnes, also known as Chinese artichokes,' Perdita added, for the benefit of Janey and William, who were following at a safe distance.

Perdita tipped out the soil and then sought for the pearly pink tubers. 'It's like digging for gold,' she said.

'Who would have thought that that dried-up crusty old thing could have turned into something this wonderful?' said Lucas.

'I know,' said his beloved, fondly. 'And the crosnes are pretty amazing too.'

KATIE FFORDE

Katie Fforde and I met after we had attended a meeting of the Romantic Novelists' Association, an organisation that devotes a lot of its time to developing new writing talent. Katie takes an active role in the association, which she says helped put her on the road to becoming a successful novelist. 'I owe a lot to the association,' Katie told me, over a glass of wine and canapés in a London wine bar. 'I had been trying, unsuccessfully, to write romances for Mills and Boon for years but it wasn't until I submitted a proposal for a novel to the RNA's New Writer's Scheme that my career took off. They helped me to find an agent, who encouraged me to write my first novel, *Living Dangerously*, which featured in a WH Smith Fresh Talent promotion.'

At the time Katie Fforde was a full-time mother, with two children at school and a toddler at home. 'I used to write mainly in term times but I would have to steal the time—even if it was only for an hour a day. Now, that my children have grown up, I try to write a thousand words a day, but I can't sit at my desk for hours at a time. My creative energy is quite short and I need to take time out to do other things: work in my garden, watch television and be with my family.'

It was while watching a television programme that Katie Fforde was struck with the idea for *Thyme Out*. 'I was watching a series called *A*

Woman Called Smith in which the name Smith is picked at random out of the phone book. This particular episode featured a woman called Frances Smith who runs a market garden, growing specialist salads and other vegetables, and sells them direct to London chefs. I decided to write to her and she was not only an inspiration for my novel, but was an enormous help with the writing. I gave my heroine, Perdita, all her energy and skill and ability to know what would make money, and what would take too long to grow or not be special enough. I went to visit her and her husband in Kent and spent a most stimulating weekend with them. She told me about a new vegetable called a crosnes, very difficult to grow but worth a fortune if you can. Of course it had to go into my book.'

Katie is also a great fan of cooking programmes and feels inspired by them to try exotic recipes herself. To get the professional kitchen scenes right in *Thyme Out* she went to a local restaurant and asked if she could watch them in the kitchen. 'But I couldn't just stand there doing nothing so I asked for rubber gloves and cleaned the pans. I was amazed that all the pans were little, as many dishes are individually pan-fried. It just goes to show that if you don't do the research you can get it wrong.'

What other advice would Katie give to anyone with ambitions to write fiction? 'Perseverance,' she says. 'It took me ten years between starting and getting into the bookshops. It takes some people longer. Because you're not an "overnight success" it doesn't mean you won't get there eventually.'

Jane Eastgate

❧

Freya is almost sure that Michael is
the man for her and and is all
prepared for him to propose marriage.
But Michael has different ideas. Over
dinner he announces that he thinks
they should just be friends.
Reeling from the shock and unable to
go home to their shared flat, Freya
knocks on the door of the only person
in New York who she is sure will be in
on a Friday night—Jack, a man she
knows too well to ever fall in
love with.

❧

Chapter One

FREYA PEELED OFF her clothes and stood in her underwear, contemplating her reflection. She wanted to look her best for Michael tonight. There had been no time to go home to change; she must make do with this cramped ladies' room beneath her office. Her new dress hung from the cubicle door: a cool $1,000-worth of palest pink that shimmered with a tracery of opalescent beads—a Cinderella dress chosen to make her as feminine and delicate as a porcelain doll. That was the look she was aiming for, less *femme fatale*, more . . . *femme*, plain and simple.

'Let's go somewhere special,' he had said over breakfast on Monday morning. 'Somewhere we can talk.' Questions had exploded in her head, like popcorn in a hot pan. Freya had choked them back. But all week long she had carried his words around with her. Was this 'It'? Was she about to become Mrs Normal, grouching about schools and the state of her suburban lawn?

She began to make up her face—a pencil to darken the pale arches of her eyebrows, mascara to bring her light blue eyes into focus. Which lipstick? Scarlet Woman was out. So, frankly, was Vestal Virgin. Ah-hah, Crimson Kiss, that was more like it. She slid the colour over her lips, then bared her teeth, satisfactorily white against the red.

But what if she was wrong? Maybe Michael just wanted to finalise plans for their trip to England. Freya cocked her head to fix an earring, considering this possibility. No, she decided. Michael was a lawyer and habit was his middle name. Every January he bought his suits in the sales, always two, always Armani, either navy or charcoal. He called his mother on Sunday evenings. There was nothing unpredictable about him. If he wanted to 'talk', he must have something important to say.

Balancing precariously on one flamingo leg, then the other, Freya slid on sheer stockings, then stepped carefully into the precious dress and drew it up her body, shivering at its silky opulence. A hidden side zip pulled it snug around her small breasts, miraculously creating a discreet cleavage. She slotted her feet into flat shoes, with the faintest sigh of regret for those strappy four-inch heels she'd seen in a 5th Avenue store. It was too bad that Michael wasn't taller. She reminded herself sternly that successful relationships were founded on compromise.

A few adjustments, a mist of perfume and she was finished. Did she look the part? Freya found her brain flooding with words she had never associated with herself: *fiancée, engagement, honeymoon, Mr and Mrs . . . Daddy and Mummy*. She grabbed the washbasin with both hands and peered in the mirror. Narrow pointed face, skin pale as buttermilk, long arms and legs—too long? She was as tall as many men: 'giraffe' they had called her at school. Could somebody really *love* this person—for ever and ever, amen? As she smoothed back her newly cropped hair, so fair it looked almost colourless in this light, she caught sight of her left hand, with its bare ring finger. Her expression sobered. It was nice to be wanted. It was wonderful to be loved. She wasn't twenty-nine any more.

Yes, Michael was the one, she was almost sure.

The restaurant Michael had chosen was a new and very expensive place on the edge of the Village, so confident of its must-go status that Freya walked past it twice before spotting the tiny engraved entry phone. She leaned on the buzzer, and immediately the door was opened by an angelic young man with a peroxide crop. She found herself in a waiting area where voluptuous sofas flanked a *faux* fireplace and there were Georgian-style urns on the mantelpiece. Shallow steps led down into the dining room.

As the young man led the way, Freya scanned the tables. On one of the banquettes, perched somewhat stiffly between lime-green bolsters, was Michael. She made her way down the steps, waiting for him to notice her. When he did, he looked startled, almost shocked: very gratifying. He leapt up from his chair to greet her with a kiss on each cheek.

'Freya, you look wonderful!'

'I know.' She put her hands on his shoulders and laughed into his eyes, then stepped back so that he could admire her properly. 'It's the new me. Don't tell me, you thought I was *born* wearing trousers.'

'No, no.' Her exuberance seemed to disconcert him. 'I mean, you always look fabulous.' He pulled the table out so she could sit down opposite him, and resumed his position. How adorably lawyerly he looked, with his square, handsome face, serious brown eyes, and wavy hair clipped close. They would love him in England. She wondered if he'd already bought her a ring, and if so where he was hiding it.

A waiter drew a bottle from a cooler by the table.

'Champagne?'

'Absolutely.' Freya shot Michael a sparkling smile. 'Are we celebrating?'

'Well . . .' He looked bashful. 'It *is* Friday night.'

Freya held her tongue. After five months of living with him, she knew that Michael's favourite Friday-night routine consisted of gourmet take-out, a video and early bed. But then he did work very hard.

As the waiter filled her glass, Freya was surprised to see that the bottle was already half-empty. It was unlike Michael to drink alone. He must be gathering his courage.

'So how was your day?' she asked.

'Fine. They're holding a meeting next month to vote on the new senior partners. Fred thinks I have a good chance.'

'Fred always says that.' Freya popped a couple of chargrilled pistachios into her mouth. Then she saw Michael's lips purse and quickly added, 'But I'm sure you do. King of the divorce courts, that's you. Hey, look at this.' She pointed to the menu, hoping to distract him from her lapse in tact. 'Beggar's Purse, *seventy dollars*. What can it be?'

'Some kind of pancake, I think, with caviar inside. Seems a lot to pay for fish eggs, doesn't it?'

'Not if it's beluga. My father took me to St Petersburg once, when he was working at the Hermitage, and we went to this special dinner. I was about twelve, and it was the first time I'd ever tasted caviar, but I've never forgotten it. Total heaven. Go on, try it.'

'Fish gives me a bad reaction. I think I'll go for the soup.'

'Good choice.' Michael always had soup.

There was an awkward pause. Freya suppressed a twinge of irritation. But Michael had always been shy; she must let him go at his own pace.

It was his shyness that had caught her attention in the first place, that evening at an uptown gallery. Michael had come to the opening with his boss and the boss's ghastly wife, one of those pampered Manhattan ice-queens who liked to think of themselves as a patroness of the arts. Freya was recovering from a bad relationship and she knew she exuded misery and defeat. From her vantage point in a corner, Freya had watched Michael's super-polite behaviour as he was dispatched to fetch wine. She was impressed by his good humour. Observing his open, masculine face, free of cynicism, the thought had occurred to her: Why can't I fall for a nice man like that?

Later Michael confided that he had dared to approach her only because she looked as lost as he felt. Galleries were not his scene; he had no talent for social chatter. When it turned out that the boss's hospitality did not extend to dinner, Michael had asked Freya out instead.

It had been a slow, old-fashioned courtship, especially by Manhattan standards—flowers, exhibitions, walks in the park. Fifteen years in New York had taught Freya the art of detachment—from the drunks and crazies, from the loneliness that came in the small hours and the men who said they'd call and never did. It was nice to feel attached. Michael's apartment on the Upper West Side was blissfully warm and comfortable. Freya spent more and more time there until one day—and it was shaming to admit that she couldn't remember the exact details—they became lovers. Soon afterwards Michael persuaded her to move in altogether. And she had liked that too. The simple domestic pleasures of shopping and cooking, that relaxed moment at the end of the day when they would exchange news of what had happened since they parted in the morning, made her feel that she was at last having a grown-up, normal relationship. Now they were almost like a married couple. Very like a married couple, Freya realised, for Michael had been talking to her for some time and she hadn't heard a word.

'. . . so I said, "OK, we'll shut you down." That shut him up.' Michael looked triumphant. 'But that's enough about me. How about you? How's Lola?'

'In Milan, thank goodness.'

Lola Preiss was Freya's boss, a woman of unspecified Central European origins and legendary reputation, whose gallery on 57th Street attracted punters with a million or so to spend on big-hitters like Warhol, Lichtenstein and Stella. Three years ago, after years of dogged drudgery in half the museums and galleries in New York, learning about everything from framing and lighting to printing techniques, while simultaneously developing her own 'eye', Freya had been rewarded by an offer to set up Lola Preiss Downtown; her brief was to seek out and develop young artists. She loved the work, and it would have been a dream job but for Lola's monstrous ego, which made her interrogate Freya over every decision she made and publicly claim Freya's successes as her own.

'So has it been a good week?' Michael persisted. 'Sell any big ones?'

Freya rolled her eyes. 'Michael, you don't measure art by the square yard.'

'I know that. I was just taking an interest.'

'Sorry.' Freya bit her lip.

The waiter brought wine and food. Over her truffle salad, Freya told Michael about her appointment that afternoon with a client sent by Lola, who had arrived an hour late and turned out to be a complete time-waster.

'I hate that type, don't you?' she burbled on. 'All Rolex watches and phoney European accents, and leering at you as they talk about the role of art in breaking sexual taboos.'

'Not a lot of leering goes on at Reinertson and Klang, I'm afraid.'

'Glad to hear it! I wouldn't want you running off with Mrs Ingwerson.'

'Mrs Ingwerson is fifty-four years old.' Michael's tone was cool. 'And the best secretary I've ever had.'

'Joke, Michael!' Freya gave her fork a humorous little flourish. He certainly was slow on the uptake tonight. Over his shoulder she caught sight of a couple leaning close to smile into each other's eyes, their faces lit by a glow of candlelight, their legs entwined under the table. Wasn't that how it was supposed to be? She felt a tremor of disquiet.

The waiter cleared their plates and brought the main courses while Michael began telling her, at some length, about some article he'd read in *The Times* about the mayor's controversial policy on underage crime. Freya nodded at appropriate moments while her mind raced along its own track. Romance wasn't everything, she told herself. It was juvenile to expect to be swept away by passion. Mature relationships were founded on companionship and mutual respect, not to mention cash flow and a nice place to live. You had to take the long view. Freya pushed her fish nervously round her plate. One man—*this* man—for the rest of her life, 'till death us do part': it was a scary idea.

Michael cleared his throat. 'Freya. I've brought you here tonight for a special reason. I have something to say, and something to give you.'

'Really?' Uh-oh, was this it? Freya felt herself flapping helplessly like a fish in a net. 'But, you know what, I'm still hungry,' she gabbled. 'I've just got to have one of those irresistible-looking chocolate things.'

'OK,' Michael said curtly. He waved over a waiter.

'What about you? The berry pie sounds good. Or the sorbet.'

'I don't want to eat. I want to talk.'

'Oh. Right.' Freya grabbed her wineglass and drained it.

Michael smoothed his tie down his shirt-front. 'These last few months we've been together have been some of the best of my life,' he began. 'You've opened my eyes to so many new things. I want you to know that I think you're a terrific person.'

323

ROBYN SISMAN

'You're a terrific person too,' Freya responded chirpily.

He ploughed on as if he hadn't heard. She realised that he'd rehearsed this speech. 'I've been thinking about the future. I'm thirty-six now, and I know what I want. I'm ready to settle down soon. If I get the partnership, I'll be able to afford to move. A house out of the city, Connecticut maybe, or some place upstate. Who knows, I might even take up golf.'

'Golf?' squeaked Freya, beginning to panic.

'And I want someone to share that life with me.'

Freya suddenly saw herself trapped behind a white picket fence with a frilly apron glued to her waist.

'Home. Stability. Shared interests,' Michael intoned. 'And kids, one day.'

Behind the picket fence there now appeared a scrum of yowling toddlers with jammy faces. Freya could actually feel her biological clock whirling into reverse. A hand placed her dessert before her—brown goo in a creamy lake. Her stomach heaved.

'These are the things I see happening, things I'm looking forward to, things I want to share with another person.' He stared at her intently, almost fiercely.

Quick! Head him off. 'Could we order some coffee?' she croaked.

'In a minute. There's something I want to give you.' He was patting his pockets. Any minute he was going to produce the ring!

'There's no rush. Let's leave it till tomorrow.' Freya cast around wildly for inspiration and caught sight of the canoodling couple. She leaned low across the table. 'Why don't we go home,' she cooed, 'and make mad, passionate love?'

'You don't understand.' Michael had now taken whatever it was out of his pocket. He pressed the object into her fingers—a small, square box.

Freya opened it. Inside was a gold signet ring engraved with the monogram MJP. Michael Josiah Petersen. She knew this because she had bought him the ring herself.

She was completely at a loss. She took out the ring and turned it round in her fingers, then looked into Michael's face for guidance.

'We've had such great times together.' Michael's voice was thick with emotion. 'But—'

But? Freya's head jerked up. But what? What was going on here?

'—but I think it would be better if . . .'

'If what?'

'Well, I think it would be better if we could be . . . just friends.'

'Friends,' she echoed. *'Friends?'* she repeated loudly.

There was a dull splat. It was the ring, dropping from her lifeless fingers into the chocolate dessert.

Chapter **TWO**

WALK. DON'T WALK. Signs flashed. Headlamps dazzled. Traffic revved and roared. Freya strode up Broadway, heels clacking, long legs scissoring in leather trousers. A piece of crushed material dangled from one swinging fist. From time to time she swished it angrily, like a lion tamer with his whip. People got out of her way.

Bastard! How dare he ditch her like that? He'd led her up the garden path, then pushed her headfirst into the muck heap. 'I think you're a terrific person,' she mimicked to herself, waggling her head like a crazy. So *terrific* that he'd taken her to the most fashionable restaurant in town for the pleasure of dumping her in public. Her eyes blurred, and she stepped out into the street without seeing that the lights had changed.

A clash of car horns made her jump. Automatically Freya responded with a rude gesture and kept walking. She sniffed fiercely and swiped the heel of her hand across her cheeks. She hadn't cried in front of anyone since she was fifteen years old, when her little sneak of a stepsister had peeked through the keyhole of her bedroom door and then run to tell the household that Freya was a crybaby. Well, not any more. Freya had chosen this city *because* it was the toughest in the world. Manhattan was a place where you walked fast and avoided eye contact.

OK, so she was back to square one. So what? She'd been alone before. She was used to it. It was better than staying with a man who didn't love her. She wasn't doing that, not even for one night.

For after itemising the reasons why she wasn't right for him, Michael had been insensitive enough to suggest that she stayed on in his apartment until she found a new place, and had accused her of being 'emotional' when she refused. That's when she'd got up and left the restaurant—just cut him off in mid-sentence. There was no way she was going to let anyone see her get emotional. Anyway, she didn't need Michael's charity. There were alternatives to hanging around like Little Miss Grateful, sleeping on Michael's couch and demurely passing him the skimmed milk at breakfast time. 'I have plenty of other *friends*,' she'd told him pointedly.

The bad news was, they were all out. She'd made some calls from the gallery, when she returned to take off that stupid dress and change back into her work clothes. But it was still only ten o'clock on a Friday night, when most normal people were out having a good time—even Cat, her best friend, who had complained to her this very week that she hadn't been on a date in months. So where was she? Freya shrugged. It was no big deal: she would try later from her mobile. If the worst came to the worst, she could check into a cheap hotel. Freya pictured the desk-clerk's leer as she arrived in some seedy, ill-lit foyer, a lone woman with no luggage. Her scorching pace faltered. Where was she?

Union Square opened up ahead of her. It was a warm night, June 4, with the first promise of real summer, and the place was bustling. By the fountain in the middle of the square some guys had set up an *ad hoc* band—saxophone, double bass, guitar, a singer in a worn top hat. Behind them the city reared into the night sky, sparking like a perpetual firework display. The husky voice of the singer drifted out across the square.

Freya came to a halt and wrapped her arms across her chest. Under her fingers, she could feel the delicate beading of the pink dress. Abruptly she turned her back on the music and the view. Her eye fell on a large garbage container. She strode over to it and in a sudden, savage gesture stuffed the dress inside, between newspapers and crushed styrofoam cups and cigarette butts, pushing it deeper until the delicate chiffon began to rip, and red goo from pizza cartons smeared across the fancy beadwork. So much for her foolish female fantasies.

Twenty minutes later she was in Chelsea, standing outside the basement door of one of the seedier-looking town houses, a paper bag clasped under her arm. The window overlooking the narrow front yard was barred and curtained, but a light shone from inside and she thought she could hear the hum of voices. It was the first Friday of the month, right? Some people never changed. Freya pressed the doorbell.

She heard an inner door open, a casual male shout, the sticky tread of sneakers on bare tiles. A shadow loomed behind the panel of coloured glass. Then there was the click of a lock, and light streamed onto her face. Standing in the doorway was a tall, loose-limbed man with a haystack of blond hair, holding a drink in one hand. His eyebrows rose in surprise. Had she done the wrong thing? What if he was holed up with some babe? Then he shouted, 'Freya! I don't believe it!' and drew her inside with an easy hug. He smelt of bourbon.

'Hiya, Jack.' She stepped back from his embrace. 'You're still running the game, aren't you?'

'Sure. Come in.' He grinned at her. 'We can always use another sucker.'

'Sucker yourself!' She followed him across the chequerboard floor, squeezing past a bicycle propped against one wall. 'Who tricked you out of a full house that time with a lousy pair of nines?'

But Jack was already pushing open the door to the living room with his foot. 'Hey, everybody, look who's here!'

The scene was so familiar she didn't know whether to laugh or cry. In the centre of the room was a big round table covered with a stained cloth and littered with beer bottles, cigarette papers, pretzels, coloured poker chips, dollar bills, overflowing ashtrays, and pizza cartons. Smoke hung in a visible cloud below the globular ceiling lamp. And there they all were, the old crowd—Al, sitting backwards astride his chair, rolling a joint; Gus, doing his fancy double shuffle; Larry, counting his chips. There was another man, too, a stranger in a black shirt, with dark eyebrows and a challenging stare. The tableau held for a split second, then jerked into life as if her entrance had broken a spell.

There was a general hubbub of greeting. Someone went to the kitchen to get more ice. A glass was pressed into her hand. Larry bounded over and gave her a bear hug, his springy hair tickling her chin. These were her real friends.

'I didn't know you let women play.' A sardonic voice cut through the chatter. It was the stranger, still sitting at the table.

Jack gave his disarming laugh and hooked a heavy arm round Freya's shoulders. '"Women", no. Freya, yes. This here's my oldest friend, Leo. Freya's one of the boys.'

'She'll clean you out if you aren't careful,' added Gus.

'But I'm always careful.' He got up to shake Freya's hand in a formal manner, introducing himself as Leo Brannigan. 'So you're the famous Freya?' He scrutinised her with interest.

'I suppose so.' She laughed.

'Jack used to talk about you. You're English, aren't you?'

'Yes.'

'But you live in New York.'

'Yes.' He was still holding on to her hand.

'Are you married?'

'*No!*' Freya withdrew her hand and glared. What *was* this? 'Are you?'

'Of course not.' He gave an amused half-smile. Freya wasn't sure if this was a put-down or a very slimy pick-up.

'OK, Al, your deal.' Jack's voice was suddenly brisk. He brought Freya a chair and counted out a pile of chips at her place. 'One-dollar ante, fifty-dollar limit, dealer's choice.'

Freya knew the rules: number one was no girly chitchat. That suited her fine. In one swift movement she reached into the paper bag, drew out a bottle of Southern Comfort and plonked it on the table.

They started with five-card stud. As soon as Freya gathered her cards into her hand she felt focused, alive, confident. She loved this moment, when her world shrank to a pool of light and there was nothing but the clack of chips, the whisper and snap of cards, the clink of a bottle against glass. 'Poker isn't a game,' her father used to say; 'it's Greek drama: man against Fate. Never crow, and never whine.' Well, she wouldn't. She poured herself three fingers of Southern Comfort, took a deep slug, and blanked out Michael and the whole disastrous evening.

Lady Luck was with her and she played like a witch, finessing winning hands out of the air, varying her play to fox the opposition. Every time she remembered Michael's pitying eyes, or the fact that she had no place to sleep tonight, or that her life was a mess, she simply took another little drink. It worked a treat.

She dropped a stack of chips into the pot. 'See you five,' she said, 'and raise you . . . twenty.'

Gus slapped down his cards in disgust. 'Fold.'

'Me, too,' sighed Al.

'She's bluffing!' protested Jack. He pointed his finger at her. 'If you win this hand I'll—'

'You'll what? Fly me to the Caribbean? Give me a signed copy of your book?' Freya held his gaze. They were both grinning, enjoying this.

'I'll buy you dinner at Valhalla's on your birthday.'

'But that's months away!'

'So?'

'You'll forget.'

'No, I won't. November 7th, right?'

'Wrong. It's the 8th.'

'That's what I said.' His blue eyes danced. 'The 8th at eight—who could forget that? It'll be a special rendezvous, like that movie—'

'Yeah, yeah, I know. Bogart and Bacall in *Key Largo*.'

'Not *Key Largo*.' Leo was emphatic.

'Wasn't it Cary Grant and whatsername?' offered Gus.

'Whatever,' Freya said impatiently. Her fingers tingled. She wanted to finish this hand. She nodded at Jack. 'I accept the bet.'

'If you lose, you pay,' he warned.

'Of course.'

'OK, everyone. I want you all to bear witness.' Jack counted out his chips and placed them ceremoniously on the table. 'See you,' he told Freya.

Freya laid down her cards with an elegant ripple of the fingers. 'Three of a kind. Queens.'

'Shit!' Jack slumped over the table in mock despair and flipped his cards to show her a flush in clubs.

When they broke for coffee around midnight, Freya found she was more than a hundred dollars up. She felt great, high on adrenalin and alcohol. She stood up, stretching her arms wide to ease her back muscles, and went into the kitchen. She couldn't find a cup, so she washed one up from the collection of dirty dishes in the sink. Once the coffee was ready, Jack took the pot round, pushing through the crowd with his big shoulders, joking with everyone.

When he reached her, she leaned back against the worktop and held out her cup. 'You're a pig,' she told him, gesturing at the kitchen.

'I'm busy,' he countered. 'My mind is on higher things.'

'Does that mean the novel's going well?'

'A work of art can't be rushed.'

'I wouldn't call three years a rush. How many missed deadlines is it now?' She caught his eye. 'OK, I'll shut up. Tell me about Leo. I haven't seen him here before.'

'He started that magazine—Word—remember? The one that published my story about the boy in the storm?'

Freya nodded. 'You got fifty dollars and bought a bicycle.'

'Yeah, well now he's a literary agent doing million-dollar deals.' Jack rubbed a hand through his hair. 'He thinks I have talent.'

'Of course you have talent. You also have an agent. You're not thinking of leaving Ella after all she's done for you?'

'No . . .' Jack said uncertainly, looking put out. He set down the coffee pot and dug his hands into his pockets. 'So how's Mark?' he asked.

'Michael.'

'Whatever. Do we gather that he's let you come out to play tonight?'

'What kind of a question is that?'

'You're getting awfully snappy in your old age. Poor old Martin was probably happy to get rid of you tonight, so he could settle down with some nice, restful briefs.'

'Michael.' Freya glared at him. 'At least he does a real job. Some people have to earn their living, you know.' She pushed him out of the way, and returned to the card table. She wasn't in the mood to be teased.

When they started playing again, Freya's luck changed abruptly. Her pile of chips dwindled to nothing; she drew some more from the float and wrote an IOU. She folded early in one hand, and took her cellphone into the hallway to telephone Cat, who would surely be home by now.

'You have reached Caterina da Fillipo. Please leave your name and number, and I'll get back to you.'

Freya groaned. 'It's me,' she announced, after the beep. 'I need you. Call me on my mobile the minute you hear this. *Please.*'

When she returned to the poker table, the men were all talking about someone she didn't know, a guy who worked on Wall Street and was fabulously successful. She reached for the Southern Comfort, but all it did was fuzz her brain. In a round of five-card draw she misread a six for a nine, and made a fuss when she lost. She found she was out of chips again, and signed another IOU.

At the end of another disastrous hand, Freya rested her head on the table and closed her eyes. She felt terrible. Why had she come? She'd lost all her money and made a fool of herself. She wanted to go to bed.

Bed!

'Wait a second,' she croaked, trying to straighten up and focus. Someone was dealing the cards, floating them across the table. 'I have to make a call.' She groped for her phone and started pressing buttons. Nothing happened. She banged it on the table and tried again. 'Stupid thing won't work.'

'Maybe that's because you're trying to make a telephone call from a pocket calculator.' Leo's voice was as dry as the Sahara.

Everyone found this hilarious. Freya heard their donkey laughter. She saw Jack grinning openly at her from across the table. Aflame with alcohol and bad temper, she threw the calculator straight at him. It crashed into his glass, splashing drink all over him.

'Freya! What do you think you're doing?'

'Fuck off, Jack. It didn't even touch you.'

Something weird was happening to the room. The walls were billowing in and out like sails. The floor was tilting.

Someone bent close beside her. 'Are you all right, sweetheart?'

'I'm fine,' she mumbled, and passed out.

The bed was hot and sweaty. Sunlight glared through thin curtains. Somewhere a fly was buzzing. Jack groaned, turned onto his stomach and buried his face in the pillow.

The buzz came again: not a fly, but the doorbell. Jack opened an eye and squinted at the bedside clock. It was almost noon. He rolled over and levered his body into a sitting position and pulled on a pair of jeans over his undershorts. He added a cleanish white T-shirt, raked his fingernails through his hair, and stumbled to the front door. On the way, something bit into his bare foot. Hopping and cursing, Jack dislodged a metal bottle top from the soft flesh and flicked it back onto the floor.

On his doorstep a pretty young woman was smiling up at him.

Automatically, Jack smiled back. It took only seconds to recognise her as one of his students from the creative writing seminar he taught on Tuesday evenings, Candace Something-or-other. They had gone out for a drink after class last week.

'I hope it's OK to drop by,' she began shyly. 'You said the other night that if I was in the neighbourhood . . . We were going to do some more work on my structure, remember?' She gestured at her chest, which was ample and deliciously rounded, and after a moment of confusion Jack saw that she was clasping a bundle of books and papers. 'But if this is a bad time—'

'No, no.' Jack found his voice. Dark hair fell to her shoulders in a glossy wave. Her skin was smooth and glowing. 'It's a perfect time. Come in.' He stepped back to let her pass inside, inhaling a fresh smell of soap.

'Beautiful glass,' she said, admiring the etched panel in the door. 'I love these old places. They're so full of—'

'Shit!' Jack recoiled from a rancid blast of last night's fumes as he opened the living-room door. 'Wait here a minute, will you?'

She stopped obediently in the doorway. Moving swiftly, Jack pulled open the curtains, then toured the room picking up bottles, glasses, ash-trays and other jetsam, which he piled higgledy-piggledy onto the centre of the table. With an expertise born of practice he then flipped up the corners of the tablecloth, drew them tight to create a giant makeshift sack, and carried the whole clanking mess out to the kitchen. Returning, he opened a window, flipped over the seat cushions of the couch and patted one invitingly. 'Sit down. I'll make some coffee.'

Candace was leaning against the doorjamb, watching him in frank amusement, a tip of pink tongue curled against her upper lip.

'What's so funny?' he asked.

Her smile broadened, revealing straight pearly teeth. 'You are.'

Jack decided this would be a good moment to tuck his T-shirt into his jeans. 'Party last night,' he growled cryptically.

'I guessed.' Candace swayed over to the couch, sat down and crossed her bare legs. She gave a dreamy sigh. 'I love parties.'

'Not that kind of party.' Jack set her straight. 'This was a boys' night. Cards and booze and all that bad stuff. You're much too young and innocent for that kind of thing.'

'I'm twenty-two!' Candace protested.

'Exactly.'

Jack retreated to the kitchen, smiling to himself: young girls were so adorable. While the coffee heated, he ducked into the bathroom, located some headache pills and washed them down with a whole glass of water. Then he squeezed out a gob of toothpaste and squelched it around his mouth with his tongue. That was better. Body cleansed, his memory followed suit, and now he remembered how Candace had approached him as he was leaving the seminar room. He must have given her his address and some vague invitation.

When he returned with the coffee he found Candace examining his shelves.

'All these books!' Her tone was admiring. 'I can hardly believe you've read them all.'

Jack could hardly believe it either. 'Publishers send me things for endorsement. And I do some reviewing.' He shrugged modestly, slopping coffee.

'Here, let me do that.' Candace took charge of the tray, pouring coffee from the pot, while Jack sprawled in an armchair.

'So this is the home of Jack Madison,' she said. 'You can't imagine how exciting it is for me to see how a real writer lives.'

Jack glanced vaguely around the familiar room. Piles of old magazines were stacked on the floor. 'It's kind of messy, I guess.'

'Creativity is messy. Writing is just so involving, I'm beginning to discover that. If my room-mate talks to me I'm, like, "Leave me alone, I'm thinking."' She paused. 'Do you find that?'

'Absolutely.' Jack felt a prickle of familiar panic. He did not have writer's block; he was just allowing time for his novel to ripen in his imagination.

'But maybe you don't have a room-mate to bother you?' Candace cocked her head enquiringly.

'What? Oh no. I hate sharing with other people.'

'Even . . . women?'

'Especially women. All those fights about the garbage, or who finished the milk. I like to be able to do what I want when I want.'

Candace nodded. 'I have a favour to ask.' She took a pen out of her bag, then reached towards her pile of papers. Jack's heart sank. He didn't want to spend his Saturday in textual analysis of someone else's dreary prose.

She held something out to him. 'I know it's corny, but would you . . . ?'

Jack was gratified to recognise the collection of short stories that had launched his career. 'Aw, you shouldn't have wasted your money.'

'I found it on sale, reduced to half-price. Wasn't that lucky?'

Jack frowned. This was not something authors liked to hear. He turned to the title page, took the pen Candace offered and thought for a moment. Then he wrote 'Candy is dandy', and signed his name with a flourish. He closed the book and handed it back.

Candace hugged the book tight, so that her breasts plumped up above the stretchy top she was wearing.

'Listen,' Jack said casually, 'are you doing anything tonight?'

'Me?' Candace's eyebrows rose in surprise. 'Not especially. Why?'

'I was thinking—you could leave me your script to read, and we could talk about it over dinner.'

'But it's Saturday night.' Her lips curved flirtatiously. 'You must have plans. Isn't there somebody—?'

'Nobody,' Jack said firmly. 'Not a thing. No plans, no ties, no—'

A sudden commotion interrupted him. There was a yelp of pain and a muttered tirade as a whey-faced figure limped into view, wearing nothing but a striped shirt Jack vaguely recognised. He stared. It was *his* shirt. And the woman inside was Freya. He'd forgotten all about her.

''Scuse me,' she croaked. 'Oof!' She winced as the slanting sunlight hit her face and flung up a protective hand, then shuffled blindly across the room, depositing a metal bottle top on the table as she passed. Then there came the slam of the bathroom door and the sound of throwing up.

'I have to go now.' Candace was already on her feet. The sparkle had gone from her face.

'But you've just come!' Jack sprang out of his chair, blocking her way. He wanted to strangle Freya. 'Look, you haven't even finished your coffee. Sit down.'

Candace shook her head. 'I need to do some shopping. And you're busy.'

'No, I'm not. Oh, you mean *her*?' Jack sounded incredulous. 'That's just someone who came to play cards last night and got drunk.'

'You said it was a boys' night.'

'I don't think of Freya as a *girl*.' Jack chuckled at the very notion. 'She's an old friend. An old, old friend. I mean, really old.' He swallowed. 'Practically forty.'

Candace's eyes darted to his. She looked suitably shocked.

'Personally,' Jack lowered his voice, 'I think it's kind of sad when someone of that age gets out of control and has to be put to bed *in the guest room*, don't you?'

Candace shrugged.

'Actually, my study. It's so frustrating. I haven't been able to do any work all morning. The sooner I can get her out of here, and back uptown with her boyfriend, the better.'

'That's up to you.' Candace tossed her hair. 'It's none of my business.'

'Good. So are we meeting tonight?'

'I don't know . . .'

'Come on,' Jack drawled persuasively. 'Why don't you write down your phone number? When I've gotten rid of Freya I'll give you a call.'

'I don't know,' she repeated. 'I might be busy after all.'

'Write it down anyway. Just in case.'

Minutes later, Jack was standing on the sidewalk watching Candace's tilting hips as she receded down the street. Everything about her signalled availability. Well, why not? he thought—so long as Freya hadn't ruined the whole thing. Jack scowled. *Thanks, Freya, you're a pal.*

Back inside, Jack looked around for her. But it seemed she had gone back to bed with her hangover. He was sorry that Freya didn't feel well, but Michael must take care of her. Jack headed for the telephone. Then his expression sobered. What exactly was the etiquette of calling up another man to inform him that his girlfriend had just spent the night in your apartment?

Pondering this problem, Jack slumped into a chair by the telephone and flipped idly through his address book. The pages were worn and dogeared, each one crammed with names and numbers. He could remember when the pages were crisp and white and empty, the leather binding a sensuous, glossy tan stamped with his initials—a going-away present from Lauren, his stepmother, 'for all the wonderful friends you'll make'. Now the book was a satisfyingly fat compendium of publishers, movie theatres, girlfriends, favourite bars, magazine editors, libraries, pool clubs, restaurants, bookstores—and friends, of course. Freya's name sprouted all over the 'F' section. He'd never known anyone who moved as often as she did. The very first entry, now crossed through, gave the address of that leaky old boarding house in Brooklyn where he'd come looking for a cheap room his very first week in New York. An image flashed up of long blonde hair fanning out around her upside-down face as she leaned over a top-floor banister to call out to him.

In those days Freya had struck him as an impossibly superior being, a sophisticated twenty-five to his raw twenty-two. She knew where you could fill up on soup and bagels for five dollars, which flea markets sold the cheapest furniture, how to sneak into openings and gorge on canapés and champagne for free, which movie theatre let you see the picture twice around to keep warm. She'd introduced him to 'the gang'—a group of would-be artists, actors, musicians and writers who shivered together through the winters, dragged their mattresses onto roofs and fire escapes in summer, and assured one another they were geniuses. From the first Jack had enjoyed her sharp wit and independence of mind. There had even been a time, one night years ago, when he'd . . . Jack frowned. He did not wish to revisit that humiliating occasion.

Returning to the address book, he leapfrogged swiftly from one Freya entry to the next—uptown, downtown, this boyfriend, that boyfriend, this job, that job. Yes, ten years was a long time. They were still friends, would surely always be friends—but he had his own life to lead, and she had hers. He found Michael's number and dialled.

'**A** *wisp of silver strayed diaphanous beneath the moon, suspended in the inky well of night. Watching it, something dark and primitive stirred in Garth's loins, and he emitted a groan of longing, like the honk of a lonely goose . . .*'

It was midafternoon. Over the last couple of hours Jack had done the dishes, cleaned up the living room, left a cup of tea by the bedside of a comatose Freya, and taken out the trash. Now he was lying on the couch under the large window, sneakered feet comfortably propped on the far armrest, a sheaf of papers on his chest. From what he could make out, *Forbidden*—world copyright Candace Twink—was a story of doomed love set in the Civil War, featuring a feminist version of Scarlett O'Hara and a black slave apparently familiar with existentialism.

What was he going to tell her? Sometimes, Jack privately wondered whether creative writing could be taught. But he needed the money. He wrote reviews and magazine pieces for the same reason. His allowance simply wasn't enough to live on any more. Jack thought resentfully of his father, with his beach house and his mountain house as well as the Madison mansion, his expensive cigars and even more expensive wives. Jack's allowance barely covered the rental for this apartment; but when he tried to ask for more, all he got was the suggestion that Jack got himself a 'real' job.

Still, there were compensations. He leaned his head back against the armrest of the couch and closed his eyes, trying to picture the shape of the evening. First he'd take Candace for drinks at Z Bar, where they could sip cocktails on the roof terrace. It would be important to get the business part over at the beginning, so pretty soon he'd take out her script and give her his critique. Then, over the second cocktail, he'd suggest one ruthless cut—dropping the subplot about the amputee, for example—something to get her emotions going. They'd fight, she might cry, he'd apologise, they'd make up, and afterwards they'd move on to some dark, funky restaurant, then back to her place.

Satisfied with his plan, Jack returned *Forbidden* to its folder. After all that work he was starving; he would make himself a sandwich. He got up from the couch, stretched his arms wide and yawned, sucking in his breath so vigorously that it made a curious noise in his throat. Hark! Was that, perchance, the honk of a lonely goose? He tucked his fists into his armpits and flapped his elbows experimentally.

'Taking off somewhere?' said a voice.

Jack whirled round. 'Oh, hi, Freya.' He tried to turn the flapping into a vigorous rib-massage. 'Uh, feeling better?'

'Fine.' She was fully dressed in last night's clothes, bag over her shoulder, ready to go. 'I just came to say goodbye, and thank you. I'm sorry to have been such a nuisance.'

'That's OK.' Her formal manner caught Jack off guard. He scanned her more closely. 'Can I get you some coffee? Aspirin?'

She shook her head. 'I'd better get back.'

'Right.' Jack hesitated, wondering how much he dared question her. Freya always acted as if her private life was a state secret. 'Back where?' he ventured finally.

'Home, of course.'

It was the 'of course' that did it, uttered with such condescension that Jack was piqued into saying, 'Why don't you call Michael? He must be worried about you.'

Immediately he regretted his cruel impulse. Freya's face closed tight, like a fragile sea creature poked with a stick. She was unzipping her bag. 'I'm sure I must owe everyone money from last night.'

'Afraid so. Don't worry, I paid for you since you were . . .'

'Asleep.' She pulled out her wallet.

'Whatever. The total's kind of steep—two hundred and forty-seven dollars.'

Her hand froze. 'I don't seem to have my chequebook on me right now. Is it OK if I pay you back next week?'

'Well, of course it is!' What was the matter with her?

'Thanks, Jack.' Her face softened, but only for a moment. 'I'm sorry about this morning, by the way. I hope I didn't interrupt anything.'

It seemed to Jack that her eyebrows arched in a knowing way. 'That was one of my students,' he said reprovingly.

'Really? Are you teaching her the ABC?'

Jack glowered. 'I'll come and help you get a cab.'

'No! I mean, thanks, but I think I'll hop on a bus.' She half turned away, hesitated, then stepped towards him in that decisive, long-legged way she had. They kissed cheeks. 'Thanks for the game, and thanks for the bed. See you soon.'

'See you,' Jack echoed, following her into the hall. He opened the door for her and watched her walk up the steps to the street and then off along the sidewalk. He wondered where she was going. Some friend? Another man? She obviously didn't want to tell him, and he knew better than to ask. Fine. He shut the door.

Cheese and peanut butter, he thought, with a smidge of piccalilli, corn chips on the side and an ice-cold beer. Yum. His mouth was already watering. He headed for the kitchen, yanked open the fridge door and started assembling ingredients. What a mystery women were. He'd known Freya for over ten years, yet she wouldn't tell him she'd split up with her boyfriend; whereas Michael, whom he'd met about twice and didn't even like, had told him right away. Men were so straightforward. Jack still didn't know the exact reasons for the break-up, but it was pretty clear that Michael wasn't expecting Freya back. When Jack had protested that Freya was sick and needed somewhere to go, Michael had responded, 'You're her friend, you take care of her.'

Of course, that was impossible. He had a novel to write. Jack ran a forefinger round the inside rim of the peanut-butter jar and put it in his mouth: sensational. Anyway, you might as well try to take care of a sabre-toothed tiger: Freya did exactly as she pleased, and always had. Jack flicked a splodge of piccalilli on top of the cheese, pressed a piece of bread on top to complete his sandwich, and took a large bite. The real conundrum was how Freya and Michael ever got together in the first place. The guy had no style. He had actually complained to Jack that the bill at last night's restaurant had come to $365, 'not including tip'. Jack chuckled. He loved that—Michael's entire character summed up in three words. In fact, it was so good that he wanted to write it down. Taking his sandwich with him, he walked through to his study so he could scribble a note for his 'Ideas' file.

When he opened the door, the first thing that caught his eye was the narrow divan bed. Normally a repository for papers, it was a vision of tidiness. The bedspread lay flat and scrupulously symmetrical; in the centre was a neat pile of folded sheets, with his striped shirt and a ten-dollar bill on top. Next to the money was a note: *For laundry—F.* Jack picked up the note, smiling at the familiar, cryptic signature. What a funny person she was. He remembered the surprise party she'd organised for Larry when he got his first job in TV; the scores of old movies the two of them had seen together, legs hooked over the seats in front, sharing popcorn. The nagging guilt he'd been trying to ignore all morning exploded into some much larger emotion—concern? affection? shame? When he asked her where she was going, she'd said 'Home, of course.' Except Freya didn't have a home. Her family lived thousands of miles away in England. Michael had thrown her out. She was alone in the loneliest city in the world. And he was supposed to be her friend.

Jack tossed the remains of his sandwich onto his desk. Stupid woman! Why did she have to be so proud? He hurried to grab his keys and ran to the front door. Wait a minute—what about his bicycle? Jack manhandled it outside. Then he half scooted, half hopped down the path and up to the sidewalk, bumped down into the street and, swinging his leg over the bike, raced off in the direction he had seen her take.

He wove his way perilously across the stream of traffic and pedalled head-down towards 7th Avenue and the downtown bus-stop. This is crazy, he told himself. She could be walking on any of a dozen different streets. She could be in a coffee bar. She could have caught a cab after all—except she probably didn't have any money. *You're a bastard*, Jack told himself, as his ancient bike juddered and squeaked.

When he was four years old his parents had divorced, and his mother had taken him and Lane, his baby brother, to live with her in Atlanta. He didn't remember his mother much—she was out a lot—but Jack remembered being happy. Then one day he learned that his mother was to marry again and was going to live somewhere far away. She wanted to take Jack with her, but his father wouldn't allow that. Shortly after his seventh birthday, Jack remembered the arrival outside the house of a big shiny car, and his father, a stranger tall and golden as a god, laying a heavy, claiming hand on his shoulder, saying, 'Son, I've come to take you home.'

At the next block Jack swooped left, joining the stream of traffic. Shit, he could see a bus ahead of him, letting out a pair of gym-bunnies with their sports bags. By the time he reached the bus, she had one foot on the first step of the bus, one hand on the rail.

'Freya! Wait!' he called.

She looked around, blinking, and her eyes focused on him. He'd have said she'd been crying if he didn't know that Freya never cried.

'Jack? What's the matter?' she said.

There was no time for tact. 'I know about Michael,' he bawled across the line of people waiting to board the bus. 'I called him this morning. You haven't anywhere to go, have you?'

Freya's mouth opened and closed. 'Yes, I have.'

'Oh yeah? Where?' Jesus, she was stubborn. He rolled the bike forward, balancing on his toes. 'Come and stay with me. Just until you get yourself fixed up.'

'No, Jack. You've got your writing and all your . . . students. I'd cramp your style.'

'No, you wouldn't.' Of course she'd cramp his style!

'Hey, Romeo, get lost!' barked a voice. It was the driver, mirrored sunglasses flashing. He bared his teeth at Freya in a sinister leer. 'Come on, lady. Make my day.'

Freya leapt back onto the sidewalk. The doors closed behind her with a swoosh of compressed air, and the bus took off.

'Have you got a place to stay?' Jack demanded.

'Not yet. But—'

'Then come home with me.'

No answer. Her eyes were lowered, her lips pinched tight.

He wanted to put his arm round her, but he didn't dare.

'There's grease on your jeans,' she said at last.

Jack smiled at this typical evasion. He turned his bike round, making a big production of it, giving them both time. Suddenly he had an idea. 'Frankly, Freya, I need the rent.'

That got her attention. 'You're not serious, are you?'

'Perfectly serious. Twenty dollars a day, two weeks absolute max.' He held out his hand, palm upwards. 'Deal?'

She wavered for about five seconds, then gave his palm a decisive slap. 'I warn you, I'm hell to live with.'

Jack nodded. He could well believe it.

(Chapter) Three

'MEN ARE SUCH PIGS.' Cat's dark eyes glowed with sympathetic indignation. 'So then what happened?'

'Well, after he'd fished out his stupid ring and made the waiter bring him a bowl of water so he could clean it up, he told me I wasn't committed to him. Can you believe it? The creep dumps me, then twists the whole thing around so that it's *my* fault!'

Freya and Cat were sitting opposite one another in a cramped restaurant in Chinatown. A teapot and two cups, pale blue with pink dragons, steamed between them. It was Monday lunchtime. The courthouse, where Cat spent a lot of time in the course of her work as a family lawyer, was just round the corner. Cat was supposed to be working, but like a true friend she had cancelled an appointment to hear Freya's tale of woe.

'When I think of all the hoops I jumped through for him!' Freya continued. 'Drinking skimmed milk because of his cholesterol count, pretending I liked those dreary operas he took me to.' Her brow cleared momentarily. 'One good thing: at least I won't have to sit through that bloody *Ring* cycle.'

'At the Met? Freya, those tickets are like gold dust. How can you not like Wagner? He's so romantic.'

'Not the R-word. Please.' Freya pressed a hand to her forehead.

'Of course. I'm sorry.'

A Chinese woman in worn slippers halted by their table and gave a surly jerk of her head to show that she was ready to take their order.

'I'll have a number five,' said Cat. 'What about you, Freya?'

'I couldn't eat.'

'Of course you can eat. Now hurry up and decide.'

Freya stared at the inscrutable menu. A Bloody Mary with extra Tabasco was what she wanted, but they didn't serve alcohol here.

'You choose,' she said. 'Nothing with more than four legs.'

When the waitress had gone, Freya sank her chin in her hands and fixed Cat with a mournful look. 'Be honest, Cat. Why didn't Michael want to marry me? What's wrong with me?'

'Nothing!' Cat was gloriously emphatic. 'You're gorgeous, smart, funny. What's wrong with *him* is the question.'

'I find the only man in New York who actually wants to commit—but he doesn't want to commit to *me*. Why not?'

Cat considered. 'You don't think . . .?'

'What?'

'You don't think he could have found another woman?'

'Michael? Don't be ridiculous.'

'In that case, he probably got cold feet. I blame the media. Every time you open a magazine, there's another article about how desperate women are to get married. No wonder men are scared. Ten years ago it was HIV; now it's single women: the new plague. Run for your lives!'

Freya giggled, forgetting for a moment how miserable she was. Cat always made her laugh. They had met years ago, at a tap-dancing class of all places, where Cat had broken her ankle while attempting a double pick-up. Freya, temporarily homeless, had ended up taking care of her and sleeping on her pullout bed. She had discovered that Cat's Latin temper and Columbia-educated mind concealed the most generous heart she knew. Cat adored her family, a huge Italian-American tribe based in Staten Island. She had a passionate social conscience and contributed hours of free legal work to those who couldn't afford the fees. Now it was Cat who cooked Freya meals when she was down, listened to her moans about Lola, and picked up the pieces when some man let her down. Cat was a real friend and Freya trusted her absolutely.

The food came with indecent speed, confounding any pretence that it had been freshly made. Freya took a tentative bite.

'Maybe it was a mistake to walk out on Michael.' Cat was thinking aloud. 'I mean, if you'd stayed at the restaurant and talked through the situation, he might have changed his mind.' She shot Freya a speculative look. 'Even now, he could be reconsidering. Just think. It could still all be yours: house, children, Connecticut, station wagon, country club—'

'Stop trying to torture me.'

'Ah-hah! I thought so. Admit: you liked the *idea* of getting married.'

Freya glowered. She didn't want to admit anything of the kind.

'I'm sorry, sweetie.' Cat reached out impulsively for her hand. 'I'm sorry it didn't work out with Michael. But you could be awfully disparaging about him. You never even let me meet him.'

'I know.' Freya was embarrassed. For some reason she was always secretive about her emotional life. Anyway, Cat would have scared the pants off Michael. She shrugged. 'You'd hate Michael. He's so straight.'

'But you wanted to marry him?'

Freya squirmed under Cat's challenging gaze. She probably did want to marry someone, sometime. The fact that she might have rejected Michael in the end was beside the point; he hadn't even given her the option. 'Well, I thought I did,' she muttered. 'Mind you, he was never exactly King Kong in the bedroom.'

'Really?' Cat was agog. 'You mean . . . technical problems?'

'No, the equipment worked. Let's just say that I think he must have read about the importance of foreplay in some magazine.'

'But foreplay's my second-favourite part!'

'Depends how it's done. With Michael it was a bit like going to the dentist. You know, the hygienist cleans your teeth and tells you all about her vacation in Florida, and then you rinse and spit, and spit and rinse, until you think "For Chrissakes, get out the bloody drill!"'

Cat yelped with laughter, making heads turn. 'That's so cruel.'

'What are these crunchy bits?' Freya poked moodily at her food.

'Probably ginkgo nuts, or lotus seeds. Every dish has a perfect balance of yin and yang. I haven't had a single cold since I started coming here.'

'Maybe that's what's wrong with Michael—too much yin, or too little. He's always blowing his nose, or asking me if I have a Kleenex. It drives me mad. Drove,' she amended.

There was a thoughtful pause. 'You know, Freya, needing a Kleenex and not having one doesn't mean you're a wimp.'

Freya slapped the table. 'For me, it's simply not sexy. End of story.' She glowered at her friend. 'You're too nice. Promise me, you'll never marry someone just because you feel sorry for him.'

Cat fixed Freya with a portentous stare. 'I'm not going to marry anyone,' she announced. 'It's official.'

'What do you mean?'

Cat wiped her mouth carefully with a paper napkin.

'I've made a policy decision. I'm not dating any more. The fact is, *I don't need a man.* I have a good job, enough money, my own apartment. Frankly, I'm not at all sure that the ideologies of marriage and feminism mesh. No. I have seen the future as a single woman—and it works.'

Freya couldn't help feeling sceptical. Anyone could see that Cat was made to have a husband, a home and a tribe of children to manage.

'What about love?' she asked.

'Pure make-believe. I see husbands and wives every day in my work, and the truth is the men beat up their wives, steal from them, cheat on them. I've got a case right now of a woman in her *seventies* who's suing for divorce on the grounds of unfaithfulness.' Cat sighed.

'What about kids? You love children.'

'There's a fertility clinic right in the building where I work. All I have to do one day is get out of the elevator at the fifth floor instead of the ninth, and I could walk out pregnant.'

'Hmm.' Freya tried to picture herself proud and free and single, an Amazon towering above the petty squabbles of the sex war. 'What about sex?' she said.

'You don't need a husband for that,' Cat scoffed. 'No. The fact is that women want romance, affection, fidelity, children, and an adult mind to engage with. Men want sex, unquestioning admiration, no responsibility and a regular turnover. There's no synergy.' She lifted her chin defiantly. 'I can't tell you how relieved I am since I made this decision.'

Freya stared thoughtfully at her friend, at her vibrant, expressive face, her creamy skin and mass of curly black hair, her voluptuous figure. 'If you've given up dating,' she asked, 'where were you on Friday when I needed you?'

'At my sister's, baby-sitting. I gave Tonito his bottle and sang him a song, then I had two vodka martinis and reheated *spaghetti alla matriciana*, watched *When Harry Met Sally* for the umpteenth time, and fell asleep on the couch.'

'The perfect evening.'

'I rest my case.' Cat looked smug. 'Now listen, sweetie, I'm sorry I wasn't home Friday, but you're welcome to come and sleep on my couch for as long as you want. I'd adore it.'

'Thanks, Cat, but I might as well stay at Jack's, now I'm there.'

'Is that the big blond guy who was at the beach party last year?'

'If he was carrying a six-pack of nymphets, probably.'

'Mmm-mmm.' Cat smacked her lips in a vulgar Italian manner. 'Maybe you should introduce me properly one day.'

Freya frowned. 'You just said you were off men.'

'I said marriage was an untenable position for a feminist. I can always research my theory.' Cat's eyes sparkled.

'Well . . . just so long as you understand that Jack is not marriage material.' Freya felt it was her duty to warn her friend. 'If you wanted to go dancing, say, or see an old film, Jack would be the perfect partner. In all other respects his knuckles are still scraping along the ground.'

'But you like him,' Cat pointed out.

'I'm different. I'm immune.'

'I see. Well, stay with him if you want to, but be careful.'

'Of what, for heaven's sake? We're just friends.'

'Men are funny. They see you wandering around in a bath towel, or hanging out your underwear, and suddenly they want to *pounce*. It's an instinct thing.'

Cat was checking her watch. 'Sweetheart, I hate to say this but I really must go.'

'I'll walk you back. And I'm paying. No arguments.'

Outside, Freya hooked her arm into Cat's and gave it a squeeze as they set off down the street. Maybe Cat was right. Here they were, two single women together, perfectly happy. No husbands to irritate them. No children to rush home to. Just friends. Suddenly Freya felt optimistic again. She had taken this afternoon off work so that she could sneak into Michael's apartment and grab the clothes she needed while he was safely at the office. Then she would start looking for somewhere to live, and figure out what to do about England now that Michael had let her down. Somehow the future would sort itself out.

Freya lifted her head and looked about her. The morning's rain had cleared, leaving the air summery and fresh, a good ten degrees cooler than yesterday. Sunlight filtered through a silvery sky, bouncing rainbow reflections off the World Trade Center in the distance.

Freya gasped. '*Quick!*' She yanked Cat backwards and turned to duck into the shelter of the nearest building entrance.

'What's going on?' Cat shook her off.

'It's Michael!' she whispered. 'You don't think he followed me here, do you?'

'Which one?'

'Tan briefcase, blue shirt, crossing the road.'

'Hmm. Nice suit.'

'Bugger his suit. What's he doing here?'

'He's a lawyer. That's the courthouse. And I'm Einstein.' Cat smirked.

Freya watched the dark figure retreating and was shocked to realise that, beyond a desire to remain invisible, she felt absolutely nothing.

'The important question,' said Leo, 'is how you're going to position yourself.'

'Right here on this barstool seems pretty good to me.' Jack grinned, and tipped a bottle of beer to his lips.

The truth was, he was hellishly uncomfortable on the moulded plastic seat, raised on its slim chromium stalk to an awkward height that left him pawing alternately for the footrest and the floor. These things weren't made for someone of six foot four. But he wasn't about to complain. When it came to a free lunch he could take the rough with the smooth.

This was Club SoHo, a new members-only media hangout. Jack had read about its glitzy membership—screenwriters, actors, agents, producers—but this was the first time he'd been inside.

'I'm serious,' Leo persisted. 'People don't have time to figure things out for themselves any more. You have to tell them what to think. Get the juices flowing. Connect.'

'"Only connect",' Jack muttered vaguely. 'Who wrote that?'

Leo plucked at his tie, a bold snakeskin pattern aggressively teamed with a crimson shirt. 'No idea. I never went to college.'

This was a daring admission from someone in the literary world. Jack was curious. 'How come?'

'No time. No money. I came to books late. But I'm making up for it now.' Leo gave a sly grin. 'Let's go eat.'

The dining room was on the first floor, plain but stylish, lit by three high, arched windows overlooking the street. On the way to their table, Leo stopped to say hello to a man who turned out to be Carson McGuire. His first novel had been on the best-seller list for weeks. Everyone said it was a masterpiece. Jack hadn't read it yet.

In the flesh McGuire was unprepossessing: squat, fortyish, Bruce Willis haircut. Yet the sheen of success was upon him. His cheeks were plump and smooth, his jacket uncreased, his body language subtly assertive. With him was a tempestuous-looking young woman with

slanting cats' eyes and a thrilling acreage of bare flesh. Jack was beginning to feel painfully conspicuous in his jeans and shabby jacket when
Leo at last turned to include him in the conversation.

'Carson, do you know Jack Madison? He wrote that terrific collection,
Big Sky, a couple of years back.'

'For sure.' McGuire did the professional handshake/eye contact
number. 'Great book. Nice to meet you, Jake.'

'Yes. Thank you. Uh, great.'

What wit! What suavity! Carson McGuire would certainly remember
him. Jack lumbered after Leo to their table, feeling as ridiculous as a
dancing bear.

'Great guy, Carson,' said Leo, once they had taken their seats.
'Absolutely one of my favourite clients. I *think* I'm just about to clinch a
Hollywood deal for him, but don't tell him, huh?' Leo winked.

'How would I? We don't move in the same circles.'

'You will, Jack, you will.'

Leo spoke with such confidence that Jack felt ashamed of his sulki-
ness. He made an effort to rise above it. 'A movie deal, Leo: that's wonderful. Carson's a lucky man to have you for an agent. Good taste in
women, too.' He cocked an eyebrow at the dark temptress.

'That's Mercedes. She's a model, from Venezuela or somewhere.
Carson's married, of course. Still, while the cat's away . . .' He shot Jack a
man-to-man smile.

'Yeah.' Jack chuckled. 'Cute mouse.'

'By the way, what happened to that poor woman the other night?'

'What poor woman?' Jack's smile faded.

'Your fancy English friend who threw the calculator at you!'

'She's fine.'

'Got rid of her OK, did you? Some ditzy woman once passed out like
that at my place, and I caught her crawling into my bed at five in the
morning. I told her, "If you're sober enough to get here from the couch,
you're sober enough to go home." I put her in a cab, quick, before she
started getting ideas.'

'Freya's not like that.'

'Come on, Jack, once they pass thirty they're all like that. Hormones
in overdrive, bodies in freefall, careers a little shaky. They put those soft
pussycat paws on you and suddenly—ouch!—in go the claws.'

Jack gave a weak laugh. Freya was probably moving her things into
his apartment at this very moment. 'Freya's just a friend.'

'They're the worst. They think they "understand" you.' Leo grimaced.
'They worm their way in by making you dinner, or doing little favours

like stocking your fridge or taking your stuff to the repair shop. One minute they're telling you that they'll always "be there" for you; the next, they're always *there*, period.'

'Ha ha.' Jack wished Leo would order some more booze.

'Secretly, of course, older women *hate* men. They know we can wait for ever to get married and have children, whereas they have to do it by the time they're forty—and they *can't stand it*. It blows their equality theory to hell. I like to stick with the under twenty-fives, myself.'

Jack grinned, remembering Candace. 'I'm seeing an adorable twenty-two-year-old at the moment.'

'Way to go.' Leo reached across to give him an approving punch on the arm. 'Now, what are you drinking?'

A pretty waitress took their order and brought a bottle of wine. To Jack's relief, Leo began talking about the publishing industry. Jack watched his sharp, clever face and emphatic hand gestures, half listening to an energetic commentary on takeovers, book fairs, six-figure deals.

'. . . you see, in the old days publishers relied on good reviews to sell a book—but who gives a shit about reviews these days? Nowadays it's like the movies: the pitch is everything. You have to make a book sound hot, irresistible, must-have.' Leo paused as a waiter placed their order on the table. 'So, Jack. Tell me about your new book.'

'Oh. Well it's, you know, OK. Going well, in fact. Slow, but—'

'What's it called?'

'*The Long Summer*.' Saying it aloud was painful. 'At the moment.'

'Good title. Don't change it. Contemporary setting?'

'Yes, but it sort of weaves back, you know, into some family, uh, history.' Jack busied himself with a mouthful of guinea fowl.

'Sounds fascinating.'

'And there's a kind of love story except it doesn't—well, anyway, a love story. Kind of.' Jack grabbed his wineglass and drained it.

'Wonderful. I can't wait to read it.' Mercifully, Leo changed the subject. 'How do you like the club?'

'Great spot. Is it easy to get membership?'

'Almost impossible. But I know the owner. I could probably swing it for you. You want to get in soon, though, before they increase the fee.'

'How much is it now?'

'Four thousand dollars.'

'Whoooh! I think I'll have to wait for my inheritance.'

'With your talent? I could get you an advance tomorrow, so big you wouldn't have to worry about such things.'

Jack stared at Leo. Could he really do that?

'Of course, I know you already have an agent,' Leo said. 'Ella Fogarty, isn't it?'

'She's . . . I . . . We go way back.'

'A really nice woman, no question. I admire your loyalty.' Leo leaned across the table. 'Listen to me, Jack. You have talent. You are going to be a star. All you need is a little help. If you want it, I'm here. Understand?'

Jack met Leo's intense gaze and nodded solemnly. 'Thanks. I—I'll think about it.'

'You do that. Now, what about dessert? I recommend the *tarte tatin*.'

Chapter Four

FREYA TWISTED HER KEY in the familiar lock and pushed open the door of apartment 12B. She took a tentative step inside.

'Hello?' she called out.

But of course there was no answer. Michael was safely at work. She had the place to herself.

Swiftly she crossed the living room and opened the bedroom door. Everything in here was the same—the clutter of bottles and make-up tubes on her chest of drawers, her kimono hooked on the back of the door. Freya walked over to the window and leaned her forehead across the glass, staring out. This was what she had always liked best about the apartment: its calming view over Riverside Park and across the Hudson River to the smokestacks of New Jersey.

She sighed. Another era over. Why was it that her life no longer seemed to progress? When she looked back over the last few years, there seemed to be no development, just one damned thing after another: another man, another job, another apartment.

Freya blinked her eyes and hauled herself back into the present. She dragged a chair over to the closet and reached for her two suitcases, old friends, stacked on a high shelf. When she yanked them down, dust and debris showered onto her head and drifted to the floor. Damn. She fetched a dustpan and brush to sweep up the mess, and a long apron to protect her clothes, then dusted off her hair and tied an old cotton scarf washerwoman-style around her head.

She put her suitcases on top of the bed, lids flipped open. First, the essentials: passport, underwear, shoes. The passport was easily stowed in her handbag; her extensive collection of fancy lingerie and footwear, however, required an entire case to themselves. Freya sat on the lid and bounced out the air until it shut. She filled the other suitcase, staggered to the elevator with both of them, and stowed them downstairs in the doorman's cubbyhole until she was ready to take a cab to Jack's. On the next trip she fetched a bulging dress-bag. By this time she was feeling dishevelled, and grumpy with hunger. She stood in the kitchen and chomped eight Ritz crackers in a row. Her eyes roved around the neat, familiar room. She pictured Michael in his striped apron, sleeves rolled up, meticulously chopping and measuring. He was a good cook, whereas she was useless in the kitchen.

Swallowing hastily, she grabbed a couple of plastic shopping bags and did a final sweep of the apartment, dropping in small items—bottles of goop from the bathroom, the new Matisse biography she was reading, some favourite sounds from the rack by the stereo.

Last of all she located her handbag and the two items that she had laid ready on top of the chest of drawers, now empty and otherwise bare. One was a small framed photograph of her mother. Paris, Place Vendôme, 1972—the last week, possibly the last day, Freya had seen her. For a moment Freya held the photo in her palm, staring down at it. The carefree eyes smiled back. Her mother had been only thirty-one when she died. Freya stroked the cold glass with a fingertip, then carefully slotted the picture into an inner pocket of her bag.

The other item was an airline wallet containing two tickets for England, one for her and one for . . . well, who? The wedding was less than three weeks away. Freya felt a burst of anger that Michael couldn't have waited a bit longer to ditch her. She couldn't go alone; she *couldn't*. Her imagination raced ahead, conjuring up scenes of embarrassment and humiliation—and that's when she remembered the hat. She had bought it specially. Climbing onto the chair once again, she foraged in the clutter of overnight bags, rolled-up posters and exercise weights until she came upon a smartly striped box.

What was that? Freya froze, arm arrested in midair. She could hear a distinct metallic scuffling, horribly like the sound of a key in a lock. Instinctively, she crouched low and slid off the chair. It couldn't be!

But it was. Freya felt a faint draught of air as the apartment door opened. She heard footsteps, the rustle of shopping bags, then a slam loud enough to make her jump. She checked her watch: barely five o'clock, much too early for Michael. She grabbed the dustpan and brush, and holding them before her like shield and dagger, edged cautiously into the corridor.

An elderly woman was hanging something up in the hall closet. She wore a neat, old-fashioned suit of celery green, its pleated skirt falling modestly to her plump calves, and had a nimbus of fluffy white hair sculpted like a meringue. Freya must have made some small sound, for the woman turned suddenly, saw her, and clutched the pussycat bow at her neck. 'My goodness! You practically scared me to death!'

Freya stared. Who was this person?

Whoever she was, she seemed quite unabashed. 'I thought you came on Tuesdays,' she said, closing the closet door with a firm hand. She advanced on Freya, head high. 'Do you speak English?'

Freya opened her mouth, but no words emerged.

The woman aimed an index finger at her own heart. 'I,' she said, slowly and distinctly, 'am Mrs Petersen, Mr Petersen's mother.' She thought for a moment. '*La madre de Signor Petersen. Comprendo?*'

Freya's brain raced. What was Michael's mother doing here? And why was she speaking in mangled Spanish? Freya knew nothing about Mrs Petersen except that she was divorced, worshipped her son and had consistently refused to acknowledge Freya's existence.

'Oh, never mind. Come with me.' Mrs Petersen beckoned commandingly and bustled towards the kitchen.

Freya hesitated. Did she really look like a maid? She caught a glimpse of herself in a far mirror, complete with dustpan, apron and knotted headscarf, and allowed herself to be led zombie like into the kitchen where Mrs Petersen demonstrated exactly how she was to defrost the fridge, empty and wipe clean the food cabinets, and polish the kettle. Next stop was the bathroom, where Freya was instructed to disinfect the tiles and scrub the toilet.

'*Si, si.*' She nodded meekly.

When they reached the bedroom, Mrs Petersen eyed the open closet, and its line of bare hangers, with satisfaction. She checked that Freya's chest of drawers was empty, ran one dustometer finger across the top, and grimaced. Freya noticed with dismay that her handbag was sitting on a chair next to the chest. Giving a theatrical gasp, she ran across the room to screen the bag, and pointed open-mouthed at the empty closet. 'Pliss, hhhhwhere ees Mees Freya?'

'Gone.' Mrs Petersen gestured like someone shooing geese. '*Vamoose.*' Freya crossed herself.

'No, no, Juanita, or whatever your name is, it's all for the best. *No bueno muchacha. Artista.*' Mrs Petersen frowned. '*Inglesi.*'

'Ah.' Freya sighed in condolence.

Mrs Petersen was now rifling through her son's clothes, pulling out his suits and laying them on the bed. 'I want all these to go to the cleaners, understand? *Launderio*.'

'*Si*.' Did the woman think Freya carried the Black Death?

'You get started, then. I have some calls to make. *Telephonio*.'

Freya listened to the retreating tattoo of Mrs Petersen's heels. Then she took off the apron, folded it, and placed it in the middle of Michael's bed, with the apartment key on top. Quickly she assembled her belongings—bag, plastic bags, hatbox—wondering how she was going to sneak out of here. From the living room Mrs Petersen's voice rose in a girlish gush. Evidently she and an old friend had been telephonically reunited. Freya lurked just out of sight in the bedroom doorway, waiting for an opportunity to escape.

'. . . not too bad. I have the maid here, getting everything back into shape. I think I'll rearrange the furniture, too. It's so important for Mikey to have a fresh start, with no reminders.'

Mikey? Freya rolled her eyes.

'. . . of course it was his decision, Myra. You know I never interfere.'

Ha!

'I know what's right for my son: a nice American girl, somebody young and fresh who can make him a lovely home.'

Freya ground her teeth.

'He told me she never cooked him a real breakfast, not once. She wouldn't even sew on a button for him, though she's been living off him for months.'

By now Freya was burning with indignation. How could Michael have been so disloyal? She glared malevolently round the bedroom, centre of their supposed togetherness. Her eye fell upon the pile of clothes that Mrs Petersen had instructed her to take to the cleaners.

'. . . I imagine it was one of those, you know, *physical* things. But that always wears off, doesn't it? Which reminds me . . . *And where do you think you're going?*'

These last words were addressed to Freya, who was walking boldly across the living room to the front door. Wedged between her arms and chin was a great heap of Michael's suits, under which she had contrived to conceal her own possessions.

For explanation, Freya nodded at her overflowing armful. '*Si si por favor y viva espana hasta la vista*,' she gabbled frantically, trying to open the apartment door with her little finger.

The door yielded explosively, nearly toppling her backwards. She headed for the elevator and stabbed the DOWN button. *Quick!* she prayed, glancing back at the door of 12B, which had slammed behind her and so far remained shut. As soon as the elevator arrived Freya leapt inside, threw everything on the floor, and pressed L for Lobby. A few minutes later she tumbled into Joe's Dri-Kleen and dumped Michael's suits in a slithery pile on the counter. Her arms ached. She felt sweaty, untidy and unattractive, and extremely angry.

'Name?'

'Petersen.' Freya spelt it out for him, impatience rising.

While Joe filled out the tickets, Freya rested her elbows on the counter, scowling at a sign that read: REPAIRS ON THE PREMISES. JUST ASK! What was she doing here? What kind of a person took her ex-lover's clothes to the dry-cleaners, at the behest of her ex-lover's mother, who thought she was the cleaning lady? An idiot, that's who. How dared Michael complain about her to his mother?

'I forgot to say,' she said, 'all the trousers need shortening six inches.'

'Okey dokey.' Joe picked up his pen again.

He copied down her instructions obediently, and handed her the tickets. She stuffed them into her pocket. She would post them to Michael so that he could collect the suits. It was a pity she couldn't be present when he put one on. She pulled open the door to the street.

Jack opened the door of his bedroom. He was wearing a sleep-creased T-shirt and faded undershorts with a lipstick kiss imprinted on the right buttock. After steadying himself on the doorjamb, he launched himself on a trajectory that should, with luck, lead him across the north side of the living room and round the corner to the bathroom. Walking on autopilot, he successfully negotiated the corner and biffed the bathroom door with the heel of his hand, as he always did. Normally it flew open with a satisfying *pop!* Today it nearly broke his wrist. It was locked! He recoiled sharply and cradled his arm, panting with the pain.

'Out in a sec,' chirruped a voice, a female voice: Freya. He kept forgetting she was here.

Next there came the hiss of water, which meant that she was only just beginning her shower. Women always took for ever. Muttering to himself, Jack stomped through the kitchen and unlocked the door to the back yard. He took a couple of paces across the cracked concrete and peed vigorously onto a patch of dandelions.

Something was fluttering at the edge of his vision. Jack turned his head and gaped. A makeshift washing line had been strung out across one corner of the yard. From it dangled various flimsy wisps of female underwear. This was awful. What would the neighbours think? Jack winced his way across the rough terrain, snatched the garments off the line and took them inside. To his surprise he found the bathroom already vacated and exuding warm, scented steam.

He shut himself in, only realising once he was inside that he still held Freya's underwear. He dumped the pile on the toilet seat, then ran water into the basin and lathered his face with shaving foam. He dipped his razor into the warm water, and cut a long swath through the foam. Ouch! Whimpering softly, Jack bathed his stinging cheek in cold water, then peered in the mirror to examine the damage. One side of his face was covered with tiny red pinpricks beginning to exude blood. What had happened to his razor? But he already knew the answer. He flung open the bathroom door.

'Freya!' he bellowed.

'Morning, Jack,' said a voice about three feet away from him. 'I was about to make some coffee. Want some?' She was standing at the entrance to the kitchen, immaculate and aloof, already dressed in a zippy career-woman suit.

Jack brandished his razor in the air as if he was about to lasso a steer. 'Have you been using this to shave your legs?'

'I might have. Oh, all right, I did. Sorry. I left mine at Michael's.'

'Then buy yourself a new one. Look at my face!'

'Sorry,' she said again, but she didn't sound properly penitent.

'And you locked the bathroom door. I practically broke my wrist on it. I need my hands. A writer is like a concert pianist.'

She folded her arms and gave him a smile he didn't altogether like. 'Which wrist, oh, Toscanini?'

'Huh?'

'Which wrist sustained the near-fatal injury? The one you're waving your razor around with, or the one you're using to prop up the wall?'

Jack glowered and turned to go back into the bathroom.

'Love the shorts,' she called after him.

Jack slammed the door, readjusted the shower head to its harshest setting and stood under the drumming water. It was only a temporary arrangement, he reminded himself. 'Two weeks,' he'd said, 'two weeks *max*.' If today was Tuesday, that meant only nine more days of cohabitation. *Only* nine days? Only *nine* days? Only nine *days*? He closed his eyes and tipped back his head. Water ran down his face like tears.

The best policy was simply to avoid one another. So far, he'd managed this rather successfully. Jack's mood brightened as he recalled how he had persuaded Candace to come out with him on Saturday night, as he'd known she would. The evening had gone pretty much according to plan. Candace, in a skimpy black dress, was even prettier than he had realised. Out of the black dress, she was sensational. At the end of the evening he had escorted her home, learned that her room-mate was fortuitously absent, and decided to stay.

Jack stepped out of the shower and grabbed a towel to frisk himself dry. Candace was a sweet girl, too. When they finally got out of bed, she'd insisted on making him waffles and maple syrup for breakfast. He didn't especially like waffles, but he'd enjoyed watching her make the effort for him. After that, frankly, he'd become restless. Candace's apartment was tiny, its windows looking straight into other windows or at blank, dirty walls, and it made Jack feel claustrophobic.

Jack's thoughts reverted to Freya. He still hadn't got round to telling Candace about Freya moving in. But he'd been busy. A man couldn't do everything. Wrapping the towel round his waist, he returned to his bedroom to dress. As he pulled on his usual jeans and comfortable shirt he sniffed appreciatively at the smell of coffee and toast. There were *some* good things about having a woman about the place. He arrived in the kitchen, determined to be good-humoured, and looked around for his cup of coffee and his plate of toast. Neither was to be seen.

'Didn't you make me any toast?'

'Hmm?' Freya was sitting on the only stool—his stool—and appeared to be totally absorbed in reading the newspaper—his newspaper.

Jack cleared his throat testily, making his point. When she didn't react, he began to fix his own breakfast, rustling the plastic bread bag and banging the toaster loudly enough to shame her into an apology.

Sure enough, her head suddenly lifted. 'Listen to this: Bliss and Ricky have split up!'

Jack waited a few withering seconds. 'And who, may one enquire, are "Bliss" and "Ricky"?'

'Bliss Bogardo the supermodel, Ricky Radical, the rock star. Have you been living in a cave?'

'I prefer not to clutter my mind with trivia. Now, might I trouble you for the sports section?'

She gave him a look, then disengaged the relevant pages and handed them over. Silence followed while Jack poured himself some coffee, put his plate of toast on the table and set the paper next to it. He opened the refrigerator door and closed it again.

'Where did you put the milk?'

'All gone, I'm afraid. There was only a teensy bit left anyway.'

Black coffee. Jack hated black coffee. He would have thrown it down the sink if he weren't above childish gestures. Instead he heaved a chair from the living room and seated himself at the rickety table. He reached for the butter—at least she hadn't finished that too—and spread a generous amount across his cooling toast, aware of Freya's critical gaze.

'You certainly like butter.'

'Yes. I do,' he said evenly.

'Frightfully fattening.'

'Are you trying to tell me something?'

'No.' She crunched into her second—third?—piece of toast. 'Though you have put on weight since I first met you.'

Automatically Jack sucked in his stomach. 'That's muscle.'

'Muscle!' Freya cackled with merry laughter.

Jack picked up the paper and held it in front of his face.

'I've been thinking,' said a voice behind his paper. 'If I'm going to be staying here for a bit, we need to establish some ground rules.'

Jack flapped the paper and read on.

'I mean, people who share a place usually have house rules . . . Hello? Are you there?'

'*What?*'

'Don't you want to give me instructions about garbage and laundry, and who does the dishes or cooks dinner?'

'No.'

'What about cleaning? That bathroom's a health hazard.'

'Cleaning is not one of my interests.'

'What about bringing people home?'

'I usually go to their place.' Then the full implications of her question struck him. He lowered his paper. 'You mean—*you?*'

'No. Rudolph the red-nosed reindeer.'

'Well . . .' Jack was flummoxed. Was Freya really intending to bring another man *here*, to his apartment, to his study, to his inner sanctum, and—and—*fool around*? She'd only just broken up with Michael. Where were her standards? 'I guess we could let each other know beforehand if we wanted . . .' He coughed gruffly.

'Privacy?' She pronounced the word the English way—'priv' to rhyme with 'give'.

'Pry-vacy,' he corrected.

'Righty-ho. One more thing: I'd like to make some contribution to the household. I thought I'd try to get to the market today—stock up the fridge. Is there anything you'd particularly like?'

'Peanut bu—'

Jack bit back his words. *Stock the fridge*. Wasn't this what Leo had

354

warned him about? The older woman, the supposed 'friend' who wormed her way into your life and never left?

'No! Do NOT go to the market.'

She gave him a mystified look, then shrugged. 'OK. You go. I hate buying food anyway.'

Jack also hated buying food. How had he got himself into this mess? He watched grumpily as Freya got up and put her cup and plate into the sink—unwashed, he noticed. At least she was going. Jack returned to his paper. Peace at last.

But instead of leaving, Freya opened the back door, looked into the yard and shrieked.

'Someone's stolen my underwear!'

'I brought it in.'

'*You* took my underwear? Why?'

'Because—because it was dry!'

'So where is it?'

'I—uh, I think I left it in the bathroom.'

'And why exactly did you need to take my underwear into the bathroom with you?' Freya's voice was suddenly steely.

Jack slammed down his paper. 'I didn't *need* to. I forgot I had the damn stuff. Jesus, Freya, stop looking at me as if I'm a pervert.'

'I'm not!'

'You are!'

'I'm not.'

'For Chrissakes, are you ever going to work?'

'Right now. Don't be so touchy.'

'I'm not.'

'Are.'

'Not.'

'Are, are, are.'

Freya seemed to think this was an amusing game. Jack clamped his lips together, refusing to be caught again. Now she was leaving the kitchen. In a minute or two she would be gone.

But she wasn't. First she brushed her teeth, then she disappeared to her room for what seemed hours, then she came out, uttered a feminine little *tut!* of surprise as if she'd forgotten something, went back in, came out. Her footsteps clacked across the floor and she reappeared in the doorway, armed with her briefcase, standing stiff and straight.

'I just want you to know how much I appreciate your having me here.' She spoke with the cheery spontaneity of a Greek messenger announcing a massacre in Sparta.

Jack grunted.

'Perhaps, as a gesture, I could make you dinner tonight?'

Ohhh no. She wasn't going to catch him that easily. 'I'm going out.'

'Alternatively, I've noticed a number of broken electrical items in my room. If I could assist you by taking them to the repair shop—'

'No.' These women were as cunning as fiends. 'I like them that way.'

'You like broken irons?'

'Definitely.'

'And broken alarm clocks?'

'Passionately.'

'And broken—?'

'I like everything except broken records. Stop nagging, Freya. If I wanted a wife, I'd be married by now.'

Hah! That got her. She tossed her hair, what there was of it, and turned on her heel. She was leaving! Click-clack, click-clack went her shoes—one of the five thousand pairs she had stashed in his study. He heard the front door open, the sound of traffic from the street, then . . . nothing. Time ticked by as he awaited the blessed slam of the door. It didn't come. What was she waiting for? Unable to stand the suspense, he lurched up from the table and strode out to see what was going on.

There she was on the threshold, head down, leg crooked to support a big, lumpy bag in which she was rummaging. Why did women buy bags that size if they could never find anything?

'Oh, Jack,' she said in a vague, maddening way, 'do you have any quarters for the bus?'

'No. I do not have any fucking quarters for the bus!'

She raised her head. There was a shocked look on her face. He almost wondered if he had hurt her feelings. But then she shouldered her bag, stepped outside, and turned to present him with a phoney smile.

'Goodbye, darling,' she cooed. 'Have a wonderful day at the office. Aren't you going to kiss me goodbye?'

Jack slammed the door in her face.

When Freya returned from work that evening, she was relieved to find the apartment empty. After Jack's deplorable bout of bad temper this morning she realised that Cat was right: men and women were not designed to live together in harmony. Besides, his absence gave her a chance to make some essential domestic improvements. She carried a large bag through to the kitchen and banged it down on the counter. From it she took a can of scouring powder, a bottle of bleach, a scrubbing brush, cleaning cloths, rubber gloves. Mess was one thing; a shower cubicle where you could scratch your name in grime was another.

She hurried to change her clothes, not wishing to be caught by Jack in the middle of this demeaning job in case it gave him false notions about the roles of the sexes. The sight of her room was depressing. Small to begin with—a single bed at one end, Jack's desk under the window at the other—it was now absurdly cramped. Stacks of shoeboxes took up most of the floor space, along with the suitcase she used as a chest of drawers. Her clothes hung high above the bed from a heating pipe. Tomorrow she'd get up early so she could buy *The Village Voice* hot off the press, and check out the apartment rentals.

Within a few minutes she had tidied away her work clothes, pulled on a T-shirt, ancient jogging pants and sneakers, and was standing in the shower in a snowstorm of scouring powder. She hefted the big scrubbing brush and set to work. It was surprisingly satisfying. Nothing could be duller than routine cleaning, but visible dirt was a challenge. After half an hour of steamy labour the light- and dark-grey tiles were revealed to be white and black, the toilet foamed with a sinister froth of chemical blue, and she could read the manufacturer's name on the whisker-free basin. Since she was now so dirty and the bathroom so clean, it seemed a good idea to market-test her handiwork by taking a shower. She had just finished rinsing shampoo out of her hair when the doorbell rang. It was almost certainly Jack, too lazy to face the effort of getting his own key out of his own pocket. Freya took no notice. Stepping out of the shower, she dried herself and slipped on her kimono, and was twisting a towel around her hair when the bell sounded again. The idiot must have forgotten his key.

She slapped her way to the front door, leaving a trail of damp footprints. But it wasn't Jack. It was a young woman.

Freya put up a hand to steady her towel turban. 'Yes?' she enquired.

'Is—is Jack at home?'

'No.'

'Oh . . . He said to meet him here.'

'What for?'

'It's creative writing night. We're going together.'

'How sweet. You'd better come in.'

Freya stepped back and opened the door wide. She recognised the girl now. It was Little Miss ABC, Jack's 'student' from the other morning. With her cute, plump cheeks and flirty skirt, she looked about seventeen. As she jiggled past on high-heeled sandals, Freya retied her kimono tightly around herself and followed the girl into the living room, watching her scan the apartment with a proprietary air, as if to check that Jack was indeed out. At length she turned back to Freya and gave her a pert, lip-gloss smile.

'I'm Candace,' she announced.

'The perfect name. I bet Jack calls you "Candy", am I right?'

'Sometimes.' Candace flushed. 'What's that smell?'

'Cleanliness. Marvellous, isn't it? And before you ask, no, I am not the maid.'

'Who said you were?' Candace looked ruffled. 'I saw you here on Saturday. Jack said you were an old friend. He didn't tell me you were *living* here.'

'Men.' Freya rolled her eyes. 'They're so forgetful. Now, if you'll excuse me, I must hobble back to my knitting. Help yourself to anything you want—Diet Coke, lemonade, milk and cookies . . .'

And with that Freya escaped to her room, cheeks flushed, lips set in annoyance. She disliked being caught at a disadvantage. Why hadn't Jack warned her? A glance in the mirror showed her unattractively naked face, her turban askew, the fraying silk at the neck of her kimono. Freya scowled at her reflection. She threw off the kimono and rapidly started to dress in her favourite jeans and a skinny black top. She slicked her damp hair behind her ears and began to apply make-up. When she returned she found Candace charmingly posed on the couch, head bent over Jack's copy of Aristotle's *Poetics*.

'Only me,' said Freya. At least the girl had the book the right way up. Freya fixed herself a bourbon on the rocks, and perched on the arm of a squashy chair, swinging one long leg. Candace stared at her warily.

'You're Frieda, aren't you?' she said.

'Almost. Eight out of ten. Actually, it's Freya.'

'Jack said you live uptown with your boyfriend.'

'I did.' Freya's smile hardened.

'So what happened?'

Freya hesitated. She did not need to explain herself to this pinhead. 'If you must know, he wanted to get married and I didn't.'

'Oh, I admire you,' Candace paused, 'for making such a brave decision.'

Freya frowned suspiciously. 'What's so brave about it?'

'Just . . . I mean, at your age . . .' Candace lowered her eyes.

Freya folded her arms. 'Are you implying that's the last proposal I'll ever get?'

'I didn't say that. My Aunt Rochelle didn't get married until she was forty-two. She never had children, of course. And she's divorced now.'

'What an inspiring story. Thank you, Candace.'

They sat in silence. Candace looked at her watch. 'He's late,' she said.

'Jack's always late.'

'How long have you known him?'

'Ten years. And you?'

A holy expression came over Candace's face. 'You can't measure a relationship in time. Not chronological time, anyway.'

'Oh well, if it's *chronological* time you're talking about . . .'

Candace wasn't listening. Her full lips parted in a secret smile. 'When he walked into my first class I almost died,' she confided. 'Isn't he just the handsomest man in the whole world? Those blue eyes.' Candace gave an ecstatic shiver. 'Plus, I felt so in awe of his talent.'

Freya crunched an ice cube.

'At the beginning I wasn't sure he even noticed me—as a woman, I mean. But then I sort of bumped into him after class, and I felt this incredible *connection* . . . even though he's so much smarter and deeper and—'

'Older?'

There was the sound of a key in the lock. Both women's eyes swivelled to the living-room door. They waited in silence, listening to Jack manoeuvring his bike into the hall. Candace moistened her lips and shook back her hair in preparation for his entrance.

The door opened and Jack ambled in, sliding his wire-rimmed glasses into place with a forefinger. For a split second Freya saw him through Candace's eyes—hunky and appealingly dishevelled. Then she almost laughed out loud as Jack caught sight of them both and halted abruptly, as astounded as if he'd found Hitler *and* Stalin in his living room.

'Well, well, well!' He was suddenly as jovial as Santa Claus. 'My two favourite women. Together! How—how wonderful!'

'I know. Isn't it marvellous?' Freya mimicked his rapturous tone.

Jack shot her a dirty look, and rubbed his hands with hectic bonhomie. 'So!' he enthused. 'I guess you two girls have met!'

'We two girls certainly have.'

Candace could resist him no longer. With a tremulous cry, she launched herself from the couch and almost ran to throw her arms round Jack's waist. Freya watched deadpan as Candace gazed up at him adoringly, a darling little daisy turning its face to the sun.

Jack mussed Candace's hair with a casual hand, then disengaged himself. 'OK, everyone!' he cried, his jollity control still on maximum. 'I'll just, uh, get my papers, and we'll go!'

'W—we?' faltered Candace, staring at Freya in panic.

'No, no.' She waved a hand. 'You young people run along and enjoy yourselves. I want to stay home and give my dentures a good soak.'

The two of them quickly made their escape. Freya could hear them going down the path—the slow rumble of Jack's voice, Candace's happy, answering giggle. Then there was silence, and the long evening ahead.

Freya topped up her drink, slotted a Billie Holiday tape into the stereo, and flopped onto the couch. On the floor beside it was the inevitable teetering pile of Jack's magazines, mostly copies of the *New York Review of Books*. She hoisted a handful onto her stomach, and shuffled through them idly. Names leapt out at Freya from the magazine covers—Updike, Roth, Isaiah Berlin, Velázquez. How could a man who revelled in the intellectual fireworks of these articles spend his leisure time with the Candaces of this world?

Freya suspected it was sheer laziness. There was something about Jack that made women drop into his hand like ripe fruit from a tree; he didn't have to bother to pick them. She remembered when she had first seen him, fresh off the plane from North Carolina. Those were the days when she was mixing with a bohemian crowd and living close to the breadline. Jack had strolled onto the drab set of their existence, with his beautiful leather luggage and that old beat-up typewriter he was so proud of, looking like Robert Redford in *Barefoot in the Park*. He'd been so young, so eager. So polite! He said he was going to be a writer.

It hadn't taken long to scuff him up. They'd all teased him like crazy—for his beautiful shirts, his rich daddy, the slow rise and fall of his accent. Jack took it all in good humour. His family was rich but he wasn't, he said; he'd had a big bust-up with his father and for the time being, anyway, he was one of them. Freya took him under her wing. Jack was funny; he was generous with what he had; he wasn't ashamed to be enthusiastic; and he was serious about his work. She liked him.

And he liked her. But that was all. He was too young for her. It was tacitly agreed that they would be friends. And they still were. Freya turned back to her magazines and flicked idly through the pages. She was glad she'd never got involved with Jack. He was good fun and good company, but his relationships with intelligent women never seemed to last long, probably because he couldn't stand the competition. Men liked intellectual challenges, and they liked attractive women: they just didn't like the two in combination.

Or did they? Freya's attention sharpened as she reached the back pages of the *Review* and discovered the 'Personal' advertisements. *Yale grad seeks attractive, cultured companion for excursions to theatre, exhibitions, country and—who knows?—more private places. Bogart in search of Bergman. Let's play it again.*

Freya sat up excitedly and looked around for a pen. This could be the answer to her problem.

'*Lover man, oh where can you be?*' wailed Billie. Freya didn't exactly need a lover man, but she did desperately need a man, and she needed him within the next two weeks. Readers of the *New York Review of Books* were bound to be a cut above the usual lonely hearts; these men would be respectable, educated, sophisticated.

It was worth a try. All she needed was one lucky strike. Freya found the three most recent issues and started to compile a short list.

Suddenly brisk, Freya gathered together her bundle of magazines, got up from the couch and walked purposefully across the living room. Jack's computer was in her room, the room that she *rented*. If she used it to send out one or two teensy email messages he could hardly object.

Chapter Five

THE SHIP CAME INTO THE HARBOUR.
Hmm
The ship entered the harbour.
Better, but—
The ship ploughed into the harbour.
Oh yeah, brilliant. He'd made it sound as though the ship was demolishing the harbour. Jack put his finger on the DELETE key, and pressed hard. He checked his watch. Hey, time for coffee!

Twenty minutes later he was back where he started that morning, staring at a blank screen. He had long ago passed his publisher's deadline for delivery of his new novel. He must hurry up! The story was in his head, somewhere, a jumble of fragmented thoughts, but the words wouldn't come.

Jack looked at his watch. He'd give anything for the phone to ring and someone to invite him out for a long oblivious lunch. Maybe he'd feel more sparkling when he'd had something to eat. In the kitchen he compiled a sandwich—ham, cheese, dill pickle, mustard, a couple of shots of Tabasco—then he carried it into the living room and turned on the TV. It was important to keep abreast of popular culture. He could hardly work while he was eating, could he? Oh look!—*Buffy the Vampire Slayer*. He slumped back contentedly. He had just stuffed the last of his sandwich into his mouth, when the phone rang. Jack levered himself out of his chair, zapped off the sound and sidled across the room, keeping his eyes on the screen. He picked up the receiver.

'Hi! Is Freya there?' It was a man's voice.

'No,' mumbled Jack, still chewing.

'Will she be home tonight?'

'Guess so.'

'OK, I'll try later. Tell her Max called, willya?' He hung up.

Five minutes later, exactly the same thing happened, except the man was called Norman. Jack felt a flicker of irritation. He was not Freya's secretary, after all; he had work to do. As soon as he found out what happened to Buffy he'd—Damn it! The phone again. A man named Lucas claimed to be calling from his 'limo'.

'Who are you, by the way?' asked Lucas. 'You the gay one?'

'*No!*'

Jack slammed down the phone. How could a man work with such interruptions? He turned back to the television screen. On top of everything else, he'd missed the climax of the show. He switched off the set and returned to his office in a sour mood. Freya's things cluttered his space—dresses hanging hither and yon, her perfume hung in the air. A man needed order if he was to work efficiently. Suddenly Jack caught sight of a sprawl of magazines under the bed, and let out a hiss of outrage: she'd stolen his *New York Review of Books*! She'd even left half of them folded inside out. Jack snatched them up angrily, and a loose piece of paper fluttered to the floor. He stooped to pick it up and carried it over to his desk.

It was the draft of an email. As he began to read, a smile of glee spread across his face. It seemed that Freya was on the hunt for a new boyfriend to torment.

To: ....
From: Freya c/o jackmad@aol.com
Subject: Dating

I saw your ad in the New York Review of Books. *If you are interested in having dinner this weekend with a tall [**attractive** crossed out, **slim** crossed out], blonde, professional woman [**35** crossed out, **33** crossed out, **29** crossed out] in her thirties, then contact me and convince me why we should meet. Telephone............ evenings only, email <u>midnight to 7am only</u>.*

PS. If a man answers the phone, that's my room-mate. He's gay.

Jack smashed his fist on the desk. How dare she give out his email address to a bunch of lonely-heart losers? How could she contaminate his computer, sacred repository of his most precious thoughts and ambitions, with her tawdry *billets-doux*? Who was she calling gay? She'd even given out his telephone number!

The phone rang again and he let out a roar of fury and charged into the living room like a bull into the ring. He snatched up the receiver and shouted into it, '*She's not here!*'

'Jack? Is that you?' A man's voice. 'It's Michael Petersen here. You OK?'

'Fine, fine.' Jack forced out a genial chuckle. 'In another world, I guess. Writing is so absorbing.'

'Pardon me for interrupting the great work, but I wanted to get your address. There's some mail I need to send over to Freya.'

Jack dictated his address in a laboured, grudging tone. Why couldn't the guy call Freya and interrupt *her* work? Then he had a brainwave. The sheer beauty of it made his scalp tingle. He would persuade Michael to *take her back!* Jack could barely restrain a shout of hysterical joy. With difficulty, he modulated his voice.

'You know, she's not herself. I think she's missing you.'

'Really.' Michael's voice was unaccountably cold. 'Allow me to tell you what happened in my apartment on Monday.'

Jack listened in awed silence. It seemed that Michael's mother had suffered some kind of nervous breakdown following a bizarre encounter with Freya in Michael's apartment. Mrs Petersen had since checked into the Plaza and was consoling herself with shopping and room service, at Michael's expense. There was worse to come.

'Six *inches*?' Jack repeated, when Michael reached the final catastrophe of his story. 'That's—that's terrible.' Unfortunately, a guffaw escaped him as he pictured a finicky, besuited Michael revealing an expanse of executive hosiery and hairy calf.

'Obviously you find Freya more amusing than I do,' said Michael. 'Some of those suits cost a thousand dollars apiece. I'm thinking of suing her.'

'Good idea.' Jack's tone was robust. 'Not that I don't adore Freya, but I admit she can be pretty headstrong. It's always the same with women: they're wonderful creatures, until you try to live with them.'

'Don't think you can patronise me, Jack Madison. I'm telling you, Freya's a disturbed person. You want to watch out.' With that, he hung up.

Jack returned to his desk and turned on his computer. He pulled up the file he'd been working on. Now let's see: *The ship was in the harbour* . . .

Jack's eyes strayed to Freya's draft. *Convince me why we should meet—*

how typical of her lofty manner. He pitied the poor sap who fell for that line. A thought struck him. Three men had ignored Freya's instructions to telephone in the evening: what if the emailers had done the same? What if there were some replies she hadn't seen? Jack scented revenge. He began tapping keys, then clicked the mouse.

Eureka!

Hi, babe! Couldn't wait 'til midnight. How did you know blonde is my favorite color!!! I am six feet tall, rugged, around 40, with my own funeral parlor business. I adore fur, long legs, oysters, and dead bodies (just joking!!!). I can meet you anytime, anywhere this weekend. Tom.

Jack flipped in fascination through several more until he found the final one. It was personalised with a little icon at the top, which Jack recognised as a portrait of Shakespeare. Immediately below was the heading: 'Bernard S. Parkenrider, Associate Professor, BA, MA, PhD'. Jack gave a snort.

Dear Freya, la table est reservée! I look forward to meeting you tomorrow (and tomorrow and tomorrow, as the Bard would say!). Yours in great expectation, Bernard.

Well, well. Freya deserved to be taught a lesson. She had abused his hospitality, and intimidated his adorable little Candace. He sat for a moment in silent concentration. His mind moved with a speed and infernal ingenuity he hadn't achieved in months. Within ten minutes he had registered a new hotmail address, laid out a rough imitation of Prof. Parkenrider's absurd Shakespearean letterhead, and composed a poem to Freya, which he sent purportedly from Bernard. Then he invented a message to Bernard from Freya.

Dear Bernard, I am so thrilled to be meeting a genuine scholar! I want to hear EVERYTHING about your work. You may like to know a little more about me before we meet. Besides my 'artistic' inclinations, I like to think of myself as an intellectual—though of course I enjoy fun. Among my interests are men's fashions and German opera. I also have a keen interest in footwear. My friends joke that I am rather bossy and always like to have the whip hand (!), but I'm sure you can deal with that. Freya.

PS I adore hairy legs!

Jack rubbed his hands. That should spice up their romantic little tryst. He reached for the mouse and pressed SEND.

Freya turned off 5th Avenue and walked briskly towards Madison on high, spiked heels. It was a warm evening, and she felt good to be out in the Friday night bustle, with somewhere to go and someone to meet. Apart from one evening at Cat's, she'd been stuck in the apartment all week, prey to Jack's grouchy temper and oafish humour, until she was screaming to escape. Jack wanted her out tonight anyway: Candace was coming over to 'cook dinner' for him, ho, ho. It had given Freya considerable satisfaction to inform him that, as it happened, she had a date already.

'Oh yeah?' Jack's incredulous smirk had been intensely irritating.

'Yes. I'm meeting a professor of English literature at a Japanese restaurant. It will be nice to have some intellectual stimulation, for a change.'

This, apparently, was so hilarious that Jack could only raise sceptical eyebrows, as if Freya's experience could hardly match the kind of 'stimulation' he was anticipating with Candace. Men were so crude. Distracted by their own sweaty animal grapplings, they did not understand the importance, to women, of the life of the mind.

Thankfully, there were exceptions. Freya repeated to herself the words of the advertisement that had initially sparked her attention. *University professor, 39, cultured, humorous, battered but unbowed, seeks superior female for invigorating encounters.* She had at once pictured an attractively rumpled figure in corduroy, with amused eyes and a wry smile. They had since spoken on the phone, and she had been struck by his polite manner and his flattering eagerness to meet her.

His name was Bernard, pronounced the American way with the emphasis on the second syllable. Ber*nard* was an educated man, mature but not old. If he turned out to be unsuitable for her purposes, she would at least have enjoyed an evening of intelligent conversation.

Here was the restaurant. Freya pushed the door open and stepped inside. The manager consulted his book to check whether Professor Parkenrider had arrived.

'This way, please. The gentleman is waiting.'

They passed the sushi bar, where a man in white was slashing vegetables to ribbons one-handed, and headed for the sleek ebony tables beyond. From one of them, a lone figure rose to greet her.

'Bernard?' Freya put out her hand.

Instead of shaking it, he clasped her hand in his and raised it to his lips with a gallantry that Freya told herself was charming. 'Ah, Freya. We meet at last.'

'Yes. Hello.' Freya reclaimed her hand. 'Shall we sit down?'

As she settled herself at the table, a quick glance confirmed her first impression. Bernard's looks were not immediately prepossessing. He had pale, pouched eyes and straggly, reddish-brown hair that curled behind his ears. Over a white nylon shirt stretched across his sloping chest, he wore a vivid tie and—yes—a chocolate-brown corduroy jacket. If he was thirty-nine, she was Pollyanna: fifty was more like it.

Bernard picked up a jug and poured *sake* into the small cup in front of Freya. 'Come, let the festivities begin!'

Freya took a sip, resisting his efforts to clink cups.

'So tell me, Bernard.' She kept her voice light and brisk. 'Where exactly do you teach?'

Bernard cleared his throat. 'At this present time,' he began, 'I am attached to a small but elite junior college in southern New Jersey. My duties are more of a bibliographic nature, involving the cataloguing, purchasing, issuing and recalling of diverse printed materials.'

'You mean, you work in a library?'

'To be sure.' Bernard nodded ponderously. 'At all events, that is my *job*. My *work* involves lucubrations of a quite different order.'

'Lucu-what?' Freya gave a perky laugh, trying to lighten the atmosphere. Bernard seemed very serious.

'From the Latin *lucubro, lucubrare, lucubravi, lucubratum*, meaning to labour by lamplight. I refer, in short, to the work of Shakespearean scholarship on which I am embarked. A small thing, but mine own.'

'Shakespeare! How fascinating. You must tell me all about it.'

After half an hour, Freya had to admit that she had condemned herself to dine with a twenty-four carat, *bona fide* bore. The seaweed and shrimps had come and gone with agonising slowness: when Bernard opened his mouth it was not to eat but to pontificate. Now a platter of raw fish dotted with rice mounds sat between them. As Freya listened to his interminable catalogue of Shakespeare's use of phallic imagery, she feared that by the time the platter was empty she would have died of boredom. She glanced enviously at the lively groups around her.

'. . . And here's another example: "When *icicles* hang by the wall, and *Dick* the shepherd *blows* his *nail*, and Tom bears *logs* into the *hall* . . ."' At each key word Bernard paused to shoot Freya a glance loaded with innuendo.

Freya stood up abruptly. 'Excuse me a moment.'

In the ladies' loo, fortunately empty, she pulled faces at herself in the mirror until she felt almost normal, then she crept out and hovered in the passageway until one of the waiters passed by.

'Psssst!'

He came over, polite but dubious. 'I need a taxi,' Freya told him, pressing a ten-dollar bill into his hand. 'Urgently. In fact, *now*.'

Then she fluffed out her hair, assumed an innocent smile, and returned to the table under Bernard's unnerving, gloating gaze.

'Wonderful shoes,' he commented, as she sat down. 'Are they as painful as they look?'

'Not really.' Freya shrugged. 'I like wearing heels.'

'I mean, painful for anyone you stepped on.'

Freya stared at him. His mouth hung open in a slack, suggestive smile. 'Why would I want to step on people?'

Bernard gave her a sly wink.

'And stop winking at me!' she hissed.

'Mercy, mistress.' Bernard threw up his hands in mock surrender. 'I like this game.' He licked his lips.

Freya drummed her fingers on the table. Where was that taxi?

Bernard reached across to place one moist hand on top of hers. Then, with a portentous cough, he pushed out one leg from beneath the table, and twitched up his trousers to reveal an expanse of naked calf. He waggled his eyebrows suggestively.

Freya removed her hand and stared in disgust at the skin brindled with gingery hairs. 'Do put that horrible leg away,' she said crossly. 'People are staring.'

Bernard gave her a waggish look. 'The lady doth protest too much, methinks.'

At that moment, Freya heard the words she had been waiting for. 'Miss, your cab is here.' Unfortunately, so did Bernard.

'Are we going back to your dungeon?' He rubbed his hands.

'*We* are not going anywhere.' Freya threw some dollar bills on the table. 'I am going home. Alone. You seem to have got some kinky idea about me. I don't know why or how, but—'

'From your email, of course!' Bernard was loudly indignant.

'Keep your voice down. All I said was that I was tall and—'

'No, the second one. The hairy legs . . . the whip hand . . . artistic . . .'

'You've confused me with someone else,' Freya snapped. So *that* was what he had meant by 'invigorating encounters'. She rose to her feet and glowered down at Bernard. 'I did *not* send you a second email, and I am most definitely *not* interested in kinky sex.' She turned on her heel and strode towards the entrance, her cheeks hot with embarrassment. Heads turned curiously as she passed.

When she opened the door to the street she was confronted by a wall of water falling from the sky, as if a giant had upended a colossal bucket. Her cab glowed like a beacon of hope.

'Drive!' she shouted, as she plunged inside.

'You tell me where we're going, and I'll drive.' The cab driver folded the newspaper he'd been reading with maddening nonchalance.

'Anywhere! Just drive!'

There was a rat-tat-tat on her window. A sodden Bernard loomed at her through the misty glass.

'Downtown!' she shrieked.

The cab shot into a gap in the traffic and Freya sank back damply against the seat and closed her eyes, thanking God for her deliverance.

Half an hour later, dressed in a singlet and shorts retrieved from her locker at the gym, Freya had bicycled four gruelling miles while remaining in exactly the same place. Sweat gathered at her temples as she vented the frustrations of the evening on the chrome and rubber machine. God, another hill. Freya strained at the pedals.

Now for the treadmill. She adjusted the setting and started walking at a fast, steady pace, pumping her arms, trying to obliterate the vision of Bernard's moist mouth and yearning eyes. She should have stabbed him with one of her spiked heels—except he would have enjoyed that. Freya increased the speed and began to run. Fuelled by oxygen, her brain moved up a gear. What could have made Bernard suppose that she was into punishment? What was all that about a second email?

Freya's pace faltered, and she almost toppled backwards off the running machine. *Bloody Jack!* So that's why her messages didn't immediately show up on the screen; she'd blamed her own unfamiliarity with his computer, but the real reason was that he'd read them first. It wasn't Bernard who'd sent the silly poem that had made her smile; it was Jack, making a fool of her. Freya upped the speed again, pounding the smooth, sliding rubber under her feet. Sweat poured down her body. *Just you wait, Mr Jack Madison III.*

After showering and changing, Freya found that her legs were trembling from exhaustion. She trudged to a coffee bar, ordered a cappuccino and three cinnamon doughnuts, and sat on a high stool at the window, watching the trickle of raindrops. Tonight had been a mistake. Even Jack, it seemed, had correctly decoded Bernard's advertisement; though it was hard to understand why he should have wanted to play such a cruel joke on her. Anyway, who cared?

Freya leaned her head on one hand and stared into her coffee, eavesdropping on a conversation between two women behind her, evidently a mother and daughter. Listening to them, Freya felt a pang of longing. For most of her life she had fantasised about having a real mother, someone who would love her unconditionally and give her refuge when she needed it. Sometimes she talked to her mother in her head. *What do you think?* she'd ask about some new boyfriend. *Is this how it was with you and Daddy?* But there was never any answer. She didn't have a mother, she had a stepmother.

Freya had been thirteen years old when her father told her that he and his new friend Annabelle were getting married, and that they were all going to live in a big house in Cornwall. Her first reaction was simple astonishment. How could he want to change the unique perfection of their life together? For the last seven years, there had been just the two of them. In term-time she went to school while he researched and wrote his books in the large, untidy London flat. In the holidays they travelled together in Europe, visiting museums, churches, libraries and the homes of her father's art historian friends. 'You can come too,' her father had told her, when she begged not to be left behind, 'so long as you never complain of being bored.' And she hadn't. Her father talked to her, took her to dinner with him, asked her opinion of buildings, food, people. He taught her to play chess and poker and solo whist.

There were women, of course. Her father was a handsome man. Freya had taken a certain pride in his conquests, knowing they could not last. For an unseen third accompanied them wherever they went, the memory of a loving, laughing woman who had risen early one morning to buy croissants for breakfast, failed to look the right way crossing the rue du Bac and died instantly under the wheels of a delivery truck.

Annabelle, too, was a mother—of Natasha, aged three. Freya's father explained that Tash had no Daddy, just as she had no Mummy, so they were joining up to make a new family. Freya, who loved her father more than anyone in the world, accepted it. At the Register Office in London she stood behind him clutching the stiff, wired handle of her brides-maid's bouquet and watched his blunt-tipped fingers, familiar as her own, slide the ring onto the hand of another woman. *So this is marriage.*

At first it was almost OK. There was the excitement of a new bedroom and a new house—an extraordinary house near the tip of Cornwall, big enough to get lost in, with a maze of a garden that fell in a green tumble to the shingly edge of the sea. There were barns and a crumbling dove-cote and a small chapel, cold as winter. To begin with, there had been nothing to object to about Tash, a portly three-year-old with a direct stare and a snotty nose. It was easy enough to outrun her, or hide from her tiny despotic presence. *Tash up! Tash banana! Mine!*

Freya's first shock had been Annabelle's request, polite but firm, that she should knock before entering her father's bedroom, now also Annabelle's bedroom. Next was the decision to send Freya to boarding school, as no local school was deemed ' appropriate'. Freya hadn't complained; she hadn't wanted to upset her father.

In Freya's absence at school, Tash dominated the household. As the only child of a woman who had already suffered one tragic loss, and the stepchild of a man trying hard to pull his new family together, Tash was cosseted and indulged. She resented sharing the spotlight. Freya couldn't believe that a small child could be so manipulative and malevolent.

One holiday she returned to find that Tash had started to call her father 'Daddy'—and he did not correct her. His betrayal was like a knife in her heart. Instinctively she began to turn her gaze elsewhere. She studied hard, developed her own interests, retreated into secrecy. The summer she left school, she took a job as an au pair in New Jersey. The plan was that she would return in the autumn to start at university; instead, she had discovered New York, and stayed.

Freya's thoughts drifted off, conjuring up images of how her life should be, or could have been, or might be, until the rattle of cups alerted her to the fact that it was almost midnight. She paid her bill and caught the uptown bus home.

The lights were out in the apartment. To be on the safe side, Freya inserted her key with silent stealth and, once the front door was open, took off her shoes and tucked them under her arm. All was quiet. She tiptoed into the hall and waited for her eyes to adjust. The living-room door was open. She could make out humps of furniture in the half-dark; a green pinprick light indicated that the stereo had been left on. She was moving forward to turn it off when she was halted by a tiny sound, the merest breath of a sigh. Someone was in the room.

Freya stood still, nerves tingling. Just then a car entered the street. Its approaching headlights cast a fuzzy, sulphurous glow through the curtains. As in a slow-motion dream, Freya made out the saggy couch where it appeared that some strange, shadowy beast lay sprawled in sleep. There was an orange flash as the car passed, and all became clear. Jack lay with his back to her, naked. She caught a blond spark of tousled hair, the gleam of one smooth shoulder flexed to hold an almost invisible Candace, the tangle of four legs crooked into the sofa's embrace. Candace's small, ringed hand rested intimately on the muscled curve of his buttocks.

The light disappeared, eclipsing the coupled figures and leaving Freya blind. But the image remained vivid in her mind. She was aware of her heart urgently beating. It was the surprise, she told herself. Moving as quickly as she dared, almost hurrying, she entered her own room and closed the door.

Chapter **Six**

'Sshhh!' hissed a voice.

Freya, who was standing at the kitchen sink, elbow-deep in dishwater, twisted her head to find Candace glaring at her from the doorway. In the full force of daylight, without make-up and enveloped in Jack's dressing gown, she looked very young. Her toenails were painted dark plum.

'He's trying to sleep!' she protested.

Freya hoisted a handful of cutlery out of the water, held it in the air for a few pointed seconds, then dropped the lot onto the steel drainer.

'Who?' she asked, when the jangle had subsided.

'Jack, of course! His head hurts, poor baby. I think he's sick.'

There was a moan from Jack's bedroom, and at once, with a cheep of distress, Candace fled from the room.

Within a minute she was back. 'Do you have any orange juice?'

Freya dried her hands on the dishcloth, considering this question. 'I have orange juice, yes. Jack does not. He likes us to shop separately. That means I shop and he doesn't. Where's my coffee, by the way?'

'Oh. Was that *your* . . .?' Candace's voice trailed into silence under Freya's glowering gaze.

'Great! Fantastic!' Freya snapped her dishcloth angrily. She stalked to the fridge and threw it open. In one swift movement, she grabbed the juice and plonked it on the counter.

'There! To you, Candace, I grant the freedom of the orange-juice carton, to do with as you will.'

Candace's brow wrinkled. 'Does that mean I can take some to Jack?'

'Yes, yes, yes, yes, *yes!* God! It's not as though he can't afford the stuff. Bloody Jack Madison the bloody Third.'

'The Third?' Candace paused in her search for a glass.

'Ridiculous, isn't it? You'd think he was royalty. He probably is, down on the ol' plantation, with the magnolia a-blossomin' and the bullfrogs a-croakin'.' She cocked her head. 'Uh-oh. Was that the Master's voice?'

Candace scurried away with her precious juice, leaving Freya to flick her hair in irritation. The idea of playing piggy-in-the-middle with Jack and Candace all weekend made the blood thrum in her ears.

Earlier, from her vantage point at the sink, Freya had noticed that someone had set out some tatty deck chairs in the back yard. It was a sparkling day, the sky washed to a clear cerulean blue by last night's rain. Fetching the newspaper and a pile of envelopes from the hall floor, she carried them outside and settled herself in the hot sunshine. She leafed through the post, mostly dull-looking brown jobs apart from a thick, cream envelope addressed to Jack. She turned it over, and idly rubbed a thumb across the embossed flap, which proclaimed the sender to be Jack's father. With any luck he had decided to disinherit his son.

There was one item for her, a large padded envelope redirected from Michael's address. Freya's face tightened. Tash had never written to her once in all the years she'd lived in New York. Freya ripped the envelope open and pulled out a glossy magazine. Good grief!—*Country Life*. She flipped through the pages until she found a card covered in huge scrawly writing: *Daddy said I should send this to you. See p. 51.—T.*

Freya pursed her lips and turned to the relevant spot, where she found a full-page colour photograph of Tash on the girls-in-pearls page. *Country Life* had always featured a portrait like this—the English middle-class equivalent of a *Playboy* centrefold—which advertised the charms of a well-born or aspirant young lovely, usually on the occasion of her engagement or marriage. No wonder Tash was thrilled. Freya smoothed the page flat and stared stonily at Tash's flawless young skin, her greeny-hazel eyes innocently wide, the showy ring oh-so-casually prominent on one perfectly manicured hand. Underneath the portrait was the usual formulaic caption: *Miss Natasha Penrose, 25, only daughter of the late Mr John Huffington and Mrs Guy Penrose of Trewennack, Cornwall, is to be married to Roland Swindon-Smythe, only son of Mr and Mrs Barry Swindon-Smythe of The Shrubberies, Totteridge Common, Essex.*

Reading the announcement in black and white made Freya catch her breath in panic. The wedding was exactly two weeks away, and she had nobody to go with. *What was she going to do?* She slammed the magazine to the ground upside-down and picked up today's newspaper instead, hoping to distract her thoughts. But suddenly Jack stumbled out from the kitchen and slumped in a chair. 'Urghh,' he said.

Freya ignored him—the cheap, slobbish, cruel, selfish bastard.

He stretched noisily and let out an uninhibited yawn. The silence ticked by. Freya waited. Finally he asked, in a carefully casual voice, 'How was your evening?'

'Sensational, thank you.'

'Really?' Jack's eyes widened in surprise.

'Pure poetry. There's nothing like a man who worships the ground you walk on—particularly if it's his own body. Excuse me, his own *hairy* body. Though those handcuffs need some new padding.'

Jack was looking at her in alarm. 'You're kidding.'

'Of course I'm kidding!' Freya jumped to her feet and began thwacking him about the head with her newspaper. 'How dare you set me up with a pervert?'

'I didn't—ow!—set you up. You answered the ad yourself. It was your choice. Stop that!' With mortifying ease, Jack relieved her of the paper and held her at arm's length. 'I don't get it, Freya. Can't you even last a week without a man?'

'Look who's talking!' Freya twisted out of his grasp. 'You can't let even a *day* pass without picking up some woman—however feeble-minded.'

Jack bared his teeth in a taunting smile. 'Maybe it's not their minds that interest me.'

'Where's the "maybe" in that? No wonder you can't write any more, Jack. You're about as intellectually challenged as a piece of plankton.'

His eyes flickered. 'At least I don't need to scour the lonely hearts ads.'

They glared at each other.

'I almost forgot.' Freya reached into her shorts pocket. 'Last week's rent. Thank you so much for the privilege.' She tossed a wad of dollar bills in his general direction.

After a pointed pause, Jack bent to pick them up and folded them with exaggerated care. He sagged back into his chair and considered her through eyes narrowed against the sun. 'You're really not going to like yourself when you read my novel,' he told her.

'You can't put me in your novel. That's libel.'

'A woman like you.'

'What happens to her in the end? After she's raped by the pervert.'

Jack's face clouded over. 'I don't know. Speaking of libel, I had a talk with Michael yesterday. Someone mutilated his wardrobe. He's thinking of suing.'

'He wouldn't dare.'

'Gives the word "lawsuit" a whole new meaning, doesn't it?'

'Hi, everybody,' chirruped a voice. 'I've made us all some lemonade.'

Candace tripped out to them with a tray, fully dressed and restored to bandbox perfection—lips glossed, hair smoothed, and no doubt manicured, waxed, depilated and hygienically sprayed in all problem areas. Freya looked down at her bare legs and scuffed trainers. Time to leave.

'Thank you, Candace.' She took a glass and drained it. 'You don't mind if I borrow Rosinante, do you, Jack?'

'Yes, I do.'

'Rosie who?' Candace frowned suspiciously.

'Rosinante is Jack's pet bicycle,' said Freya, 'and after you, Candace, the thing he loves most in the world. It's named after Don Quixote's horse.'

'Oh, right. Don. He was in *The Waltons*, wasn't he?'

'Come on, Jack.' Freya kicked him, none too gently, on the leg. 'It's in your interest: I'm going to check out some apartments.'

He looked up sharply. 'You're moving out?'

'Are you begging me to stay?'

'Let me know when I can crack open the champagne.'

'Is this your sister?' interrupted Candace. She had picked up the magazine which Freya had stupidly left lying open.

'Stepsister,' Freya agreed shortly.

'Let's see.' Jack held out his hand. Obediently, Candace gave him the magazine and draped herself over the back of his chair, her cheek next to his, so that they could read it together.

Jack examined the photograph, and whistled. 'I thought you said she was a schoolgirl, Freya.'

'She was. She grew up.'

'I'll say.'

'Look, Jack!' Candace pointed excitedly. 'It says she's getting married! Isn't that amazing?'

'An event of truly world-shattering significance.' Freya snatched the magazine out of Jack's grasp and slapped it shut. 'You do have your own post, Jack.' She bent down and scooped up the small pile. 'Or is this some new kind of group therapy where we all get to paw through each other's letters? There's one here from your father. Shall I read it aloud?'

Jack looked at her with dislike. 'Take the bike,' he said.

'What?'

'I said, take the goddamned bike!'

Freya hesitated, then tossed the letters at his feet. 'Fine,' she said.

Bicycling forty-odd blocks from Chelsea to Central Park on a hot Saturday was madness; to do so on Jack's clanking, three-speed antique, amid crazy traffic and death-jets of pollution, was the kind of suicide mission Freya was determined to enjoy.

Back in the old days she had bicycled everywhere—but that was because she was penniless. Even now, her bank balance regularly tipped into minus; since the pink dress and poker disaster she hadn't dared open a statement. And if Michael seriously intended to sue her . . . Freya groaned. She'd call Cat this afternoon and unleash her on the case.

Freya rose in the saddle as she pumped steadily northwards on an incline invisible to the eye but palpable to the calves. Block by block the character of the urban landscape changed—from synagogues to churches, diamonds to books, theatres to office blocks, from rich to poor and back again, while the buildings rose and the wedges of sky narrowed. Heat pulsed from granite and bounced off glass. Tourists and Saturday shoppers dawdled at crossings. Freya put her head down and pushed on, counting off the landmarks. She passed the Museum of Modern Art, with its trio of bronze Venuses that were unquestionably female in form, but headless, armless and enormous. Was that secretly how men saw women? She thought of Candace's ample curves and Bernard's yellow-toothed leer; and heard again the tremor of amusement in Jack's voice when he enquired about her date. She had lied when she told him she was going to look at apartments. She was going to the park for some privacy, so she could plot her revenge.

Sweaty and breathless—but alive—Freya at last crossed into the park. Slowing her pace, she slipped gratefully onto the tree-shaded cycle track and continued on in search of an unoccupied spot. Dismounting faithful Rosinante, Freya wheeled her through the bushes and laid her against a tree. She sat down on a shaded patch of worn grass and took a deep, cooling swig of water from her water bottle, then reached for the rucksack she had carried in the bicycle basket. From it she drew a pen and notepaper. Then she began to write. After several efforts, she had the letter as she wanted it. Finally, she took a fresh sheet of paper and wrote, in erratic lettering:

You think your such a big shot, but be warNed—the FORCES OF DARKNESS are gathering. I know what's going on with you and Her. If she gets an A and I don't, you will be Punished for GROSS moral turpatude and SEXUAL favors. Nobody can be aloud to stand in the way of my GENIUS. So watch your step. Or else.

Freya reread the letter and smiled with satisfaction. She liked to think of Jack torturing himself by trying to identify the perpetrator out of so many suspects. She folded the letter in two, slid it into an envelope and wrote out Jack's name and address in the same misshapen style. Then she took a stamp from her wallet, licked it, and stuck it on at a deranged angle. That should fix him. Suddenly exhausted, Freya lay back against the tree trunk and closed her eyes. The park was extraordinarily unpeaceful. Dogs barked, children whooped, lovers giggled in the dusty bushes. Freya endured it until a mountain-biker burst sweatily from the bushes and ran over her foot. Serenity was what she wanted; she knew the perfect place. On her way she'd post the letter to Jack.

The room was cool and silent. The paintings that surrounded her—by Gainsborough, Romney, Reynolds, Hogarth—exuded English eighteenth-century confidence and calm. The Frick Collection never changed, though occasionally items were moved around; the paintings were old friends. Wandering through these graceful rooms in the company of El Greco, Vermeer, Holbein, Titian, she felt simultaneously soothed and refreshed. There was a smile on her face as she stepped out onto 70th Street, only to discover that Rosinante's rear tyre was flat.

In a street off 2nd Avenue Freya found a big old garage smelling of rubber, with a row of bicycles parked on the sidewalk and a throng of muscled youths inside, clinking spanners and conferring over spinning wheels. As she took her place in the queue for the counter, her fingers slipped on the handlebars and Rosinante lurched sideways, ramming the person in front.

'I'm so sorry,' said Freya.

'It's OK.' It was a young man, with a friendly smile. 'What's the problem with your bike?'

'Flat tyre.' Freya sighed with self-pity.

'Is that all? Why don't you fix it?'

'Well. I . . . er . . . don't have the equipment. It's not my bike.'

'Sure you do.' He showed her a pouch strapped behind the seat.

'I thought that was a first-aid kit,' Freya admitted.

He laughed as if she'd cracked a terrific joke, revealing perfectly straight, dazzling white teeth.

'Listen,' he said. 'Let's go back outside, and I'll fix it for you. They'll charge you crazy money to do it here. Come on.'

Freya followed him outside and watched him lean his own machine tenderly against the wall. Then he came over and took the bike from her hands. He flipped it upside-down. He certainly seemed very fit.

'Shit, that's heavy! It's a real museum piece,' he muttered, fiddling with some kind of metal tool. 'Wonder how old she is. Got to be before 1973 because that's when they put casings on the offside wing nuts.' He shot her a dazzling grin. 'That's even older than me!'

Freya made a rapid mental calculation. He must be eight years younger than her, at least.

A group of bikers swooped out of the garage. Someone called, 'Coming to the park, Brett?'

The young man glanced at Freya. 'Maybe later.'

'Please don't stay because of me,' she said quickly. 'I can easily get the bike fixed inside.'

'Nah, it's OK. I want to. We can talk.'

376

So Freya perched on a fire hydrant and listened to him talk, watching his lean fingers move skilfully around her bike. Brett was an actor—well, mainly a waiter and bar person, if he was honest, though as a matter of fact he was opening next week in a challenging production—a non-speaking role, unfortunately, and unpaid, but still, it was a start. He'd only been in the city ten months, sharing a loft space in the West Village with three others—strangers to begin with, but a great bunch.

Listening to him, Freya felt an ache of nostalgia. Brett's enthusiasm about the details of her own life was infectious. It was 'cool' that she was English; 'really cool' that she ran a gallery. When she told him she was temporarily living in Chelsea, he thought that was cool too. Meanwhile, the glances he gave her confirmed the flattering truth that he found her attractive. Freya's heart was as light as a bubble.

At length Brett righted the bicycle in triumph.

'Marvellous.' Freya stood up. 'Thank you so much.'

'No sweat.'

His hand rested in a proprietary way on her bicycle seat. When he squeezed it gently, she felt a fierce leap of lust.

'Well . . .' she said.

Brett grinned at her, looked off into space, glanced back, bounced on his toes, ducked his head.

'I was going to take a loop round the park,' he said. 'Maybe get a drink. Hang out. Want to come?'

Freya thought of the crowds, the noise, the heat, and her aching legs. She thought of Jack and Candace on the couch.

'Why not?' she said.

Chapter Seven

MICHAEL HURRIED OUT of the elevator and down the hall, the trousers of his ill-fitting new suit flapping round his ankles. He was late, and he couldn't find the right office.

'Excuse me!' He flagged down a young woman. 'Can you tell me how to find Suite 719—the Birnbaum case?'

Her eyes gave him a quick up-and-down scrutiny and returned to his face unimpressed. 'Do you mean Blumberg?' she enquired.

'Atshoo!' Michael sneezed heavily. 'That's it: Blumberg.'

The woman gave him directions and Michael hurried on, wiping his sore nose with a handkerchief. He hated this kind of situation, where he had to take over a case with no notice and no background knowledge of the participants. But Fred Reinertson, his boss, had been rushed to hospital and had specifically requested that Michael handle the case. Michael was unsure whether this was an honour or a test. Either way, his partnership could depend upon his performance.

He was representing Mr Lawrence Blumberg, aged seventy-six, against his wife, Mrs Jessica Blumberg, aged seventy-four. It was not the kind of high-profile divorce case normally handled by a senior partner, but there was some family connection with Mr Blumberg which Fred had chosen to honour with his personal services.

Here was Suite 719 at last. Michael gave his nose a last-minute blow, and opened the door. An elderly man with sparse grey hair and a doleful expression was sitting in the small reception area.

'You the young fellow from Reinertsons?'

'Yes, that's right, Mr Blumberg.'

'You're late. Jessie's already in there.' Mr Blumberg nodded his head towards another door. 'With her lawyer—a woman. Seems a very commanding young lady.' His expression implied that he did not necessarily feel the same way about Michael.

Michael hid his irritation with a professional smile. 'I'm sure you and I will be more than a match for them.' He sat down next to Mr Blumberg, and took a folder from his briefcase. 'Now, if we could just run through a few points before we go in . . .'

Mr Blumberg was extremely definite in his instructions, but so long-winded that it was a good ten minutes before Michael was able to lead the way to the inner office. He knocked once, and opened the door. It was the usual unadorned room, furnished with chairs and a small conference table, where two people sat facing him. Mrs Blumberg was handsome and stern-looking, with snowy hair pinned in a bun. Next to her was a much younger woman, presumably Mrs Blumberg's attorney; though Michael noted, with fleeting disapproval, the unlawyerly flamboyance of her brilliant turquoise shirt and riot of jet-black hair.

Michael adopted his best smile. 'Good afternoon. I'm so sorry—'

'What do you think you're doing here?'

To Michael's astonishment, the young woman with the hair had leapt to her feet and fixed him with an accusing glare.

'I'm Michael Petersen, from—'

'I know *who* you are,' she said in tones of loathing. 'What I asked was why you're here.' She kneed her chair out of the way and stepped towards him. 'Let me tell you, I will not have you interrupting this meeting so that you can slap some ridiculous lawsuit on one of my clients.'

Michael stood frozen in the doorway. What lawsuit? Which client? She must have mistaken him for someone else.

'Michael Petersen,' he repeated stubbornly, 'from Reinertson and Klang. I'm here to represent Mr Blumberg.' Belatedly, he stepped forward, allowing Mr Blumberg to enter the room. 'Mr Reinertson's been taken sick,' he added.

'Oh.' Far from offering him an apology, the mad woman folded her arms and glowered.

'And you,' Michael scoured his sluggish memory, 'must be Ms da Fillipo.' He tried to inject a cheery note into his voice.

She tossed her head as if this was obvious. 'You say you're here as Mr Blumberg's attorney—instead of Fred Reinertson?' She seemed unwilling to accept this fact. 'Why wasn't I informed of this substitution?'

'Didn't our office—?'

'No, they did not.'

'Well, I apologise for that, naturally, but . . . *atshoo!*' The sneeze shook him from head to toe. 'Excuse me. I'm so sorry.'

Ms da Fillipo's smouldering brown eyes rested on his face for a moment. Then she dropped her eyelids, turned on her heel and returned to her place next to Mrs Blumberg.

Michael had hardly sat down with his client before she rapped a pencil on the table. 'OK, let's get started, now that Mr Petersen has condescended to join us. The purpose of this meeting, as you know, is to talk through your reasons for wanting a divorce and, if you are resolved on such a course, to reach a settlement.'

'But I don't want a divorce,' Mr Blumberg said mulishly.

'Well, I do,' said his wife. 'He's having an affair with Mrs Lemke from upstairs!'

Mr Blumberg groaned and smacked his forehead, as if this ground had been gone over many times. 'All I did was ask her if she remembered how to foxtrot and—'

'What kind of a woman dances with strange men in her kitchen in the middle of the day?' Mrs Blumberg demanded darkly.

'Now, Jessie: Doris is sixty-five years old,' protested Mr Blumberg.

'Doris, is it now? Well, pardon me.'

'She just moved into our building. I was being neighbourly.'

'Neighbourly! Is that why you snuck out to have lunch with her?'

'I did not sneak.'

Back and forth they went. Michael was amazed at their passion. Privately, Mr Blumberg had conceded to him that for two brief weeks he'd had 'a crazy thing' with the widowed Doris, though the craziness had consisted of little more than a kiss on the cheek and the odd bunch of flowers. Mr Blumberg couldn't see why he had to apologise. Mrs Blumberg felt betrayed and wanted her pound of flesh.

'I just want to get divorced,' she said, terminating the argument.

The discussion moved on to an examination of the Blumberg assets and the settlement to which Mrs Blumberg might be entitled. Then Ms da Fillipo uttered the words, 'And what about Pookie?'

'Pookie's *my* baby,' said Mrs Blumberg stubbornly.

'Well, I'm keeping her.' Mr Blumberg stuck out his chin.

Michael was floundering. He tried unobtrusively to peek through his notes. 'Let's see . . . What exact kind of, uh, baby, are we talking about?'

Three pairs of eyes regarded him with scorn.

'You might at least have done your homework,' Ms da Fillipo said coldly. 'Pookie is a five-year-old pedigree Highland terrier, purchased *in person* by my client, as the breeder will testify.'

'Paid for with *my* money,' Mr Blumberg pointed out. 'Jessie doesn't have any money of her own; she's never worked.'

'Never worked? *Never worked!*' Ms da Fillipo flung back her head. 'The woman who has made your home, who cooked your dinner, who bore your children; the woman who tended to you when you were sick and gave you the warmth of her body at night—*for fifty years*: how can you say that woman has never worked?'

There was an intimidated silence. Michael tried to remember what he knew of this da Fillipo woman: nothing, except that she worked for a family law partnership that had a radical reputation.

'Isn't that just typical of men?' she continued, in a quiet, sinister voice. Unnervingly, her laser gaze now moved to Michael. 'Does the woman not contribute to your life who shares your bed, who puts up with your musical tastes even when she doesn't like opera—'

'Opera?' both Blumbergs chorused in surprise.

'—who drinks skimmed milk because of *your* dietary requirements—'

'Skimmed milk?'

'—and endures your sexual inadequacies?'

'Jessie! How could you?'

Michael's head was spinning. It was almost as if she was talking about himself and Freya. But how could that be?

'You pursue this woman.' Ms da Fillipo thundered on. 'Then one day—*pfff!*—you decide you don't need her any more. So what do you do? You take her to a *public place* and cast her off.'

'But Jessie left *me*,' objected the old man.

'Of course I left you! You were having an affair with Mrs Lemke.'

'You cast her off, I say—homeless—'

'Ms da Fillipo,' Michael rose to his feet. 'I wonder if we might step next door for a moment?'

'Gladly,' she answered, glaring at him.

Michael crossed to the door and held it open with elaborate politeness, then stepped after her into the outer room. Behind him he could hear Mrs Blumberg wailing. He closed the door firmly.

'Now.' He rounded on Ms da Fillipo. 'Would you please tell me what's been going on in there?'

'Don't play the innocent with me.' Her eyes flashed. '*I know everything*. And I am not embarrassed to tell you to your face that you have treated Freya abominably. If you dare to sue her over those trousers, I shall defend her personally, to the Supreme Court if necessary.'

Michael looked down on her in perplexity, mildly disconcerted by how small she was, close to. His brain struggled to figure out how she knew so much about Freya and his trousers. How come this Caterina da Fillipo was taking it all so personally? *Caterina* . . . The penny dropped with a clunk. 'You're Cat!' he said.

'Of course.' She eyed him defiantly, arms clasped tight beneath rounded breasts. Somehow he had never imagined Cat looking like this.

'Well, listen, Ca that is, Ms da Fillipo—I am not, as it happens, intending to sue Freya, and I consider it highly unprofessional of you to allow personal feelings to interfere with a case of law.'

'Oh, do you?' Her chin lifted; her eyebrows soared: it was one of the most expressive faces he had ever seen. 'Well, I'm glad to hear that you've backed down over the lawsuit. That's something, at least.'

'I haven't "backed down". I never even—'

'And I cannot agree that personal emotions are irrelevant to a case of law. That's the difference between men and women: for me, divorce is about people; for you, it's all about money.'

Suddenly Michael was almost angry enough to slap her. 'How dare you presume to tell me what I feel? As a matter of fact, I think divorce is a tragic, cruel, painful business. Yes, I make money from it—and so do you. I'm proud that I, for one, can keep my emotions under control.'

Michael stopped, stunned by his own outburst. His nose was running. He groped for his handkerchief.

'Here.' Cat handed him a folded Kleenex from her skirt pocket.

381

'I'm *never* going to get divorced.' Michael blew his nose with a loud honk. 'The thing to do is to pick the right person—and stick.'

'You didn't stick with Freya,' she pointed out.

Michael jerked his head in exasperation. 'I didn't ask her to marry me either.' He added, more quietly, 'I don't think she wanted to.' Now that his explosion of anger had subsided, Michael felt foolish, exposed. 'Let's get back to the case, shall we?' he said. 'So far, there aren't any real obstacles to a smooth divorce except this dog business.'

'"Dog business",' mimicked Cat. 'You can't even say "Pookie" out loud. You think it's sissy.'

'No, I don't.'

'Say it, then.'

Michael rolled his eyes. This was absurd. He had never met such an unreasonable woman. 'Pookie,' he grunted.

Those fierce brown eyes stared into his, and suddenly a kind of craziness swept through him. 'Pookie, Pookie, Pookie. I love you, Pookie. Come to Mamma, Pookie. Stop crapping on the carpet, Pookie.'

Cat's mouth had gone a very peculiar shape. She was laughing!

There was the rattle of a doorknob, and a voice growled, 'Are you two people interested in our case?'

'Of course we're interested, Mr Blumberg,' Michael replied smoothly. 'In fact, we were just discussing a pertinent legal technicality.'

'Hmph.'

They had returned to the table and resumed negotiations when a sudden trill sent both Michael and Cat scrabbling in their briefcases for their mobile phones. The call was for Michael.

'Mikey! Thank goodness I've reached you.'

His mother: that was all he needed.

'What seems to be the problem?' he said.

'I want you to come over right away. It's sweltering in this room, and I can't get the air conditioning to work.'

Michael swung away from the table and hunched over the phone. 'Are you sure you turned it on correctly?' he asked in a low voice.

'Speak up, Mikey. You're mumbling.'

'Can't you get room service to fix it?' he asked, painfully aware of six eyes watching him, and six ears listening.

'They're so busy. I don't like to bother them.'

'Mother, it's a hotel. That's what they're for.'

Michael could feel sweat breaking out on his forehead. He put his thumb over the earpiece of his phone, and stood up. 'Excuse me, Mr Blumberg . . . Mrs Blumberg . . . Ms da Fillipo. This is an, um, emergency call. I'll be right back.' With that, he escaped into the outer room.

'Mother, will you please stop shouting? I am in the middle of a business meeting. I can't come now. I'll see you at dinner, as we agreed.'

Michael cut the call, snapped his cellphone shut, and leaned his head against the cool wall. His nose was running and his eyes itched. He gave a bracing sniff, squared his shoulders and re-entered the room.

An extraordinary scene met his eyes. All three of them were sitting cosily together on the same side of the table. Cat held a handkerchief to her eyes as if she'd been crying; the Blumbergs sat solicitously on either side of her.

'Well, young man.' Mrs Blumberg gave him a stern look. 'I think you owe Caterina here an apology. All lovers have quarrels, even old stagers like us.'

Lovers! Michael looked wildly at Cat, whose eyes commanded silence.

'You have to learn to say you're sorry,' continued Mrs Blumberg. She smiled across at her chastened-looking husband. 'Imagine: we were actually thinking of getting divorced after fifty happy years.'

'Imagine,' Michael repeated. He had no idea what was going on.

'Well,' prompted Mrs Blumberg, 'aren't you going to apologise to Caterina?'

There seemed nothing to do but go along with this pantomime. Michael looked at Cat, and swallowed. 'I'm very sorry.'

'That's OK.' She seemed equally embarrassed by this charade.

'Well, go on, give her a nice big hug.'

After a small hesitation Michael stepped forward, and Cat rose from her chair to meet him. He held his arms out stiffly, and she leaned her head against his chest. Automatically his arms closed around her. She felt warm and womanly under his hands. *Caterina* . . . the syllables sang in his head.

'All right, that's enough,' joked Mr Blumberg.

Michael relinquished his hold and Caterina stepped back.

'We'll leave you now, so you can be alone,' said Mrs Blumberg. 'Come along, Lawrence.'

Michael waited until he heard the outer door close, then turned to Caterina. 'What happened?' he demanded. 'What did you say?'

She moved to the table and started gathering up her papers. 'All I said was that you'd broken off our engagement.'

'Our *what*?'

'I told them that your mother didn't approve, and was trying to make you give me up.' She flashed him a defiant glance. 'I had to think of something for the Blumbergs' sake. It was quite clear they didn't want to get divorced. I thought we might as well all stop playing games.'

'But just now—you were crying!'

'That's my party trick. I can cry on demand.'

'I see,' said Michael. He didn't, in fact, understand a single, solitary thing, except that a few minutes ago there had been an impossible tangle, which this extraordinary woman had somehow pulled into a smooth ribbon of silk.

'Well . . . thanks,' he said.

She caught his eye and smiled. The transformation was astonishing.

Michael opened his mouth. 'At*choooo*,' he said.

'You want to take care of that sniffle,' Caterina told him calmly. 'What you need is some Vitamin E to get those antibodies going. There's a good health store not too far away. I'll write down the address for you.'

With the passionate energy that seemed to infuse everything she did, she tore a strip off her yellow notepad, scribbled something in a bold hand, then folded the paper and handed it to him. 'Now, I must rush.'

'Thank you. Uh, Ms da Fillipo . . . Caterina—' Michael broke off.

'Yes?' She shot him a glance of cautious curiosity.

'I, um . . .' Michael frowned. His mind was blank. Then he had an inspiration. 'I'd be very grateful if you would clear up this misunderstanding about a lawsuit—you know, talk to Freya.'

'Sure.' Suddenly she was cramming her belongings into her briefcase and busily snapping the catches. Moving like a small, vivid blue whirlwind, she was gone with a wave of her hand.

Chapter Eight

'I THOUGHT THE PART where Mack chopped up his mother was a little clichéd.'

'That was *intentional*, Mona. It's an ironic commentary on the banality of violence in our society.'

Lester was wearing a tie over an obsessively well-pressed shirt. Jack wondered: could Lester have written the threatening letter? He forced himself to concentrate. His gaze travelled around the faces at the seminar table, drawing their attention. 'Let's look for a moment at character development in "Big Mack". Who wants to comment on that?'

As usual, Nathan began to shoot his mouth off. Meanwhile Mona began to clean her nails with a hairpin. Jack studied her bony profile; maybe *she* had written the note.

The letter had arrived yesterday. Fortunately, Freya had gone to work by then, so there was no one to witness his shock. He had screwed it up and thrown it away. But all morning, while he tried to write, he found his thoughts dwelling uneasily on its threatening malice. He wondered if a similar letter had been sent to his employers. Part of his training course to become a creative writing instructor had included a lecture on 'appropriate' behaviour. Jack hadn't paid much attention. It occurred to him now that he might have been rather stupid. Teachers had to be squeaky clean. They didn't dare even shut their office doors during an interview with a student, for fear of accusations of sexual harassment.

Jack glanced at Candace, sitting right down the other end of the table, uncharacteristically silent and demure, and felt a twinge of exasperation. Without mentioning the note, Jack had told her that they must be more discreet; but not that she should impersonate a nun. Everyone must have noticed that she hadn't opened her mouth all evening. Feeling his eyes on her, Candace glanced up and blushed deeply. Jesus!

Jack smoothed back his hair. Relax. What did it matter if he lost this job? It was only money. Why the hell shouldn't he form a relationship with a consenting adult of twenty-two?

Re-entering the discussion, Jack steered it deftly onwards until the class concluded that 'Big Mack', despite its imaginative strengths, hadn't quite 'worked'. He looked at his watch. There was still an hour left of the three-hour session. 'OK. Exercise time.'

The class groaned.

'I want you to spend the next forty minutes writing a scene that moves me. You can write a poem, or a scene of dialogue, or even a letter. Just be honest. Look into your hearts and write.'

After a certain amount of fuss the students settled to their task. A pleasing, concentrated stillness fell on the room. Through the high windows, streetlights glowed in the night sky. Jack looked around the square room with its institutional blue paint, and contemplated his class—his twelve disciples—slouching, doodling, writing, chewing their pens. He felt his heart expand. He *did* like teaching. He liked the arguments and the jokes, and the intense satisfaction when a student's comprehension opened like a flower. He didn't want to lose this job.

His own desire to be a writer had been slow and stealthy. His had not been a literary household, but as stepmothers and stepfathers came and went, he had learned to read the emotional temperature and to record it in his head. When Jack was ten his father had married Lauren. She had gusted into their lives, bringing with her trunkfuls of books and the fresh, tantalising whiff of a different world. Lauren read aloud to him, explained new words and concepts. Jack's relationship with her had survived the inevitable divorce some years later, and Lauren had encouraged him when he began, tentatively, to commit some of his imaginings to words.

For Jack, writing was a liberation, like discovering an extra limb or a new dimension. He loved the notion that a good writer could create anything he liked, and make the reader believe it.

Except he was blocked. Stymied. Stuck. Perhaps he *was* a fraud, a one-book wonder. He remembered with a flicker of anxiety that it was this weekend that his father was flying up to New York for a series of business meetings the following week. There had been the usual two-line letter, typed by his secretary, informing Jack of this fact and stating that he would be free to see his son some time on Sunday. It irritated the hell out of Jack the way his father always assumed that Jack himself would be free. Dad didn't rate writing as 'work'. When Jack had proudly presented his father with a copy of his book, the first fruit of his labours, his father had merely flipped through the pages and commented with a chuckle that Jack could have produced a million of these by now if he'd been working at Madison Paper, the paper mills that were the foundation of the family fortune. Maybe if his next book got onto the best-seller list—or won the Pulitzer!—his father would finally stop jeering.

At the end of the session Jack collected up the students' efforts and distributed copies of a piece for next week's discussion. When Candace handed him her paper she surreptitiously showed him the palm of one hand, on which she had written 'See you Saturday!' As Jack rattled homewards on the subway, he was relieved not to have her chattering at his side. Emerging from the subway station, he began to compose a scene in his head: a dusky summer's evening, two people in a restaurant—himself, say, and a mystery woman. He could see the woman leaning towards him, her face beautiful and fierce, her expressive hands cutting the air as she—Wait! Here was the pizza place. Jack pushed the door open and sniffed appreciatively. He was starving. He'd grab a slice and take it home to eat in the back yard. As he debated what to choose, his thoughts turned to Freya, wondering if she'd be in the apartment when he got back. Probably. She didn't seem to be having much of a social life at the moment. Poor old Freya.

Suddenly Jack had a marvellous idea: why didn't he buy her a pizza, too? He knew what she liked. It would be a peace offering. Jack pictured his arrival at the apartment. She'd be washing her hair or watching TV; she wouldn't have bothered to eat, so she'd be hungry, and grateful. They'd sit outside and talk. It would be like old times.

Freya could bear it no longer. She shifted her weight off one numbed buttock, uncrossed her legs, and recrossed them the other way. The seat beneath her let out a loud creak, and the guy in front of her twisted his head to glare.

'Sorry,' she mouthed.

She returned her attention to the stage, where an actor dressed as a Buddhist monk had been standing in the same spotlit position for the last twenty minutes, eyes lowered, palms pressed together. So far nothing else had happened.

Wait, she could hear something: a low, rhythmic hum like a fridge in the night. Very gradually, body parts began to emerge from the darkness of the wings, eventually revealing a group of very solemn young men and women dressed in sarongs and shifts made of drab sacking. Brett was not among them.

Freya's fingers tightened on her rolled-up programme as her mind drifted back to last Saturday and the image of Brett's back view cycling ahead of her. There had been ample opportunity to take in the athletic, pumping legs and the broad back, with its peekaboo strip of bare flesh, flaring out from taut, slim hips. Once they were in the park he had slowed his pace and started to do tricks for her—riding no-handed, slaloming along the track with a graceful weave of his body, turning back with a grin to check that she was watching. Freya laughed and began to copy him, and soon they were playing follow-my-leader. It was fun, flirtatious, exhilarating. By the time they stopped, breathless with laughter, they were halfway to intimacy.

'Come on, you crazy girl. I'll buy you an orange juice.'

'No way. I'm buying.'

And they'd fought about it; and that was fun, too. Once they were in the juice bar, there didn't seem much to say. Freya liked it that way. Sitting opposite each other, he smiled at her and she smiled at him as they sucked frothy, fruity slush through straws. Of course he was ridiculously young. But did age really matter? In her heart, Freya felt no older than twenty-three. It was a relief to jettison all that baggage of career and family and failed relationships to be, well, just a 'crazy girl'.

Freya blinked, and refocused her vacant gaze on the stage. A slow drumbeat began. The actors stopped what they were doing—all but the monk, who was still praying—and turned their faces wonderingly upwards. Was it going to rain? The drumbeat speeded up and grains of rice—real rice—began to shower onto the stage. Oh, right: the harvest. Released from their sluggish trance, the actors began to whirl and leap and stamp in a frenzied dance. After a good five minutes of this they catapulted themselves offstage and into the wings, until only the monk remained, impassive under a final trickle of rice. Freya remembered now that the play was called *Grains of Truth*. Aha!

The drum stopped abruptly. Into the stark silence that followed, stepped Brett, dressed in a saffron-yellow loincloth and carrying a long wooden rake over one shoulder. Freya leaned forward. He walked with slow solemnity to the centre of the stage and lowered his rake to the floor in a graceful curve. His body had been covered with gleaming make-up and the golden light that streamed across the stage accentuated every bone and muscle. Now *this* part of the show was very effective, Freya thought approvingly. Evidently others thought so too, for they watched in rapt attention while Brett circled the stage with his rake, sweeping the rice into a pleasing spiral pattern. When at length he reached the front he straightened up and lifted the rake back onto his shoulder. There was a final *bong*! from the drum, then the rest of the cast emerged from the wings in a dignified procession and lined up on either side of him. It was the end.

The small theatre erupted in generous applause. Freya let go of her programme and clapped enthusiastically, sitting tall in her seat, her eyes on Brett. When he caught sight of her, he lost his composure and had to hide his face by bowing prematurely. Freya laughed aloud with delight.

The stage emptied and the theatre filled with the bustle of departure. When she reached the foyer, Freya ducked into the ladies' loo to check herself out in the mirror: ripped, faded jeans teamed with an immaculate white T-shirt. She had opted for the dressed-down look. Was this right?

At the stage door she joined a small scrum of hangers-on, and gave her name to the guy on the door. A few moments later Brett burst out of the exit, still in his costume, glowing and gorgeous, adrenalin pumping from every pore. He threw his arms round her.

'Wasn't that *great*?' he demanded. His skin was hot against hers.

'Fabulous.' It came out in a croak.

'I wasn't sure you'd come. When I saw you there I couldn't believe it!' he gabbled. 'Listen, I'll be a few minutes. Will you wait?'

'Probably.' But she was smiling.

'We're all going over to Julio's to celebrate. I'll be as quick as I can.' He bounded off, then pivoted neatly in the doorway and fixed her with a slow-burn look. 'Don't go away.'

Freya shook her head. As if she could.

Julio's turned out to be a scruffy, studenty tapas bar. In the noisy confusion of their arrival, Freya made her way to the bar and quietly paid for two bottles of champagne before taking her place next to Brett, now dressed in black jeans and a soft blue shirt, hair still gleaming from his shower. Everyone talked at once. What would the reviews say? Oh God, it was too agonising to think about.

The champagne arrived, provoking an excited whoop and a flurry of speculation. When the waiter indicated who had bought it, eyes swivelled curiously to Freya, then to Brett.

'This is Freya, everyone,' he announced. 'She came to see the show.'

There was a tiny, awkward pause. Freya saw that her extravagant gesture had been misjudged. It set her apart: someone richer, different—a sugar mommy. She grabbed her glass and raised it. 'You were all fantastic,' she told the blur of young faces. 'Here's to'—her memory stumbled sickeningly, then righted itself—'here's to *Grains of Truth.*'

The toast was taken up enthusiastically, everyone clinked glasses, and to Freya's relief the hubbub continued.

'Hey, that was really nice of you.' Brett's voice was low and warm in her ear. She turned her head to find his eyes inches from her own. The open collar of his shirt had slid sideways, revealing the smooth skin of his shoulder. She wanted to go to bed with him. *Now.* He gave her a brief kiss on the cheek. 'Thanks,' he said. He smelt of clean, male skin.

The table filled up with small plates of olives and shrimps and smoked ham and things on sticks, and the champagne was succeeded by a rough red wine that rasped her throat. Conversation about people she didn't know, and things she didn't want to know, dinned in her ears. She was aware of Brett's proximity, caught within his magnetic field. Every time he accidentally brushed her arm or her leg, a current of desire jolted through her. She drank steadily.

The party was in full flow when she felt a gentle squeeze on her leg. 'We could go if you want.'

Freya bit her lip. 'Could we?'

Five minutes later they were standing outside in the hot night.

'So . . .' Brett scuffed his sneaker back and forth on the sidewalk. 'Don't you live somewhere around here?'

'A few blocks away,' Freya agreed. She stuck her thumbs in the front pockets of her jeans and examined her toecaps, suddenly as awkward as a farm boy. 'You want to walk me home?'

Brett's smile widened. 'Sure.'

They walked a few yards in silence. *Do you have a girlfriend?* Freya wanted to ask. *Do you think I'm attractive? How about coming to England with me?*

'There's an audition coming up for *Cats*,' Brett began.

'Do you know, I saw that in London on opening night.'

'But . . . wasn't that way back in the *eighties*?'

Whoops. Freya's brain whirled with mental calculations. Brett must have been—yikes!—seven or eight years old, a kid on a bike.

'School trip,' she explained blithely. 'I can't have been more than thirteen. Or twelve, even. Eleven or twelve. I might as well confess I probably *am* a little older than you . . . Almost thirty.' She sneaked a glance at his face, waiting for his reaction.

'Who cares?' Brett turned to her, looking genuinely surprised that she should think it mattered. He smiled into her eyes and dropped an arm round her shoulders. 'I like you,' he said. 'That's all that matters.'

'Good.' After the tiniest beat Freya slid her hand round his back, as she had ached to do for hours, and curled her fingers round his hip bone. They walked on together, body to body, striking sparks. The silence sizzled between them. Freya's skin tingled where his arm grazed the back of her neck.

She stole a glance at his profile—at the sweet curve of his lips and smudge of dark eyelashes. His body felt warm and solid under her hand. She remembered the sight of his slatted ribs and flat stomach disappearing into the saffron loincloth. Yes, this was the answer: a younger man, eager and unspoilt.

Outside Jack's house she stopped and turned into the curve of Brett's arm. 'We're here,' she told him. 'You could come in for a drink, if you like.'

His eyes met hers. 'I like.'

On the way to the basement, she had noticed with relief that the windows were dark—not that it took a genius to guess that Jack would be staying out with Candace after his class. Even if he came back late, and caught her canoodling in the darkness with a young whippersnapper, so what? Freya unlocked the door and led the way inside. She turned on a table lamp—nothing too bright—slotted Billie into the stereo, kicked off her shoes, and went into the kitchen to pour their drinks.

'Great place!' called Brett from the living room.

Freya raised her eyebrows. As usual, Jack's apartment was a tip. But to someone sharing a room with three others it probably looked like a palace. 'It belongs to a friend,' she called back. 'I'm between apartments at the moment, so I'm using his guest room for a couple of weeks.' She paused. 'He's out tonight.'

When Freya carried in the drinks, Brett was sitting on the couch. She walked across to him in her bare feet, invitation in her eyes.

'Here you go.' She leaned down to hand him his glass. At the same time he made a clumsy lunge at her arm, to pull her down next to him. Freya half sat, half fell onto the couch. Drink splashed down her front.

'Whoa! What are you doing?' she giggled, putting down the glasses. 'I'm soaked.' She flicked at the moisture on her T-shirt, and saw how her nipples swelled visibly through the wet material.

Brett saw too. His face grew intent. Suddenly his musky weight was on top of her, pressing her back against the couch. His lips found hers, warm and insistent. Freya closed her eyes and surrendered with a sigh, opening her mouth beneath his. Her hand slid up over his shoulder to cup the back of his neck. She felt him plucking at her T-shirt, and almost smiled at his eagerness. But the touch of his fingers on her bare skin made her catch her breath. Her back arched as his hand travelled upwards; she gave a sigh of pleasure. She reached down to yank Brett's shirt free, hungry for the feel of his body against hers. She wanted more. Everything. *Now.*

Suddenly Brett pulled away. 'What was that?' he asked.

'Nothing!' She grabbed him back.

But even as she spoke, she heard it too—a scuffle in the lock, then the sound of the front door slamming.

'He-e-e-re's Jackie,' swooped a horribly familiar voice.

Freya barely had time to straighten up and pull down her T-shirt before the living-room door swung open and Jack entered, stage left, carrying two pizza cartons balanced high on one palm. 'Larks' tongues for her ladyship!' he announced. Then he spotted Brett, and his face changed. He lowered the pizzas to a more conventional position. There was a charged silence.

'What are you doing here?' snapped Freya.

Jack did a comic double take. 'I, uh, live here . . . don't I?'

'This is Brett,' she told him coldly.

'And I'm Jack,' said Jack. 'Freya's room-mate. I'm gay.'

'Oh, right. Hi, Jack.' Brett sketched a nervous wave. He was now crouched on the very edge of the couch.

'Kind of dark in here.' Jack flicked on an overhead light and dumped the pizzas casually on the central table. 'Anybody hungry?'

'No!' Freya scowled.

'You don't mind if I go ahead?'

'Yes, we do. Can't you eat in the kitchen?'

Brett jumped up from the couch. 'It's time I was leaving anyway.'

Freya wanted to scream with frustration. 'Don't be silly. You only just got here.'

'The night is young,' agreed Jack, dropping a hunk of *quattro stagione* into his mouth. Even sitting down, he dominated the room. 'I could show you the video of me fishing.'

'No, really,' Brett stammered. 'I'm on the early shift at Bagels R Us. I should get some sleep.'

Jack cocked an eyebrow. 'You a cook, Brad?'

'*Brett!*' Freya almost stamped her foot.

'No, a waiter—well, an actor, really—at least, trying to be.'

'An actor!' Jack greeted this news with enthusiasm. 'You really should stay. Freya's probably too modest to tell you this, but she's quite an expert on the plays of Shakespeare.'

'Shut up, Jack!'

What had put him in such a vile mood? It was unbearable to watch him turn Brett into a shrinking schoolboy.

'He's joking. Take no notice.' Freya smiled at Brett and took his hand. 'Come on, I'll walk you to the door.' She closed the living-room door firmly behind them, shutting Jack out, then opened the front door.

'Jack is an oaf,' she explained, stepping outside with him. 'Needless to say, he's not gay, nor does he possess a fishing video—just a weird sense of humour. Now, where were we?'

She leaned back against the brick wall, half hoping to continue where they left off. But it was no good. Brett was twitchy and self-conscious. 'I'll call you,' he said.

'Thanks for a wonderful evening,' she replied, and they kissed cheeks. But it was an empty ritual. The romance had gone.

She watched him walk up to the street, then stormed back into the living room, slamming both doors behind her, and plonked her hands on her hips. 'How *dare* you?' she shouted.

Jack looked up innocently from his pizza. 'What did I do?'

'You know perfectly well what you did. You scared him away. How could you do that?'

'I'm sorry. I didn't know it was such a big deal.'

'I didn't say it was a big deal. I just like him. I'd like to see him again. I'd like him to have stayed longer.'

'Oh.'

'What do you mean, "oh"?'

'Nothing.'

'Come on, Jack, you always mean something. You said "oh" as if you were surprised.'

Jack chomped carelessly. 'It simply struck me that he seemed some-what on the youthful side. To tell the truth, I wondered at first if he'd got lost on the way home from school and was waiting to be picked up by his mommy.'

'I knew it!' Freya grabbed the back of a chair to steady herself. '*You* go out with someone ten years younger, but that's just hunky-dory because you're a man. But if a woman does it—how tacky, how embarrassing, what could he possibly see in her? The truth is, Jack, you're selfish. You do whatever you like, but you don't want anyone else to have fun.'

'Well, if you really want to fool around with some—'

'His name's Brett. Not Brad or Brat or any of the hilarious alternatives I know you can dream up when you're pretending to write your so-called novel. Brett. B-R-E-T-T. Aged twenty-six, if you want to know.' She blew out a furious breath. 'At least I'm not screwing one of my own students. You can get fired for that, you know. Sexual harassment, gross moral turpitude . . . Where is the little munchkin, by the way?'

The words froze on her lips as Jack's head snapped up. 'It was you!' he exclaimed, his face dark with accusation.

'What was me?'

Jack rose from the table with a crash. 'Don't give me that "what was me?" crap. Who else would use a phrase like "gross moral turpitude"? Jesus, Freya, I've been having nightmares about that letter.' He flung one of the pizza boxes at her, spattering her with tomato sauce.

'How could *I* do that?' She flung the box back. 'Who set me up with that Bernard creep?'

'You know your problem?' Jack jabbed a finger. 'You're jealous.'

'*Jealous?*'

'Yes, jealous. Because I can get any woman I want, and you can never hold on to your men.'

'You don't "get" *any* women, Jack. They get *you*—if they're stupid enough to want you.'

His face tightened. They were both breathing like prize fighters.

'Isn't it time you moved out?' he asked. 'I said two weeks, tops.'

'I'll call Cat. She'll have me.'

'You do that. Meanwhile, let's stay out of each other's way.' Jack strode towards his bedroom. 'If I need to tell you anything, I'll write you a note.'

'If I'm *very* bored, I might read it.'

Jack turned in the doorway and shook his head in disgust. 'I can't believe I ever liked you.'

'You used to be different.'

'I used to be a lot of things.' He banged the door behind him.

Chapter Nine

'MS DA FILLIPO, is it all right if I go now?'

Cat looked up from her desk to see her new assistant, Becky, hovering in the doorway, her bag already hooked over her shoulder.

'It's just that it's my boyfriend's birthday,' Becky explained. 'There's going to be this big dinner, and I need to get dressed up.'

Cat checked her watch, amazed to find that it was getting on for six o'clock. 'My God, what happened to today?' she demanded. 'Of course you can go.' Cat beamed her warmest smile. 'Have a great evening.'

'Thanks.' Becky's voice was breathy with relief. Just before she made her escape, she turned back and added politely, 'You, too.'

Cat nodded. She could tell that Becky found it inconceivable that an unmarried woman heading for forty, living alone, wedded to her career, could possibly have a great evening. As it happened, Cat was meeting her brother for a movie and dim sum, and looking forward to it. She glanced out at the sky, sallow with heat and humidity, and decided to go home first to freshen up. She shut down her computer, packed up her briefcase, and checked her desk for anything she might have forgotten. Her eyes rested for a moment on the bunch of flowers that had arrived yesterday, accompanied by a card that read: 'With so much gratitude— and good luck with your young man!—Jessica Blumberg.' She turned and marched towards the elevator.

It was, of course, out of the question that Michael Petersen could ever be *her* 'young man'. That would be unforgivably disloyal. Michael Petersen had dumped her best friend without warning. Cat stabbed the DOWN button. The brute! She couldn't imagine what crazy impulse had made her invent that silly story of a broken engagement. Maybe she had felt sorry for him because of his cold.

The elevator doors slid open. Cat wedged herself into the crowded car. To be scrupulously fair—and she prided herself on her fairness— Michael wasn't quite as obnoxious as she'd imagined. He wasn't bad-looking, either. Those nice brown eyes were deceptively warm and honest, and she'd always liked that kind of hair—thick and springy, with a kind of kink to it. In actual fact, when Mr Blumberg had made them hug each other she had felt a spark of attraction—well, more of a thunderbolt. It was just as well she had given up men for good. Imagine being engaged to a guy like that! Yes, imagine . . .

She gave a start when the elevator bumped to a halt, then walked briskly through the lobby. *Get real, Caterina.* Apart from anything else, Michael would never go for her. If he hadn't thought Freya good enough, with her gorgeous legs and classy accent, he was hardly going to fall for a dumpy Italian from Staten Island. She would put Mr Michael Petersen right out of her head.

But as she pushed through the revolving door to the street, the very first person she saw was Michael. He was standing a little way down the sidewalk, gazing distractedly into the sky as if he was trying to memorise something. Cat's heart tapped a Fred Astaire number in her chest. She bolted back inside and hid behind a large pot plant. Fumbling for her sunglasses, she slid them onto her nose and peeked out cautiously She was not hallucinating. It was definitely him. What was he doing here? There was only one way to find out.

Cat came out of the door like a bullet and marched right up to him. 'What are you hanging around here for?'

Michael gaped at her. A slow smile of amazement lit his face. 'I—I was waiting for you.'

'Why?' snapped Cat. He wasn't good-looking, he was gorgeous.

'Caterina . . . could we go somewhere for a cup of coffee?' Michael gestured vaguely at a coffee shop across the street, but his eyes were fixed on hers with mesmerising intensity.

'OK,' Cat heard herself say. Quickly she tried to regain control of the situation. 'But not that place. Let's go around the corner.'

Café Ole was the usual affair of white walls, blond wood, hissing steel machines and classical music on the sound system. Michael insisted that she sat down at a small table, then he brought two cups over on a tray. He had nice hands, with clean, blunt nails. When he sat down opposite her, his physical presence seemed overwhelming. Her painfully sharpened perception registered the weave of his shirt, the spirals of his ears, a shallow cleft in his square chin.

'So what did you want to talk to me about?' she demanded.

'Well . . .' Michael put a sugar lump in his coffee and stirred it about fifteen times. 'I wanted to thank you for helping me out with the Blumbergs the other day.' He looked up and smiled at her admiringly. 'You were fantastic.'

'I was insane!' Cat tossed her head, but she couldn't help feeling a glow of pleasure. 'Jessica Blumberg sent me some flowers.'

'I got a bottle of wine.'

Cat wondered if he had also got a card wishing him good luck with his 'young woman', and felt a blush flood upwards. 'Well, you've thanked me now.' She gave a businesslike nod.

'And I also wanted to talk to you about Freya.'

Freya. Of course. 'What's to talk about? You dumped her, and she's very upset. Those are the plain facts. As her best friend, I feel very uncomfortable even sitting here drinking coffee with you.'

'I didn't "dump" Freya!' Michael protested. 'I wanted to tell you about Freya because of what you said the other day. You seemed very angry, and I—well, I don't want you to think badly of me.'

'I see.' Cat's heart began to thump. She couldn't take her eyes off him.

Slowly and hesitantly he began to explain why he had ended the relationship as he had. The plan had been that he and Freya would go together to this wedding in England—Cat must know about that. She nodded. But as the date approached he had felt increasingly uncomfortable. He knew in his heart that the relationship had no future; and he had genuinely thought that Freya sensed it too. To accompany her to England, and be presented to her family as her 'partner', would place them both in a false position. So he had decided to take the initiative and discuss the situation with Freya. Of course, he had messed it up.

An extraordinary sensation came over Cat as she watched Michael's face and listened to his halting account. She *knew* this man. How and why was a mystery, but she could read the contours of his mind and heart as if she possessed a map. She ached to reach out and touch him. Instead, she smiled into his eyes and said again, 'I see.'

Michael leaned forward. 'Is she *very* upset?'

Cat struggled to recapture her sense of righteous indignation on Freya's behalf, but there had been such a radical shift in her perception that she couldn't. Anyway, hadn't there been a breathy phone call about some hunky young guy on a bicycle?

'She'll get over it,' Cat said briskly.

'It was my own mistake,' Michael admitted. 'That first time I saw her, she looked so beautiful and lost. I had this . . . fantasy, I guess, of making her happy.'

'You're a romantic,' Cat told him. Suddenly, she felt indescribably happy herself.

'Am I? No one's ever called me that before.' He smiled with such warmth that Cat's defences melted further. It wasn't disloyal just to *talk* to Michael. She'd tell Freya that the two of them had met—but that's all.

Michael and Cat began to talk about law—where they had studied, how they liked their jobs. The conversation caught fire. Michael leaned across the table to her, eager and bright-eyed, completely transformed from the man she'd encountered with the Blumbergs two days ago.

'What happened to your cold?' Cat asked suddenly.

'Gone! I went to that place you recommended, and they gave me some amazing stuff.'

'Really? You went there?'

'Of course.'

Cat felt ridiculously flattered.

'You know, it's so funny we never met before,' Michael said. 'I used to hear about you all the time: Cat this, Cat that.'

'And I used to hear about you. But Freya's always been secretive.'

'Maybe she didn't think we'd get along,' Michael suggested.

They looked at each other. Neither said a word, but the truth rose warm and palpable between them. They got along just fine. Cat felt she could sit here with him for ever.

'Oh my God!' she exclaimed, looking at her watch. 'I have to go. I'm meeting someone.'

'Oh.' Michael looked completely crushed. 'Of course. I see.'

No, he didn't see, the great lummox. 'I'm meeting my kid brother.'

'Brother,' Michael echoed, cheering up.

'Youngest of five. Now, where did I put my briefcase?'

'It's here.' Michael reached down for it. 'I wish I'd been part of a big family,' he said. 'I'm the only one.'

Another door opened in Cat's perception. She had the sense that Michael had been on his best behaviour all his life—devoted son, good grades, solid job. Yet there were other, more passionate impulses straining to break free. She stood up reluctantly. 'Time to catch that subway.'

Michael jumped to his feet and asked politely if he could walk her to her stop. He opened the door for her, and insisted on carrying her briefcase. Oh, this was so regressive! Cat loved it. And she loved the way he used her real name. 'Caterina' was someone much more feminine and mysterious. Unconsciously she began humming a tune that had been playing in the coffee shop—the duet from *La Bohème*.

Michael stopped dead in the street and turned to her. Speculation leapt in his eyes. 'You like opera?'

'Of course I like opera. I'm Italian.'

'Even . . . Wagner?'

'Especially Wagner.'

He sighed, as if a weight had slid from his shoulders. 'That's good. Because it just so happens that I have an extra ticket for the *Ring* cycle.'

JACK: *Called Cat today, but she was in a meeting and couldn't talk. Says she'll ring me back. Please explain the situation if she calls when I'm out.*

For the second time this week I've come home to find a plate of melted butter on the kitchen table. After breakfast PLEASE remember to put it back in the fridge. (That's the big white thing in the kitchen.)—F

FREYA: *So that's the refrigerator. No wonder my laundry never comes out clean. Trust you're using 'home' in the purely temporary sense of the word. No word from Cat. The meter's running . . . J*

JACK: *Spoke to Cat at last. She's dying to have me stay with her, but her neighbour's cat puked on her fold-down bed and she's having the mattress cleaned. So I can either stay here until Wednesday, when I'd be leaving anyway, or move into a hotel. Let me know which.*

By the way, Michael is NOT suing me about his trousers. Cat ran into him at some law thing and asked him straight out. So screw you. F
PS Did anyone call?

FREYA: *So Cat's cat opened the bed all by himself! Smart pussy—or the least convincing excuse I've ever heard.*

Since you ask so prettily, OK: next Wednesday LATEST.

No, anyone did not call. Actors are busy fellows: all those yodelling classes and hair workshops. J

JACK: *Your father rang—what a charmer! I understand genes often skip a generation. He wants you to go over to his hotel for cocktails at 6.00pm on Sunday—call his 'usual suite' to confirm. He invited me too—said I sounded 'a delightful young lady'. Can't wait to meet him. F*

FREYA: *Don't get excited: Dad will flirt with a baked potato if there's nothing better around. Besides, you're way too old for him. But thanks for passing on the invitation; Candace and I will be delighted to accept.*

Garbled message on machine from Tash—about bridesmaids, I think. Laughed so hard trying to picture you in pink satin I missed most of it.

Oh—almost forgot. Your young gentleman caller called. B-R-E-T-T (though I understand the final 't' is silent). He wonders what you're doing Saturday night. I said you'd probably be washing your hair. Or was it Bernard? No, Brett, I'm almost sure. Anyway, it began with B. J

JACK: *Here's my rent money. Thanks for another wonderful week. F*

PS. Steven Spielberg called—wants to buy movie rights in Big Sky. He left a number, but I didn't have any paper so I wrote it on my hand. Then I washed your dirty dishes . . . Silly me!

PPS. It was Brett.

Strawberries . . .? Or raspberries?

Freya barely hesitated before adding both to the mounting pile in her shopping cart. She gave a happy sigh. It was Saturday morning. Seven hours from now Brett would be picking her up at the apartment for a night out—their first real date.

She had woken early, wound tight with anticipation. By eleven she had worked out at the gym, eaten breakfast, spied a fabulous dress in the window of a Village boutique and bought it, and returned to find the apartment silent and Jack apparently asleep. Still brimming with energy, she had decided on a trip to the food stores to stock the apartment with goodies. It was not, after all, impossible that Brett could still be around tomorrow, or for some days (and nights) to come. A healthy young man like that needed feeding. She was tasting salamis at the deli counter when she felt a tap on her shoulder.

'Hello, Candace,' she said, surprised. 'How are you?'

Candace stuck out her tongue.

Freya flinched. 'Yeuch! What's that?'

'A tongue stud.' Candace looked smug. 'It's a surprise for Jack. He wouldn't let me see him all week because of the teacher/student thing. So I thought, why not seize the opportunity?'

'Wasn't it horribly painful?' The silvery chip was embedded like a gob of fat in Candace's purplish tongue. Freya decided to forgo the salami.

'Jack's worth it. Actually, I came in here to buy him coffee and stuff for breakfast. You guys never have anything to eat in your apartment.'

'We do now.' Freya gestured at the cart. 'In fact, I'm very glad you turned up, Candace. After I've bought some cheese, you can help me carry everything home.'

Candace responded to this request with surprising enthusiasm. She was a good-natured girl, Freya realised, even if her elevator did not quite reach the top floor.

'How's Jack?' asked Candace, while Freya fretted over the ripeness of the *Torta di San Gardenzio*. 'I didn't want to call him because my tongue was swollen and made me talk funny.'

Freya frowned. 'We're not on speaking terms.'

'That's too bad. I thought you were such good friends. Jack's told me all about you—how you came to New York without any money and put yourself through art school, and how you two lived in the same rooming house and always went to the movies together.'

'My goodness, Candace, are you planning to write my biography?' Freya didn't know whether to be annoyed or flattered by the extent of Jack's revelations.

'I was jealous,' Candace confessed. 'Crazy, isn't it? I kept pestering him, until he explained why he could never feel that way about you. But you two should make up. Let me talk to him. He could at least be grateful that you're buying all this stuff for the apartment.'

'Well, it's not exactly . . .'

But Candace had spied the magazine rack and darted away. She rejoined Freya at the check-out, and even tossed in twenty dollars towards the bill. They walked back together, arms wrapped around big brown bags, sunglasses slipping in the heat.

'They say it could get up to ninety today,' said Candace. 'I'm like totally smothered in sunblock.'

'Gorgeous, isn't it?' said Freya, daydreaming about Brett and tonight. Her new dress was short and strappy, in a shade of aquamarine she knew suited her, made of a strange, stretchy fabric that glistened like fish scales. She wondered if she should buy some of that fake-tanning stuff to warm up her pale skin. She sneaked a glance at Candace's skin for comparison, lavishly exposed by a scarlet mini-dress with bows tied at the shoulders, and a generous impulse slipped past her guard.

'I think I should warn you: Jack's father is in town, and he's invited you and Jack for drinks tomorrow evening. At the St Regis.'

'The St Regis!' squeaked Candace. 'The one with all the marble, and a little brass house for the doorman?'

'Jack's father has a special suite.'

Freya watched the implications sink in. After a pause Candace asked, 'Are the Madisons—I mean, are they an *old* family?'

'God, no! But stinking rich. Mind you, Jack's dad must be slashing his way through the family fortune with all his alimony payments; he gets divorced on a regular basis.'

Candace was silent—probably nervous, poor thing.

'Don't worry.' Freya gave Candace an encouraging smile. 'I've spoken to Mr Madison on the phone, and he sounds delightful.'

'I think I'll wear my black.'

'Perfect. I'm sure he'll love you.'

Back in the apartment they deposited their groceries on the kitchen floor. There was no sign of Jack; his bedroom door was still shut.

'I told him I'd be here by noon.' There was an edge of exasperation in Candace's voice. She went into the living room and reappeared shortly with a music tape in her hand, which she held up for Freya's inspection.

'How about this?'

Freya grinned. 'Yep, that should do it.'

Within five minutes Jack appeared in the doorway, sketchily dressed in jeans and T-shirt, aghast to find the apartment rocking with music and the kitchen floor strewn with bulging shopping bags.

'What's going on?' he growled. 'How can anyone be expected to write the great American Novel?'

'Hello, Jack. Were you writing? We thought you were asleep.' Candace flashed him a smile and then caught Freya's eye and giggled at her own boldness. 'Still, now that you're here, you can help us put away all these wonderful groceries Freya's bought for you.'

'What?'

Candace pulled something at random from one of the bags—a package of rice—and dumped it into Jack's hands. 'Food,' she explained. 'For you. All you have to do is put it away.'

'But I don't even know where—'

'In here,' said Freya, who had stationed herself by a cupboard on the far side of the kitchen. 'Come on, chuck it over.'

'And I'll stash the cold things,' Candace volunteered. She pulled open the fridge door and stood beside it, smiling expectantly at Jack.

But at that moment 'Saturday Night Fever' pounded out of the stereo, and a sudden madness overtook them all. Candace started it by waggling her hips to the music and beckoning to Jack like a siren. Infected by the beat, Freya copied her. Thinking of Brett and tonight and how she'd look in the aquamarine dress, she laughed into Jack's outraged eyes and undulated her long body.

With a sudden grin, Jack capitulated. In a flash he had bent to one of the grocery bags, armed himself with a banana and a cucumber, and was stabbing the air, John Travolta-style. Candace whooped with delight. After that, there was no holding him. He shook packets of dry pasta like maracas. He clashed tins, juggled grapefruit and spun frozen pizza on one finger. Freya lobbed things higgledy-piggledy into the cupboard with a huge grin on her face. She'd almost forgotten that Jack could be like this. And he did have a great bum.

When the track had finished they collapsed at the table, laughing and out of breath. 'So what are we doing tonight?' Candace asked Jack.

'Whatever you want. See a movie. Grab something to eat. Why, do you have something special in mind?'

'Yes, I do.' Candace straightened. 'I think it would be a lovely idea if we invited Freya to join us.'

'*What?*' Jack and Freya pounced as one.

'Look how friendly you two can be if you only make an effort.'

'Thanks, but I have plans,' Freya said coolly.

'Why, what are you doing?'

Freya gritted her teeth. 'I am going out, Candace. With a man.'

'Oh yes, so you are!' said Jack. 'Freya has a new boyfriend,' he stage-whispered to Candace.

Freya blushed. 'We're taking the train out to Coney Island, as a matter of fact. Very tacky, Candace. Not your scene at all.'

'But I adore Coney Island!' Jack protested. 'I haven't been there for— well, probably not since I went with you, Freya.'

'I've always wanted to go to Coney Island,' Candace announced.

'No,' said Freya, feeling trapped.

'A double date!' Jack enthused. 'I think it could be a really, like, bonding experience.'

'I said no! And that's final.'

'He was a left-hander, of course—tall guy, graceful as an acrobat—and he hit that ball clear over the lights in right field.'

'Sounds a cool game, Jack. There's something about left-handers that gives them that extra edge. Do you remember when the Tigers . . .?'

The two men moseyed on down the boardwalk, beer cans in hand, blind to the gaudy funfair delights around them and totally ignoring the two women who trailed at their heels.

'How can you call it the *World* Series when no other nation even plays baseball?' Freya yelled at the men's backs.

At the sound of her voice, Brett and Jack turned politely. 'Hmm? What's that, Freya?'

She toned down her glare. 'I was wondering: are we going to do something, or what?'

A split-second glance of understanding passed between the two men. Brett came over and took her hand. 'Of course.' He smiled at her. 'What do you want to do?'

'I dunno,' she murmured, swinging his hand.

She wanted him to tell her she looked beautiful. She wanted to put her lips to that boyish groove at the back of his neck, where a soft duck-tail of black hair met tanned skin. She wanted to laugh and be silly. She wanted to fall in love. Or something.

Freya had suggested Coney Island to Brett because it was cheap and different, and because that's where she'd often gone to have fun when *she* was twenty-six. Its glory days as the 'World's Largest Playground' for New York's huddled masses were long gone. But at night, when darkness hid the litter and peeling paint, the combination of bright lights and the slow lap of the ocean gave it a kind of magic. Freya showed Brett her favourite landmarks—the sea-serpent humps of the old wooden roller coaster; the lights of Rockaway Point across the inlet, with the black ocean beyond, rolling its way to Europe.

'I can't believe you've never been to England,' she told him, as they leaned elbow to elbow on a railing, staring out to sea. 'It's absolutely brilliant for theatre. You'd love it. If you, er, won a free air ticket, you'd go, wouldn't you?'

'Of course—depending on my work.'

'Oh, yes, of course. *Grains of Truth* is closing on Wednesday, isn't it?'

'Thanks for reminding me.'

'I'm sure you'll land another part soon,' Freya said.

But not too soon, she added silently. The spare plane ticket to England still lay snugly next to her own in the airline wallet in her bag. She could just see herself at Tash's wedding with Brett on her arm. *Twenty-six, actually*, she'd say, if anyone asked.

She now set herself to the task of being the life and soul of the party, with particular reference to Brett. She dragged them all into the Hall of Mirrors. Then they rode on the Dodgems, swirling giddily around the black-rubber floor to earsplitting technobeat. Eventually their meanderings brought them beneath the huge wooden piers that supported the roller coaster. They could hear the escalating rattle of cars speeding overhead, then a chorus of screams as they plummeted downwards.

'The Cyclone.' Jack rubbed his hands in anticipation. 'Hold on to your stomachs, folks.'

But Candace put down her tiny, sandalled foot, scarlet nails and all. Nothing would induce her to step inside one of those death machines.

'Well, I'm going,' Jack declared.

'So are we,' said Freya firmly, looking at Brett.

He ducked his head. 'You go. I'll stay and keep Candace company.'

Before Freya could protest, Jack had bought two tickets and was leading the way up to the waiting cars. Freya followed grumpily. This was not at all what she had planned.

They strapped themselves in and sat in silence, waiting for the cars to fill up. Freya fiddled self-consciously with her dress, trying to stretch it down over her thighs. Every time she moved, it gleamed with a silvery light. It was funny that no one had been moved to compliment her on it. Was it too short, too tight, too teenage?

The car began to move, ratcheting its way up the first steep incline, hoisting them into a sky now truly dark, with a sliver of moon hanging high over the ocean. At the top it wobbled perilously for a few gathering seconds. Eyes squeezed tight shut, Freya gripped the safety bar as the car tilted sickeningly into a nose dive. There was thunder in her ears;

wind rushed into her open mouth. Up and down and up and around they went; then again, that thrilling leap into the sky. She felt as if she could fly all the way to the stars.

The roller coaster slowed at last, and trundled back to its starting point. Freya let out a shaky sigh and blinked her eyes open.

'I've just thought of a scene for a novel.' Jack's breath tickled her ear. 'A proposal of marriage on the Cyclone. Wouldn't that be great?'

Freya turned to look at him. His hair stood up on end, as if he'd been electrocuted. 'You know your problem, don't you? You're a fantasist.'

'I'm a writer.'

Writers write, Freya almost said. But she was in too good a mood to start a quarrel. 'And I'm starving,' she announced, climbing out of the car.

When they emerged into the crowds, Candace and Brett were nowhere to be seen.

'Maybe they've eloped,' said Jack.

Then Freya pointed up some steps to the boardwalk, where a group of black teenagers was dancing in a tight, jittery circle to some unseen source of music. 'There they are.' The two white faces bobbing at the edge of the circle were easy to pick out. 'Come on, let's join them,' she said, hurrying ahead.

But when she reached the group, she didn't have the nerve. She watched Brett twirl his limber body, arms high in the air, while Candace jiggled and swayed. When the track ended, Brett threaded his way over to her. 'That was fun,' he said breathlessly.

'Time for dinner,' Jack announced, taking command. 'My treat.'

He set off down the boardwalk with Candace, casually holding the back of her neck between thumb and forefinger. For the first time in years, Freya longed to be cute and kittenish, so that Brett would drape a proprietary arm round her, too, instead of bouncing along beside her.

The lights and noise of the funfair receded, until all they could see, when they looked back, was the glow of the big wheel, pink and purple against the black sky. Suddenly everyone around them was white and speaking Russian: elderly couples walking their dogs; young girls in tight, chattering groups; middle-aged women in halter tops and mini-skirts, looking for Saturday night excitement.

'This is incredible!' exclaimed Brett.

Freya smiled back. 'Russian emigrés started settling here back in the fifties. They call it Little Odessa. I thought you'd like it.'

They came to a strip of beach restaurants, with tables outside, crowded with families and festive parties. Freya spotted an empty table, and they sat down. Jack took charge of the ordering: vodka, eggplant caviar, potato salad, smoked eel—'And herrings,' Freya reminded him.

The food arrived in a succession of small dishes. Freya explained each one to Brett, and popped delicacies into his mouth. Conversation flowed back and forth, until around midnight the singing started—jolly, rhythmic songs involving repetitive choruses and clapping. Then dancing broke out, eventually sweeping all four of them into a ragged line that hopped, bopped, kicked and sang its way round the tables. Freya held on to Brett's waist. His shirt hung loose; her thumbs grazed his warm, smooth skin. She closed her eyes and pressed her cheek against his bouncing back. Her head spun. It was time to go home.

Not for nothing was the train back into the city known as the Trans-Siberian Express. The view was monotonous, the journey interminable, and the other passengers as cheerful as transported prisoners.

'You don't mind if Brett stays over?' she had asked Jack in a private moment during dinner.

'Candace is coming home, you know. There won't be much privacy.'

And when they finally tumbled into the apartment, Freya felt the awkwardness of their situation, as the four of them stood blinking at each other in the overbright living room. It was two in the morning and the long journey home had taken the gloss off the evening. As Jack had hinted, the geography of the apartment was not conducive to privacy.

'Who needs a drink?' demanded Freya.

But Candace had already grasped Jack by the waistband of his trousers, and was pulling him backwards towards his bedroom. 'You're coming with me, lover boy.'

Jack spread his hands helplessly. 'When you gotta go, you gotta go.' His smug expression seemed to linger even after the bedroom door had closed behind the pair of them.

She fixed a couple of drinks in the kitchen and carried them back out to Brett, who was sitting on the squashy arm of a chair. From Jack's room came a high-pitched giggle and the squeak of bedsprings.

'So, Brettskowich.' She ruffled his hair. 'Alone at last.'

The door of Jack's bedroom opened, and he emerged, loosely wrapped in a towelling robe, long belt trailing. 'Still here, Brett?' he said, and headed for the bathroom.

Brett stood up. 'I think—'

'So do I.' Freya seized Brett's hand and led the way to her bedroom. 'Let's go in here. Then we won't be bothered.'

She flicked the door shut behind them, and leaned her weight against it. Light slanted in from the street, throwing Brett's face into shadow. His eyes glittered as he turned to look at her.

'My agent says I'm perfect for the juvenile lead in musicals, but I don't want to get typecast. What do you think?'

'I think you'd be wonderful.' Freya wriggled downwards on the bed, and stretched out one long leg to touch Brett's thigh encouragingly with her bare foot. Pity he still had his trousers on. 'Someone with your looks—and your talent—is bound to be successful.'

'You're just saying that.' He gave her foot a playful caress, sending desire shooting up her body. But almost at once he pulled his hand away again, looking nervous.

A throaty cooing was coming from Jack's bedroom, which Freya took to be Candace in the throes of passion. Initially, Freya had found this irritating; now she was beginning to hope that Brett would take the hint, but so far the noises from next door had had the opposite effect. Brett seemed to prefer to perch cross-legged at the end of her bed while she leaned against a pillow at the top end. Somehow she must signal her availability. She stretched her arms languorously above her head and gave a deep, sensuous sigh. Brett looked up. She smiled.

'Ready for bed?' he enquired.

Eureka!

'Aren't you?' Her body was turning to soup in anticipation. 'Why don't you come up here so I can examine you properly.'

Brett laughed uncertainly, as if she had cracked an obscure joke.

If the mountain would not come to Muhammad . . . Freya curled herself slowly onto all fours and crept panther-like down the bed. When she reached Brett she gave a soft growl, sat back on her haunches and slid one hand between the buttons of his shirt and onto the flat, hard plain of his stomach. Brett tensed.

'Relax . . .' she told him.

Her fingertips traced the silky arrow of hair leading downwards. She found the dip of his belly button and stroked it gently. Next door, the coos were turning into deeper moans, interspersed with excited yelps.

Brett gave a nervous laugh. 'I'm not sure—'

'Forget about them.' Freya's voice was soothing. 'They don't matter.'

'I don't think—'

'Don't worry. You'll be fine.' Freya reached for him again. He was so warm, so smooth, so firm, so—

With a suddenness that shocked her, Brett broke away and stood up. 'Guess I'll go home now.'

'What?' Freya blinked at him from the bed.

'It's late. I should get back.' Brett started to tuck in his shirt.

'But—why?'

'I feel . . . uncomfortable.' Brett ducked his head. 'I don't fit in here. I don't want to get into anything . . . heavy, you know?'

Freya struggled to decode this. Was he put off by the activities next door? Didn't he *like* sex?

'You're not gay, are you?'

'No!' His chin came up. 'And I'm not a toy boy either. You pat me on the head like I'm six years old, and then you expect—'

'*What?*' Freya stared at him, aghast. She could decode this all right. He was telling her she was too *old*. 'Right.' She stood up in one swift, smooth gesture and looked Brett in the eye. 'That's pretty clear.'

'Wait.' He put a hand on her arm. 'What I mean to say is, I like you. I like talking to you. But maybe we can be, you know, just friends.'

'Sure.' Freya managed a shrug. 'I'm going on holiday next week anyway. I might give you a call when I get back.'

'Great.'

She opened the door of her room and led the way across the living room to the hall, where Brett had left his bike. She could read his hurry and his relief in the way he unslung his helmet from the handlebar and laid his hands on his beloved machine. She prickled and stung and smarted with humiliation. Unlocking the front door, she held it open.

'Well, goodbye,' he said awkwardly, as he pushed the bike past her. She could see him wondering if he should give her a peck on the cheek. This was excruciating. She folded her arms across her chest and stood back.

'See you, Brett.'

'Bye.' He disappeared into the night.

For several moments Freya stood on the threshold, breathing hard. Why did men always want to be 'just friends' with her? She gave the rubbish bin a kick. Even her friends didn't want to be friends with her any more! Look at Cat, who had fobbed her off with the feeblest excuse and wasn't returning her phone calls. As for Jack . . .

Freya closed the front door and stood in the living room, listening. All was quiet. She pictured Jack and Candace drifting off into satisfied sleep, and stamped her foot. Worse than everything would be Jack's triumphalism when he discovered that Brett had fled.

Unless . . .

Freya prowled around the living room, trying to psyche herself up. 'Mmm,' she began tentatively. 'Aah . . . ooh . . .' She leapt onto the couch and padded squashily up and down. 'Oh, Brett,' she projected throatily in the direction of Jack's bedroom. 'That's so *gooood.*'

Freya located a broken spring in the couch, which twanged in a deeply satisfying manner. She began to bounce up and down on it, flinging her arms about for good measure. 'Ah . . . aaah!' She teetered across the couch's fat arms and along its back, hurling herself onto the seat with an uninhibited cry. 'Oh *yes*! . . . oh, Brett . . . oh—'

A shadow moved at the periphery of her vision. She froze. It was a person, carrying a glass in one hand.

'Having a good time?' enquired Jack.

Chapter Ten

JACK'S FATHER HAD ALWAYS been a stickler for the outward forms of social behaviour. A true Southern gentleman, he liked to claim, was invariably punctual, courteous to the ladies, and mindful of 'dressing nice'—by which he meant a jacket, tie and real leather shoes with laces. It was therefore a well-judged twenty minutes late, wearing an open-necked shirt and sneakers, with Candace scurrying disregarded behind him, that Jack timed his appearance in the bar of the St Regis Hotel.

Because it was a Sunday, and still early in the evening, the panelled room was sparsely populated. Even if it had been packed to bursting, Jack could have located his father simply by searching for the figure of a waiter deferentially bowed over one of the tables. Sure enough, there in the far corner his father was comfortably ensconced at the best table in the place, shooting the breeze with some butler-type in white gloves.

Candace grabbed his arm. 'Is that him?' she whispered.

'Yep.' All day she'd been pestering him for details, until he'd finally snapped, 'He's just my dad. You'll see.'

Now she gave an approving murmur. 'Isn't he handsome? He looks just like you.'

'Well, he's not.'

As he approached the table, Jack experienced a confusion of filial emotions—defiance, resentment, guilt, and a kind of familiarity that approximated to affection.

His father rose from his chair, as tall and as broad as Jack, looking pleased to see them. His moustache had been newly clipped; his thick white hair was scrupulously parted and combed: a handsome man, indeed, though he had turned sixty-five.

'Jack, my boy. Good to see you.' He clasped Jack's hand warmly.

'And you.' Just in time, Jack bit back the 'sir' that had been drummed into him from an early age. 'This is Candace.'

His father's face intensified with interest. He liked women, and they liked him. Jack had protested that there was no need for Candace to get all dressed up just to meet his father, but he couldn't help feeling gratified by her glossy appearance in a subtly sexy black dress.

There was the bustle of seating themselves and deciding what to drink. Jack's father suggested a glass of pink champagne to Candace; both became positively rapturous about the fact that she'd never tasted it before—how thrilled she would be to try it, how honoured he was to give her the opportunity. Just to be annoying Jack ordered a beer.

His father was telling Candace about how the hotel had been built for John Jacob Astor, with crystal from Waterford and marble from France. 'I'll get George to show you around in a little bit. Would you like that?'

Candace wriggled her shoulders and said she would love it. 'And is Mrs Madison here with you?' she enquired.

Jack's father looked surprised; then his eyes crinkled into laughter, and he went through an absurd pantomime of patting his pockets. 'Nope. Don't believe I've got one with me today.' He winked at Candace. 'Already got four wives scattered across the country—and that's four too many. Cost more 'n a decent fishing boat these days.'

Candace gave him a look Jack could only describe as saucy. 'You're not telling me you prefer fish to women, are you, Mr Madison?'

He patted her knee delightedly. 'Well, now. That depends on how much of a fight they put up.'

Jack twisted his glass round and round, his face stony. He was long used to his father's high-flown gallantries, but that Candace should flirt back seemed a betrayal.

'I don't know how you all survive up here,' marvelled his father, 'with the noise and dirt, living in those little bitty cells you call apartments.'

'I know what you mean.' Candace sighed wistfully, as if her true spiritual home were a country mansion patrolled by servants. 'I'd love to visit the South one day.' Candace leaned forward confidingly. 'You have so much history—and all those beautiful trees!'

'You'll have to get Jack to bring you down for a visit.'

'Oh, would you, Jack?' Candace turned to him in a swirl of perfume. Jack took another sip of beer. 'We'll see.'

They made small talk while Candace sipped her champagne. When her glass was empty, Jack's father summoned George, the waiter, to take her on a private tour of the hotel.

409

'Man's talk,' he explained to Candace with a wink. 'You understand?'
'Of course.' .

He withdrew his eyes with difficulty from her sashaying back view.
'Pretty girl.'

Jack nodded his agreement.

His father waved over one of the under-waiters to bring more drinks.
This time Jack ordered bourbon. Mentally he rehearsed his speech: the
cost of living in New York, the incompatibility of writing fiction and
journalism. But before he could find an opening, his father leaned easily
back in his seat and began to speak.

'I'm glad we have this chance to talk, son. There've been some
changes at Madison Paper, and I think it's right to let you know what's
going on in the business, even if you've never shown much interest.'

'It's not that I'm not interested, Dad. It's only—'

'I know. You've chosen to do things differently. That's why I want to
talk to you, bring you up-to-date.'

His father began to drone on about foreign competition and new markets. Jack stopped listening to the words. He thought he knew where this
was leading. Sure enough, his father began a long ramble about their
search for a new board member, someone he could trust—

'Dad, stop right there.' Jack raised his palm. 'I know you're thinking
of my own good, but I can't come home to help run the business.'

His father burst into a loud guffaw. 'You! Run the business!'

Jack was shocked. 'Well . . . isn't that what you're asking?'

His father brought his laughter under control. 'Jack, you've been up
here in New York *ten years*. What could you possibly know about running a paper business? No, I wanted you to know that, as of next
month, we'll be inviting your brother Lane to join the board.'

'Lane?' Jack pictured his brother in his high-school football outfit,
with massive padded shoulders and a helmet masking his features.

'I know he never got the grades you did, but he understands paper.'

Lane? As far as Jack remembered, Lane never understood anything.

'There was a time when I hoped and prayed you'd come home to
Madison Paper, but you haven't, and it's too late now.'

Jack nodded, his mind in a whirl.

'Up to now, I've given both you boys allowances to help you get on
your feet. Lane's been learning the paper business, and you—well, I
guess you've been learning your "business" too.' His father chuckled at
this quaint notion. 'Of course, Lane is younger than you, but he'll be
getting his board stipend now, so it all balances out.'

'What do you mean?' Jack was floundering. 'What balances out?'

'I mean that I'll be terminating his allowance at the same time I terminate yours.'

Jack tried to get a grip. 'When were you thinking . . .?'

'Next month is the last payment.'

'*Next month?*'

His father gave a shark-toothed smile. 'Madison Paper is a business, not a gravy train. We can't carry passengers.'

Jack's turmoil must have shown in his face. His father frowned. 'You're not in any kind of trouble, are you, son?'

Jack looked him in the eye. 'No.'

His father's expression relaxed into a bantering grin. 'You mean you always dress like a bum? Beats me. New Yorkers used to have such *style* . . . Like her,' he added, his eyes lighting up.

Jack turned round to see Candace approaching them. He stood up at once, rocking the table. 'We have to go now.'

'Aw, so soon?' His father rose courteously and took Candace's hand, smiling down at her. 'Maybe you'll both join me for dinner tomorrow?'

'I don't think . . .' Jack began.

'That would be lovely,' Candace said simultaneously.

A sense of hopelessness and failure washed over Freya. Ever since the Michael episode she had experienced one humiliation after another—and she had a horrible feeling they were all her fault. Nothing was going right in her life. She was sick of camping in the corner of someone else's study in someone else's apartment. Living with Jack, whom she'd always got on with—*always*—had turned out to be a nightmare. But the real nightmare, her overriding obsession, the thought that made her prickle and snap with panic, was the knowledge that in two days she was going home for Tash's wedding. Alone.

The apartment was silent when she let herself in, and almost as stifling as outdoors. With a sigh, Freya pulled off her shoes and made straight for the kitchen, where she took a beer from the fridge, flipped off the cap and drank from the bottle. She undid the top two buttons of her dress and rolled the bottle across her skin. It would almost be worth going to England for the pleasure of being positively cold in midsummer. Almost . . . Abruptly, Freya set down her beer bottle on the table and headed for the bathroom, unbuttoning her dress as she went. She stood under the cold, cascading water, forcing herself to concentrate on the things she had to do before she left town. Today was Monday; her flight left on Wednesday night. She must try to cash in the spare air ticket.

She'd told them all—boasted, if she was honest—about bringing a 'friend' with her. Everyone knew what that meant: a lover certainly, possibly a long-term partner.

Freya stepped out of the shower and towelled herself briskly. She was a tough New York cookie now. Of course she could cope with Tash's wedding alone. She heard Cat's bracing voice saying, '*I don't need a man.*' Quite right. Wrapping herself in the towel, Freya picked up her clothes and was walking past Jack's bedroom to her own when she was startled by the sound of Jack clearing his throat.

She paused by his closed door and called out, 'That you, Jack?'

'Yep.'

'What are you doing?'

'Nothing.'

'That sounds fun.'

Silence. She shrugged, and continued to her room. By the time she had changed into shorts and a faded blue cotton top she was hot again. She went to retrieve her beer and found Jack in the kitchen, a chair pulled up to the open fridge and his bare feet propped on the bottom shelf. He didn't even look up.

Freya put a chair alongside his. He moved his feet over to make room for hers on the shelf, and they sat for a while in silence.

'Weren't you and Candace supposed to be having dinner with your dad tonight?'

'Yep.'

'So what happened?'

'Couldn't face it.'

'Ah.'

Freya stole a look at Jack. What was the matter with him? She'd have said he was sulking, except Jack wasn't a sulker.

'So where's Candace?' she fished.

'I let her go by herself. Dad's going to show her his old haunts.'

'Lucky Candace.'

Jack shrugged, as if he didn't care what Candace did.

'Hey.' Freya nudged his foot. 'I'm not doing anything tonight. You're obviously not doing anything. Why don't we go to the movies?'

'I don't feel like it. You go.'

'Don't be so boring.'

'I like being boring.'

'Oh, come on.' Freya stood up and gave his chair a shove. 'It's no fun going alone. Get up, you great lump. Let's go and see what's on. You can cheer me up with your lively personality and sparkling repartee.'

'Uh,' said Jack. He wriggled his bare toes. 'I'd have to put some shoes on.' He made this sound on a par with climbing Mount Everest.

'So get them! Chop chop.'

Freya went to get her shoes and her bag, and waited outside for Jack to lock the front door. They walked down the street together, keeping to the shade of the spreading trees that were just coming into blossom.

Their first stop was a big bookstore on 7th that was blissfully air-conditioned. Jack went in search of *The Village Voice*, so they could check the listings. Then they walked away from the store, stopped under an awning and huddled close, scanning the newspaper. Suddenly Freya exclaimed and stabbed the listings page. 'Look! *High Society*.'

'Fluffy,' objected Jack. 'Fluffy fluff-fluff.'

'Romantic,' Freya corrected.

'*Bing Crosby?*' Jack's eyebrows rose incredulously.

'Frank Sinatra,' she reminded him. 'Grace Kelly . . . in a swimsuit.'

'OK, you win.'

They sat in the back row of the half-empty cinema, legs propped up on the seats in front, fingers absently picking popcorn out of a carton wedged between them. Their crabbiness melted as the film spun its magic out of the darkness, enveloping them in the sunny, madcap dottiness of a 1950s society wedding. It was the perfect choice. When the credits rolled, they stumbled to their feet with foolish, faraway grins and wandered outside to stand on the pavement, taking time to readjust to the heat and rush of the city.

Jack took off his glasses and folded them away. He smiled down at her. 'Hungry?'

Freya gave a languorous, Grace Kelly shrug. 'Maybe an ice cream at that Italian place on Broome Street?'

'Café Pisa? That's on Mulberry, not Broome.'

'No, it isn't.'

'Yes, it is.'

Eventually they found the narrow entrance, marked by a browning evergreen in a tub.

'Ha! Broome Street,' said Jack.

Freya waved airily. 'It must have moved.'

They pushed past the narrow bar, where old men sat on stools drinking grappa, and walked out into a courtyard festooned with coloured lights. They ordered ice cream and coffee and sat in companionable silence under an umbrella. Jack twiddled the ashtray round and round. Freya leaned her head in one hand and drew patterns in the dusty tabletop, waiting for him to tell her what was bothering him. Finally he turned to her. 'My publishers want to cancel my book contract,' he said.

'What?' She straightened with a jerk.

'There's some new broom in the company whose mission is to sweep away the old inefficiencies—of which I am apparently one.'

'God, Jack. Can they do that?'

It seemed that they most certainly could. Jack had missed his deadline. The new regime were also demanding the return of the money Jack had already received—and spent.

'The real bummer,' said Jack, 'is that Dad has chosen this moment to cut off my allowance.'

'He hasn't!'

'So I can't pay back the money. Nor can I afford to live while I finish my book.'

'That's awful, Jack. I'm sorry. What are you going to do?'

'I don't know. I'll have to give up the apartment, maybe leave New York for good. Get a job.' He raked his fingers through his hair. For the first time Freya noticed two faint lines scored across his forehead.

'At least you don't have to worry about me,' said Freya. 'I've found a sublet.'

'You're moving out?' He sounded surprised.

'Yep. I'll take all my stuff away on Wednesday and dump it in the new place, ready for when I get back from England.'

'Oh yeah . . . England.' Jack frowned. 'I forgot about that.' He scraped up the last of his ice cream and dropped his spoon in the bowl with a clang. 'Well, that's my life down the drain. What's your excuse?'

'My excuse for what?'

'For your peculiar behaviour over the past couple of weeks. You're worried about something. I can tell.'

'No, I'm not.' Freya stuck her chin in the air. 'And there's been nothing "peculiar" about my behaviour.' Apart, she admitted privately, from answering lonely hearts ads, picking up young men, writing anonymous letters and simulating sex.

Jack gave her a look. 'You can't fool me,' he said.

In the end she found herself trying to explain the problem of a single woman of a certain age attending the wedding of her much younger sister—worse, stepsister—without an escort. It was uphill work.

'What's the problem?' Jack was mystified. 'Someone will pick you up when you get there.'

Freya eyed him. 'Who exactly do you think is going to pick me up?'

'I would.' He grinned.

'No you wouldn't—not when the place is crawling with scrumptious twenty-five-year-olds.'

'Ah. I take your point. But I'd still pick you up.' He smiled winningly. 'Speaking of scrumptious twenty-five-year-olds, why don't you take Little Lord Fauntleroy with you?'

'If you mean Brett, that's over.' Freya folded her arms primly. 'No, I shall go alone. At least that means I won't be encumbered when I meet Mr Perfect. Correction: *Lord* Perfect.'

Jack frowned. 'You can't do that.'

'Why not?'

'You might stay in England and I'd never see you again.'

'So? You're the one who's talking about leaving New York.'

'Yeah, but—'

'In a few months' time maybe neither of us will be here.'

Jack looked momentarily shocked by this thought, then gave a hopeless shrug. 'You're right.'

'Mind you, I'm still holding you to my birthday dinner, wherever we are. A bet's a bet.'

'The 8th at eight.' Jack nodded. 'I'll be there.'

'Unless I've already become Lady Perfect.'

'And I'm giving my acceptance speech for the Pulitzer.' He gave a cynical grunt. 'Seen any flying pigs recently?'

Freya suddenly felt utterly defeated. She sank her head back to stare into the rusty-black sky, its pale stars almost eclipsed by the city's electric glow. Once, she had had long blonde hair, fizzing energy, a thrilling succession of jobs and men, friends, parties, a beckoning mystery future. Once, Jack had been the handsomest, luckiest man in New York, bursting with talent. And now look at them. Jack was broke, with his career on the skids; and she was a pathetic thirtysomething too scared to go home to a wedding without a man in tow. They had reached the end of the track, last stop on the line.

Suddenly Jack was jabbing her arm, repeatedly and painfully, with one finger. 'I've had a brilliant idea,' he announced.

'Stop that!' She swatted his hand.

'Listen.' He pulled his chair close. 'You want someone respectable to come to this wedding with you, right?'

'Yes.'

'Someone good-looking and male?'

'Definitely.'

'Well, then.' He sat back in his chair and folded his arms.

'Well, then what?'

Jack raised his eyebrows as if the answer was obvious. She raised hers, to show him it was not. He spread his hands. '*Me.*'

Freya stared at him, then burst out laughing. 'Don't be ridiculous. I'm supposed to be going with a *boyfriend*.'

'So? Why couldn't I pretend to be your boyfriend for a couple of days.'

'Four days. Thursday through Sunday. We'd be sharing a room. You'd have to hold my hand, and gaze into my eyes, and pretend you thought I was wonderful.'

'But that's my best thing!'

'And you'd have to be charming.'

'I *am* charming!'

'Look at your clothes.'

'I have real clothes—I just don't wear them.'

'And your hair.'

'But my hair's always been like this!'

'Exactly.'

'What if I cut it . . . just for you? Snip, snip . . .'

Freya tried not to smile. 'You just want an excuse to escape your problems,' she said severely.

'I want to help you.' He reached out and caught her hand in his, startling her. 'We could help each other,' he amended.

His mouth curved in a familiar, teasing smile. But his blue eyes were serious. She felt his palm against hers, and the firm grip of his fingers. *Jack*, she thought. *Jack?* Her eyes met his.

'You're on.'

Chapter Eleven

'NICE BED.'

Jack bounced on the four-poster bed, dislodging a shower of small particles from the tattered hangings. He lay back, chuckling softly.

'Glad you like it.' Freya unsnapped the catches of her suitcase. 'You'll be able to admire its finer points from over there'—she pointed—'on the *chaise-longue*.'

Jack raised himself on one elbow to squint at an angular piece of furniture that looked like a cross between a prison bunk and an old-fashioned dentist's chair.

'Aw, come on. I'm way too tall. I'm not sleeping on that thing.'

'One of us has to. We're only *pretending* to be a couple.'

'That's a relief. I don't know how much more of this warm together-ness I can take. Hah! Missed!'

Jack reached down over the edge of the bed to retrieve the missile Freya had thrown at him: one of her shoes. (Eight pairs she'd brought with her—*eight!*—as he'd discovered when he'd offered to carry her suitcase at the airport.) He turned the shoe over in his hands, wonder-ing at the fragility of the high tapering heel and the slender straps. He tossed it over to her. 'Here you go, Cinderella.'

Without comment she put it in the massive carved wardrobe and continued unpacking. Jack decided to do the same.

She'd been wound tight as a spring ever since they landed. For the first hour of the long drive to Cornwall, he'd barely glanced at the pass-ing landscape; his eyes kept straying to the speedometer of the hired car, which scarcely dropped below ninety. Freya drove the way she did everything—fast, defiantly, with an edge of danger. He hadn't dared to mention the word 'lunch', and finally took refuge in sleep.

He'd woken in midafternoon to the astonishing sight of a line of high-tech windmills cresting the hill before them, arms flailing. Freya announced that they were now in Cornwall. Jack put on his glasses and looked about him with interest. At first sight, Cornwall seemed slightly spooky, a mixture of forbidding moorland and grim, granite towns. Gradually the landscape softened into a patchwork of spreading mead-ows grazed by piebald cows. Mile by mile, the horizon seemed to flatten itself and recede into a silvery haze. Jack felt expectancy bubble within him; they were approaching the sea.

'Next hill,' said Freya, reading his mind, and sure enough, at the next rise in the road, there was the heart-lifting sight of a sweep of sparkling water, darkening to slaty blue. She glanced over at him and smiled.

Soon afterwards they turned off the main road and entered a maze of lanes that plunged into woody ravines and skirted narrow, secret creeks. Jack rolled down his window and sniffed the sweet English air. A high midsummer sun shone out of a blue sky. He took it as a good omen.

At a dip in the road, Freya turned into an entrance flanked by stone posts. 'This is it,' she said, and gunned the car up a narrow, wooded lane. They followed this for at least half a mile, at length shooting out of the woods and rattling over a cattle grid. Open pastureland dotted with sheep sloped away on either side and tucked itself into dark folds of wood. Dead ahead, shaded by elegantly clustered trees, lay a large manor house of grey stone. Jack's eyes widened. There were decorative gables romantically covered in creepers, and a huge central window, two storeys high, studded with small panes of glass like a panel of diamonds. A forest of brick chimneys sprouted from an undulating roof of weathered slate.

'You never told me you lived in a place like this.'

'I don't. I live in New York. This is my stepmother's house.'

Freya whizzed round the back, through a stone archway, and into a courtyard with dusty cars randomly parked, a washing line strung with dishcloths, a lopsided tub of geraniums and a few scurrying chickens. The slam of car doors summoned no grander personage than a waddling black labrador, whom Freya introduced as Bedivere.

She led Jack down a dark passage lined with muddy boots and empty wine bottles, and brass hooks laden with coats and hats, fishing nets, coiled rope and dog leads. They entered a large room with a beamed ceiling, bare stone floor and windows on two sides. Jack blinked in the dusty sunlight. It seemed to be a kitchen, though not of a kind he recognised. A big wooden dresser stood against one wall, crammed with jugs and plates. There was a deep, square stone sink with tarnished brass taps. In the centre of the room a long oak table was laid for five. Something was simmering on an old-fashioned stove, and a delicious smell of cooking filled the room.

'Outside, probably,' Freya said cryptically. She strode across to the open window, and—as if this was perfectly normal—climbed onto the sill by means of a sturdy block of wood, evidently placed there for this purpose, and jumped down the other side. Jack clambered after her, with the sensation of stepping through a looking glass into an enticing wonderland. He found himself in a small garden, enclosed by high green hedges and quartered by stone paths.

Freya strode towards a shadowed archway in the hedge, then turned to wait for him. Jack could hear female voices raised in argument. He took her hand, pulled it through his arm and they walked through the archway together.

Ahead of them stretched a long, level lawn freckled with daisies. A spreading cypress cast its shade onto a huddle of striped deck chairs and a wrought-iron table bearing a tray of drinks. No one noticed them at first. Two women stood with their backs to them, each leaning on their croquet mallets as they watched a man in a Panama hat bending to position his ball by one of the white hoops. He straightened, shaded his eyes and gave a joyous shout. 'Freya!'

She tugged Jack forward a few paces, then stopped uncertainly.

The man hurried towards them. He was tall and lean, and so like his daughter that Jack almost laughed aloud: same oval face, same long nose and oblique smile. Only the colouring was different; Freya's eyes and hair must come from her mother.

'Here at last.' Freya's father wrapped his arms around her in an eager, uninhibited hug. 'How marvellous!' He stroked her hair in a tender gesture and beamed.

'Hello, Freya. Lovely to see you.' This must be Annabelle, a handsome, matronly woman in a flowery, calf-length skirt and white blouse. Her dark hair was striped with grey, and held off her broad brow with a hairband. Her face was worn, but pleasant. She didn't look like a wicked stepmother. Freya allowed herself to be kissed on both cheeks.

The younger woman hung back, swinging her mallet. She was a pretty brunette with high colour, full lips, and slanted eyes that met Jack's knowingly. She wore white trousers cut off below the knee and some kind of sleeveless top that displayed smooth, rounded arms.

'Hi, Freya.'

'Hi, Tash.'

They kept their distance, looking at each other with appraising eyes and tight smiles. *Ouch!* thought Jack.

Jack felt his arm grabbed again. 'This is Jack,' Freya told them all, with an air of defiance. 'My—friend, Jack Madison.'

'Delighted to have you with us, Jack.' Freya's father stepped forward smoothly. 'I'm Guy Penrose, and this is my wife Annabelle. Now: let me introduce you to the mystery of Pimm's. A strange English drink, but I think you'll like it.'

With some relief Jack strolled with him to the drinks table. They stood, talking easily, while the shadows lengthened and birds arrowed through the sky. The drink was like a punch, chock-a-block with fruit and sprigs of mint. Jack drank thirstily. The tiredness of the journey dropped away. He began to enjoy himself.

Tash was fluttering her fingers in Freya's face. 'Don't you want to see my ring? It's rubies, you know. Cost a fortune.'

'Oh, yes.' Freya bent to study it. 'It's lovely, Tash. Really nice.' Her voice wasn't exactly warm, but Jack could tell she was making an effort.

'Guy, darling, why don't you help with the suitcases while I see to dinner?' said Annabelle. 'I expect you two would like to change after your long journey.'

'Good idea,' Jack agreed heartily. 'A quick shower, and I'll be ready for anything.'

But there was no shower. The bathroom bore little resemblance to any bathroom Jack had ever seen. There was a gigantic bath with clawed feet in the middle of the room, with a cold tap marked 'Hot' and a hot top marked 'Cold', as Jack discovered the hard way.

Freya had led him through a hallway as big as a barn with an intricate timber roof. They had passed along a warren of corridors and then up back staircases to this vast bedroom with its gloomy furniture and tattered carpeting. Freya acted as if it was all perfectly normal, but Jack couldn't work out if the Penroses were very rich or very poor. Never mind. He would piece it all together. He might even get a novel out of it. Meanwhile, it was illuminating to observe Freya in her native habitat.

Jack had never seen her so nervous. He couldn't tell whether this was because of her family, or because of him. It was, admittedly, a little strange to be alone together in the bedroom they would have to share.

Freya turned over for the millionth time. She had tried every conceivable position on this wretched *chaise-longue*, and they were all torture. It was now nearly two in the morning, as she knew from hearing the clock on the stairs chime every bloody quarter of an hour.

Outside, a screech owl was doing what screech owls do best. Inside, a gentle, rhythmic snore emanated from Jack, fast asleep in the four-poster. Freya sat up irritably and glowered in his direction. The moon was full and the curtains worn. She could see his head blissfully cradled in a downy mound of pillows, and the great sprawling lump of his comatose body. How come he was there, and she was here?

She slumped back onto her bed of pain. It was her own fault. Jack had insisted that the bed was more than big enough for two, but she hadn't cared for the frisky manner in which he had made this suggestion. It was her idea that they should preclude further argument by tossing a coin for bed privileges, and she had lost. Now she cursed Jack for accepting his win so easily. A real gentleman would have protested.

But Jack wasn't a real gentleman; he was only pretending. Freya brooded darkly on his pretence at dinner tonight, when he had shamelessly wormed his way into everyone's good graces. 'Let me carry that for you, Mrs Penrose . . . Terrific cigar, Mr Penrose.' There he'd sat, utterly at ease, in a dark blue shirt and pressed trousers she'd never even seen before, with his new haircut, entertaining them all with stories about his home town. Her father even fetched up a bottle of special port from the cellar, as if Jack were Mr Nice Guy instead of a mean, selfish, heartless, *sleeping* beast.

Freya threw off the eiderdown and stood up. She'd had enough. She stomped over to the bed and scowled down at Jack. He was lying on his back now, right in the middle of the bed.

'Jack,' she whispered experimentally.

Not a flicker. Freya hesitated. What would it matter if she borrowed a teeny corner of the bed, just for a few hours? She placed the heel of her hand against Jack's pyjama'd shoulder, and pushed. He rolled obediently away, leaving a nice, empty space for her. Freya climbed in.

Ohhh . . . heaven! Freya sank her head back on a pillow and stretched her legs luxuriously. The sheets were deliciously warm from Jack's body, and gave off a faint masculine smell, sweet and comforting as freshly baked bread. She was comfortable and sleepy and warm. Really, she felt quite . . . marvellous. Her eyes closed. Her mind began to drift.

She remembered that it had been autumn. The streets had been spangled with leaves as yellow as Jack's hair when he'd yelled up to her window the news that he had sold his first story. She had bounded down the stairs to tell him that she too had marvellous news. She had at last wangled her green card, the precious document that allowed her to do a proper job in America, with a proper salary, instead of slave-labour for slave wages. On the strength of their old friendship, new wealth, and imminent fame, they'd decided on a joint celebration dinner at a ritzy restaurant. Jack had dug out a tuxedo, she'd tarted herself up in a dress and high heels, and they'd taken a cab, like a couple of swells, all the way to the smart uptown address. They'd ordered lavishly, clinking glasses in regular self-congratulatory toasts. They'd talked and argued and laughed until it was time to pay the outrageous bill and tipsily return home. Jack had accompanied her to her door, they'd said good night—and then he had spoilt it all by suddenly lunging at her and declaring that he wanted to go to bed with her. There had been no romantic preamble, no attempt at courtship. She'd said no, of course. Who did he think he was? Freya had no desire to be just another notch on his bedpost. Jack had been surprised at her rejection, then angry. The episode had never been mentioned since, though the memory of it was like a tiny thorn in their friendship.

Freya gave a tiny, silent giggle. Here she was, after all these years, in bed with Jack Madison. It wasn't so bad. Of course, he was asleep. Freya gave a languid yawn. There was something she must remember: oh yes, to wake up early. Absolutely. No problem.

Jack woke with a tremendous sense of well-being. Every muscle was relaxed, each limb exquisitely heavy; his very bones felt refreshed. For a while he lay utterly still in his warm cocoon, letting consciousness seep back, incapable of even the minor muscular effort of raising his eyelids.

Gradually he registered clues to his whereabouts: no traffic noises, no sirens, just the soothing drone of a distant lawnmower. He could smell sweet, fresh grass and frying bacon. A golden light danced at the rims of his closed eyes, promising a sunny morning. There was a complacent smile on his lips as he opened his eyes, rolled his head across the pillow to look woozily about him. Someone was in his bed!—a female someone, with short, tousled hair of a pale gold colour.

Jack leapt out and stood on the bedside rug. The *chaise-longue* was bare. On the floor next to it, the eiderdown in which Freya had wrapped herself last night lay in a discarded heap. Struck by a sudden thought, Jack gazed wildly down at his own body: he was still wearing both halves of his pyjamas. He tiptoed to the other side of the bed and peeked at Freya's face. She was sound asleep. The sheet covered her almost to the chin; he couldn't see what she was wearing. Surely he'd remember if . . .?

How quietly she slept. She lay on her side, one cheek nudging her pillow, the other faintly flushed and sheened with sleep. Jack couldn't help smiling a little to see her so silent and unguarded. As if conscious of his scrutiny, she took a sudden deep breath. Jack jerked away, but all she did was wriggle into a new position. Jack decided to escape to the bathroom to consider his position.

While hot water filled the bathtub at a grudging, gurgling trickle, he took off his pyjama jacket and lathered his face with his shaving brush. Worried eyes stared back at him from the mirror. This was not the first time he'd woken to find a woman unexpectedly in his bed. But Freya! This was worse than embarrassing; it was unthinkable.

Jack squirmed at the unwelcome memory of a blunder he had made, years ago, when the two of them had gone out to celebrate the sale of his first story. He'd never met anyone like Freya before—beautiful, quick and clever—with her tart English tongue and her air of sophistication. Back then, he'd been an eager twenty-three or -four, thrilled to be out on a date with her. They'd talked and laughed, and he'd drunk perhaps one Armagnac too many. Afterwards, he'd escorted her home to the scruffy rooming house and said good night. He'd walked down two flights of stairs, then turned round, walked back up, banged on her door and, as soon as she opened it, blurted out, 'I want to go to bed with you.'

Ouch! He had nicked the underside of his chin. Jack ran the cold tap and dabbed at the tiny cut. The water in his bath had now reached the eight-inch mark. He stepped out of his pyjama bottoms, climbed in and slid down against the curiously grainy surface. *I want to go to bed with you.* Jack closed his eyes. How crude. After a moment of cool silence, she had arched her fabulous eyebrows at him: 'Don't be ridiculous, Jack. I'm far too old for you.'

The memory made him sit up in a swirl of water and reach for the soap, just for something to do. He rubbed it vigorously across his skin. An ice-maiden, that's what she was—or so he had told himself, though her serial love affairs suggested that she was nothing of the kind; it was just him she didn't fancy. Fortunately, she had never mentioned the incident again; he hoped she had forgotten.

So what about last night? Could he? Did she? The awful truth was, he couldn't remember a thing about last night. He'd have to take his cue from Freya.

He climbed out of the bath and dried himself off, then wrapped the towel round his waist, tossed his pyjamas over one bare shoulder and unlocked the door. Let's see: down those funny back stairs, then right— or was it left? He was thoroughly lost when a cheeky voice behind him said, 'Morning, Tarzan. Sleep well?'

Jack turned round to see Tash, semiwrapped in some silky pink thing, giving him an appraising stare.

'Uh, yeah. Thanks.'

Her pussycat smile suggested that *she* knew what he'd been up to all night. He put a hand to his towel, to check that it was secure.

'Your bedroom's that way.' She pointed. 'See you later, alligator.'

Freya was lying against a high, white bank of pillows, wide awake and looking straight at him. There was a dreamy smile on her face.

'Hi,' he offered tentatively. 'Did you, uh, sleep well?'

'Mmmm. Wonderful . . .' Her eyelids drooped rapturously, leaving slits of sparkling blue. 'Of course, I wasn't exactly *asleep* the whole time.'

Jack nodded sagely, wondering what the hell that meant. He jerked a thumb towards the *chaise-longue*. 'How was the . . . ?'

'Hideous.' Freya gave a delicate shudder. 'You were right, Jack. The bed was a *much* better idea.'

Jack swallowed.

She wriggled down in the bed and heaved a voluptuous sigh. 'Oh, Jack, wasn't last night unforgettable?'

Jack's eyes bulged. 'You bet!' he agreed heartily.

As the silence lengthened, he became painfully aware that this was an inadequate response. Freya's smile faltered.

'Don't tell me you don't remember?'

'Well . . . I feel grrreat.' Jack thumped his chest, Tarzan-style. 'But the details kinda escape me.'

'Oh, Jack, how could you forget?' Her voice throbbed with reproach. 'The masterful way you stole all the blankets . . . That mighty snore, like the call of a wild stallion . . .'

By this time Freya was laughing so hard that she had to climb to her knees, gasping for breath. The bedclothes fell away, revealing that she had been dressed in jeans and T-shirt all along.

'Very funny,' said Jack. He should have known. He *had* known. He walked with dignity to the wardrobe and took out a shirt, while his mind raced to invent a swift revenge. Coolly, he began to do up his buttons. 'At least I don't talk in my sleep,' he said conversationally.

'What?' Freya stopped chortling. 'I never talk in my sleep.'

'Have it your own way.'

'What did I say, then? Tell me!'

'All right.' Jack clasped his hands in a maidenly fashion, fluttered his eyelashes and assumed a ludicrous falsetto. 'Oh, Jack,' he fluted, 'how handsome you are. Oh Jack, Jack—be gentle with me. *Oof!*'

A pillow hit him smack in the face. He threw it back. She threw another one. Soon a full-scale pillow fight was under way. Jack's aim was better, though, and during one foray he managed to score a direct hit, knocking her off-balance. He pumped his arms in triumph, momentarily forgetting the insecure arrangement of his towel. He felt it loosen and slither to the floor. Meanwhile, Freya grabbed wildly at one of the bed-hangings, which suddenly shredded loose from its attachment and collapsed on top of her. She fought her way out of its dusty folds, emerging just as Jack whipped his towel back into position. Around them a snowstorm of feathers drifted slowly to the floor.

Their eyes met in a truce.

'Breakfast?' said Jack.

They found Annabelle in the kitchen in sergeant-major mode, bifocals on nose and clipboard in hand. While Freya made toast and scrambled eggs for herself and Jack, a succession of young people flowed in and out of the room, taking orders about marquees, flowers, caterers, cars and bed linen. A dozen extra people were staying in the house tonight, including a pair of bridesmaids and Roland's parents. Roland and his mates had been booked into a local pub. They would be coming by train from London and would need to be collected from the station.

Jack persuaded Annabelle to stop pacing and sat her down next to him with a cup of coffee. Then he borrowed her pen and somehow reduced everything to five headings on a single piece of paper. He ringed one of the headings, labelled it 'F and J' and passed the list back to a dazed-looking Annabelle. 'We'll be back around six,' he told her.

The jobs for which Jack had volunteered included dropping by the pub, collecting an order of fresh fish from a village Freya had intended to show Jack anyway, and picking up Roland and a couple of his friends at the station late in the afternoon. In other words, they had the day to themselves.

Freya drove down to the whitewashed pub overlooking the estuary, where Roland and his friends were to be billeted, and checked that all was in order, as per Annabelle's instructions. Then she wound her way westwards towards the sea, taking tiny back lanes hemmed in by hedgerows that cascaded with honeysuckle and dog roses. The sun was high and hot in a clear blue sky. She took Jack on a detour past her favourite church, right on a sandy beach. Then she looped inland and dropped back to the village where the fish man had a shop on the cobbled quayside. Boats bobbed low in the small harbour ringed by grey cottages. Having dealt with Annabelle's order, Freya added a small one of her own: fresh crabmeat stuffed into two crusty rolls, which she packed into a knapsack already containing a bottle of water, a bag of juicy plums and swimming things. Her plan, endorsed by Jack at breakfast, was to walk from the village along the coastal footpath to a beach, where they could picnic and swim.

The narrow footpath snaked up and down, through waist-high bracken and brambly hedges, over windswept cliffs, skirting shingly coves, until they stood high above a curving stretch of smooth sand, lapped by an inviting blue sea. They scrambled and slithered down a precipitous rocky path and at last, hot and dusty, collapsed onto their chosen spot on an almost empty beach. A shallow cave in the cliff provided a sliver of shade for the picnic and enough privacy for Freya to change at once into her bikini.

'Last one in's a rotten egg,' she shouted childishly as she sprinted across the sand and splashed into the waves. 'Lovely,' she called to Jack, clamping her teeth against the icy cold. She watched him plunge in after her, and crowed with laughter when he reared out of the water again with a bellow of protest. She stayed in just long enough to prove how tough she was, then they chased each other down the sand until they were warm.

They ate their lunch sitting on their towels, watching distant fishing boats wink their way to a hazy horizon, then lay on their stomachs, soaking up the sun and playing noughts and crosses in the sand. They talked in a desultory way about childhood holidays, friends they had in common, movies they had seen, and whether it was better to live in the country or the city, until sunshine and the slow rustle of the waves lulled them into contented silence. It was only when Freya felt Jack's cool shadow fall across her, and heard his voice reminding her of the time that she realised she had been asleep. On the walk back, she let Jack go ahead, hypnotically watching his tanned calves and battered sneakers march ahead of her. She felt drugged with sunshine.

Back at the village, they stowed styrofoam boxes of fish, packed in crushed ice, into the boot of the car and headed towards the railway station. Freya had never met Roland. All she knew was that he was twenty-nine years old and did something well-paid in property development. But when the train arrived, there was no mistaking the three young men who erupted noisily onto the platform, gaudy shirts hanging out of baggy shorts. It was a five-hour train journey from London, and they looked like they'd used every one of them for drinking. Having loaded a baggage cart with cases, two of them pushed it down the platform at a swerving run, chanting 'Here comes the groom', while the third, presumably Roland, perched precariously on top. Dark-haired, white-skinned, with heavy-lidded eyes, he was good-looking in an insolent way. When Freya introduced herself, Roland eyed her bare legs and told her she could pick him up any time, *hurgh hurgh*. His friends were called Jamie ('rugger bugger', Freya said to herself) and Sponge (blond curls, public school, posh). Without Jack she would never have got the luggage loaded and the three men squashed, protesting, into the back seat. Once inside, Roland demanded silence while he made an important business call on his mobile phone.

Freya pressed her foot on the accelerator. She didn't much care for Roland's swaggering air. But presumably Tash loved him, or at least wanted him. In some ways Freya could make sense of the match. Roland had the money; Tash had the country-house credentials. They were both greedy and ambitious. He would do deals; she would shop and lunch and oil the wheels of his career. They would be stylish and successful. It wasn't the sort of life that appealed to Freya, but perhaps it might make Roland and Tash happy. She glanced at Jack, and was amused to see him cock an eyebrow towards the back seat and roll his eyes at her in silent complicity.

Back at the house, Freya lay on the bed and snoozed while Jack took a bath. When he returned they swapped round, though Freya was back in the bedroom within half a minute. There was a spider on the wall above the toilet—a huge, black one with a zillion legs, waiting to leap onto her bare neck. She was going to have to wait until it disappeared.

'Oh, for heaven's sake.' Jack marched her back to the bathroom, where she hovered outside while he trapped the spider between cupped hands. He chucked the spider out of the window, gave her a withering look of masculine superiority, and withdrew.

By the time Freya returned to the bedroom, Jack had disappeared, tactfully giving her a chance to dress for tonight's party. She stood by the bedroom window and tilted her face to her hand mirror. Her cheeks were faintly sunburnt, but none the worse for that. She decided to leave her skin as it was. Make-up and hair completed, she wriggled herself into her dress—the aquamarine fish-scale number she had worn to Coney Island—and sat down at the dressing table.

There was a soft knock on the door.

Freya grabbed a comb. 'Yes?' she called casually.

'Only me,' said Jack, opening the door. He ambled into the room, then paused as he registered what she was wearing. 'Oh . . . the mermaid outfit.'

'It's too bad if you don't like it,' Freya said defensively.

'Who said I didn't like it?'

She saw that Jack was wearing a pair of immaculate white jeans and an electric-blue linen shirt. His tawny-blond hair was clean and combed, swept back from his broad, tanned face. He came over and stooped low, shoulder to shoulder with her, surveying them both in the mirror in a way that Freya found disconcertingly intimate.

'The perfect couple,' Jack pronounced with a smile.

She thought he was mocking her, and got quickly to her feet. 'I want to give this to Tash, then we can join the party.' She picked up a large gift-wrapped package from the bed, where she'd put it ready.

They found Tash and Roland in the library downstairs, surrounded by the spoils of marriage: monogrammed bath towels, crystal marmalade jars, Italian espresso cups, Egyptian cotton sheets, and other essentials of modern living. Tash was wearing a flimsy, slithery dress that could have been a slip or a nightie—fuchsia pink with a turquoise bra underneath. She knelt on the floor, flushed with excitement, ripping off wrapping paper under the admiring gaze of her girlfriends. Roland sat behind his bride-to-be on the sofa, languidly smoking a cigarette.

As soon as there was a gap in the proceedings, Freya stepped forward and handed her parcel to Tash with a smile. Tash tore off the wrapping.

'Golly, what is it?' She passed it over her head to Roland. 'By the way, everyone, this is Daddy's daughter by his first wife. And that gorgeous hunk is her boyfriend, Jack. So hands off, girls!'

'It's a painting,' Freya kept her voice light, 'by a young artist I handle. Stick it in an attic, if you don't like it, but I'd advise you to hang on to it. It could be valuable one day.'

Roland was looking at it with his head cocked on one side, then on the other. 'Which way up's it supposed to be?'

Tash giggled, and darted a look at Freya. Her eyes glowed like coals.

Freya tried to smile. As soon as the focus of attention shifted elsewhere she met Jack's eye and retreated through the French windows.

'Well, *I* liked it,' said Jack. 'It's a portrait, isn't it?'

'Of course it is!' Freya folded her arms tight. 'Why does she always have to be so vicious?—"This is Daddy's daughter by his first wife"—She can't even bring herself to say my name out loud. Bloody hell, I tried so hard to give her a special present.'

'Let it go,' said Jack. 'She's probably a little jealous of you. Her daddy is really your daddy, and she knows it. You're taller than her, smarter than her and you have a gorgeous hunk of a boyfriend like me. Who wouldn't be jealous? Come on, let's check out the party.' He put his arm round her.

'What are you doing?' Freya wriggled her shoulders.

Calm blue eyes looked down into hers. 'I'm pretending,' Jack said smoothly. 'This is a party, and you're my girl. Remember? This is how normal couples behave.'

'Oh. Well. All right.' Freya allowed herself to relax fractionally into the warm crook of his shoulder. At least Jack was tall, so that she could wear proper high heels.

A steady procession of cars was rolling up the long driveway. From all directions, people were emerging from archways and sweeping across lawns to funnel down the broad path leading to the courtyard where the party was being held. At the entrance to the courtyard, a line of eager teenage girls and boys, recruited from the village, held trays of drinks. On a mown square of grass at the centre, a jazz band was playing. Along one wall a line of charcoal braziers glowed red, ready to barbecue the fish she and Jack had collected earlier. Next to them were trestle tables laden with sticks of bread, bowls of salad and wedges of cheese, punctuated by sheaves of wild flowers in garden buckets—simple but festive.

Inside the high hall, with its ingeniously timbered roof and flagstone floor, Annabelle had achieved wonders. There were tables draped with pink paper tablecloths and decorated with flowers. A large area had been covered by a temporary dance floor; above it pink and silver balloons printed with 'Natasha' and 'Roland' hung down from the rafters. Beyond this, at the far end of the room, was a stage, where two men were setting up loudspeakers and a karaoke machine. Freya followed Jack up the steps where he engaged the men in conversation about amps and fuses and peered curiously at the karaoke equipment.

The hall was beginning to fill up with guests carrying platefuls of food. There seemed to be about a hundred people altogether, mostly twenty-somethings from London, who had been billeted all over the surrounding countryside in cottages, hotels, pubs, spare rooms, mattresses on floors and even tents. Shrieks of excitement rose above the general buzz; jazz was superseded by funk-rock from the speakers; a tantalising smell of grilled fish wafted in from outside. She saw Jack signalling to her that it was time to collect their plates of food and eat. Freya was assailed by an unfamiliar sensation: she was happy.

As the girl in the hippie-chick outfit yowled her way to the end of the song, the audience hooted and clapped their approval. Freya nudged Jack to pass her some more white wine, and washed down her last mouthful of raspberries and cream. She felt well-fed and mellow, comfortably hemmed in by the warm bodies of Jack on one side, and Sponge on the other. Opposite sat two interchangeably pretty bridesmaids called Polly and Lulu, both in black sleeveless dresses. It turned out that Sponge was Roland's best man, and endearingly nervous about his duties. Over dinner, they had all tried to help him with tomorrow's speech. In fact, Jack had practically written the whole thing for him on a paper napkin. Sponge was much impressed to learn that Jack was a published writer.

Jack was on good form tonight, Freya thought, leaning her head on her hand and watching him with a lazy smile. And his haircut suited him. He looked pretty good. In fact he looked great. Her heart softened. Impulsively, she pulled him close and kissed him on the cheek.

He turned his head. His smiling blue eyes, disconcertingly close, rested on hers for a moment. They held surprise, and something else she couldn't quite decipher.

Eventually, the karaoke ended and the guests deserted their tables to unleash their high spirits on the dance floor. Gallantly, Sponge asked Freya to dance with him and she accepted. She felt the warm, anonymous press of bodies, and saw how her dress shimmered in the flashing lights. She caught sight of Jack dancing with one of those bridesmaid girls. Hmmm.

When she went back to her seat for a rest, everyone else had disappeared. Freya poured herself another glass of wine and frowned at the table, empty now except for crumpled paper napkins, glasses, bottles and a litter of crumbs. She was beginning to feel painfully conspicuous when someone draped an arm round her shoulders and slumped into the chair next to her.

'Hello, sis,' slurred Roland, breathing into her face.

Freya recoiled from the fumes. He pulled his chair closer. His shirt was unbuttoned. Sweat glistened on his skin. He patted her thigh. 'You're a little cracker,' he told her. 'Fantastic legs. Come on, let's dance.' He grabbed her hand and staggered to his feet.

Freya gritted her teeth. If it had been anyone else she would have told him to get lost; but rejecting her stepsister's chosen partner might look like sour grapes. She allowed him to lead her into the press of bodies. Almost at once the music slowed to a smoochy number. Roland reached out and pulled her close, pressing every sweaty inch of his body to hers. He glued his sticky hair to her cheek. His hand groped her bottom and squeezed slowly, suggestively. She couldn't bear it.

Quite suddenly, Jack was standing there with a big, bland smile on his face, and his hand resting affably on Roland's collar. His teeth gleamed in the lights as he spoke into Roland's ear. The next thing she knew Jack was steering her away.

Freya smiled into his face with relief. 'What did you say to him?'

'I told him they were playing our song.'

'Yuk. That's so corny.'

'You have no romance in your soul.'

'Where have you been, anyway?'

'Looking for you.'

And with that, he drew her into his arms. Freya relaxed against him and clasped her hands round his waist. She rested her cheek on his shoulder and gazed through half-closed eyes at the blur of bodies and shimmer of lights. His shirt smelt good.

When the tempo changed into the pounding, irresistible beat of a familiar old song, they stepped apart spontaneously and carried on dancing. Freya undulated her arms and writhed her body. Jack spun and stamped. They advanced and retreated and circled, mimicking each other's gestures, laughing at the sheer silliness of it all. When they took a break and returned to the table for refuelling, Freya felt flushed and charged with energy.

'This is such . . . fun!'

'That's because you're not angry.'

'Angry?'

'Tight. Wound up. Snap, snap, like a vicious little crocodile.'

'Is that how you see me?' Freya was stung.

'Not tonight I don't.' Jack drained his glass. 'Tonight you are a goddess. Freya, goddess of love and beauty. Come on, let's dance.'

They plunged back into the hot pack of gyrating bodies. Freya saw Tash and Roland clasped tight in a passionate snog, and Sponge leaping about with one of the bridesmaids. Jack deserted her for a moment and reappeared with a protesting Annabelle, whom he coaxed into a kind of slow rock'n'roll, while Freya leaned against the wall and watched with a smile. You could see why women found Jack attractive. He was tall, athletic, masculine—all that stuff. Then there were those flashing blue eyes, that looked as if he had just thought of a marvellous idea or was about to make a joke. No one was more fun to be with than Jack, when he was in a good mood. Look at him twirling Annabelle about, his thick hair now a little rumpled. He'll never go bald, she thought irrelevantly. *However*: it was important to remember that Jack preferred young girls and she was three years older than him; that flirting was as natural to Jack as breathing; that he was here to *pretend* to be crazy about her.

When Annabelle withdrew from the dance floor, flushed and trying vainly to push her hair back into place, Jack reclaimed Freya and didn't let her go for the rest of the evening. Fast numbers, slow numbers, old favourites whose words they shouted aloud: they danced and drank, and drank and danced, until suddenly the music finished, the lights stopped flashing, and the party was over.

Freya stumbled out into the courtyard with Jack, dazed by the sudden darkness and cool air. Fairy lights sparkled in the trees. A double line of flares lit the path to the house. Jack held her hand loosely as they were swept along with the crowd. There was a babble of voices shouting goodbye, arguing over car keys and who was sober enough to drive. Freya saw Annabelle trying to round up Roland and his chums in the drive, and shepherd them out to a waiting minicab. Then the noises receded as she and Jack veered off towards the house. They walked up stone steps and onto the terrace. The lawn was silver, shadowed by the looming shapes of clipped bushes.

'*Ah-woooh!*' Jack was howling at the moon.

Freya gave him a shove. 'You're drunk.'

'Who cares?' With a sudden grin Jack pulled her into his arms and waltzed her along the terrace.

'Stop!' She stumbled against him as her ankle twisted, and one of her shoes came off. She bent to retrieve it. 'Bugger. The heel's loose.'

'Uh-oh. Looks like I'm going to have to pick you up and carry you.'

Freya laughed in his face. No one had carried her since she was about eight years old. 'Don't be ridic—'

'Stop saying that!' He made a grab for her. Freya swerved out of his reach and took off along the terrace at a lolloping, peg-legged run. He chased after her. She darted in through the French windows, across the library and into the hall. As she reached the bottom of the staircase, her stockinged foot slid on the wooden step. She grabbed the newel post, breathless and dizzy, and swung herself round defensively to face Jack.

He reached out and picked her up, just like that. 'Light as a feather,' he pronounced, staggering wildly around the hall.

Freya put her arms boldly round his neck. 'OK, carry me, you he-man. Let's see how far you get.'

He shifted her weight a little and began to climb. Moonlight streamed through the big window at the turn of the stairs. Freya stared dreamily at his profile. What nice ears he had. She blew playfully on the hair at the nape of his neck. When he reached the landing, he paused.

'Out of breath already?' she teased.

He turned his head and kissed her. The shock of it ripped through her. Her eyes closed, then flew open.

'Freya,' he whispered. His voice was full of longing.

'Jack . . .' She put her fingers to his face. It felt soft and hard, smooth and rough, familiar, yet as new and exciting as a wild frontier. Suddenly she wanted to touch every part of him—his ears and his neck and the line of his eyebrows and that corner of his mouth that curled up when he was secretly amused. She slid her feet to the ground, staying within the strong clasp of his arms, feeling his body against hers. Then she wound her arms round his neck and kissed him back.

It seemed that her being split in two, so that her mind floated free in a haze of anticipation, while a drumbeat of desire propelled her body upstairs. She felt the reassuring bulk of Jack's body, his thigh hard against hers, his breath on her hair. The bedroom was bathed in moonlight. Without any conscious wish or effort she was lying down, eyes shut, arms stretched wide on a bed that tilted and swayed beneath her. Then Jack's weight was on top of her. She smiled and ran her hands down his back, feeling the ripple of his ribs under her thumbs. He pulled down the straps of her dress, then raised himself off her. Her eyelids fluttered open. He was kneeling astride her. He was undoing his shirt.

Wait . . . Undoing his shirt? Was this right? No . . . *Yes!* But the warning voice grew louder. This was Jack—her old friend, lover of Candace and a thousand interchangeable others, past and future. She was heading down a blind alley: she would get hurt. Freya put her hands flat against his chest. 'I don't think this is a good idea.'

Jack seized her hands and was kissing her palms. 'Of course it's a good idea,' he murmured. His eyes were half closed, his face sharp and concentrated with desire.

'No.' She pulled herself out from under him, into a sitting position. Jack reached for her—blindly, possessively. She put out a hand to ward him off. 'No,' she said again. With a supreme effort she managed to swing her legs over the edge of the bed and stand up. She was trembling. She couldn't stop. It was embarrassing. She held on to the bedpost. 'I think I'm a little drunk, and so are you. Let's not do anything we'll regret.'

'*I* won't regret it,' Jack said fiercely. He slid from the bed and smoothed his hands over her shoulders. He was trembling too. 'Come on, Freya, let yourself go. We've been wanting to do this for years.'

'I have *not*.'

It was a lie. She wanted to. Oh, how she wanted to. Her body was ripe and ready as a juicy fig. *It's just sex*, she told herself. She didn't want to have 'just sex'—not with Jack.

But that's what it would be. On Sunday he'd go home to Candace; she'd be no more than another name on the list. With an effort as great as slamming down a steel shutter, she made herself say, 'It's been fun pretending, Jack, but I think this game has gone far enough.'

'I'm not pretending! And neither are you.' His thumbs dug into her arms.

'Let's not forget about Candace.'

Jack tossed his head at this irrelevance. 'Freya—'

'We're friends, Jack. That's all.'

'It's not all!'

'For Chrissake, let me *go*!' She was almost weeping.

His fingers tightened painfully. Then he flung her away from him. They stared at each other in distrust.

Jack's eyes narrowed to glittering slits. His mouth twisted. 'Well, what a little cock-teaser you are.'

Freya's head snapped back, as if he'd hit her. Her nose prickled with tears that she commanded herself not to shed. Vulnerability made her caustic.

'You and your cock. That's all you think about. The only reason you want me is because I'm *here*.'

'That's not true!'

'You don't really want a woman like me. Someone who talks back. Someone who doesn't think every single thing you do is a miracle. And I don't want someone who screws around. So let's not get started, OK?' She could hear her own breath, ragged and harsh, and made an effort to calm her voice. 'I'll sleep on the *chaise-longue*,' she said.

Jack punched the air in fury. 'You don't think I'm going to stay here, do you? Just climb into bed like a good little boy, while you lie sanctimoniously on the other side of the goddamned room? Jesus, Freya! You really have got ice in your veins.'

He backed away from her. He was buttoning his shirt, his fingers fumbling, sliding, slipping. Anger flowed out of his powerful body. He jerked open the door. His mouth twisted in a parody of the smile she loved. He cut the air with a mocking sweep of his hand.

'The bed's all yours.'

Chapter Twelve

HE OUGHT TO HAVE passed out by now. Why the hell hadn't he? Jack slopped more whisky into his glass and raised it to his lips. The smell made him nauseous. He slammed down the glass and paced up and down the library, kicking errant scraps of silver ribbon and crackly paper out of his way. He was so . . . *angry!*

His first impulse had been to leave—to jump in the car, drive straight to the airport and go home. To hell with Freya and her family and this stupid wedding! But the car keys were in Freya's bag upstairs; returning to the bedroom was too humiliating to contemplate. Instead, he'd tramped around the dewy gardens for the better part of an hour, irritatingly shadowed by an inquisitive Bedivere. But his efforts to calm his mind and exhaust his body had proved futile. All he'd got was wet feet.

He *hated* her, yet he couldn't get her out of his mind. Freya running down the beach in her bikini, long legs gleaming with sea water. Freya dancing in her mermaid dress. The feel of her in his arms, the tender lift of her chin as she'd raised her head to kiss him. And the kiss itself . . .

Jack groaned aloud and circled back towards his drink. Thank the Lord for alcohol. When at length he'd returned to the house, he'd remembered the couch in the library, big enough to sleep on, and a tray of drinks at his elbow, and found his way here. Now he slumped onto the worn cushions and sank his head in his hands. He needed to sleep. But he couldn't. Resentment boiled inside him. How could she do that to him? Not once, but *twice*. What did the woman want? *Come here, Jack. Go away, Jack. Isn't this fun, Jack? No, don't be ridiculous.* Push, pull, push, pull, until he was dizzy, exhausted, frustrated and furious. When he thought of how he had put himself out for her, abandoning his work, flying thousands of miles to take part in this ridiculous charade, and she couldn't even—! And why bring Candace up? He hadn't even thought of Candace since he'd been here—not once!

Jack jumped up from the couch and began pacing again, looking for distraction. The room was full of shelves of books—clothbound, leatherbound, jacketed. He moved along the shelves, looking for something taxing and intricate. Ah, Henry James: *The Golden Bowl*. That should do it. He placed the book by the couch, then collected all the cushions he could find for his sore head. Grunting, he bent down to unlace and remove his damp shoes. The bottoms of his trousers were wet, too. Maybe if he hung them over a chair to dry, he could use those huge wedding-present bath towels as a makeshift covering. He was starting to unzip his fly when the sensation of being watched made him turn round.

A woman was standing in the open doorway. For a moment he thought it was Freya. Then the figure stepped out of the dimness and came into focus.

'Can't you sleep either?' said Tash.

Jack gave a noncommittal grunt. As she strolled over to him, he saw that her feet were bare and her dark hair loose and tousled. She was wrapped in the pink thing she'd worn this morning.

'Ooh, lovely, you've found the booze.' She gave him a conspirator's smile.

'Uh, yes. I'm afraid I helped myself. Hope that's OK.'

'Course it is, Jack! What's ours is yours.'

'Thanks.' Her friendliness was cheering. 'Here, let me get you a glass.'

He poured her a drink and sat down on the couch. Tash clambered onto the other end and relaxed with a small sigh, tucking her legs beneath her. She raised her glass in a playful toast.

'Here's to my last few hours of freedom.'

'Freedom,' echoed Jack. Yeah, he'd drink to that.

'Just think: by tomorrow evening I'll be Mrs Swindon-Smythe.' Tash giggled. 'It sounds frightfully grown up.'

'You're a brave girl.'

'Don't say that! I've got butterflies in my tummy as it is. Still, I suppose Roley's got the essentials, so what the hell?' She gave a larky grin. Her wide eyes gazed cheekily into his. She was a sexy little number all right. Lucky Roland.

'So tell me, Jack. What are you doing down here all alone? Has she chucked you out for some frightful misdemeanour?'

'Who, Freya? Nah.' Jack waved a casual hand. 'I just . . .'

'You just what?' she asked teasingly. 'Forgot your condoms?'

'No.'

'Don't tell me: you attempted something more exotic than the missionary position, and she freaked.'

Her outspokenness embarrassed him; irritated him; excited him. His eye fell on the navy-bound volume by his side. 'Actually, I came down to get a book.'

'A book! Golly, what an exciting sex life you two must lead. Do you always take off your shoes before reading aloud to her, you kinky thing?'

'Shut up, Tash,' Jack growled.

'Oops, sor-ree. Do I detect a lovers' tiff?'

'No, you don't!' Jack banged the arm of the couch. 'We're not lovers!'

There was a long pause.

'Really?' Tash's voice sharpened with interest.

Jack passed a hand across his aching head. He didn't have the strength to pretend any more. 'I may as well tell you.' He put down his whisky glass. 'Freya and I are just friends. We've been friends for years. She wanted someone to come over here with her, and I agreed. End of story. We've never—' he broke off.

'What, never?' Tash smiled incredulously.

Jack shook his head.

'But you tried tonight, and she slapped you down?'

Jack looked away, saying nothing. It was humiliating to realise how he'd demeaned himself: the haircut, the smart clothes, buttering up Freya's family, pretending to go upstairs to bed together, then sleeping separately. Revealing his humiliation to this warm-blooded, uninhibited young girl made him feel like an impotent old fool.

'Poor Jack.' Her voice was like molasses. 'Perhaps you need some . . . cheering up.'

Jack turned his head and looked at her. She was eyeing him over her glass. She really was very pretty, with her shiny dark hair tumbling around her face, and soft skin flushed like a ripe fruit. He could see the swell of her breasts at the opening of her robe, and the nipples that pressed through the thin, shiny material.

Tash put out the pink tip of her tongue and slowly licked the rim of her glass, watching him with dark, dreamy eyes.

'Don't tease,' he said.

'Why not?' Her full lips pouted. She stretched out one smooth, bare leg and inched it across the couch and onto his lap. Her robe fell away, exposing a creamy thigh.

'Because I'm tired of games.' He gripped her foot, halting its progress.

'I love games,' Tash said huskily.

He could feel her toes stroking him, pushing his zip wider and wider. His body began to hum. 'Why are you doing this, Tash? You're getting married tomorrow.'

'That's why. One last, lovely taste of freedom. With lovely, lovely Jack.' Tash put down her glass. Keeping her eyes locked on his, she loosened her robe and wriggled it free of her shoulders. Her breasts sprang towards him, just asking to be stroked. She arched her back and smiled. 'What do you think?'

Jack was beginning not to think anything much. 'I think . . . you're a very naughty person.'

'It takes one to know one. I should think you could be very naughty indeed.' Her voice dropped to a throaty whisper. 'Come on, Jack. No one will find out. It can be our secret.'

The tiny corner of his brain that was still functioning told Jack that this was unusual behaviour for a bride-to-be. Still, if she wanted to, who was he to argue? It was just sex. He liked sex. He loosened his grip on her foot and let it roam, up and down and around. His fingertips slid up the inside of her leg. When he reached the soft, incredibly silky skin of her thigh, she eased her legs apart, and leaned back. Jack pushed aside the last concealment of her robe. He could see everything. His heartbeat began to accelerate. He'd been badly treated. He was owed.

Tash put one hand out to her glass and dabbled her middle finger in the whisky. When she took it out, he could see the liquid running down and gathering in heavy, golden drops.

Maddened by her teasing, Jack launched himself on top of her. He heard her give a crow of pleasure, and felt her hot little hands slip under his loosened trousers.

Jack spread his fingers across the swelling flesh of her breasts. He thrashed his legs, trying to kick free of his trousers, and the two of them tumbled together off the couch. Tash fell on her back among the crumpled sheets of wrapping paper. Her fingers reached up and tore at his shirt. Then she half sat up and pushed at his shoulder to roll him onto his back. She smoothed her hands greedily over his chest, along the hard curves of his shoulders and arms. Her cat-like face creased with pleasure. 'You're much too good for my big sister,' she murmured, and lowered herself on top of him.

She knew lots of tricks. Her slick body squirmed and squeezed and arched, until Jack grabbed hold of her and pushed her onto her back. Tash reached up for him; he pinned her arms behind her head and pulled her tight. Thought dissolved into sensation. Then he heard her ratcheting breath, fast and on a rising pitch. He opened his eyes and saw her head tilt and her mouth widen. Some instinct made him jam the edge of his hand into her mouth to muffle her cries, while her body rippled beneath him. The savagery of her sharp little teeth made him plunge faster, deeper. One, two, three, four . . .

It was over. Jack lay with his full weight on top of her, eyes closed, mind empty, heart racing, his skin hot and sparking with sensation. Gradually his muscles relaxed, his breathing slowed. He rolled away with a groan.

He heard the delicate chiming of a clock. Consciousness returned, sudden and shocking. He lifted his head. His white trousers dangled over the edge of the couch, one leg inside out. *The Golden Bowl* had fallen to the floor and lay face down, its pages splayed open.

Jack raised himself clumsily on all fours. He looked at Tash's pink and white body, sprawled like a puppet's. He saw the glint of her half-closed eyes, the slack mouth he'd been too frenzied to kiss. A length of ribbon, silver etched with wedding bells, was caught in the tumble of her hair.

Freya filled the kettle with water and plonked it on the Aga. Where the hell was he?

Probably sulking somewhere. Bloody men. Yes, all right, perhaps she had been a bit come-hither last night. But they were supposed to be pretending: that was the whole point of bringing him here. OK, *OK*: so she'd got a little overexcited. She'd had a lot to drink. And Jack was an attractive man; she'd never denied that. But she had not come all this way to have a one-night stand with Jack Madison!

Freya poured boiling water on her Earl Grey tea bag. Where were his priorities, for God's sake? The wedding was only hours away. And she wanted to know what he thought of her hat. It was a sizzling lime green, extravagantly brimmed, and probably visible across five counties. Yes I AM the older sister, it proclaimed—the glamorous one from glamorous New York, with the glamorous man—Buggeration: she'd spilt the milk.

There were quick steps in the passage. Annabelle burst in, her hair in rollers, eyes glassy with frenzied concentration.

'Has that kettle boiled? Freya, you're a saint. Now, where did I put the Swindon-Smythes' tea tray? Just look at the time! Oh dear, oh dear.'

And out she went again.

Freya sipped her tea. It had begun. She could look forward to an entire day of this lunacy, until the blessed moment when Tash would toss her bouquet into the crowd and drive away. And unless Jack turned up, she would have to endure it all alone.

'Good morning, darling. Had a good sleep?'

Her father entered the kitchen at a sprightly pace, freshly shaved and smiling, hair curling damply from his bath.

Freya raised an eyebrow. 'All spruced up to give away your daughter, I see.'

His eyes rested on hers for a moment. 'Crumpet or toast?' he asked mildly.

'Neither. I'm not hungry.'

'Nonsense. Sit down and have some breakfast with your old dad. Tell me what you've been up to.'

'What, now? You're far too busy.'

'Plenty of time yet. I've hardly seen you since you arrived.'

There was a flurry of footsteps, and a figure whirled through the kitchen and towards the scullery. 'Darling, have we got any soya milk? Will skimmed milk do? I wonder. I hope they aren't expecting a cooked breakfast. Those girls aren't even awake yet. And the hairdresser will be here any minute. For heaven's sake, Guy! Have you forgotten Tash is getting married today? You can't just stand there!'

'Why not?'

Annabelle gave a shudder of exasperation and zoomed off.

'See what I mean?' said Freya.

'Best to lie low for a bit. She'll blow herself out. Tell you what, let's take a tray into my study. No one will bother us there.' He hesitated. 'Or would you rather go back up to Jack?'

'No,' said Freya, suddenly galvanised into activity. She strode across to a cupboard. 'Marmalade or honey?'

'Let's be devils and have both.'

The study was a beautiful room, high-ceilinged yet cosy, a perfect square of panelled walls with a fireplace on one side and a mullioned window on the other, looking out over a sweep of lawn to the meadows beyond. Freya carried in the tray and her father cleared a space on his desk, a mahogany monstrosity covered with a familiar clutter of books, papers and journals.

'Glad to see you haven't got any tidier,' she remarked.

Her father chuckled and closed the door. He lowered himself into an armchair and watched Freya busy herself with his plate and mug.

'How nice to be waited on by my daughter! Come and sit down and tell me what you're up to in New York. How's the job? Is the art world as dotty as it seems? Are you happy?'

Freya folded herself into an old leather armchair, balanced her mug on the arm and began to answer his questions—the first two, anyway. She was conscious that her answers were grudging, but why should she have to reveal every little detail of her life? He wasn't really interested, anyway. He had Annabelle and Tash to think about. As she spoke, her gaze hovered on the cluster of framed photographs displayed on the bookshelf behind his head, the same collection he'd had for years. One showed him and Annabelle on their wedding day, flanked by Tash and herself. They were all smiling except her. How clearly she remembered puzzling over why her father needed Annabelle. Wasn't she enough for him? Now the question almost made her laugh aloud. On the one hand, a gawky schoolgirl peering warily from behind that awful fringe; on the other, a full-figured woman sexually in her prime, with a child to prove it. Everything came down to sex, in the end. Jack's voice floated back to her: *What a little cock-teaser you are*. She *hated* Jack.

Her father, sensing her inattention, turned to look at the photos. His face softened. He reached out a long arm and picked one up.

'Ah, look at you.' He tilted the picture to show her. 'That was taken the very day you were born. You were so tiny, yet you had an absolutely definite personality, as powerful as a magnetic force field. Extraordinary! You have no idea how I felt when I first held you in my arms. I wanted to protect you from everything. I already dreaded the day when I'd have to give you away to some husband who couldn't possibly deserve you.'

Freya prickled with irritation. 'Though as it happens, it's Tash you're giving away,' she pointed out.

His smile faded. His face sagged with sudden weariness. She had hurt him. He lowered the photo to his lap with a small sigh.

'Tash is Tash, and you are you,' he said. 'I've done my best to be a father to her, but you're *mine*. You're special. I've always loved you and I always will love you. You're not to mind about all this wedding palaver. It has nothing to do with you and me.'

Freya gave a vague smile. She felt abashed at his warmth. She didn't know how to respond.

'I know I'm a tactless old idiot,' he continued. 'It's not important who gets married and who doesn't. But—well, I suppose the time has come when I'd like you to find someone special to care about, and to care about you—not so you can have the status of marriage but so that you can experience the big things of life. Companionship. Commitment. Sharing. Children. They . . . stretch one.'

Freya pursed her lips. Did he think she had never considered these things too? Had *ached* for such experiences—enough to pretend to herself that she wanted to marry Michael, whom she didn't even love. 'I don't think I'm the domestic type,' she said flippantly. 'Anyway, I haven't found the right man.'

Her father looked at her. 'You seem to get on very well with Jack. I like him.'

'Jack's all right.' Freya shrugged. 'He's just—' She broke off. She'd nearly said he was just a friend.

'What happened to the chap we were expecting—Michael?'

'Oh, that's all over,' Freya said breezily.

'And now you like Jack and you're living with him. That's right, isn't it?'

'Ye-es.'

'You don't sound very certain.'

'Well . . . Jack's a bit of a playboy.'

'Perhaps he needs somebody fierce and sensible to sort him out.'

Freya ignored this. 'Playboys are fun, in their way. At least Jack never bores me.'

'What, never? Darling, you must bag him at once!'

'For God's sake, Daddy, it's not a big thing. Not like you and Mummy. We quarrel all the time.'

Her father's eyebrows soared. 'Do you think Karina and I never quarrelled? We'd hardly been married a month before I stormed out, saying we'd made a dreadful mistake and might as well get divorced at once.'

Freya was shocked. 'Why? What happened?'

'Heavens, I can't remember now.' Her father laughed at the very idea. 'People have to express their frustrations, you know.'

'But—but you loved her, didn't you?' Freya faltered.

'Of course I loved her. And she loved me. Loving someone doesn't mean that they're perfect, just that you see them clearly, flaws and all, and love them anyway. Karina was fierce and impetuous and stubborn—like someone else I know. I loved her for being the way she was, and sometimes I suffered for it too.'

Freya pictured Jack's face last night, when she'd told him she was only pretending. For a moment her bravado wavered. What if she had made a mistake? What if he had spent as miserable a night as she had? She looked down at her plate and fiddled with her toast crumbs. 'And if you had a quarrel—a bad one, I mean—what did you do?'

'Apologised. Forgave each other. Made up.' He grinned suddenly. 'That was the good bit.' He leaned towards her eagerly. 'It's so lovely to talk to you, darling. I wish I saw you more often. I was thinking of coming to New York in the autumn. I'd love it if we could spend some time together.'

Freya frowned. 'It'll be the auction season.'

'Not the whole autumn, surely.'

'I suppose Annabelle wants to do her Christmas shopping?'

'Actually, I rather thought I'd come alone. It's you I want to see—if you can spare the time.'

His humility made Freya faintly ashamed. Part of her longed for them to be together, but it wasn't that easy. She couldn't allow it to be that easy. She glanced back at the photograph of her father on his wedding day. He had chosen his life, and she had chosen hers.

'Well, think about it.' Her father, suddenly brisk, hauled himself out of his chair. He peered long-sightedly at his watch. 'Ah. Just time to take Bedivere for a run.'

Freya noted the time with a fresh spasm of panic. The wedding was due to start in two hours. Where was Jack?

The tide was going out. Each wave slurped up a mouthful of shingle, then sprayed it back onto the beach in an undulating line. Jack had no idea how long he'd been sitting here: long enough for the sun to rise over the far shore of the estuary and stab its brightening rays into his eyeballs; long enough for him to have reached a decision.

He was leaving. As soon as the wedding began, he would sneak back up to the house, gather his belongings and go. Freya would make up some kind of story to cover his departure; she was good at deceit.

He didn't want to think about last night. He wasn't particularly proud of his antics in the library with Tash. But he'd been drinking, and she had come on strong. Anyway, what did it matter? In a couple of hours she'd be married. As for Freya . . . If she didn't want him—and last night she had made it painfully clear that she didn't—she could do without him altogether. It was too painful to continue with this absurd charade as her partner, especially during the festivities of a wedding. He felt wrung out, hung over, let down and fed up. He was going home.

Jack let his collection of stones trickle through his fingers and struggled unsteadily to his feet. Even this small effort brought beads of sweat to his forehead. His legs were leaden. Behind him rose the lush greenery of the garden through which he'd plunged, on a steep zigzag path, to escape the waking household. The house was invisible from here; he could no longer remember where exactly the path had emerged. Trudging back across the shingle, he took the first opening he saw.

The narrow track climbed steeply. Jack could see that it had once been much wider, with broad steps carved out of the soil and shored up with logs. But the logs had rotted; the vegetation pressed close, closer, until he could barely discern the path. He was wondering whether to retrace his steps when he heard a crashing noise in the undergrowth. He paused. It was coming nearer. Were there wild boar in England? Jack quickened his pace. The crashing got louder; he could hear fierce panting. The path ended abruptly, and he found himself teetering on the brink of a ten-foot drop, overlooking a sunken pit. Then a black labrador burst out of a thicket and cantered towards him, tail waving, and a voice called, 'Ah, well done. You've found Lethe's Leap.'

Jack turned to see Freya's father striding towards him, swinging a stout stick. The tilt of his head and his amused half-smile were so like Freya's that Jack suffered a wrench of recognition.

'Named, of course, after the river of forgetfulness in the Greek underworld,' Guy continued. 'One leapt in and forgot all one's responsibilities and the conventions of decent behaviour. Where you're standing is effectively the diving board.'

Jack stared down at the rough rectangle of weeds edged with broken stone slabs. Comprehension dawned. 'It's a swimming pool!'

'"Was" is the operative word. I shouldn't think it's been used since the fifties. No doubt Freya's told you the colourful story of Annabelle's inheritance?'

Jack frowned. 'Freya tells me nothing.'

'I know the feeling.' Guy gave a wistful sigh. 'Never mind. I'll fill you in while we walk back.' He paused, and added courteously, 'Unless you have other plans?'

Jack was suddenly conscious of his dishevelled appearance and the oddity of his presence here, alone. 'No, I was just—'

'Splendid.'

Guy set off at a brisk pace along a curving track that took them out of the garden and up into wilder woodland. Jack loped alongside him, only half listening to Guy's history of the house and the Ashleigh family who had owned it for centuries. He was trying to figure out how to avoid being shepherded back to the house and into a confrontation with Freya. But gradually the story claimed his attention.

It seemed that in the 1920s the house had passed into the ownership of Frederick 'Fruity' Ashleigh, a 'confirmed bachelor' with a taste for lithe young men, whom he imported in droves for house parties of legendary debauchery. 'He's the one who had the swimming pool built,' said Guy, 'presumably as an excuse to get his young friends to take their clothes off.'

Fruity's particular friend was a young man twenty years his junior, known as Bunny. 'The two of them set up house together, spending half the year in Cornwall and half in London. Despite spectacular quarrels and rampant infidelity on Bunny's part they were a devoted pair, and when Fruity died childless he willed the house to Bunny. But Bunny took himself off to London, where he behaved very badly in Soho, by all accounts, and left the house to crumble. In due course he died himself—keeled over in a pub. Not being the most practical of men, he had failed to make a will. After many months and an extortionate legal bill, it transpired that his nearest living relative was Annabelle.'

'I see.' Jack's head was pounding, but it seemed polite to make a contribution to this conversation. 'So, uh, Annabelle is no relation at all to the Ashleighs?'

'None whatsoever. We met shortly after she inherited the house. Her husband was dead, she'd a small child to look after and hardly any money. She'd tried putting the house on the market, but no one would touch it. So in the end we decided to take it on together. The house is still a bit of a muddle, as I expect you've noticed.'

'No, no. It's very . . .' Jack trailed off as he saw Guy's eyebrows rise in a sceptical expression that was extremely familiar to him. He gave a sheepish smile. He liked this man. 'It's delightful,' he said firmly.

At last they reached the top of the hill and paused to catch their breath. A magnificent view unrolled in all directions. Behind them, the sea was now visible in a shimmering strip beyond the trees. Across the valley, the house lay tranquilly in a green pool of mown lawns. Immediately below them, snug in a wooded dip, was a small stone chapel in a neat enclosure of iron fencing. Jack could see figures bustling in and out, carrying flowers. He remembered the wedding.

'Yes,' Guy mused, 'the house should see us out.' He paused. 'Goodness knows what Tash will do with it.'

The mention of Tash sharpened Jack's attention. 'So all this goes to Tash,' he said slowly, 'not Freya.'

'Yes. That's a bit of a problem.'

Jack scuffed the grass with his shoe. In what way was it a problem? Did Guy suspect him of being a fortune hunter?

'I don't think Freya's interested in the house,' he said coolly.

'Good Lord! Neither do I. I only mean that I don't like her to feel excluded. She's not, of course. She's the one who stays away.' Guy sighed. 'I don't know if you've noticed, but Freya is rather an independent sort of person.' Jack's mouth twisted. Yes, he had noticed. 'She wouldn't take any money from us when she went to New York—insisted on making her own way. It's as if she fears things will be taken away from her unless she controls them herself.'

'Mmm.' Jack was beginning to feel uncomfortable. He was here on false pretences and didn't deserve Guy's confidence.

'Unfortunately, things *have* been taken away. It's a terrible thing for a girl to lose her mother. One tries to compensate but . . .' Guy jabbed at the ground with his stick. 'I don't think she's ever forgiven me for marrying Annabelle. She doesn't seem to understand that Annabelle isn't a substitute for her—nor could Freya ever be a substitute for Annabelle.' He looked up at Jack. 'I sometimes think that's why she hasn't settled into a relationship of her own.'

Jack avoided his glance. He wasn't playing this game. 'I guess she hasn't found the right man.' He shrugged carelessly.

'Very probably. It would take someone of special qualities to make Freya happy. Shall we walk down?'

Jack stomped after him, feeling disconcerted and irritable. Freya wasn't his concern. She didn't want to be his concern. So it was irrelevant whether he possessed 'special qualities' or not. He glowered at Guy's boots, trying not to think of how he had abused this man's hospitality.

'I'm very pleased Freya brought you over,' said Guy, turning to him with a friendly smile. 'We don't get to meet her men friends. She likes to keep her life compartmentalised. Still, I expect you know that all too well, since you're living together.'

What? Jack's head snapped up.

'She was telling me about it this morning.'

This morning?

'She said you didn't bore her. I must say I was impressed.'

'But—'

'Oh, don't worry. It's not for me to approve or disapprove. In fact, I'm glad she has someone to care for her.'

'Yes . . .' Jack pictured her face when he'd shouted at her last night.

'She reminds me of those cats who climb out on a limb and can't get back. You see, I'm not there to rescue her.'

Guy's face was so sad and tender that Jack was moved. He felt suddenly light-headed. He pictured Freya alone at the wedding, eyes watchful, alert to any slight. *Oh, Freya* . . . She was so stubborn, so mistrustful. How could she have thought he was 'pretending' last night?

'I'd better get a move on,' said Guy. 'Annabelle will be flapping. It's a man's job to stay out of the way until the last moment, then lend a calming presence, wouldn't you agree?'

Jack didn't answer. He was watching a distant car winding its way up the drive. There would be plenty of cars dropping people off and going away again. It shouldn't be hard to get a ride to the station.

'Well, I'll see you up at the house. Come along, Bedivere. By the way,' Guy thwacked a bramble into submission. 'I don't wish to be personal, but I do happen to know an excellent cure for a hangover.'

Chapter Thirteen

THE CHAPEL WAS FILLING UP. Above the dogged drone of the organ came the rustling, flapping, cawing sounds of gathering guests. Jamie was on duty at the door, dashing in striped trousers and black tailcoat, handing out service sheets.

Freya looked at her watch: three minutes to go. In her heart, she had not seriously believed that Jack would stand her up. But he had. Here she was, sitting in the front pew with a ringside view of the event she had dreaded for months. She bent her head to the service sheet.

His suit still hung in the closet; his shaving kit and toothbrush were in the bathroom: she had checked. But Jack himself had disappeared. Where was he? She clamped her jaw tight.

The organ music broke off. A roar of chatter rose briefly to fill the void, then hushed to an expectant whisper. Roland stood up, his features rigid. Sponge put his hand once more to his pocket, checking that the ring was still there. Reverend Thwacker took his place at the head of the aisle, glasses flashing fiercely in a stray sunbeam. On Freya's right, Annabelle, a vision in peach, slipped a hankie out of her sleeve, preparing for a gush of maternal joy. The organ gave an asthmatic wheeze, gearing itself up for the entrance march. Freya turned her head and caught a distant glimpse of Tash, deceptively virginal in off-the-shoulder ivory. She became vaguely aware of a commotion nearer to hand, a murmured tut-tutting, a voice saying 'Excuse me, ma'am . . . Thank you, sir'. It was Jack.

For a moment she couldn't think of anything to say. He looked wonderful. His suit was perfection. His shirt was crisp. His tie dazzled. His hair gleamed like old gold. Her spirits soared.

'What kept you?' she said.

Before he could answer the organ erupted into the triumphant peals of the 'Entrance of the Queen of Sheba'. There was a rumble as everyone stood up and turned to admire the bride. Freya rose, too, shoulder to shoulder with Jack, inhaling his masculine smell of shaving soap. Her eyes slid sideways to search his face. He smiled his easy smile.

'Great hat.'

Having decided to honour his promise to Freya, despite the way she had treated him, Jack intended to enjoy himself. His hangover had miraculously receded. Sunshine, champagne and a complacent awareness of his own noble behaviour had restored his good humour. He escaped from the muggy warmth of the marquee and strolled out onto the bright lawn, pausing only to allow a pretty waitress to refill his glass.

So this was an English wedding. He must make some notes. The house rose in front of him, its curlicued gables sharply profiled against a serene blue sky. Guests assembled at the entrance archway to run the gauntlet of the reception line in the hall and emerged, a few yards along, from the French windows of the library, where the wedding gifts were on munificent display. There were flowers everywhere, spouting from urns by the front entrance, tumbling from pots placed by the guy ropes of the marquee, colourfully bunched on the damask-covered tables where, it seemed, lunch would shortly be served.

He began to circle the marquee, a pink-and-white-striped affair like an outsized jousting pavilion, eavesdropping on conversations.

'Absolutely riddled with dry rot . . .'

'. . . bonus last year was seven and a half K.'

'Prada, actually.'

'No, no, you haven't changed *a bit*. It's simply that people look so different in hats.'

At that moment Jack caught sight of Freya emerging from the house and stepping across the lawn like a racehorse. She was looking sensational in some dress thing that was cut low at the top and high at the bottom: his favourite kind. He liked the way her hat emphasised her elegant neck and cast intriguing shadows on her face. He raised his hand to attract her attention and caught her smile of relief.

'Where have you been?' he called out, as she approached.

'There's been a flap about the cake. I was helping Annabelle.'

'That's nice of you.' He put his arm round her waist and gave her an approving squeeze. He felt her resistance, and tightened his grip. It gave him an ignoble thrill to know that, having brought him here for precisely such play-acting, she could hardly rebuff his intimacies in public.

He let go of her for a moment to swipe a glass of champagne off a passing tray, then handed it to her with a smile and clinked his glass to hers. She was smiling.

Freya put down her dessert spoon with a contented sigh. The lunch had been delicious, the wine plentiful, the company amusing. She felt soothed by the hum of conversation, and pleasantly lethargic in the warm air trapped inside the marquee. Jack was on cracking form. It was relaxing to listen to the familiar cadences of his voice and feel the presence of his arm resting casually across the back of her chair.

She had misjudged him by thinking he would let her down. His disappearance had been perfectly understandable: his masculine pride was hurt, and it had taken him time to recover. She remembered what her father had said that morning about forgiveness and compassion, and decided to be especially nice to him. Jack had recently suffered two major blows: first the loss of financial support from his father, then the cancellation of his book contract. Then he had made a pass at her—probably out of some psychological need to assert himself—and she had rejected him. For a moment Freya pictured his face in the moonlight when he had kissed her—when she had kissed him. She straightened in her chair and crossed her legs. The point was, she reminded herself, that she and Jack were friends again.

Her thoughts were interrupted by a peremptory clinking of cutlery on glass, a signal for silence.

Jack turned to her. 'What's happening?'

'Speeches,' she said curtly. This was a moment she had been dreading. She watched her father rise to his feet, swallowing her jealousy as she prepared to listen to him praise the bride.

It was a good speech—affectionate and urbane, with an edge of that self-deprecating humour she loved. He was welcoming to Roland. He praised Annabelle. He paid tribute to Tash's real father, who had died so young and whose relatives he was delighted to welcome today. He was gracious and courteous. Freya could not help feeling proud.

'. . . and another way in which I am lucky is that I do, of course, have *two* daughters. I am particularly pleased that my daughter Freya is able to be with us today, along with her friend Jack. For those of you who don't know, Freya leads a very successful and fulfilled life in New York. She is the best of companions as well as a beautiful young woman—thanks to her mother, I may say. I love her, and I am proud of her. This event would not be complete without her presence. Thank you for coming, darling.'

Freya bent her head to hide her face. Her heart was full. He had not forgotten her.

His speech came to an end and now Roland stood up to embark on his long list of thankyous. As Freya's father sat down, Freya turned to Jack, and found that he was watching her. He smiled reassuringly, as though he could read her mind.

The audience was laughing now. Roland had sat down. Heavens, it was good old Sponge! She must pay attention. 'Marriage is a field of battle,' he was saying, 'not a bed of roses.'

How strange. That was just what her father had been trying to tell her this morning, about his marriage to her mother. Perhaps she'd been pursuing quite the wrong idea of relationships, expecting them to meet some ideal of perfection and destroying them when they didn't. Now she thought about it, a bed of roses sounded rather insipid. For a moment she glimpsed an alternative view of men and women as sparring partners, continually testing each other's strengths—combative but not destructive, knocking each other into shape.

'. . . to Roland and Tash!' Damn, she had missed Sponge's speech, though his huge grin indicated that it had been a hit. Freya raised her glass in a toast and took a sip of champagne, enjoying the fizz on her tongue. Impulsively she turned to Jack and clinked glasses with him. 'Thanks for coming, Jack. It's made all the difference.'

Jack and Freya were sitting together in a saggy old swing seat half-hidden in a cave of yew, lazily watching the guests crisscross the lawn. The cake had been cut. Roland and Tash had gone upstairs to change. The sunshine still held, bestowing a mellow glow on the proceedings. After the speeches Freya had mentioned to Jack that she was thinking of inviting her father to New York for a visit, and was surprised by his immediate enthusiasm. 'He'd love it!'

'I say, Jack, do you know anything about cars?' It was Sponge, holding the hand of a pretty girl in blue, and looking anxious. He and Jamie were titivating the going-away car with the usual 'Just Married' paraphernalia. Jamie had somehow engaged the steering lock and no one knew how to free it. Jack said he'd see what he could do, and Freya waved him off.

She sat alone, idly swinging, and rested her head on the faded cushions. She closed her eyes. It was nearly over. She had survived. In fact, she had positively enjoyed herself. Having someone to accompany her had made all the difference. She wondered if she and Jack would be able to sneak off this evening for a walk to the pub and a quiet supper together. The swing seat squeaked protestingly as Freya sat upright, jolted by a shocking realisation. How blind she had been! The issue of whether she had a companion for this wedding—an issue that had tormented her for so long—was, she suddenly saw, absurdly trivial. What had made the difference was one particular man, a man who took care of her and made her laugh, a man she knew with the intimacy of long friendship, a man she liked—perhaps more than liked . . .?

A hubbub broke through her thoughts, and she noticed that all the guests were now milling towards the driveway at the side of the house. She strolled over, looking out for Jack, though there was no hurry. She would have plenty of time, before they returned to New York, to examine this new, exciting idea that swelled within her.

Tash had changed into a summer dress splashed with poppies; she looked pretty and excited. Freya saw her hug Annabelle and step into the open-topped car. Roland sat importantly at the steering wheel, a cool dude in shades. Someone was passing round a basket of rose petals to throw; other people had bought their own confetti and were busy ripping open packets.

Roland sounded the horn and Tash stood up on the passenger seat, holding something high in the air: her wedding bouquet. There was a murmur of excitement from the crowd. Tash scanned the faces below her with a slow turn of the head. Her words floated across the air. 'Where's Freya? Where's my big sister?'

Freya felt a prickle of embarrassment, tinged with anger that Tash should draw attention to her in this manner: her 'big' sister, still unmarried. She had no wish to scramble for the trophy bouquet, even if it was tossed straight into her hands. But her hat was like a big green 'Go' sign. Already Tash had seen her. She had climbed down from the seat and was walking forward with a smile on her face. The crowd parted.

'Aah, how sweet.'

'What a generous girl.'

Their words brought Freya to her senses. This was Tash's version of an olive branch; she could at least accept it graciously. She stepped forward to meet Tash halfway. Tash pressed the bouquet into her hand, then pulled her into a sisterly embrace. Freya bent down to hug her back. She felt Tash's arm snake about her neck and the smack of breath in her ear as Tash whispered, 'Jack's a big boy, isn't he?'

Freya jerked with shock. Her head whipped back so that she could look into Tash's face, which radiated such malicious triumph that Freya was left in no doubt about her meaning. She tried to pull away, but Tash held tight. 'Pity he's not your real boyfriend,' she spat.

Then her armlock loosened. There was a gleam of teeth, the glint of narrowed eyes and she had gone.

Freya rocked on her heels. Blood thumped in her ears, louder than the cheering voices around her. 'Good luck!' they called. 'Goodbye!' She saw a blur of waving hands. The air exploded into colour. There was the growl of an engine, the spatter of gravel, a clinking of tin cans. She was icy cold. If she moved, she feared she would fall over and splinter.

Something was digging into her palm. It was the stiff wired handle of the bridal bouquet.

The last shreds of confetti spun and drifted to the ground. The crowd cleared. Jack saw Freya staring straight at him. Her hat turned her face into a Cubist portrait of fractured light and geometric shadows, and he thought with wonder and affection of all the different women hidden behind that single configuration of features: scornful goddess, brash poker player, resentful little girl; the clever woman who kept her brain—and her tongue—sharply honed, the gorgeous creature running down the beach. He realised that he wanted to kiss her.

'Freya,' he called.

She turned and walked away in slow motion, like a figure in a dream who cannot hear however loud you shout.

'*Freya!*' He loped after her.

'Excuse me.' A female voice shrilled in his ear. 'Aren't you Jack Madison?' A manicured claw gripped his arm.

'I'm sorry.' He was conscious of musky scent and a confection of tinted hair. 'There's something I have to do. I'll catch you later.'

But Freya had disappeared. He'd lost her. He thought she'd been heading for the house, and hurried inside. It was cool and silent. He peered into the empty library, then retraced his steps to the kitchen. There was the slow drip-drip of a tap. Bedivere lay pressed to the Aga; he gave a civil thump of his tail. 'Where is she?' asked Jack.

He thought he heard a tiny sound from beyond the kitchen, and wandered down the cluttered passageway, looking through doorways. She was standing with her back to him in a kind of pantry room, doing something at the sink.

He smiled with relief. 'Freya, I wanted to—'

'*Get out!*'

She spun round and something hit him low in the stomach. Jack clutched it instinctively—something pulpy and damp—but it was Freya he was looking at. She had taken off her hat. Her face was grey.

'What is it, sweetheart?' Jack was appalled. 'What's the matter?'

'How *could* you?' she shouted. 'When you knew how I felt. How could you just—*fuck* my little bitch of a stepsister?'

Jack swallowed. This was bad. 'It just happened,' he said. 'It wasn't my idea. I was trying to get some sleep in the library and she—'

'Tash, of all people! What's wrong with you, Jack? You're like a dog that has to sniff at every lamppost.'

'It wasn't like that! She practically seduced me.'

'Oh sure.'

451

'She did! She came right in and took off all her clothes—'

'Bollocks, Jack. Do you really expect me to believe that? On the night before her own wedding?'

'It's the truth.' He gestured helplessly. 'I'm sorry. I was mad at you.'

'You even told her that we weren't really a couple. Imagine how great that makes me feel. Imagine how much fun it will be for her to stick the knife in for years to come. But hey—who cares? Jack Madison got his rocks off, and that's what matters, right?'

'It wasn't like that.' Jack felt as if he'd been caught by a sudden wave and was tumbling blindly in its murky turbulence. He struggled to find his footing. 'It didn't mean anything.'

'It does to *me*!' Freya slammed her own chest with her fist, so hard that he heard the thud of knuckle on breastbone. A sudden tenderness made him want to put his arms round her. But her teeth were bared. Her eyes blazed wide. 'What kind of a friend are you? I ask you to do *one thing*—pretend that we're a couple, for four lousy days. But you can't do it—one temptation, and you cave in. You're pathetic, Jack!'

'Now wait a minute. *You* were the one who pushed me away. It would never have happened if we'd—'

'Oh, for Christ's sake, grow up! "It didn't mean anything." "It wasn't my idea."' Her mimicry was savage. 'I don't give a shit who you have sex with. This isn't about Tash. It's about you. About what a useless human being you are.'

Her words poured over him—burning, unstoppable.

'Everything's always someone else's fault—your dad, your publisher, Tash, me. You always take the easy way out. You want constant adulation without making any effort to earn it. All the advantages in the world have been showered on you, and you've squandered every one of them. You're too spineless to commit to *anything*—whether it's a woman, or a friend, or even your own writing.'

'That's not fair!'

'Isn't it?' Her face twisted with contempt. 'Let me tell you the truth, Jack. You're a spoilt dilettante living on Daddy's money. You'll never finish your novel because you're too lazy! You will never be a real writer, because you have no respect for the human heart.'

Freya let out a shuddering breath. There was a long silence. Something was hurting. Jack looked down and saw what she had thrown at him. It was a bunch of flowers—roses. A thorn had drawn a trickle of blood.

When she spoke again, it was with a quiet hopelessness that was more damning than her anger.

'I opened up my whole life to you, Jack. I thought you were someone I could rely on. Someone I could trust. I thought we were *friends* . . .'

Her voice broke on the word. Her head drooped. Jack saw that she was crying. A great cavity opened in his chest.

She looked into his face. Her eyes were raw with tears. 'I keep trying to like you, Jack, but I *can't* . . .'

He stepped forward. 'Freya—'

'Get away from me!' She gave a violent swing of her arm, and nearly fell. She gripped the edge of the sink. 'Get out! Out of this house and out of my life. I never want to see you again.'

Because it was a weekend at the start of the summer season all the flights to New York were full. Jack had ended up spending the night in Heathrow Airport.

Finally, midmorning on Sunday, he had been offered a last-minute seat on some Middle Eastern airline, and had handed over his credit card without even bothering to ask the price. He wanted to be out of the airport before Freya turned up for her own flight—the one he would have accompanied her on if everything hadn't gone wrong.

He felt tired and sick at heart. Though he longed for oblivion, sleep was impossible. Reeling with shock, he'd packed his bag, propped an adequately brief thank-you note to Guy and Annabelle on the kitchen table, and slunk out of the house like a thief. But now answers and explanations clamoured in his head, demanding expression. Jack shifted this way and that on his seat, edgy with frustration. Finally, he reached down for the rucksack he had stowed under it, drew out a pen and his writer's notebook and began to write.

> *Dear Freya,*
>
> *I know you'll want to scrunch up this letter when you see who it's from—but don't. Just for once, listen to what someone else has to say.*
>
> *Yes, I slept with Tash. It was an incredibly stupid thing to do. Maybe it's not an excuse to say that I was angry and drunk, or that she deliberately set out to seduce me, but that's the truth. I'm not proud of myself. I don't regard Tash as a 'conquest'. I'm sorry it happened.*
>
> *But, Freya—let's be honest. Can you give me any good reason why I shouldn't sleep with Tash, or with any other woman? You don't want me: that's crystal clear. You threw me out of the bedroom—remember?*

Jack paused, and frowned at the words he had just written. Freya's words were now flooding back to him in a strong, stinging tide, filling him with rage.

The real truth is, your pride is hurt. You don't want me, but you wanted everyone at that wedding to think that I wanted you. Doesn't that strike you as a little unfair? Why don't you think about other people, for a change? Your poor father, for example, who obviously adores you. Are you still blaming him for marrying another woman more than twenty years ago?

And what about me? We've been friends for so long. OK, I stand rejected. Throw away ten years of friendship if you want. I have other things to think about.

Like what? Jack asked himself, as he stabbed an emphatic, black full stop into the paper. His pen hovered, and then began to race again across the notepad: *I'm sorry you don't think much of me as a writer. It's good to know the truth after all these years. You don't understand how hard it is to write a book—to reach right down into the depths of oneself and—*

And in that moment Jack did reach down into the depths of himself. He slammed down his pen, closed his eyes and sank his head back on the headrest. All he could see was Freya's crumpled face and the tears in her eyes. He had hurt her. He had made her cry. Freya *never* cried. He could justify himself to kingdom come, but nothing could eradicate the pain in her face, and the knowledge that he had inflicted it.

The real truth tore at his heart. Freya was right. It wasn't the sex with Tash that mattered; it was his betrayal of Freya. She had trusted him, and he had delivered her into the hands of her bitterest enemy.

And she was right about his book. It was his own fault he hadn't finished it. She might even be right about his talent.

Jack reached out his hand to smother the page in front of him and crush it into a tight ball. He squeezed it in his fist, tighter and tighter, smaller and smaller.

'*I keep trying to like you, Jack, but I can't . . .*'

He didn't blame her. He was a failure.

'*I never want to see you again.*'

Well, fine. She wouldn't.

Freya had only one thought in her head when she arrived back in New York, and that was to see Cat. Cat would understand. Cat would open a bottle of something and sit up late with her, listening for as long as it took. Cat would help Freya to tear Jack to shreds. Together they would denounce Tash as a slut and a snake. At last Freya would be able to give vent to the rage and misery that she had been forced to keep hidden, a smouldering, spitting, crackling furnace inside her.

She had told the family that Jack's father was seriously ill—a heart attack—and that Jack had flown straight home to be with him. She was almost certain that her own father didn't believe her; there were too many holes in her story. (Why hadn't she gone with Jack, to comfort him? Why hadn't she at least driven him to the station?) Freya saw that he was wounded by her reticence, but she could do nothing.

She had cried practically all the way back on the plane—hating herself for this display of weakness, embarrassed by the curious gaze of other passengers, but too tired and wretched to stop. In a daze, she had taken a cab into the city and let herself into her new, charmless apartment: two boxy rooms and no view, overwhelmingly silent and empty. The belongings she had brought over from Jack's last week stood in a forlorn pile on the bedroom floor. There wasn't a scrap of food in the fridge. Outside, it was raining.

She stayed only long enough to take a lightning shower and change into clean jeans and a shirt. At the last minute she called Cat to make sure she was in—though where else would Cat be at nine o'clock on a rainy Sunday evening? The number was busy, and Freya was too impatient to wait. Besides, if Cat was talking on the telephone, that meant she was home. Freya threw on her raincoat and plunged out into the street, head bent against the rain. Cat's apartment was only a few blocks away. Freya practically ran the whole way. Finally she pushed through the door to Cat's building and raced into the elevator.

Now she was outside Cat's door, ringing the bell. *Quick, Cat! Hurry!* But nothing happened. She rang a second time: still nothing. She leaned her cheek against the door and moaned in despair. *Where are you?* Then she sniffed—and sniffed again. Was that or was that not the pungent aroma of Cat's legendary *spaghetti alla putanesca*? Freya rang the bell again, and started to pound on the door. 'It's me!' she yelled. 'Let me in!'

Almost at once she heard movements, then the click of the lock. The door opened, and there was Cat—familiar, wonderful Cat. Freya stumbled into the apartment and threw her arms round Cat's neck. 'Thank God you're here!'

Cat tottered backwards under her weight. 'What is it? What happened?' She steadied herself on Freya's shoulders. Her eyes swept over Freya's face and bedraggled hair, wide with concern. 'You haven't been attacked, have you?'

'Much worse.' Freya began pulling off her raincoat. 'You won't believe what happened to me in England.'

'But you're not hurt? I mean, physically.'

'Well, no.' Freya glanced at Cat, slightly perplexed to be taxed on this point. 'But I've had the most ghastly time.' She tossed the raincoat onto a chair and swept back her wet hair.

'Freya—' Cat began urgently.

'I *hate* men, Cat. Don't you?'

'Well, that's just—'

'Let's get a drink, and I'll tell you what happened.' Freya brushed past Cat, leading the way round the corner of a tall bookcase that divided the entranceway from the rest of the living room.

'Freya, *wait!*'

Afterwards, Freya recognised that she had absorbed multiple impressions in a single second—the unusually dim, romantic lighting; Cat's small dining table set for two, lit by a flickering candle; the warm smell of cooking; a sound behind her that was part gasp, part guilty moan; the belated realisation that Cat was far too stylishly dressed for a normal Sunday-night chill, and had deliberately not answered her door at the first ring. But at the time, all she felt was simple astonishment. There was a *man* in Cat's apartment. And that man was Michael. He stood stiffly between her and the dining table from which he had obviously just risen, for he was still clutching a linen napkin.

Freya and Michael stared at one another in shocked silence. Freya could not make sense of his presence here. Then Michael's gaze slid to a point beyond her, and his expression subtly altered. Freya whirled round, just in time to catch the same expression on Cat's face. It was a look of complicity—of utter, naked intimacy. Freya's eyes darted from one to the other. Cat and Michael. Michael and Cat. Her best friend and her ex-lover: together.

'Whoops,' she said, attempting a laugh.

Cat was coming towards her, reaching for her hands. 'Sweetie, don't be upset. Let me explain.'

'We were going to tell you as soon as you got back from England,' Michael added, stepping forward to stand beside Cat.

'The thing is, there was nothing to tell—not at first.'

'I only met Caterina a couple of weeks ago.'

Caterina?

'Everything's moved so fast.'

'It's a surprise even to us.'

The word 'us' gave Freya a piercing sense of exclusion.

'I've been almost crazy with guilt.' Cat stared up at her with pleading eyes. 'But I couldn't help it. These things happen. Please don't be upset.' She tugged at Freya's hands, trying to get through to her. 'I couldn't stand it if you were upset.'

Freya drew herself up, tall and dignified. 'Why would I be upset?' she enquired, disengaging her hands. 'You're both free agents. It's nothing to do with me. Look, I've had a long flight, and I'm tired. And your dinner's getting cold.'

'Fuck the dinner! Stay and talk with us,' Cat begged.

'Maybe another time, OK?' Freya took a step backwards and sketched a stiff wave. 'Have a nice evening,' she said carefully. Then she retreated swiftly round the bookcase. There were footsteps behind her, and a beseeching call from Cat, but now Freya had her palm pressed tight against her mouth and couldn't have answered even if she'd wanted to. She grabbed her raincoat from the chair, pulled open the door and ran to the elevator.

As soon as she reached the lobby, Freya bolted out into the dark street. But having got there, she stood stock-still in the middle of the slick sidewalk, not knowing what to do or where to go. She felt utterly bereft. People streamed past her as she stood in the rain. They muttered and shouted at her to get out of the way, yet still she didn't move. She had a sudden, fearful vision of this whole, huge sea of humanity receding further and further until she was left standing quite alone. She sensed that this was a turning point. Either she could retreat to her silent apartment and lock herself in, alone and safe; or she could go back up to Cat and Michael, dispel the shadow she had cast on their happiness, and readmit herself into their lives. Freya hugged her coat tight as the rain spattered and bounced. Which was it to be?

Chapter Fourteen

JACK SLOWED THE CAR on the rutted track, braked to a halt, and reached for the piece of paper on which he had scrawled directions to the cabin. He'd been to the mountains before. The Madisons had a place down near Asheville, the summer playground for moneyed Carolinians where Jack had spent vacations swimming and rafting with his brother Lane. As a student, he'd come roistering up here with friends, to ski in winter and hang out in summer. But he'd never been so far north before, and he'd never come alone. This part of his home state was known as the

High Country, the Lost Provinces, or simply 'out there'. He was beginning to see why.

Jack gazed out across the scene with a flicker of misgiving. Blue afternoon shadows lay on the steep, wooded hillsides. Down in the valley the grass looked smooth and soft as billiard-table baize. A dark, snaking line of pine and dogwood marked the course of the New River, and far in the distance he caught the greenish gleam of its rushing passage. The country was beautiful, but wild and lonely. The resort towns had petered out. For the last several miles he'd climbed steadily along winding dirt-and-gravel roads, past lonely farmsteads with their big red barns and grazing cattle. He'd burned his boats now. His apartment was in the hands of a realtor; his belongings were in storage—all except the things in the trunk of his car. The car itself he had hired at the airport in Charlotte, and would return to the nearest drop-off point as soon as he found an old jalopy to buy. Studying the map again, Jack concluded that he was on the right road, unpromising as it looked. He pulled on a battered fishing hat to shade his eyes from the sun, and pressed on.

It hadn't taken him more than twelve hours back in New York to realise that he had to get out of the city. After Cornwall, Manhattan's frenetic pace jarred. The double-whammy of losing his allowance and his book contract meant that he couldn't afford to stay anyway. Most tormenting of all was the knowledge that Freya was only a mile or two away, despising him. He could almost sniff her corrosive contempt in the grimy air. *Lazy . . . spoilt . . . dilettante.*

What he needed, he decided, was a writer's retreat—nothing fancy, just somewhere peaceful so he could shut himself away and concentrate on his novel. His stepmother Lauren lived in Virginia now, in a pleasant, comfortable house; it occurred to Jack that her guest room might be the perfect place, and he called her up to suggest it. To his chagrin, Lauren did not share his enthusiasm for this plan. Still, within twenty-four hours she'd called him back with a proposal. A friend of hers owned an old vacation place up in the mountains that had been in the family for generations. There was no electricity, and her friend wasn't sure exactly what state it was in, but Jack was welcome to stay there rent-free so long as he repaired the house and made it secure. Jack had accepted eagerly.

A hand-painted sign was coming up on the left and Jack ducked his head to peer through the windscreen. 'Feed Store,' he read. Good. He felt a surge of excitement; the adventure was about to begin. And here at last was the private track, so overgrown that he almost missed it. He heard the crunch of pine needles under the tyres and gunned the car up a sudden incline. He rounded one bend, then another, then coasted to a stop as his foot slid off the accelerator in shock. Ahead of him was a miniature forest of shoulder-high hogweed, above which he could just discern a sloping tin roof swathed in creepers and the upper half of rough log walls. It was a shack, a wreck.

Switching off the engine, he swung the car door open and climbed out. Silence enveloped him like a shroud, and for a moment he experienced something akin to panic. Then he pulled himself together, excavated the carjack from the back of the car, and used it to beat a path to the narrow raised porch and lever off the defensive planks from the front door opening. Behind, the door itself hung ajar off broken hinges. Jack took a step inside.

He was now standing in a biggish room, maybe fifteen feet by twenty, with a roughly sawn floor and walls. At one end was a square pine table and a rickety gas stove; at the other, pulled close to the stone fireplace, were two chairs and a couch with the stuffing half torn out of them. There were drifts of dead leaves and a choking layer of dust. Jack discovered two small windows, covered by makeshift shutters, and a further door that led into a tiny back room, furnished with a bare bedstead, a plain country chair, and a splintered rail that must once have been used for hanging clothes. That was it.

Jack went back outside and sat on the porch steps, fighting down his dismay. He wondered about trying to find an inn or a hotel, just for tonight, but it would be dark in an hour. Anyway, that would merely postpone the problem, and he didn't have money to squander.

He used the remaining span of daylight to gather a stack of brushwood, reconnoitre a source of water, and sweep out the cabin with a surprisingly serviceable broom located in a lean-to shed. When the mosquitoes began to bite and the bats to swoop, he exchanged his shorts for jeans, pulled on an old sweater and carried a selection of items from the car to the cabin. By the time he had finally wedged the broken door shut, the sky was black as pitch. Jack built himself a fire, more for light and comfort than warmth, and sat on his sleeping-bag in front of it, munching his way through a mega-sandwich and two apples, while he made a list of all the things he would need to buy tomorrow. Around ten o'clock it began to rain. Raindrops pinged on the tin roof and dripped through multiple leaks. The chimney smoked ferociously. Jack took off his shoes and slid fully clothed into the sleeping-bag, resting his head on his folded jacket and staring into the flickering flames. Arthur Miller, he remembered, had built his own cabin before moving into it to write *Death of a Salesman*. Jack conceded that he was not Arthur Miller, but his Madison pride was seeping back. He would not be beaten.

It took him five days to make the cabin habitable. He fixed the water pump, scythed the hogweed flat and piled it in the woods, patched up the roof and rehung the door. He replaced the mosquito screens and cleared the chimney of birds' nests. In the small, sleepy local town he bought a secondhand stove and fridge, plus the gas canisters to fuel them, and invested in three brand-new kerosene lamps. He solved the problem of a bed by slinging a hammock across one corner of the cabin, and was almost getting used to sleeping in it. The small back room he turned into his study, with a desk made from an old door propped on sawn rounds of pine logs, securely nailed. Parked outside under the trees stood his new vehicle, a wheezy pick-up.

Finally he was ready to start writing. His old portable typewriter sat square and neat on the makeshift desk, alongside a high stack of virgin paper and several folders containing his notes and unfinished script. Jack made a ceremony of his first day of real work. He got up early, shaved in front of the mirror he had hung on a tree outside, fixed himself coffee and a ham-and-eggs breakfast, dressed in shorts and a clean T-shirt and seated himself in his bare wooden cell. Pumped full of hope and determination, he reached for a folder and took out the familiar script. Ah yes. 'The ship was in the harbour . . .'

Five hours later, Jack slammed his hand on the desk in frustration and strode outside to the front porch, glowering at the magnificent view. He was still stuck. The story was there, but he could not breathe life into it. For the rest of that day and the next two days Jack wrestled with the problem. Sweat poured off him as the July sun beat on the tin roof and turned his study into an oven. He cursed himself for all the hours he'd wasted back in New York when he could have been writing in comfort, with all the conveniences of air conditioning and a computer. Time was ticking by. His money might just last for three months. This time, his deadline was immovable.

On the fourth day he rose at first light, pulled on his hiking boots, slung a rucksack over his shoulders, and set off into the woods. Morning cloud hung thick and damp over the trees. The pine-spiced air was alive with the whistle of birds and gurgle of cold, clear streams. His eyes absorbed the scenery, as a strengthening sun turned it from misty sepia to vibrant colour, but his mind was focused on the story he was trying to write. It hung there like a hologram: he could see it, but he couldn't feel it. As the miles passed and the path wound upwards, Jack's thoughts began to drift—childhood memories, scenes from movies, and then—without warning—Freya. He had been trying to shut her out of his thoughts, but suddenly she was achingly close. He could feel the bouquet in his hands, the prick of thorns; he could see the twist of her body as she clutched the sink. *You have no respect for the human heart.*The memory brought shame and tenderness, regret and self-doubt in a powerful, swirling mix.

He climbed on automatically towards the bald pate of a granite mountain-top that was his goal. Finally he reached the summit, panting a little, and stood to admire the landscape that unrolled beneath him to a hazy horizon. He was struck by its ordered perfection. Seen from this vantage point, the terrain that seemed so confusing at ground level now assumed an irresistible logic. He could see how streams connected with rivers, why farmers had shaped their fields to certain precise patterns, how the interlocking hills created a mirror image of interlocking valleys. He wished he could discern the structure of his novel this clearly.

In that instant, Jack's thoughts about writing and his feelings about Freya connected, striking a spark of insight that flamed into life and illuminated his whole book. He saw that in worrying over structure and theme he had forgotten the human heart of his story—forgotten it because he had refused to look into his own heart for so long. He sat down on the bare rock, overwhelmed by a sense of release and excitement. Instead of stifling all these unwelcome emotions—guilt, envy, pride, doubt—he would face them, and harness the insights they brought to drive his narrative forward. Ideas, scenes, whole passages of dialogue began to race out of his brain, like fishing lines that had finally hooked onto something live.

It was late afternoon by the time Jack returned to the cabin. He washed hastily, throwing off his clothes and upending a bucket of spring water over his head. Then he dressed and hurried to his desk, grabbing a hunk of bread and a piece of cheese on the way. His muscles ached but his brain was jumping. He placed two lamps on either side of his type-writer. Even as he was sitting down, connections snapped together in his head. Fleetingly he wondered where Freya was. Then the conscious thought of her was swept away under an intoxicating rush of words. Placing his work-scratched hands on the keys, he began to type.

Freya was in Chelsea, having spent the afternoon poking around disused garages and run-down warehouses. Two weeks ago Lola Preiss had announced her intention to move the downtown gallery out of SoHo. Several of the cannier dealers were moving up to Chelsea and Lola didn't want to be left behind. She had instructed Freya to draw up a short list of likely sites.

Now it was after five. There was no point going back to work.

Instead, she walked out to the end of one of the old shipping piers and stared at the river for a bit, then retraced her steps and began to thread her way through small leafy streets, aiming vaguely for the subway station. Everything looked very familiar—the decorative wrought-iron hoops round the trees, the potholed sidewalk. She did, in fact, seem to be in Jack's street. She hoped he wouldn't be looking out of his window. She did not wish to see him. But so long as she stayed on the opposite side of the street from his apartment, she'd be safe.

Glancing across, she saw that there were builders at work on something, cluttering the kerbside with their usual paraphernalia. Soon the neighbourhood would be full of bankers, and its character would change. As she drew closer, her idle nostalgia sharpened to surprise. It was Jack's house that was under reconstruction; specifically, it was Jack's own apartment that was being gutted. What was going on?

Without pausing to think, Freya dashed across the street and asked the builders if they were working for a Mr Madison. Nobody knew, but they were pretty sure some new people were moving in.

Freya gripped the front railings and stared into the empty shell of the apartment she had known so well. Now that the first shock had passed, she realised that there was nothing strange in the fact that Jack had moved. He'd said he couldn't afford to stay. She told herself that it was silly to feel unsettled. It was of no interest to her where Jack had gone. Jack was a bastard. She never wanted to see him again.

Never. The word seemed to reverberate in her chest. She saw the long months stretching ahead—July, August, September . . . Surely he'd come back in September, to start his teaching courses?

But what if he didn't? What if she had driven him away for good? She couldn't even remember the name of his home town. Oakville? Oakland? Oh, what did it matter? She stepped straight off the kerb at 10th Avenue and almost collided with a cyclist, who swerved wildly. Freya wondered what Jack had done with Rosinante. *Where are you?* she shouted angrily in her head. But there was no answer.

Jack had settled into a routine now. Every day he got up with the birds at dawn, washed, dressed and did the necessary chores. Then he wrote right through the day until five, when he went out for a long evening hike or a swim in the stream, and sometimes caught himself a trout for supper. At night he'd settle by the fire and revise what he'd written that day and make notes for tomorrow. Then he'd climb into his hammock and be asleep by ten. He felt healthy and energised and the routine kept him focused. Slowly the pages were building on his desk.

Saturday afternoons were the exceptions, when he spruced himself up and jumped in the pick-up for a brief return to civilisation. First, Jack would check to see if he had any mail waiting at the post office, though there usually wasn't, because hardly anyone knew he was here. Then he'd shop for food and supplies. Once or twice, as he passed the display of postcards, he'd thought of sending one to Freya—just a one-liner, a signal. But what could he say? After shopping, at the unfashionably early hour of six o'clock he'd go to the Barbecue and Pickin' Parlor, where he'd eat a mountain of chicken, ribs, beef and pork, served on a wooden, pig-shaped platter with creamed corn, biscuits and gravy. Then he'd stagger back to his truck and drive home to read by the fire.

Today was a sizzler, even though a new bronze veil on the upper mountain slopes warned that autumn was already on its way. Jack parked the pick-up on the main street and headed quickly for the shade of the post office with its clanking fan.

'Looks like you're Mr Popular today,' said the man at the counter when Jack finally reached the small window, and he handed over three letters. Jack took them over to a corner, feeling curiously uneasy as he noted that his father, Lauren and Candace had all chosen to write to him at the same time. He decided to open Candace's letter first. He slit open the envelope, and took out what was evidently a long and important communication.

Dear Jack, he read. *I'm afraid that the news I have to tell you will come as a terrible shock . . .*

Chapter **Fifteen**

Three months later

'DON'T BE NERVOUS.'

'*I am not nervous!* . . . How do I look?'

'You look fabulous and beautiful—and radiant and serene—and all the other things a bride's supposed to be.'

'What about my hair? I hate November: New York's always so windy.'

'Your hair is perfection. We're in a cab, remember?'

'What if he isn't there?'

'He'll be there. Stop fiddling with your bouquet.'

'But I was so mean to him!'

'And he was horrible to you. You've forgiven each other. That's what love means.'

'I think I'm going to faint.'

'You are not going to faint.'

'I really love him, you know.'

'I know.'

The church was stuffy and the bride late. This was the third time that the organist had played 'Jesu, Joy of Man's Desiring'. Jack felt hot and constricted in this ridiculous outfit. He could feel the stock around his neck pushing his chin into an aggressive tilt.

Still, he'd promised Candace, and he'd promised his father. He had to go through with it.

'OK: deep breath. Are you ready?'

'You go first.'

'Don't be silly.'

'Take a peek. Please. For me?'

The door to the church stood ajar. A modest aisle paved in coloured tiles led through rows of seats, packed with murmuring guests. At the far end a man waited, rigid with anxiety, staring at a colourful representation of the Crucifixion. Freya smiled. Michael turned his head, and his face flooded with such joy and relief that her eyes pricked with tears.

'We are gathered together to join this man and this woman in holy matrimony, which is an honourable estate . . .'

Jack caught his stepmother's eye. She winked, and for an instant his tension relaxed. Lauren had been the last wife but two: his father had never taken marriage very seriously.

Yet the solemnity of the service made it hard not to take marriage seriously. Love. Fidelity. Fortitude. Endurance. It felt quite different to be up here at the altar instead of sitting among the congregation.

'Do you, Candace Marie, take this man to be your lawful wedded husband . . .'

Jack snapped to attention. His big moment was coming up. *Where was the ring?*

'Do you, Michael Josiah, take this woman to be your lawful wedded wife—to have and to hold from this day forward?'

'I do.'

Freya looked at his face, so proud and excited. She had never seen his brown eyes glow like this, or such a tender curve to his smile. Love was truly amazing: powerful, irresistible, unpredictable. Who could have guessed that out of all the women in the world, the right one for Michael would be her dear friend Cat, whose face shone with the same happy confidence as she repeated the marriage vows?

Freya felt humbled. How little she knew of human nature. Here were two people she could have sworn would dislike each other on sight; yet they had slotted together like a key in a lock, opening the door to a new future together. It looked so easy. *If only* . . .

'I now pronounce you man and wife.'

A chorus of uninhibited sobs broke out behind her. That would be Cat's mother and the other da Fillipo women. Italians were so emotional. A cascade of glorious, liquid music poured from the organ loft. Freya ducked her head and glared at the tips of her exquisite new shoes. Just for a moment, she was feeling rather Italian herself.

'Congratulations, *Mrs Madison*.' Jack bent to kiss the bride.

Candace smiled at him triumphantly. She was practically airborne on a waft of gauzy white material—veils and trains and other stuff he couldn't name. There was no sign of the tongue stud today.

Across the street half of Oaksboro—the half who hadn't been invited to the wedding—crowded the sidewalk in a scuffle of red and yellow leaves, and peered from the windows of red-brick storefronts. It was just late enough in the afternoon for the football game to be over. What could be more interesting than to loiter in the last rays of a dying November sun, memorising every last detail of the latest Madison bride? Jack wondered what they made of it all.

'Come on, everybody.' Jack winced at the commanding boom of his father's voice. 'Let's go back to the house and *celebrate!*'

'Sweetie, how can I ever thank you?' Cat threw her arms around Freya. 'You've been wonderful.'

'Don't be silly. I just—'

'No, she's right.' Michael gave Freya's elbow an appreciative squeeze. 'We'd never have got this organised without you. You've done a great job.'

'Nonsense. Thank *you* for giving me the chance. I've loved doing it.' Freya smiled. She hadn't done this much smiling for months.

They all stood beaming at each other until Freya pretended to remember that there was something vital she must check, and managed to shoo Michael and Cat away to join their guests. She watched them go with mingled affection and relief. It wasn't that she *minded* that Cat and Michael had fallen in love. She hadn't minded helping Cat to choose her outfit, compile her wedding-gift list, order the flowers, arrange the reception. She hadn't even minded being a bridesmaid. It was just a little . . . painful. There was still a slight awkwardness between the three of them, though they did their best to pretend otherwise.

Freya was glad now that she had gone back up to Cat's apartment that terrible, rainy night, though it had taken every scrap of courage she possessed to put her own misery aside, and absolve Cat and Michael of guilt. She was proud of herself for behaving so well.

On the home front, she had finally signed a rental lease on a long-term apartment and redecorated it herself. It was a lovely apartment with a sunny aspect and heart-lifting views; there was even a small spare room for her father, who was coming to visit next month.

At a personal level, although Freya had told Cat about Jack and Tash—and Cat had denounced Jack in a very satisfying, robust manner—she hadn't gone on and on about it. It seemed selfish to wallow in misery when Cat was so happy; Freya had made a big effort to redirect her energies into showing how delighted she was for her friend.

Freya lost herself in the crowd, chatting and trying to suppress memories of the last wedding she had attended. This was Cat and Michael's day, and she wanted it to be perfect. At one point she caught sight of the pair of them together, Cat talking animatedly while Michael watched mesmerised. Cat was carrying her nephew Tonito on one hip, his fat legs tucked comfortably round her waist. She glowed with happiness. Freya was prepared to bet that Cat would be pregnant within the year.

Freya kept herself busy, checking that the food and drink were circulating, that there were enough chairs for the older guests, and helping to fill glasses for the toasts. Then everybody gathered close, someone rapped on a table for silence and Cat's father stepped forward. His dark eyes raked the room. 'I have only one question,' he growled. 'Why did it take her so long?' Freya listened with affection as he talked about Cat's character and achievements—her big heart, her fighting spirit, her tiny forgivable flaws—until, with an old-fashioned formality that she found moving, he took his daughter's hand and placed it in that of her husband's.

After the speeches, time seemed to hurtle forward. A car had been booked to take Cat and Michael to the airport; they were flying to the Caribbean. There were suitcases to be taken downstairs. Cat and Michael slipped upstairs to change.

While she waited for them to reappear, Freya noticed Cat's grandmother sitting alone, apparently overwhelmed by the noise and bustle.

She must be well into her eighties, poor thing. Freya walked over and stooped low. 'May I bring you something?'

The old woman took her hand gratefully and drew her into the next chair, glad of someone to talk to. In her eccentrically accented English she told Freya what a marvellous party it was, how handsome she thought Michael, how lovely Cat looked in her wedding suit. Mrs da Fillipo stroked Freya's hand while she talked.

'You are not married?' she asked.

The question took Freya by surprise. She looked down at her ringless fingers, suddenly jolted out of the comfortable mundanity of small talk. 'No,' she said shortly.

'But why not? You are so pretty.'

Freya tossed her head. 'Men aren't everything.'

'That depends on the man.' The faded eyes peered shrewdly into her own. 'You have never been in love?'

Freya felt her lip tremble. *Please stop!* 'Oh, love,' she shrugged. 'It's such a silly word. I mean, how can you tell?'

Mrs da Fillipo smiled and patted her hand kindly, as if they both knew Freya was talking nonsense. 'The first time I saw my husband,' she said, 'was at his engagement party to someone else. But that didn't stop me.' She chuckled. 'A woman always knows. And when she knows, she must *act*.'

'But . . . it isn't always easy to know what to do.' Freya dropped her flippant tone and met the old lady's gaze frankly.

Mrs da Fillipo gripped her hand tight. 'You must follow your heart,' she urged. 'You *must*. Gianni and I were married for fifty-six years. I miss him every day.' Her kind, creased face clouded with sorrow. Freya swallowed hard.

'Oh, look!' she said brightly, pointing at Cat and Michael, who had reappeared in casual holiday clothes and were making their sentimental farewells. Cat came over to say goodbye to her grandmother, and Freya gave up her seat to allow them some privacy.

Finally the bride and groom were ready to leave. They stood together at the front door, with guests gathered around them in a tight circle to wish them well. 'Goodbye, everybody!' shouted Cat. With a theatrical wave of her arm she tossed something into the air.

The bouquet sailed up to the ceiling high above Freya's head, where it seemed to hang for long seconds. Then it spun downwards in a whirl of cream and gold and bronze. Freya saw its tiny petals catch the light and turn into a shower of sparks. Down it came, faster and faster. Oh no! It was heading straight for her. Surely someone else would catch it? *Please*.

But no one did. At the last moment she put out her hand and caught it. *Aaaah* . . . sighed the crowd. *Bravo!*

Freya stared into the tender open hearts of the flowers. They were so beautiful. Her fingers tightened on the stems. Then she burst into tears.

There was a ripple of consternation. Freya covered her face with her hand. *Please . . . no! Don't do this, Freya*. But she couldn't control the gasps that jerked her shoulders and tore at her chest.

'Sweetie, what is it?' Suddenly Cat's arms were around her.

'Nothing,' Freya sobbed. Everyone—*everyone*—was watching. She was ruining Cat's wedding. How could she?

'Tell me,' Cat asked gently. 'What's the matter.'

'I don't *know*,' wailed Freya. 'You go. Please.' She flapped her hand.

'I'm not leaving you like this.' Cat's voice was low but firm. 'Come on, we'll go somewhere quiet and talk.'

'You'll miss your plane, Mikey.' Mrs Petersen's chiding, singsong voice sliced through the silence.

Cat's head snapped up. 'The plane can wait!' she answered back. She put a protective arm round Freya's shoulders and shepherded her to the doorway, where Michael hovered anxiously. As the two of them stumbled past and headed for a door marked LADIES, Freya saw Cat and Michael exchange a look. Michael nodded. He'd wait.

Then Freya was in a tiled room that smelt of air freshener. Cat sat her down on an upturned waste bin and crouched in front of her.

'What is it?' she demanded. 'Who upset you?'

'Nobody.' Freya wiped her nose with the back of her wrist.

'Here, let me get you a Kleenex.' Cat rummaged through her capacious handbag, discarding items on the floor until she found a travel-pack of tissues, which she tore open and passed to Freya. She waited until Freya had blown her nose, then grasped her hands.

'Oh baby, maybe we should have waited longer.'

'No, no.' Freya shook her head. 'It isn't anything to do with you and Michael.'

'Then what is it?'

Freya thrashed her head from side to side. The wave of feeling that had been gathering inside her all day—for weeks—for months—finally broke. 'It's . . . *Jack!*' she burst out.

'Jack?' Cat rolled onto her heels. Her eyes were wide. Her hair practically crackled with shock. 'As in "that bastard Jack"?'

'He's not a bastard.' Freya blew her nose loudly.

'I don't get this.' Cat frowned. 'I thought you told him you never wanted to see him again.'

'I *know* . . .' Freya wailed. 'But I think he was The One.'

'Oh, sweetie . . .'

'And now he's *married!*'

'*What?*'

Freya ground the heels of her hands into her forehead. 'It's all my fault. I drove him away. And now I'll never see him again.'

Ever since that day in Chelsea, her fury and humiliation had begun to abate, to be replaced with a gnawing curiosity. Where was he? What was he doing? What was he thinking? She replayed the events in Cornwall over and over again. It hadn't been all bad. Some moments had been good. In fact, some had been *marvellous*. She couldn't stop thinking about him. By September, she'd been desperate enough to search for the phone number of the Madison home in Oaksboro (Oaksboro! that was it), and then call. But her call had been answered by a housekeeper. Freya asked tentatively if Jack happened to be there. *Not right now*, came the answer. *He's out to dinner with his fiancée, Miss Twink.* Freya couldn't believe it. She had scrolled through the local papers on the Internet until she'd found the announcement for herself. It was true.

There was an urgent rap at the door. 'Caterina! . . . *Aeroporto!*'

Cat shot furiously to her feet. 'In a minute,' she yelled.

Freya made herself stand up, too. She caught sight of her blotched face in the mirror above the basin, and tried to pull herself together. 'You must go, Cat,' she said. 'It's your wedding day.'

'Fuck the wedding day! My best friend needs me.' Cat threw her arms around Freya and held her close.

There was another knock, gentler this time. 'Uh, darling? The car's outside. When you're ready.'

'I'm coming.' Cat beamed at Freya. 'Isn't he wonderful? Now wash your face. You look terrible.'

While Freya obediently splashed water on her eyes and cheeks, Cat repacked her handbag: passport, paperbacks, mineral water, vitamin capsules. 'Oh look,' she said, 'I picked this up at the bookstore.'

'What?' Freya peered blearily at Cat's reflection. Cat was studying something in her hand. It looked like an invitation.

'Hmm,' said Cat, reading. 'Fifth Avenue . . . very upscale . . . November 8th . . . the day after tomorrow. *Perfect!*'

'What's perfect?' Freya turned to look and gave a cry of repugnance. 'No way!'

'Yes! Don't you see? It's a sign.'

'But that's my birthday! I don't want to go to a bloody singles evening on my birthday.'

'What else are you going to do?'

Freya opened her mouth and closed it again.

'Promise me you'll go, or I'm not leaving.' Cat looked so bossy that Freya couldn't help smiling.

'I promise,' she said.

'Oh, sweetie.' Cat's face softened. She drew Freya into a fierce hug. 'You never know. Look at Michael and me. Anything can happen.'

Chapter Sixteen

JACK STEPPED OUT of the office building and paused for a moment to flip up the collar of his overcoat. While he'd been inside, the sky had darkened from overcast grey to soiled black. Yellow lights blazed and blinked around him. There was the grind and screech of congested traffic. Jack savoured the tainted air while he considered what to do next. He allowed himself to look at his watch, though he knew almost to the minute what time it was. An inner clock had been ticking in his head for days, for months, getting louder and more urgent until now he could think of nothing else but what might—*might*—happen tonight.

He still had an hour to kill. If he took the subway he could be at his destination in twenty minutes—but then what? He decided to walk. Shoving his gloveless hands into his pockets, he slotted himself into the pedestrian traffic and headed south.

It was good to be back in the city. He felt energised by the rush of people on this ordinary Monday evening—young and not so young, fashionably thin and grotesquely fat, glamorous in fur coats, wretched in stained track suits. He liked the feeling that he belonged, that he was one of this elite band of gutsy survivors.

For it seemed, from what Ella had said to him this afternoon, that he had succeeded on one front, at least. His agent had looked him in the eye, laid a reverent hand on the script he had mailed off from the little country post office two weeks ago, and pronounced it 'wonderful'. The best novel she'd read all year. 'Dramatic', 'moving', 'memorable', 'original'. Even the publishers who had cancelled Jack's contract were backtracking wildly. Ella didn't care to put a figure on the probable advance, but she was confident that it would be 'substantial'. The book was good, and he had completed it. That was enough. No one could call him a 'dilettante'. Right at the end he worked practically night and day. He'd had to, in order to finish in time for the wedding.

His pace slowed as he reached a bookstore. The windows were brightly lit and artfully styled, spilling over with desirably packaged books on every subject. One window was devoted to a single title, a first novel which had been rapturously praised and lavishly publicised. Nestling among the books were blown-up photographs of the author, a young man with movie-star looks. Jack stared at the cocksure face, waiting for envy to kick in, but he felt only a swell of sympathy. *A great beginning, kid: make sure it's not the end.*

'Hey, man, watch your back!' He heard a shout and the clink of bottles as a delivery man trundled a handcart past his heels and swivelled it towards the glass entrance. The bookstore must be putting on some kind of shindig—a book reading or an author signing. Jack hitched up his trousers, wondering whether to go in and see.

He checked his watch again, feeling his ribs contract around his lungs. The long countdown was almost over. The bookstore might offer a welcome distraction for the twenty minutes still to go. But what if she was already waiting? Jack shifted from foot to foot, making up his mind, while his breath puffed miniature clouds into the frosty air.

They were so confident, so smiley, so bloody efficient! Chat, exchange card, move on; chat, exchange card, move on—as if they were harvesting a crop, on piecework. Did they then go on a dating binge, or hoard the cards as some kind of illusory insurance against loneliness?

Freya took another sip of her tepid white wine and gazed into the middle distance with a half-smile on her face, as if she wasn't really part of this sad, singles group, but merely sightseeing. Her dress was sleeveless and severely cut, but made out of the softest possible leather, with buttons all the way down the back; she wore very high heels of a purply colour so sensational that it would have been criminal not to buy them. This was quite wrong. Freya didn't fit. All the other women wore business suits with sensible hemlines and nice white blouses. This was turning into one of the worst evenings of her life. She thought of Cat, downing cocktails with the man she loved amid whispering palm trees.

The party was taking place on the bookstore's cavernous first floor. The lights were bright, the temperature stifling. Freya wasn't in the mood for this. She didn't have the energy to start from scratch yet again.

However, she had promised Cat so she must make an effort. Freya straightened her shoulders and braved the chattering hordes. If only Jack was here. If only she hadn't said those terrible things to him. If only he wasn't *married*. Freya could think of no explanation of why Jack had married Candace. Could she be pregnant? Had Jack's father forced him to marry her? Was there some Madison inheritance dependent on marriage?

The touch of a hand on her elbow made her jump. 'Well, well,' said a familiar voice, 'if it isn't the woman who mistook a pocket calculator for her mobile phone.'

It was that literary agent, Leo Brannigan, smiling in his irritatingly superior way. He was wearing the cool-media-person's uniform of casual jacket and immaculate T-shirt. 'How's it going?' he asked with a leer. 'I hear these evenings are great for pick-ups.'

'Oh, I'm not with this lot.' Freya trilled with laughter at the very idea. 'I just, er, came in to buy a book and, er, decided to sneak a free glass of wine. It's my birthday,' she added, as if this were an explanation.

'Oh yeah?' Leo looked unconvinced.

'What about you?' she countered. 'Found any nice girls?'

'*Me?*' Leo's dark brows snapped together. 'No, I've got one of my writers downstairs signing books. I'm just hanging out till he's finished.'

'It's not . . . Jack, is it?'

'Who? Oh—*Jack*. No. Wish it was. He decided to stay with Ella Fogarty.'

Freya nodded. Good for you, Jack, she thought.

'No, I missed a trick there.' Leo gave Freya a brooding look, as if it was her fault. 'I just hope Ella knows how to extract the right level of advance. These publishers are such tightwads.'

'Mmm.' What was he talking about?

'The word is, it's very good. Even better than *Big Sky*.'

Freya tried not to goggle. Jack had finished his book! She took a slurp of wine to cover her surprise. 'I always knew he'd do it,' she croaked.

'It didn't look that way back in the summer,' said Leo. 'Even though I tried getting him on my list I wasn't sure he'd ever perform. Then something happened to him, I don't know what.'

I do, Freya thought. Her heart sang.

'Maybe it was the marriage,' Leo suggested.

'Bollocks!' Freya exclaimed. Catching Leo's startled glance, she added, 'I mean, I don't see why that should have any impact on his writing.'

'Well, I do. I'd say that was a real punch in the balls.'

'Would you?' Freya smiled brightly. *What* was a punch in the balls?

'I mean, from the old man,' continued Leo helpfully.

Freya frowned. 'What, you mean cutting off his allowance?'

'The guy had an *allowance*! Jeez, these spoilt rich boys. No, I mean the business with the girlfriend. The one he married.' Leo's tone implied that she was a half-wit. 'What a great story. There's a novel right there.'

'You think so?' Freya was utterly mystified.

'Well, sure! You introduce your girlfriend to your father, and the next thing you know they're getting married. It's your worst fucking nightmare.' He cackled maliciously.

Freya stared at him, open-mouthed. There was a strange noise in her head, like one of those complex 3-D puzzles clicking into place. The very week she'd left for England with Jack, Candace had gone out on the town with Jack's father. Jack's father liked women. Candace liked money. Candace wanted to *be* someone. Leo had said 'father'. Freya took a gasp of breath as the glorious, miraculous, obvious truth arrowed into her brain and finally hit the bull's-eye. Candace had married Jack Madison *senior*! Which meant . . . *which meant that Jack wasn't married after all!!!* She burst into hysterical laughter.

Leo was looking at her as if she'd finally flipped.

'I just think it's terribly funny,' she explained. *He wasn't married!*

'You women are so callous.' Leo shook his head in disgust. 'Just think how upset the poor guy must be about it.'

'Don't be daft!' Freya scoffed. 'Jack wouldn't care who married her. She's a bimbo, for heaven's sake. Jack's much too good for her. I mean, he's so . . . talented and so . . . funny . . . and nice and handsome and—'

'Oh, I get it . . .' Leo gave her a sly look. 'I heard you'd moved in with him for a while. But you couldn't get your hands on him because of this other girl, right? Now the field is clear, you can start chasing him again.'

Freya drew herself up tall. 'I was never chasing Jack,' she informed him with dignity. 'We were just friends.'

'Oh sure,' he said sceptically. 'Then how come you're not with him now instead of hounding poor single men?'

'What?' He'd lost her again.

He sighed at her stupidity. 'Didn't you say it was your birthday?'

'So?'

'You know: you and Jack—the bet? Don't tell me you've forgotten.'

Freya stared at him. Her heart was beginning to pound. Of course she hadn't forgotten. The scene had replayed a thousand times in her mind.

'*The bet!*' she shrieked, so loudly that the room hushed for a moment and everyone stared. Her mind whirled. The 8th at eight. *Today*. Oh God, he might be there now!

She grabbed Leo's wrist and looked at his watch. Nine fifteen. He'd think she wasn't coming—that she didn't care—that she'd meant it when she said she never wanted to see him again. *Oh Jack, wait!*

The waiter pounced on Jack's empty glass and shot him a dirty look. Jack had lingered for almost an hour over two Bloody Marys; outside, there was a queue waiting for tables. Yet again the waiter asked if he should open the champagne; yet again Jack told him to wait.

How much longer? Jack had spent many hours of his life waiting for women. In female terms, Freya was barely late at all. Candace, for example, had kept his poor father waiting in the Oaksboro church for forty-five minutes—and that was for her own wedding. But she had turned up in the end. They were on their honeymoon now in Candace's dream destination, Las Vegas.

Her note had been lying on the hallway floor of his apartment when he got back from Cornwall.

You bastard! Harry from upstairs told me where you've gone and who with. I always thought there was something between you and Her. Well, I have too much respect for myself as a woman to play "second fiddle". It is time for me to focus on my own life-goals and fulfil my potential as a human being. DON'T call me.

It had not immediately occurred to Jack that Candace's 'life-goal' might be to marry his own father. Once he'd recovered from his surprise, the news of the marriage seemed entirely appropriate, though even he was struck by the single-mindedness with which Candace had embraced her destiny. Jack now suspected that, even as she'd composed her note of dismissal, Candace's eye had been firmly fixed on a prize infinitely more valuable than himself. He had accepted his father's offer of the role of best man, 'to show everybody we're still friends', as his father put it. 'Everybody' meant the whole of Oaksboro and practically everyone Jack had ever known. He was in no doubt that they all knew exactly how the happy couple had met. The story of how a man approaching seventy had stolen his own son's girlfriend was too good not to broadcast throughout every bar and hair salon in the county.

Oddly, the potential humiliation of this situation had produced the opposite effect. Contemplating Candace in her wedding creation, her left hand locked tight into the crook of his father's arm and displaying several thousand dollars' worth of diamond ring, Jack had felt no jealousy at all, only a faint sadness that this was her narrow definition of happiness. He felt sorry for his father with this absurdly young trophy wife, who was unlikely to make him any happier than his previous four. Jack wanted to do things differently.

Still, it was going to take some getting used to, having Candace for a stepmother. Jack longed to tell Freya the whole story. He knew how hilarious she'd find it. But she wasn't here.

Jack looked at his watch: 9.15. She must come. *She must!* Every time the door opened he had looked up, hoping it would be her. He'd secured one of the most desirable tables, in a quiet corner, romantically lit. He'd enjoyed choosing the champagne (dry? brut? *pink??*), and ordered it at once so that it would be waiting for her in its frosted bucket. He ached to see her face—her smile, her eyes, her lips.

Tonight had been his real deadline for months. Valhalla's, the 8th at eight. Jack gripped the edge of the table, so tight that his thumbnails whitened. He wanted her here—*now*. He missed her company and her laugh; he missed her cleverness and her fighting spirit; he even missed their arguments. Ever since Cornwall he'd been unable to think about any other woman: again and again he'd found himself waking from vivid erotic dreams; his mind full of her eyes, her breasts, her legs . . . She'd once said to him, 'You don't really want a woman like me.' But she was wrong. Freya was the *only* woman he wanted.

Here was the waiter again. Jack waved him away and checked the time: 9.30. He was kidding himself. She wasn't late; she had never intended to come. The flame of hope that had been burning inside his heart flickered one last time and went out.

Jack glanced again at the champagne resting in the bucket beside him, and the sheaf of flowers waiting on her chair. Then he signalled to the waiter to bring him the bill.

Where were they all? Cars raced towards her, headlamps blazing, paintwork rippling with reflected light, but she couldn't see a single cab. Wait! There was one. Yes! She stepped off the kerb and waved wildly. Thank God! Then, to her fury, it stopped about ten yards before reaching her and someone else got in. Freya shook her fist as it shot past. She pictured Jack in the restaurant, waiting for her, wondering if she was coming. Frantic with impatience, Freya turned and began to walk.

Was she kidding herself? Would he really remember the bet after so many months? Even if he did, would he turn up after the terrible things she'd said to him? She could see the crisscross flash of 34th Street ahead of her. It was already 9.30. Should she give up? There was a ringing in her ears, drowning out the sounds of the street. Into the muffled hush, as clearly as if old Mrs da Fillipo were standing right next to her, came the words: *A woman always knows. And when she knows, she must act.*

Freya broke into a run, long coat tangling in her legs, high heels stuttering on the sidewalk. She remembered the terrace in the moonlight, when the heel of her shoe had come loose, and how Jack had picked her up in his arms. A flame of desire licked through her. She had known then, but she hadn't trusted her heart. She had let fear of rejection and her own stupid pride stand in her way. But she knew now. And she was suddenly certain that, against all the odds, against reason or probability, Jack was waiting for her. She would race into the restaurant, breath-less—she could see his incredulous smile. She'd be smiling too. She'd walk right up to him and say . . . What would she say? The words formed in her mind, words she had never allowed herself to speak aloud. *I love you.*

A cab! She waved at it desperately and it stopped. *Thank you, thank you, thank you.* Freya fell back against the seat, amazed at the idea she had just admitted into her mind. She loved him!

At last! Here was the long plate-glass curve of the restaurant. There was a queue outside, figures huddled into coats, stamping their feet. Freya squashed dollar bills into the cab driver's money tray, and raced to the door of the restaurant.

'Hey, you! Get in line!' called a belligerent voice.

'I'm meeting someone,' Freya tossed over her shoulder.

She pushed her way into the entrance, into the clatter and roar of a restaurant at peak hour. A crowd of people was clustered two and three deep around a long chromium bar. She barged her way through and walked straight into the sea of tables, head swivelling this way and that. Her heart slammed at her ribs. Where was he?

'Excuse me, miss, do you have a reservation?'

'I'm meeting someone,' she repeated, stepping further into the room. She felt a chill of panic. He *must* be here.

'May I have the name?'

Freya turned reluctantly, taking in the professional smile.

'Madison,' she told him, with a tiny thrill at saying the name aloud.

'If you'd just come with me . . .?'

Freya followed him to his smoothly sculpted lectern, and held her breath as she watched his forefinger skim down the open pages of his reservations book. 'Madison. Here we go,' said the man.

Yes! Freya could have kissed him.

'But that table was booked for eight o'clock.' The man put out his hand to stop a young woman who was passing. 'Suzie, this lady was supposed to be meeting Mr Madison, table twelve. Do you happen to know if he left?'

Suzie was looking curiously at Freya. 'He gave me some flowers— said he didn't need them any more. He left maybe twenty minutes ago.'

Freya gave a sigh of defeat. 'OK. Thanks.' She turned away.

She walked back past the bar and pushed her way outside. Instinctively she swung away from the lights and laughter, and walked alone down the dark street.

Jack had kept his promise. He had waited for her for almost two hours. He'd bought her flowers. This time she had disappointed him as bitterly as he had once disappointed her. Freya's eyes squeezed tight at the thought of what she had thrown away. *Just* friends? What was so 'just' about it? What could be more exciting and intimate than being with someone who knew what you were thinking almost before you thought it, who caught your jokes and tossed them back in an instant, who knew all your likes and dislikes, who saw into the dark corners of your heart and liked you anyway—and who also happened to be wildly sexy. Freya had always fancied Jack—she could admit it now—but it was the friendship that was dazzling.

Freya gave a despairing sob. She didn't even know how to contact him. He could be anywhere—*anywhere*—in this teeming city.

She blinked. Something was bothering her at the extreme edge of her vision, an intermittent, flickering light. Freya turned her head. Across the street was a fluorescent sign. *North by N rthwest*, she read. The second 'o' had slipped and was dangling by a cable, spitting sparks. Freya stared. It was a cinema. *North by Northwest* was one of Jack's favourite films.

Before she knew it she had stepped off the kerb and was walking across the street. A ticket lady sat in a glass booth, eating popcorn.

Freya bent her head to the narrow slot. 'Excuse me, has anyone bought a ticket in the last half-hour or so? A man?'

The lady stared at her with bored eyes. 'You want ticket?'

'OK.' Freya took out her wallet and handed over a note. What was she doing?

'Movie almost finished,' the woman said, sliding Freya's ticket across.

Freya ignored her. She crossed the dingy foyer, drawn by the music—panicky violins and the bang of drums.

She pushed through the doors and stopped, blind in the sudden dark. On screen, Cary Grant was clinging to a rockface with one hand; the other gripped the hand of a blonde woman dangling in space, about to fall towards pine trees far, far below.

Freya scanned the audience as her eyes adjusted to the dark. There were perhaps a dozen figures scattered through the rows. None of them was Jack. She turned to go. She felt desolate. It had been stupid to think she could find her way to Jack, just because she loved him.

Wait a minute! There was a lone figure right over the other side, his legs propped on the seat in front. It was Jack. Freya felt her heart would burst. She hurried round the walkway and down the far aisle.

On screen the couple were now in each other's arms on the upper bunk of a train compartment. The woman was wearing white pyjamas. 'This is silly,' she laughed.

'I know. I'm sentimental.'

Freya reached the row where Jack was sitting, one seat in from the end. He hadn't noticed her yet. His face was unguarded, his expression wistful. Freya melted with tenderness. She began to tremble.

But when she spoke, her voice was light. 'Is this seat taken?'

Jack looked up. His face flooded with astonishment and delight. He reached for her hand, holding it as if he would never let go, and flipped down the seat to draw her close. His eyes smiled into hers. 'I've been saving it for you,' he said.

ROBYN SISMAN

Although Robyn Sisman was born in America and lived in Illinois until she was six, most of her life has been spent in Britain. This Anglo-American upbringing, coupled with her marriage to an Englishman, writer and biographer Adam Sisman, has given her a refreshing perspective on transatlantic relationships—something she has used to good effect in her three bestselling novels, all of which have a British heroine and an American hero. In *Just Friends*, the fact that Freya and Jack are different nationalities is just another of the differences between them that makes their relationship so lively.

'The inspiration for *Just Friends* came from lots of different sources,' Robyn said, speaking to me by phone from her home in Somerset. 'In fact, one early spark came from watching an old Hollywood film called *His Girl Friday*, starring Cary Grant and Rosalind Russell. The characters are divorced but still friends. They have a great sparring relationship—full of chemistry. That's what I wanted to achieve in *Just Friends*.'

Robyn was also interested in exploring the modern phenomenon of the thirtysomething woman who can't find a man, so much discussed in the media at the moment. 'I wanted to write a novel that looked at why women and men find it difficult to make a commitment to relationships. I think it's very hard for today's women. They have their own careers, their own money, their own homes and have to be quite tough to survive.

But the downside of that is that it's difficult for them to be open enough to get involved in a relationship.'

Robyn Sisman moved to Somerset six years ago with her husband and two daughters, Flora and Charlotte. Before that the family lived in London, and while she admits that at first she missed living in the city a great deal she says that, 'there are lots of advantages to living here, especially for the children. I love it when they come home from school and rush out to the swing in the garden or the trampoline.'

The idea behind the move was that they would buy somewhere in the country that was large enough for both of them to have their own offices in the house. 'Which we do, but I just can't seem to work in mine,' Robyn admits. Instead she rents an office nearby that used to be a nun's cell. 'It's quite a peculiar arrangement. It is part of a convent that was built in nineteen fifteen and it's like a country version of industrial units. I rent a tiny office where I have my computer, kettle, heater and so forth, and I go there and just get completely caught up in my book.' She is already hard at work on her next book and with two writers in the family life can get hectic, especially when they both have a deadline approaching. 'It works terribly well for us. We enjoy it—mostly,' she laughs.

Sally Cummings

Printed and bound by Maury Imprimeur SA, Malesherbes, France

601-009-1